Inside

Scott M. Hoffman

DORRANCE
PUBLISHING CO
EST. 1920
PITTSBURGH, PENNSYLVANIA 15238

Dorrance Publishing Co
585 Alpha Drive
Suite 103
Pittsburgh, PA 15238
Visit our website at *www.dorrancebookstore.com*

ISBN: 978-1-4809-2595-3
eISBN: 978-1-4809-2181-8

Inside

"C'mon, Bobby, let's go! We've got to get going!"

"I'm coming, Dad! Just another minute!"

Jimmy Williams sat impatiently on the living room couch in the one-bedroom apartment in which he, his wife, Karen, daughter Mary, and son Bobby lived on the northwest side of Chicago.

"For Christ's sake, Bobby! How long does it take an eight year old kid to get ready? You're not a broad, who has to fix her face! C'mon!" Jimmy barked out.

Jimmy was forty-seven years old, stood five feet, ten inches tall at a very strong 160 pounds. He had wavy black hair with a tinge of gray running alongside his temples. His hands were thick and powerful; hands I once saw tear apart a deck of cards with a smile on his face.

Jimmy was not a man who waited for life to come to him, he seized it with those strong fingers and shook it, ripped it apart until it did exactly what Jimmy Williams wanted it to do; nothing more, nothing less.

"Sorry, Dad. Sorry it took me so long. Sorry I wasn't ready on time."

"Enough with the sorrys already," he said, his eyes piercing his son's right through the glasses he wore.

His eyes were like bullets—ready to come out of the chamber of a gun. They were dark brown eyes with a ring of a blue hue around them. Those intense eyes could drive a shivering feeling into the heart of your soul, leaving it scorched, just a flickering flame that has no more feeling of any self-worth.

1

I had seen many a man cower when he fixed those eyes on them. With laser-like efficiency, they were Jimmy's spokesman; no questions asked, no answers given. Everything was understood.

"I just hope you are more efficient as an adult than you are as a kid. You've got a long fucking way to go!" he said.

Then a smile started to ease across his face as he looked at me. It was as if the morning sun was just starting to rise; awakening from its sleep, rubbing its eyes so the rays would become definitely bright hues, gaining strength with each passing second, until reaching a vibrant bright yellow. The rays making you believe it's a great day look, as it stretched across the horizon.

Jimmy's smile was now crisscrossing each cheekbone, working its way down to the sides of his lips. "Yeah, Bobby, I guess you're a kid once in your life, and an adult the rest of your life. So, enjoy the kid time," he said.

He said goodbye to my mother, who was in the kitchen baking chocolate chip cookies for later. My mother was a quiet, soft spoken woman. She had dark black hair, was five feet three inches tall, and weighed 110 pounds. When she wanted to get her point across to the children, all she needed was to give them the mother's stare. What the stare telegraphed to my sister and me was, 'whatever you're thinking about, it better be on the right side of the street, because if you go to the wrong side of the street, I will make sure you don't cross that street again.'

Jimmy kissed her warmly on the cheek, kind of like the kiss you get in 6th grade; not threatening, just the acknowledgement that I think you're kind of cute and maybe we could go for ice cream sometime.

Jimmy and Karen were ultimately married for sixty years before Jimmy died. There was a love affair that was not bound by an alarm going off at 6:00 A.M. every day, telling you it was okay to let your feeling of love begin for that day. No, their love was non-stop over six decades of marriage. Jimmy never let the love die at any time. Every birthday was remembered, every anniversary was remembered, and every Mother's Day was remembered. Gifts were always given for these days. He never forgot Valentine's Day or Christmas.

To Jimmy, Karen was always number one. There never was a two or three. As a child, it was refreshing to see them over and over, just looking in each other's eyes, holding hands, and saying I love you without saying a word.

Over their entire sixty-year marriage, love never left the equation. Even in their eighties, they walked down the street holding hands like giddy teenagers.

When his eyes met hers, their emotions answered all questions. "Do you love me?"

"Yes," her eyes said. "I love you."

His eyes said, "Yes, I love you." Their lips never moved. Near the end of his life, Jimmy told me the only regret he had was that he couldn't marry Mom again and start all over with his princess.

As we walked to the car this crisp March 1956 day, my organized crime education was about to begin.

"Dad, where are we going?" I asked as I climbed into the front seat of our 1949 Chevy. The Chevy was originally red, but Jimmy had it painted a light green. He had it painted he said because a red car would draw a cop's attention. "Never buy a red car." He said, "It stands out to a cop and that's the car he'll stop."

Jimmy's first brand new car was a 1961 Chevy Biscayne, which was light brown. I never bought a red car.

At that point in my life, I did not know what my dad did for a living. I heard my mom's sister Sarah say that he had a union job. I didn't know what that meant, but soon I would learn about what he really did for a living.

Dad started the car while putting on the heater. He said to me, "You got your hat, Bobby?"

"Yeah, Dad, I found it. It was in my coat pocket. That's why I took so long looking for it." This bland conversation about a kid's hat was my father's way of getting to the subject he really wanted to talk about.

"Bobby, we're going to this place. It's actually a club where women dance. And the men will drink and tip the dancers as they dance in front of the men. It's...ah, ah...what they call a... ah, ah...strip club." He finally got the words out. Now, at eight years old, I did not know what he was talking about. I just looked at him; my eyes were trying to connect with what he was saying, but to no avail. I didn't know what to say, so I just sat quietly in the car.

"Bobby, we're going there, because I have to collect money from someone at the club," he said. "You see, Bobby, in Chicago there's this family I belong to. It's sort of like our family, but it's not like our family in the sense that these guys are not blood relatives. You know what I mean? Bobby, they're like family to us, but not in a sense like you, me, Mom, and Mary."

"Sure, Dad, sure. Sure, I know." As I looked at him, I really did not understand what the hell he was talking about. I was just confused about this family that's *not* our family, but is supposed to be *like* our family. At eight years old, I was not Albert Einstein, so where's this going?

"This family, Bobby, in Chicago, they are known as the Outfit. They are... ah, ah, ah...what you would call part of this...ah, ah, ah...thing called organized crime. You understand so far, Bobby? I mean it's...ah, ah...a lot I'm telling you...ah, ah...you understand what I'm saying?" Jimmy asked.

All of the sudden, at that point my, eight-year-old brain matured rapidly to that of an eighteen-year-old person. I was no longer in the third grade at

Rowley Elementary School in Chicago. *Holy fucking shit! Holy mother fucking shit! My father is in the mafia!* is how my brain broke this down.

Jimmy Williams, my father, is in the mafia. Jesus, Mary and Joseph! screamed my brain. *What the fuck? Wait until I tell my friend Jeff Greenberg, he ain't going to believe it.*

The reality still was that I was an eight-year-old kid with an eight-year-old's brain, so this family organized crime stuff was way beyond my radar screen, but I just listened to Dad for now, waiting to hear the next bit of instruction.

"You see, Bobby, most kids don't know what their fathers who are in 'the life' do in the life. So, if you decide you really, really want to go into the life, I'm going to show you what the life is all about. You'll see everything so you can decide whatever you want to do, either be with the Outfit or not," Jimmy said to me.

Wow, oh wow! Here I was, a third grader at Rowley trying to learn penmanship from Mrs. Kinski, and Dad is going to give me an education that will last a lifetime; an education that will show me how the dark side of the world works.

In the coming years, I was to become educated about gambling, the local bookie operations and Las Vegas; loan-sharking, also known as shylocking; extortion, labor racketeering, money laundering, drug trafficking, mob prostitution run out of hotels and separate locations; pornography, which included both adult and child movies, adult bookstores, phone sex and companion services; taking care of 'our friends,' which were politicians, judges and cops by paying them off; fixing professional boxing, horse racing, college basketball, placing bets for professional football and baseball players; controlling Hollywood through making sure the unions were taken care of so television and movies could be made; and other assorted illegal activities, which also included stock manipulation, stolen securities, forgeries, embezzlement, any type of scam, and oh, yes, one more thing…murder.

I learned about street taxes—how much and on what businesses. Most of all, I learned who to trust and who not to trust. Jimmy would constantly drill me about the various personalities I would meet in the world.

Yes, my Outfit education was going to become very extensive, far greater than any classroom. I was to find out with money, and the Outfit could generate millions, anyone could be reached, no matter who you were. When I say anyone, I mean anyone. That included 'Corporate America,' Congressmen, the FBI and yes, the President of the United States. I saw it time and time again on different levels.

Corruption has no boundaries. Everyone involved is an equal partner, no favorites. The rules are simple—someone gives, someone takes. A hand never goes away empty.

We drove down Pelling Avenue, which bordered Gibson Airport, which is in Chicago, and the northern suburbs of Gabriel and Vermont Park. Pelling Avenue was dotted with small industrial buildings, and in between, you would find 'entertainment clubs,' as Jimmy referred to them. They were not on every block, but there were quite a few as I peered out of the car window, enough that they were a source of income worthy of the Outfit's interest.

The clubs were housed in small one-story buildings, mainly flat roofs with, in some cases, neon signs with the name of the club that, at night, would flash across Pelling Avenue.

We pulled into the back of Club M and parked behind the back door, where we proceeded to ring a sort of knobby bell affixed to the side of the door.

A young guy, maybe in his mid-twenties, came to the door. "Bobby, I want to introduce you to Jimmy Ruffino, he works here at Club M," Jimmy said. Jimmy Ruffino eagerly stuck out his hand, and I shook it.

There wasn't anything I could remember about Jimmy Ruffino that stood out in my mind. A slender built guy with a cigarette dangling from his lip, he was just starting out in the life then, but as the years went by, he moved up and up until one day there was no more Jimmy Ruffino. When I mentioned his name to someone in later years, I got the 'who are you talking about' look. Jimmy who?

They never found Jimmy Ruffino's body. With the Outfit, you never really knew what happened to the guys. For some reason, they disappeared, never to be seen again—here one day and gone the next. Sometimes, they would make up a story about why the guy vanished. Usually it was a lie.

The nature of the club with their various licenses for entertainment, liquor, food, cigarette machines, etc., etc., did not allow Jimmy to bring me in the front door. I was a minor and if there was some type of inspector, or Cook County Sherriff's Police checking IDs, they would have their hand out, expecting ten bucks to be put in it to keep their mouth shut about a minor in the club.

Until I was twenty-one, I never went in the front door of any club; I stayed in a backroom, but there wasn't anything I didn't see.

In the car before we went into the club, Jimmy told me the street tax for entertainment clubs was five percent of the weekly gross. What did you get for your money? Well, what you got was you remained in business. No one bothered you. Protection money became my first day's Outfit education piece of knowledge.

I stayed in the backroom, watching the action through an open door as Jimmy, along with Jimmy Ruffino, went to see the club owner Dave Szymanski, who Jimmy later brought back and introduced to me.

Jimmy told me before that any one guy he introduced me to should be addressed as Mr. So and So. Never call him by his first name. If the guy was married, address his wife as Mrs. So and So. Never call her by her first name. If someone said it's okay to use their first name, then I could do it.

"Bobby, now if it's not his wife, don't say nothing. Keep quiet, you understand, Bobby? You don't know what kind of relationship he's got, and maybe you say something that upsets the broad, it don't take much to upset some broads. So, you don't want him to get mad at you, because the broad is mad, and he don't want to hear her mouth, because then you got a big fucking problem that could turn into a bigger fucking problem.

"You got it kiddo? You understand, Bobby? Once these guys who got tempers get hot about this and blow up, you might be lucky to only get a crack in the face and be able to walk out of the place, or it could get worse."

"Don't worry, I completely understand, Dad." It was my first experience with Outfit etiquette. Who knew the members of the Outfit were such gentleman? Yah, right!

"Nice to meet you, Bobby. You can call me Dave."

"Nice to meet you, Mr. Szymanski."

It was Tuesday night in the club, about 7:30. The place seemed dark to me, but this was my first time in a club, so maybe this is how it was. The bar was a half circle. The place was not real busy, as the club's business was more from 9:00 P.M. until 2:00 A.M., closing time.

There was piped-in music. It was lively, the kind you could dance to. The girls were dancing to the music above the bar on a somewhat elevated stage. The stage had dark, mahogany-stained boards that supported the girls, and there were two light silver poles at each end of the stage.

Three girls, wearing no expressions on their faces, shook their loosely covered breasts and rolled their hips. Their body language, gyrating to the music, was strictly an enticement, a fantasy for men to ogle and dream, only a dream, about sexual acts with the girls.

The girls wore G-strings that teetered on nudity, some more athletically inclined in their dancing than others. They earned a small hourly wage plus tips. Ten percent of their tips were given to the club owner.

Men would look mesmerized at the girls, sipping their watered-down drinks. When the girls wanted their tips, they got close enough so the men could stuff dollar bills into their tops. Some men would leave a tip on the stage and not get near the girls. They didn't want to ruin their dream.

At first I was thinking, *what type of girl does this? Is she a vertical prostitute?* I pulled back on the trigger a bit, and realized they might have to support their kids or help with a sick mom or dad. I learned that day to never make any hard and fast rules about anyone until you know the 'why' part of their life. A judge can't decide the case until he hears all the evidence. So, I never prejudge someone.

As I would talk to the girls in the times I was in the clubs, my resolution became the right street to walk down as I found out people need to earn a living...point, game, set, and match. There would be no pontification from me on moral righteousness. You earn a buck however you can because you need to. If you don't take care of yourself, who else will? I treated the women with respect and they did the same toward me.

The money made in any strip club is basically from the liquor. Some places might serve sandwiches, which would serve as an additional income, but that was more the exception than the rule. The clubs would serve beer, but when it came to the mixed drinks, they watered down those drinks and, as less liquor was used from the bottle, made money for the club.

The clubs would water down the drinks a bit to keep the customers drinking more. There was a bouncer or two to make sure the customers didn't harass the dancers. Just drink, drink, and drink is what the clubs wanted you to do.

To the Outfit, a strip club was a source of money laundering. Any cash business such as strip clubs, or b-girl (bar girl) bars, in which a fifty-cent beer became a five-dollar beer, and a woman would sit next to the customer, nuzzle up to him and get real flirty with him so he would buy the woman a beer or mixed drink at the exorbitant prices charged; restaurants and regular bars; or any business in which cash is used are good money laundering sources.

Cash from Outfit businesses, generally of the illegal nature, is mixed with cash from legit businesses, showing more receipts than actual business. Cash leaves no trail so it's very difficult to trace.

Dave Szymanski walked back into the backroom with Jimmy, where I was waiting. He had a thick, white envelope and before giving it to Jimmy, he looked at me. It was a nervous look, anxious look, as sweaty moisture rimmed around his lip.

"Don't worry Dave, Bobby is okay. He's a quiet, shy kid who's been told to keep his mouth shut. He's a student trainee," Jimmy said with the tinge of laughter.

"Okay Jimmy, okay. I'm just not used to kids in here, you understand," Dave replied.

"Yeah, I know, Dave, but he's got to learn if this is what he wants to do for the rest of his life," Jimmy said, staring at Dave.

"Fine Jimmy, fine. Fine." He then gave Jimmy the envelope. Jimmy, in turn, gave Dave a white envelope from the sport jacket he was wearing.

"Work it Dave, work it!" Jimmy said.

"Okay, Jimmy, sure, sure. I'll work it like always!" Dave said.

I watched in total amazement, like two ships passing in the night, but instead of exchanging pleasantries from one captain to another, Jimmy and Dave were exchanging hard, cold cash, US currency, to increase the Outfit's bottom line.

The money Dave got was to be laundered. Dave would create more receipts than drinks or food that was sold. That money would be washed with the rest of the club's cash, thus earning a bigger five percent next time when Jimmy came for his collection.

The Outfit would be taking in more money from the club, and the laundered money could not be accounted for by the Cook County State's Attorney's office, the Feds, or anyone. It was out of sight for a while, only to resurface as part of a bigger profit.

Phew! Mrs. Kinski, my third-grade teacher at Rowley Elementary School, needs to incorporate this type of math, besides learning about multiplication tables and decimals in our math studies.

"Bobby, I got to go to the bathroom. See that guy over there?" Jimmy was pointing to a big, strong-looking kid in a black Ban-Lon shirt. "That's Danny Carci's kid, Petey," Jimmy said. "I'm going to talk to him for a couple of minutes." He said, "Dave, it's okay for Bobby to wait here."

"Yeah, yeah, Jimmy. Bobby can wait here," Dave said.

As I waited for Jimmy, Jimmy Ruffino brought one of the dancers into Dave's office and then left. Dave closed the door, but not completely, so I could see and hear what was going on in the room.

"Look, honey, for whatever reason, you're not lighting these guys up with your stage performance so they'll buy more drinks. You know, spend more money, so we can make money." Dave Szymanski said to her, "I'm going to give you a joyride." I was thinking *what the hell is a joyride?*

Dave walked over to a small refrigerator in his office, opened the door and took out a small vial with some liquid in it. He then went to a cabinet where he had a container of closed syringes. He took one syringe out and took the top off, and stuck it in the vial. I was not sure how many cc's he put in the syringe.

He told the dancer to pull down her bottom attire and bend over. She complied, and he took the syringe and plunged it into one of her cheeks. She winced a bit. She straightened up and adjusted her bottom attire. He put the vial back in the refrigerator, and threw the syringe away in the garbage can.

"Wait about five minutes; it's a sort of upper...amphetamine...that'll get your motor going. Now you'll be up on the stage making us some money," he told her. "You feeling okay? Just sit here and wait a bit," Dave said.

"Yeah, yeah, I'm okay!" While slapping her ample bottom, she said, "I'm glad I'm not boney down here."

The sweat beads started to moisten around the hair of my neck. *What just happened here?* I was thinking. *I mean how? Come on, he's no doctor. Will she be okay? I got to tell someone. What if she gets lightheaded or feels like she's going to pass out; come on, who's going to help her?* I was thinking. *She's still a lady.*

Then I composed myself and remembered about keeping my mouth shut like Jimmy told me. In the life I was going to see things that would scare me, shock me, amaze me, hurt my feelings, be extremely repulsive, and leave me utterly disgusted, at times. But, always remember to keep your mouth shut. When in doubt, follow rule number two, which is to follow rule number one—keep your mouth shut.

Jimmy came back to the room after talking with Petey. "Let's go, Bobby, I've got to make another fast stop at another bar," he said.

As we walked back to the car, my legs felt heavy; no bounce to the step, no left, right, left, right cadence. My mind was numb. My brain was telling the rest of my body, "You guys won't believe what I just saw!" My brain, with nervous anxiety, spilled out the events that just happened.

My nervous system, like children in a kindergarten class sitting in a circle on the floor listening to the teacher read a story; quickly broadcast the events the brain was telling to the rest of my body after patiently, like the kindergarten kids, listening wide eyed to every detail.

"Holy crap!" my legs blurted out after hearing the special breaking news the nervous system had told in a conference call to all of my body parts. The leg muscles, who reported to my legs, were told by the legs that, on orders from my blood, "Make Bobby work harder and harder to walk." My legs told the leg muscles not to deviate from blood's orders, or there would be disciplinary actions taken.

"Bobby, Jesus why are you walking so slow! For Christ's sake, you're not ninety years old, come on! Step it up, kid!" Jimmy said.

"Okay, Dad. Sorry, sorry," I mumbled.

I reached the car as my legs fought me every step of the way. Each step felt like I walked a mile. Once in the car, I replayed in my head what I saw in the club that night.

Here was an eight-year-old kid in a strip club, who saw women wearing practically nothing on their bodies, dancing and gyrating to music; men looking blankly at women, a drink in front of them, sometimes yelling, "C'mon, baby, shake what God gave you," referring to their breasts; some guys smoking, some not, reaching with dollar bills, crumbled or folded, trying to shove them into the upper part of whatever the hell you call what the dancers were wearing.

I saw Jimmy give Dave Szymanski a white envelope with money, not sure how much, and Dave give Jimmy a white envelope with money, not sure how much. I saw Dave shove a needle full of something into a dancer's ass to make her have some drug-induced happy feeling, so she would dance better. Thus, making the customer happy, which translated into him buying more watered-down drinks, and the club made more money. There were these two poles on each end of the stage where the dancers did something; if I told you what it was, I would probably be arrested. Just another day at the office.

We drove further south on Pelling Avenue to a bar called The Well. It was a b-girl bar and, like Club M, we parked in the back of The Well that had a small, maybe five-car lot, which was private for the bar big shots. The patrons parked on the street. We went in through the back door, which was unlocked.

Jimmy introduced me to Sam DeSale, who was the owner. "Hi, Bobby, nice to meet you!" he said in a rather loud, booming, vibrating voice. *You probably could hear Mr. DeSale in Milwaukee, Wisconsin, with that type of voice!* I thought.

You would think in a b-girl bar all the women at the bar would have pretty faces with shapely figures. Well, this was not the case at The Well, or any other b-girl place I was ever in throughout my life.

There were some cases meeting the pretty standards, but a lot of them were just average looking, really nothing you would look at once, twice, or three times. However, with makeup on and under dark lighting and having a friendly voice, I suppose the men were just looking for someone to talk to. The woman's looks didn't matter as long as he was comfortable with her.

I learned a b-girl didn't have to be pretty, just touch his arm, put her hand on his shoulder long enough for him to think she actually cared about him, or slowly rub his thigh ever so slowly, calculating in her mind how many rubs it would take to create an affectionate feeling so he would buy more drinks at the highway robbery prices being charged. She would sit next to him and listen to his stories and laugh at his jokes. She would make him feel special. She would give him the attention he wasn't getting at home.

Guys go to strip clubs and b-girl places because something is not right at home. If they were happy, they would be at home. A single guy going to one of these joints is one thing, but a married guy, c'mon; home is where your loving wife and children are waiting for you. Why wouldn't you want to be home with your loved ones? I learned for some men, home is the last place they wanted to be.

The male species can huff and puff, throw his chest out, be the alpha male to everyone else, but once a woman begins using her physical game plan on a man directing his testosterone north from south, east from west, he melts into a gooey, and Jell-O like substance, letting her hands formulate her next action. It does not matter if she looks like the current Miss America, the latest, hottest Hollywood starlet, or death warmed over, she will now be able to make him respond to those important four words that are used in the b-girl bars, "How about another drink?"

If his verbal response is slow, she then moves in closer for the kill, slowly and subtly letting her breast rub against his shoulder, attached to the one arm that will take out the wallet, or money clip, and buy more drinks. Yes, she knows the breast will close the deal. It works over and over as men think the touches of her breasts are pre-game sex, sort of the warm-up before the actual sex games begin later that night somewhere, someplace, they hope.

"Sure!" he says. "Let's have another drink!" She smiles and calls the bartender over, and the hunter has now become the game. He is no longer stalking her. She now has the trophy; him. She now knows a spigot of money will start pouring, buying more drinks, thus, bringing in more money for The Well, and the Outfit knows this, too. The drinks will be watered down to make sure he keeps buying and buying, like at the strip club.

At the end of the night, there will be no sex, only an empty wallet as another sucker supports the Outfit.

Jimmy met with Sam, only for a few minutes. I watched as Sam gave him a rubber banded white envelope, which had an undisclosed amount of cash that made the corners of the envelope bulge. After Sam gave Jimmy the envelope he said, "Bobby, I got something for you." Christ's sake, I hope it wasn't a b-girl from the bar.

"Here, here." He handed me a small light red sucker.

"Thanks, Mr. DeSale," I said. I figured I better take it as I did not want to hear Jimmy's mouth saying, 'Don't refuse these guys or you'll piss them off, and if you're lucky, you'll only get a crack in the face' crap again.

"You're welcome, Bobby!" Mr. DeSale said.

Before we drove home, Jimmy turned to me and said, "Bobby, I know you saw a lot of stuff tonight. I know it ain't right for a kid to see all this stuff, but damn it, if you want this life, you got to see this life has bumps, warts, and whatever the hell else. I'll talk to you more about this, as time goes by, I will go over things! Don't worry, things are blurry now, as they should be, but we'll go over and over things so you'll understand how things work." Jimmy then leaned over and kissed me on the cheek.

Somehow that kiss made me feel better, I think, but I was not about to bet the ranch on it either. My first day seeing an Outfit operation made me feel I was in for quite an Outfit education. I sensed being an adult was a lot tougher than it looked.

The next day, Jimmy took the money he collected from the strip club and b-girl bar to Dean "Double D" Dragonetti, who ran the day-to-day operations of the Outfit. Jimmy was Dean's consigliere; Dean's right-hand man, who did whatever Dean assigned to him, including Dean's order that someone should be killed, or as it was referred to 'being whacked'. Jimmy would have to organize the hit.

Once an order is given, it must be carried out—no deviation, no changing what the order is; just take care of it or you become the next order. Not every order is about killing someone. Orders could be given ranging from meetings known as sit-downs, to paying someone off for doing something.

Jimmy had known Dean since they were each seventeen years old. He knew Dean's explosive, violent, sadistic temper, and once Dean was on a roll about something or someone, Jimmy just sat in a chair and listened and listened and listened.

Dean was not a smiley, feel good kind of a guy. He was foul-mouthed, dirtier than a toilet with his crude language. Constantly spewing f-you, f-this, f-him, and other assorted phrases with 'f' in front of them. I guess this was part of Dean's management style. Funny, I don't think you learn this type of management style when you are studying for your MBA in Finance from a business school.

He was a textbook bully. You were afraid to be in his company, and you were afraid not to be in his company. I have to say, with me, he was always nice. While Jimmy didn't have a trusting soul, I think down deep Dean trusted Jimmy more than Jimmy would admit. Though with the Outfit, trust was like Chicago's weather—wait five minutes and it will change.

Jimmy laughed when I asked him once if Dean's height—which was maybe 5'7"—if the wind was blowing right, played a role in his behavior. You know the Napoleon complex. "He was like Frank Nigri, an old timer from the 1930s who died years ago," Jimmy said. "You see, old Frank was about 5'4", and he believed if you whacked a short guy maybe under five foot ten, who would miss him?" Jimmy chuckled.

I remember the first time I went to Dean's house. After we walked up the steps there was a doormat on the landing outside the front door. Normally, people have a doormat that says WELCOME. Dean's doormat read GO AWAY.

Dean was a ladies' man. His daughter Marie was born out of wedlock. His eyes were always darting around the room, looking at the women in the room until he saw the one he wanted. Then his eyes narrowed, and like a lion hiding in the weeds, his body sprung up and he walked over to her, and the conquest ritual began.

His women were legendary; a lot of Hollywood actresses knew this extremely powerful man ran the day-to-day operations of a criminal organization known as the Outfit. With just a stare at a movie honcho, he could put them on their way to fame and fortune. So, they had no qualms trading a night for the jackpot of Hollywood.

He did whatever to whomever, whenever. He technically reported to John Ricci, but Dean was his own man, calling the shots as he saw fit. I believe if Ricci stood in front of the train, Dean would run him over. Ricci was one of those guys who stayed in the background and took his cut from the street crews. Ricci, to me, was a paper boss; he could give an order on someone and it would be carried out, but as he got older, he distanced himself from most people.

Dean was one person I definitely called Mr. Dragonetti. He feared no one. Besides doing whatever the capo (boss) wants you to do, a consigliere functions not only as an advisor, but is also the eyes and ears for the boss on the street. And, if the boss is not functioning as a boss should, there would be calls for him to be whacked for incompetency. Yes, you heard me right. A boss could be ordered killed. One of the reasons for which a consigliere could order a hit would be if the boss was or appeared to be a homosexual.

Here's the convoluted thought process in organized crime, ladies and gentlemen. A boss, a double hit for being gay; yet, a gay member of a street crew, who was a good earner—meaning he brought in a lot of money from criminal activities—would be told to keep it off the street, do it on the side somewhere behind closed doors. So, the so-called brains of a street crew, the boss, could be whacked for being gay, but not a street crew member. Go figure, huh?

After Dean met his demise years later, I asked Jimmy if he ever thought, as the consigliere, to call for Dean to be whacked for something, I don't know, maybe being bi-sexual or some other quirky behavior.

"Are you fuckin' for real, Bobby?" he said. Jimmy's voice grew stronger. "That thing about whacking a boss, who in their right fuckin' mind is going to try that?" he said. I could see Jimmy's body language was accelerating quickly. It was like, "Gentlemen, start your engines," at the Indy 500. He began to pace, arms outstretched, palms up, fingers gyrating back and forth.

"Holy crissakes. Once you would tell one guy in the crew, one fuckin' guy in the crew, you want to whack a boss, he would run as fast as his legs could carry him to the boss and rat you out. You would never get another 24 hours in your fuckin' life," Jimmy said. "You are gone, history. You are cemetery-ready, if you know what I mean, Bobby. I dunno who ever came up with that idea about whacking a boss, but if a consigliere does try it, he pretty damn well better make sure he can do it, and do it goddamn fast, right away...

boom…right now, this second. Don't let the shooter or shooters be able to take a shot, because if word gets out, you become the 'late Mr. So and So,' you understand, Bobby?"

Sure, a consigliere has a lot of power, but he has to know his territory. He's got to make sure the landscape is right before he does something. I remember Eric Lito; he was a made guy, a boss of a West Side crew that was a good earner, bringing in good money on gambling, loan-sharking, and prostitution. Dean was told by someone Eric was gay, so he called Jimmy in.

"Jimmy, find out about Eric Lito. Someone told me he's a little light," then Dean raised his arm and bent his wrist down as if to indicate to Jimmy that Eric was gay. "You know, if he's a fag…well, let's just see before we make a decision," Dean said.

Jimmy had a tip that Eric hung out in the Stallion Club, a gay bar on the Near North Side. Jimmy went to the Stallion Club one night. It was around 2 A.M., closing time. He saw Eric come out of the club holding hands with a guy, then he stopped and kissed the guy. Eric was in his late 40s and this guy looked to be no more than 30 years old.

The Outfit, in the 1950s, '60s, and '70s, had control of the gay bars and gay clubs. The gay trade was a big money maker for them as they were getting at least a 50% take from each place. The feelings in the Outfit toward gays back then were very closed; no one talked about it. It could get you whacked. A gay guy in the Outfit would never dare think about coming out. Being gay meant being discreet during those years; the Outfit could expose you to whomever they wanted, and, thus, could make your life a living hell and still whack you.

Being gay today, while still not easy, compared to the '50s and '60s, is better. People still need to be tolerant of someone who is gay. God gave them feelings just like you and me. They are human beings just like you and me, who should be treated with dignity and respect.

Through control of the Chicago alderman of the ward in which gay bars and clubs were located, the Outfit had the political muscle to control all the required licenses needed to keep the places open. The Outfit had the political muscle through the alderman who was a friend who did favors for the Outfit in return for money to keep the Building Department inspectors and Health Department inspectors away.

The aldermen, through their power, could turn the inspectors on to you like a mid-summer rain storm that comes down in buckets by having the doors of your establishment closed. By having the inspectors write up a mountain of violations of the Building & Health Code Ordinances that would force you to stop your business from being a business anymore. Thus, the Outfit ran your business. Either you danced with them or danced with no one.

Jimmy always taught me to find the strength of the situation. Whatever it is, take it and put it in your back pocket. Pull it out when the time is right, so then you could broker yourself a better deal than the one you had before. If you have the strength, you have the power to force the other person to do what you want them to do, not what they want to do. It's like the Golden Rule—whoever has the gold, rules.

Having to tell Dean about Eric Lito's gay status, Jimmy knew he had the Outfit's financial involvement with the gay bars and clubs in his back pocket, but could he convince Dean the Outfit's earned money was stronger than one man's sexual proclivities. Uncertainty filled Jimmy's mind as he didn't know, would Dean even listen to what Jimmy had to say.

"Well, Jimmy, what did you find out about Eric Lito?" Dean quizzed Jimmy. Jimmy only had one way to play it, so he told Dean what he saw.

There was a deafening silence between Dean and Jimmy. They sat in Dean's office, which was in Italiano's Restaurant. They looked at each other eye-to-eye. A conversation was being held between the two, but no words were spoken.

Their thoughts were rapidly filling the office, but not a word was said. As each second passed, both men faced each other, just looked and looked at each other, allowing the conversation to be batted back and forth in each other's mind. Each one knowing the spoken word would impact the outcome of someone's life, though not a word was spoken.

Their bodies listened to each other defend their own position one thought at a time. Dean, then Jimmy; Jimmy then Dean...not a word was spoken. Point-by-point, information was articulated through their body language that only someone in the life could understand. Each man, one a made member and the boss, the other an associate member, both of Chicago's powerful crime family, were going to let their emotions make the closing arguments as to what the fate of this human being would be. Not a word was spoken.

"You know, Jimmy, in the life, we've got certain rules. Like, you can't physically touch a made guy unless it's authorized, otherwise you get whacked. We got a rule about being gay," Dean said.

"Dean, you're right, we got rules. If you're gay, you get whacked, but in some cases, you have to look at how that rule affects the bigger picture of an organization," Jimmy countered.

"So, let me get this straight. You're saying to forget about the rule, if the need of the organization is bigger than the rule. Is that what you're saying?" Dean asked. "Yeah, that's what I'm saying," Jimmy said.

"So fuck the rule," Dean said.

"Not really. You just have to apply it when the action stands alone by itself. Eric is a good earner. We whack Eric, and the organization loses dough it might or might not make up with someone else, so the Outfit suffers," Jimmy coolly but directly said, looking eyeball-to-eyeball at Dean.

"The basis of the Outfit's existence is to bring money into the organization," Jimmy said. "By letting a rule be broadly applied, we hurt ourselves. Once the money stops coming in, that money no longer can make us more money," he said.

"Listen to me, Jimmy, and listen good. You tell Eric to keep whatever the hell it is that he's doing off the street. Don't do it in public. Make that real fuckin' clear to him—don't do it in public. Use a motel, hotel, his place, the confessional box in a church. I don't give a fuck; just not in the street. You clear on this, Jimmy? This is the end of it. I don't want to hear another fuckin' time about Eric and his gay boy," Dean said.

"It couldn't be any clearer," Jimmy said.

This was why Jimmy was the consigliere.

In 1968, Eric Lito was honored at the Charlemagne Hotel on the Northwest Side by Dean Dragonetti, and the Who's Who from the Outfit. Wives were invited to this affair; no girlfriends were allowed. Too many potential fireworks if each met the other. Eric was honored for his outstanding service to the Italian community.

The FBI was not invited, but they came anyway, taking pictures, of course, of everyone. I think Eric gave a couple of bucks to the Mother Scaloppini's Home for the Aged. Maybe that was the Italian community he helped.

In 1988, Eric died of congestive heart failure. He always made sure he kept it off the street.

Unlike the five organized crime families in New York, which were always fighting for territories, Chicago had one leader with control over the various street crews, and that was John Ricci. He was the Chairman of the Board.

Dean Dragonetti ran the day-to-day operations of the Outfit, and while he would meet with Ricci to discuss matters, he had a free hand to pretty much do whatever he wanted.

Anthony "Tony G" Galante ran Las Vegas and Hollywood for Ricci. He would meet when necessary with Dean, but he was Ricci's guy, making money for Ricci. A small man in stature, his appearance was one that outwardly appeared to be unassuming, almost like 'maybe-we-can-slip-one-by-Tony type of personality. Galante was the quietest of the three as far as temperament. Don't be fooled. Galante did not reach his level of authority by being the unassuming type. Galante was not a wallflower. He was a big time player.

Galante would cut his losses very quickly if you were not bringing in the money the way he wanted. Bodies piled up during times of his reign; sometimes, it seemed like the deaths were occurring in an assembly-like style during those periods.

He got his point across, and others in the Outfit knew, he being from the Capone era, was not shy about ending your life expectancy sooner than an actuarial table predicted. Galante set the rules of the game, and you better make sure you played them exactly that way. Monday followed by Tuesday, no deviation; do not freelance with Galante, otherwise 'ex' was going to be put in front of your name…as in what happened to Mr. So and So? Oh, you mean the ex-Mr. So and So.

To many people, Galante appeared to run the Outfit, but Galante quietly, efficiently, and smoothly always made sure Ricci knew he was the ultimate team player. The one thing the Outfit didn't put up with was showboating. They never liked someone to stand out who might draw the Fed's attention. Getting your name in the paper too much could mean the next time your name was in the paper, it would be in the obituary column.

Before Dragonetti was chosen to oversee the day-to-day operations of the Outfit, he ran the Northford Street crew. Jimmy then was an underboss for Galante overseeing his street action, the gambling, loan-sharking, extortion, and money laundering that was done in Chicago with the Las Vegas and Hollywood money. Chucky "Crooked Finger" De Polle was Galante's consigliere. De Polle had a broken finger from playing softball as a kid, thus, the nickname.

Whomever Jimmy worked for, that's where his loyalty called home. As later on with Dean, Jimmy had a good rapport with Galante. Galante always jokingly said Jimmy was an Italian by injection. "Working with us Italians got in your blood," Galante would kiddingly say to Jimmy.

Jimmy had started out 30 years ago as a 17-year-old kid driving a beer truck before Prohibition in the 1920s for Al Capone's boys. He would drive the truck to Milwaukee, Wisconsin, which was carrying the illegal booze to be sold there. Who do you think rode shotgun with him? You guessed it, Dean Dragonetti. Dragonetti actually carried a twelve-gauge shotgun, keeping it on the floor in case they had a problem driving to Milwaukee. It was not uncommon for another gang to stick up and hijack the truck. If a rival gang hijacked the truck, Capone lost money, because then that gang would sell the illegal beer for their own profit.

The Northford Street crew, starting with Capone, was the strongest street crew in the Outfit organization. So, it came to be the power structure at the top of the Outfit flow chart was always dominated by Northford guys.

Ricci was in charge of Northford after Capone went to prison in the early 1930s.Galante was head of Northford after Ricci ascended to the very top of the Outfit organization in the late 1930s.

While other street crews would boast about how tough and strong and smart they were to anyone who would listen, the Northford boys still called the shots.

Practically everyone involved in some capacity with the Outfit that I have come across in my life was either a made member, associate member, our friends, politicians, judges, and cops, or any other assorted wannabes, who all told me Jimmy was smart. With the Outfit, smart, if not handled right, could get you in trouble. Some guys figure a smart guy has the boss's ear, so if the smart guy is not around, they could get the boss's ear. I'd seen guys get whacked for being too smart for their own good.

Jimmy just had the uncanny ability to always see beyond his nose. Outfit life, at best, is a balancing act, and Jimmy knew how much to put on the scale so it stayed balanced. He looked at how small things affected the bigger picture. He taught me to start at the end and work backwards with any problem. Look at the consequence and then look back to see what led up to the end result. When someone praised Jimmy, to me, my sense of pride and admiration grew by leaps and bounds, because they were talking about my dad. Not someone else's dad, but my dad.

Sure, Jimmy was like all us mortals. He wasn't perfect and had questionable judgment at times, but he was never convicted of any crime, nor did he ever go on trial for committing something that was illegal.

When I was nine years old, the FBI walked him out of the apartment in handcuffs, taking him to FBI headquarters for questioning. He looked back at Karen, and told her to call Gary Rosenthal, Jimmy's attorney. A few hours later that day, maybe six or seven hours later, he would be back at home and not charged with any crime.

There were a couple of times when Jimmy was called before a Grand Jury who were looking into alleged Outfit activities. He pled the Fifth Amendment on each and every question asked of him by an Assistant United States Attorney. The Feds were always suspicious of Jimmy, but there's a big difference between suspicion and evidence.

"Bobby, remember, there's your story, my story, and the truth," he said. He never believed anything at face value. Especially with the Outfit, where lying was so ingrained, you had to excavate very deeply at times when searching for the truth. "Always research the question before you give the answer, Bobby. Sometimes, the truth is going to hurt, but you might save someone's life," he would tell me.

Jimmy was not a big advocate of murder. Sure, if the order was given to him, he had to carry it out by making the arrangements as to who the shooter or shooters were going to be, when and where the hit would take place, the amount of money to be paid for the hit, and all other associated details.

"Listen, Bobby, this is important. They," meaning the Feds, "can get you on not paying taxes and murder. Hey, it's in black and white—if you don't pay your taxes, they got you. What are you going to say if you sign a tax return, and it ain't legit, or you don't file a return at all, and they can prove you got income? They got you on income tax evasion and maybe conspiracy to commit income tax fraud. I mean, baby, it's over if they're able to show hidden income that you didn't report. You see where this is going, Bobby?

"The Feds have the manpower to check every financial activity; they gotta look at a lot of paperwork, but if they can put it together, then they can make a case. So, Bobby, always pay your taxes. It's one of the easiest ways to get convicted. How did they get Capone? Right…income tax evasion. They never convicted him on one damn murder…not one!

"Murder, Bobby, that's a whole different story. I mean, remember, Bobby, there's no statute of limitations on murder. The Feds can go after you 10, 20, 30 years later, but guys don't think about that. Often they do things on emotion, not reason. Look, once you put three in the hat, for the rest of your life you are a marked man, and they can legally go after you."

"I don't understand. What's this 'three in a hat' stuff?" I said.

"Oh, yeah, I'm a little ahead of myself. My fault, Bobby," Jimmy said.

"Once the order is given to whack someone, a lot of killings are done with the shooter, or shooters firing three shots in the back of the guy's head. This way he never sees the shooter or shooters, and say he lives, who's he going to identify? He ain't seen the faces of the shooter or shooters who actually shot him," Jimmy said.

"Oh, I see what you're saying," I said.

"The first thing you learn about organized crime is it does not matter what city or wherever it takes place. Everything, and I mean everything, is about money. Without money, they cannot bribe a politician to get government contracts, zoning changes, get their kid a government job, etc. Without money, they cannot bribe a judge to throw out a case on a legal technicality, etc. Without money, they cannot bribe a cop to not show up in court on a case, get inside information, especially from the Chicago Police Department's Organized Crime, Gambling, Vice and Narcotics Units, and help from the FBI.

However, not many guys would listen to Jimmy about paying their taxes. Their criminal minds could not see they were actually convicting themselves by not paying taxes or filing a tax return. They made a case by not following the law for the Feds in that all the Feds had to do was subpoena and go through document after document after document. Once the Feds had their evidence, then…bingo…indictments, convictions, and prison time followed very swiftly.

I faithfully pay my taxes every year, whatever I owe, per my return prepared by Ira the accountant.

Nor, did they listen to Jimmy about giving the order to whack someone. "He's gotta go, he's gotta go," they would say, but was murder the only option? Jimmy would suggest a sit-down, giving the guy 'X' amount of Gs, and telling him, "Move to Florida or someplace out of Chicago; you're done with the Outfit. Keep your mouth shut, and you'll live to be an old man. If you still want to be part of the Outfit organization, St. Matthew's Cemetery on the Southwest side of the city is where you'll be conducting business," Jimmy would tell these guys. Surprisingly, few of these guys who he did talk to about office arrangements at St. Matthew's ever asked Jimmy to repeat himself after he preached the good life to them.

These times were rare exceptions, rather than the rule. Bosses like Thomas "Cute Tommy" Covelli would make a decision, not talking about any room for negotiations, only this guy has done such and such for a period of time, he's gotta go.

Sometimes guys got whacked because lies were told about them. Someone wanted someone dead, so they made up a story. There were times guys got killed for reasons that weren't legit. In someone's mind, the guy had to go, so he went.

I remember one such case. Norman Gaspermonte, a boss, liked the wife of one of his street crew members, Tommy Responto. He liked her so much, he made up a story that Tommy had sticky fingers. He was pocketing some of the gambling money, according to Gaspermonte. He gave the order Tommy should be whacked based on the lie he told. Tommy was hit, and Gaspermonte played the role of the caring friend in order to woo Tommy's wife. She fell for all the phony insincerity Gaspermonte threw at her over a period of time, and they eventually got married.

Years later, she wound up divorcing him as he turned out not to be Mr. Faithful to her. Still, Tommy got whacked only because Gaspermonte wanted his wife.

Jimmy realized, with some people, discretion is the better part of valor. He wasn't going to stick his neck out for someone whose neck was to be sliced and diced, because some capo said so. That was the decision, then so be it; no appealing the decision to the United States Supreme Court was going to change the outcome. Jimmy went along, if he was involved, making the necessary arrangements and staying far away from what was going to happen.

Street crews had the autonomy to make their own decisions, but they better be bringing in the money. Loss of revenue equaled loss of autonomy. Also, a change in leadership at the top of the crew would brew if the money did not come flowing in.

If things were not going well financially for a capo, he's brought in for a sit-down meeting. He was basically told the numbers had to be where they should be in the next couple of months or travel accommodations would be made for him to St. Matthew Cemetery. Some carrot and stick approach, huh?

John Balencenti, an old-time street boss, was a distant cousin of Michael "Nutty" Naturo. Naturo immediately took over control of the organization after Capone went to jail. Naturo only lasted a few years as boss, as he died of throat cancer. John Ricci, who was Naturo's underboss, became the boss of the bosses, *numero uno*, replacing Naturo. John Balencenti, a long-time member of the Northford crew, became the boss of the crew.

Balencenti was boss of the crew for many years and ran a successful crew during those years. The problem with being the boss of the Northford crew was you were always under the microscope. Since the Outfit's upper management primarily came from Northford, they set higher standards for that crew. Any slippage in revenue from the crew brought a response from the higher ups, as the bottom line was still the bottom line.

Gussie, as everyone called Balencenti, was summoned to a catering place called Chateau D'Ville. The crew's numbers had started a downward trend, and Dean Dragonetti wasn't happy. Meetings like this were held in the backroom of Chateau D'Ville late at night, long after the customers left.

Chateau D'Ville, while known for its catering business, did serve dinner seven days a week also. It was the place for Italian weddings, bridal and baby showers; other organizational affairs like Knights of Columbus and Lion's Club events; charitable organization fundraisers for Mother Scaloppini's Home for the Aged; and other worthy charities.

In Chicago, you would be hard-pressed to find an Italian family that did not have an affair held at Chateau D'Ville. Tony's wedding was held there, Ann Marie's baby shower was held there, Rocco's First Communion was held there, and Outfit meetings were held there.

Chateau D'Ville was the place where Outfit members were told to have their weddings, their bridal and baby showers, their children's First Communion parties, and any other of their family affairs. No discussions about using another place…you were told this was the place you were going to use, so just go ahead and make your reservations. To the best of my knowledge, no one ever said 'no.'

In lieu of the Outfit business, owner Oscar Mele, whose wife was a cousin of John Ricci, did not care who used the back office after hours. He gave them a key and counted his money. As usual, he was just another spoke in the never ending Outfit wheel.

Jimmy was at the meeting with Gussie, Dean Dragonetti, and Timothy Robitle, one of Dean's lieutenants, was also there.

"You know, Bobby, Timmy Robitle was one of those guys that, with five guys behind him, acted like a real tough guy, but one-on-one, hell, he couldn't even take a broad. I'd bet my money on her," Jimmy said.

"Tough guys, Bobby, never have to advertise and make themselves out to be one tough son of a bitch. Their actions will show people how tough they really are, and when they walk into a room, their presence will be felt by all," he said.

I kind of got the feeling Jimmy didn't think much of Timmy, and I don't think he was on Jimmy's Christmas card list.

"Gussie, your numbers have been falling off a bit the last two months," Robitle said to Gussie. "Gussie, your numbers are usually pretty steady. Maybe your boys on the street are getting a little fuckin' lax. What are they doing...fucking off and not collecting our money?" Robitle said, his voice starting to rise.

Dean and Jimmy sat quietly for now. Robitle was going to carry the lead on this job appraisal meeting. Timmy thought this was his time to shine in front of Dean. Dean's letting him go after Gussie, so Timmy thought Dean had confidence in him and would push him up the Outfit corporate ladder. Let's see how much confidence Dean really had in Timmy.

The Outfit hierarchy got ten percent of the combined weekly take from the street crews, which was a steady income, while waiting for additional money to come in from all other directions. This was the seed money the Outfit executives needed to maintain other illegal activities. With cash on hand from the street crews, illegal activities could be financially taken care of such as gambling, loan-sharking, prostitution, and money laundering, to name a few. In turn, these and other illegal activities would produce larger revenue for the Outfit.

The Feds would estimate that the Outfit was a one hundred million dollar operation, but I can tell you it was a lot higher than that.

"I mean, Gussie, we ain't going to take this shit. If your guys aren't producing, start cracking the mother fuckin' whip on them," Robitle said.

Still, Dean and Jimmy said nothing; just sitting in their chairs listening to Robitle make his case. Robitle, in reality, was just a mere mouthpiece, yapping away at Gussie. What he said really had no bearing on the final decision. Dean was letting him play the role of a stalking horse, sort of a legman, who gets the information the boss wants.

Gussie sat in his chair, hands folded in his lap, stoic, looking at Robitle, listening to each word, absorbing them, and waiting for his turn to defend himself. Robitle finished the conversation as he looked at Dean's face, and he got that slight nod of Dean's head, signaling to him to get quiet and sit still, which he did.

Turning his body so it faced Dean and Jimmy, Gussie started his rebuttal. He was an old war horse, a veteran in the Outfit's ways. For all it was worth, he would try to let Dean know he was not going down without a fight.

"I've started a high stakes poker game at the Star-Lite Motel," Gussie said. "It's going to be bringing in bigger money for my street crew. These are some high rolling Vegas guys who are looking for some local action besides their Vegas trips. I'll have one of my guys at the Star-Lite, and he'll take ten percent off the top of the pot, each and every time. Next month, my numbers will be up just based on the Star-Lite gambling," he said.

Dean listened, but didn't comment one way or the other, just looked at Gussie, peering at him, waiting to hear what else he had to say.

"I've had the boys do more auto thefts; the better cars—Buicks, Cadillacs, and maybe a sports car, when possible," as he tried to make a joke. "I told them to stay away from the poor man's cars—Chevys and Fords." Neither Dean nor Jimmy laughed.

"Once we get the cars, we take them to Vinnie Ignato's chop shop, where they are fixed up to be sold down South," Gussie said.

From my experiences with chop shops, stolen high-end Chevys and Fords were better sold cars in the South than Buicks and Cadillacs.

"Cars in the chop shop are given new State of Illinois plates that are gotten through a contact in the Secretary of State's office that steals them, and is paid so much per plate he steals. Once the cars are driven down South, the plates are removed before the cars are sold. A phony registration is set up in Illinois so everything is bogus from the start. A highly mixed sulfuric acid is used to burn off the vehicle identification number (VIN).

"Stolen tires are put on the car, and whatever maintenance is needed is done on the car, usually it's also painted another color. Then presto, like it came off the assembly line in Detroit, it is driven to Kentucky, Tennessee, Alabama, or somewhere else in the South, and the car is dropped off at a mob-controlled used car lot where the car is sold to some unassuming customer.

Chop shops are a very lucrative business, but the nature of their business requires more time to ultimately get the money back to Chicago. While Gussie paints a brighter picture in terms of bringing in more revenue from a chop shop operation, and the numbers might reflect increases down the road, Jimmy knows Dean wants action now. Down the road is down the road.

"Look, Gussie," Jimmy said, "you need to raise the juice." In loan-sharking or shylocking, whichever you prefer, the interest on the loan is known as the juice.

Generally, gambling and loan-sharking walk down the aisle hand-in-hand, as the gamblers need money to support their gambling habit, so they visit a loan shark to get the dough. However, I can tell you this for a fact; you get business guys who, maybe, for some reason have a bad credit rating or also cannot get a bank loan, who visit loan sharks.

Loan-sharking is not confined to a specific element of people. If you need money, the sharks, they're there for you. The juice you will have to pay far exceeds the principal of the loan. Hey, beggars can't be choosers, right?

Guys that need quick money, for whatever reason, come to loan sharks. Maybe they have over extended their credit, credit cards are maxed out; maybe they've been playing the big shot role, living beyond their means, trying to impress their honey, but they come, needing money.

There are some guys who have champagne taste on the beer salary, and when the beer goes flat, they got a problem. Believe me they always walk in the door knowing full well the situation in which they have put themselves. There are no surprises in the loan-sharking business; we give, you better pay, or else.

"What are you charging on your loans?" Jimmy asked Gussie.

"Well, the basic six for five; once the juice is over ten Gs, I add a couple of points," Gussie said.

"Start charging three points on five Gs and up," Jimmy said.

Dean liked what he heard. You could see in his face the look of financial fear evaporate into a slight feel good smile. *Nah, Jimmy is making the Outfit world right*, Dean's thinking.

"Good plan, Jimmy," Dean said. "Yeah, I like it. The other things, they'll come into play later, but the juice will pour quicker for us right now."

"The business guys, Gussie, who you deal with, when they can't pay the juice, what are you doing, a 60/40 split if they have to make you their partner?" Jimmy questioned.

"Yeah, I do a 60/40 split if they can't pay the juice, then I become a silent partner, of course, getting the 60. They get the 40 and still run their business. I don't know a fuckin' thing about their businesses, and I don't want to know. All I want is the money owed to me from the businesses," Gussie replied.

"Well," Jimmy said, "make it a 70/30 split on their business. We'll just bleed the business until we get our money. Who knows, maybe this guy can run a business on his thirty percent. I mean, I guess it could happen. If he owns a building, factory, or warehouse where he runs his business out of, we'll burn the place down at the end to get the insurance money. We can get Harry "The Bomber" Sarcino to light it up and…poof…like magic, we make the place disappear," Jimmy said.

Dean's face had that stoked smile painted from ear-to-ear, getting brighter and brighter, the more he digested Jimmy's plan. Dean's eyes were illuminated now with total brightness. Gussie thought he would now be back in Dean's good graces, as he would follow Jimmy's plan.

"Okay, Jimmy, thanks for the help. Yeah and, Dean, you'll see...next month will look better," Gussie said, as everyone rose from their chairs.

"Yeah, Gussie, I feel it's better already," Dean said, as everyone shook hands and started to leave.

Gussie got in his car. Timmy, Dean, and Jimmy walked to their cars, which were parked directly behind the Chateau D'Ville. As Timmy opened the door of the black Cadillac that he drove to the meeting, Dean turned to him. Jimmy stood off to the side.

"Timmy, start looking for Gussie's replacement. Let me know who you have in mind," Dean said.

"Right, boss," Timmy countered with.

"See ya, Jimmy. Thanks, as always. You pulled the chestnuts out of the fire," Dean said.

Jimmy wondered at what point Timmy would be looking for Jimmy's replacement. With the Outfit, job security could be good for 24 hours. You gotta stay on your toes with these boys, as you never can tell what might happen.

In the corporate world, the executives would have been pleased that Gussie would be implementing a plan. He would be told, "We'll meet again in six months and review your status." In the Outfit world, good plans do not always equate with a good standing with your boss, as he has other plans for you.

"You see, Bobby, gambling and loan-sharking are married. Each one is the other's partner for life. They never get divorced or live separate lives. They live on and on, decade after decade, as if they remain eternally young," Jimmy said.

"In Chicago, Bobby, we have a certain way we do loan-sharking. Now, most guys generally do six for five, which means that if a guy comes to us and wants to borrow, say, five hundred dollars, we charge six hundred dollars of interest. That's where you get the six for five," he said. "So, the next week, the guy owes us eleven hundred dollars principal plus the juice, I mean the interest. Follow me so far?" Jimmy said.

"So far," I said.

"You can also go seven for five, which is the same as six for five, except the juice is higher. I mean, interest," he said.

"You can say juice. That's what it is," I said.

"Okay, okay, I'll stick with juice. No reason to be skipping back and forth on the term," he said.

"No, okay, getting back to the guy who owes eleven hundred bucks, he ain't going to have the eleven hundred the next week. I mean, if he's borrowing five hundred plus the juice, how in the hell by the next week is he going to pay back eleven hundred? It ain't gonna happen. So, now we know we got the guy and we start piling on the juice," Jimmy said.

"So now the guy is told the following week his eleven hundred dollar loan is going to be twenty three hundred dollars. The juice is now twelve hundred added to the eleven hundred, making the total twenty three hundred up to that point. You still are working on the six for five, but as the total loan jumps higher each week it ain't paid, the juice doubles each week. The juice is always higher than the principle. So by the third week, the loan goes from twenty three hundred dollars to forty seven hundred. The juice is twenty four hundred.

"You follow me, Bobby? See what I'm saying? I mean, if you got a question, just say so," Jimmy said.

"I'm okay. I'm following what you're saying," I said. *Boy, this is sure different than learning multiplication tables*, I thought.

"Here are some other ways guys loan money out," Jimmy said. "For starters, on the original five hundred dollars, you can go six for five with two points, meaning the points are a percentage, so two points is two percent. So the loan is six for five with two points. In this case the two percent is added to the original principal; same thing for seven for five with two points.

"Also, you can just go straight points. Say a five hundred dollar loan is five points or five percent, which would be five percent juice each week added to the total each week." As Jimmy spoke, he rattled off the numbers in almost one continuous breath.

"Now, Bobby, to make a loan really grow," and Jimmy stood up from his chair, lifted his arms up from his sides, palms turned over facing up, he raised the palms upward, "you add points once the loan is at a certain number," he said. "Once a loan is, let's say, at ten thousand dollars or 10 Gs, you add maybe three or four more points of juice to be figured in each week, which is added to the doubling of the juice, which still happens each week.

"Bingo...the loan starts growing faster each week than weeds in the grass in the backyard," Jimmy said, with a slow rising smile crossing his face.

"Anything you want to ask? I mean...you know...I threw a lot of numbers at you, and...uh, uh...if you got a question, just ask," Jimmy said, shrugging his shoulders.

Here I was thinking very well, maybe a few Outfit guys would finish high school, most dropped out when they were 16, which is the legal age in the Chicago Public School system to drop out. Yet, here they were, like fuckin' Albert Einstein when it came to these juice numbers.

They keep this stuff in their heads, rolling it out time after time, as you can see, client after client, but really victim after victim. *Though really, these guys were adults, and know what the story is when they come in for a loan,* I thought.

One thing with the Outfit, they don't go door to door looking for business, making cold calls. People always come to them, so if you go to a loan shark, it's really 'buyer beware.' And if you're not aware, they will make sure you are aware. They are the educators in Real Life 101. Their class assignment is simply pay or else. The 'or else' is planted in the client's brain in the first five minutes of the conversation.

The or else will be diagrammed very vividly so the client will sit frozen in his chair; his blood, for the moment, getting thinner. I often felt that some guys liked to talk about the or else more than the conditions of the loan. It was the oral fine print to which the client better listen.

The or else was more than we'll break your legs. It was dropping in the conversation the mentioning of the names of your wife and kids. "Oh, by the way, how are they doing?" you would be asked. The Outfit let you know they would make it personal if they didn't get their money. That was the or else part the client clearly understood.

Usually the client would try and pay something each week, though the loan would continue to swell week after week. I mean, this is where I saw guys with businesses lose them to the shark. The loans got too high, and the client's only resolution was to give up a percentage of his business.

Once in a while, a shark would take jewelry or rare coins in lieu of a cash payment. Most guys, in the case of jewelry, didn't take it too often as it meant you had to fence the jewelry to convert it to cash. Sharks wanted cash, as you got to remember, the street crew members had to be paid, and their pay came from criminal activities such as loan-sharking.

I remember seeing a $10,000 loan grow to $300,000, and it was paid off. Not by the client. No, the guy's father liquidated all of his stock and bond investments to pay for his kid's gambling habit. The poor father, and that's what he became as he only had his Social Security checks to support him and his wife after cashing out the investments and giving the money to his son.

How does a fuckin' son do that to his father? I mean, I understand the father's point. He's afraid his kid will get beaten up, so he coughs up the dough to help his son. I get all that, but I mean, damn, let the sorry-ass kid take a beating. Here you are, working your ass off for maybe 40 years or more, you invest your hard-earned money to put you on Easy Street when you retire. You and the missus plan on getting away to Florida for a couple of weeks each year in the dead of a Chicago winter, using the retirement money. Now, here comes your asshole son, who by the way, was in his mid-40s, not some kid, but an adult who screws up your life forever.

I hope he at least said thank you, Dad, and gave him a hug with meaning behind it. I know someday I'll be a parent and have kids, but if my son ever gets involved with a shark, he's on the island by himself, and he better figure out how to get to the mainland. If you call me, sonny boy, it's going to be, "I can't hear you. We must have a bad connection." Then I'll hang up, and no money, not one goddam cent, will be sent to you.

Jesus, I pray I have girls. I know they give you other problems, but at least they don't get involved from a loan standpoint with sharks. I never saw a shark have a woman as a client.

"Now, Bobby, when a guy don't pay on his loan, we have, uh, guys who pay him a visit to see why he ain't paying," Jimmy said. "They're called juice collectors. I mean, they're told what the guy owes, and how if he ain't paying anything, even a hundred a week or something, then we gotta know what's going on," he said.

"In some crews, Bobby, and this is not for every crew, there's a set-up man. He goes along with the juice collector, the muscle, but when they get to the client's house, he leaves the juice collector in the car.

"He goes into the client's house, and I'm telling you, Bobby, some of these guys could win an Academy Award for the acting job they do. They'll walk in all nice and syrupy, sweetness, dropping drop by drop from their throat up through their lips, words coming out that give the client the feeling he will only see bright sunshine in his life.

"'I'm here to help you,' they start out by saying with a programmed 'I'm your friend' smile cemented on their faces. I mean, this is Sales 101—always have a smile on your face. A client can't turn down a smile.

"'We've got this slight…uh…slight problem. No big deal here, not something we can't work out, right, Mr. So and So?' the actor says. 'Now, I know you can't pay the whole loan. My boss knows that if by some miracle you can do that, it would be just wonderful. So, let's figure out, you and me, just how we are going to start to lower the debt ever so slowly,' the loan actor says. 'Maybe, with a tiny bit more effort, you can raise that number in the coming weeks. I know you will really try hard to raise the number even by a few dollars, but this is a great, great start.'

"If the client doesn't give a number, starts to talk around it, says he'll try, but does not commit to a number, then the actor takes the discussion in a different direction.

"Ever so gently he says to the client, 'Come over here to your door,' and the client gets up from his chair and walks over to the door. The actor opens the door and puts his right arm around the client's right shoulder, still keeping that folksy front going with an 'I'm your friend' smile on his face.

"When the door of the house opens, that's the signal for the big bruiser to get out of the car. He stands in front of the car, hands folded in front of him in a downward position, and since it's daytime, he puts on his sunglasses. The juice collector strikes a menacing pose, jaw clenched, body pointing right in the direction of the client, ready to unleash its fury once he's told to do so.

"There's no body language suggesting any warmth coming from the juice collector's body. His body language puts forward the need to be fed violence through the absorption of punches, kicks, maybe the use of a baseball bat or lead pipe to the body of the client. The beating of the client, for now, will feed the violent antagonistic nature these men possess. It will fill up the body, calm it, let it kick back and enjoy the brutality of one human being pounding another human being into submission. The fullness in the body will last until the next beating is required to keep the wild animal content.

"Today, the juice collector is a prop, just part of the act. Just give it your Hollywood tough guy look today, but no action will be forthcoming from you. Your belly will not be filled today.

"'See that guy out there?' the actor points with his left index finger raised, pointing to the juice collector, still keeping his right arm around the client's shoulder. 'Now, Mr. So and So, if we can't work out a number, and I really believe we can, I know some guys need to think it over, but we need to agree on a number, otherwise that guy in front of the car will be coming to see you next week by himself.' The juice collector raises his right arm and makes a fist with his right hand. Looking at the client, he takes his right fist, brings up his left arm and slowly taps his right fist into the palm of his left hand. The or else will commence, and it will stop only when I say it stops.

"'I don't think you'll want to see him, because there will be no conversation with him,' the actor says. 'So let's go back into your very nice house, sit on the couch, and work out a number, okay?'

"At this point, a shaken client, head down, bowing to the Outfit demands, walks into his house as the actor still keeps his right arm around the client's shoulder. As the actor closes the door with his left hand, he smiles at Mr. Violence in front of the car. The smile says everything is okay.

"The client and the actor work out a number. The actor shakes hands with the client, and leaves with the juice collector to play his role for the next client.

"Bobby, the fear of fear is the greatest tool one person has over another. Once you have a person afraid, and by subtly easing his family into the conversation, the fear heightens. Then, you have control over the person and you will get him to do what you want him to do.

"Like I said, not every street crew has a set-up man. Some just send the juice collector out to the client," Jimmy said. "The juice collector is always aware that the purpose is to get the client to pay on the loan. If you beat him, he might not be able to work to earn money to make some type of payment."

"So they role play," I said.

"Yes, but they're the bad cop. There is no good cop, so they have to put fear into the client very directly. So the juice collector uses vile, tough talk first to scare the client into paying," Jimmy said. "Yeah, yeah, sure clients do get smacked around, even beaten at times, to get the point across," he said. "Examples have to be made so other clients will react in fear, but the boss wants to see money, so the juice collector has still gotta bring home the bacon. So the juice collector plays a role to see how far he's gotta go," Jimmy said.

Nearly twenty-five years later, the Feds offered a guy the opportunity to enter the Witness Relocation Program if he would cooperate with the Feds and allow them to make audio and videotapes of the conversations between him and a juice collector discussing payment of a loan.

This client, like most of the other clients, would never be able to pay back the full amount of the loan. The juice would be way too much on top of the principal to allow a completed payment.

The client, fearing for his life and his family's lives, accepted the Fed's offer and eventually he would testify in a trial. With audio and videotapes and hearing the client corroborate what a jury heard and saw, the Feds got their conviction as the jury found the juice collector guilty of extortion.

For the client, though, it meant having to relocate to a new area and be given a new identity. If the guy had a young family, it was tough as the kids were pulled out of school. The guy would be leaving his mom and dad, sisters, brothers, cousins, and friends all behind him, not being allowed to communicate with them. His wife would have to leave behind her family and friends.

The Witness Relocation Program is run by the United States Marshal's Office. When someone goes into the program, they are assigned an FBI handler to ease them into their new environment.

I know what you're thinking, and I was thinking that myself. Isn't a guy still in danger? Won't someone come looking for him? From my experience knowing people in the program, you're okay as long as you stay in the program. If you leave the program, then you might be vulnerable to be harmed.

Guys you have testified against either die in prison, or if they do get out, are old and have no more members in a street crew left to go after you.

Let's face it; a lot of people don't like change. I don't like change myself, so pulling up stakes is not an easy thing for people in the program to do, especially if they're close to their family. On the other hand, you have no choice, because if you stay in Chicago, you and your family are a target.

You are assisted in getting a job as the Feds aren't going to pay your freight forever, so they have to get you situated with work. The program relocates the client, or anyone else who enters the program, to areas west of the Mississippi River. You could be in Austin, Texas; Phoenix, Arizona; Tacoma, Washington; Boise, Idaho; Sacramento, California; or anywhere else the Feds want you to go. No one was ever sent out East. Like you're going to send a Chicago guy to New York? Yeah, right.

Once in the program, you have to learn your new name. I remember when Sal Cilintro entered the program, he had to write his new name on a piece of paper and keep it in his wallet so he could take a peek once in a while to remember his new name.

The Feds keep tabs on you, especially during the first year. For some Outfit guys, leaving their former profession back home could mean looking to continue a similar lifestyle somewhere else. You would be surprised how many Italian guys get Irish names. Though, did Sal Cilintro really look like Jimmy O'Brien? Yeah, in your dreams.

Maybe because there are so many Irish men and women in law enforcement, maybe the Feds feel Irish names like O'Brien, O'Malley, Fitzpatrick, Hogan, McDougal, McCormick, O'Farrell, etc. would put you on the righteous road and cleanse your soul of all its misgivings, and you would then walk the line of the straight, virtuous. Well, it could happen, right?

"This law they passed, this RICO law, Bobby, you're going to see a lot of rats now, guys are going to rat out other guys to get less time," Jimmy said.

"Remember what I'm telling you. If someone goes to jail, you tell their family he's going to college. You never, ever say he's going to jail. It's always he's going to college. You got it?" he said.

"Yeah, I got it," I said.

"Well, now with this RICO thing, I dunno what you really can say. I mean, you can't say he's going to college. He's leaving Chicago for good if he rats out a guy," Jimmy said.

"It's just, Jesus, this is going to make an impact. I know you always had to watch guys, keep an eye on them, but now you can't trust anyone," he said. "It's a changing world, Bobby. You gotta adjust and adapt to what's going on around you," Jimmy said.

The RICO Act, formally known as the Racketeer Influenced Corruption Organizations Act was passed in 1970 by Congress. While the law's intentions were to prosecute the Mob, the Feds have used RICO to prosecute non-Mob people in other job titles in the business world. While RICO prosecutions are known for criminal prosecutions, a person can be charged in a civil case. The award could be as high as triple the amount of the original lawsuit if a party is found guilty.

Federal prosecutors now armed with RICO could build racketeering cases by putting under that racketeering umbrella gambling, loan-sharking, extortion, money laundering, conspiracy to commit murder and other criminal activities. Racketeering is when one extorts money or advantages through threats of violence, blackmail, or by unlawful interference with business or employment.

Sounds like we're looking at the Outfit's playbook. So, for you people, when asked what racketeering is answered all of the above, meaning gambling, loan-sharking, etc., you guys get a gold star. For the others of you who didn't answer correctly, well, you'll just have to go to summer school.

The penalties under RICO are stiffer—more prison time and, if convicted, you have to serve 85% of your time. If you get convicted of murder, then under RICO, it's life, no parole. Hell, I should have become a lawyer.

Jimmy was right. In years to come, RICO created a lot more rats, maybe as many rats as the guys the Feds were going after.

"You see, Bobby, it's the old story—if you throw enough darts at the board, something's gotta stick. This is what the Feds try and do with RICO. They figure if we charge a guy with enough counts, something's gotta stick for a conviction," Jimmy said.

Shortly after RICO became law, Gino "Big Gino" Camolli, when he was being arrested by the FBI and was told he was being charged under RICO, asked the FBI agent, "Who's Mr. RICO?"

Often juice collectors were doubling as contract killers. Guys such as Wally Grabac, Larry "Larry the Piano" Scabullo, Gaetano Ponsieto, Phillip "Philly Dog" Drave, and others of their ilk would wear a juice collector's hat, and then flip it off to put on their hired killer hat when appropriate.

"Was the reason these guys did juice collections that there were not enough hits to be done?" I asked Jimmy.

"Yeah, Bobby. It's not like you go to the office at 9:00 A.M. and the boss says, 'Today, Bobby, you will be assigned a hit to do.' Guys have to do juice because, in reality, a hit will occur infrequently as you don't always know when it's going to happen. It depends. Some years more guys get whacked than others," he said.

"You can't figure what your income is going to be from year to year solely based on murders," he said. "You need a steadier income. Guy's got bills to pay, families to support, so juice provides the bridge until a hit comes along. Sure, guys can get a no-show city, county, state, or union job, but a lot of these guys aren't even cut out for that," Jimmy said. "They're only good for working the street," he said.

"Look, a guy, if he's lucky, might be in the life, you know, thirty, forty years. Who knows, maybe longer, and maybe he's done, let's say for the sake of this conversation, twenty hits. Some guys might do more, some less, so figure it maybe they don't even do one a year over their Outfit lifetime," Jimmy said.

"There's plenty of guys doing hits, so he ain't the only game in town. There's competition. In setting a price, sometimes you get a guy who really needs the dough, so if you tell him five Gs, he's okay with it. Other guys try and bump you up another five or ten Gs. They got to be careful, too. I mean, if I go back to Dean and tell him Wally Grabac wants, say, ten Gs more than what Dean wants me to pay him, you know what Dean will say. 'Fuck him; tell him this is what he gets. This piece of shit who we're whacking is only worth what we tell you he's worth, and tell him a hit can go both ways,'" Jimmy said.

"Bobby, I would never tell Wally the last part of what Dean said, because I don't want him looking over his shoulder. Then he's not concentrating on the job he's supposed to do, and we can all get fucked up," Jimmy said. "I'll just tell him the price, and if he's still unhappy, I'll say, 'Wally, no hard feelings. I'll look for someone else.' Then he'll counter with, 'No, no, Jimmy. It's okay. Sure, I can live with that price.'

"Wally knows he doesn't want to be a pain in the ass," Jimmy said. "Then no one will want to hire him for a hit, and bang, there goes the extra five or ten Gs he would have gotten. Pretty soon someone will say, 'Why do we need this guy at all,' and bang, the order's given on Wally. Bye, bye, Wally," Jimmy said.

Grabac, like others in the profession of murder, could care less about taking the life of some guy destroying the life of his family…in effect, killing them emotionally.

"Once a guy, Bobby, pulls the trigger on someone the first time, every time after that is routine," Jimmy said. "Murder becomes like brushing your teeth every morning. Oh yeah, you want me to kill someone? Sure, sure, fine. I'll just follow the normal routine like I always do with these guys," he said.

To Grabac, murder was a job, just like collecting juice. Grabac was a frozen, solid, cold-blooded, mean, stubborn, ruthless son of a bitch, who feared no one. He was the type of person who needed to be caged twenty-four hours a day so he would never, ever have the opportunity to hurt someone.

When I was 12 years old, Jimmy sent me out with Wally on a juice loan collection. By the age of 12, I had gone out on twenty-five to thirty juice loan collections with many more to come. I already had the questions memorized that would be asked. I had seen quite a bit of pain inflicted in some of the previous collections. The beatings were often vicious, more than a couple of punches thrown.

In the beginning, my body became physically distressed, especially when seeing the blood. I would feel nauseous, edgy, my t-shirt mopping up the sweat beads running for their lives from my pores, a vibrating heart of an anvil slugging my brain. As I would go out again and again on juice collections, my body toughened up.

My body felt that boot camp was over and I could begin to handle the emotional stress better each time I went out. I reached a point where I became indifferent, rather callous to what I was seeing. Another beating was becoming another beating.

Though most of the clients got the verbal message real quick and made arrangements to pay something, when this happened, the hormones in my body jumped out of the pew screaming hallelujah, hallelujah, the Devil has left the building. We'll have peace for another day.

The house Wally and I were going to was in Clayton. Clayton was a suburb northwest of Chicago—an upper middle class community where families were raised far away from the streets of Chicago. Clayton High School would see 90% of its annual graduating class go on to college.

As we drove through the cul-de-sac, I looked at the homes. They were spacious four-bedroom homes that made me wish I lived in one of them. At least, I would have my own bedroom. Well, you can't blame me for wishing.

The house was on a 60-foot lot and set back on the lot away from the street. There were a row of green bushes near the front window on the first floor. From the outside, it looked like the bedrooms were upstairs.

Wally drove into the driveway, which was a shiny, jet black asphalt, slightly winding type of driveway. He parked the car, and we went and knocked on the door. After a couple of knocks, I could see Wally was getting annoyed. He started to rapidly press the doorbell.

"I'm coming. I'm coming," a woman said, as she approached the door. The door opened and a woman with a smile on her face and her belly sticking way out (I don't know how many months pregnant she was, but I guess she didn't have much more time until the baby was due) greeted us. "Can I help you?" she sweetly said.

"Yeah, yeah, I'm looking for Mr. A.," Wally said. I don't really remember the client's name, so he'll be Mr. A.

"Well, he's my husband, and he's at work. Can I help you?" she said in a very innocent way.

"Sure your husband is not home?" Wally questioned her as he walked by her, entering the house. I followed behind and looked at the nice furniture in a spotless house. It was the typical upper middle class suburban dwelling that you see in the Chicago area. Everything in the house appeared to be neat and orderly.

I glanced to my right and noticed a picture of a young bride and groom in the frame perched on a coffee table. I was thinking *how did he get himself caught up in this mess?* Why didn't he think about what his actions would do to his marriage?

"No, he's not home," she said.

"Well, I'll just look around," Wally said, as his eyes started to roam around the first floor of this two story house.

"I just said, he's not home," her voice starting to get firmer.

"He owes money. I'm going to take a look in the kitchen," Wally said, as he started walking to the kitchen. He came back after a few seconds in the kitchen.

"What do you mean he owes money? We pay our bills on time," she blurted out.

Wally started walking through the first floor of the house. He opened a couple of closet doors. *Maybe the guy's hiding in a closet*, Wally's thinking. He didn't find Mr. A. in any of the closets, so he started to trot up the stairs to check the upstairs rooms.

"Sir, sir, I don't know why you are here. My three year old is napping upstairs. Come downstairs right now," she said, bristling at Wally. Her voice had the pay attention to me tone. Wally had his routine on these collections, and no one was going to change his course.

He went upstairs and took a look around, as he wasn't up there for an extended period of time, then trotted down the stairs.

Watching all of this, I was starting to get a bad feeling about what was going to take place in this house. I could smell his scent on the prey, looking for the intended victim.

His eyes were starting to narrow. A major storm was coming. Dark, ominous clouds signaling a storm loomed over the house. His 6' plus, over 200-pound body was getting prepared to telegraph a message. I could just feel it coming.

I had seen Wally in action before, but only with guys; never with a woman. I was preparing myself for the upcoming tornado, but how do you really prepare for it? All you can do is just hopelessly stand on the sidelines and watch another mauling. Maybe, just maybe, he'll believe the wife and we'll get out of here without a physical confrontation.

"Is he in the basement?" Wally asked sharply, in a clipped voice.

"I told you, he's not here. Now, I'm going to call the police," she said. No longer wanting to be part of something she didn't know anything about, she started walking to where the phone was on the kitchen wall. Wally swung into action, grabbing her right shoulder with both hands and flung her down with such a mighty force that she fell on her back so hard, her body bounced and then it settled back on the floor. She was on her back looking into the eyes of God's mistake.

He raised his right foot and started to pump his size 13 foot into her pregnant belly. Her defenseless belly was exposed to his reign of terror. His foot, with each pump, gained speed and momentum—one, two, three, four—I couldn't keep up with the number of times his foot forcefully pressed into her stomach. His foot came crashing down on her belly time and time again.

"Stop, please! Please, stop! Oh God, please stop!" she cried to him between agonizing moans. Her face was getting flushed. The color in her face ran as fast and as hard as it could to get away from this inhumane punishment he was giving her. Fear was frozen in her eyes as she lay on her back.

I couldn't believe what I was seeing. A lady, a pregnant lady, face contorting with pain. God, where are you? Save her!

He drew his foot back, cocked it, and then he fired a burst of kicks in staccato-like fashion into her stomach. Her belly was shaking from this rampage. Then he paused for maybe a couple of seconds, and he continued his machine gun-like, short kicks, again and again into her flesh. Her banshee-like screams reverberated throughout the house. I looked away as it became too painful for me to watch. My stomach was tied up in a million knots as my stomach acid was gurgling.

Wally's face looked like one of those scary, very menacing Halloween masks. His face was boiling with rage—red-faced, eyes enlarged—so intimidating, they made you ask for permission to live; a menacing body language coming at you for your final existence as a human being. The full fury of his explosive temper raging was now out in full force for all to see.

He stopped kicking her as the rage in his body had reached its destination. The bus made its final stop. He looked at her; didn't say a word, just looked at her.

She lay on the ground, carnage beaten by the conqueror as blood started to seep out of the right corner of her mouth, while moaning for help that would come from no one.

The blood came out very slowly as if it was trying to make sure the rage was really over. The droplets of blood carefully and cautiously oozed out into the light of day. Each droplet looked at another as if to ask, is it safe to come out? "Yeah, it looks safe. Just be careful," one said to the other.

I stood there motionless. I felt like a freakin' zombie in a horror movie; except this was not a movie, it was real life Outfit in action. Nothing moved in my body, not one blink of an eye or muscle in my leg; not a damn thing moved or was close to moving in my entire shell-shocked body.

Finally, my brain, which went through an internal apocalypse diagnostic checklist, relayed the message the rest of the body wanted to hear, "We're safe. We're okay, start your body functions effective immediately."

As Wally went to check the basement for any sign of Mr. A., I looked down at her. Her breathing was heavy, grabbing for air. I thought *was the baby okay?* Who the hell knew at this point?

I turned and ran to the bathroom on the first floor. I took a towel and ran a few drops of cold water on it and ran back to her. I had never seen anything like this in my life. Who does this to a woman, forget about her being pregnant? This is a woman, no explanation needed; you don't act violently to a woman.

"My baby, my baby," her voice getting louder with each call to her child. I bent down and wiped the blood away from the corner of her mouth. "Take very slow breaths. Just breathe slowly," I said to her as I tried to calm her down, fearing if she started to scream again Wally would come back, and the 'Wally Show' would begin again.

I held her left hand with my right. I dabbed the corner of her mouth where the blood was coming from with the towel using my left hand. While speaking slowly, trying to comfort and assure her that everything was going to be okay, she looked at me with those dull brown, lifeless eyes, not speaking to me at all. I looked, but I didn't want to look at her stomach. The skin was crimson red, extremely lacerated. You could see bruises and welts. If this was how the outside of her body looked, what was the inside of her body like? The thought was too horrific to imagine.

I worried even more about the baby's health. I wondered how did the baby survive this violent tornado, which came rushing at it? Maybe a better question was, is the baby still alive?

Her breathing got better. The breaths became longer, more sustainable as she followed my instructions. She was in serious, obvious pain; her face grimaced with even the slightest movement in her body.

At this point, I didn't know what to expect. When Wally came back, would we just leave or would the violence start all over again? Would he kick her? Would he choke her? Would he punch her? Just wondering what this psychotic bastard would do next gave me a nervous, uncertain, jagged feeling throughout my body.

As I looked at her, and thought about what I had just seen one human being—or so-called human being—physically do to another human being, the reason for all this mayhem popped into my head. It wasn't about her husband owing money. It was Wally, simply put, liked what he was doing. He got his kicks, his own personal high from hurting people. Violence was Wally's drug. When he got it, he liked the high it gave him.

He would probably commit the act of violence, the terrorizing, the beating, instilling a calculated fear in the person's soul that never would be deleted…all of these things for free. Yeah, he would do all this for free, just to satisfy a warped, disturbed behavior that not only would inflict pain, but to satisfy a thirst in his soul to pillage a person's body so his own ego would sit on the Outfit's throne as the high and mighty. The hearing of his name or seeing his face would impact a victim to pay whatever they owed to avoid his evil conduct, and keep their medical costs down.

In my lifetime, I've known a lot of Wally Grabac's. And no, it's not just a job for them. They might say that, which they often did. It was that these juice collectors and contract killers were sick, perverted, mentally unstable people, who got one big old-fashioned high by doing what they did for a living.

Someone's life meant nothing to them. Someone's family and the turmoil they caused for that family meant nothing to them. Only the fact that they deemed themselves the Outfit's anointed 'almighty' to do whatever they wanted, to whomever they wanted mattered to them.

Yeah, who in their right mind is going to kick a pregnant woman in the stomach? Who in their right mind hits a woman, period?

I folded the towel so I could put it under the lady's head for some elevation. I thought maybe it would help her body relax a bit.

"Okay, okay, let's go," Wally said, as he came back to me, not even looking at the carnage he left behind. Now the rush was on to get out of the house, which we did. The calmness in his voice was amazing to me. I learned these animals of the wild streets of Chicago could turn the violence switch off just as easily as they could turn it on.

When we got inside the car, Wally put both hands on the steering wheel after putting the key in the ignition.

He turned and looked at me. He had his 'Gee, did I do something wrong?' look on his face. "What did ya see?" he said, looking straight in my eyes. His pupils were sharpening. There was still a little smoldering of violence in them.

"You were being polite to her, just asking a few questions," I said passively, as I didn't want to ignite a violent spark in those eyes.

"Nothing else? You didn't see nothing else?" he asked quickly, spitting out the words.

"No, nothing that I can recall. You know, when women are pregnant, they have good days and bad days," I guess I said to him.

"I guess," he said with a sigh, his voice dropping in tone, sounding like a traditional 'whatever' type of response that someone says when they don't know what else to say. Then he started the car, and we pulled away from the curb. From that point until he dropped me off at the apartment, the subject of what occurred at the woman's house was put on the shelf. He didn't talk about it as I sat in the car looking out the side window, wondering if I was ever going to be a kid, or had I hopscotched into adulthood.

I don't know whatever happened to the woman, her baby, or what her husband said when he found out what happened to her. The police were never called as Wally was never arrested. Oh yeah, there's one small, minor, insignificant detail to this story. The guy increased his weekly juice payment. I wonder why?

Being in the life was not for the faint of heart, do-gooders, or anyone else with kindness in their soul. Only evil filled out the application form.

Eight months after Gussie Balencenti's management review, Tim Robitle was now ready to tell Dean Dragonetti, who he would recommend to replace Gussie. After doing an exhaustive search and reviewing the candidate's credentials, as Tim put it, he was ready to make his recommendation. Drum roll please. It turned out to be Tim Robitle. Wow, what a surprise, huh? Like saying it never snows in Chicago.

Gussie, while all of this management maneuvering was going on, figured during these past months his numbers improved enough to put him in better standing with Dean. Dean played the Outfit's game of let Gussie think he was on better terms, allowing the months to go by, but Dean's mind was made up eight months ago that Gussie would go. He could care less, at this point, what Gussie's numbers looked like.

"You see, Bobby, Timmy is a lieutenant for Dean, so if he's looking to move up higher in the organization, he's got to run a street crew," Jimmy said. "Can he run a crew well? That's another story," Jimmy sarcastically chuckled. "Being a lieutenant to a capo is like being a street consultant, in a way," he said.

"I mean, the boss tells you what he wants you to do, then you go out and everyone on the street knows that whatever they got to do is coming from the boss. So, you go into a situation, and like a consultant, you make recommendations," Jimmy said. "Then you leave it up to whomever you're talking to, to do or not to do what you've recommended. If that guy doesn't do what you recommend to him, which is coming directly from the boss, he's in the jackpot, not you," he said.

"Running a street crew is different. You call the shots," Jimmy said. "You're not the lieutenant; you're the guy sending the lieutenant on the street with some type of order. You're now responsible for everyone in the crew. You can't walk away if you don't like something," Jimmy said. "You gotta be able to straighten something out when it needs to be straightened out."

"If you got what it takes to be boss, it'll show. And if not, it'll show that, too," he said. "If you run a good crew, and you're a good earner, the higher ups will take notice and you will find yourself in their good graces, which means you'll get more from them," Jimmy said. "Maybe you'll get more territory, more authority over things. You see, the more they trust you, the closer you get to the inner circle.

"But you gotta remember, Bobby," Jimmy said, pointing his right index finger at me, "the elevator goes down as quickly as it goes up." He said, "If you screw up on something, or the higher ups are unhappy with the way the money is coming from the street crew, or some other reason, you will wind up being in the jackpot like Gussie." Jimmy continued, "The Outfit doesn't look kindly on someone they are unhappy with. They don't give out too many second chances."

Dean, Timmy, and Jimmy met at Roll-On Bowling Alley, a twenty-four hour, seven day a week bowling alley, open even on Christmas Day. The place later became a discount store, and I think it's a beauty supply store today. It was a Tuesday night, and Timmy made his case to Dean about replacing Gussie. Dean listened as Timmy told Dean he would bring the numbers up to Dean's satisfaction. He would be more aggressive than Gussie in finding additional revenue sources.

After Timmy finished, Dean looked at Jimmy for some guidance. When a boss gives the eye to the consigliere, it means the boss isn't buying what someone is trying to sell him. "Timmy, sit here. I want to talk over a couple of things with Jimmy," Dean said. Dean and Jimmy got up and walked to a backroom that was next to where the brooms, mops, and cleaning supplies were kept.

"What da ya think, Jimmy?" Dean asked. Now Jimmy knew he had to choose his words very, very carefully. He had to be careful and cautious, because if he talked negatively about Timmy, and Dean didn't make Timmy the boss of the street crew, then Timmy would know what came from Jimmy was the reason why he didn't become the boss. Timmy then would be out to go gunning for Jimmy to prove to Dean he could do the job.

Jimmy's life would be on the line. Since the Outfit plays with two-headed coins, the other side of the coin is Jimmy has to be careful as maybe Dean likes Timmy and wants to make him the boss of the street crew. Either way, Jimmy has to watch his words with extreme care.

"Timmy's been your lieutenant for, what, 14 years? He started out as a driver, and he did work his way up with you," Jimmy said. "I mean, of course, until someone gets the job, you don't know how they're going to perform. The only thing, Dean, is that Timmy was never made; he was not a member of the Outfit. He was an associate," he said.

To be a made member of the Outfit, there's a requirement that both of your parents have to be Italian 100%; no half Italian, just 100%. Then someone will sponsor you and you go through the ceremony. Jimmy never could become a made member, because his parents were not Italian. Timmy, while having both of his parents being Italian, was never sponsored by Dean to get made.

There is no timetable on when to be made. It could happen in your 20s, 40s, even 50s. There have been street crews run by non-made guys, but the respect of the crew toward the boss is a lot different if he's made, which is the point Jimmy was making. They gotta perform regardless if the boss is made or not, but it's the way they perform that matters.

At one time, to get made, you had to make bones. That meant you had to kill someone to show that if you had to kill, you could. Later on, guys became made members without having to kill anyone.

I know this is going to sound crazy, but sometimes in a rare instance, guys would be riding in a car, and they would give a prospective made member a gun and tell him to go shoot that guy walking down the street. The car would stop, the guy would get out, and some unsuspecting guy just walking home maybe from work who had no beef with anyone was whacked. The shooter would grab the dead guy's wallet and watch to make it look like a robbery.

This was not a common practice to shoot a stranger. Generally, to make bones you had to kill someone who, somehow, was involved with Outfit business. In killing a stranger, you didn't actually know who the stranger was. You might be killing someone who has juice, who should not have been killed.

So, the Outfit tried to avoid killing strangers, though there were times when it did happen. There was a rule in the Outfit that you didn't shoot cops and kids. They were on the endangered species list, but if a guy wanted to, he would kill either one, but strictly at his own risk. No one supported killing cops or kids in the Outfit.

"Look, Dean, I think, and it's your decision as always, but make Timmy an acting boss, see how it goes. If he works out, then if you want, you could have Timmy made, so he could become a member of the Outfit. Then you could remove the acting title and make him the boss of the crew," Jimmy said.

From experience, Jimmy knew with the Outfit you had to make sure north connected with south, and east connected with west. If something wasn't connecting, you had to find out why. When dealing with the Outfit, you were always on a slippery slope, and they made sure there was enough grease on the slope so your footing was not stable.

"Right, right. I agree, that's how we'll handle Timmy," Dean said.

"This way, too, the crew will feel that if they can work with Timmy, they'll deliver for him. And if everything works out okay, then Timmy's the right man for the job. But, in the back of the crew's minds, if things aren't working out, they'll think he's only acting anyways, he's not the boss," Jimmy said.

"So this way, if Timmy doesn't work out, you can justify getting rid of him, and the crew will say, 'The higher ups see what we see,'" Jimmy said.

"We've whacked guys before without justifying it," Dean said.
"Yeah, I know. That's true, but you ran a crew, I was a crew member at one time, and the thing is you want to have the money flowing from the crew's activities," Jimmy said. "The Outfit is always in the black. We are never in the red," Jimmy said.

"If guys are moaning and bitching among themselves about the boss, they can lose the edge on the street," said Jimmy. "It's like the water from Lake Michigan, it's gotta flow nice and smooth, no choppiness, just a nice smooth flow all the way down the lake. "You don't want guys losing their edge," he said.

Dean paused as he took a few steps walking in the supply room area and turned his back on Jimmy. "Yeah, if the guys are unhappy, we get fucked up on the street, and that creates a problem," he said, still not facing Jimmy. Turning to face Jimmy, he said, "I'm giving you the order on Gussie. We'll go back and tell Timmy he's acting boss. That's it for now. We want to see how he performs. No talking about making him a made member. None of that now. If he don't produce, why fuck around having him made," Dean said.

"Okay. I was thinking ten Gs for Gussie," Jimmy said.

"Nah, he's in his 70s. He could drop before we hit him. Make it $8,500. That's good enough. Who ya got in mind?" Dean asked. "Well, I was thinking one shooter, Nick Minto," Jimmy said.

"Okay. Nick's okay, but tell him we want three in the hat, Jimmy. And, yeah, Jimmy, I want you and Timmy to be in the other car waiting for Nick. This way it'll be confirmed with you guys there," Dean said. "Who's going to be the wheel?" Dean asked.

"George McCruthen," Jimmy said.

"Yeah, Georgie the Wheel, he got us out of some tight spots in our younger days with his driving skills. Yeah, Georgie is okay," Dean said.

"So, do you want to do eight Gs for Nick and five hundred for George?" Jimmy asked.

"That's okay, now let's go back and tell Timmy," Dean said.

They went back to the table. Dean told Timmy he gave Jimmy the order on Gussie. Once Gussie was whacked, Timmy was told by Dean he would become the acting boss of the street crew. Timmy nodded in agreement. He was beaming with pride, knowing he was the acting boss of the crew. Smiles appeared all around the table for everyone.

"In business, Bobby, when an executive is let go or resigns, which is practically the same thing, they get severance pay," Jimmy said. "They get so many weeks of pay and that's it. In the life, it doesn't work that way. You can't just let guys go like that," he said. "They might rat you out to the Feds. Who knows what they'll tell the Feds."

"But why Gussie, he's a nice man? I asked. "I remember when he bought me an ice cream cone or gave me a piece of chocolate."

"Bobby, in the life it's all about money. We're not so different from business. How long does a sales manager keep a salesman if he don't sell? Think about it," Jimmy said.

"Yeah, but the sales guy, he don't get killed," I said.

"But listen, if the sales guy ain't selling, he's killing the business, so he's gotta go," Jimmy said.

"So Gussie is killing business, so he has to be killed," I said.

"Sort of...yeah...sort of the same thing in a way," Jimmy said. "In the life, if you're not bringing in the business, that's killing the business on the street," he said. "If you're killing the business on the street, you're killing the money. Then we have no money to operate," he said.

"In the life sure has some strange logic," I said.

"The logic, or whatever you want to call it, keeps us in business," Jimmy said.

The pit of my stomach had this weak, gnawing feeling. It was a restlessness churning in my stomach wall, bouncing off each side of the muscles lining my stomach, knowing Gussie Balencenti was not going to be alive much longer. I thought about the kindness Gussie had shown to me, and I didn't want to see anything bad happen to him.

I realized in Jimmy's philosophy of In the Life 101, while I didn't agree with it, it came down to the survival of the fittest. Gussie was no longer fit enough to survive.

"Isn't Gussie supposed to get a sit-down meeting? You always told me a made guy can't be whacked before a sit-down. An associate member can be hit without a sit-down, but Gussie was made," I questioned.

"We had our sit-down, me and Dean, that's it," he said.

"Wait a second," I countered. "Gussie wasn't there."

"He didn't have to be," Jimmy said.

"Isn't it a rule a made guy has to be at the sit-down?" again I asked.

"Look, I'm telling you a rule is not a law," Jimmy said. "A law is like something passed by the State of Illinois. Say you steal a candy bar, you get caught, you're convicted of the crime, and now you go before a judge." Jimmy's voice was starting to get an edge to it, more vocal, starting to become prickly. "He sentences you to what he thinks is appropriate under the law. He tells you you're not getting put away in jail, even though the law says you could be sentenced to serve jail time," Jimmy said. "He tells you you're going to be sentenced to have to walk around for the next seven days with your finger up your ass," Jimmy said. "That's your punishment, as the law allows a judge discretion in sentencing someone," he said. "That's a law. A rule has no legal guideline; it's how we apply it. So yeah, Gussie got his sit-down," Jimmy said.

In years to come, I would see how rules would be twisted, bent, cracked, broken, and manipulated by those making the decisions in the Outfit. The rules were rules of convenience. If it was convenient to apply them as you wanted them to be, then the rules were convenient. It didn't matter if the rules were applied fairly to all. They were applied however the Outfit wanted them to be applied.

When a guy became made during the ceremony, one of the rules he's told he must uphold is that he must be faithful to his wife. Well, I could have become a millionaire if I would have placed a bet on that one for every time I saw a made guy cheat on his wife. Never once that I can recall was a made guy taken to task about his infidelity. So, whether it was a rule about faithfulness to your wife, or a sit-down for a made guy, the Outfit decision-makers used selective memory in applying the rule.

Jimmy began to make the final arrangements for the final chapter of Gussie's life. He arranged a meeting with Nicholas "Quick Nick" Minto in the parking lot of the Stadium restaurant. Nick Minto started out as a driver and gofer in Gussie's street crew when he was 18 years old.

Nick Minto, who was 5'8" tall and had a slight kind of wiry build, was another one of the string of high school dropouts who hung around with the wrong crowd—the criminal crowd—and started his life walking down a criminal street. He'd steal cars and do minor street stickups while in his teens. He was sent away to Charleston Juvenile Hall a couple of times when caught after committing a crime, as in those days, he was still considered a minor.

He got chummy with Chuck "Lucky Chucky" DeSalvo who, while not in Gussie's crew, knew him, and recommended Nick to Gussie. Gussie took Nick in, and, thus, Nicky's criminal seeds were planted in the Outfit.

Nick was uneasy at his meeting with Jimmy. The money Jimmy offered was fine, using George McCruthen as the wheelman was fine, but what was not fine in Nick's mind was the killing of Gussie.

"There is no doubt about it, Gussie's gotta go?" Nick asked in a questioning voice. "Yeah, his crew is not performing the way they should," Jimmy said. "You've talked with Gussie, had a sit-down with him about his crew?" said Nick, still warily.

"We had a sit down with Gussie, Dean, and me, and frankly, Dean didn't think Gussie could run the crew well enough to bring in the money we expect, so he gave the order," Jimmy said.

"Where was the sit-down?" Nick asked.

"Chateau D'Ville," Jimmy said.

"That was when Dean gave the order?" Nick asked.

"Yeah, he told me after the meeting," Jimmy said. "That's why I'm here, to see you as I told Dean I thought you were the right man for the job," Jimmy said.

"You really skated on this sit-down issue. The sit-down at Chateau D'Ville was not about Gussie getting whacked. It was about his job performance," I said to Jimmy.

"Jesus, Mary, and Joseph, what is it with you, Bobby, and this sit-down thing," Jimmy's voice getting irritated with me. "We had a sit-down; we made a decision, period. I don't want to hear anymore crap about this sit-down stuff, okay?" Jimmy said. "I know you like Gussie, but you gotta put your feelings on the shelf and take care of business," his voice calmed back to its normal tone.

"Okay, drop it, okay?" Jimmy said.

"Okay," I said.

The Outfit has this verbal bob and weave; it likes to justify its actions so it uses it when necessary. It reminds me of the time I asked Big Louie Convente to get me four tires for my car. He said sure, told me how much they cost, and we agreed on a price. The tires were hot, as they had been stolen from a tire store.

About a week later, I get a call from Big Louie that he has the tires, and he'll bring them over, and I'll pay him what our agreed price was. Big Louie brings the tires over and I figure I'll ask him to change the tires on the car. When I see the tires, I've got one question, "Big Louie, where is the air in the tires, they're all flat," I said.

"Bobby, you didn't say you wanted air in the tires. You just asked for four tires, so I brought you four tires. If you wanted air in the tires, you should have asked for air," he said, with a God-given straight face.

Sit-down...yeah... the Outfit gave Gussie a sit-down, but he never asked for a sit-down about being whacked.

"Nick, now if you got a problem with whacking Gussie, tell me now. It's you who started with him, and maybe you don't want to finish him," Jimmy said.

"If I say no, then I'm the next order given by Dean. Right, Jimmy?" Nick said.

"You said it, not me," Jimmy smiled, as he responded to Nick. Nick let out a deep tension relieving breath. "Jimmy, okay, I'll do it. Just let me know where and when you want me to whack Gussie," Nick said.

In the life, when an order is given by the boss, it doesn't matter if he's running day-to-day functions of the organization, or he's the boss of the street crew, or any other higher up, you carry out the order no matter what. It's game, set, and match—that's it.

Jimmy would tell me time and time again, "You don't go against the order. You might not like the order, but it has to be carried out."

Nick had no choice. If he refused the order, Jimmy had to go back to Dean and tell him Nick said 'no' to carrying out the order. Jimmy did not want to do that since he recommended Nick. Dean would look at Nick as a poor choice and give the order to whack Nick. In Dean's eyes, since it was Jimmy recommending Nick, and Nick didn't work out, this could diminish Jimmy's standing with Dean. With the Outfit, moving down the pecking order was ill advised.

In the life, you never want a boss to have any doubt about your abilities, whether it's to advise the boss, collecting street money, whacking someone, or having to deal with him in any other capacity. If that happens, the boss figures why do I need this guy around, and he makes an example of you to the others by getting rid of you via an order. This move by the boss gets everyone's attention that this is the big leagues and you play by my rules.

Sometimes I think screwing a broad was easier than dealing with the mind games you play in the Outfit. Well, though with a woman, you know what I mean, what the hell, there's no sense in getting into that subject. Women… they're a whole other story.

"Bobby, you're going to come along with me when Gussie gets whacked," Jimmy said. "We won't be in the same cars as the others. I'll drive my own car and park a little bit away from the hit. You gotta see this, Bobby, if you want to be in the life," he said, "because this is the part of the life you gotta be able to stomach if you want to be in the life."

I gulped. Here I was, 13 years old, and I was going to see someone get whacked.

"Dad, are you sure you want me to go? Are you sure?" I asked.

"Bobby, if you decide you want to be in the life, this is part of the life you have to see, because if you can't stomach this part of the life, you won't be able to function in other parts of the life. It's like a guy who wants to be a cop. He's in the police academy training to be a cop, and when they get to the part of the training where they teach you to shoot a gun, he freezes and he doesn't fire his gun at the target," Jimmy said.

"He ain't going to make it as a cop, because no matter how many times the instructor yells fire, he never pulls the trigger, so they gotta send him home and tell him forget about it," Jimmy said. "Same with being in the life; you gotta be able to perform this violent behavior by either carrying out the order or giving the order," he said. "If you can't, then being in the life is not for you," Jimmy said.

I knew Jimmy was right, but good God, having to witness the taking of one's life when you're 13 years old was not something over which I was jumping for joy. Sure, I had seen a lot of beatings up to this point, but I had never seen an actual murder. Oh well, I guess you just have to chalk it up to another form of education, if you wanted to be in the life.

There was an old Italian tradition that on Sunday, by let's say around 2 P.M., everyone in the family assembles at Mama's house to eat Mama's delicious cooking. The sauce used on the spaghetti always tasted better when Mama made it. The second helping of spaghetti always tasted better at Mama's. It was a time-honored tradition that every Sunday you went to Mama's to eat, have a glass of wine (the kids got cokes to drink), hear some corny jokes from Uncle Luigi that you heard a million times before, but still made you laugh, and be with people who loved you dearly.

The kids would be running through the house playing, and after the meal, men would play cards. While playing cards, they would debate politics, current events, sports, and argue who was the better heavyweight fighter, Cassius Clay or Rocky Marciano.

"Clay, that big mouth, no way he could have beaten Rocky," one would say.

"Forget about it. No one could beat Rocky. Man, he never lost to anyone. He was the champ," another would say.

It was a time when everyone still lived in the neighborhood. Uncle Tony and Aunt Barbara lived next door to Mama. Uncle Angelo and Aunt Connie lived across the street, Cousin Joey lived two blocks away; everyone was family, ready to be there for you. Aunt Angela would wear different hairstyles on a Sunday and Mama would say to her, "What are you trying to look like, Sophia Loren?" with a smile on her face. Cousin Carmen would bring lots of different girls to Mama's house on Sundays, and Uncle Lou would ask him if he was Frank Sinatra or what, shaking his head.

If you had any family disputes, they were left outside of Mama's house on Sunday. Once inside Mama's house, you knew Mama would laugh with you and cry with you. Mama's love on those Sundays expanded to all. If conversations started to get heated, Mama would use her safety net, "C'mon on, let's eat." That would break up any bad will that was starting to brew. Mama loved all and all loved Mama.

The older you got, you realized how smart Mama was. Maybe Mama didn't have a formal education, like a college degree, but on Sunday, she had a doctorate in family. She knew how to say it and when to say it. When you raised your kids, you relied on a lot of Dr. Mama's principles of life that you learned on those Sundays. When you would be out with family or friends, you would remember what Mama would say on Sunday when she would sit at the table with her family. "It's never the money you spend when you're out, it's the people you are with that make it a good time," she would say.

Sundays in Mama's house you learned to make mistakes, pick yourself up, and try again. How many times did you hear her say a failure is something that didn't work this time, but the biggest failure was never to make that attempt again? On Sundays, in Mama's house, you learned to be a person.

As Mama got older and started to need some help in the kitchen, daughters and daughter-in-laws would cook some of the food and bring it to her house on Sundays.

When Mama died, sometimes one of her daughters would continue the Sunday tradition by telling everyone in the family this is what Mama wanted—keep the family close by getting together on Sunday. As time passed from one generation to another, the tradition began to evaporate. The younger ones in the family got married and moved to a place called the suburbs and the older ones in the family began dying off. With two working parents or a single working parent with kids, it was hard enough to get a cooked meal during the week let alone get a family meal on Sunday.

It was a good tradition. Family was with family, and it kept a family close, or as close as they could be. I guess some people didn't have time to be family on Sunday. However, some families did keep the tradition alive.

The Outfit, even in its craziest of crazy moments, felt the tradition should be honored. The tradition is what Jimmy wanted Gussie to have one last time. Gussie's hit was now scheduled. It was going to be after Gussie went to his daughter's house for the tradition. Gussie's belly would be full of the pan fried meatballs, and spaghetti with the sauce prepared the same way Gussie's mama made it time and time again, Sunday after Sunday. His palate would be drenched in red wine.

Gussie would go out of the life having gone through the tradition with a fulfillment of the good memories of his earlier Sunday life. Jimmy would make sure Gussie had a proper send off, his final bow before the curtain came down on his life. There would be no more Sunday tradition for Gussie as the Outfit's tradition would be his last.

I dreaded thinking about the Sunday, when it would come, knowing I would have to face it as there was no Plan B. This was it, a life would be taken, and the world would merrily go on, not missing a beat.

I was hoping for a snow day, so the hit would be cancelled, but it turned out to be snowless on that Sunday. The hit was set for the last Sunday in January. Gussie usually left his daughter's house by about 6:30 P.M. The time of the hit was important, as it would be nighttime at that time of the year, so if there was someone else on the street, they probably would not be able to identify the shooter in the darkness of night. Outside of maybe someone walking their dog, really, how many people are going to be walking down the street on a cold, raw January Sunday night in Chicago anyway? Probably not too many.

The gun used would be a .22 caliber with a silencer. Nick Minto would put on a black ski mask just before he got out of the car. Even if someone was walking down the street, they could not identify Minto because of the ski mask. He would approach Gussie from the back walking in normal steps, not running after him, which might create a noise, then forcing Gussie to turn around and actually see his killer. The gun would be held pointing straight down alongside Nick's right leg, held in Nick's right hand.

George McCruthen, the wheelman, would drive the car slowly on the street following Nick. Once Nick got close enough to Gussie, he would tap the top of his head with his left hand. George would put the car in park, and he would press down on the accelerator, racing the engine to drown out the noise of the gun shot, even though a silencer was being used. The racing of the engine would not only muffle the popping sound that a silencer makes, but it would muffle the sound of a scream from Gussie once he was shot.

The plan called for Nick to raise his right hand and fire the gun rapidly at the back of Gussie's head, putting three in the hat. Nick would turn, run to the car, get in the front seat and George would shift the car to drive and take off down the street at high speed. Nick would take off his mask, turn his head toward Tim Robitle, who was sitting in the back, and say, "Hi, boss."

Jimmy told Karen he was taking me along, as he said we were going to visit someone and we would be back later. Karen had a pretty good idea that Jimmy was involved with the Outfit, but never knew for sure what he did for them. I was nine years old when the FBI came to the apartment, put Jimmy in handcuffs, though they didn't arrest him. They were just taking him downtown for questioning.

Jimmy turned to Karen and said she should call Larry Rosenthal. Larry was Jimmy's lawyer. She did and several hours later, Jimmy was home. I didn't know then, since it was late afternoon on a Wednesday when the FBI took him, that later on in my life, I saw when the FBI arrested guys they came usually at 5:00 A.M. Other times when the FBI wanted to talk with Jimmy, they would come around dinner hour.

Karen had that look on her face after calling Larry Rosenthal that told me she knew Jimmy was part of the Outfit, but she was not going to talk about it. I kinda wished she had spoken about what she felt about Jimmy's other family. We could have gotten this mob stuff out in the open. I know I would have felt a whole lot better getting this Outfit life off my chest. Karen turned and walked away from me, not uttering a word about Jimmy and the Outfit. Here I was, nine years old, and I gotta fill in the blanks, and I don't know where to begin.

The only thing Karen said to Jimmy was whatever he was doing, to keep it out of the apartment. I'll say this for Jimmy; he never conducted mob business in the apartment with anyone.

Before we walked out of the apartment, Jimmy told me to wait a second as he went back to the bedroom and into a closet. He came back and we went to the car. As we were sitting in the car, he reached under his coat and pulled out a .32-caliber handgun and put it in the glove compartment of the car right in front of me.

I just stared at the black handgun, utterly amazed at seeing it. I didn't even know Jimmy had a gun. *What's going on here*, I was thinking. *Are we going to be in a shootout or is someone coming after us? Just what the hell is happening here?*

Jimmy started the car and pulled away from the curb. Looking straight ahead, he started talking to me. "Whenever you make a plan, you always got to figure something could go wrong. Nothing is foolproof. You gotta be ready, so when it happens, you can correct it right then and there," he said.

My body filled with anxiety. *What did Jimmy mean 'if something goes wrong'? The plan looked error-free to me; every detail was planned for…*I thought *what was he talking about?*

I figured I better ask as I was in the car, and I better not be involved in the 'if something goes wrong' part of the equation. "What could go wrong?" I asked Jimmy, with a pensive look on my face.

"I'm not saying something will go wrong, but maybe Nick gets second thoughts and don't pull the trigger. The order still has to be carried out," he said, in a matter-of-fact kind of tone.

"So, you would carry out the order if Nicky doesn't?" I nervously asked.

"Yeah…yeah, I would have to do it, but don't worry, nothing will go wrong," Jimmy said in a reassuring voice.

Composing myself I said, "Okay, it's just…you know…I've never been through this whole process, and I want to be sure neither one of us gets hurt."

While driving, Jimmy reached over and with his right hand; he placed it on my left shoulder and gave it a couple of pats. "You're a good son, Bobby. Thanks for caring. You'll see, everything will go smooth," he said. I started silently praying to God, hoping he was in the neighborhood, and he would hear my silent cries for help.

Gussie's daughter lived on the far Northwest Side of the city. Every house was on a 30-foot lot, with lawns full of snow in the winter. I pictured in the summer how the lawns would be manicured, with happy boys and girls playing in front of their houses. Even in the winter, the streets were very clean. Every-thing looked neat on this block. *Nothing appeared to be out of place, very orderly,* I thought. I sort of wished I lived on this block.

We drove past the car. I think it was a Plymouth—maybe blue—that had George at the wheel; Nicky, sitting shotgun in the front next to George; and Timmy sitting quietly in the backseat, waiting for things to start cooking.

Jimmy pulled alongside and everyone looked at everyone, but no one spoke. I looked right directly in Nick's eyes. Did they look strong, confident, or were the pupils looking unsure, not totally with the program? Maybe the pupils had their own sit-down and decided this shooting was not going to happen.

Nicky stared at me. I stared right back at him. His eyes didn't back away from our visual confrontation. His eyes looked hard and direct, even to blink was a chore at this point. Those intense brown eyes had been down the killing street before. I could see the pupils had been accessories to the crime of murder in the past. This was not virgin territory to them.

They were rock solid, we've done this before, and we will do it again was the vibe I got. Nicky was not going to flinch on this hit. His eyes closed the deal. Nicky's eyes gave their stamp of approval as this hit was okay to do.

Jimmy parked the car, maybe three spots ahead of George's car, both cars facing north as we were on a two-way street.

"Nice neighborhood," I said.

"Yeah, a lot of cops and firemen who have to live in Chicago live in this area," he said.

"Cops? Cops live here? Maybe right on this street?" I said, starting to panic as I could feel uncertainty in my body. "They could, like, look out their window or walk down the street and see us."

"Nah, don't worry. That's why we're doing this hit at night in January. Who's going to be walking the streets on a night like this?" Jimmy asked.

"But," I said.

"But what?" Jimmy said.

"But nothing," I said. *I'm a minor,* I was thinking. *I'm not doing the killing, so why should I make such a big deal about this? They can't put a kid in jail, or can they? Maybe I can come up with an illness. I'll call it 'killitis,' and tell Jimmy I'm going to have to miss this hit. Just use a sick day for me. Dream on, Bobby, dream on.*

At a few minutes past 6:00 P.M., the front door of Gussie's daughter's house opened. She gave her father the last kiss of his life on the left cheek of his face. It would be the kiss he carried to his grave.

"See ya next Sunday. If something comes up during the week and you need me, just call me," she said.

"Sure, baby girl, sure," Gussie said. The Sunday tradition had come to an end now. Another tradition was about to begin.

Jimmy started the car and gave two headlights flashes, which George saw. The flashes were the signal to begin the operation. Jimmy looked at Gussie, then looked in his rearview mirror to see if George got the signal. George started his car. Nicky put on his ski mask and checked the silencer on the gun one more time.

Gussie started to walk down the street to his car. His daughter shut her front door, and Gussie's life clock began rapidly descending the remaining seconds of his life.

Nicky got out of George's car and began walking behind Gussie, gun at his side. George pulled away from the curb slowly, no headlights on, following Nicky at a very slow pace, barely creeping along.

When Nicky got close enough to Gussie, he tapped the top of his head with his left hand. George pulled the car up parallel to Nicky, put it in park and raced the engine. Gussie started to turn to see what the noise was.

I was feeling shaky as I looked out the driver's side mirror as this whole scenario was playing out right in front of me. My hands started to quiver, so I brought them together, the left hand trying to comfort the right hand, and the right hand trying to comfort the left hand; two grieving souls trying to find a place of solace in the violent world of the Outfit.

The right hand saying to the left hand, "If we hide, maybe it'll go away; this violent act will pass away from us, and we won't become mentally disfigured from seeing it."

The left hand saying to the right hand, "Please hold me as tight as you can; don't let me go. Give me strength to carry on after this viciousness is concluded. Please, hold me tight."

It happened quickly with Gussie starting to turn. Nicky raised the gun, shooting Gussie three times in the back of the head. Gussie's body began free-falling, hopelessly out of control, arms starting to rise upward, blood pouring out the back of his head, with the body contorting in a spinning motion, and spiraling to the pavement. His body hit with a thud, arms now downward, splattered on the cement, blood profusely running as fast as it could from his head into some nearby snow on the sidewalk, turning it into a red snow cone.

Nicky stood over him and shot Gussie once in the face, then darted to the car, quickly got in the front seat, and pulled the ski mask off. George put the car in drive and sped off. Nicky turned his head to Timmy and said, "Hi, boss."

Jimmy looked straight out his side car window at the motionless body. He put the car in drive, and we drove away.

I wanted to speak, but the words were not coming out of my mouth. My neck had become wet with a slippery type of perspiration on the back of my shirt collar. I really didn't know what to think at this point.

As he was driving back to the apartment, Jimmy said, "Well, that's it," with no real emotion on his face. I could see as I looked at him that he had done this murder thing over and over before in his life. So, until the next hit, it was story over, close the book, and move on. He had lost his violence virginity a long time ago.

I hadn't done this before. This was the first time in my life I saw someone get killed. Saying, well, that's it, wasn't going to cut it with me. *We're going to talk about this, Jimmy, you and me. Fuckin' a, we're going to talk about this right now.*

"Why?" I asked Jimmy.

"Why what?" he said nonchalantly.

"Why was Gussie really killed?" I asked.

"Look, Bobby, sometimes there's a plan behind the plan, and that's all I'm going to say," he said.

This profound statement about a plan behind a plan made absolutely no sense to me. What the hell was he talking about? At this point, knowing Jimmy, I figured it was best to back off. No sense getting him angry as he wouldn't tell me anything more about this plan behind the plan. I was already upset, so he might say something that'll upset me even more. *Let it go, Bobby. Someday I'll find out about this plan behind a plan, but today is not the day.*

When we got home, Karen looked at me. "You okay, Bobby? Something bothering you? You look like something is bothering you," she said.

Mother's always have this mother's sense when something is wrong with their children. They can smell a problem a block away. They look at you with those mother's eyes, trying to dissect what's going on in your head.

"Nah, I'm okay," I said, slowly turning away from her.

The next morning I was up early as I didn't have a comfortable night's sleep. I kept replaying what happened to Gussie in my mind. I then got dressed. I went outside to get some air, and the newspaper boy just delivered the *Chicago Review* to the house next door to our building.

I walked over and picked up the *Review* off the stairs. "Mob Hit" in big, brazen bold black capital letters was the screaming headline that jumped out at me on the front page. There was a picture of the police around a body, though you couldn't really see Gussie's body that clearly. But, of course, I knew it was him.

The story said a neighbor walking his dog at about 9:30 P.M. found Gussie lying in a pool of blood. The story talked about reputed mobster John "Gussie"

Balencenti being shot three times in the back of the head and once in the face. The police said they had no suspects.

I put the paper back down on the steps. No need to read any more of the story. I knew what happened as I was there to see it in person. Some reporter was not going to tell me what happened. Walking back into the apartment building, I wondered what Timmy's first hit as a boss was like.

Watching your first Outfit murder was like having sex for the first time. It was awkward, you were far from being smooth, but at least you were no longer a virgin, and maybe the next time, and the time after that, and the time after that, you would feel more secure about your visual performance.

In the next twenty-six months, the following events occurred. Nick Minto was shot, gunned to death. His body was found in a dumpster in the alley near Peakway Avenue. George McCruthen was found slumped over the steering wheel of his car in his garage after he had been strangled to death.

A person who had just parked his car in Lot P near Devon Airport on the South Side smelled a foul order as he walked past a car in the lot. As he got closer, the smell grew stronger. He reported what he smelled to someone at the airport, who in turn called security. Security went to Lot P, opened the trunk as the driver's side door, while closed, was not locked, and they flipped the side latch. Tim Robitle had been shot three times in the back of his head and three times in his chest. The body was decomposing, and when the police arrived, they felt the body had been in the trunk maybe two or three months.

The police called Tim's death a mob hit, like the deaths of Nicky and George. The murders are still open on the books as the police never made any arrests in the cases. In police lingo, the cases are unresolved.

During the twenty-six month period that the murders took place, I was trying to put the puzzle together, why this happened to Nicky, George, and Timmy. It's not like five years had gone by. All the action happened in a twenty-six-month period. As with any story, there's a story behind the story, but what was it?

It was a warm spring-like Sunday morning in April when Jimmy asked me to help him wash his car. As we were drying the car with our soft cloths in typical Jimmy fashion, out of the blue he started talking about the murders of Nicky, George, and Timmy.

"Bobby, look, here's what happened," Jimmy, while rubbing his neck with his right hand, said. "About a month before Gussie was scheduled to be hit, Tim Robitle tells Joseph "Joey the Mouth" Scornavaco that he's going to get a big promotion, and this promotion was the beginning of his climb to someday run the Outfit. Telling Joey the Mouth is like telling the world," Jimmy said.

"Joey's like a radio station—he broadcasts it to whomever he thinks will benefit him," Jimmy said. "So, he tells his captain Peter "Little Pete" Lambertini, figuring maybe he'll score some points for himself that Tim got plans to run the Outfit. Joey the Mouth leaves out the part about Tim saying one day he would run the Outfit, not this minute. Maybe Joey the Mouth had a beef with Tim and conveniently left out the future part to stick it to Timmy. I don't know. Or, it was Joey the Mouth hearing what he wanted to hear, and that's the story he told Little Pete. I can't say for sure," Jimmy said.

"Little Pete figures he better push this story up the ladder as he doesn't want to get whacked for knowing something he should have told somebody," Jimmy said. "Little Pete tells Frank "Frankie Maestro" Maestrovatta, a lieutenant in the Park Avenue street crew. Frankie Maestro tells his capo Felix "Phil G" Grappo."

It sounds like a bunch of women at a coffee klatch, I was thinking.

"Phil G tells Martin "Marty One Time" Pointui, a consigliere for the Tampa Avenue street crew."

So, when is someone going to have the balls to tell Dean, I was trying to figure out? Marty One Time calls his brother-in-law Robert "Bobby Short Stack" Prolovene, who owns an insurance company that processes phony teamster medical claims so a check will be cut to each employee for each phony claim. Bobby Short Stack tells Marty One Time he better call Jimmy Williams. Now, finally Dean will hear about it. This, boys and girls, was the normal way guys communicated in the Outfit. Now you can see why things happened to guys that shouldn't have because of misinformation.

"Once Marty One Time called me, I started questioning him," Jimmy said. "So I had to speak with everyone, but most important Joey the Mouth."

"Jimmy, my right hand to God, that's what he said. He's going to run the Outfit, and this promotion is the first step," Joey the Mouth said.

"What if God is left handed?" Jimmy said as a joke, but Joey the Mouth didn't pick up on it and stuck to his story.

"What did you do then?" I asked.

"Well, there's this diner Timmy liked to go for coffee, and he was friendly with the waitress who often served him, so I decided to go talk with her," Jimmy said.

The waitress was young, working at the diner to earn some spending money while attending college. She recognized Jimmy.

"Hi, Mr. Williams," she said.

"You have a good memory," Jimmy said.

"I recognized you from the times you have come in the diner with Mr. Robitle," she said.

"I know Mr. Robitle often talks to you. Did he recently talk about any business plans?" Jimmy asked.

"He said something about getting a promotion, which would lead to running a business, but he wasn't specific about his plans, so I just congratulated him and that was it," she said.

"Maybe he's just keeping everything as a surprise," Jimmy said. "Well, we'll just have to plan a surprise for him," Jimmy said kiddingly.

"Yeah, I guess so," she said.

Jimmy, pulling out his wallet said, "I know your time is valuable, so here's five dollars for your help," as he took out a five-dollar bill and handed it to her. "One thing we don't want to do is spoil Mr. Robitle's surprise, so let's keep this conversation between just you and me, okay?" Jimmy said.

"Gee, thanks a lot for the five dollars, and don't worry, my lips are sealed," she said.

"Good, thanks for the information," Jimmy said.

"The waitress had no axe to grind. She had no reason to lie, Bobby; so she actually corroborated what others have said," Jimmy said.

"Without knowing what Tim said about the future," I said to Jimmy, "maybe Tim was talking about running the Outfit down the road, maybe ten years from now, not today as everyone seems to be saying."

"With the Outfit, Bobby, the future could be today. Bobby Williams is here in the morning," and Jimmy, snapping his right middle finger and thumb together, "Bobby Williams is gone by night," Jimmy said. "I'm sure Timmy had thoughts about running the Outfit, which lots of guys do, but in the jungle you gotta strike first once you have all the facts, or you might be the one swallowed up," Jimmy said. "The longer Timmy thinks about it, the more he's going to want it, and you don't know when and who's going to get whacked along the way," he said.

"You gotta make the play when the play has to be made," Jimmy said. "In your professional and personal life, there are times you have to make the play when the play has to be made," he said. "The boss comes to you with a work assignment maybe no one else wants to do, so now you gotta make the play when the play has to be made to show the boss you can do it, and do such a good job, he looks at you differently now. He's got confidence in you, so maybe you'll get better work assignments. And who knows, maybe a promotion," Jimmy said.

"You meet a nice girl, you start dating, one thing leads to another, you love her, she loves you, and now you gotta make the play when the play has to be made. If you don't ask her to marry you, you could lose her. So, you gotta decide if you want to make the play or not. See what I'm saying?" Jimmy asked.

"I do, but what if you're making the wrong play with Tim?" I asked.

"All you can do is make sure the information walks a straight line. If the information starts to stagger or develops curves, you gotta find out why before you make a play," Jimmy said. "With Timmy, I think I got it straight," Jimmy said.

Jimmy called Dean, and he told Dean he needed to see him. When they met, Jimmy told Dean about what he'd heard from people concerning Tim's plans.

"Oh, is that so?" Dean said.

"Yeah, that's what he said, according to what I've been told," Jimmy said, looking right in Dean's face.

"Well, if that motherfucker thinks he's going to be running the Outfit someday, it ain't going to fuckin' happen…not today, tomorrow, next week, or next fuckin' year," Dean said. "No, he fuckin' thinks that he's going to whack me or somebody else to get the job, fuck him. We're gonna take him out; he's no fuckin' good," said Dean.

Jimmy listened, as once Dean got going, you just stood there and let the emotion spill out on to the street. It would then evaporate into the cement and a cooling period occurred, then Dean could be talked to after that.

"Well, we'll go through with our plan to whack Gussie, use all the players just like we planned, tell Timmy he'll be acting boss, and let some time go by. Then, we'll get rid of everyone involved—Nicky, George, and Timmy," Jimmy said. "With everyone gone, no one can point any fingers at us; we're in the clear," Jimmy said.

"Sound okay so far?" Jimmy asked.

"Yeah, Jimmy, I like the plan," Dean said.

"Then, once we're ready to move on everyone, we'll call in Alphonse DeLeo, the underboss of the crew, talk to him and we'll make it sound to him like it's his idea to get rid of Timmy," Jimmy said. "You know, like we'll say to him Timmy's not really going to be bringing up the numbers of the crew, and we got it from a reliable source Timmy is going to whack someone in the crew to make an example of someone, so everyone better start performing better," he said.

"We'll come up with a couple more lies to stoke Alphonse up. By the time we get through with him, Alphonse is going to see it's a game of survival, and Timmy's got to go," Jimmy said.

Dean gave Jimmy a sideways glance as he turned his head slightly to the right.

"So, then we tell Alphonse to come up with a plan, we'll give it lip service, and we'll tell him he'll be the boss of the crew after the hits go down," Jimmy said.

"You know, Jimmy, if I didn't know better, I would say you were going after my job," Dean said sternly, and then a smile rose on his face. A smile that was sunshine and warmth rolled into one. The type of smile that was the okay smile,' yeah, we're cool' smile, 'you know what you're doing' smile, and 'I'm with you' smile. Not the smile that behind it was 'I'm going to take care of you, you're the next order, see ya'—the vile murderous type of smile.

Dean nodded his head up and down a couple of times. "Yeah, we'll do what we have to do, so go ahead and do it," he told Jimmy.

Ah, so now I knew what Jimmy meant by the plan behind the plan. I thought Alphonse "Allie Boy" DeLeo never had an original thought in his head, and I mean never. He did just whatever everyone else did before him. Not only did he have tunnel vision, but he lived in a deep mental tunnel, oblivious to the real world of the Outfit. He was the nephew of Fred "Freddie Boy" Partipillo and rose up the ranks for that reason and that reason only. Freddie Boy ran gambling and loan-sharking on the Southeast Side of Chicago and nearby Hammond, Whiting, and East Chicago, Indiana. Freddie was a made guy with blocks and blocks of juice, which commanded respect in the Outfit.

Hell, I think Allie Boy had to use his uncle's juice to make it out of kindergarten; otherwise he still might be there. Once you put a thought in Allie Boy's head, he would do it, and that's exactly what happened. Allie Boy was one of those robotic types in the Outfit. Once you programmed him, he did what you wanted. So, on the street, everyone thought it was Allie Boy who hit Nicky, George, and Tim; that he was behind the plan.

Maybe Allie Boy was smarter than they thought. When Allie Boy walked down the street after the hits, people gave him the "Hi, Allie, how's it going?" greeting as they wanted to be in his good graces.

Allie Boy, they figured, was now a rising power, a man you better pay deference to when you saw him. God forbid you didn't want to get on his bad side. Allie Boy knew this also as he would swagger down the street, shaking hands with those minions who wanted to make sure Allie Boy knew they would kiss his ring to maintain a good standing with him.

This was how Jimmy and Dean wanted it to be. Their hands were scrubbed clean of the murders as Allie Boy would wear the crown, not them. The question would be for how long.

"So, Gussie was kinda like the fall guy?" I asked.

"In a way, but Gussie was being hit for other reasons. But to get Tim, it had to be done that way," Jimmy said.

"It seemed Gussie was in good standing after the sit-down at Chateau D'Ville," I said.

"Bobby, Gussie was losing control of the crew. He should have taken action sooner when the money wasn't coming in like it should," Jimmy said. "At the sit-down, he was trying to play catch up," he said.

Moving up the corporate ladder in the Outfit, becoming a boss was what a lot of guys strived for. I saw it many times where a guy started out as a driver for someone and years later became a boss. The one thing you had to remember was that if you want to become a boss, never tell anyone you want to become a boss.

There's this feeling in the Outfit—maybe even paranoia—that someone is out for your job. If you are a good worker in the organization, someone will see what you're capable of doing, and, thus, will become your juice. They will push you up, giving you more visibility to the higher ups.

Then you will start to move up. Jimmy often told me that if there's something that is important to you, keep it to yourself. Never tell anyone. If you tell just one person, that person can tell others and then you've got a problem. If you are the only one that knows, no one can hurt you, so be careful what you say and to whom.

It was a lesson well learned. Never let your mouth get you in trouble by telling a secret. The killing of Gussie was just a bridge to really get Timmy. Timmy wasn't the first guy who said he wanted to run the Outfit, but telling someone who then let others know was going to get Timmy a reserved spot in St. Matthew's Cemetery, courtesy of the Outfit.

Unfortunately for Nicky and George, they were standing on the bridge when it needed to be blown up. With the Outfit, Timmy forgot the gospel— hear no evil, see no evil, and speak no evil. If you don't remember the gospel, then follow the teachings of the Outfit in its purest form—keep your fuckin' mouth shut.

With everyone gone, the slate was clean. There was no one left who could read between the lines and figure out who called the shots on this one and caused a problem for those who did. The Outfit mentality on this one was one for all and all for one, no one was going to get a pass, and no one was going to be alive. It was your vanilla-flavored, dead men tell no tales scenario, which was licked out of a sugar cone by the Outfit. The Outfit always excelled at cleaning up after themselves.

Prostitution run by the Outfit was done in both the city and the suburbs. While bars were used quite a bit for the meeting between the girls and the johns, hotels and motels were the places used for securing the oldest profession.

Ernest "Ernie M" Marciano ran the downtown and Near North Side prostitution in the city. Prostitution was a cash business, which continually, like drugs, brought in money for the Outfit. There were generally no slow seasons, though the Thanksgiving/Christmas period could be, I guess, considered a slower time.

Money was needed for holiday gifts for his wife and kids, so after those expenses there was not much money available until January for a john's sexual needs. However, some guys would still need their sexual fix, so they would go to the prostitute before Christmas to get their end of the year physical gift. If it meant spending a little less on holiday gifts, the family be damned, his sexual needs were more important than their happiness.

When a john's wife was pregnant, he would schedule more time for sex with the prostitute. I never knew a prostitute who was not happy to hear the john's wife was pregnant. To the john, his wife's pregnancy seemed to fuel the need of intimacy that much more. Maybe he felt physically distant from his wife as the no sex rule applied during the pregnancy period.

The prostitutes would offer their congratulations in the most heartfelt way, if you get my drift. The girls put out a little more effort knowing the john was either a first-time dad, or one with children and just adding to the family.

The prostitute would talk sweetly to the john, telling him how wonderful it was that he was a father, and what a stud he was. This cooking of the emotions by the prostitute paid off in the john being in a good mood and, after sex, leaving the girl a bigger tip.

The financial breakdown for prostitution was a 60/40 split, where the Outfit got the 60% and the girls got 40%, plus tips. The downtown hotels used were The Carolina, Chicago Inn, and Madrid, which while not the top of the line places, were clean and tidy. The owners of the hotels had mob ties. They were located on a side street—places the johns felt at ease being in, as they didn't have the hustle and bustle of the more well-known hotels—and offered a discreet atmosphere, giving the johns cover to enjoy their horizontal dances.

The building's outer appearances were maintained. You would not see chipped paint or any resemblance to a building that needed repairs. Prostitution, like any other business, must be marketed properly. Johns had to be made to feel comfortable in their surroundings, which the hotels made sure was the case. An unhappy john and an unhappy Outfit were both bad for business.

The rooms were cleaned every day, furniture would be polished; the decor would be kept immaculate. These hotels were not the seedy type you would see in a Hollywood movie. They were used by the Outfit to sell a product, so image was key. The john saw a good outer product, thus, when he met the girl, he was already sold on the product the Outfit was selling.

Mob prostitution, like other mob interests, needed help from our friends the politicians, judges, and cops to exist. In this case, it was the cops. Roger Moreland was the Commander of the Chicago Police Department's Vice Unit. His sergeant was Darryl McPherson.

Both Moreland and McPherson were friends of the Outfit. Roger was paid three thousand dollars a month, of which he gave Darryl one thousand dollars a month to act as his bagman. Darryl would meet with Ernie on the last day of the month to pick up the cash.

The money bought protection from Roger. He made sure his officers left the inside of the hotels alone. If the vice officers saw a woman, who was a prostitute, soliciting potential johns for a ten dollar trick on the street in the vicinity of the hotels, the pavement princesses were quickly hustled off the street. There was to be no outside sales near the hotels, as Roger knew this and was being compensated to keep the streets clean of any competition. The Outfit had a monopoly on hotel prostitution, and no one was going to break it. Vice cops were very efficient in whisking away any street competition that might interfere with the inside money being made by the Outfit. With the girls on the street, it was now you see them…now you don't.

When Roger needed to make a vice bust, he and Ernie would set one up at the Evergreen Motel, a place on the Near North Side of the city that was close to Outfit-controlled regular bars, b-girl bars, and strip club joints.

Roger would call Ernie to let him know he needed to make some arrests. If the vice unit doesn't make any arrests, why are they needed?

Ernie would set up the bust for a weekday, usually Wednesday, though he would move it around between Monday and Thursday. There was never a bust on Friday, Saturday, or Sunday. Those days were off limits. You never wanted to interfere with the weekend, as its volume made it a busier time than the weekdays; hence, more revenue for the Outfit.

Though, with johns you never could be sure when they would come. You had some guys who came during lunchtime, some straight from work late in the afternoon, and others came after they had dinner with the wife and kids. Some guys had a special day during the week or weekend. Doctors liked to come on Saturday or Sunday morning. They would use the excuse they have to see patients in the hospital, which their wives bought. So, they came at those times and got their sexual prescription filled by the girl, then they drove back home and played the role of a loving husband for the rest of the day. I guess medical school didn't cover this type of anatomy.

When prearranging the Vice busts for Roger, Ernie would often use people off the street to act as johns. He would pay guys to pretend they were a john, and when the guys were arrested, they would be listed as John Does for the police report. He would pay these guys ten dollars apiece. Ernie tried to avoid real johns from getting arrested. If real johns got arrested, it was bad for business. Since the cases for the fake johns and prostitutes were generally dismissed by a judge, the fake johns had no worries about having a criminal record.

When Vice made arrests, the cases would be generally assigned to a judge who was a friend. Ernie had judges who used the services that the girls provided, so the Outfit had them in their pocket. The Outfit didn't worry about Vice arrests, since they controlled the judges who handled these cases.

A judge for Vice cases was paid two thousand dollars per case. Since every arrest was a separate case, the judges could make ten thousand dollars or more in a day. Depending on the volume, the cases could be divided among a few judges.

The Vice cops who made the arrests wouldn't show up in court and the judges would dismiss the case. When making the arrest, the Vice cop would do something that he knew would cause a judge to dismiss the case. So, if the Vice cop was told to go to court, the judge would use the technicality to dismiss the case. Examples of this were a Vice cop not giving the arrested parties their rights or not having any probable cause to arrest anyone.

A judge would give the Vice cop a pretend admonishing about how he handled the case. The Vice cop grinned at the judge, as all parties were told they were free to leave. Another show ended in the Cook County legal system.

Many a time, I would be a spectator in the courtroom, watching the proceedings, sitting there just waiting for the reason to come up for the judge to do his 'bye-bye gig' to the case. I usually knew the reason, so to me it was fun to know the final outcome before there was a final outcome. I can still hear in my mind a judge piously announcing the reasons the case would be dismissed. Sometimes, it was hard for me to distinguish if the criminal was the one wearing the tan Department of Corrections uniform or the one wearing the black robe.

Each of the hotels had a madam to supervise the girls and collect the money from the girls. Sometimes the money would be kept in a cigar box; other times a metal container, which would be locked with a latch in the front. The madam was responsible for the money after she collected it from the girls. She would pay the girls what they were owed later that day and keep the rest for Ernie or one of his boys to pick up. The madams in mob prostitution had been working girls previously, so they knew how prostitution was supposed to run.

Ernie or two of his associates John "Big John" Duermi and Daniel "Danny C" Culle would go to the hotels, usually at 2:00 A.M. or so, to collect the money. They would take their sixty percent of the money and leave the remaining amount for the madam to distribute to the girls. Ernie would pay the madams separately. They would earn three to possibly four thousand a month, depending on the amount of money produced by the girls. Some madams had more girls than others in their stable. Some girls were more productive than others, so things had to be factored in when determining a madam's pay.

Ernie and the boys would watch for a drop off in money. Some nights might be more or less, which was okay as long as the money was in a range. If they saw wide swings in the collection of the money, they would talk to the madam about how many tricks were being turned by each girl that day. Ernie and the boys would inquire if there were any problems between the johns and the girls. Unhappy customers could mean their unhappiness was reflected in the revenue. It was the old adage—Is everyone happy?

As the girls would turn in the money from each john, the madam would have to keep track of each girl's amount separately. She would write the information down on flash paper. Flash paper was the type of paper used by bookies to keep track of the bets placed by each customer.

If there was a bust by the cops or Feds, the bookie would run to the bathroom, and throw the flash paper in the toilet. As soon as the flash paper hit the water, it would disintegrate, breaking apart, and the handwriting would smear as the water soaked the paper.

The bookie would flush the paper down the toilet, and it was goodbye evidence, see ya. The bookie would be like a magician and make...puff...all gone, never to be seen again. The flash paper was purchased at stores that sold magic paraphernalia as magicians used it as part of their act. The Outfit was a large account at these stores.

With the flash paper, a madam, if need be, could quickly dispose of vital information for which a prosecutor would be looking. The madam, who besides supervising the house of ill repute, was a little bit of everything to the girls. Maybe a mother they never had, maybe a priest for them to bare their inner most feelings to, maybe just a good friend to sit down with over a cup of coffee to hear them bitch about something. Yeah, a madam had to fulfill a lot of maybes with the girls, but the one maybe role that they had to be was a disciplinarian.

When the money dropped off, the madam had to talk to the girl or girls involved. Since most madams were prostitutes themselves, they used the same stories to their madams about the money, so you were not going to tell a madam some excuse she didn't use herself. Blaming the weather for a drop off in money just was not going to warm their madam's heart to give you a pass. The old weather story had two chances of surviving—slim and none, and slim left early.

If a girl wasn't producing enough money, the madam would talk to her, a sort of verbal warning. After the talk, if the girl didn't improve, she would let Ernie know. Ernie or the boys, on Ernie's direction, would go visit the girl. They didn't play nice. They would use a coat hanger, covering the bottom base of the hanger with cotton so it left no marks, and they beat the girl on the back part of her thighs.

I witnessed many beatings and I still cringe today at the thought of a woman getting beaten. Each hit of the hanger caused a stinging feeling to the girl's thighs. She would promise to do better, as she begged them to stop. The more she begged, I watched them become more sinister. They swung the hanger quicker, causing more blows to be given.

Helplessly, I watched until they reached the pain threshold that satisfied their violent standard. The blows then became a trickle and then they stopped for good. She fearfully got the Outfit's message from its crayon mentality, bring in more money or else the next time you'll wish it was just a coat hanger.

After getting their assignment, a girl's production rate improved dramatically. Their client list grew as they became more aggressive at the pickup spots. The only respect the Outfit showed to a woman was if she was good in bed. To the Outfit, a woman was a broad, never understanding they were both one in the same. A woman should be treated with love, respect, dignity, and make sure she doesn't fall off the pedestal.

The rates for the girls' services ranged from one hundred to five hundred dollars an hour; a well-heeled john would be paying the high end rate. Ernie told the madams what the rates were and, while he did set parameters as to what a specific john would pay—a lawyer, judge, doctor, businessman, any type of professional guy, etc., had a certain rate—he allowed the madams some flexibility.

The madams could use their discretion on the johns. What a john did for a living would be taken into account by a madam when charging a john his hourly rate. Since the johns were repeat business, they would be paying the same rate each visit. The madams often knew more about the john's finances than his wife.

The madam would tell the girl what the charge was going to be, so she knew what her cut was going to be. Since the girls were also working for tips, they would work the john in a little more caring way by talking to him in a kind, sweet, reassuring voice to relax him, even while they had sex with him. By using this ploy to relax the john, he would find the sex more pleasurable and, maybe, she could get a little higher tip to offset the loss of income from a lower hourly rate. Another way of raising the tip was for the girls to praise the john's sexual ability; make him feel like he's the best, even if he wasn't.

Remember, boys and girls, it's always about the money. She doesn't care about him physically or emotionally. She only cares about the money. I've seen some girls refer to a john as Mr. Ten Dollars or Mr. Twenty Dollars based on his tip—no first or last names.

The first thing a madam thinks about when a girl's income drops is she might be pocketing some of the hourly charged money. Since it's happened before, it's not an unusual thought to circulate in a madam's head.

So, the madam talks to the girl to clear the air about her skimming money. The girl always denies it at first, but the madam, through her interrogation, gets the girl to finally admit the fact that she's been pocketing money from the hourly charge. Once that is cleared up, the discussion continues. The girl tells the madam her business has fallen off, she's got bills to pay, a kid to support, whatever reason the girl can come up with as to why she took the money.

The girl will have to pay back the money she's taken; what she is supposed to receive from the hourly charge will be held back to help pay back the money she took.

Mob prostitution was not going to reach into its heart and pull out the 'forgive and forget card' and hand it to the girl. Mob prostitution, being one of the Outfit's children, was taught to believe in the cause and effect principle. The girl caused the problem. Now she must receive the effect of the consequences.

Once the madam finished talking to the girl, she ordered her to stand up and pull down her outfit, letting it fall to her feet. The madam would take the disciplinary coat hanger out of the drawer and get out of her chair. She would walk around behind the girl and start hitting her, first many times on the lower back of the calf muscle of the right leg, then moving to the left leg, repeating the blows.

I've seen this happen on many occasions, being in the room when it took place. Watching the madam dole out the physical discipline to the girl was very disturbing to watch. I would shudder as I watched girls fight back the tears after the beating. The blows of the coat hanger would sting and burn the skin. While the blows did not leave marks, they left the desired message, getting the point across—this is our business, not yours, so hands off our money.

The coat hanger becomes the dominant force attacking the weaker skin. The skin must submit to the attacks as it has no defense against the merciless thrashing it is absorbing. It signals the brain, *when, oh when will it stop? Please tell me, God, when will I stop being dehumanized?*

The brain bites its tongue and says, *soon, soon, my child, be brave, be brave.* The brain helplessly listens to the cries from the skin saying *no more*, just waiting for the squeals of anguish to stop from the skin. Finally, the moment happens, there is silence. The skin's voice is quiet. No more, no more of this brutality.

"Bobby, I know seeing a girl get beat with a coat hanger was upsetting to you, but the girl's gotta bring us all of our money. She can't take any of our money. Besides, she's gotta bring in money, and if talking to her doesn't work, then she's gotta get beat," Jimmy said.

Damn right it's bothering me, I was thinking. *This is a woman we're talking about—a living, breathing woman—and you still do not hit a woman no matter what, so don't try and give me some Outfit bullshit logic trying to justify hitting a woman. You don't hit a woman, do I make myself clear? I'll put it on repeat in case you missed it, you do not hit a woman.*

"I know, Bobby, I always told you that you have to be respectful to a woman. It bothers me, too, to see a girl get beat, but...uh...uh...business is business. And, if a madam's gotta beat her at that point, the madam's just doing her job. If the madam doesn't do her job, then Ernie or one of his boys will do far worse to her than what the madam would have done," Jimmy said.

"So, you're telling me the madam is just following orders," I said.

"Right," he said.

I was thinking *when did the state of Illinois become Nazi Germany?*

I know working for the Outfit is not like working for Sears or some big corporation where, if there's a problem, an employee would be talked to by someone in personnel after being referred to personnel by the immediate supervisor or something like that, depending on the company policy. For crissakes, we're talking about hitting a woman. What company condones that? With the Outfit you are talked to once, and if the problem doesn't go away, then they take action.

With this wonderful management style, even if you think you are doing the right thing, their definition of right could be completely different than yours. I've seen cases where a girl does improve after the initial talk with the madam, bringing in the right amount of money, but still gets beaten because some psycho twisted brain that lacks any type of reasoning power says that since I had to tell you to improve, you get beat. The Outfit's brain message is we hired you for a job, do the job the way it's supposed to be done at all times. If I have to tell you how to do the job, then you suffer the physical consequences, got it, sweetie?

The Outfit was never keen on caring about someone's feelings. Their management style was based on three simple principles—fear, fear, and fear. The problem with this was the Outfit's interpretation of the Harvard School of Business management approach was you never knew what triggered which repercussion to anyone. Since I don't believe Harvard or any other business school teaches psycho management, the Outfit created their own course on this one. You still don't hit a woman.

Ernie was very particular when it came to making sure the girls were drug free. The madams knew they had to send the girls for a random blood test some time during the calendar year. The girls were told when they were hired, other than a prescription drug, no illegal drugs were to be used.

Some girls listened, some didn't. That's why there could be a turnover of girls as drugs were their downfall, in many cases. Since the girls had their own places, and would show up for work at their designated times, they were pretty much on the honor system.

Ernie wanted the girls to be pristine. He wanted them to project that wholesome girl next door image. These would be the type of girls a guy could bring home to meet Mom. The girls in Ernie's mind would be a combination of Mother Theresa and Miss Hot Pants. What they did vertically for a living should not deter from the image of a rosy-cheeked, fresh-faced, nice girl who had the pure rich soul of a Girl Scout.

While some girls, when they started working for Ernie might have fit that image, after working in the world's oldest profession for a while, that image became more hardened. They became the type of girls a guy would bring home to meet Dad.

The johns had to use condoms, which the girls always provided, unless the john brought one with him, which didn't generally happen. There wasn't going to be any john going bareback, none of that stuff. No condom, no sex. Got it, buddy?

"You see, Bobby, prostitution is like Las Vegas. We're portraying a happy atmosphere, a fun time," Jimmy said. "With the johns, you want them to feel good about the atmosphere, comfortable in their surroundings, good about the girls, and good about paying top dollar for sex," he said. "Look, let's face it, if a guy has a good home life, forget about the sex for now, he won't be coming to use our services," Jimmy said.

"When did you become a therapist?" I snickered.

"Nah, it just stands to reason, a happy marriage fuels a happy sex life," Jimmy said.

"What about a single guy? I mean, you get single guys who come to the girls," I quizzed him.

"Who knows, maybe a single guy is shy, doesn't have friends who can introduce him to girls. The introverted type, maybe a loner, who knows," he said. "But I'll tell you this, whatever the reason, he goes away happy, just like the married guy, because we get his business over and over, again and again. We fill his sexual tank just like everyone else," Jimmy said.

"Okay, Dr. Jimmy. I'll see you for my next appointment," I laughed.

The business of pleasure, which the Outfit ran, was very, very customer friendly. The Outfit wants you to enjoy yourself, tell your friends how much fun and enjoyment you are having, so maybe they want to come and have some fun, too. Let's all play in the pool together. As long as everyone has fun, who cares about the financial and emotional cost.

However, there is one dark, black, thickly topped-off cloud blocking the beautiful brilliant, carefree sunshine beaming into this sexual utopia. There is a victim. Someone does get hurt, so I'm sorry, but I'm going to have to stop the sexual merry-go-round. The family is the victim.

The wife and children suffer not having the undivided love they should be receiving, and the money being spent on a person who works vertically for a living, rather should be spent on them.

I understand that for some guys, not every marriage is a winner, but not every wife is some maniacal bitch from hell, either. There are tons of wonderful, beautiful, kind, loving women out there who, simply put, are the ideal mate. They're out there, guys, just waiting for you.

When it comes to reasoning what is really good for them, the johns use their penis as the barometer. Sex becomes the standard that some guys use in determining what a relationship should be. Fellows, you're making a big mistake using sex to replace happiness. A few moments of sex with a paid vertical princess will never replace a lifetime of happiness with the true princess in your life. She's the one that's there when times are good, and she's the one that's there when times are bad. She will be there for you as you are her one and only love. Don't become sexually blinded, or you will be the one missing out on the best of what life can offer with someone who will give you her best of what she has to offer.

Unfortunately, I've seen the 'wow, I had a great wife and blew it' syndrome play out like a thought strictly on repeat, over and over, after she somehow finds out about the sex being carried on outside of the house and divorces him.

Sometimes, in my life's experiences with watching johns destroy their marriages, I think it comes down to this—some people marry the wrong person for the right reasons. The reasons for marriage are supposed to be love, honor, cherish, respect, devotion—all the factors that are the emotional structure of what builds and defines a marriage. So, those are the true components of the marriage and are the right reasons to marry someone. Some guys, by their actions of not being faithful to their wife, didn't get the memo and, therefore, become the wrong guy for her.

It wasn't as hard as you think for the Outfit to find prostitutes. Ernie would drop in with either Big John or Danny C accompanying him to some of the bars on the Near North Side.

These bars were not controlled by the Outfit, but still had the action, so Ernie would get friendly with the bartenders and would ask them which girl at the bar was working that night. Ernie would dangle a twenty dollar bill in the bartender's face as bait. Once Ernie got the information, he smiled, put the money on the bar, and said, "I'll see you next time."

The bartenders were always eager to help Mr. Marciano out with the information he wanted, as a twenty is a twenty. Pretty easy money, huh?

"Hi, Mr. Marciano, what can I do for you tonight," they would chirp in an orchestrated fashion. Their voices were programmed, so as soon as Ernie and Company walked in, they parroted what Ernie wanted to hear. Hum, that twenty sure is a tasty cracker.

The bartenders saw the way Ernie and his boys carried themselves, asking about which girl was working tonight, that these guys had to be Outfit guys. So, as long as he was putting out a crumb or two, they would swallow them up before Ernie took his business somewhere else. Keep Mr. Marciano happy was their mantra, and the twenties would reign down on them from this Outfit Santa Claus. They were like children getting a new toy on Christmas Day, all bright-eyed, ready to please their master.

There were some girls who, after listening to Ernie's proposal about working for him, gave him the, "I'll get back to you," line. They realized this was Mob prostitution we're talking about, and they would take a pass, forget about it, nope, not for me. They would continue to work solo at the bar, keeping their independence. They walked away.

Actually, I give those girls a lot of credit. They looked danger in the eye and got the hell away from it. However, these girls were in the minority as more often than not, a girl would succumb to Ernie's proposal about making more money, having a better life, no one will bother you, all the trappings that purred sweetly in a girl's ear, but left a stench that smelled of trouble. She did not walk away and, thus, began her mob prostitution career.

Mob prostitution was how the Outfit made its friends beholden to us. The politicians, judges, and cops had sexual appetites that had to be fed. From the very first feeding, they became manipulated slaves, pawns to be moved back and forth by the Outfit to provide any favor the Outfit wanted. The Outfit used its tight sexual grip on its friends to be the criminal organization that movies were made from.

Without corrupt officials clearing the streets for the Outfit to skip down those streets and pass out criminal goodies, there would be no Outfit. The Outfit's muscle would lose definition, become flabby, and who fears flabby? So, sex was the thread that neatly tied the corrupt buttons in place. Sex was the one thing the Outfit knew could get it anything it wanted. It always did and always will.

The friends' names, along with the names of other johns, were kept in a black book held by the madam. Then, if favors were needed by the Outfit, Ernie would consult the book to see who would perform the favors. Its friends had no choice but to jump through the Outfit's hoops. If word got out about its friends' sexual exercise programs, they would be ruined. Their wives would divorce them, careers would be washed into Lake Michigan, friends and colleagues would treat them as social outcasts—everyone would just run away from them.

In a way, the Outfit didn't want to go public with its friends' sex lives, because once they went public, they would have to start over with someone new. Publicity was never included in the Outfit's repertoire. Too much of it could get you whacked. A new dog would have to be trained. So, the Outfit held the threat of what it could do if its friends didn't comply with Outfit wishes over their heads. Tick, tick, tick with the information bomb just hanging over their heads, its friends knew the Outfit ran the game, not them.

There was one customer who never came to the hotels. This customer would receive a house call visit to his home from one of the girls. This customer would not even pay for his girl's services. He got her services pro bono. Ernie never took a penny from this customer.

Our Lady of Perpetual Worship, while not only was it the neighborhood Catholic Church, it was also known as the Outfit's church. Guys would come back to the old neighborhood with their wife and kids, Sunday after Sunday, to sit in a pew all dressed up in their Sunday suits, and the wife and kids also dressed up sharper than sharp, to pray to the Almighty.

Pew after pew would have a mix of the common neighborhood folk, and the criminals that were in the life. Not the good life the neighborhood people tried to lead, but the illegal life the Outfit members committed themselves to.

It was interesting to see good sitting next to evil. Did the Outfit think when God handed out his blessings, by sitting next to the good people, they would be included with the good people? Sort of a one blessing fits all. I don't think so.

When it was time for the collection baskets to be passed down the aisles, while the good people might, if they had it, put in five dollars, the Outfit boys would put in ten dollars. If the good people put in ten dollars, the boys would put in twenty dollars. The Outfit, even in this house of worship, where every mortal is deemed equal in God's eyes, had to make sure through their donations that God would respect them for the power they were.

When the Outfit boys felt they needed God, he better damn well remember they were the ones who made Our Lady of Perpetual Worship a stronger financial parish. The Outfit boys, in their eyes, were performing a form of sacramental loan-sharking, and God would have to deliver the juice by granting them whatever they wanted from him. God, to the Outfit, was added to the list of its friends, probably in a special religious category.

If God did not deliver on the Outfit's requests, it could cut off the money and the good people of Our Lady of Perpetual Workshop would suffer. The money used in the Christmas food drive would stop. The money used to buy new prayer books would stop. The money used to fund the sports programs that would keep the kids off the streets would stop. Money used in other programs would stop. The Outfit's money could go from a green light to a red light in a flick of a switch.

As the money from the Outfit was put in those wicker baskets on Sundays, even the Almighty, with all his power and the might that he had, knew that if he did not deliver the juice, he would just idly watch good parishioners lose their beloved programs. "Damn the Outfit," he muttered under his breath.

Every Sunday, Ernie Marciano brought his family for the 10:00 A.M. Mass to Our Lady of Perpetual Worship to pray. As Ernie entered Our Lady of Perpetual Worship, he would greet his Outfit parishioners with handshakes, and the Outfit greeting, "How ya doing?" to each and every one.

As the Marciano family settled in on the dark brown hardened wooden bench-like seating, Ernie would look straight ahead, eyes focused at the individual standing behind the podium on the stage. It was time for the service to begin, and it was to be led by the customer.

Father Thomas McAvoy, known to everyone in the church and the neighborhood as Father Tom, stood behind the podium, and spoke loudly and firmly into the microphone, telling the parishioners, saints and sinners alike, to please be seated, the service will begin.

Father Tom was a huge hulk of a man at 6'3", 225 pounds, with muscles on top of muscles, who got your attention quickly. With brown hair starting to gather some gray along the temples, and exceptionally clear, light blue eyes, this 50-year-old man drew approving glances from the females in the pews. Their eyes followed his every movement on the stage. This man of the cloth was a chick magnet to them. If only he wasn't a priest; he was one fine catch, they sighed.

Father Tom was from the neighborhood, played high school football for St. Leonard's and after high school, he decided he wanted to spread God's word, so he became a priest.

He worked out regularly at the local health club, and once in a while on a Saturday night, he would take off his collar, leave it in his church office, and go visit Emerald Isle. Emerald Isle was a neighborhood tavern where a lot of his old football teammates from St. Leonard's would hang out. The Isle, as everyone called it, was where St. Leonard alumni would come to swap stories about bygone days.

Father Tom's buddies would relieve their past high school years with stories, some stretching the boundaries of truth. They would tell bad jokes as they wanted to be together in their own liquid parish. Father Tom would be right in the middle of them, telling stories and laughing at the jokes. He was a regular guy at heart, just yearning to be one of the guys—not Father Tom, but Tommy from St. Leonard's.

His yearnings to be a regular guy included the need for female companionship, which was on his checklist. Father Tom, while he dressed in a different uniform, still had the same feelings about women as other men did. He just wanted the soft, sweet smelling body of a female next to him. He wanted her scent to drip into the pores of his skin.

Father Tom's pleasing personality, along with his physical attributes, under different circumstances would have been an easy sell to any woman. It would not have been a question of if he would meet a woman, but rather which one of the litter would he choose.

He talked with Ernie about how difficult it was as a man of the cloth that he would, for the rest of his life, have to remain celibate. This was the door opener for Ernie. He could solve Father Tom's problem of companionship, plus gain some brownie points with the Church for future use when needed.

The Outfit never felt a problem could not be solved. How they solved the problem took on some often bizarre and unorthodox methods. In solving a problem, the only thing the Outfit had to do was figure out how it benefitted the Outfit.

Finally, after several conversations with Father Tom, Ernie convinced him that he could discreetly have one of the girls come to Our Lady of Perpetual Worship on Wednesday afternoons, and there would be no charge for her services; it would be free.

"You could say it's a counseling session," Ernie said.

"Well, uh, I guess if you put it like that, Ernie, I suppose it would be okay," Father Tom said.

"I mean, whatever you do, it's your business, Father. I mean you decide how things are going to go, okay?" Ernie said. "Look, Father," as Ernie raised his right hand and crossed himself, "we're men, and we have needs, sometimes physical, sometimes emotional, and those needs have to be taken care of," he said.

Father Tom sighed as he knew he had taken an oath of celibacy when he became a priest. In becoming a priest, celibacy was part of your commitment to God that could not be negotiated. The Vatican wanted it that way, and that's the way it would be. There was no one to appeal to. Either you accepted celibacy or you did not become a priest. Father Tom was just going to have to somehow navigate around celibacy.

Ernie decided on sending Janet Travers to see Father Tom. Janet was not your normal prostitute, if there ever was a normal prostitute. Janet had been a Chicago Public School elementary teacher for six years.

She met Ernie in a bar one night and after talking to him, she thought she would try it for kicks. *It was, maybe, only going to be one night, one guy, then back to teaching the next day*, she thought. Well, it's now seven years later, and a lot more guys than one.

Janet was a petite woman, 5'2", 110 pounds, who used her intellect quite a bit with the johns. When the johns asked for her, they referred to her as the broad with the brains. She would hold conversations with them about numerous subjects, especially the johns who were having problems with their kids in school.

The johns would listen as Janet told them what educational programs were available for them to get their kids into, depending on what the problem was. They were always thankful and showed their appreciation by giving her a bigger tip.

A lot of Janet's sessions were spent talking to the johns with, maybe, a little sex happening near the end of the hour. If a john just wanted sex, then the conversations never happened. He was still the customer, so she had to comply with what he wanted as her tip was at stake.

Ernie felt Janet was the ideal match for Father Tom, and let him know that coming Wednesday she would come to Our Lady of Perpetual Worship by 2 P.M. Wednesday was a good day for Father Tom, as he was alone that day in the church. His secretary was not in that day, so he and Janet would be able to have time together alone.

When Janet walked into Our Lady of Perpetual Worship, she and Father Tom stood frozen, looking at each other. He had taken off his collar to avoid the formal look. As they looked at each other, she smiled at him. Oh, that warm melting of the ice smile a woman gives a man. Father Tom felt the vibe. The smile she gave, oh yes, he felt it.

The smile mesmerized him as he couldn't even say, "Hi, I'm Father Tom." She sensed his hesitancy and walked up to him, taking both her hands and held his hands in hers. "Hi, I'm Janet Travers," she said. He said hi to her.

Father Tom had a bedroom in Our Lady of Perpetual Worship as he lived in the church. Somehow, after seeing Janet, he did not think it was appropriate to take her there. There was something about Janet. Maybe it was her smile. Maybe it was the brightness illuminating in her big, beautiful brown eyes. Maybe it was just Janet. Whatever Father Tom was feeling about Janet, the bedroom seemed out of place at this moment. Celibacy was safe for now.

He walked her into the sanctuary where they would sit in the last row and talk.

"Let me help you with your coat," he offered.

"Such a gentleman," she said coyly, while maintaining a smile.

They looked in each other's eyes as they sat and exchanged stories, keeping the banter light between them. As the seconds turned into minutes, Father Tom's feelings for Janet started to quickly climb the emotional thermometer. As his feelings grew stronger, he liked being in Janet's company. She relaxed him with her easiness. She relaxed him with a soft, clear, sweet sounding voice that removed his anxieties, opening the door and letting them go play somewhere else. And, she relaxed his body, making him feel like a complete man once again.

During the conversation, he held her hand for a moment, skin to skin, flesh to flesh. It was a brief physical encounter; his way of making a bond with her. He got gratification from the warmth of her hand. It made him feel like he was Tommy from St. Leonard's out on a Saturday night date.

He released her hand, not wanting to hold on to something that might not be sustainable. Maybe she didn't like some stranger she just met holding her hand for a longer time than she wanted. So he backed off, letting go of the precious female hand and its dangling fingers.

As soon as he let go, they both looked directly in each other's eyes. A second or two or three passed. No words were spoken; just visual emotions flashing from him to her and her to him. Their body language bounced their emotions off of each other.

She spoke, starting to tell him about a humorous incident when she taught second grade. She moved her body a little closer to his. While continuing to talk to him, she slowly took his right hand, the hand that had formerly held her hand, and placed her right hand over his. She held his hand delicately, not gripping it, but rather letting her hand guide her emotional feelings directly to his hand.

Hands are the bridge connecting a love emotion. Watch two lovers walk down a street holding hands, maybe talking, maybe not. They convey their love to each other by transmitting the love vibe through their hands. Their hearts reach out to their hands to transmit a love signal in three simple words—I love you.

Janet and Father Tom continued their conversation as she held his hand until he glanced at his watch, realizing the hour was just about up.

"Ah, I guess your time is about up," he said.

"Really? It went so fast," she said, removing her hand from his.

They both stood up. He helped her with her coat as she maintained her radiant smile. Even though it was winter outside, in the sanctuary it felt like a hot July Chicago day.

At this point, Father Tom wasn't sure what to do. He really wanted to hug and kiss her, thanking her for helping him retrieve his manhood. With celibacy peering over his shoulder, Father Tom decided it was best to take the conventional road.

"Thanks, Janet, for a great afternoon," he said, as he extended his hand to shake hers.

"You're welcome, Father Tom...er Tom. I'm not sure what to call you," she said, extending her hand as they shook hands.

"You can call me Tom," he said, with a smile stretching across his face. They walked to the front door of Our Lady of Perpetual Worship. He started to open the door. They stood face to face.

"See you next week," he said hopefully, as his voice had a question mark stuck in his throat. Would she say yes? Would she say no? He wondered. *Please, God, you see I've been a good Catholic boy. Encourage her to say yes*, he hoped.

While maintaining that ongoing smile, she said, "See you next week," and walked out the door.

Father Tom walked back into the sanctuary. He looked at the stained glass window of the Virgin Mary in the sanctuary and thanked God for his guidance. *You won't be sorry you helped me, as I will always be true to my beliefs*, he told God. He realized he had gotten sex without having sex. He had gotten generic sex, mental and emotional sex, that while it was a substitution, it was still as gratifying as any physical sex could be. His celibacy was still intact, no problem. Holding hands, no big deal. He did that with grieving parishioners upon their loss of a loved one, so that didn't break the celibacy window.

Janet had given him his sexual salvation that he needed to feel like a man should fee. It was the companionship he wanted. It was the companionship he got.

Janet went back and told Ernie, who had paid her the two hundred dollars she would have charged Father Tom for the hour, that from now on she wasn't going to accept Ernie's money. It was going to be for free between her and Father Tom.

For the next several years, Father Tom and Janet met every Wednesday at Our Lady of Perpetual Worship at 2 P.M. They talked, they laughed, they giggled, and they even held hands. Celibacy, which had been perched on Father Tom's shoulder, eventually got off and walked away. It had no reason to stay as Tommy from St. Leonard's had become the complete man he wanted to be.

Parishioners noticed a different Father Tom. He smiled more. His sermons on Sunday become more enthusiastic. After the services, his greetings in the hallway to the leaving parishioners were more humane. There was a softness in his eyes.

Maybe he had a girlfriend, some of the parishioners whispered among themselves. Father Tom was a different man. He was receiving the one thing he really always wanted and that was to be with a woman. While he knew that he could never have the physical sex, because that would cross the celibacy line, and once crossed he would have to turn in his collar and give up being a priest, he was able to build a sexual standard that both he and the Catholic Church could sit in agreement on. It would work for him, and he hoped it would work for the Catholic Church.

Being a priest was the life he wanted, and being a priest is what he would remain. Tommy from St. Leonard's was back. Maybe spreading God's word, but he was definitely back.

Our Lady of Perpetual Worship became a better place because Father Tom became a happier spiritual leader. He got the verbal and emotional sex he needed to fuel his soul. He was able to make his dream come true, and how many of us really can say we made our dreams come true? For to chase a dream, you have to have a dream.

When dealing with the Outfit, the boys have a saying…We've got a hook in you. It means they control you, they own you, and they make you do what they want you to do.

Ernie now had his hook in Father Tom. By providing Janet to Father Tom, he guaranteed Father Tom's loyalty.

"You know, Father, sometime in their lives friends of mine will have to hold services at Our Lady of Perpetual Worship for the loss of their loved ones," Ernie said.

"Some might say the loved one didn't always lead a clean life, if you get my drift," he said. "So I just wannabe sure everything goes smooth on your end when that day comes. I mean, they are Catholics, baptized and all, so that should make it okay, right, Father?" Ernie, in a rather direct voice, said.

"I don't see any problem, Ernie. They're still God's children no matter what their past is," Father Tom said. "I'll perform the service, and go to St. Matthew's Cemetery to say the prayers for them at the burial," he said.

"Good. Good. Great, Father. Wow, that's great. Thanks, Father," Ernie said, while pumping Father Tom's hand. Even in the House of the Lord, the Outfit had juice.

When a loved one in an Italian family died, more often than not, they would use Gondere Funeral Home to have their loved one prepared for their final resting place. The Italian community in Chicago relied on Gondere Funeral Home to provide a proper burial for their loved one.

Jake Gondere's father, in the early 1900s, started Gondere Funeral Home from scratch. Enrico Gondere came from Northern Italy to America, landing in Chicago to live with a cousin. He had virtually no money, spoke practically no English, yet worked and worked and worked as hard as he could when he got a job at Sweeney's Funeral Home, mainly picking up dead bodies from residents in their homes and hospitals. Since old man Sweeney had juice with a couple of aldermen, Sweeney's would get calls from the city morgue to pick up bodies that were not claimed by anyone.

Enrico would be sent over to the morgue to pick up the bodies as Chicago taxpayers wound up paying for the funerals. Sweeney would bill the City of Chicago for his services. Sweeney paid off the aldermen, and the city paid off Sweeney. Enrico learned that, in Chicago, corruption fed off the dead.

He stayed at Sweeney's ten years, learning every phase of the funeral business. A shy type of guy, he was introduced to Lucianna Paoeli by a mutual friend of both, and they went out for an ice cream cone the next night. One date led to another date and another, and after two years of courting her, Enrico proposed marriage to her.

"The manicotti could get cold waiting for you," she teased him as she accepted his proposal. She knew Enrico was the one for her right from the ice cream cone date.

It was his drive, his passion to wanting to succeed in life that drew Lucianna's attention. To become what he wanted to be in the country that opened its doors to him, and let him arrive in Chicago with only one word in his vocabulary, which was 'success.' That's what captured Lucianna's heart—his drive that, while being an immigrant, he would become successful in this, which offered opportunities that existed nowhere else in the world but America. The stairway to success would not be easy, but Enrico, no matter how tired or defeated he was, he would put one foot in front of the other, and balance himself on each step. Step by step, he would climb to reach the top of the stairs, and gain the success he wanted for him and Lucianna.

"I will never let you down," he told Lucianna. "I will fight harder today than I did yesterday for you," he said. "You are my world and I will give you a world of prosperity so you can have a good life," he told her.

Shortly after their marriage, Enrico decided he wanted to open up Gondere Funeral Home. He went to Stanton Finance Company to talk with the owner John Stanton about getting a loan. The property Enrico was looking at was owned by Stanton Finance Company. John Stanton was a crusty guy in his late 50s, who lived a few blocks from his business. He had no family, so the business was his family.

"Listen, Gondere, you miss one monthly payment, just one on the loan, and I'll call in the loan. You understand?" he said in a gruff, harsh voice. When he approved Enrico's loan application, he told Enrico he did not want to have to foreclose on a funeral home. "You seem to be a hard worker, so I'm approving the loan on that fact as you have no collateral at this point to support the loan," Stanton said.

"I don't approve a loan without collateral, but there is something about you, Gondere, something in your personality that I think will make you a success," he said.

"Don't worry, Mr. Stanton. I will never miss a payment," Enrico said confidently.

Enrico was as happy as he could be after leaving Stanton Finance Company with an approved loan. He immediately filled out the paperwork required by the City of Chicago to become licensed. He went downtown to City Hall to hand in his paperwork the next day.

Enrico worked day and night, many times going home for dinner, then coming back to the building to rehab it to get it ready for approval by the city's building inspector, who would have to okay that the building met the proper building codes before Enrico could open for business. Lucianna was concerned Enrico was working such long hours, but he told her it was his labor of love.

Several months later, he called the city to schedule a building inspector to check the building as he had completed the needed construction work.

Bob Luken, the city's building inspector, praised Enrico's work as he walked through the building. Luken stopped by an air shaft. "I'm not so sure about this," he said as he looked at the air shaft. Having watched Mr. Sweeney grease the aldermen to get favors, Enrico learned in Chicago it's what is put in someone's palm or not put in someone's palm that could make or break your business. The Chicago style of doing business rubbed off on him.

Enrico took a couple of bucks out of his pocket. Maybe this will help your decision," he said as he put the money in Luken's palm. Luken looked back up at the air shaft and said, "Mr. Gondere, everything in the building passes, so I'll recommend your license be approved." Enrico learned how to make some juice that day.

"Why is it after all these decades, city building inspectors still keep getting caught taking a bribe? Doesn't anyone learn from the previous inspector who got caught?" I asked Jimmy.

"I guess they have itchy palms," he said.

Enrico had just about depleted his savings that he and Lucianna were living on. Enrico proudly felt he was living the 'American Dream.' A kid with nothing in his pockets but a dream comes from Italy to Chicago, and with hard work, extreme dedication, and a fierce effort to succeed. Gondere Funeral Home becomes his dream come true. Gondere Funeral Home opened for business, and Enrico began his quest to become a hero to Lucianna.

The first four years, Enrico was struggling financially to keep Gondere in the black. Business was coming in, but not much volume and slowly. He worried a lot then about paying Mr. Stanton, paying his employees, and supporting Lucianna.

He walked home one night after work, his head down, and his footsteps had no pep in them as they trudged along the pavement. He showed all the signs of a beaten man. The cash flow was very weak, and as he walked up the stairs to the apartment, he knew he was going to have to look Lucianna in her beautiful eyes and tell her he was a failure. Gondere was going to have to close his dream; their dream would be buried under a pile of hope he once held so tightly. A pile of hope he squeezed every day for her and only her, to lead the life the wife of a successful businessman should enjoy. He wanted her, when she walked down the streets of Chicago, to hear people say, "There goes Mrs. Gondere. What I wouldn't give for her life."

Once inside the apartment, he glumly looked at the love of his life, Lucianna. There was stillness in his voice. His vocal chords were waiting to be prompted to react.

"How did your day go, honey?" she cheerfully said.

"Well, I've had better," Enrico said.

She took him over to the sofa where they sat down, and she held his hand.

"Enrico, I went to the doctor today to get the results of a test I took," she said. "I wasn't sure, so I didn't want to say anything until I got my results, and I'm pregnant," she blurted out.

"Lucianna! Lucianna!" he joyfully said as he reached over and hugged her.

"What, what, we're going to have a child? My God...my God...I...I don't know what to say," he said. "I'm going to be a daddy. You've given me the greatest gift I could ever ask for," he said so exuberantly, the words were coming out in rapid fire response filling the apartment with utter joy.

"When, when is the birth going to happen? Are you alright? Here, here, sit back on the sofa and rest," Enrico said.

"I'm three months pregnant, so six months from now we will be a complete family," Lucianna said.

The status of the funeral home would have to wait. Enrico did not tell Lucianna about the financial difficulty the business was in. *Now was not the time. Now was a time for basking in the happy thoughts about the impending birth of their child. It was all they should be thinking about*, Enrico thought. Whatever it took, he was going to make Gondere's not only exist, but be successful.

Enrico now had to think for three, not two anymore. Somehow, someway, he would turn the business around at Gondere's. But how, that was the unanswered question swirling around in his head.

A few days after finding out he was going to become a father, Enrico, sitting in his office, started to ponder the future, and at that point the future looked bleak. What, oh what was he going to do?

A man walked into Gondere's who was going to change the gloomy future into a very, very illuminating future for Enrico. Freddie Torrino, who some in the neighborhood called unsavory, entered Enrico's life.

Freddie came to Gondere's to seek their services for the passing of his mother. The arrangements were made, and Freddie was very impressed by Enrico's professional approach in the preparation and all other pertinent details for his mother's funeral. Enrico made Freddie feel like his mother was a very special person, and Enrico took great pains in making sure all of Freddie's requests were honored.

A week after the funeral, Freddie came back to see Enrico. "Bringing me more business, Mr. Torrino?" Enrico jokingly said. "Enrico, please call me Freddie," he said.

"Sure, okay, Freddie," Enrico said.

Freddie Torrino ran a gambling and loan-sharking operation. In a few years, he would join up with a guy who moved to Chicago from Brooklyn, New York, one Mr. Alphonse Capone, and become part of Capone's mob.

"You don't seem very busy," Freddie said.

"Yeah, well I'm still trying to build my business," Enrico said.

"I'd like to help you," Freddie said. "I'm going to talk to some of my friends, and see if I can get them to use your services."

"Wow! That would be great. Thanks. Thanks a lot," Enrico said.

"It's my pleasure to help you as you never know, maybe someday you can help me," Freddie said.

"Sure. Sure, anything. You name it," Enrico said.

Freddie smiled as he was putting the hook in Enrico so smoothly and effortlessly, Enrico never felt a thing.

By the end of the month, Gondere did twelve more funerals than the previous month. Business was starting to really pick up. At first, most of the funerals were coming from the business community in the neighborhood, taking care of their loved ones. Then, Enrico started to get a lot of neighborhood customers, the Joes and Janes that populate a neighborhood.

Freddie put out the word that Gondere's was to be used for funerals, and if someone used another funeral home instead of Gondere's, he wanted to know why.

There was one guy in the neighborhood who did use another funeral home. Once Freddie found out about this, he sent a couple of his boys to pay this guy a visit. They beat him up enough so when people in the neighborhood saw his bruised face and cut lip, they got the message loud and clear what would happen if they didn't use Gondere's.

Enrico was unaware of Freddie's tactics. He just watched the money as it came. If there was ever such a thing, a funeral home became a happy place to be around. The money saw to that.

While Gondere's no longer was in the red, it started to put month after month's revenues in the black. While the business was prospering, finally the blessed day came for Enrico and Lucianna. They became proud parents of a boy they named Jake.

About a year later, the business, which appeared to be nearly extinct, was flourishing. Enrico had saved money so he now had enough money to make a down payment on a small three-bedroom house. He and Lucianna looked at houses and found one that suited their tastes and purchased it.

On Sundays, Enrico and Lucianna would go to Mass at a church that had just been open for a few weeks. Like anything new, the church sparkled. Our Lady of Perpetual Worship was where Enrico prayed, not only for the health and well-being of his family, but to give thanks to God for blessing him with a growing and successful business.

Word spread to other areas of the city where there were Italian communities about Gondere's. As Jake Gondere in later years would say, in business word of mouth can make you or break you. As Gondere's reputation grew, business started to come in from different Italian neighborhoods in Chicago, which increased the volume of business.

Outfit families were bringing their loved ones to Gondere besides the neighborhood people. Enrico's balance sheet was getting stronger and stronger with help from the Outfit, who buried loved one after loved one at Gondere's.

While in high school, Jake worked when he could side by side, learning the funeral business from Enrico. Soon, Jake was going to learn another side of the business that would teach him what it was like to deal with mobsters.

Freddie had become part of the Capone mob, which in taking over the rackets in Chicago, would bring Enrico a different type of business than his normal one.

Freddie grew to a bigger wheel status for Capone and one morning he went to see Enrico.

"Good morning, Enrico," Freddie said, walking into Enrico's office.

"Hi, Freddie. What can I do for you?" Enrico asked.

"Enrico, I've known you many years. I was here when you were really struggling with trying to make the business go, and I was glad to help you any way I could, so your business could succeed," Freddie said.

Now here's where the hook, which was put into Enrico years ago, is about to be pulled by Freddie.

"You see, Enrico," I am a member of Mr. Alphonse Capone's organization, and, well, we are reorganizing our businesses, and because of that certain people will be eliminated," Freddie said.

Enrico stared at Freddie, wondering what he was talking about. Since he still had to find out what Freddie was talking about, he quietly listened as Freddie continued speaking.

"I've got to ask you a favor, Enrico. We'll work out the financial details as to what you have to charge for your services later, but I need you to make people disappear so their bodies will not be found," Freddie said in a much softer voice than he normally spoke in.

Enrico didn't know what to say. He was completely stunned by what Freddie wanted him to do. Finally, after composing himself, he spoke. "I'm, I'm not sure what you want me to do," Enrico said. "Are you talking about burying dead people?" he said.

"Yeah. I just want you to like make the bodies go away quietly, somewhere where they won't be found," Freddie said.

"Well, let me think about this," Enrico said.

"I'll come back and see you in a week," Freddie said.

After Freddie left, Enrico sat in his chair nearly thirty minutes, thinking and thinking about what he should do. *These are not loved ones who died. These are people the Capone mob was going to kill, and Freddie wants me to help him dispose of these corpses in some manner,* Enrico thought.

He's asking me to do something that's illegal. What if I say no? Do I have a choice? He could start bad mouthing me to the Italian community, and then there goes the business. Everything I have worked for will be lost. How would I support Lucianna and Jake if I lose the business? For every reason Enrico could think of for saying 'no' to Freddie, he thought of reasons why he should say 'yes' to Freddie.

Enrico decided he must talk with God first before he made any decision to help Freddie or not to help him. Every Saturday afternoon at 4:30 P.M., there was time allotted for confessional at Our Lady of Perpetual Worship. Enrico decided to go on the upcoming Saturday.

As he got in the small box, ready to talk to Father Collier about what was on his mind, he realized he would have to talk about committing a sin in the future rather than trying to get forgiveness for an already committed sin.

Father Collier, a priest for nearly forty years, sat in the adjoining confessional box and opened up the slot between his box and Enrico's. "I am here for you," Father Collier told Enrico.

"Father, I ask for your forgiveness as I am about to commit a sin—a sin that once I commit it, I will not be able to stop committing it. I will repeat it over and over again," Enrico said.

"My son, the Almighty has forgiveness in his heart for sinners," Father Collier said. "For the sinner who goes through the pain and anguish of committing the sin once, twice, three times, the number does not matter. God will forgive the act of sinning as you come before God asking for his forgiveness as one of God's children. Even though it is a sin you have committed, God knows to maintain his flock of children, he must forgive one of his children," Father Collier said.

"Without a flock there will eventually be no family, and God has always perceived the need of having a family so children can grow into that family and marry and have their own family," he said. "A flock needs to evolve from one generation to the next, otherwise how do we sustain the world?" Father Collier said.

"So, even though you will be committing a sin, since you are part of God's flock, he will always love you, you will have his undying love into eternity and his forgiveness," Father Collier said.

"Thank you, Father," Enrico said.

Enrico got up and left Our Lady of Perpetual Worship, knowing he would have God's love and forgiveness, even though he would be helping Freddie do something illegal.

As Enrico walked home, a biting wind coming out of the north had dropped the temperature as the evening air grew chilly. Enrico put his hands in his coat pockets while walking wearily, carrying a heavy heart. While the Catholic Church handed him a 'free to sin card,' Enrico thought about his role as a father in raising Jake. *Fathers are supposed to teach their sons the life of honesty and morality*, he thought. *What type of a father am I by showing him how to sin? I guess, in my son's eyes he won't hold his father so dear*, Enrico said to himself.

Enrico reached into his pocket for the key to open the front door of his house. Before he walked into the house, he took out his wallet to look at a baby picture of his son. *Remember me, how I was, not how I turned out to be*, he said as he looked with troubled eyes at the picture. Putting the picture back in his wallet, Enrico knew he had to come up with a plan to satisfy Freddie.

Over the weekend, Enrico thought and thought about how he could get rid of the Outfit's murder victims. Finally, after much deliberation, he came up with an idea that on Monday, he would need Jake's help to implement.

On Monday night, Enrico took Jake into the display room where customers would choose a coffin for their loved ones.

"Jake, I'm going to have to help Mr. Torrino, so let's take out the padding in the coffin where the body is placed," Enrico said.

It pained Enrico to include Jake in helping Freddie. He was teaching his son how to become a criminal in the funeral business.

This isn't what a father is supposed to do as Enrico became disgusted with himself. Yet, he had to make the play when the play had to be made; otherwise, Gondere's would be hurt financially as Freddie would retaliate. He carefully explained to Jake that sometimes in business you have to cut a corner.

Jake listened and helped Enrico remove the padding from the coffin. Enrico saw at the bottom of the coffin there was a panel and, if he removed it, there was space for another body. Enrico removed the panel and climbed into the coffin, crawling into the area below where a body would lay right above it. At 5'8" and weighing 170 pounds, Enrico fit into the space. He saw where the space could be expanded to fit someone over six feet tall.

"This is what we're going to do," Enrico told Jake after climbing out of the coffin. "When Mr. Torrino calls us to pick up a body, we will remove the panel and put the body in that area. When we have another customer, we will put that person in the upper area of the coffin like always."

"You mean we're going to bury two people in the same coffin," Jake questioned.

"Well, technically we will be burying two, but only the body on top will have a wake and services," Enrico said. "Thus, the origin of the double coffin originated in Gondere's, and to the best of my knowledge, existed nowhere else in any funeral home in Chicago at that time.

The next day, Freddie came to see Enrico who told Freddie about the double coffin plan. Freddie was ecstatic, congratulating Enrico on a brilliant plan. Freddie would be charged the cost of preparing the body and their pickup charge for the body, unless the body was brought to Gondere's.

Freddie happily agreed to the charges, and soon thereafter, bodies started to appear from Freddie and continued appearing long after Freddie died. The police never could find bodies of presumed missing mob-related murders in a lot of those cases. If the police had looked at the burial sites at St. Matthew's Cemetery, they would have found a lot of the boys. For the rest of Enrico's life, the hook remained solidly entrenched in his back and Freddie and others after him made sure the hook stayed firmly in place.

Unknowingly, Italian families who thought they were just burying their loved one were burying someone else's loved one also. It became a joke between Enrico and Jake that if you buried one, you got the second one free in the same coffin. The double coffin was continued by Jake after Enrico died of a heart attack when Jake was in his mid-30s, for Jake's hands were to become as soiled as Enrico's were from accepting the dirty money during his lifetime.

"You know, Bobby, Jake once told me when Pops got involved with Freddie Torrino, I thought how could he even think of doing that type of business with him. I was in high school, so what did I know about business? Don't get me wrong. I loved Pops, but still was that what you want to teach your son about right and wrong?" Jake said. "So what happens when Pops dies, I continue doing the same damn thing for the same damn people," he said. "I guess the meatball rolled off of his plate onto mine," Jake said wistfully.

The only one of Jake's four kids who went into the business with him was Billy, his youngest son. The double coffin business, while unsteady, as you didn't know when a body would turn up, was a real money maker as Jake would actually be getting two charges of services for one coffin. Since the Outfit paid in cash, Jake never reported that income and basically had free income to do whatever he wanted with it. I guess when it comes down to it, money beat honesty. Money is the big mouth everyone listens to.

Jake was always nice to me. I remember when Jimmy would take me along when he had to see Jake. Jake would walk me over to DeCleo's Bakery and buy me an Italian cookie. Boy, were they hard. I had to dunk them in some milk to soften them up, which I still do today.

I would go to a lot of wakes with Jimmy at Gondere's. We would go up to the casket, view it, turn and offer condolences to the family members, and Jimmy would then look at Jake. Jake would give Jimmy the nod that the body of whomever was in the lower area of the coffin.

I still remember my first wake. I was maybe nine years old when I saw the double coffin used. The Outfit guy who was put in the lower part of the coffin was Anthony "Tough Tony" Capriano, a bookie who supposedly was seen talking to a guy who looked like a Fed. Since none of this was checked out by Arnold "Arnie Boy" Nardulli, the boss of the street crew who gave the order to have Tough Tony whacked, Tony might have been killed unfairly.

As usual, it could have been some guy running his mouth in hopes of getting Tony's clients. You would see guys trying to steal other guys' clients all the time. A guy could have made up a story telling Nardulli that Tony was talking to a Fed in hopes of taking over Tony's gambling operation. Since research was not one thing the boys excelled at, Tony could have been whacked just so someone profited from Tony's death.

If someone told a story about someone to a boss, not every boss took the time and effort to check out the story to see if it was true or not. There were some bosses that did check out the story, and a few lives were saved because of it.

Nardulli, however, was one of those bosses who just went with one story. A lot of bosses went with one story, because they wanted to. For whatever reason, and God knows there were a lot of them, a boss wanted the guy whacked. A right reason, a wrong reason…just clip the guy, it didn't matter; so the order was given and that was the end of another life.

"Bobby, in life, you always check things out. There are three stories— mine, yours, and the truth. Two of those stories gotta match. Until they do, you never jump to conclusions on anyone," Jimmy said.

What Jimmy taught me went beyond the Outfit. It spilled over into my life, in general. It was the 'don't leap before you know what you're leaping into philosophy.'

I had this strange, weird feeling as I walked up to the casket with Jimmy. Here was some total stranger lying in a coffin, and Jimmy and me are pretending to be sorry while Tony is in the lower portion of the coffin. The first time you go through this, it leaves you uncomfortable. But the more I did it, I got pretty good at putting on a face of sorrow. Once, even some stranger's family member hugged me crying, telling me I would be okay in time, and I would have the stranger in my soul. After doing these wakes enough times over and over, I tried to give a sincere feeling of sympathy to the loved ones. My acting skills improved with each appearance.

When an Outfit guy died of natural causes, a regular wake and funeral would be held at Gondere's Funeral Home. The FBI agents would snap pictures of the Outfit guys going in and out of Gondere's. It was just the Outfit guys who had to disappear who went in the double coffin. I wondered if the Outfit guy underneath someone got along with his partner. There were Outfit guys who literally wouldn't kiss this guy's ass. Maybe there was trouble at their final destination. All this funeral stuff creeped me out.

Gambling for the Outfit, as was true for mob families in other cities, was their bread and butter, meat and potatoes, when it came to income. Going back to the Capone era and before gambling money, which created the need for loan-sharking, was what the Outfit built their foundation on for other illegal activities.

Gambling was what the Outfit knew, and it was what they trusted. Gamblers come back time and time again with that magic stardust in their eyes that this…this will be the time I'll be a winner. Sure, you and I know that this financial panacea gamblers are looking for will not happen. Of course, there are some winners, just like the lottery. Someone…and I emphasize "someone"… will be a winner, but the house never loses. Quick, name a casino that has filed for bankruptcy. What's the matter? Cat got your tongue? Yeah, I thought so. Can't name one, can you?

For the Outfit, this is one addiction that helps guys in the life buy a house, put their kids through college, and buy a new car. Hell, they look at it as good for the economy.

Mob gambling for the Outfit was divided up into non-Las Vegas and Las Vegas operations. The local gambling operations would be seen in the various street crews. Those operations consisted of betting on college and professional football; some college and professional basketball, though, Chicago did not bet as heavily as New York did on the college and pro games; professional boxing; horse racing, the flats meaning the thoroughbreds and trotters meaning harness racing; video poker where the Mob gets 50% of the take from the machines mainly in backrooms of bars and restaurants; high stakes poker games in downtown hotels; and in later years, offshore gambling sites.

With computerization occurring at a much later time, online video poker became just a modern day form of mob gambling. The owners of the online sites were mob affiliated. There was another form of mob run gambling—kind of like marinara sauce meets an egg roll—sort of East meets West.

In Chicago's Chinatown area, fan-tan,—a card game in which players must build in sequence upon sevens and attempt to be the first one out of cards— was mob run. Harry "Handsome Harry" Chang, who was a top official of the Chinese Businessman's Association, which was very prevalent in Chinatown, ran fan-tan for the Outfit.

He had games going in bars and restaurants, and the Outfit got 5% right off the top for each game played. Nice money, huh? The winner of the game would be told the House takes 5% of the pot.

The Outfit, being the trusting sort that we knew they were, had someone watching Harry. Michael "Lover Boy" Rossi, who oversaw mob gambling also in the Lancaster neighborhood on the Southwest side of the city, was who Harry reported to.

Michael, with his jet black hair, good looks, sharp suits, and easy smile was a natural for the ladies. He was a ladies' man who treated the girl he was with at the time as the most important person in North America, and the women just loved the attention. Did they care he was married with three kids? Nah. Did Michael care that he was married with three kids? Nah. He chased, and the women loved to be chased. Michael was a made guy in the Outfit, which meant you couldn't screw with him, but he sure tried to screw a lot of ladies.

I gotta say, when you were in his company, he was a fun guy, laughing and joking with the waitresses in a restaurant. I remember lots of times when I was with him in a restaurant; he would snatch up the check before I could get my hand on the table.

He was a big baseball fan, especially the Chicago White Sox, and he would always rib me about my Cubbies.

"Hey, Bobby, do the Cubs have a team this year, or do they still play baseball up there in, what do you call it, the Northside?" he would say with a smirk on his face. He took me to a lot of Sunday Sox games, even though I promised God I would remain a Cub's fan. The Sundays on the South Side were good for me as they got me away, at least for a few hours, from watching the Outfit games.

As long as you didn't get involved with Michael's' business, you were fine. I learned over time with my involvement with Outfit guys, you had to be on guard for their multiple personalities. Sweet as sugar could turn into vile as vinegar quicker than quick with them. Their sociopathic and psychotic behaviors were always right outside the front door, which could walk right into your life whenever the Outfit opened up the front door and let them in. With the Outfit, you never knew when this would occur. Even God would scratch his head when trying to figure out this behavioral switcheroo.

Even when playing the role of Mr. Nice Guy, Michael knew business was still business and had to be taken care of. Michael sent his boys to Chinatown to make sure he got his cut of the Chinatown gambling action. If Michael didn't get his money from Harry and send the big boys what they were supposed to get, they would make sure he would be meeting women who would come to visit him at St. Matthew's Cemetery. So, Michael made sure the leash was wrapped around Harry very, very tightly.

Harry, who when he would meet a woman, would introduce himself as Handsome Harry Chang, though I never remember Hollywood knocking on his door offering him a contract, had another habit. He always used the word 'okay' when he talked to you.

"Harry, what time is it?" you would ask him.

"It's, okay, 3 P.M., okay," he would say.

"Harry, how's your day going?"

"Okay, okay, it's okay."

"Harry, go screw yourself!"

"Okay, okay, I will. Okay."

Harry was always a body in motion. He was one of those guys, who when sitting on a chair, would be tapping his foot. I'm not sure what the beat was that Harry was listening to, but it gave him that nervous edge.

Maybe it was his involvement with the Outfit, not known for their sea of tranquility, which kept his motor running. With the Outfit, it was one strong, powerful wave after wave, crashing violently against the shoreline. Those powerful waves scared and frightened people into fearing for their lives. The waves eroded whatever confidence people had in withstanding them. You better make sure you do what they want, and then they will throw you a life preserver jacket to wear as long as you do what they want. If you don't do what they want, your life preserver jacket will be ripped off you, and you will be thrown into the freezing water of Lake Michigan, never to be seen again.

By being involved with the Outfit, Harry's nervous system was on high alert every day. It never had a day off. It could never just kickback on the sofa and have pleasant thoughts of, let's say, a nice winter vacation in Florida. Harry's nervous system was fearful and timid, trying to anticipate what the Outfit would want or do. His whole body was impacted by his line of work.

Harry had four restaurants—Johnny Kong's, The Eggroll, Chinese Valley, and Mr. Lee's—that had daily fan-tan card games where tables were set up in the backrooms of each place. He had several bars, notably Panda Lounge, Kitten's, Pacific Inn, and Suzy's, where not only was fan-tan played, but Harry had Chinese girls offering their services to the customers in some of the bars. The girls he used as prostitutes were in their early 20s with pretty faces and nice figures.

"Okay, Bobby, you have to have the right package when it comes to the girls, okay." Harry would tell me. "Okay, they gotta attract the men, so they gotta fit the package. You know, young, firm, make a man take a second look, maybe a third look, okay," he said. "If the guy likes the package, he'll want to buy it, okay," Harry said.

"So you're telling me a guy isn't interested in the girl's brain?" I asked, with a sly, teasing smile on my face.

"Okay, ya, sure, as long as it mixes with her breasts and butt, okay, then it will work," Harry said. "Okay, no ugly; ugly, is bad for business," he said.

The whole time I was having this conversation, I was thinking *Harry actually believes what he's saying is true. The crazier thing is he might be right.*

Chinese men attracted to the women in the bars paid for their services gladly. You could see the excitement flush their faces.

Harry used a small hotel, the Aviator, for the lovemaking to occur. The Aviator was considered an SRO (single room occupancy) hotel with fifty to sixty full-time residents who lived there. They paid a set weekly amount of rent, and they lived in, basically, one room, which had a bathroom and a tiny kitchen area. If you picture a studio apartment, then you can visualize what the one room looked like at the Aviator. There always seemed to be a few vacant rooms, which Harry's girls would take the customers to for the paid fun and frolic. The front desk personnel referred to these rooms as Mr. Chang's playrooms.

The Aviator was owned by an opium dealer named Dennis "Fat Dennie" Fong. Fong was about 5'8" or 5'9" tall and weighed a little bit over 200 pounds.

He was a heavily muscled guy with large bulging forearms and huge rippling biceps. His head looked like it had been plopped down on top of his massive shoulders. I know he had a neck, it's just I don't remember seeing it. I think his neck was somewhere between Chicago and Indiana.

Fong had small, dark brown, beady eyes. When he looked at you, his eyes were located directly on your face like bullets to be fired at you from a gun. He never smiled. His face always had a mean, contemptuous look. He didn't like you, and you didn't like him.

When he sold his opium, he always wore a sports jacket to conceal his gun. He wore a shoulder holster with a big barreled gun inside of it. I'm no gun expert; maybe, it was a Winchester, but I'll tell you this, the longer you looked at the barrel, the bigger the barrel got.

Harry and Fong had a business arrangement. Harry would use the Aviator, and Fong sold opium in the bars run by Harry. So everyone's operation was neat and tidy. Harry paid off the 5th District Police Commander John Carroll one thousand dollars a month to stay away from the fan-tan games, the girls, and the Aviator. While Harry did not have any Italian blood in him, by working for the Outfit, he became an Italian by injection.

Harry was on the board of directors of the Aviator. Normally in corporate America, men and women are chosen to sit on the board of directors of a corporation based on their longstanding business experience. Companies want the best business minds to help make a company successful.

Outfit run businesses tend to have a different corporate mentality when it came to their board of directors. The Aviator's board of directors was comprised of Harry and Eddie the maintenance guy who worked at the Aviator. That's it, just the two of them sat on the board.

I once asked Eddie the maintenance guy what was his role on the board of directors.

"Well, let's see, Mr. Chang told me that he would be the chairman of the Finance and Strategic Planning Committee, and I would be a member of that committee," Eddie said. "Mr. Chang told me I would be the Chairman of the Building Support Committee, but since he wasn't going to be on that committee until he got someone to put on the committee, it would be an inactive committee," Eddie said.

"Did you know anything about finance and strategic planning?" I asked Eddie.

"Nope. I'm Eddie, the maintenance guy. I didn't know anything about that stuff," Eddie said.

"What did you and Harry discuss at a board meeting?" I asked.

"Well, we never had a formal meeting. Mr. Chang, once in a while, would come up to me and tell me something about what he was going to do," Eddie said. "After telling me what it was, he would ask me if it was okay and I said, 'Sure, Mr. Chang. It's okay,'" he said.

"What happened next?" I asked.

"Mr. Chang said, 'Good, the committee passes the order of business,' and then he walked away," Eddie said.

"Let me get this straight. You had no formal meetings, either monthly or quarterly, so no minutes were ever taken because there were never any formal meetings," I said to Eddie.

"You got it," he said.

"Did Mr. Fong play any role with the board?" I asked.

"It's funny, because Mr. Fong, while the owner, let Mr. Chang kind of make a lot of decisions. Mr. Fong stayed in the background, other than telling me nice job for something I did. That was it," Eddie said.

"I mean, when I told my wife I was going to be on the board of directors, she jokingly called me Eddie the Big Shot. I'm just a nobody, just a guy who fixes a toilet that doesn't flush or a faucet that drips water, and Mr. Chang wants me to be on the board of directors. It made my chest swell up with pride," Eddie said with a little moisture in his eyes.

Eddie the maintenance guy might not have been some hot shot trader at the Chicago Board of Trade or Chicago Mercantile Exchange. He might not have been a financial whiz at some big financial company. Eddie the maintenance guy was a downright decent human being. For every one dollar you paid him, he gave you back two dollars with his loyalty and hard work. He came to work during the cold, snowy winter days. He came to work during the hot, humid, taxing summer days. He came to work when he was sick. He stayed late if he was working on something that had to be completed. He was an employer's employee.

The one thing that made Eddie the maintenance guy different than the Harry Changs of the world, is that Eddie's dignity could never be bought. So, for the men and women who have to work for a living, which is practically all of us, when you're having a tough day at work, think of Eddie the maintenance guy who was always true to himself and stood tall in what he believed.

Two of Michael Rossi's boys, Charles "Needle Nose" Gnoche and John "Little John" Sarli, paid visits to Harry's places on a daily basis. They made sure Michael got the gambling money due to him, and also made sure that everything ran smoothly at the restaurants and bars.

They would check with Harry to find out if he had any problems. As with any of the Outfit activity, you wanted the money to flow in the door. The Outfit never wanted to see choppy waters. They would smooth out the ripples real fast.

"Hey, Harry, how's it going?" Charlie Gnoche asked one Tuesday afternoon.

"It's okay, but there's this one guy—he comes in to play at Johnny Kong's—Mike Ling, who's been saying we rig the fan-tan games," Harry said.

"Is that so?" Johnny Sarli said.

"Yeah, it's okay. I mean I don't think it's a big problem, okay? You know, just a guy talking, okay," Harry said.

With a smile, Charlie said, "Why don't you give us his address and we'll discuss this matter with him."

"Yeah, sure, okay, I'll give you his address. I mean, I guess he's got a slight gripe, okay, and maybe he'll feel better once he gets it off his chest, okay," Harry said.

"Oh, he's going to feel a bit better," Johnny snickered.

Charley and Johnny went to see Mike Ling, who lived in Chinatown. They rang his doorbell, and he came to the door and opened it.

"Mr. Ling, we want to have a little discussion with you," Charlie said. Johnny pushed Mike with such a force that Mike fell backwards into his sofa as they walked in, Charlie closing the door. Mike sat straight up in the sofa.

"Listen, Mr. Ling, we understand you got a beef with the fan-tan game at Johnny Kong's," Charlie said.

"Now, Mr. Ling, we're going to make that beef go away so you can become all smiles again and continue to enjoy playing fan-tan at Johnny Kong's," Charlie said.

Charlie reached down and cupped his right hand under Mike's chin, pushing Mike's head slightly upward. Johnny threw a hard fast-moving punch into Mike's stomach.

"Johnny, he's starting to feel relieved of that beef already," Charlie said.

"Yeah, the medicine is starting to work; but you know, this might be the type of beef that requires a couple more shots to get it out of your system," Johnny said. With that, Johnny fired two more right hand punches BAM, BAM, into Mike's stomach.

Mike was in severe pain, but with Charlie cupping his chin, Mike could not speak let alone scream out as the pain was scorching his stomach, and he had no release mechanism for the pain to escape.

"Shhh, shhh, Mr. Ling. The medicine works better when you don't fight it," Charlie said.

"A few more, Johnny, and I'm sure Mr. Ling will feel a whole lot better," Charlie said. Johnny saw a metal ashtray, picked it up and hit Mike repeatedly in the stomach. Mike started crying from the pain.

"Ah, tears of joy, Mr. Ling. That's good to see. Mr. Ling, I think you've had enough medicine," Charlie said.

"In a few days, Mr. Ling, you'll go back to Johnny Kong's and continue your normal activities," Charlie said, as he removed his hand from under Mike's chin. "No more beefs, Mr. Ling, right?" Charlie asked.

Mike, holding his stomach with both hands as the throbbing pain in his gut kept contracting over and over again, nodded his head up and down.

"You see, Mr. Ling, if this medicine doesn't work, then we'll have to come back and prescribe a stronger dosage," Charlie said.

The doctors of pain walked out, leaving Mike to curl up on the sofa, holding his stomach, tears streaming from his eyes down his cheeks, now knowing the street medicine practiced by the Outfit made you feel worse, not better. I can hear them now, the mothers of Charlie Gnoche and Johnny Sarli, bragging to whomever would listen about their sons, the doctors.

It was a rainy Thursday night when I went with Jimmy to the western suburbs to see Marjorie Rossi, Michael's wife. It had been about a week since the sentencing of Michael and others. As we drove to the house, I kept hearing this country and western song in my head when I thought of Marge Rossi. It was called *Stand by Your Man*. For nearly twenty years, Michael Rossi ran gambling in Chinatown, and for nearly twenty years, he had been cheating on his wife.

After a four-year investigation, the Feds got convictions in the Chinatown cases. Michael Rossi was convicted of racketeering under the RICO law for gambling, loan-sharking, extortion, and money laundering, and was sentenced to eighteen years. Charles Gnoche and John Sarli were convicted of racketeering under RICO for gambling, loan-sharking, and extortion, and were sentenced to twelve and ten years, respectively. Dennis Fong was convicted of racketeering under RICO for conspiracy to commit murder, money laundering, and drug trafficking, and was sentenced to thirty-five years.

The Feds were only able to make their cases based on the cooperation of one person. The FBI convinced Harry Chang that cooperating was more appealing than a twenty-year prison sentence. Harry wore a wire and recorded conversations with everyone. He testified at the trial after the tapes were played for the jury. Harry received full immunity and, after testifying, entered the Witness Relocation Program and was sent to Northern California to begin his new life.

As we pulled into the circular driveway, I gazed at this immense five-bedroom house. This was Marge's dream house, where she, Michael, and the kids had moved nine years ago.

Michael was always a live, large kind of guy. He made the big money and he spent big on the family and his ladies. The question now, with Michael going 'away to college,' where was the money going to come from to support Marge?

Truthfully, Jimmy was the only one who ever cared about the wife and kids of Outfit guys. Once Michael got indicted, everyone ran away from him. This was very typical in the Outfit; you find out your so-called friends drop you very quickly from the Christmas card list. No one called Marge to offer any support, except Jimmy. This is why the Outfit wives all adored Jimmy, as they knew he cared about their well-being.

Jimmy had his faults, but he was loyal to the wives and kids, because as he would tell me, "I got a family, too."

Michael's legal fees were what ate up a good portion of his money. Defense lawyers like Jerry Crandall don't come cheap. When a lawyer goes to court, his hourly rate is double. The trial lasted seven weeks, so there were a lot of billable hours.

Marge met us at the front door. She was tall, about 5'8", thin, and pleasant woman with collar-length brunette hair. She always dressed stylishly and wore a lot of silver jewelry. Other Outfit wives would compliment her on her outfits, saying they wished they were thin like her, to be able to look so good. Today she was plain looking.

She first hugged Jimmy, then she hugged me. She escorted us into a very large, open-looking living room where we sat and talked. Her face had an anxious look to it. I wouldn't say it was a sad look, but a look of concern.

"Marge, I'm sorry Michael is going away to college," Jimmy said to her.

"Thanks, Jimmy," she said.

"You've got some palace here," Jimmy said, as we looked around the living room. Marge had it decorated well enough. The Queen of England could live here.

Jimmy exhaled a deep breath. "Marge, did Michael have any money left after legal expenses and other bills?" he asked.

Marge tightened her lips and let her tongue moisten them lightly. "You know, Jimmy, Michael handled all the money. He gave me money for the house and kids. I mean, I supported Michael's financial decisions, but right now I've got, maybe, three hundred dollars in my checking account," she said.

"Marge, you got a great place here," Jimmy said, looking around, "but the reality is you can't afford it."

"I know, I know," Marge said.

"I know your youngest one is still living at home with you, but you're going to have to put the place up for sale," Jimmy said.

Marge looked directly at Jimmy, hoping there was another way to get enough money to keep the house.

"Now I know you're going to need a job, so I've been working on that," Jimmy said. I sat quietly in my chair, absorbing the conversation. "I have spoken to John DiOrsini who is a big labor guy on Chicago's Labor Council. John and I go way back. I remember when he was a truck driver and worked his way up in the union, eventually becoming president of his local. So, I explained the situation and here's what we'll do, if you say it's okay to do. I mean I want you to be happy," Jimmy said.

Marge, who was fifty-one, fifteen years younger than Michael, knew she had to work to support herself and her youngest child. She listened intently as Jimmy continued talking.

"William Spenneto is the president of a local that represents warehouse workers. You will be his secretary," Jimmy said.

"That's right up my alley. I went to secretarial school and I was working as a secretary when I met Michael," Marge said.

"Okay, fine, but here's the deal. While you will work as a secretary, you will have a union title Assistant Warehouse Technician I, and you will be making eight hundred fifty dollars a week to start," Jimmy said.

"This way, besides taking out for Social Security from your check, they'll take out union dues, so if you work twenty years, you'll get Social Security and a union pension," Jimmy said. "You'll be starting at more money than a secretary, plus you'll get union raises per the contract and you'll get insurance," Jimmy said.

"You gotta keep this under your hat. Don't tell anyone. No one's gotta know," he said.

"If you say it's okay, I'll get the ball rolling for you, but I want to make sure you are okay with all of this...you know...you're happy," Jimmy said.

Marge hugged Jimmy and started to cry. "You're so wonderful for doing this for me. Thank you. Yes, yes, of course, I'm happy. I accept what you have offered me," Marge said.

"Good. I'll make the phone call to get things going as it'll take a month, then you'll start the job," Jimmy said.

"Look, there's one more thing. You need money now, so I was thinking, I'll get you four thousand dollars. Does that cover your mortgage, food, and other bills?" he asked.

"Yes, oh yes, that more than covers it," she said gleefully.

"Okay, I'll get you the money in a couple of days, but just put enough in your checking account to pay the mortgage. Pay cash for everything else until you start working. You don't want to show a lot of money all of a sudden in your checking right now," Jimmy said. "If you have any money after you start working, then you can add it to your checking slowly, not all at once."

"Wow, I never would have thought of that. Thanks for the advice. I'll follow it," Marge said.

"I also spoke with Lynn Pastore, John P's wife who is a real estate agent, and she told me she would gladly help you sell your house and help you look for another place," Jimmy said. "If it's okay with you, I'll leave her phone number with you," he said.

"Sure, sure, it's okay," Marge said. "I will definitely call her," she said.

"Now this is just a suggestion, it's still up to you. Whatever money you have left after selling the house and paying the mortgage, which I mean, let's face it, that's where most of the money from the house will go...I would buy a two-bedroom condominium for cash," Jimmy said. "You'll be responsible for assessments, which are generally monthly taxes, and your regular monthly expenses. This way you won't have a mortgage over your head, and you won't have to worry about losing your place," he said.

"You figure it's like paying rent, but more secure for you," Jimmy said. "I mean, I'm only suggesting this, it's your decision, but at this stage of the game, why not make it easier on yourself? You'll have to watch your expenses as you won't have the money for your life right now, but you can still have a life. You're attractive, still young. Fifty-one is not old. You'll date, maybe meet a nice guy, things will pick up for you," Jimmy said. "If you need anything fixed around the house, call me. I'll come over and take care of it for you," he said.

As Jimmy finished talking, Marge, with both her hands, held his right hand. I looked in her eyes. They had been reincarnated. They had come back from despair and death. They were alive; they were dancing to their own beat. Marge's whole body was picking up on that beat. Her smile was coming back. She was coming back to the woman I knew.

"I really love this place, but what you're saying about a condo is probably the practical thing for me to do at this stage of my life," Marge said. "I'll call Lynn and set up an appointment with her. And, as much as I hate to do it, I'll put this place up for sale and ask her to help me find a condo I can financially handle," she said.

"Jimmy, you've been so good to me; very sweet and reassuring. You treat me like a princess," Marge said. "I can now see why the other Outfit wives adore you," she said. She then leaned over and kissed him on the cheek.

"If you decide to take a vacation from your wife, Karen, you can always park your shoes under my bed," Marge said.

I gulped.

"Thanks, Marge, but Karen has me tied up in an iron clad, long-term contract as I'm her exclusive one and only love, and I sort of like it that way," Jimmy said. They both started to laugh as we all got up from our chairs.

Marge looked at me. "You're very lucky, Bobby, to have a father like Jimmy. Guys like him are few and far between," she said.

"Thanks, Marge," I said.

We said our goodbyes at the front door. "If I need some advice on something, is it okay to bother you?" Marge asked.

"It's never a bother. Just call me and we'll talk things over," Jimmy said.

Marge opened the door, hugged Jimmy, and then hugged me. "See ya, Jimmy," she said.

"See ya, Marge. Keep your chin up. Everything will turn out just fine," Jimmy said.

"Goodbye, Mrs. Rossi," I said.

As we walked out the door, Jimmy turned to face Marge. "Marge, there's one more thing," he said.

"What's that?" she asked.

"Don't get involved with dating any Outfit guys, okay?" Jimmy said.

"Sure, Jimmy. I won't, unless they're like Jimmy Williams," Marge said, with a coy smile on her face.

Jimmy shook his head and laughed, and we started walking to the car. "Bobby, when you meet the man who can understand women, let me know. We gotta talk to him before he becomes a multi-millionaire, because he's going to have knowledge that guys will pay big dough to find out," Jimmy said.

"You'll be the first to know," I said.

In my lifetime, the times I walked away from Outfit situations in which I had a happy feeling were very few and very far between, practically non-existent. If they weren't killing or beating you, they were crushing your world. You gave them what they wanted, or you felt their hellfire wrath strike you down. But in this one rare existence, I felt only positive vibes for Marge Rossi. She was going to make it; she would be okay. Her safety net was being held tightly by Jimmy.

As we drove away, Jimmy started talking to me, and what he told me he would tell me again and again. We talked a lot about it over the coming years, and I never forgot it.

"Bobby, always remember that you have three types of health. You have physical, mental, and financial. All three have to be in good standing; they all have to be in sync with each other," Jimmy said. "If you don't have good financial health, it will affect your physical and mental health, and that's the health most people don't think about. You stop people on the street and ask them about their financial health and they're going to look at you like you're from another planet," he said.

"Michael Rossi was a high living type of guy. He made big bucks and he spent big bucks," Jimmy said. "That's okay. I mean, if you're making the dough, you spend it, fine," he said. "But Rossi never did a financial checkup for Marge and the kids. He was spending a hell of a lot of money chasing women," Jimmy said. "That money could have gone to his financial health so Marge and the kids would be in good shape," he said. "So, you see, Bobby, Rossi's life changes, he's going away to college and where does that leave Marge? It leaves her in one big financial hole," Jimmy said.

"Sure, I have access to some Outfit money, so I can help her a little, but the point is, look at how poor financial health affected her physical and mental health," said Jimmy. "Compare Marge to what she was like when we walked in, and what she was like when we left…big difference, huh?" Jimmy said.

"Big difference," I said.

"You know why, because her financial health improved. She gained confidence that financially she was going to be okay," Jimmy said. "Never let your financial health get low. It's like changing oil in the car; you gotta keep an eye on your financial health. Make sure you check it a couple of times a year," Jimmy said. "You'll have a much happier, healthier life if you do," he said.

"Remember, Bobby, when you're gone, you can't manage your wife and kids' financial health from six feet under," Jimmy said. "Take care of the family, Bobby. They're your only priority in life," Jimmy said.

Jimmy stopped talking, and I looked at him thinking *I wonder how many sons are lucky enough to have a father teach you about your health? Probably not too many.*

The Las Vegas operation was where the big money was going to come from twenty-four hours a day, seven days a week. The 'suckers,' as Jimmy called them, would come to the casinos to help some guy in Chicago earn a living by gambling. In comparison, Las Vegas was the entrée, and the local Chicago action was the side dish.

Even though Bobby Berman, who was a New Yorker and a protégé of New York's legendary Sid Glickenstein, came up with the idea of gambling places in the desert in the late 1940s, it was Chicago who became the dominant player in Las Vegas. Maybe, it was the distance between New York and Las Vegas. Maybe, New York felt they had enough action in the New York/New Jersey area. Maybe, they felt Las Vegas was just a flash in the pan and would not last. Whatever the maybes were, the New York families never developed Las Vegas like Chicago did. New York had their hotels with casinos, but they watched from a distance as Chicago made Las Vegas the place to go to have fun, and help make the Outfit financially stronger than they ever imagined.

New York approached Las Vegas as an afterthought, rather than seeing it the way the Outfit did, as a constant drenching money stream running back to Chicago.

Las Vegas, like Florida, was considered in mob circles to be open. It was no specific mob family's territory. Any mob family from anywhere, which included

New York, Chicago, Philadelphia, Boston, Cleveland, Detroit, and Kansas City, to name a few, could operate in Las Vegas. In the 1990s, Detroit and Buffalo were the major players after the Feds got convictions against Chicago, Cleveland, and Kansas City bosses. The Detroit and Buffalo families were not around too long as the Feds got convictions against their bosses.

As Chicago started to take control of Las Vegas by the late 1950s, other families aligned themselves with Chicago. Chicago gave them money to build their places and Chicago became partners with other families. Chicago expanded beyond its own hotels, getting revenue from the other hotels they were connected with. So, as you can see, money was being sent back to Chicago in various ways. The state of Nevada and the Feds didn't know or even think about the millions of dollars they would never get from the skimming that took place.

They were like kids in the summer who would watch other kids ride the new bikes they had gotten the previous Christmas. What about their bikes? Where was the money for their bikes? Sorry, kids, just walk a couple of blocks down from your street, and you'll see some older guys wearing fancy suits, having huge pinkie rings that the sun reflects its rays off of and expensive black automobiles. That's where your money for your bikes went.

Jimmy, at the time Las Vegas was starting to develop, was working as an underboss for Anthony "Tony G" Galante. Galante decided he wanted to go to Las Vegas to eyeball the town for himself. After walking down Las Vegas Boulevard, which was where the strip would grow to immense proportions over the years, he saw the potential where the Outfit could make lots and lots of money from Las Vegas. He knew Chicago and Las Vegas were going to become the best of friends over the decades.

When Galante got back to Chicago, he had a meeting with Chuckie De-Polle, his consigliere, and Jimmy. Galante told them about the potential he saw in Las Vegas for the Outfit, and he wanted some feedback from them about developing an operation in Las Vegas.

Chuckie really didn't grasp the magnitude of what Las Vegas could do for the Outfit's bottom line. He was hesitant on endorsing Las Vegas. He favored staying with the local action in Chicago. It was what he knew; it was successful, so why change? In his mind, status quo was a good thing.

"Tony, maybe we should wait a bit with this Las Vegas thing. Let's see if it can stick or will it just never take off. Let's see if New York can make a go of it in Las Vegas first. I mean, we got our local stuff here that carries us, so I dunno, maybe we wait and see," Chuckie said.

Tony tapped the table top with his right hand on the table, and his right index finger moving up and down. He had a stern look on his face, and he didn't seem real happy with what Chuckie said.

"Jimmy, what do you think?" Tony asked.

"From what you're saying, Tony, Las Vegas has the potential to be a gold mine for us. You gotta figure people from all the other states, and who knows, maybe people from foreign countries, will come to gamble in Las Vegas," Jimmy said. "Since no other families are really out there, we could become the dominant force. Look, we don't want New York to get a foothold there," he said. "We gotta create the right atmosphere to draw the crowds," Jimmy said.

"With your Hollywood juice, we could bring in live entertainment where people see a performance, and afterwards go back to the casino in a good, festive mood, and gamble some more," Jimmy said. "Making them happy will make them be ours for the taking," he said. "Keeping the sucker happy is good for business."

"With the additional revenue we get from Las Vegas, we can expand our operations in Chicago and other places, making us more powerful than we already are," Jimmy said.

"I think we should start with one hotel, take money from our gambling and loan-sharking operations, and if we have to use money from somewhere else and build the hotel, then let's see what happens," he said. "We'll have our people from Chicago out there running the place," Jimmy said.

Tony stopped tapping his finger and he started to smile. "Yeah, I like your thinking, Jimmy. I like it a lot," Tony said. Tony looked directly at Chuckie, but did not speak to him. While still looking at Chuckie, Tony said, "Some people can see things, some can't."

"Okay, Jimmy, get the money thing going with the street crews you oversee, and we're going to build one damn fine moneymaking casino," Tony said. That's how the Monroe, the Outfit's first hotel was built, to be followed by El Casa, and then their premiere *numero uno* place the Terrablanca.

After the meeting, Jimmy and Chuckie were standing in the parking lot outside by themselves. "You motherfucker," Chuckie blurted out. "You're an underboss. I'm the consigliere. You should have backed me up in the meeting. What the fuck is your problem?" Chuckie heatedly said.

"Tony asked me what did I think, and I told him what I thought, and he liked what I said better," Jimmy said, keeping his cool.

"Now, Jimmy boy, you have fucked yourself up real good. I ain't gonna forget this and I'm going to get you for this, got it motherfucker?" Chuckie said.

They both parted ways from each other, walking to their cars. Chuckie DePolle, in that moment of heated and explosive volcanic anger, signed his own death certificate. He might as well have called up Gondere's and made the funeral arrangements.

In the life, as soon as someone says, "I'm going to get you," you got to get him before he gets you. You are now in the Outfit's jungle, and it becomes the survival of the fittest as to who walks out of the jungle and who doesn't.

Jimmy knew, at this point, Chuckie was now going to look to make him the scapegoat for something, so then Chuckie would gain stature in Tony's eyes. Making Jimmy a scapegoat would allow Chuckie to pursue having Tony give the order on Jimmy for him to be whacked. Chuckie smiled to himself, rubbing his hands together in glee as he thought all he had to do now was come up with a plan to get rid of Jimmy. Jimmy was smiling, too, as he had his own plan, ready to go live with it.

Jimmy called Dean, and they set up a meeting at Chateau D'Ville. When they met, Jimmy told Dean about the meeting with Tony and Chuckie, what Chuckie said about Las Vegas, and then what he said about Las Vegas. Then he told Dean about what Chuckie said to him outside in the parking.

"If Chuckie goes after me...who knows...maybe Tony next, then you. He's got to go," Jimmy said. By putting another log on the fire of paranoia, Jimmy felt Dean would bite, which he did, and now they had to talk about a plan. In the Outfit, all you had to do was stoke the fire of paranoia that someone was out to get you so they could move up in the organization, and bingo, that person was not going to finish out the current calendar year. Their life was deemed to be over as they had become a problem that was going to be corrected in a short order.

For Chuckie DePolle's family, his wife, Lois, and their six kids, it would become their own atomic bomb. Its explosion was going to greatly impact them in not only losing a husband and father, but where the money to live on and to pay the bills was going to come from. No one was going to care about them and their needs once Chuckie was gone.

Chuckie DePolle's family was going to find out the Outfit was, basically, throwing their lives in a garbage container to be picked up by the garbage men and removed from the Outfit family. The DePolle family's lives would be chilled by the cold hard attitude the Outfit takes when you are no longer part of the Outfit family. People in the Outfit would avoid any contact with the DePolle family. If you were to ask an Outfit guy about the DePolle family, his response would be, "Never heard of them. Who ya talkin' about?"

I always felt sorry whenever I saw something that was going to hurt the wife and children. It wasn't their fault, yet, they would pay a steep financial and emotional price for being connected to the Outfit. They became yesterday's news very quickly. The Outfit washed their hands thoroughly of them as they did not want the virus of caring about someone to permeate their body.

"Never put yourself in the jackpot, Bobby," said Jimmy. "Once you put yourself in the jackpot, you've isolated yourself from everyone," he said. "No one is gonna help you. They run from you because, frankly, you ain't gonna be around much longer. You've become a debit and not a credit to the Outfit. You gotta look in the mirror, because the guy you see is the guy who put you in the jackpot; no one else but you," Jimmy said.

"So, once you're in the jackpot, that's it. It's done. You're through?" I said.

"Well, you could get out of the jackpot. I mean, it's happened, but then you got the trust issue," Jimmy said. "A guy gets down on his hands and knees and promises his wife he'll never cheat on her again, and maybe he won't, but can the wife trust him? That's the unknown answer."

"So when Chuckie mouthed off to you, he put himself in the jackpot and in a way put a hit on himself?" I said.

"Yeah, you could say so. I mean, if Chuckie got a pass, could he be trusted?" Jimmy said.

"Jimmy, you're right. We gotta do something about Chuckie," Dean said. "Maybe his eyes are bigger than his stomach, and he thinks he can move up in the organization, which he can't. He put himself in the jackpot on this one. He's gotta go. We gotta pin something on him that will stick with Tony so he'll give the order on Chuckie," he said.

"Dean, why don't we use our friends at the FBI to help us?" Jimmy said. Jimmy's plan was starting to unfold.

"How so?" asked Dean.

"We can have our two friends, agents Glenn Dalton and Mark "Duke" Slater go see Tony with a picture of Chuckie that they have on file," Jimmy said. "Then they ask Tony if he knows Chuckie. Tony might say he does or doesn't know him. That don't matter, because Glenn and Duke will say Chuckie told them he knows Tony," Jimmy said.

"Ah, so since the Feds tell Tony Chuckie told them he knows Tony, Tony will think maybe Chuckie is going to rat him out to the Feds and, thus, he'll give the order to have Chuckie whacked before he actually rats out Tony," Dean said.

"So, if I got this right, we drop info on Tony that Chuckie's a rat and Tony better get rid of this motherfucker before the Feds get him to rat Tony out," Dean said.

"Yah, correct. So far on all points," Jimmy said. "Then you'll call Tony and set up a sit-down with him. At the sit-down, you'll tell him the same story that the Feds came to see you, and wanted to know if you knew Chuckie, as Chuckie told the Feds he knows you," Jimmy said.

"Beautiful. This sounds better by the second, "Dean said. "Okay, go ahead and call Glenn and Duke. Let's get this going. We can't give that piece of shit Chuckie any time to come up with something," Dean said.

"Thanks, Dean. I'll take care of it," Jimmy said.

"No, thank you, Jimmy," Dean said.

Jimmy called Glenn and Duke, who for a couple of hundred dollars each implemented Jimmy's plan. Tony met with Dalton and Slater, and told them he didn't know Chuckie other than playing cards with him. After meeting with the agents, Tony called Chuckie in for a sit-down meeting. "What did you tell the FBI?" Tony snarled at Chuckie.

"FBI? What FBI? I never talked to no FBI," Chuckie said.

"Then why did the FBI come and see me and show me your picture, telling me you know me," Tony said.

"I didn't talk to the FBI. I swear on my mother's grave, I didn't' talk to the FBI," Chuckie pleaded. Even in death, a poor mother still is her son's mother when he needs her. I guess a mother once in your life, a mother the rest of your life, even in the hereafter. God bless the moms.

According to Jimmy's plan, a week after the FBI paid a visit to Tony, Dean was to call Tony to set up a sit-down. Dean was going to tell Tony the FBI came to see him, showed him a picture of Chuckie and told Dean Chuckie said he knew him. This was being done to reinforce in Tony's mind that Chuckie should be whacked, as the FBI was giving the impression Chuckie was going to rat out Tony, Dean, and maybe other Outfit guys.

A meeting was set up for Dean and Tony at Bowlarama, a bowling alley that was open twenty-four hours a day, seven days a week. Jimmy called Larry Gustafson, the owner, to arrange the meeting, which would take place in a back office not far from where you would rent bowling shoes.

Bowlarama was a popular bowling alley, especially to conduct Outfit business. Jimmy always made sure there were a lot of parties for the kids of Outfit guys held there. Jimmy also arranged for Outfit friends to form their bowling leagues there. It was the right hand helping the left hand and vice versa.

Larry was always cooperative when Jimmy called…very cooperative when it came to the needs of the Outfit boys.

"Sure, Jimmy, no problem at all. Next Monday night. You need a room? Sure, take any one you want. If I can be of any additional help, just let me know," Gustafson said.

Dean arrived first, giving Larry the wave and walked back to the office. Tony came in about ten minutes later, gave Larry the wave, and walked back to the office.

"Last week the FBI came to see me showing me a picture of Chuckie De-Polle, and telling me he says he knows me. What the fuck's up with that?" Dean said. "Of course, I said I don't know him," he said.

"They did the same thing to me," Tony said. "Damn if I know what the fuck Chuckie's pulling."

"It sounds to me like we got a rat," Dean said.

"Yeah, he gave me the bullshit about swearing on his mother's grave he didn't talk to the FBI, but now it's the same fucking thing happening to you," Tony said.

"Yeah, how many fuckin' times has he used his old lady's grave with that one?" Dean said.

"Look, Tony, if it was just you or just me, that's one thing, but goddamn it, it's both of us, so to me he's a rat who's going to take us both down," Dean said. "The only good rat is a dead rat," he said.

Tony paused for a while. "You have to remember, Tony picked Chuckie to be his consigliere, so it comes down to a reflection on Tony. If he made a wrong choice with Chuckie, that might show a sign of weakness in his leadership among other Outfit guys; any visible weakness in the Outfit doesn't last very long and neither do you.

"Well, I need to check this out some more," Tony said. "I mean, right now it don't look too good for Chuckie, but I want to check out a couple of things first. But, if this is what Chuckie is doing, I'll give the order," Tony said.

"That's fine. Okay, yeah. I'm okay with what you gotta do. You gotta make sure. Just let me know what you're going to do, because we don't want this to spread, and then we gotta deal with more fuckin' rats," Dean said.

"Sure, sure, I'll let you know," Tony said.

They got up and walked out together. On the way out, they each gave Larry the wave and left Bowlarama.

Dean was confident he sealed Chuckie's fate. Tony never defended Chuckie, and that's not a good omen for Chuckie to live a long life.

Tony decided he was going to drive over to Chuckie's house and have a talk with him in the car. As he parked the car a few houses down from Chuckie's house, he saw two Chicago cops walk up to Chuckie's front stairs. He recognized both of them.

Jack Nolan and Francis Majera were both from the Organized Crime Unit. Neither one of them were our friends, as Nolan and Majera were straight cops who pursued Outfit guys very intently. They hated the Outfit and they tried to make as many cases as they could against the Outfit. Since they were here to see Chuckie, this could be another reason in building a stronger case against Chuckie. Tony was not feeling too good about Chuckie at this time.

Tony remained in his car, looking out the front window, knowing maybe Nolan and Majera were coming to see Chuckie about something unrelated to what Tony came for, but even so, was Chuckie still ratting someone out for something? Tony stayed about fifteen minutes more, replaying everything over in his head. *Talking to Chuckie would be futile*, he thought, *as Chuckie would just deny, deny, deny.* Tony started his car and left. His mind was made up. He made his decision. Nearly forty-eight hours later, Tony called Dean and told him he's giving the order on Chuckie.

Dean called Jimmy and asked him to come over. Jimmy went over to Dean's house, and after Dean told him about Tony's phone call, they celebrated with a bottle of red wine.

"Didn't you feel bad about setting Chuckie up?" I asked Jimmy. "Nah. You see, Bobby, guys like Chuckie...you have to make the play when the play has to be made. You have to take him out, because if you don't, he will come after you," Jimmy said. "Never wound a guy; always kill him," he said.

"When you're in the life, you really can't trust anyone, because people are only loyal to whomever benefits them, and if Chuckie would have gotten Tony to believe that I had to be hit because of something I supposedly did, then I'm a dead man," he said.

"Chuckie was the one who said he wasn't going to forget, and he was going to get me after the meeting that we had about Las Vegas with Tony," Jimmy said. "All he had to do was keep his mouth shut and nothing would have happened to him. But no, he had to put me on notice that he was coming after me," Jimmy said. "He fucked himself. He's got no one to blame but himself," Jimmy said.

"I know, but he's got a family," I said.

"Sure he's got a family and he should have thought about his family before he opened up his mouth," Jimmy said. "In the life, something bad happens to someone when they do something they're not supposed to be doing, don't do what they're supposed to be doing, or have their own agenda," he said.

"This ain't hopscotch. You can't jump back over the line once you have crossed it. That's why you have to think before you speak or do something," Jimmy said. "The only way you can beat all of this is if you're the only one holding the gun," Jimmy said. "Since that ain't gonna happen, because there's more of us than you, you gotta remain in the shadows and don't bring any attention to yourself," he said. "Keep it on the shelf," Jimmy said.

"Yeah, yeah, I know," I said, letting out a sigh. "It just doesn't feel right that the wife and kids pay the price for his actions, but that's life, I guess," I said.

Jimmy just looked at me. It was one of those times when your father gives you the 'learn from it' look and they're telling you something without speaking.

Chuckie was told by Tony he was going to be sent on a trip to Las Vegas with Joe Aruti and Joe's twenty-two year old nephew John Scataratico, known as "John Scat." John Scat would become a prolific killer for the Outfit in later years. For now, he was just going on a trip to Las Vegas with Uncle Joe and Chuckie to check out the construction of the Outfit's first Las Vegas hotel, the Monroe. Work on the Monroe had started so Chuckie never thought it was unusual to be sent to Las Vegas. As far as Chuckie knew, the trip was legit. Except the one thing he didn't know was that he was not coming back to Chicago.

Jimmy had recommended Joe Aruti to Tony Galante as the guy from the Outfit who should be overseeing the building and running of their hotels, first the Monroe, then the El Casa, and finally the largest of the three, the Terrablanca. Over the years, Joe, and later different guys, would be sent to Las Vegas to make sure everything went smoothly with the Vegas operations.

Guys would be shuttling back and forth between Chicago and Las Vegas, specifically bringing back skimmed money from the casinos.

Joe Aruti was the type of guy who would roll up his sleeves and do the Outfit's heavy lifting, such as juice collections, beatings, murder—anything that the job required. Joe always wore the Outfit face—sober, a dark-looking evil, an intense look that would destroy you in a blink of an eye. Joe was forty-two years old when he became the Outfit's first Las Vegas guy in the early 1950s. Jimmy's juice with recommending Joe for Las Vegas held him in good standing with Joe. Nearly twenty-five years later, when Joe took over and ran day-to-day Outfit operations after Dean's demise, he never forgot how he got there and who got him there.

On a Thursday, Chuckie, Joe, and John Scat would leave for Las Vegas. Before leaving the house, Chuckie gave Lois a strong, defiant, direct to the point kiss. Their lips did not just meet and bounce off each other. Their lips stayed together, hung together for that final, passionate moment they were never going to have again.

This was not some quick wake up kiss. No, it was the defining moment between two adults who are never going to see each other again, as a caressing moisture slowly spread across their lips. The kiss was reassuring, as two lovers skipped across a love bridge they crossed many years ago in their life.

They kissed as one united in their passionate emotion for the internal love they felt for each other. The kiss was as right today as their marriage had been for both of them.

The last kiss between two lovers is not scripted or videotaped. No, it's real, it's live, it's happening right now in this moment. The softness of the lips meet for the last time in a cascading theme of I love you to each of them. It will be the kiss burned into eternity as no other kiss will be remembered, like the last kiss.

"I'll see ya in a few days," Chuckie said as he released his embrace of Lois.

"Have a safe trip, hon," she said, looking into the same eyes she looked into when they were seventeen-year-old kids trying to get the first kiss right.

Her hero was going off to a war he was never going to win.

By the third day in Las Vegas, Joe told Chuckie they were going for a ride.

"Bobby, whenever someone says to you, 'We're going for a ride,' take your own car. Never drive with anyone, because you ain't coming back," Jimmy said. "That's why I always take my own car at all times, no matter what," he said. Probably, I always take my car whenever I go somewhere for the same reason. Jimmy instilled in me an uncomfortable feeling about riding in someone else's car. I don't feel comfortable in someone's car, especially when they say, "Let's go for a ride."

Joe drove about twenty miles outside of Las Vegas, directly into the desert with Chuckie in the front passenger seat, and John Scat sitting in the back seat. The car stopped, and the three men got out in the darkness of the night, in the quietness of the desert.

As they drove, Chuckie sensed this was no business trip. There was nothing to look at out the car window but desert—no people, no cars, no animals, nothing. He thought about Lois and the kids. He was already missing them. How would Lois handle raising the kids without him? Question after question started entering his head. They filled his brain rapidly. There were too many questions coming in; they created a mental flooding of thoughts in Chuckie's head. *It's too late, not enough time to answer those questions*, he thought. The door is now closing to the brain; the questions will die from lack of answers.

After getting out of the car, Chuckie turned to Joe. "Is this it?" he asked. "Yeah, this is it," Joe said. A loyal soldier, who gave his life to the Outfit, was going to be fatally discharged with no planned homecoming for him.

John Scat, who stood behind Chuckie, pulled out a .45-five caliber gun from his coat. He fired three shots into the back of Chuckie's head. Chuckie fell down in sort of a spinning motion, landing face down. John Scat bent down, turned Chuckie over and fired three more shots in the chest area near the heart. It was over in a matter of seconds.

Joe and John Scat buried Chuckie in the desert where, in the years to come, many more Chuckie's would be buried.

The dirty work was done. Tony named Lou Barano, an old timer who was friendly with Jimmy, as his consigliere. Barano was a quiet, go along type of guy who kept his mouth shut. That's why he lived to be an old timer.

Two years later, John Scat, at the age of twenty-four, was recommended by Uncle Joe to go through the ceremony and become a made member of the Outfit, which he did. Joe Aruti continued making trips to Las Vegas to oversee the running of the Monroe and coordinate the building of El Casa and Terrablanca.

Lois had a hole in her heart that could never be filled. A week after Chuckie was supposed to come home and did not, she eventually filled out a missing person's report with the Chicago Police Department. She knew her man, her husband, the father of their children, and the love of her life was taken from her by the Outfit. The Outfit went into its 'hear no evil, speak no evil, and see no evil' mode concerning Chuckie as the months ticked by. No one spoke Chuckie's name. Only a grieving widow remembered what he meant to her, not what he had become; a guy whose mouth got him buried in the desolate no-man's land of a desert in Nevada.

The backbone, the moneymaker for any casino, whether it's in Las Vegas or a state that has legalized gambling, is the slot machines. There's a reason why a casino has two, maybe, three thousand slots, though a lot of casinos probably have fifteen hundred to two thousand slot machines. The profit margin for a slot machine is 60 to 70 percent. Yup, you heard it right, 60 to 70 percent. So, now you know why the casinos load up their buildings with slot machines. The payouts on the slots in Las Vegas were set. You would get casinos that would advertise a high payout ratio or high percentage to lure customers into their casino. So, sure, some people who win big now and then were good for business. A big winner made people think if they played the slots at that casino, they could become big winners, too. However, most slot players, unbeknownst to them, are part of the 60 to 70 percent profit.

"Like bees to honey, the suckers can't wait to play the slots," Jimmy said. "Well, I guess they like paying for someone's kids' college education, someone's remodeled kitchen, someone's second car, someone's girlfriend. Yeah, God bless the suckers for their generosity," Jimmy said, as sarcasm, drop by drop, dripped from his mouth.

Before computerization of the slots, certain machines would be fixed to payout what the Outfit wanted. A technician, by hand, would set the payout ratio.

The technician would go to the casino by 6 A.M. and make the adjustments on the designated machines long before the customers in larger numbers who came to play later in the day were present. Some machines would be set to only pay out 75 percent of the incoming money to the slots. Some machines might be set to pay out 80 percent, and the rest of the machines would be left untouched just paying out what they had been previously set to pay out.

With computerization of the slots and video poker machines, payout ratios could be set with the software being used rather than making manual adjustments. The slots could be programmed and put on a network. Each machine could generate a report showing what amount of money has been played in each slot and what each machine paid out. Also, the report could show the usage of each machine to see if there was a heavier usage time when more money was played, thus, determining when and what the payout ratio should be.

I'm not saying any of the corporations that run the casinos today are doing any of this, but why do the casinos have so many slot machines? I think any of you who made it past kindergarten can figure it out. Jimmy always said, "Let the suckers build the pot, then you take the pot." The slots were the pot built by the suckers that the Outfit took.

"I'm not here to ruin your fun if you go to Las Vegas or your state licensed casino gambling establishment play the slots, video poker, and any other computerized games; go ahead and enjoy yourself. If you want better odds at winning and at least have a better chance against the house, stick with blackjack, table poker, craps, or any table game, which are not computerized, as of yet.

I suppose there could someday be a blackjack machine that deals you on a screen one card face up and one card face down. The one face down only you can see, and the house can only see theirs. You would bet accordingly, putting your money in the machine and pressing the bet button. If you wanted another card, you would press the card button for another card. After the hands are completed, the machine would deal new cards to the players and the house.

Yeah, it's all futuristic, and I've given a simplified method, but if Gerard "The Brain" Delcamo was still in the life, he'd have a machine up and running and, believe me, it would be rigged in the Outfit's favor. Gerard was the Outfit's electronics guy and along with Frank "The Wiretapper" Lipinski, circumvented many an electrical alarm system in their day, allowing Outfit guys to get inside buildings, warehouses, and private homes to steal merchandise and sell it to a fence who sold the hot merchandise to customers. The electronic duo allowed Outfit guys to bypass bank electronic security systems and commit late night bank robberies after the banks were closed.

After serving two separate stints in prison, one a four-year sentence and years later a six-year sentence, both for electronic fraud, Gerard went to work for an electronic security company. Who better than him to advise customers on electronic security measures? It takes a thief to know a thief.

Gerard was always grateful for his Outfit education, as it helped him get a high paying job. I never thought of the Outfit as a corporate talent developing organization, but for someone like Gerard, the Outfit was a career builder.

The slot machines in Las Vegas were generally emptied by 3 A.M. on a daily basis. Their money, plus all other gambling money from the casino, would be taken to a backroom known as the 'count room' in each of the three Outfit run hotels. Tony Galante determined the percentage, which was pretty much in line with the 4 percent street tax on construction jobs, and a 3 percent street tax imposed on mob controlled restaurants and bars in Chicago.

You figure the Outfit was getting 21 percent a week right off the top from each of their hotels. Since everything was in cash, no one knew for sure how much the Outfit was skimming, but I can tell you this, for the next nearly thirty years, in which the Outfit was in Las Vegas, no one associated with the Vegas operation ever took out a mortgage to buy a house or car loan. Everything was paid in full with cash.

"See, Bobby, back then in the 1950s, we were kinda feeling our way around Las Vegas," Jimmy said. "I mean, no one really knew anything about casino gambling in a sense, because we ran a different kind of gambling operation in Chicago," he said. "We were into bookmaking, where guys placed bets with a bookie on sporting events," Jimmy said. "Don't get me wrong, what we did in Chicago helped in Las Vegas, but we were not running a casino operation like New York did in Havana, Cuba, back then," he said.

"We knew gambling, that's for sure, but to make it work on a Las Vegas type operation, some things were trial and error. Just like some people worked out in Las Vegas and some did not," Jimmy said.

"The Outfit guys were fast learners," I said with a smile on my face.

"With us, if you were not a good student, the discipline was a lot more severe than having to go to a detention class," he said with a laugh.

"Thank God Tony Galante had the juice in Hollywood as we were able to bring the stars in to perform as the headliners at our places," Jimmy said. "By bringing in the stars, people wouldn't become bored just gambling," Jimmy said. "They would go see a show, then come back to the casino and gamble some more," he said.

"By controlling the unions in Hollywood and Las Vegas, Tony built up a lot of IOUs and when he had to, he called in his marketers to help Las Vegas grow and grow," Jimmy said.

"Could Las Vegas have made it on its own without the Outfit?" I asked.

"Yeah, I think so, but the profits would have been a lot less. We knew we had to create Las Vegas into a special place, a unique, one-of-a-kind place where people were treated special and felt special and wanted to come back again and again," Jimmy said.

"Everything had to run smooth, no riff-raff allowed, everyone treated like kings and queens, and if there was a problem, it got straightened out real quick," he said. "The deal with the cops there was you take care of the outside, we'll take care of the inside," Jimmy said. "You never wanted anyone to leave with a bad taste in their mouths," he said.

"That's why everyone was trained to be polite, walk around with a smile on their faces, mingle and be friendly with the customers," he said. "You wanted the customers to feel like they were in a safe, secure, fun atmosphere. Just sunshine all over the place," Jimmy said.

"It was an image, because while the customers were happy, we would be off skimming money to get our cut," Jimmy said. "Vegas was never meant to be the real world. It was about making the customers feel like they were living the high life," Jimmy said. "Making them for a few days have the pleasure of champagne taste on the beer salary," he said.

In college I took this one marketing class as an elective, and I thought about the Las Vegas operation from a marketing standpoint. I was going to do my term paper on Vegas, but I figured the professor wouldn't believe what I wrote. So, I said forget about it and didn't write it, and picked another topic. The Outfit was ahead of their time in marketing Las Vegas...way, way ahead of their time.

To get licenses for the Outfit casinos, Tony Galante, with involvement from Dean Dragonetti, used legit business people to form corporations. While the guys on paper were legit, they were really known to Tony and Dean. Nevada State Gaming Commission was not going to issue licenses to Outfit guys, hence, the need of forming corporations. While the corporations got licenses, their involvement was in name only.

The corporate guys got a nice amount of money each year from the Outfit as compensation, but they were just figureheads with no actual power over the operation. Clean was needed to get a license and, as far as the Gaming Commission was concerned, they were clean.

Tony Galante put in permanent bosses Alex "Skip" Richardson at the Monroe, Charles "Cuckoo Charley" Baretta at the El Casa, and Rocco "Rocky the Mechanic" Durso at the Terrablanca to not only run the places, but to oversee that the money owed to the Outfit got to the Outfit without problems. These guys ran the casino part of the hotel operation, while they were also responsible for hotel operations. They hired people with hotel experience to run the hotel part of the operation. The hotel people reported to the casino boss of each hotel.

The hotel people were pretty much left to run the hotel operation on their own. The casino guys, unless there was a problem, kept their hands off that part of the operation. On a daily basis, the casino guys would check with the hotel guys if everything was running smooth. The hotel guys knew who the boss was, and were mindful of that fact.

The casino operators designated who would be the couriers that would deliver the money to Chicago. The couriers, or 'messengers' as the bosses called them, were lower level Outfit guys from Chicago who lived in Las Vegas and traveled back and forth to Chicago. Every two weeks, money would be taken from Las Vegas and sent to Chicago.

The money was taken daily from the gambling activities where it was first counted in the count room of the hotels. Then the money would be put in duffel bags and transported to a main storage area, which was a warehouse about five miles from the hotels. If you drove past the warehouse, you would think it was a corporate warehouse. There was a phony corporate sign on the building to make the place look legit, which it wasn't. The money would be locked up in storage trunks inside the warehouse and held there until the money was moved to Chicago.

There were always two Outfit guys inside the warehouse for protection. There were a total of six guys who worked three shifts of eight hours apiece. The warehouse was staffed 24/7, even holidays. The men had handguns and shotguns at their disposal.

The warehouse was supervised by an Outfit guy named Frank "Smokey" DiGree. DiGree was a short, nervous, chain-smoking guy. He would talk to you while the cigarette dangled from the corner of his mouth. It would bounce up and down as he spoke. The job, as you can imagine, was very nerve-racking as the correct amount of money better be in those trunks, otherwise Frankie boy was going to be dangling somewhere.

The couriers would bring the money to the warehouse in sealed envelopes in which the money had been counted, and the pit boss signed off on the envelope and dated it. The pit boss's signature was an acknowledgement of the dollar amount inside the envelope. The pit boss would write down the dollar amount on the outside of the envelope. The amounts in the envelopes would slightly vary with each envelope.

Once the couriers got to the warehouse, both guys inside the warehouse signed, dated, and wrote the time received on the outside of the envelopes. Then the courier walked over to the trunk and opened up the trunk with his key. His key was the only key used, as there were no keys in the warehouse. After putting the envelopes into the trunk, the courier closed and locked it, and left. The Outfit's system, pertaining to the skimmed money from the casinos, was designed so if there was a breakdown in the system, they could track who was responsible for that breakdown. No one person was totally responsible for everything. The cake was made up of many slices.

You and I are thinking the same thing – Wow, what a temptation to steal some money, but everyone knew the rules in this money game. You get caught stealing money, you get buried in the desert, or as some guys referred to the desert as St. Matthew's West. Yet, that didn't always stop someone from trying.

When the couriers were to remove the money, which was removed by the oldest dated envelopes from the warehouse still sealed, they met the pit boss at a designated place. He opened the envelopes, counted the money again to make sure it was all there, and put the money in another sealed envelope, signed it, dated and wrote the dollar amount on the back of the envelope. He would repeat the procedure for each envelope. The money then began its journey...off it went. It arrived in Chicago and was given to Jimmy, who turned it over to Tony Galante.

Tony would distribute the money to designated people in the Outfit. The Outfit never stopped believing in Santa Claus. As long as they had Las Vegas, they celebrated Christmas every two weeks.

The state of Nevada never knew how much tax revenue they lost as the hotels only showed the state auditors what they wanted them to see. Since everything at that time, really— until the slots and video poker machines started accepting credit cards and were computerized much, much later—was in cash. Customers brought cash so they could gamble with cash. The customers would go to a designated area in the casino and buy a rack of coins equivalent to the cash they were spending to gamble on the slot machines. If they wanted fifty dollars in coins, they paid fifty dollars in cash at the money window. Years later, customers could use credit cards to gamble by inserting them in the new slot machines equipped to handle that type of transaction. One thing the boys always did was update the slot machines to find a better way to make money for themselves, not for the customer.

The Nevada State auditors had no paper trail to follow. What they saw in cash reports generated by the hotels was all they could audit from. While the gambling revenue was enough that the state of Nevada never enacted a state income tax, the state missed out on the millions of dollars skimmed by the Outfit and other crime families in Las Vegas.

Sure, in later years the Internal Revenue Service changed the way hotels had to report earned income, so it forced the hotels into developing different types of financial reports, but that was not until sometime in the early 1980s. For nearly thirty years, the Outfit had Outfit accounting reporting, working for them as they would be always receiving the credits and never took any debits. The Las Vegas operation under the Outfit followed their accounting principles of 'you can't audit what you don't show.'

They were damn good at their jobs. No hotels went bankrupt, none of the workers, unless there was a cause to fire them, lost their jobs or were 'laid off,' as the Outfit put it. They helped build Las Vegas into a thriving community that enhanced economic opportunities for all. Which, I suppose is okay, but I am not sure if the Las Vegas Chamber of Commerce would want to promote the illegal methods, which the Outfit did rather conveniently, making non-legit business practices the norm.

The lure of money is the one temptation that potentially can cause a problem in any business. Money paws at you, it caresses you. Oh baby, just a little tiny drop of currency coming my way will make my life secure and full of sweetness. Someone at some point will decide, nah, it's only a few bucks, who's going to miss a couple of dollars. Then their actions put them in a very precarious state of mind. In other words, they put themselves in the jackpot.

I've seen the Outfit tolerate certain things that surprised me, and they let the thing pass with no action taken. However, the one thing the Outfit did not tolerate was the loss of revenue, because someone had sticky fingers. You take money from the Outfit, they inflict harm on you.

In Las Vegas it was easy for a guy to get caught up in the life of broads, booze, and gambling. It was a safe haven for the weak minded. If you let yourself go to the fast lifestyle in Las Vegas, you better have some fast money in your pocket to cover the costs incurred by that lifestyle.

Before you knew it, the financial house of cards would tumble down on you, and you would start to steal from the money which was right in front of you day after day. Guys who would steal money in Las Vegas practically had the same stump speech. "I was going to pay it back," they would say, as if they had any intentions of paying back the money.

Now, you weren't going to pay back the money you were stealing, because you had no way to pay it back. C'mon, who ya kidding? Otherwise, you wouldn't have stolen the money in the first place. You would have had the money to pay off your debts, otherwise, why risk getting a permanent time out from the Outfit.

Rocky Durso, when he moved to Las Vegas from Chicago to run the Terrablanca for Tony Galante, brought along John "Johnny the Sparrow" Pasenti, a trusted top aide in Rocky's street crew. Johnny was made the night pit boss at the Terrablanca.

The Terrablanca, while being the Outfit's largest hotel, was also its best revenue producer. A lot of money was generated in the casino, which found its way to a back room to be counted by Johnny.

Johnny was divorced and, at that time, didn't know anyone to socialize with. Night after night, Johnny carefully counted the gambling money in the count room. He took the necessary amount for the skim, put the money in the envelope, signed it, and sealed it. He repeated the procedure until the total amount of money was taken, envelope after envelope. There was nothing at this point to indicate he was not doing his job. Night after night, he saw great sums of money come into the count room, but he maintained his financial celibacy, and just counted the money. He had no thought process, at that time, to steal any of it.

A little more than a year later, Johnny started to talk to one of the cocktail waitresses. Paula was a local girl whose family left Oklahoma in the 1930s because of the Dust Bowl. She was too young to have any recollection of Oklahoma, so as far as she was concerned, Las Vegas was the only home she ever knew.

One day Johnny, near the end of her shift, asked her if she would like to have a drink with him at a quiet bar a couple miles from the Terrablanca. She said 'yes,' and they went to a bar that was frequented by the locals. No tourists came to a place like this.

As Johnny said, it was a quiet place where you could talk and feel relaxed. The seconds turned into minutes, the minutes turned into an hour, and before they knew it, a second hour passed. They just talked and talked. It was just a general conversation that two people have when they meet the first time; but, yet, while not revealing much about each other, it revealed they both cared for each other.

They only had one drink apiece, but the conversation flowed back and forth between the two, thus, no more liquor was needed to get them talking.

Johnny only said he was employed like her at the Terrablanca, but never talked about his ties to the Outfit. He told her he was forty-one and divorced with no kids. She told him she was twenty-six, had never been married, and hadn't had many dates as there had never been that one special guy in her life.

"Maybe we could go out for breakfast one day soon," Johnny said as they were leaving the bar.

"Yeah, I'm off Tuesday. How about then? Is that okay with you?" Paula asked.

"Sure, that would be fine," he said.

From the breakfast date it moved to a dinner date and from there they started dating on a regular basis. At this point, Johnny was okay financially. There weren't a lot of clubs around, yet, in those days or expensive restaurants, so they would go to the movies a lot. Since the movies were cheap back then, Johnny wasn't spending a lot of money on their dates.

The weeks started to fly by and the relationship was gaining strength to the point where Johnny felt confident to take her to his apartment. For the first time in their budding relationship, they made love together in that one-bedroom apartment.

Johnny waited until he felt the moment was right. He didn't want to push her, thus, risking that she did not want him and the relationships might fall apart. No, she wanted him alright and was very happy to make love with him, and he could feel it in her body as he embraced her.

Love for both of them that night was very pleasurable. It was something both of their bodies had been waiting for, patiently standing in the line for love, and when it was their turn to perform, they did it with honors. Their bodies moved in sync...she on him, he on her. This was not high school love-making. This was two adults creating a sexual high with their bodies.

Both of them reached the level of satisfaction that was needed to begin to move on to the next plateau in this relationship, for if their lovemaking effort failed, the relationship might have been put on life support. Without healthy, satisfying sex, a relationship can face a steep mountain to climb. A poor bed-room performance is never forgotten by either party. A failing grade in bed can lead one or both of the participants to look for someone who can perform at the top of their class, and not have to be sent to sexual summer school to brush up on their skills.

Following that night, Johnny started to think maybe he needed a little more money to do some nice things for Paula. He wanted to show his deep love to her by getting her better gifts. That is where the trouble began and ultimately snatched his life from him. Johnny Pasenti's death watch was just beginning.

Back in Chicago, Johnny, in his younger days, participated in and ran floating crap games. Johnny figured that he could make some extra money by shooting dice at the Terrablanca. After his shift was over, he would walk over to the dice table and begin his quest to make more money to spend on Paula.

Craps is a game in which a lot of money moves very quickly. It is a game that, if you have never played it, do not play it now. First, go by the craps table and watch how it's played. Learn the game, learn how to place your bets, but never...and I mean never...just start playing without knowing what you're sup-posed to be doing. Hotels will teach you how to play. All you have to do is ask at the front desk.

The reason you have to know what you're doing is you can win big money or lose big money in a very short time frame. More often than not, you will lose more than you win, so pay close attention to the game. Remember, it's your money. Take it from one who has spent many an evening at a craps table, losing his money more than winning.

"Bobby, always let the suckers build the pot, then you take it," Jimmy would tell me. "Whether it is craps or poker or any other game, sit back," he would say. "The suckers think they got a chance, so let them make the money for you by building the pot, then you snatch it for yourself," he would tell me. Jimmy taught me Las Vegas was a suckers' town. Without the suckers, Las Vegas would have been a sleepy-eyed town in the desert where the ranchers came on a Saturday night to get a drink.

Johnny, like a lot of dice throwers, made some money in the beginning. The money to be made is on the percentage bets you make on the person throwing the dice. A couple of simple examples of this are, say, you bet 3-1 the shooter will throw under ten, or 6-1 he'll throw over ten.

Johnny liked throwing the dice. He felt he was controlling his own destiny. He was making money for Paula and nothing was going to stop him from winning money for her. With his winnings, he would buy her the better things in life that he felt she deserved.

The problem with gambling is when you go from, "I'll just play with one hundred dollars; that's my limit and if I lose that, I'm done for the day," to an obsession where you're gambling every day, the odds work against you. You lose more than you win. I've seen it a million times. People think they're going to beat the house. It won't happen. Instead of walking away, they think no, I'll turn it around, and so they continue gambling far longer than they should have.

"Bobby, there's one way you can beat the house in Vegas," Jimmy said. "If you win, let's say, five bucks, you put it in your pocket and walk away," he said. "You've got your winnings in your pocket, and Vegas is out five bucks, but people don't do that," Jimmy said. "They keep gambling and eventually the odds work against them. When you go to Vegas, remember, it's a vacation; relax and enjoy yourself. Just gamble your limit, don't let them take your last dime," Jimmy said. "Otherwise, Vegas will give you a hearty handshake, and say, 'Thanks, sucker, for giving me your money,'" he said.

Johnny's good fortunes at the dice table started to turn against him. He began to risk more money on his bets in hopes of winning more money. As the losses started to grow, he started to drink more like the drinking was going to make him an instant winner. Yeah, right. Drinking and losing parallel each other, driving you to a deeper, blacker hole. Once in that black hole, no one hears your screams for help. People just walk by that black hole and shake their heads at the fool who is stuck at the bottom.

As the losses continued to mount, Johnny did not have the money to cover them. He built up a lot of IOUs and the Terrablanca was holding these markers over Johnny's head, making him start to think about an alternate plan to come up with the money to cover the markers. He knew it wouldn't be long until Rocky Durso got wind of his markers.

He went home one night, deciding not to gamble that night, but rather to think over what would turn out to be a deadly wrong move on his part. As he lay in his bed, he said to himself, *I've got a way out of this. I'll just borrow some money from the Terrablanca when I count the money collected from the day's gambling proceeds. I'll just take enough money to cover my markers. Once I clear my markers, I'll pay back what I owe to the Terrablanca from my paycheck. The Terrablanca really won't be losing any money. They'll get it back, so for a while they won't have it, but it'll come back to them. I mean, who's going to be mad? It's not like I'm not going to pay it back*, he reasoned.

The problem with plans that are built on sand is they have no substance. The fool who thinks this plan is going to work is delusional and believes the plan has no holes; its success is guaranteed, he tells himself. Johnny was making himself believe the fantasy could be turned into reality. So who becomes the fool?

A wide, beaming smile plastered Johnny's face. This was going to be the right move. *I'll be square with everyone*, Johnny told himself.

Wrong move, Johnny…wrong freakin' move. Once Rocky Durso finds out you stole money from the Terrablanca, which is like stealing from him, you're going to have one unhappy capo. An unhappy capo and your life expectancy become comingled. You get my drift? In other words, you better make plans to have that birthday party of yours real soon. Don't wait for the exact date, because you ain't going to be around when the real day comes.

The funny thing about all of this is Paula wasn't what you would call a high maintenance type of girl. Anyone who met her always described her as "the girl next door," clean cut type. She was thrilled just to go to a movie, but in Johnny's mind he felt she should have more, a lot more of the nice things in life.

"When a man meets a woman who he likes, gets along with…uh…compatible…that's the word I'm looking for, he sometimes can go overboard in his affection," Jimmy said. "Not all guys are like that, but there are some who are afraid of losing the good thing they've got and start spending a lot of money on the woman, buying expensive things, hoping they won't lose her," he said.

"Kinda like the champagne taste on the beer salary," I said.

"So, once you put yourself in the financial jackpot because of what you're spending on her, some little guy in your brain punches the stupid button and you do something stupid," he said. "Stupid is stealing money from the Outfit for crissakes. This is what we do for a freakin' living. It's like a kid playing against an adult. Who's going to win that one, because the kids' chances are slim and none, and slim left early," Jimmy said.

"You don't beat the master at his own game. You only beat yourself," he said.

"Johnny was holding a losing hand and should have folded immediately," Jimmy said. "The trick, Bobby, is never play a losing hand. Get out of the game before it costs you," he said.

The following day, Johnny went back to work. Like every other workday, at the designated time, he went to a backroom in the Terrablanca to count the money from the day's gambling take. This day, however, was going to be different, as he would count the Terrablanca's money for the Outfit, and also count the money he was going to steal. Two separate piles of cash would be on the table.

After counting out the money he needed, he put a rubber band around the cash and put it in his pocket. The remaining cash he put in an envelope, sealed it, wrote the dollar amount on the outside of the envelope, signed it, dated it, and it was business as usual, just like any other day.

Johnny let out a sign of relief as he sat in the chair. *Mission completed*, he thought, and no one was the wiser. He shook his head slightly and chuckled to himself. *Man, I'm glad that's over.* He got up from the chair and walked out of the room, feeling all that financial pressure he was under just exited his body through the pores of his skin.

The anxiety ran out of his body full throttle. There was no stopping the high he was getting, knowing he could erase those markers. His shoulders were straight back; there was confidence in his step. This was the Johnny he wanted to be. He couldn't wait to see Paula, as she was going to see Johnny the way he saw himself—confident, assured. Yeah, get ready, baby. The Johnny you wanted was the Johnny you're going to get.

Among all of this self-appreciating high Johnny was feeling, at the moment, there's always someone who is going to let the air out of your balloon. No plan is always a safe plan. The sun-bleached sky can turn rapidly into dark as night storm clouds about to unload a torrential downpour on your parade.

Johnny, take cover. Run, Johnny, run! Find somewhere so the storm will not make a direct hit on you. Hurry, Johnny, the seconds of your future are being chased by the storm. There's not much time left. It's coming, Johnny. It's closing in on you, Johnny. Oh, my God…it's going to hit.

One of Tommy Lasciola's jobs at the Terrablanca was to review what the security camera recorded in the room where Johnny counted the money. Lasciola was another one of Rocky Durso's Chicago boys who worked at the Terrablanca. The camera was installed up in the ceiling light fixture to watch the activities occurring in that room only. The camera was Rocky Durso's eyes in the room to make sure no money was stolen.

Tommy and Rocky Durso were the only ones who knew the camera was in the room. The camera, which in those days did not have the clarity the ones today have, so the images on the film were grainy, yet, you could still make out images and see the faces of the people in the film.

Normally, the film Tommy looked at day after day was the same. He would see the pit boss count the money with nothing special to look at. Then he looked one day at the images of Johnny on film. Tommy looked and looked at those images. Johnny had no idea there was a camera in the room, so he didn't know Tommy, who used to hang out with him in Chicago, was looking at Johnny's epitaph in that film. Tommy played the tape again and again and again, at least ten times he played the tape. He wanted to make sure what he saw on the tape was really what was happening in the room. He wanted to make sure the evidence he had on his friend Johnny to be not only convincing, but it must be conclusive, no doubt about it.

After playing the tape those many times, Tommy was ready to see Rocky. He had his evidence. It was going to be goodbye, old friend. Tommy called Rocky.

"Boss, could you come upstairs? There's something you gotta see on the films from the counting room," Tommy said.

"Sure, sure, I'm coming up," Rocky said.

Tommy played the film from a projector for Rocky. "Play it again, Tommy," Rocky said. Play it again, play it again, play it again," Rocky said, over and over, each time his voice grew with stinging anger in it.

"Again, Boss?" Tommy asked.

"No, I've seen enough," Rocky said disgustedly.

The film showed Johnny counting out two piles of money. The pile on which he put the rubber band showed him putting that money in his pocket. The other money from the Terrabalanca went into a sealed envelope like it was supposed to.

Tommy stopped the projector and looked at Rocky.

"I've known Johnny for a while," Tommy said.

"You were just doing your job, Tommy. I'll handle it from here," Rocky said. "Go back to work," he said. "Tommy, this is between you and me. Not one word to Johnny."

"Sure. Right, Boss," Tommy said.

When it comes to the Outfit's financial business that comes first. As far as friendships go, they wait in line for their turn. Sometimes friendships dissolve while waiting their turn as it becomes a game of survival at that point. I use my friend to survive is how one friend treats another.

Rocky sat in the security room, knowing he had two choices. Call Johnny in and tell him he's fired and to get lost or give the order for Johnny to be hit.

To the average working Joe or Jane, you would call Johnny in, tell him he's fired, and either he gives back the money he took or you will call the cops.

Well, that's the difference between the Outfit and normal people. Normal people have a concern that things need to be handled in a professional manner, as with them, violence never enters the room. The Outfit could care less about what type of manner is used. They know one type of manner and that will be used. This is not a 'please and thank you' organization. Outfit etiquette dictates they want to make sure having sticky fingers is not contagious, so others will not attempt to be another Johnny with their money. So, street justice— not something taught at Our Lady of Perpetual Worship—will be used for the book of social graces learned by the boys on the hard streets of Chicago.

We're very cost efficient with personnel matters. No severance pay, no insurance money to be paid out; none of that crap. "Just see ya at St. Matthew's for the burial," Jimmy would say.

Rocky, having brought Johnny from Chicago to Las Vegas to work for him, knew people behind his back would question his management abilities. "C'mon, Johnny was his guy. Didn't he know what he got himself in for with Johnny?" they would say.

Predictably, Rocky chose the Outfit's way as that was the only way he knew how to handle this personnel matter in order to save face.

Business is always business with the Outfit. The moment you let your heart dictate to your brain, you've got big trouble. The moment your heart opens up its mouth about compassion, the brain will tell the heart to lose that thought if you want to see another sunrise. The Outfit runs from compassion. For the most part eliminate, eliminate, eliminate are the brain's marching orders. Never play another tune. "Heart of compassion toward your fellow man," the brain says, "unless I tell you, got it? If you don't play the Outfit's tune, we'll get another heart and you're fucking history," the brain said. Heart always knew how far to go with the Outfit.

Rocky Durso gave the order Johnny should be whacked, but Johnny's hit was not going to be done in Las Vegas, rather in Chicago. Rocky did not want Johnny's mess in the neighborhood. There would be other times to do a hit in Las Vegas, but not this time.

Let Johnny disappear and Rocky would show everyone else he could take care of a problem without any disruption to business. The Las Vegas strip would be bustling with folks from all over the country and the money these folks gambled in the casinos would continue to march in, not missing a beat. Outfit business would continue to flourish and Johnny Pasenti, who came to Vegas as a nobody, will leave Vegas as a nobody. It's Vegas, baby.

"Johnny, I called you in because I need you to go to Chicago to see why a couple of construction companies that I have ties with are not paying their street tax to me. You'll be briefed at a meeting in Chicago about what's going on," Rocky said.

"Sure, Boss. Glad to help you out. When do I leave?" Johnny asked.

"Tomorrow morning. There's a 10 A.M. flight booked for you. Keep me posted once you find out what's happening in Chicago," Rocky said with a very straight, legit looking face.

"Definitely, Boss. I'll be in touch," Johnny said.

Wiseguys are notorious, and I mean notorious with a capital N, liars. They lie anytime, anyplace—to your face, behind your back, after breakfast, before you go to sleep. You name the situation, there will be a lie told to fit the wiseguys' need, to make you believe the actions you are taking are the correct ones.

If you did not know a wiseguy's legal name, he would look you in the face and lie to you about that. He'll lie to a woman when she asks him if he's married, which he is. He'll lie to a woman about his employment. He'll lie to a woman when he tells her she's the only one. He'll lie to a woman when he says he loves her just to have sex with her. He'll lie to the ultimate woman in his life, his mother, about anything pertaining to his life.

So, when Rocky Durso told Johnny about a couple of construction companies owing a street tax that was a lie. Johnny, however, had no way of knowing Rocky was lying to him at that point. Johnny played the good soldier and went to Chicago, thinking he was helping Rocky. Yeah, he was helping out Rocky alright, by helping Rocky have him killed.

Johnny called Paula after meeting with Rocky. "I've got to go to Chicago on business. I'll be gone for a few days," he said.

"Oh, okay. I'm going to miss you. If you get a moment, call me. Have a good trip. I love you," she said.

"I love you very much," he said.

"Bye," she said, not knowing that the love paradise she and Johnny were building for their future would never be completed.

The next morning Johnny flew to Chicago. At the airport in Chicago, he was met by Michael Cassidy and Donald Briatte, two juice collectors who Rocky knew. After exchanging hellos and getting Johnny's luggage, they got into the car.

"Yeah, we're taking you to where someone will brief you. You'll get to know everything you need to know," Cassidy said while driving. Briatte was in the front passenger seat next to Cassidy, and Johnny sat in the back.

Cassidy kept looking in his inside mirror at Johnny. "How's the weather in Vegas?" Briatte asked, trying to make some small talk to pass some time. "It was in the mid 50s when I left, which is about right since we're in December," Johnny said. In situations like this it always amazes me how, before wiseguys are going to whack someone, they have this idle banter, a meaningless conversation going nowhere, but filling up time until the main performance happens.

No one says, "Get in the car; I'm going to kill you." No, it's, "How are you feeling? How's the family?" A bunch of feel-good things you would talk about while sitting on the porch, sipping lemonade. This phony caring when, in fact, it's just another lie buys time. That's all it does…buys time. The clock of life ticks, ticks, ticks down those final seconds of the victim's life. We never think much about time until we have very little left of this precious commodity. Yet, time is the one thing that makes us all equal. Rich man, poor man, it doesn't matter; you still get twenty-four hours a day...no more, no less. No one gets any special treatment of being given more than twenty-four hours in a day, nor is anyone penalized and given less than twenty-four hours. How you use the time is your business.

Johnny, while sitting in the backseat, was thinking about time, the time he was going to spend—hopefully, the rest of his life—with Paula. In time they would get married, have a family, buy a house with a white picket fence, have a dog named King, and they would be the All-American family.

In Johnny's mind, he was able to manipulate time into a happy, tranquil life. There was nothing bad or evil in Johnny's time; it was all good. He couldn't wait to get back to Las Vegas to begin the happy lifetime it was going to afford him.

"Johnny, you want to get something to eat?" Briatte asked.

"No, I'm okay. I had a meal on the plane," Johnny said.

The offering of a meal before you whack someone is the equivalent of a prisoner being offered his last meal before being executed. To the Outfit, killing someone on an empty stomach was just downright inhumane. You should be able to fill your belly with something you want to eat one more time, and then the murder becomes humane.

The murder, thus, becomes morally acceptable to the Outfit. A full belly dignifies the taking of one's life. See, we treated him fairly. He got a last meal of his choice. See, the body will not starve after the expiration of life. See, the Outfit cares for its victims. See, the Outfit boys can be admitted to Heaven when the time comes. God, are you seeing all of this?

Karen would always tell me God see's when you do good and God sees when you do bad. It was a piece of motherly advice given to me that, while intended to keep me on an honorable street in life, sure made a lot of sense as I got older and saw what happened to some of the Outfit boys. To the Outfit, a lifetime of doing bad should be exonerated by offering a last meal to another person you are going to do bad to. This reverse logic never plays out well with God.

"I've got my standards," God said. "I'll be damned if evil is the standard of life we are going to live by in this world I've created," he said.

"Evil will always be a part of the world, but it will never replace the good that is generated by the love, kindness, caring, and sincerity human beings possess in their souls. The neighbors who bring a hot meal to a grieving neighbor who has lost a loved one; the people who give of their own time, volunteer it to help other's at a shelter; and the people who volunteer in after school programs to mentor young children. All the good deeds performed by human beings for other human beings day after day over their lifetime," God said. "The right hand of those who have clasped the left hand of those who don't have," he said.

The Outfit's con will never exist in my eyes. Fuck the Outfit," God said.

Cassidy pulled up to an empty warehouse located on the South Side at 83rd Street and Kentucky Avenue. The company that owned the warehouse had a factory in Chicago that made industrial containers and stored them in the warehouse. When sales orders came in, the containers were sent to the customers from the warehouse.

I'm not sure, but I think the company moved to Indiana or Michigan and closed the factory and the warehouse years ago. The company never found a buyer for the warehouse. The property was abandoned, and the Outfit would use it in different capacities. A meeting could be held there, though you never saw many winter meetings, as all the utilities were turned off, nor did anyone come around during the day to talk things over.

The warehouse's main purpose was where someone was killed. The stories I'm sure the warehouse could tell, if only it could talk. There was a period of time in which the Feds were looking into some Outfit murders, and late one night the warehouse was set on fire and it burned to the ground, evidence included. I wonder who set the fire. You get three guesses. I'll give you a hint. It wasn't the Mayor of Chicago or the Cardinal of Chicago's Catholic Archdiocese.

The car doors opened. Johnny got out first from the backseat and started to walk to the warehouse. He never saw the guns under the front seats of Cassidy and Briatte. Both were .22 calibers with a silencer on each gun. As Cassidy and Briatte got out of the car, they took the guns out of the car. Both of them held the guns in their right hands and covered them inside their coats so Johnny could not see them.

Once inside the warehouse, Cassidy told Johnny he might as well go upstairs to the office and wait for someone to show up. Johnny looked around the desolate warehouse, and was starting to get the feeling something was not quite right.

"Are you sure someone is coming here?" Johnny asked.

"Yeah, sure. Someone will be here any minute," Cassidy said, while pretending to look at his watch.

"Are you really sure someone is coming here?" Johnny persisted, with a tinge of doubt in his voice.

"What, ya don't believe us? Someone's coming," Briatte said, bristling.

Johnny turned his head slowly around, moving it from spot to spot as he scanned the vacant warehouse. "Doesn't look like much of a place for a meeting. Looks more like a place to whack someone," Johnny said.

Cassidy and Briatte tightened their grips on their guns. *Johnny may be getting a little too smart for his own good*, they thought. They had their own way of how they were going to kill Johnny, and they did not want to alter their plan.

"Johnny, look, you go upstairs and if it makes you feel better, me and Donnie will go wait in the car," Cassidy said.

Reluctantly, Johnny turned and started to walk to the stairs leading up to the office. His back was turned to Cassidy and Briatte. They drew their guns and opened fire.

Cassidy fired three shots into the back of Johnny's neck, and one shot in his back. Johnny's body made a sharp descending motion and tumbled first onto the stairs and then fell face first onto the ground. Cassidy walked up to Johnny's body, kicked his body over and fired one shot into the chest area near Johnny's heart. Briatte walked over and did the same thing, shooting Johnny once in the same chest area.

They looked at each other with a slight grin. Cassidy said to Briatte, "You should always wash your hands as you do not want sticky fingers," referencing the money stolen by Johnny from the Terrablanca.

"Yeah, good hygiene is important," Briatte said laughingly.

They went out to the car to get a body bag, a couple of mops, plus cleaning solution, and a small bucket from the truck. Johnny lay on his back in a pool of blood, which drenched his body. He looked dead, appeared to be dead, but was he really dead?

Cassidy looked at Johnny. He and Briatte were told to bring the body to Gondere"s. If they were just going to bury Johnny, it wouldn't matter if Johnny was alive or not, but they didn't want to bring a live Johnny rather than a dead Johnny to Gondere's.

"Donnie, go get me the wire in the trunk. I'm going to give Johnny a Sicilian necktie," Cassidy said.

The Sicilian necktie is choking someone to death using some wire. Briatte came back with some industrial strength wire and Cassidy twisted it in his hands, got down on one knee, and put it around Johnny's neck.

"Donnie, time me. Give me a couple of minutes," Cassidy said.

"Okay, go," Briatte said, as he looked at his watch.

For the next two minutes, Cassidy strangled Johnny. He would loosen his grip slightly, then grab the wire again, applying a powerful turn on Johnny's neck several times during the two minutes.

"Okay, time's up," Briatte said.

If there was any doubt about Johnny being alive, that thought disappeared. Johnny laid stone cold dead, eyes wide open; no hint of any body movement could be seen.

Cassidy and Briatte looked at each other for a brief moment. They exchanged approving glances, nodding their heads in a slow up and down motion. They now were in unison in their belief that Johnny was dead. Briatte picked up the body bag, which was by the door, and brought it over to Cassidy who unzipped it.

"Donnie, you grab the legs and I'll grab under the shoulders," Cassidy said. They lifted Johnny's body up and nudged it into the body bag, then zipping it up.

"We'll go to Gondere's, and then we will come back and clean up the floor, "Cassidy said.

"Sounds good to me," Briatte said.

They then carried the body bag back to the car and shoved it into the trunk, which Briatte had left slightly open. Then they drove off to Gondere's to get rid of the body. For their day's work, Cassidy and Briatte got five Gs each.

When they got to Gondere's, they went in to see Jake. Jake sent a couple of his workers, who along with Cassidy and Briatte, went back to the car. Cassidy opened up the trunk and the workers took the body bag out, putting it on a cart, and wheeled the cart back inside the funeral home.

"We're all through, right Jake?" Cassidy asked.

"Yeah, I'll take care of everything. It's been paid for, so yeah, you boys are through," Jake said.

"Okay, see ya next time," Cassidy said.

"Till next time," Jake said.

Cassidy and Briatte went back to the warehouse to clean up the blood-splattered wood floor. With no DNA or technology to be used on the floor to gather a blood sample in those days, Johnny's blood would vanish from the warehouse floor. The floor would be Outfit clean, ready for the next victim.

"Sometimes, even in death, you can catch a break," Jimmy said.

"How so?" I asked.

"Well, when Johnny was taken to Gondere's to be put in a double coffin, who does that lucky son of a gun get in the upper part of the coffin? None other than an elderly priest who died of a heart attack," Jimmy said.

"You mean he got a priest as his partner?" I asked.

"Yeah, how lucky is that?" Jimmy said.

"Look, the priest can act as a mouthpiece for Johnny when he goes before St. Peter to try and get beyond the pearly gates to go to Heaven," Jimmy said.

"I mean, it's a bench trial. St. Peter will be the only one hearing Johnny's plea. There's no jury," he said.

"No way," I said.

"Yeah, you know, since a priest is a man of God, he's going to have the juice with St. Peter. The priest's got an inside track," Jimmy said.

I looked at Jimmy kind of skeptical about this revelation I was hearing.

"If it was you or me doing what Johnny did in his lifetime, we would get our ass thrown in Hell, but since Johnny's got a priest, and the priest and St. Peter are on the same team, St. Peter has got to listen to the priest while he talks about Johnny in a good way," Jimmy said.

"Bobby, I think with the priest's juice with St. Peter, Johnny's got a shot at Heaven. I really do," Jimmy said.

"What if the priest doesn't want to go along with this plan?" I asked.

"Fuck the priest if he doesn't' want to go along. We'll dig him up and whack him, so he'll be dead twice. If he knows what's good for him, he'll go along," Jimmy said.

As you can see, the Outfit's take on fundamental Christian afterlife values varies from the norm you learn at your house of worship or Bible study classes you take at your house of worship. It's fucked up.

At this point in time, I have not received a memo from Johnny letting me know the outcome of what happened. If any of you have juice with St. Peter and can find out how this saga ended, please advise.

The loss of a loved one has a numbing effect on the soul. When a loved one dies, for the grief stricken, who are trying to cope with this traumatic loss they just suffered, they are in a haze. Their world is cloudy, their feet do not know in which direction to walk, their minds are only thinking of the one who has died, who they will not see ever again.

For a mourner, their lives have been frozen at the exact moment they found out about the death. Nothing is going into the brain and nothing is coming out.

They plan for a funeral. When a concerned person asks how they are doing, they say fine, but that's a lie. No one is really doing fine during the grieving period, because grieving is reflecting on what the person meant to you, and there is no way you can simplify your emotions into one word at that moment.

Sure, time will help soothe the raw emotion a person has, just thinking about the loss of a loved one, but it will never replace what information the brain has stored about the loved one.

The person will remember when the loved one taught them how to ride a bike; when the loved one watched them play Little League baseball or soccer;

when the loved one threw the football back and forth with them on a crisp fall day; when the loved one consoled them after they lost the election for president of their eighth grade class; and when the loved one took them out to practice their driving skills before going for their driver's license. When the loved one gave them the keys to the family car after they got their license, and told them to be careful; when the loved one consoled them after breaking up with their first boyfriend or girlfriend by telling them there's plenty of fish in the sea or wait and, like a bus, one will come by in fifteen minutes; or when the loved one helped them pick out their prom dress and later their wedding gown.

The person will remember when the loved one attended the grammar school, the high school, and college graduations. When the loved one drove them to the airport or train station as they would begin their military service and, in saying goodbye, hugged them very tightly, not wanting to let go. When the loved one walked them down the aisle; when the loved one told them the importance of being a good husband and father; when the loved one told them marriage is the ultimate happiness in one's life. When they told the loved one they were pregnant, and the loved one was going to be a grandparent. When the cycles of life would go up or down, they will remember how much the loved one truly loved them.

These are the memories that will be remembered to help the person go forward with their life. While these people have the comfort of recalling their love for the departed, there are those who lose someone and never know how what was lost. A vast emptiness is in their soul that stretches for mile after mile, with no answer in sight.

It was nearly two weeks since Paula heard from Johnny. He hadn't called from Chicago, and she was starting to wonder if things were okay with him and her. She was friendly with one of her co-workers Marge, who was a few years older than her and more experienced in the art of romance than she was.

"Marge, it's been two weeks and I haven't heard from Johnny," she said.

"Maybe he's got to stay in Chicago a little longer," Marge said.

"I know, but I miss my Johnny," she said.

"Don't worry, honey. He'll be home soon," Marge said.

While she waited to hear from Johnny, Rocky Durso promoted Joe Armanetti to Johnny's position as night pit boss, which included a pay raise for Joe.

"Joe, as far as I'm concerned, you got the position full time as Johnny won't be coming back. But, for right now, the word to everyone is you are temporary, and that is what I want everyone to think, so don't say anything different, okay? Got it?" Rocky asked.

"Mum's the word," Joe said.

Everyone who worked for Johnny at the Terrablanca was told Joe was just temporary until Johnny came back. They would report to Joe in the meantime.

A month went by and still no Johnny; she was getting worried. *Maybe he was hurt, or maybe he didn't love her anymore*, she thought.

"Marge, I'm not sure what to think about Johnny anymore," Paula said.

"Go talk with Joe. Maybe he can find out what's going on with Johnny. Who knows, he might walk in today with a diamond ring and propose marriage to you," Marge said.

She laughed. *Wow, wouldn't that be great*, she thought.

"You're right. I'll go talk with Joe," Paula said.

She went to Joe's office and knocked on the door. "Door's open. C'mon in," Joe said.

She walked in. "Joe, can I talk to you?" Paula asked. "Sure, sure. Sit down," he said.

"It's been a month since Johnny went to Chicago on a business trip and I haven't heard from him. Have you heard anything?" she asked.

"Nah. You know, all they did was tell me I was taking Johnny's position temporarily and that's it. I don't know anything else," Joe said.

"It's strange. It's not like Johnny not to call me," she said.

"You know, some guys got their ways about doing things," Joe said. "Don't worry. I'm sure you'll hear from Johnny," he said.

"Well, if you hear something, let me know," she said.
"Yeah, I sure will," he said.

Paula walked out of the office and as she closed the door, Joe looked straight at her. With a frown on his face and his lips held tightly together, he shook his head and shrugged his shoulders. Joe knew Johnny was never coming back. He didn't know or want to know the details of what happened in Chicago. *Poor kid*, he was thinking, *poor kid. She lost her lover.*

"What did Joe say?" Marge asked Paula.

"Really not much. He just said he was put in Johnny's position on a temporary basis and didn't know anything else," she said disgustedly.

"Well, no news is good news," Marge said.

"I suppose, but if he was going to break up with me, why wouldn't he just tell me? I mean, this is kinda the cowardly thing to do, run away and leave me," Paula said.

"I don't know. I wish I had an answer for you, but men are not predictable. You never know what's in their heads," Marge said.

"That's for sure," she said.

A little more than a year went by. Joe Armanetti, during that time period, had the temporary removed from the front of his title, and was officially given

Johnny's position as night pit boss. After talking with her cousin who lived in Long Beach, California, Paula decided to leave the Terrablanca and move to Long Beach to live near her cousin.

Las Vegas had given Paula a bad putrid taste in her mouth. Every day she walked into the Terrablanca, she saw Johnny's face, the gleaming smile, and the warm brown eyes looking back at her. She kept hearing his voice over and over again. "I'm here, honey, right with you. I love you so much."

She told Marge she was moving to Long Beach, and she gave Joe Armanetti two weeks' notice that she was leaving her job at the Terrablanca.

"Can't talk you out of it, kid?" Joe asked.

"No, Joe, my mind's made up. I am going to Long Beach. I just gotta do it," Paula said.

"Well, you're a great worker and a good person," Joe said.

"Thanks, Joe. That means a lot," Paula said.

"You'll meet someone in Long Beach, you'll see, and he's going to be grateful to have a heck of a lady like you," Joe said.

"Thanks again. Well, I'll go back to work now," she said.

"Good luck, kid," Joe said.

Paula went back to work that day and the two weeks flew by. On her last day, she hugged and thanked Marge for being her friend. She gave Marge her address where she was moving to in Long Beach, so they could correspond and remain friends. Joe came down on the casino floor, gave her a goodbye hug, and he gave her an envelope with fifty dollars in it.

"I know we don't give severance pay, so just take it and enjoy yourself," he said.

Paula was overwhelmed with joy. She hugged Joe and kissed him on his cheek. She said goodbye to Marge and Joe, and walked out of the Terrablanca, thinking Johnny would dissolve from her mind.

She drove back to her apartment, picked up her belongings, gave the key to the building manager, and began her drive to Long Beach.

It took her two days as she didn't want to drive through the night, so she stopped at a motel. Once Paula walked into her cousin's house, she felt her new life had begun. Everything was behind her. Johnny was just a distant memory from another place in time, she thought.

Less than a month later, while looking for a job, her cousin told her the local bank was hiring tellers. She went to the bank and interviewed for a job as a teller. The bank hired her. Paula found a small studio apartment not far from the bank, and she moved in shortly after she began working. She wrote Marge, telling her all the wonderful things that were happening to her—the new job and new apartment. Life was certainly looking up for her.

One day a man came into the bank and, from that point on, they began to talk. He was a fireman with the Long Beach Fire Department, and even though he was ten years older than her, Paula enjoyed talking to him on a variety of subjects, and felt very comfortable with him. Every time he came to the bank, he stood in line by her station. Even if there was an opening at another teller, he waited for her.

Finally, after several weeks, he asked Paula out for a date and she accepted his offer. Following the first date, more dates kept coming, as a relationship was beginning to build. She had been corresponding with Marge, who was still working at the Terrablanca, and told Marge she was dating a really nice guy who was a fireman. They really seemed to enjoy each other's company, she wrote in her letters to Marge.

Eighteen months later, he proposed marriage to Paula. She happily said 'yes' to his proposal. She accepted his diamond engagement ring, and they started to talk about when they would set a date to become married. They decided to get married the following June.

Marge and her husband were invited to the wedding in Long Beach. She told Marge the day of the wedding she knew she had the right guy for her.

In the ensuing years, Paula had a daughter, her husband eventually became a captain in the fire department, and she and Marge exchanged Christmas cards every year with pictures of her family.

Her life seemed to be very fulfilling as she enjoyed raising her daughter, and had a wonderful, caring husband who saw her as his one and only true love. A beautiful fairytale life was playing out for her every day of her life.

Marge, who had left working at the Terrablanca quite a while ago, felt what her friend wrote in her Christmas cards to Marge seemed so positive year after year. Practically twenty-five years had passed since Johnny entered her life, and she never expressed any remorse in those yearly Christmas cards. She never wrote his name, mentioned him, or made any reference to him in the cards. Marge felt time had healed the love wound in her heart, and Marge was glad to see how well Paula adjusted without Johnny.

One following April, an old navy buddy friend of Marge's husband invited both of them to come from Las Vegas to visit him and his wife in Long Beach. Marge was extremely happy to go to Long Beach, because she could then see her dear friend from the Terrablanca.

While they put pictures in the Christmas cards, Marge hadn't seen her friend in such a long time and was really looking forward to seeing her in person.

Marge and her husband, after a couple of days in Long Beach, decided to drive to her friend's house. Once they got there, Marge, with her husband by her side, rang the front doorbell. Marge rang it and rang it, but there was no answer. Marge knocked on the front door repeatedly, but still there was no answer.

"Let's go around to the back of the house. Maybe someone is in the yard," she said to her husband. Sitting on a chair next to a small table was Paula's husband. His hair, while gray, was turning white and he had been retired nearly five years from the fire department.

Marge introduced herself and her husband to him as he remembered these faces from the pictures in the Christmas cards. He apologized for not answering the front doorbell, and greeted Marge and her husband, thanking them for coming.

He got two more chairs so they could sit down. "Where's your better half?" Marge cheerfully said. He looked at Marge and her husband with a freezing cold stare. The question drained the blood from his face. It diluted the pinkish hue on his face into a chalky white blank look. Marge sensed something was wrong right away. She felt uneasy, bracing herself for the something bad that was going to come out of his mouth.

"The day after this past New Year's Day, in the morning, I went to a lumber store to buy some plywood for work I was going to do inside the house," he said slowly. "I told Paula I would be back in an hour. I went and bought the plywood and returned to the house."

"When I came in the house, it was very quiet. I went into the kitchen, but Paula was not there," he said. "I figured maybe she was in the backyard, so I checked there. Nope, she wasn't there. I went upstairs to our bedroom and I was calling her name as I approached the bedroom, thinking maybe she was there."

"I walked into the bedroom and found Paula on the floor, a hand gun next to her right hand. I just froze in my tracks, seeing her body on the floor. My heart began racing. She had shot herself twice along the right side temple of her head. I immediately picked up the phone and called for the paramedics, but having seen lots of dead bodies as a fireman, I knew she was dead," he said soberly, trying to control himself. "I tried to feel for a pulse, but there was none. Her body was stretched out on the floor and I could see it had no life left in it. I tried giving her CPR, but soon realized it was futile to continue as there was no movement in her chest showing that any air was reaching her chest, allowing her to breathe. I stopped the CPR and went downstairs to wait for the paramedics."

"The paramedics came in less than five minutes and we went upstairs. I told them I tried to see if I could revive her, but there did not appear to be anything to revive. The paramedics looked at her and tried to get a pulse, and did a couple of other things, but told me she was dead. In the meantime, the police came as a police report had to be done. I felt shock waves go through my body upon hearing she was dead. Even though I knew she was dead, it was a jolt to me. God, I loved her so." He got control of his emotions and continued talking.

"I looked toward the nightstand near the bed and there was a piece of paper on top of it. I looked at the paper and it said, 'I miss my Johnny.' She never mentioned or talked about anyone named Johnny. I just couldn't for the life of me figure out who this Johnny was," he said looking down and shaking his head from side to side. "I showed the note to the police and they asked me if I knew who Johnny was.

"No, officer, I don't know who Johnny is," I said. "The police concluded the shooting was a suicide and that's what they wrote in their report. The paramedics took her body to the closest hospital where a doctor pronounced her dead and would sign the death certificate as cause of death, suicide.

"After the paramedics and police left, I called my daughter. After graduating from Long Beach State University, my daughter moved out of the house and was sharing an apartment with a girlfriend. She came right over and we were both trying to console each other. I asked my daughter, 'Did Mom ever talk about a guy named Johnny?' after I showed her the note. 'No, Dad, she never did,' my daughter said. I called the funeral home and I told them my wife's body was at the hospital and could they pick her up. They told me once they had the body, they would call me, so I could come in and make arrangements.

"A few days later, we buried her. I'm sorry I didn't let you know, but I was so upset, I didn't think about anything but her. I miss her so much," and the tears that he gallantly had been fighting while he spoke started to fill his eyes, and they began to dribble down his right cheek.

"Why, oh why, did she kill herself? We had such a beautiful life together," he said as the tears shifted gears and started running from his eyes down both of his cheeks. "I would do anything for her, anything at all. God, with all my heart, I miss her," he said, his voice starting to crack.

Marge got out of her chair, walked over, and embraced him. "It wasn't her fault," she said to him. "Sometimes we just don't have answers for these types of questions and never will," she said. "You're a good man; I know she loved you very much. Maybe God had a reason for all of this to happen. I guess I just don't know what else to say to you," Marge said.

Marge released him and he thanked her for her kind words. "Did you know this Johnny?" he asked her. Marge, seeing how emotional he was, felt the safer bet was not to tell him about Johnny. "No, no I didn't know who Johnny was," Marge said.

"I'm putting the house up for sale next month," he said. "I don't want to be here without Paula. I see her everywhere in the house. She's cooking dinner in the kitchen, she's gardening in the backyard, she's playing with our daughter in our bedroom, we're watching television in the den, yet, the reality is she is nowhere in the house," he said. "My life feels frozen when I'm in the house, lonely, quiet, not hearing the sound of her voice ringing in my ears," he wistfully said. "It's time to go," he said.

"You're right, it's time to go," Marge said.

Marge and her husband sat with him for another hour letting him talk and listened to the good things he said he and his wife did over the lifetime of their marriage as one happy couple.

Marge and her husband got up from their chairs, said goodbye, and left him. He thanked them for coming over and letting his inner feelings come out into the daylight. Marge's sadness was so low walking out that it couldn't even have been measured at that moment. *Why did it have to happen?* she kept thinking. She held her husband's arm tightly as they walked to the car.

Once inside the car, Marge thought about her dear friend and wondered if Johnny missed her as much as she missed him. Marge was never going to get an answer on that one.

"What, does the Outfit have a patent on screwing up people's lives? Here you have two people very much in love, and the Outfit screws that up," I questioned Jimmy.

"Okay, I see that, but wasn't there another way to handle this? I mean, what would you have done if you were Rocky Durso?" I asked.

"Honestly, I would have done the same thing Rocky did," Jimmy said. "You see, if the money is coming to Chicago short, who are they going to blame? It's like baseball, they don't fire the players, they fire the manager," he said.

"Rocky had to do what he did or else the order would have been given to hit Rocky, because he was responsible for money coming from the Terrablanca," Jimmy said.

"Okay, so what if Johnny had come to Jimmy Williams for advice, what would you have told him?" I asked, as I wanted to know how Jimmy would have replied to Johnny.

"If he comes to me, asking Jimmy Williams whom he doesn't report to, then I would have told him to work out a payment plan to pay off those markers with someone at the Terrablanca," he said. "Maybe it might take a couple of years, maybe longer. I didn't know what he owed, but the Terrablanca wasn't going anywhere, so something could have been worked out," he said. "Also, he had to stop gambling," Jimmy said. "This all hinges though on Rocky Durso, if he would go along with a payment plan. If Johnny didn't get caught stealing the money, sure; it's possible Rocky would have approved a payment plan. Once Rocky caught Johnny stealing the money, forget about a payment plan. That's gone. Rocky's mind was made up that Johnny was going to get whacked, and that was that," he said.

"See, when you're in the life, you have to play it straight—no curves, no angles. One plus one gotta equal two, not three," Jimmy said. "Johnny knew the game, but he wanted to play with his ball and bat, and with the Outfit it's their ball and bat, not yours," he said.

"The Outfit is not the Salvation Army. They are not a courteous and well-mannered organization. They poke you in your eye so you cannot see, they rip your soul right out of your body with one swift defiant move," Jimmy said. "When you become a made member of the Outfit as Johnny was, you pledge your loyalty to them. They are the family. You belong to them. They come first," he said.

"Johnny switched his loyalty to her and the moment you switch teams, the Outfit puts you on their shit list. That's just how it is," Jimmy said. "When you have stars in your eyes like Johnny did for her, you tend to block out the ray of reality your brain is trying to tell you, and your thinking gets screwed up," he said.

"You lose track of the reality that if you think you can get away with screwing the Outfit, then it's like everything will be okay. The world will be a beautiful place to live in all chocolate and lollipops, kindness around every corner. Well, forget about that, kiddo. That's when the Outfit comes looking for you and they ain't going to give you a gold watch and thank you for your years of service," Jimmy said.

"Get this straight, Bobby. The Outfit does not want anyone, and I mean anyone, to get between them and their money. You do that and the next step on the bus for you is St. Matthew's Cemetery, and you ain't leaving; you're staying permanently," he said.

I looked at Jimmy. I knew he was right in what he was saying. While I, in my inexperienced way, was looking for a different solution, there are times, as much as we don't always want to admit it, a son knows when his father is speaking the truth. It's just here you had two people who had become submerged in a pool of love with each other, and you could see this movie was going to have a happy ending. However, one mistake, one stupid mistake made and the Outfit, in effect, whacks two people, shattering their world into a million pieces that could never be put together by me, you, or anybody else.

The Outfit was just as responsible for her death as Johnny's. Killing Johnny, in effect, killed her as her soul was buried right alongside his. They were forever joined as one body of love, cemented together for life. The thing about your first serious love is once it's over, it's best to just put it behind you. However, for some, it can kill them.

While Tony Galante had his boys running the casinos in the Outfit's hotels, he needed someone else to make sure other parts of the Las Vegas operation ran smoothly. He needed someone to make sure there were no problems with the unions, the entertainers who performed at the hotels were happy, and to handle any other problems that would come up in a professional manner that wouldn't draw attention, thus, affecting the Las Vegas operation. In other words, he needed Barry Tigerman.

By 1960 the Nevada State Gaming Commission had created their black book. What was in the black book? The state of Nevada kept a written listing of reputed mobsters from across the country, who were not allowed in the state's casinos. If these guys were caught in a casino, the casino could lose its operating license. Today the book is computerized.

There were a few Outfit names in the book at that time, and the list of Outfit names grew into the 1960s and 1970s.

Dean Dragonetti and Tony Galante's names were in the book, so Tony knew he needed someone clean to freely enter his hotels and casinos. His choice was going to be his criminal defense lawyer Barry Tigerman.

Barry had gotten Tony acquitted of extortion and tax evasion charges brought up by the United States Attorney's Office in Chicago several years earlier. Without any doubt in his mind, after that trial, Tony felt if he ever needed someone who he could rely on, it would be Barry.

In the many times Jimmy or I talked to Barry, we both agreed he was a very, very smart man. Some people in just having a general conversation, you can tell they have the smarts, and Barry was definitely in that crowd.

Gary Rosenthal, Jimmy's lawyer, knew Barry very well as they both went to the University of Chicago Law School together, though Barry was in his third year and Gary his first year. Since both practiced criminal law and defended Outfit guys, their paths crossed on many occasions.

Barry was not a man to mince words. He was very blunt with his language. His words were strong and stinging. He didn't use profanity, but told it like it was, his version, whether you wanted to hear it or not.

Gary would always say if you wanted an excellent criminal defense lawyer, Barry was your man. And, if you wanted a cold-hearted jerk, Barry was your man. Barry's reputation on both counts always preceded him, even before he opened his mouth.

Tony went to see Barry in his law office about moving to Las Vegas, and becoming Tony's general counsel and chief troubleshooter for the hotels, casinos, unions, and any other situations requiring attention in Las Vegas.

"I need someone in Vegas with your legal skills to keep an eye on things for me, "Tony said to Barry.

"What about Hollywood and their unions? That's also part of your operation," Barry asked.

"See, that's why I need you. I was just thinking about Vegas, but you're right about Hollywood," Tony said.

"I'm always right," Barry said.

"You could be based in Vegas and go to Hollywood when needed," Tony said.

"Yes, I could do that, so let's talk about my financial compensation, because I have a practice in Chicago that is worth something. And if I'm going to have to give up my Chicago practice, the numbers have to work for me," Barry said.

"I was thinking $75,000 a year," Tony said.

You have to remember, we're talking 1960 prices of things. Gas was maybe twenty-five cents a gallon, a newspaper maybe ten cents, so seventy-five grand a year back then was a whole lot of money.

"Eighty grand to start, plus a ten percent bonus the first year, then a five percent raise every year with a ten percent bonus, based on the gross salary each year," Barry said, looking directly in Tony's eyes, his pupils locking in on Tony's pupils. Tony sighed and brought his left hand up near his lips, rubbing his lips with his hand from side to side, and then rubbing his chin.

Tony sat silently, looking at Barry for a moment. Barry continued to look at Tony, his eyes not even blinking. Tony laughed and said, "You drive a hard bargain. That's a lot to think about," he said.

"I have a practice here that I would have to give up. Remember, you came to see me, so you need me, not the other way around," Barry said sternly.

It's very rare to see the Outfit pushed up against the wall. They usually are the aggressor and they don't push, they throw you against the wall. Outside of the Feds, I can't recollect too many people forcing themselves onto someone associated with the Outfit. I learned with the Outfit, though, when they needed the mental muscle, whether it be in the courtroom or running something in their operation, they never held back on spending a buck.

Barry Tigerman had the ability to make whatever it was disappear, so when asked about it, the Outfit would grin and say what about it.

In Las Vegas, many people good naturedly would refer to Barry as the boss. I think if you spell boss backwards, double sob, that would clearly define Barry Tigerman.

"Well, okay. I'll meet your demands. When can you leave for Vegas?" Tony said.

"First of all, I have to talk Sylvia into moving to Las Vegas, and that won't be easy, since she's close with her two sisters and will be concerned with the impact a move will have on our two sons. Then, it'll be at least six months until I can close up my practice in Chicago," he said.

"I've got some trial work coming up that I have to complete, so the six months is a ball park figure. I'll just have to see. I'll let you know," Barry said.

"Fine. That's okay. I know you can't shut the door and leave tonight for Vegas as I would like you to. Okay, take your time. Just keep me posted when you know when your leave date will be," Tony said.

"I'm going to talk with Sylvia tonight, so we'll see how that goes, "Barry said.

Tony got up from his chair and shook hands with Barry. The handshake solidified the deal between him and Barry, and Tony then left the office. Barry knew with Tony's juice, Barry could run Las Vegas the way he wanted to—smart, but efficient, just keep everyone happy. Having defended other Outfit guys, Barry knew how they worked and what was expected of you when you worked for them.

When Barry left his office, he was trying to think of ways to convince Sylvia to relocate to Las Vegas. As he pulled into the driveway, lots of scenarios crossed his mind, but there wasn't one specific thought that he could develop into a compelling plan that would win Sylvia over. *Oh well, let's see how the conversation goes*, he thought.

Sylvia Tigerman, in the purist sense, was an operator, no two ways about it. When she was an underclassman at the University of Chicago, she got the bright idea to have a party at her house on the South Side one Saturday night.

She went to both the University of Chicago Medical and Law School buildings, and posted a notice on their bulletin boards about the party at her house. It was an open invitation for both medical and law school students to mingle and have fun. Sylvia did not put up a notice in any other school building. She only wanted potential doctors and lawyers at her party. Young Sylvia was looking for a future with someone whose income was going to be able to provide her with the life she wanted.

With Sylvia, a man was going to be either a doctor or a lawyer; otherwise, he was a nobody. That's what she thought of other professions. They were not up to her standards, so why bother with the peons.

That Saturday night, a second year law school student, who was talked into going to Sylvia's party by one of his classmates, went to her house. He was a shy, quiet guy who was not much of a talker, and even in his adult years, was still basically that type of a guy outside of the courtroom.

Sylvia saw him standing by himself, awkwardly trying to fit into a social situation that he was obviously very uncomfortable with. *He's the one; he's the one* her brain kept flashing in bright neon lights. *Go Sylvia, make your move, catch your financial fish. You can do it, girlfriend,* her brain kept blasting out to her.

Sylvia walked over to him.

"Hi, I'm Sylvia Feigenbaum. What's your name?" she asked. He was caught off guard that someone from the opposite sex was actually talking to him at a party. When did hell freeze over?

"Lar, I mean, Barry, Barry Tigerman," he nervously responded.

She giggled. "It sounded like you weren't sure of your name," she said.

"Your beautiful brown eyes caught me off guard," he said. That statement even shocked him. All of a sudden he went from Mr. Law School Student to Mr. Suave. *Where did that come from?* he thought.

I guess in the souls of all men, hidden deep in the subconscious room of our brain, is a Hollywood heartthrob wannabe who has been continuously practicing his scripted lines in hopes the lines will get a lady's attention, allowing him to go on the stage of life and speak them. Once the door is opened, the heartthrob rushes out the door, running up the steps of his soul to become the man he always wanted to be. Barry gave his performance that night.

After hearing Barry's line, Sylvia said, "You are quite a charmer, Mr. Tigerman."

"I'm going to law school. Uh, I'm a second-year student," Barry sheepishly said.

Sylvia smiled. She looked at where some people were dancing to the music from the record player. She kind of rolled her eyes in that direction. "Would you care to dance, Barry?" she said sweetly.

"I'm not much of a dancer," he said.

"I'll show you a couple of steps," she said coyly.

"Sure, let's give it a whirl," he said.

As they started to dance, Sylvia put her right arm around Barry's waist, holding him a little tighter than one would expect on a first dance. She kept smiling at him all the time.

"You're better at this than you think," she said.

She glided him along the floor, teaching him some dance moves.

Yes, Mr. Tigerman, I will be teaching you many things as your wife, Sylvia thought. *He was going to be the one,* she said to herself. In time, he was going to be the one.

In the romantic jungle the man is the hunter, and the woman is the game, but in Chicago, we have different types of jungles and in this one, the hunter is captured by the game.

They went on a date to go see a movie the next Saturday night. She didn't care about what movie they saw; she was with him and that's all that mattered.

She was making sure he was exclusively hers so no one was going to keep her from becoming Mrs. Lawyer. Sylvia's operation had begun and Barry was going to be spun easily and effortlessly by Sylvia into the type of man she wanted him to be. The surgery would be painless. Why, he was even going to enjoy it. He'd thank her and ask for more, she reasoned.

"You see, Bobby, there are two things a man can never beat a woman at—love and revenge," Jimmy said. "A woman will make it pleasurable for you, and then they can kill you," he said.

I never forgot what Jimmy told me about the opposite sex. The power of a female is undaunted. A smile and the right fragrance, and before you knew it, big and ugly who thought he was in charge, surrendered his authority in a very smooth transition. He never knew what hit him.

Barry and Sylvia continued dating and he became more and more comfortable when he was around her. While Barry was never going to be Mr. Excitement, Sylvia ignited a spark in him with honors that brought a balance to his social life that he never would have had. While in his legal profession, he would become a star with Sylvia by his side; he would go from a social dud to a social stud in that his social skills reached C level, which for him meant he could socially skate by.

He graduated from law school and she graduated receiving her undergraduate degree in Business Administration. I often felt Sylvia was very capable in teaching this business of life to others, especially in how to select a partner. She was a pro at that.

Sylvia's father, Sam Feigenbaum, was a tailor who owned Sam's Tailor Shop on the South Side near 53rd Street and Comanche Avenue. Sam was a man who had the foresight to find ways to better himself, and ultimately that would pay off for his family.

Sam recognized that if you take advantage of an opportunity, the rewards could be very high. As a businessman, he saw that if you helped out a Chicago politician, he would help you. Sam bought tickets to his alderman's annual dinner, he bought tickets to the annual picnic, and he donated money to the alderman's Christmas food drive for the needy that lived in the ward.

Sam and the alderman were on a first name basis. The alderman made sure his precinct workers, who had city jobs and were beholden to the alderman, used the tailor shop for whatever services were required, such as cleaning their clothes, alterations on men's and women's clothing, and repairing their clothes. The alderman also encouraged others in the ward to use Sam's business.

This is how it's done in Chicago. It's the Chicago style. You take care of me, I take care of you, and everyone else be damned. It goes from the right hand to the left hand, and from the left hand to the right hand. So in Chicago, come Election Day for any election, everyone who has been taking care of a politician in some form of graft comes to the polls prepared to try and keep the politician in office; otherwise, they'll have to start kissing the ring of someone else.

In Chicago, elections are very democratic. Everyone's single vote counts; dead or alive. It doesn't matter; your vote will be recorded. There's an old political saying in Chicago—'Vote early, vote often.' Chicago elections are not about politicians really caring about the voters as much as, 'Give me another four years to fill my pockets with payoffs so I can live the American Dream at the taxpayers' expense.' The staggering number of politicians in Illinois who are convicted and live by the commandment of corruption just proves the old political adage—'You start off as a whore, and you end up as a prostitute.' That's why politics is known as the second oldest profession.

Since Sam had juice with the alderman, he went to see him about a job for Barry. Sam knew Barry and Sylvia would be getting married, so he was actually helping his future son-in-law. He went to Alderman James Coates' office.

"Hi, ya, Sam," Jim said, as Sam walked in.

"Hi, Jim," Sam said.

"How's the family?" Jim asked.

"Good and yours?" replied Sam.

"Doing just great," Jim said.

"Jim, I gotta ask a favor. It's for this guy my daughter Sylvia is dating. I think they're getting serious about each other. He just graduated from the University of Chicago Law School this past June, and a couple of weeks ago he got a letter from the state saying he passed the Bar and is now a licensed attorney in Illinois," Sam said.

"He needs a job, right?" Jim said.

"Right," Sam said.

"Sam, you have been a loyal supporter of the 16th Ward Regular Democratic Organization in the past, and I know that you will continue to be in the future," Jim said.

"Sit right here. I'm going to call Tommy McFarland, who handles patronage for the Mayor. Let's see what's available."

"Hi, Tommy, this is Jim Coates. One of my loyal supporters has a kid he knows who's graduated from the University of Chicago Law School, and passed the Bar. What...uh...you got anything available?" Jim asked.

"Give me a second," Tommy said.

Tommy shuffled some papers. "There's a position in the Law Department as an Assistant Corporation Counsel that's open." Jim, mouthing what Tommy tells him to Sam, then puts his hand over the phone.

"How's that?" Jim asked.

"Great. Perfect," Sam said.

Taking his hand off the phone, "Okay, Tommy. I'll send the kid downtown with a letter from me. I'll put the specifics in the letter. Thanks, Tommy, for your help," Jim said.

"Have the kid come into the ward office on Wednesday night. I'm here every Wednesday night, and I'll give him the patronage letter, and we'll tell him where Tommy's office is in City Hall," Jim said. "Now, make sure he takes that letter and the one saying he's passed the Bar to Tommy's office, okay, Sam?"

"One more thing. I'm going to start an annual golf outing. I mean, even if you don't play golf, you can come to a dinner we're going to have later that night. Is that a problem?" Jim said.

"No, Jim, that's fine. I'd love to come to the dinner," Sam said.

"Good. When the time comes, I'll send over Bobby McMahon, your precinct captain, with some tickets so you can help us out, okay?" Jim said.

"Sure, Jim. When Bobby comes over, I'll gladly help out. It's my pleasure," Sam said.

Sam told Sylvia and Barry about the job. Barry, while thanking Sam, still had his nose up in the air as he wanted to work for a corporate law firm.

"Honey, look at the contacts you'll make as a city lawyer," Sylvia said. Sylvia had the knack of building an opportunity when one couldn't be found. She held Barry's arm.

"You're right. It's about the contacts," Barry said.

Barry worked as an assistant corporation counsel for the City of Chicago, prosecuting slumlords in Housing Court for five years. The last case he prosecuted before leaving the law department was a slumlord named Tony Galante. Tony was convicted and had to pay a fine

"You've got some good lawyering skills, Mr. Tigerman. Too bad they're being wasted working for the city," Tony said after court.

"Thank you, Mr. Galante, but this was my last case as I'm leaving the city and I will be joining a law firm where I'm going to practice criminal defense," Barry said.

Tony asked the name of the firm, Barry told him, and they said their goodbyes. Tony Galante became Barry Tigerman's first client at the law firm, and as they say, the rest is history. In Chicago, politics has a way of opening doors that are closed to others.

It makes me laugh when I hear Washington politicians talk about political gridlock in Congress, and how difficult it is to get things done there. In Chicago politics, I never heard of political gridlock. Is there really such a word? Maybe the Washington politicians need to spend their summer vacation in Chicago to learn how to get things done. We might even give them a letter.

"Sylvia, there's something I need to talk to you about," Barry said.

"Okay, sure, honey," she said.

"Tony Galante wants me to move to Las Vegas to become general counsel for the hotels and casinos, and to be legal counsel for some of the unions he's involved with in Hollywood," Barry said. "I would also be involved indirectly with unions in Las Vegas," he said.

"Las Vegas," Sylvia said slowly and suspiciously, the words barely oozing out of her lips.

"Yes, Las Vegas," Barry said.

"What about your practice in Chicago?" she asked?

"I would sell the practice. There are a couple of young lawyers I know and I think for the right price they would be interested," he said. "Sylvia, here's the financial compensation I'd be getting" and he enumerated what he and Tony agreed upon. "So, it's $80,000 to start, a ten percent bonus on that first salary, followed by a five percent raise every year, and a ten percent bonus to be figured on the increased salary each year."

"Honey, am I understanding you correctly?" she asked. "We'll have to sell our lovely house."

"Yes, you are correct in understanding me, and we'll buy another lovely house," Barry said.

"I'll miss my sisters," she said.

"They can always come and visit us," he said.

"I've got ten fingers and ten toes, so are there more Jews than that in Las Vegas," Sylvia said. "I'm not thrilled about not being able to get a good kosher corned beef sandwich. Is there even a Temple there to attend holiday services?" she asked sarcastically.

With a smile on his face, Barry said, "We can build a Temple."

"We've got to consider the boys, Robert and Alan. They've got school, their friends. You know, they're people, too. We can't be selfish, just thinking of ourselves," Sylvia said. "We're going to talk to the boys, we're not going to ram this down their throats, I want their input," Sylvia said.

"I understand what you're saying. We will talk to the boys," Barry said.

Sylvia was a very loving, caring mother. I will always defend her on that. The boys, along with Barry, came first with her, and if they were not happy, she was not happy. What was best for the boys was always what Sylvia wanted.

They called the boys downstairs to the family room. Sylvia let Barry explain everything as she sat quietly, waiting to speak when the time was right.

"I think this would be a wonderful opportunity for our family," Barry said, as he concluded telling them about the move to Las Vegas. In true Barry style, he was blunt with the boys about the move to Las Vegas as far as the changes they would have to make in new surroundings. The one thing he didn't tell them was he was going to be working for the Outfit, and do only what was best for the Outfit, no matter who got physically or mentally hurt.

Robert, the eldest at 14, who was the spokesman for himself and his younger brother Alan, who was 12, after listening to what Barry told them said, "If you and Mom feel this is best for the family, then Alan and I are okay with the move to Las Vegas."

"Alan, do you agree with Robert?" Barry asked.

"Yes, Dad, I do," Alan said.

Sylvia, looking at her sons, said to Robert and Alan, "Dad and I love you both very much and we would never directly do anything to hurt either one of you. I know there will be some difficult times ahead, adjusting to a new school, making new friends, and other unexpected things that will come up, because Las Vegas is not Chicago, but we'll work through the changes as a family, a loving strong united and very proud family," Sylvia said. She got up from her chair. She first kissed Robert, then Alan on their cheeks, and then walked over to Barry and kissed him on his lips.

The boys then left the family room and went back upstairs.

"We are obviously going to have to take a trip to Las Vegas to see where we want to live, and that will depend on where the best schools are for the boys' education," Sylvia said. "There's so much to do, Barry, I don't know where to begin," she said.

"Sure. Sure, Sylvia, we will go to Las Vegas," Barry said. "Don't worry; we'll work out all the kinks. You'll see," he said.

Sylvia Tigerman, in my opinion, was the 'Queen of Opportunity.' After being told about Las Vegas, her mind started to think how to make Las Vegas financially work that would benefit the Tigerman family. "Barry, the cost of living is a lot less in Las Vegas than in Chicago, and, frankly, I think there will be a lot of real estate opportunities there for us," Sylvia said.

Of the three Feigenbaum girls, only Sylvia was the one with a business head on her shoulders. Sam used to talk to Sylvia about putting it 'into the ground.'

When the Depression hit after the 1929 stock market crash, the real estate market crashed just as hard. Sam Feigenbaum, unlike most of the people who were hard hit by the Depression, due to his financial austerity, had some money. He was able to buy two apartment rental buildings for about twenty percent of their actual value. One building had two rentals and the other building had three rentals. Both buildings were in foreclosure by the bank as the building owners walked away from the buildings, as they were not able to pay the mortgages.

Sam found out about these two buildings and he spoke with a bank vice president about buying the buildings. He made an offer to the bank to buy the buildings for cash at twenty percent of their actual worth. The banks, at that time, were desperate for cash, so they sold the buildings to Sam.

"Sylvia, remember cash is king. With cash you can always make deals that will benefit you, so always make sure you save a little bit, because you never know when the cash can make an extra buck for you," Sam said. Sylvia became her Daddy's girl when it came to finances. He talked and talked to her about making an extra buck. He showed her how it was done, and daddy's girl would shine ever so brightly in the coming years.

In the next ten years, Sam acquired seven more rental buildings, ranging from nine to sixteen rentals in each building. Sam hired another tailor, as his real estate investments were not only paying off handsomely to him, but they were requiring more and more of his time.

"Sylvia, always put it in the ground," he said. "Buy real estate—buildings or empty lots. Remember, there's only so much land, and if you own the land, you can command top dollar for it," Sam said. "Forget about the stock market. Look what happened in 1929. It crashed and people lost everything, including their lives," he said.

"Buildings can be built and torn down, but the land is still needed to build on. As long as you own the land, people like developers have to come to you. That's why you put it in the ground," Sam said.

Sylvia was the originator of having a Plan B.

"Barry, this Mafia stuff, I mean, Tony Galante, who knows how long he'll be around. Either he'll get killed or go to prison," Sylvia said. "Then where does that leave you? Maybe the next guy keeps you, maybe he doesn't," she said. "You've got to become licensed in Nevada to practice law, so you can have some other clients besides this Outfit stuff," Sylvia said.

"Since you'll be representing the hotels/casinos, unions, and whomever else Tony Galante wants you to represent, you'll be meeting lots of people, and those contacts can help you build a practice," she said. "Maybe it'll be a limited practice, but a practice nonetheless. It's always better to make sure you keep a door open to walk through if one closes on you," Sylvia said.

"You're right, honey. No use having all your eggs in one basket. I'll get licensed in Nevada," Barry said.

She snuggled up to him. "Then we'll check out real estate opportunities after we settle down in Las Vegas. Since we are going to have extra money, why not let it work for us," Sylvia said.

"I always said you were the smart one," Barry said, as he put his arm around her shoulder.

They went to Las Vegas a few weeks later to see what was going to be available to them for housing and a school for Robert and Alan. Before they left Chicago, Barry called Tony Galante.

"Hi, Tony, it's Barry Tigerman," Barry said.

"Oh, hi, Barry. How ya doin'?" Tony asked.

"Good, Tony. Sylvia approved the Las Vegas move, and we are leaving tomorrow to check out housing and schools for our sons in Las Vegas," Barry said.

"Beautiful, just beautiful. Glad to hear it," Tony said.

"I'll keep you posted on the timetable of when the final move will be made to Las Vegas. Sylvia and I still have a lot of details to work out, but we are moving in that direction. Now, be a good boy and don't get in any trouble while I'm gone. I'll be back in about a week," Barry said.

"Scouts honor, I'll be a good boy," Tony said.

After Barry finished talking to Tony, he hung up the phone. He shook his head slightly as he realized Tony was never in the Boy Scouts. Another day, another lie in the life of the Outfit as the Boy Scouts of America has no resemblance to the Outfit's Boy Scouts.

Barry and Sylvia visited downtown Las Vegas on one of their travel days. Downtown Las Vegas, in those days, was a little bit on the seedy side. There were some, not many, rental properties and plenty of vacant lots. There was one small casino, but there were plans to eventually add a couple more casinos, but those were plans in the making with no definite time to start construction.

The odds were better to gamble downtown. The blackjack and poker tables had lower minimum betting than on the strip. Not many tourists traveled downtown. They stayed on the strip. You had mostly the local residents, who lived in or around Las Vegas, who went downtown to gamble. There was one small hotel named the Black Bird in downtown that usually had more vacancies then occupants in those days.

On her first ever visit to downtown Las Vegas, Sylvia listened to a tune that played over and over again in her head. It was an old tune, but one she liked and listened to a lot. The tune 'put it in the ground' was Sylvia's anthem. When Sylvia told Barry downtown had what would start out as potential and end up as a reward in her opinion after she saw downtown; Barry, at first, was skeptical.

"Sylvia, you really think downtown can make a buck for us?" he said, looking around at a lot of barren land that was looking back at him.

"Yes, Barry, I do. The strip will grow beyond what it is today and that growth will force developers to look for more and to expand, and downtown is the next place they'll look," Sylvia said.

"Okay, it's just hard to imagine this turning into that," Barry said.

There are two types of eyes that people have. They have either today eyes or tomorrow eyes. Today eyes only see what's in front of them; a form of tunnel vision. Tomorrow eyes can see potential in something, which extends beyond today. Sylvia had those tomorrow eyes, and Barry, as doubtful as he was about the downtown area, he believed from the tips of his toes to the top of his head his Sylvia could turn dirt into dollars.

Nearly eighteen months after seeing downtown Las Vegas, Barry and Sylvia bought their first rental property in the downtown area—a four-story building that had twelve rental units. A few months later, they bought a six-unit rental building and two vacant lots. This was the beginning of their numerous real estate holdings. True to her word, Sylvia, in time, watched the strip grow and, in turn, downtown grow. Sylvia's tomorrow eyes developed quite a sparkled luster to them. She came, she saw, she conquered the real estate opportunity. Las Vegas likes to leave a mark on you, and Sylvia Tigerman would leave a mark on Las Vegas that was so embedded, it would be seen by generation after generation of Las Vegas tourists.

A year after Barry moved to Las Vegas, he passed the Nevada State Bar. Besides representing Tony Galante, he started to build a legal practice through the contacts he met in Las Vegas. He represented show business people on things like the closing of a house they bought in Las Vegas, represented them on a driving under the influence charge in court, and negotiated any business deals outside of Las Vegas, among other things. When it came to negotiating a business contract with one of the Outfit's Las Vegas hotels, Barry would refer the show business people to a local Las Vegas attorney, who was a friend of Barry's. Barry would get a referral fee from the lawyer. As you can imagine, there were never any problems with the contract negotiations. The show business contacts became very lucrative for Barry.

Was there a conflict of interest between Barry and his lawyer friend? I suppose, if you put it under a microscope, you might find a flaw. Barry was a Chicago guy who cooked these deals Chicago style, adding a cup of Chicago ethics. The Chicago ethics he learned from his dealings with the Outfit were put the money in your pocket and deny any money ever existed. Chicago ethics are learned from birth. After a newborn baby is born and cleaned up, they have their palm outstretched and say, "Where's mine?"

Barry's reputation as the go-to guy in Las Vegas grew and grew. If someone had a problem, the saying was, "Go see Mr. Tigerman. He'll straighten it out," and he always did.

Robert and Alan enjoyed their new schools and started making friends with their classmates. Sylvia, when not taking care of Barry and the boys, went downtown to collect the rent money from their properties and also to look for more real estate to add to their holdings.

When Sylvia went downtown, she dressed very plain, no makeup, and no jewelry, except for her wedding band. She left her diamond wedding ring at home. Sylvia tried to fit in with the locals as much as possible, as she learned humility got you a lot farther than being flashy. The Las Vegas locals were plain, everyday folks. A lot of them were ranchers who would come downtown for an evening out. They were straight shooters as far as being honest and forthright in their behavior. The only juice they knew about was the orange juice they drank with their breakfast.

These were not Chicago people. They weren't driven by the big city life. They had to be nurtured in a different way. No gamesmanship with these people. Being humble was your key to success with them. Sylvia played the role very well. She got along well with whomever she had contact with.

She would bake chocolate chip cookies and pass them around downtown to all the folks she met. A Protestant church near downtown was in need of repairs, but didn't have the money to do the work. Sylvia went to the church, introduced herself to the minister, and offered to help the minister by fundraising for the church. The minister welcomed Sylvia's help to raise money for the church.

After contacting local businesspeople in the area, Sylvia started to hold fundraisers. The business community responded with donations and, eventually, Sylvia raised the needed money so repairs could be made on the church.

At the same time she was working on fundraising for the church, she was also raising money for the largest synagogue of its time being built in Las Vegas, Temple B'nai David. Sylvia and Barry were heavy financial contributors themselves to the synagogue. She got Rocky Durso, the boss of the Terrablanca, to contribute money to the synagogue.

"Rocky, you like kosher hot dogs, don't you?" Sylvia asked.

"Yes, I do," Rocky said.

"Well, see, you have a Jewish connection," Sylvia said.

Rocky started laughing so forcefully, tears came to his eyes as he gave her money. She left him some chocolate chip cookies and moved on to the next victim.

Sylvia's involvement with fundraising for the church and synagogue gave her the opportunities to not only develop business contacts, but contacts that could use Barry's legal services. Her business contacts helped her when she was negotiating real estate deals for rental property or vacant lots. Being on a first name basis with individual sellers or bankers who were selling the property, personalized their transactions, making the deals go a lot easier. A couple of chocolate chip cookies given out to them by Sylvia didn't hurt the process, either.

By having cash, Sylvia was able to negotiate lower prices on the real estate as the sellers were more than glad to get the instant money. Sylvia was able to avoid, in a lot of cases, having to get a mortgage, especially for the rental properties, by having cash to negotiate. Sylvia learned Daddy was right, cash is king.

Sylvia realized that her initial success in fundraising for the church and synagogue could be expanded. She talked with Barry about doing political fundraisers for chosen candidates. Since both of them were lifelong Democrats, Sylvia suggested working for Democratic candidates. Barry agreed.

"By helping Democratic candidates, we can help ourselves in the long run," Sylvia said to Barry. Sylvia had one of those twenty-four hour minds in which a second shift was mentally brought in to continue thinking of deals while she slept.

"Sure, the bigger base we can develop, the better it becomes for us, not only financially, but in building a better foundation within the community of who we are and what we can do in Las Vegas," Barry said.

"Honey, thanks for looking at the potential of the bigger picture. See, that's why I married you," she said sweetly, giving him those innocent looks from her tomorrow eyes. With two super charged egos working together, this plan had success stamped all over it.

Barry bent over and kissed Sylvia on her lips. "Well, that's another problem solved," Barry proudly said.

"Yes, honey, one less to worry about," Sylvia said.

Maybe it's in the woman's DNA, but this sisterhood has the uncanny ability to make a man think he has solved the problem, receiving all the accolades accorded to him while, in fact, it's the better half who has solved the problem, but let the problem dangle in the man's head to make him think it still exists.

I don't know how they do it, but they do it time and time again, and we men—myself, Bobby Williams included—fall for this carnival act winter, spring, summer, and fall. That old saying, 'Behind every successful man is a good woman,' needs to be changed to, 'Behind every successful man is a woman with one hell of a brain who made the man think he was successful, so he became successful.' Yeah, there's a reason women outlive men, and it's not in the water.

There was going to be a secret partner also in this political fundraising venture. Maybe this partner was miles and miles away from Las Vegas, but this secret partner was going to reap the benefits also. Tony Galante and Dean Dragonetti were overjoyed when Barry told them about the political fundraising he and Sylvia were going to do.

To the Outfit, the more politicians that could be stuffed in their pockets, the more favors they could make the politicians do for them. Barry worked for the Outfit indirectly as legal counsel, so he could be the front man, the pawn used by the Outfit with the politicians.

The Outfit would communicate to Barry what favors they wanted, and he would be the messenger sent to the politicians with their favors list. It was a plan that would benefit all the players. Everyone would be happy, as each party connected to the favor got to munch on a chocolate chip cookie. For the politician that didn't like chocolate chip cookies, they learned to like them, as a chocolate chip cookie melting in your mouth was far better than being buried in the desert, melting underground courtesy of the boys from Chicago.

Sylvia had seen how her father benefitted by financially assisting the alderman in Chicago. Her first political fundraiser, which was one of many she did in her life, was for a city councilman's race in Las Vegas. The Democratic candidate was a political nobody with very little campaign money. With Sylvia's financial help, he became a political somebody and won the election.

Sylvia saw how the financial muscle she provided to the candidate paid off. Having the most money when running for political office does not ensure you will win the election, but it sure goes a long way in bringing you up from the back of the pack to near the front of the winner's circle.

As time went on, Sylvia and Barry, who put the arm on his contacts for money, got involved financially with state races for state representative or state senator. The more fundraisers they did, the more proficient they got, and they saw more of their Democratic candidates win. They moved up, raising money for a governor's race, and then the ultimate pinnacle political office held in Nevada, the United States Senate. The Outfit had a friend in Washington, DC.

As the Tigerman's political friendships blossomed, so did the favors requested by the Outfit. One favor asked for and received was the easing of regulations in the state of Nevada.

By passing a law allowing less restrictive things to be trucked in Nevada, the state of Nevada helped the Outfit more easily move contraband that was illegal throughout the state. While the Outfit would fill their trucks with what was allowed under the law, the trucks still had plenty of room for cartons of narcotics that would be heading north to California and south to Arizona. Another Outfit favorite was to ship stolen guns to be sold in those same two states.

The change in the law meant Outfit trucks would not have to pull into designated state inspection areas for the trucks to be inspected and weighed. The Outfit trucks merrily rolled down the highway with the drivers laughing at the inspection areas whenever they passed them. The Outfit boys were giving the verbal equivalent of the raising of the middle finger to the state of Nevada. Damn those chocolate chip cookies sure tasted delicious.

"Without our friends, we wouldn't be in business," Jimmy said. "So, there's no way the Outfit could not exist without our friends?" I asked.

"Bobby, we need the juice with the politicians, judges, and cops, otherwise they could crack down on us. Tougher lawyers, tougher criminal sentencing, and more arrests would happen, all affecting our existence," Jimmy said. "Look, while these friends are small in number, compared to the number of politicians, judges, and cops when we look at the total numbers, it's those few that help us stay employed," he said. "As long as you have a buck, you'll find a hand to put it in. That's where the juice comes in. I guess you would say it keeps us solvent," Jimmy said in unbroken laughter.

"Dirty hands need to be washed with more soap," I said.

Whenever he was conducting business, Barry always wore a suit and tie, no matter if the temperature was 55 degrees or 105 degrees in public. The suits consisted of his favorite colors—black and darker black. The colors reflected his mode of operation.

He was blunt in speaking to you and did not care to repeat himself to you. After all, in his mind, he spoke the words of wisdom from the Oracle. His ego was so big that it rose above God's head, and God strained his neck to see it. He was a man who worked in the murky shadows of darkness that surrounded and engulfed the Outfit's Las Vegas operation. He was put in Las Vegas for one reason and one reason only—to make sure the Outfit's Las Vegas operation had no speed bumps put in its path. The Las Vegas operation, to the public, always wore a smile on its face. Barry's job was to make sure the circus always entertained the customers, and the customers always paid the Outfit's freight.

Near the Terrablanca, about two blocks south, a new hotel/casino was being built by a New York investor by the name of Allen Shakestein, who had ties to the Rinaldi crime family in New York.

Gus Zablocki, president of the Teamster's Local 5, which had laborers, cement truck drivers, and heavy equipment operators among its members, called to complain to Barry that Shakestein was using non-union people to build the Broadway Inn.

"Barry, you gotta do something about these non-union guys being used to build the Broadway Inn," Gus said. "We've got some Chicago boys in Local 5 who are not working because of what Shakestein is doing," he said.

"Gus, first of all, calm down. I will look into the problem, decide what needs to be done, and then once I act, there will be no more problem when I am through. Are we clear on that?" Barry said.

As he exhaled a breath of air, Gus said, "It's just I know Vegas is really going to be growing in the future, and I don't want someone pushing my boys out of the work picture now, and gaining a foothold for the future where non-union people get the jobs my boys deserve."

"Business will be done as business should be done, are we clear on that?" Barry said.

"Alright, we're clear on that. I'll wait and see what happens, and as the saying goes in Vegas, 'If you have a problem, see Mr. Tigerman,' so I'll let Mr. Tigerman handle it," Gus said.

"I couldn't agree more," Barry said.

Bill Junaway was providing the non-union help to be used to build the Broadway Inn. He, by trade, was a carpenter, and told Shakestein in their initial meeting that by hiring non-union workers, the cost of building the Broadway Inn would be a lot less. He cited the differential in labor costs between union and non-union workers would be a lot less with non-union workers on the job. Shakestein was from New York, a big labor city, so he understood what labor costs meant to a job. He agreed with Junaway about the labor costs, and he decided to use non-union workers to build the Broadway Inn.

When you move to a new town or city, you have to learn the ways of your new environment. To help the learning curve, it's always nice to make friends with someone who will show you the ropes. The Outfit was more than happy to drive the welcome wagon over to Shakestein, and if they had to, drive over him.

Barry knew calling Shakestein at this point could possibly set up a Chicago versus New York confrontation, so he decided to go after Junaway first. Barry would use Junaway as his conduit to Shakestein.

Barry went to see Junaway at his small office located in a compact two-story building near downtown that was owned by Junaway. Junaway's office was tucked away on the second floor.

"Mr. Junaway, I'm Barry Tigerman, a lawyer from Chicago representing hotels here in Las Vegas that have Chicago interests behind them, and I also represent various unions such as Local 5," he said, while walking into Junaway's office.

"So?" Junaway said, barely looking up from his desk.

"Mr. Junaway, I'm instructing you to stop sending over non-union workers to the Broadway Inn for employment," Barry said directly and firmly, his words zeroing in on the subject.

"You're what? I don't know who you are or who you think you are, but you better get outta here before I throw you outta here," Junaway said, his head rising up now looking in Barry's face.

A good lawyer, which Barry was, always knows the answer to the question he's asking. It was time for Barry to give the answer.

"Say hello to your wife, Leslie, and your two boys, Michael who's eight and Joseph who's six," Barry said, and then turned around and began walking out of the office.

Junaway's face started to turn an angry fluorescent red. "You threatening me, you son of a bitch," Junaway said as he stood up from the desk loudly enough for Barry to hear. Barry just kept on walking, a small fracture of a smile appearing on his face. Remember, this is not a naturally smiley guy. I'm not sure if he even smiled when World War II ended, but now he knew he was on his way to removing the problem, because once the family is put in the mix, tough guys aren't so tough anymore.

In the Outfit's bag of vile tricks they can use against someone, mentioning one's family is always near the top of the bag. The person can relate to his family, and by mentioning them, the Outfit's message of do what we want or else we make it personal, rings loud and clear. The implication is now deafening in the ears of the person. Items can be replaced; people can't. The Outfit feels they have hit a home run by mentioning the person's family as they have covered the bases that the person holds dear to his heart, his family. It's a question asked in a mind game, family first or not. Barry knew the answer to that question.

In nearly all instances, the person would succumb to what the Outfit wanted in order that they could walk in their home and see their loved ones every day. An empty house would be a sad house that must be avoided at all costs. There was no way around it, a person's family was priority one that could never, ever be bargained with.

Barry decided he would give Junaway a couple of days to digest their meeting. Let him swallow the references to his family and see if that would push Junaway's mental button favorably. He was hopeful Junaway would call him and tell him he would not send anymore non-union workers to the Broadway Inn.

Two days passed and Barry did not receive the phone call from Junaway. Maybe Junaway was thinking about outsmarting Barry while protecting his family. Barry decided he was going to use an old Chicago trick. If someone has a beef with someone and that person has juice with, let's say, the alderman, he will ask the alderman to have various inspectors from the City of Chicago sent to the guy's business.

Since Junaway's office was in an old building that he owned, it had the potential for a lot of code violations, as the building had some much needed repairs attached to it. The inspectors were going to have a long list of code violations that they could find. The list was going to be so chock-full of harassing goodies that Junaway's head will be spinning around and around as the costs to fix the violations mounted up higher and higher.

Barry called a friend, Las Vegas City Councilman Democrat Sean Kincannon and told him about an unsafe building he had a meeting in. "Sean, I had a meeting in a building that in, my opinion, was not safe to be in, and had numerous building code violations," Barry said. "I'm pretty experienced in noticing building code violations from my days as an Assistant Corporation Counsel for the City of Chicago, prosecuting slumlords in Housing Court." To think Barry, at first, turned up his nose at the job, and now I guess it was okay for him to lower his nose.

"Thanks, Barry, just give me the address and I will have the appropriate inspectors take a look at the building," Sean said.

"Good Sean. Also, I'm not sure if he had a business license. Maybe you can send someone out from the Department of Licensing and Collections to see if he's got all his proper licenses to run a business," Barry said.

"Not a problem. I'll have someone from that department go check that out," Sean said.

"Sean, thanks for your help on this one," Barry said.

"That's what I'm here for, to help my constituents," Sean said.

When Sean Kincannon ran for councilman, Sylvia had fundraisers for him that helped his campaign not only raise needed money, but gave him visibility to voters, which helped to secure a victory. He always said without Sylvia's help, he could not have been elected. On election night, on the stage was not only his family, but standing right behind him, a smiling, confident Sylvia, not only reveling in his victory, but knowing she had secured a new political best friend that was to be the first of many new political best friends. When Barry called these political friends to get something done, they would not only jump, but would ask 'Master' how high.

The various inspectors hit Junaway's building with a force greater than D-Day in World War II. Their pens ran nonstop as the inspectors recorded numerous code violations. *When will their pens run out of ink?* Junaway thought as he glumly watched the inspectors orchestrate an old time Chicago political dance right in front of him.

Junaway knew where this tune was coming from, but he had no juice to stop it. At the end of the day, after the inspectors left, he looked at the pile of written inspection notices which ranged from building and fire code violations to not having the proper business licenses, and realized he didn't have the money to fix the violations and make them go away. Losing the two-story building would be the end of his career of supplying non-union help to build future Vegas hotels. He didn't have the money to buy another building. Besides, Barry would just go after that building, too, he reasoned.

He shut off the lights, and head down, he painfully trudged down the aisle leading to the front door where he walked out of a building, turning back one last time to look at a life that had become his past rather than his future. Junaway was a proud man, but tonight was a defeated man.

Walking to his car, Junaway thought about the call he was going to have to make to Barry. Was there a way out of actually having to concede to what Barry wanted crisscrossed in his mind back and forth, forth and back, over and over. In the end, the answer was still the same. Since he did not have the money to fix the violations, he would have to make that phone call that was going to take away his independence as a man. He and the other non-union workers would have to sing the union song and enjoy it. Then it sunk in what would happen to his family if he tried to fight Barry. His family was the most treasured possession in his life, and he couldn't put them in any danger.

God, how he hated to make that call. No man likes to knuckle under to another man. It's not in most men's nature to concede defeat, to say I'm sorry, or apologize for a wrong deed. When a man has to admit defeat, the words move from the voice box slowly up to the lips. A part of the body does not want to concede.

The body will fight, kick, and scratch the words before they pass through the mouth. "No, no, don't do it," the body will say. "There's got to be a way we can win, not lose." The words, with a blank look, will say to the body, "Show me how we can win."

The body will slump over, its head starting to shift downward, doused by the word's question. "I can't," the body will say, and the epic struggle to preserve manhood ends.

"Mr. Tigerman, this is Bill Junaway calling you," Junaway said the next day.

"Oh, yes. Hello, Mr. Junaway," Barry said.

"I'm calling to let you know, I will not be sending over any more non-union workers to the Broadway Inn project, and I'll call them and let them know that," Junaway said.

"Good, Mr. Junaway. You're making the right decision. And by the way, I'm going to give you Gus Zablocki's phone number for Local 5. I think it would be a good idea to have you and your non-union workers join the union, as Las Vegas will be growing, and there will be a lot of work for them," Barry said.

By having them join the union, Barry stopped any future confrontation with non-union workers, as there will be none. Everyone will be in the union.

"Okay, I'll take the number," and under his breath Junaway said, "*Screw you, too, Barry.*"

"What? What did you say? I didn't quite hear what you said," Barry said.

"I said, I'll take the number and call Local 5," Junaway said. "I'll also call Mr. Shakestein and tell him I won't be sending anymore non-union help to the Broadway Inn, that the men decided they wanted to join the union," he said.

"Wonderful," said Barry.

Another win for the Outfit, as there was now peace in labor land. In future years, the phrase, "I'll see Mr. Tigerman," became as well known in Las Vegas as, "Wait until next year," the annual cry of the Chicago Cubs fan. Anyone from an entertainer to a union boss or anyone else affecting the Outfit's financial security that had a problem, punched in the 'I'll see Mr. Tigerman' command in their brain.

Later that year, after being prodded by Sean Kincannon, the City of Las Vegas went to Housing Court to seek condemnation of Bill Junaway's business property. Junaway had been given so much time to fix the violations by the city, the time had now passed, which allowed the city to go to court to seek condemnation of the property.

Junaway was notified by mail of the hearing date, but he chose not to attend as he didn't have the money to fix the violations and was resigned to the fact that he was going to lose the building.

The city won and got the building condemned. They tore the building down and removed all debris. The city put the property up for sale and it was bought for one dollar by Barry and Sylvia. They bought some surrounding vacant lots and sold all the property to O'Keefe Gaming Corporation, which built O'Keefe's Casino on the property.

Sean Kincannon's brother Jack was a real estate agent. Barry and Sylvia used Jack, which was part of the deal with Sean, to sell the properties. Jack got his commission, and the Tigerman's gave Sean a nice cash birthday present of five thousand dollars.

The next year, the Broadway Inn opened. All the local big shots were there for the grand opening. Attending were the mayor and his cronies, local businesspeople, and Allen Shakestein with Gus Zablocki, who had his arm draped over Shakestein's shoulder, and smiles were being passed around to everyone.

Standing across the street, an uninvited guest was watching. A guy wearing a tie and a black suit took in all the happiness that filled the air. He slowly turned to the east, looking toward Chicago, and knew while you could take the man out of Chicago, you could never take Chicago out of the man. Have a nice day, Outfit. Don't worry, your friend Barry will take extra special care of you in Las Vegas.

Barry Tigerman became a powerful Las Vegas icon. He would represent the interests in Las Vegas that made Vegas work for the Outfit. "What problem? I don't see a problem. Do you have a problem?" was the disappearing act he performed time and time again. He knew he could beat you in court and with the Outfit's muscle at his beck and call, could beat you outside of court, if need be. Barry always played the Vegas angles on cue.

While Barry was visibly the king of his domain to the outside world, Sylvia was the master behind the throne. They matched up perfectly as a couple. She was smart, savvy, shrewd, and to put it mildly, way ahead of her time in the friendly art of manipulation. She deserved sainthood for the way she could take any situation and reconstruct it to her advantage.

Somehow, she would repackage it, and sprinkle some sweetness on it to take away the stench that it would turn out to become. Throw in a smile, and the Tigermans would gain the advantage they wanted.

Sylvia knew how to take care of Sylvia, and while she made sure everyone ate a slice of the cake, she always made sure she got the last piece. What she did was make the play when the play had to be made. There was nothing wrong with what she was doing, as she was just watching the race after she had won.

"Bobby, the world is hell; it's tough, cruel, mean, and those are the good things. So, someone like Sylvia made sure she always wore a safety vest and wasn't going to drown. She was living in a man's world and knew she would have to fight like hell to survive. She used her resources as best as she could, because as a woman, she had to work triple hard compared to a man. I know more women are going to college and there are more opportunities today than there were in Sylvia's time, but that doesn't make it any easier. Women aren't always given the same chances a man gets. Sometimes, they get fluffed off since they are women. Women gotta make their own breaks, because the war they're fighting is being played out in an unfair world. Sylvia was one hell of a broad. I really respected her," Jimmy said.

"So do I," I said.

Barry and Sylvia, in their later years, retired to San Diego, California, where they purchased a spacious three-bedroom condominium. With the demise of the Outfit in Las Vegas, Barry would play no role for the Outfit anymore. They were gone and it was time for him to go. It took very little coaxing from Sylvia to get Barry to move to San Diego.

He and Sylvia made their money, so now it was time to enjoy it in their later years. They lived well in San Diego and enjoyed those years. Barry died in 1995 and Sylvia died in 1999. Several years before Barry died, Sylvia called her sons and asked them to come to San Diego. Both Robert and Alan were lawyers, who practiced together in Las Vegas. They were both married with children.

While they had a general practice, most of their practice was devoted to representing several hotel/casinos. The hotels in the 1980s became corporate owned, and by 1999 less than ten hotels/casinos out of about a hundred in Las Vegas had any mob ties; none from Chicago. Today, even those few remaining places where the boys once had their fingers became corporate owned.

Robert and Alan left Las Vegas early one Thursday morning and made the six-hour drive to San Diego. After arriving in San Diego, where they were greeted by Barry and Sylvia, and showing the latest pictures of their children, Robert and Alan pulled out legal pads from their suitcases and sat down with their parents in the living room.

Sylvia had already talked with Barry about the need to do estate planning. Sylvia knew that with the tax laws concerning estates, her sons and grandchildren could stand to lose millions of dollars. Sylvia was going to throw the first and only punch at the Internal Revenue Service. She was going to knock them out before they knew what hit them.

From the very first property bought by the Tigermans, Barry set up a corporation in which all properties in Las Vegas and later California were bought and sold through Tigerman, Incorporated. Barry told Sylvia that with the properties being held in Tigerman, Inc., if they were sued by someone, none of the properties would be considered as personal assets. While Barry was the president and Sylvia was the vice president of Tigerman, Inc., each son, when they turned twenty-one years old, were added to the company as directors.

"Boys, the reason I wanted to see you, and I already talked with your father about this, we need not only a will, but to talk about the estate we're going to be leaving you," Sylvia said. Barry sat patiently, quietly letting Sylvia carry the water on this one.

"Our real estate holdings have been very, very good to us," she said. "We have holdings that are worth approximately two hundred fifty million at this point," Sylvia said. "Since the estate tax will be very high, and also the capital gains tax will eat into your profits if you sell the properties, I talked with your father and, honey, correct me if I'm wrong, the best way to go from a tax standpoint is to create a foundation.

"You boys would be the directors of the Barry & Sylvia Tigerman Foundation," Sylvia said. "You both could draw salaries in those capacities," she said. "The properties would be moved from the corporation to the foundation, and the corporation would be dissolved. Am I speaking correctly, honey?" Sylvia said.

"Yes, you are," Barry said.

"Dad will identify any other assets he thinks should be put in the foundation," Sylvia said.

"I wish Sam Bernstein, the tax layer in Vegas, was still alive," she said. "Sam knew the Internal Revenue code inside and out. He knew it from any direction, north, south, east, and west," Sylvia said. "I know his son Jody took over the practice after Sam died. Hopefully, he's got Sam's smarts," she said.

"I want you boys to check with Jody about what the IRS allows when creating a foundation," Sylvia said. "We're going to do it legit. There's too much at stake to lose. Barry have I left something out," she said.

"No, honey, I think the boys understand about the foundation. As far as the will, I will write out the specifics you and I talked about, especially concerning what should be done for the grandchildren, and send a draft to the boys," Barry said.

Both Robert and Alan had been writing nonstop, taking detailed notes while they listened to Sylvia talk.

"There's one other thing, boys," Sylvia said. "Now don't take this the wrong way, but when writing the will, I want you to limit my daughters-in-law roles, only if, God forbid, either one of you dies, and my two beautiful, adorable granddaughters and my two handsome grandsons are still minors. At that time, then your wives would become legally responsible as the children's legal guardians.

"I love my two daughters-in-law, and I know you do also, but they are not blood. Marriages can come and marriages can go. They could get a bug on their bagel and start running around with a younger guy, or worse yet, a married guy. Then you boys would have a legal catastrophe to deal with, namely divorce court," Sylvia said. "They would try and take you boys to the cleaners, skinning you of your assets. So, to avoid that, their roles in the will would strictly be nonexistent except in the case, God forbid, either of you dies," she said. "I don't want your wives to have any legal access to the assets in the will, except where I have stated to you concerning your deaths," Sylvia said.

Robert looked at Alan, and Alan looked at Robert. Each brother knew what was financially at stake, so they were not about to quibble about their wives' position in the will. While blood is thicker than water, money has a way of diluting all of that.

"It's okay, Mom," Alan said.

"I understand," Robert said.

"As far as the will, Robert and I will be co-executors of the estate, so if one of us dies before the other, the remaining one of us will liquidate the assets that are not in the foundation and disperse them per the instructions you and Dad have set up in the will," Alan said.

"I will check with Jody Bernstein on the legal requirements for the foundation from a tax standpoint," Robert said.

"Where would you want the foundation set up?" Alan asked Sylvia.

"California taxes are too high, so look into Nevada to see if that is a better state for the foundation from a tax standpoint," Sylvia said. "If not Nevada, then you'll have to research which state is best. Maybe Jody can be of some help," she said.

"Okay, Mom. I'll get back to you on that one," Alan said.

"As far as Dad's stuff, his watches, and a couple of rings, that will be for both of you to decide who gets what," Sylvia said. "As far as my stuff, I'll give you a list of who gets what. I've got three safe deposit boxes full of diamond rings, gold bracelets, gold chains, gold necklaces, diamond earrings, pins, brooches, and a lot of silver things," she said. "I've got your names on the signature card, so while you are here, you can go to the bank and sign the cards so you'll have access to the boxes when need be."

"You'll work from the list I give you. None of the jewelry is to be listed in the will. Everything will go to my precious granddaughters, per my written instructions," Sylvia said.

"I want to make this perfectly clear. None of the jewelry will go to my daughters-in-law, and I mean none of it," she said defiantly. "Is this understood?" she said, eyeing both of her sons with a look so menacing even God was hiding under the table, waiting for the okay to come out.

"Yes, Mom, of course we will follow your instructions," Robert said.

God, now feeling more assured that the potential storm had passed, got out from under the table and got out of San Diego as quickly as possible, catching the next bus to Heaven. *No sense being in San Diego in case Storm Sylvia rolls in*, he thought.

"Both of you boys are on our checking accounts," Sylvia said. "Dad and I have three accounts that you can sign on. Each account has fifty thousand dollars, so I think one hundred fifty thousand dollars is more than ample to bury your Dad and me when the time comes," she said in a lighthearted way. "Dad and I are planning to be around for a while, so don't start making any funeral arrangements just yet," Sylvia said laughingly.

"Of course, Mom. Just you and Dad enjoy yourselves. It's your money and you and Dad worked very hard for it, so make each day a fun day for both of you," Alan said.

Even as the sun was starting to set on her life, Sylvia always made sure it was advantage Sylvia. She always thought like a winner and functioned like one. I can still hear her voice vocalizing in my head.

"Bobby, when an opportunity comes your way, you grab it with both hands, squeeze it, shake it, run with it, wring every bit of positive out of it that can provide a better life for you. An opportunity doesn't knock on your door every day saying, 'Here I am.' A lot of times you've got to piece A with B to get C, but don't stand and look on the outside of the opportunity, open the door, walk and fight with every last bit of strength your body has to succeed, to win and set yourself apart from everyone else.

"By succeeding, Bobby, people will know who you are and what you stand for. Then more opportunities will come your way. People want to associate with winners; losers are for the 'wait until next year' crowd," Sylvia said. "Always, Bobby, always put it in the ground," she said.

The Outfit, in a weak moment, though they were few and far between without even realizing it, can offer an opportunity for someone who realizes what he's got sitting in his lap, which can make him successful. In the meantime, others involved with the Outfit as members wonder when they are even going to get paid and have to make ends meet by committing other criminal acts, such as stickups and burglaries, so they and their families survive. Then there are those few, a select few, who munch on the successful fruits of their labor.

For Barry and Sylvia Tigerman, the Outfit gave them the chance to build their own castle in class Vegas and reign as the designated Outfit royalty, living in an amassed splendor as king and queen. Barry and Sylvia's offense in Las Vegas was very simple—make the play when the play has to be made and stay out of the jackpot. There were many who tried, but Barry and Sylvia always stood out as the model of getting what you want, when you want it. Funny, the Outfit works the same way.

The Outfit saw Las Vegas as the golden treasure in waiting that needed to expand. The three Outfit hotels—the Terrablanca, Monroe, and El Casa—saw their revenues grow from year to year, but gambling expansion was an itch the boys from Chicago felt had to be scratched. While Las Vegas was considered open where any crime family in the United States could operate, the Outfit dominated the Vegas action like no one else. They saw the desert as the golden Mecca, the first place trophy to their operation. Las Vegas brought in the big money. It was the ring the Outfit kissed. It was quite natural for them to go ahead and pursue a growth project in the 1960s that would change Las Vegas from a small town operation into an international jewel, drawing people from all over the world.

"Jimmy, we've talked about this a couple of times before, but it's time to expand Vegas by building more hotels with casinos, so we can get a bigger skim than we get now," Dean said. "I've heard from other families in Cleveland, Detroit, and Kansas City, who want to operate in Vegas, so we could partner up with them. We build the hotels and they run them, and we get our cut of the action at these places," Dean said. "We gotta figure out how to use teamster money, because once we do that, I'll call Matt Licardo, the Teamster's president in Cleveland, to get his okay. The plan has to be solid, no leaks, or Matt won't go along with it," Dean said.

"I've been thinking about how we can use teamster money for a while since we first talked about growing Vegas," Jimmy said.

"We can't just take the money from the Mid-States Greater Teamster Pension Fun and the Mid-States Greater Health & Benefit Fund without being able to replace it. You know, if you debit an account, you've got to credit the account to balance the account," Jimmy said.

Dean curled up his face, raised his lips, holding them tightly together for a couple of seconds. He then spoke, "Okay, I'm listening."

"See, as long as we have money in the funds to cover pension and health-care costs, no one will complain," Jimmy said. "No one is going to run to the Feds complaining about not getting their pension money or their doctor bills paid because, then, that's when the Feds will stick their nose in and start an investigation," Jimmy said.

"How do we avoid that?" Dean asked.

"I've been making a couple of calls to insurance companies that specialize in casualty coverage to get quotes on how much we would have to pay on a premium to get dollar coverage for the teamster funds. For example, if we pay five thousand dollars on the premium, we get one hundred Gs in coverage," Jimmy said. "Then, after the hotels/casinos are up and running, we take part of the skim we get from those places and put the money back in the fund. Once we get all our money back in the funds, we drop the insurance coverage."

"Remember, every teamster paycheck is having money taken out for union dues and medical coverage, so we are getting money continuously in the funds," Jimmy said. "When the teamsters get their new contracts, their union dues and medical coverage costs will be raised, so more money will come into the funds, and we might not have to put as much money back in the funds. The teamsters will do it for us," he said.

"If somehow something gets screwed up with the funds, the insurance coverage is our safety net. They'll cover the costs in the funds based on the amount of coverage that we are paying for," Jimmy said.

Dean, whose nature was not one to be on the quiet side, sat quietly, looking at Jimmy. "So, we take the money from the funds, but we cover ourselves with insurance in case something happens in the funds so they'll pick up the tab, and we will still be getting teamster money going into the funds from payroll deductions for dues and medical coverage. Do I have it all?" summarized Dean.

"Yes, the only other thing is figuring out the skim from the new hotels that we will be involved with," Jimmy said.

"What if we just let the teamsters put back the money into the funds on their own from their payroll deductions? No skim money or insurance money needed," Dean said.

"I mean, you could do that if that's what you want to do, but you're going to be pulling a lot of money, quite a bit of reserve money from the funds, and if a lot of retirements occur, or more people get sick than normal, you'll have a drain on the funds," Jimmy said. "I can just see someone running to the Feds screaming the funds are broke, and I lost my hard-earned money, blah, blah, blah," Jimmy said.

"How about if we tell those teamsters that want to retire, 'work or get hurt,'" Dean said.

Jimmy said laughingly, "Then the Health & Benefits Fund will definitely run out of money."

"Okay, Jimmy, it's just I hate like hell to give up any money, but I see your point. Expanding Las Vegas is going to bring us a hell of a lot more money than we get from our three places right now," Dean said. "We gotta use teamster money to make Vegas grow. I agree with you on that, since there's no other money available to cover the Vegas costs," he said.

"First, you gotta get Matt to go along with using teamster money," Jimmy said. "It's only a plan. It can be changed depending on the circumstances, so make that clear to Matt so he won't think we're not flexible to change," Jimmy said.

"Okay, I'll call him to set up a meeting in Chicago. You'll be at the meeting, too, because he might have some questions that you can answer to help get his okay," Dean said. "In the meantime, let me chew on this insurance idea," Dean said.

"Fine, just let me know when we are going to meet," Jimmy said.

The teamster funds were administered in Chicago by Howard Sanders, who had direct links to the Outfit. There was a seven-member governing board that functioned like the board of directors of a corporation, meeting every two weeks, and making decisions for both funds which could arrange how the monies of each fund was invested and spent. Sanders and his staff handled the day-to-day operations of the funds and enforced any policy that the governing board wanted implemented after approving that policy.

The seven-member governing board consisted of three seats for Chicago, two seats for Detroit, and one seat each for Cleveland and Kansas City. All of the board members had mob ties to their respective cities. At times, when voting on an issue concerning the funds, their votes reflected what the Mob bosses in those cities wanted. Mob concerns were always given priority by the board members. So, if the money had to be taken out of the funds for expansion of Las Vegas, a rubber stamp approval would take place.

Teamster dues money from their paychecks and money from their paychecks to pay the health insurance coverage would be sent to Sanders after every pay period. Sanders would put 70% of the money in the Retirement Fund and 30% of the money in the Health & Welfare Fund.

I remember Sanders telling me it was Frankie "Goose" DeTuna, a mob boss from Kansas City, who was a board member, who got the board to vote in those percentages. "When Frankie presented those percentages, a board member asked Frankie what his research was that determined those percentages," Sanders said. Frankie said, 'Let me get my research from my winter coat.' Frankie went to his winter coat, pulled out a .38-caliber gun and put it on the table," Sanders said. " 'Anyone got any questions about my research?' Frankie asked. The measure passed on a voice vote with every board member chirping 'yes.' The board, from my recollection, never had a 'no' vote on any measure at any meeting. The .38-caliber gun became the chief counsel in the minds of the board members."

As president of the teamsters, Matt Licardo had the final say where the union money went. If Licardo said the money goes to A, that's how the board members voted. Licardo only invoked his power on major projects. Generally, he kept his nose out of the lesser decisions and let the board make those decisions.

If Licardo decided to move the teamster location out of Chicago, he could do it. However, he knew to win reelection as president, he needed Chicago. The Outfit had influence in teamster locals in Milwaukee, Kansas City, and St. Louis. Chicago not only delivered Chicago votes, they delivered votes in those other cities. With the Outfit being the union powerhouse, moving the teamster location had no chance of happening.

His approval of teamster money to be used in Las Vegas was crucial. With a guy of his stature, you had to finesse him into what you wanted him to do.

This was not how the Outfit operated. You either said 'yes' to what they told you or you would hear the alternative, which would get you to say 'yes.'

Dealing with Matt Licardo meant you would have to treat him like a human being with respect. Some granule of humbleness would have to be added to the conversation. In these types of dealings the Outfit was shy, awkward, out of their element, not in the comfort zone they are normally used to. They bit their tongue and tried to play nice. The Outfit could not be the alpha force that drove their motivational engine. As much as they hated it, they would have to be the 'please and thank you, have a nice day' boys for a while. Later on, they could go to Our Lady of Perpetual Worship and fumigate their souls of such atrocious behavior during confessional. The deeds of goodness was a sin the Outfit had to dump in Lake Michigan.

A meeting was arranged to be held in Chicago the next week on a Wednesday at Chateau D'Ville in one of their backrooms.

Matt Licardo came to the meeting skeptical about what the teamsters were going to get out of this deal.

"Hi, Matt. You remember Jimmy Williams?" Dean said as Matt walked in and shook Dean's hand.

"Sure, sure, it's been a while. Hi, Jimmy. How's the family?" Matt said, as he then shook Jimmy's hand.

"Good and yours?" Jimmy said.

"Good," Matt said.

Dean briefed Matt on the financials concerning the Las Vegas expansion plan. How much money was going to be needed from the teamster funds was the center of the conversation. This was not an automatic sell. Matt was no pushover.

Matt Licardo started out in his late teens as one of those goons who the unions used to attack anyone who dared to cross a picket line from the union who wanted to work during a strike. Licardo would be lurking in the background, holding a baseball bat poised for action. From this type of work, Licardo moved on to various jobs in the union, and he worked his way up the union ladder. He was the recording secretary, treasurer, and then president of his local union. Eventually he became a national vice president and from that position, ran for president of the teamsters and got elected.

Jimmy could see from the look on Matt's face after Dean finished explaining the plan that he was not totally convinced to okay teamster money for Las Vegas. When it came to his union boys, Matt stood strong for them and was not going to allow the Outfit to push his boys around. He learned a long time ago in a Cleveland local that if you take care of the boys, they will remember when it comes to vote that it was you who got them better contracts. Your elected life would last much longer if you took care of the boys.

"Dean, what's in it for my boys?" Matt asked. Jimmy spoke up right away, because the longer there was doubt in Matt's mind, the chance of getting his approval would start to slip away.

"Jobs, Matt, that's what you would get," Jimmy said. "Not only construction jobs for the teamsters in building the hotels, but once certain permanent jobs are filled, you could then move in and organize and unionize the workers," Jimmy said. "We're not talking about building one hotel. We're talking about a few hotels, and once you get your foot in the door with those places, the union membership will grow, bringing more money to the funds," Jimmy said.

"By building a union base in Vegas, that'll give you extra money to try and unionize in other states," Jimmy said. "Look at the potential, Matt. We're going to make Vegas jump. It's going to be the place where people will want to go to," Jimmy said. "You'll see, Matt, we'll expand the strip farther and farther," he said. "The money will never stop coming in from the hotels. The money light is always going to be green," Jimmy said.

"What...uh...you trying to sell me a used car?" Matt said with a gruff laugh.

"No, just trying to get you in on the ground floor of something you'll never regret," Jimmy said.

"Well, how much money are we talking about from the funds and how is it going to work once the money is taken out of the funds?" asked Matt.

"I'll have Jimmy work out the costs after we get some numbers from some building estimators who will look over our plans," Dean said. "Since we built three hotels already, we're kinda experienced in costs," he said. "Once the numbers are ready, I'll call you," Dean said.

Dean then looked at Jimmy. "After we get your approval, there will be dummy corporations set up with people involved who have ties to the various crime families from Cleveland, Detroit, and Kansas City," Jimmy said. "These corporations will own the hotels and run them. These corporations, or in some cases private individual investors who will play ball with us, will apply for the licenses from the Nevada State Gaming Commission. From experience, I can tell you the licensing application process takes about a year," Jimmy said.

"We need to show a legit operation," Jimmy said. "The guys running the corporations on paper, at least, will look clean. They will bring in the hotel staff needed to run the hotels," Jimmy said. "The money taken from the team-ster funds will be put in the corporation's bank accounts to build the hotels," Jimmy said. "Of course, the various cities will oversee the casino operation," he said. "The families from those cities make sure the skim money taken out is done right," Jimmy said.

"If the dummy corporations start to screw around for some reason with our money, the dummies will get a one-way ticket to Dummyland, that I can tell you," Dean said. "They're going to understand from day one that they work for us, and we don't want any surprises. We want the hotels and people who come to gamble," he said. "Sure, we'll throw some entertainment out there to break up the time for the people, but our job is to get people to drop dollars in the casino," Dean said.

"We'll work on an eight percent daily skim, the families will get four per-cent, and the Outfit will get four percent, and, Matt, you'll get a lot of jobs from the hotels, which means more money for the union and more money in your pocket," Dean said.

"So, besides the union construction jobs, we'll be allowed to go in and or-ganize other workers in the hotels into the union?" Matt asked. "I know Jimmy said we could unionize inside the hotels, and as far as I'm concerned, that's got to be part of the deal," he said.

"Yeah, sure. I mean, a contract will have to be negotiated for salaries and benefits with the hotels at some point, but sure, you'll be able to go in and organize the hotel workers," Dean said. It's just the casino workers who will have to be non-union. We gotta have control over them, but outside of the casino, you can organize," Dean said.

"How about the skim money, are you going to put some of that back in the teamster funds?" Matt asked. "I don't want any of my people having a problem with their pension or medical bills. Let's make that real clear so it's understood, no one gets hurt, otherwise no deal," he said.

"Sure, we'll put some money back," Dean said, giving his best cross my heart and hope to die facial expression of innocence that money could buy to Matt. Putting money back was akin to a Chicago winter without snow. The reality of that even cracked God up.

"Then we got a conditional deal, depending on the numbers I see from Jimmy," Matt said. Jimmy would make sure Matt would like the numbers.

After seeing Jimmy's numbers, a few months later, Matt gave the final approval for the money to be taken out of the teamster funds, as Las Vegas smiled. One thing about the numbers, they are very loyal to their master and always do what someone tells them to do. Numbers always sing the tune their master wants played. They can turn a smile into a frown or a frown into a smile. Numbers live by the art of manipulation for without that, numbers would be out of a job.

The paperwork was filed with the State of Nevada's Gaming Commission early the next year to obtain gaming licenses to run casinos in the soon to be built hotels in Las Vegas, owned by corporations or individuals, all with mob ties.

A little more than a year later, licenses were given to these supposedly legit owners who all denied any involvement with the mob. The owners were all sharp guys who excelled at covering up their mob ties as the State's investigators never found any evidence of mob connections to the owners. Thus, the additional skim money from the new hotels would soon be leaving Las Vegas on a one way trip to Chicago, making the boys, at least for a while, easier to live with until their greed would grow into a bigger and bigger addiction to money that eventually got the golden goose whacked.

Since the climate in Las Vegas was more conducive to year-round construction than in Chicago, the hotels were built within a twelve to eighteen month period. They opened up with a flourish. The top entertainment was booked to perform in their main room of the hotels. Lesser known entertainers played in the lounges.

Word of mouth in any business is the best sales force you could have. People started going to Las Vegas, enjoying their trip, and would come back to their hometowns and cities, telling relatives, neighbors, friends, and coworkers how much fun they had in Las Vegas. This good word of mouth helped make the Las Vegas hotels the place to be.

The Outfit knew while good word of mouth can make a business, bad word of mouth can kill a business. The Outfit made sure the other crime families had their hotel employees trained to be polite, pleasant, courteous, and to make sure the customers' needs were taken care of quickly and efficiently.

Safety was given the utmost attention by the boys in and around the hotels. A drunken patron was immediately escorted from whatever area in which he or she was causing a disturbance. Security was made up of guys who were juice collectors, now walking around the casinos wearing a sport coat. One's sanity would have to be checked if they were in the mood for some type of physical confrontation with these overly developed bruisers, based on having too many happy spirits supplied from an over indulgence in liquor.

The hotels had security cameras in the casinos. Stories would circulate. If the boys caught you cheating, they would take you out back behind the hotel and administer street justice to your body. Since everyone knew the boys' reputation, no one dared question whether the stories were true or not.

The Outfit, who in a sense became Las Vegas' first Chamber of Commerce, wanted people to come to Las Vegas to enjoy their trip, leave with a good taste in their mouths, and go back to their hometowns preaching and spreading the Vegas gospel of fun and good times to all who would listen. The good word never included things like gambling, addiction, losing great sums of money, depression, and being fleeced by Chicago's finest, the Outfit.

Jimmy was able to get an insurance premium from a casualty type firm that would cost the Outfit two thousand dollars for every one hundred thousand dollars of coverage. So, for a million bucks worth of coverage, it cost them twenty thousand dollars. Jimmy called Dean and went to see him.

"I think coverage for five years would be good," Jimmy said.

"Nah, I don't know about five years. Maybe three years is about as far as I want to go, if I even approve this at all," Dean said.

"Okay, I'll leave the paperwork with you," Jimmy said.

"Yeah, yeah, just leave it," Dean said.

After Jimmy left, Dean took the paperwork, crumbled it into a ball and flipped it into the wastebasket near his desk. He made his decision.

None of the money taken from the teamster funds was ever put back with any Las Vegas skim money or any other Outfit money. By nationally and locally getting higher wages, which meant the union dues and health coverage deductions got bigger in their contracts and organizing more workers to join the teamsters in the ensuring years, the money raised from the teamster funds slowly found its way back home to the funds' accounts.

At no time did any teamster employee have their pensions affected or their medical bills not paid. The workers went to work, did their jobs to the best of their abilities, and never had any knowledge what was being done with their hard-earned money that was being taken out of their check for union dues and health coverage, paycheck after paycheck.

Jimmy would reinforce the saying, "Let the sucker build the pot, then you take the pot," to me over the years. Not only did the saying refer to gambling, but it also referred to people working hard for something, and someone coming in and snatching it away from you. In the case of the hardworking teamster employees, unknowingly they were the suckers, and the Outfit took the pot.

As the Las Vegas strip grew, the Outfit's involvement grew at the same pace. Smaller hotels now had to compete against the new, bigger hotels financed through the teamster funds. Some of the smaller hotels, which were ma and pa operated, got visits from the Outfit boys. The Outfit would inquire if the owners wanted to expand their hotels, since they would be facing strong competition for customers from the new hotels.

The owners were not happy to see the Outfit, but they knew competing against the well-financed mob hotels would require financial resources they didn't have. Reluctantly, when the Outfit injected two words into the conversation, "Teamster funds," the owners had to listen. The owners had heard about the Outfits reputation, so it was either play ball with them or go out of business. They would play ball.

The Outfit would provide funding for a price. The price would be far higher than in skimmed dollars. The high price would compromise the owner's integrity, shredding the moral fabric of a once proud person. The owners were born and raised in Las Vegas. They believed that if you worked hard, you would be rewarded. They went to church and raised their children with the morals they learned in church. The church never taught them, though, the sins practiced by the Outfit, so these kind, caring owners, who believed in virtue, became prey to the ways of the Outfit world.

By opening your door to the Outfit and agreeing to their terms, you have just given yourself a king-sized problem that will lead you down a street filled with potholes full of the eventual loss of your state of self-worth, control of your income as they now dictate what you can earn, and say goodbye to controlling your business forever and ever as they now are your partners.

The Outfit squeezes the life out of a business. It strangles the businesses' resources by charging too high a percentage for its payoff and, as it will become apparent, there will not be a large enough customer base to feed the belly of the business. So, the Outfit will restrict your income through these tactics as they, in effect, own the business.

The Outfit would provide limited funding as it was only going to milk the small hotels for about a three-year period, then force the owners to sell to another crime family. The Outfit would get its skim money, regardless of who the owners were. As far as the Outfit was concerned, the owners were just another employee. The hard work and loyal dedication that owners put forth in running their hotels, to the Outfit, was yesterday's news. Remember, buddy, you decided to take our money, pointing to the owners with a sneer. You want to complain? Go look in the mirror and complain to that guy. We were just helping out a fellow human being, who wanted to expand this business. "Ain't that the American way?" the Outfit would say.

With the smaller hotels, the Outfit charged a six percent daily skim and put some Outfit-type guys on the payroll to make sure the owners complied with the financial arrangements. Current employees, in some cases, were fired to make room for the Outfit flunkies.

Once the Outfit bled the hotels, where they had gotten all the money they wanted, they made an arrangement with another crime family from Cleveland, Detroit, or Kansas City to make an offer to buy a hotel from the owner. The offer would be less than the actual worth of the hotel, but it still was an offer.

The actual owner, who in theory did not own the hotel, but was running it for the Outfit, really had no other choice but to accept the offer. If not, he would be visiting the desert for a final trip, never to be seen again. That is the Outfit's way of thanking you for your years of service.

I know some of you guys are thinking, why didn't the owners say 'no,' stand up for themselves, tell the Outfit, "Goddamn it, I poured a lot of sweat into this hotel and I'm not ready to sell?" Well, since we all like to live, if the Outfit didn't use their favorite option, they had a couple of others. Since the Outfit had the juice with the city of Las Vegas, the various required inspectors could be sent to the hotels. These were old buildings with plenty of code violations that the city could use in closing the hotels. The Outfit could torch the hotels, burn them to the ground, and the owners might have to wait years to get some kind of insurance settlement. Sadly, selling was the only viable thing the hotel owners could do.

Whatever crime family bought the hotel got it at a bargain basement price. They would tear down the small hotel and put up a bigger, money-making hotel. With the new hotel, while the Outfit would get a smaller skim, the illegal pie that was going to be cut had larger slices of greed put on their plate. They would use these crime family-controlled hotels to make more money by laundering from other criminal activities, so that piece of the pie tasted that much sweeter.

With a growing Vegas strip, the Outfit created its own castle. The members became the oversized bellied kings, stuffing their faces with the green legal tender we call money.

It's often been said that some of the most beautiful women in the world can be seen in Las Vegas. It's a twenty-four-hour town where the action never sleeps. Las Vegas draws all types of people, especially women, who come to this desert town to have some action bestowed on them. There are women who not only love the action, but they crave it like an addiction that must be fulfilled. Without their action fix, they sink into a depressed state not being able to be the queen of the fake fantasy action that Las Vegas hands out. The Las Vegas action is a dreamer's dream, which never has a concrete base of reality in its blueprints.

Sally Jamesion, who the day after she graduated high school in a small Nebraska town, got in her car, leaving behind her small town life and drove to Los Angeles, trading in small town USA for the big city life. She found a job with a small manufacturing company, working as a clerk in their bookkeeping section. It was your basic vanilla nine-to-five job where the action centered on making sure the accounts were properly credited. This was not the type of job Hollywood would make a movie about.

After working seven years at the company, Sally felt the LA scene was not providing the action she wanted. Boyfriends came and boyfriends went for her, but she hadn't found that one special guy who could make her action barometer jump off the chart. She decided it was time to change actions—LA for Las Vegas. She quit her job and moved to Las Vegas, where she went to school to learn how to be a blackjack dealer.

She got a job as a blackjack dealer at the El Casa Hotel. She fell in love with Las Vegas immediately. The bright lights shining at night from the neon signs of the hotels on the strip made her body tingle. This is where she wanted to be, this is where she felt she belonged, and this was where the action was that she wanted.

She liked her job very much as she met men and women from all over the country with different backgrounds. The El Casa liked her, because she had an outgoing personality, coupled with a never-ending warm, radiant smile. She had a cute figure, which didn't hurt with the male customers, as they liked what they saw. She displayed happiness to her customers, which translated into more money gambled at the blackjack table. The customers like her, and they would make a point of sitting at her table talking to her, and they would tip her more than the average blackjack dealer got in tips. The customers became engaged with her, and they would not always think that much about their bets. With Sally joking and laughing with them while dealing the cards, she was able to get some of them to bet more than they would have. Her personality was the hotel's winning hand.

The El Casa took notice of Sally. They would sometimes ask Sally if she would extend her shift time as she was bringing in more money than most of the dealers. They would financially compensate her so she would stay a while longer at her blackjack table. Since she didn't have a family to run home to see, her time was her own. No need running out the door if she could make a couple of extra bucks.

When someone became a made member of the Outfit, during the induction one of the things you were told is that you are to be faithful to your wife and do not commit adultery, which to me always seemed strange as made guys were committing adultery as often as you ate dinner—a lot.

Jerry Marchetti was an Outfit juice collector/security guy at the El Casa. Marchetti was a made member of the Outfit who, in order to become a made member, made his bones by killing his stepfather Vic Talbot, a fence for stolen goods from the Outfit. The rumor had it Talbot was buying stolen items at too low a price and making a big profit when he sold them on the street.

The boys felt they were being cheated. Johnny Tusciolia gave the order to whack Talbot. He told Marchetti by clipping his stepfather, this would be his 'now I can become a made member of the Outfit' card.

Marchetti flushed down the toilet his family loyalty to his stepfather Talbot and clipped him. Four months later, Tusciolia recommended Marchetti to become a made member of the Outfit. Marchetti now would trade one family for another.

He was the muscle, the goon who would be paid to use his brawn, not his brain. He was the enforcer, who did not dwell on a thought process determining right or wrong. If you did it the Outfit's way, you were right. If you didn't do it their way, you were wrong. That's how Marchetti's mind worked. So, when Marchetti was told to go and collect on a juice loan, that meant the guy was probably not paying what he was supposed to, which was wrong. Therefore, Marchetti reasoned he was right if he had to beat the hell out of the guy to collect the money. He was just applying the Outfit Logic 101 that he learned on the cold hard streets of Chicago.

Marchetti was in his early thirties, was married, and had a young son. His family was living in Chicago and he called home nearly every night.

"The thing about Vegas, Bobby, if you're not careful, it can change you, because it's a different life than Chicago. The legalized gambling, the women, the whole atmosphere, and before you know it, you can get swept up into it real fast; too fast," Jimmy said.

"So, for a married guy you really gotta watch your Ps and Qs out there," I said.

"Yeah, sure, because of the constant action, there are a lot of holes, whether you're married or a single guy, you don't want to step in, because you might not be able to step out of them without paying a price," Jimmy said. "The question, Bobby, is how big is the price, either emotionally or financially, and/or both?" he said. "Remember, Bobby, when you see a hole, whether it's Vegas or Chicago, don't step in it," Jimmy said.

"Gotcha, Dad," I said.

Sally Jamesion's eyes noticed Marchetti on several occasions, often throwing a smile his way, hoping he would catch it and throw it back to her. His muscular build is what attracted her to him. Big strong guys like him made Sally feel protected—a nice, secure feeling that her body felt from head to toe.

As humans, physical attraction is what most often sets a relationship in motion. We see someone, we like what we see, and we want to pursue them. In the beginning, it's physical attraction that brings people together. As humans, we often error in that we do not always go beyond the physical attraction to see if we are attracted to the components inside of a person's soul. Physical attraction is so damn important to us, we often close our eyes to what is needed for a healthy, happy, long-term relationship. A person might not be the handsomest guy, or prettiest girl you will ever meet, but once you start talking to them, you quickly see their good inner qualities, and what they look like on the outside doesn't matter anymore.

Sally was looking for some action and she started to pursue Marchetti. She knew he was married as he wore a wedding ring, but his wife was in Chicago, so what was the harm of having a little action in Las Vegas?

Sally started talking to Marchetti every chance she got. Their conversations were friendly, as she wanted him to feel comfortable with her. Weeks went by, then after she was finishing her shift on a Thursday night, he asked her out for a drink. She accepted, and they were soon sitting at a corner table in a bar talking. He told her he was from Chicago, working security at El Casa, and said nothing else about how he spent the rest of his day.

He was honest about being married and having a son. Since she knew about his wedding ring, having seen it on his finger, she appreciated his honesty about his marriage.

Sally and Marchetti started to spend more time together. Their conversations grew longer and longer each time they met. She would say something that would make him laugh; he would say something that would make her smile. Sally could feel Marchetti's body language become more and more positive toward her.

At dinner one night, she touched his arm, then his shoulder more than at any of the previous dinners. When he would hug her, she wanted more of Marchetti, more than just a squeeze. She wanted Marchetti on top of her.

The time was getting closer for sex. She was feeling delightful, downright giddy about having sex with Marchetti. She could now see sex waving to her from a block away. *Tonight will be the night*, she happily reasoned.

When Marchetti came to her apartment, he knew she was ready for sex. After he walked in and kissed her, he said, "Let's go," and walked her to her bedroom.

They undressed and got in bed. With Marchetti on top of Sally, the sexual action began; two naked bodies together in bed, heating up each other's body temperature. He slowly, carefully, and softly started to kiss her lips. Sally's face lit up with an affectionate, pleasurable 'thank you' look. She liked the way the sexual action was beginning. It was not going to be a 'slam, bam, thank you ma'am,' as it had been with other sexual partners Sally had. She could see Marchetti had a sensitivity about sex. He had done it before; he was experienced. Here was a violent man, who created a violent world for others, being sensitive to her body.

Marchetti then, in almost slow motion, started to kiss Sally behind her right ear, ever so slowly. Each kiss was measured—once, twice, three times, then he would stop and start again. As he reached down to hold her breasts, he looked at her. They traded some kisses, and he brought his tongue out of her mouth, licking each one of her nipples. Then he guided his kisses directly on one breast, then the other.

Sally reached down to grab his shoulder. His hard muscular body began deeply pressing into hers. She could feel her sexual juices flowing, and she loved it. He worked her body now, picking up the tempo of kisses. As he kissed her stomach, the kisses ran from his lips to her belly. Her body started gyrating with sexual pleasure. Her body was divided as the upper part of her body swayed trying to stay in sync with this muscular, sexual machine on top of her. Her lower body was squirming with desire, legs flailing sideways, preparing for the sexual implosion of his raw, defined penis into her.

When it happened, it was Sally at her happiest. This was the sexual action that dotted the 'I' for her. How contented she felt with him inside of her. It was as if she felt a package of good things was placed in her body. She kissed the top of Marchetti's head. "Thank you, my love. Thank you for creating sex that I knew existed, but could never find," she said to him.

Fun, physically rewarding, and setting off brain waves that erupted into a firecracker of a beautiful fulfillment, that's how sex was with Marchetti.

Sex was good. It was the sun penetrating a dismal sky, brightening up the skin on skin affect her body had with Marchetti's body. Sex was not a debit, always a credit that could barely wait; the next time the two lovers embraced, their bodies to intertwine into an unrelenting ecstasy that would not be defined by any physical boundaries or dictated by time or location. 'Bring on the action,' Sally's body yelled out, 'just bring on the action.'

Sally knew from this first sexual experience with Marchetti that she wanted him to be her one true love of her life. The hunt was now on for Sally to capture the man she so desperately wanted.

Nearly a year later, Sally and Marchetti, who sexually were becoming old pros at perfecting their love techniques for each other, appeared to be getting ready to move up the love ladder to a serious state, at least from Sally's viewpoint. Sally's seed of emotional growth had blossomed to the point where she wanted to spend more time with Marchetti. Living with Marchetti was on her mind, but what really was on her mind was that Marchetti would leave his wife for her. Finally, she decided to meet with him to express her feelings, to open up to him that they should be together, united as one. Their sexual action showed they belonged in bed together, not only for sex, but as a compatible couple who belonged with no one else but themselves, in Sally's mind.

Marchetti came over one night and before she could even begin to talk about her feelings to him, he played Hiroshima—he dropped a bomb on her.

"I'm moving my wife and kid to Vegas permanently," he said.

Reeling from this explosion, Sally tried to quickly compose herself.

"Why? How come? What brought this about?" Sally said as she peppered him with questions.

"Well, it's rough calling them so much, and going back to Chicago once in a while, there's not much time for me to spend with them, so I figured this was the best thing to do for everyone," Marchetti said.

"For everyone?" said Sally, her face contorting into a look of worry, while angrily emphasizing the words in a loud tone of voice.

"Yeah, everyone," he said.

"Well, what about us?" she asked.

"I'm Catholic," he said.

"So what does that mean?" she asked.

"It means I ain't getting a divorce, so if you want, I'll come over when I can to see you, but the schedule will vary depending on my job and family," Marchetti said.

"No, no, that's not going to work for me," Sally said, her voice rising in frustration.

"Well, take it or leave it. If you want me to come over for sex, I will when I can, but I still have my family to see first," he said.

Marchetti had that look on his face like, 'Hey, I'm not doing anything wrong; you're the one with the problem.'

"I see where I stand. Get out of here. Just get the hell out of here," Sally said as her emotional state reached the boiling point.

Marchetti didn't say a word. He shrugged his shoulders, turned around, and walked out of Sally's life.

Marchetti, when being made into the Outfit, took an oath about not committing adultery. Yet, he went right ahead, nonstop, into doing what he swore he wouldn't do. He never had any intention of leaving his wife. He was just looking for some action.

I would see this a lot, where guys had their Vegas girls, especially the married ones. They never thought for one moment the mental and physical pain they would be inflicting on the Vegas girls, knowing they would never leave their wives, but yet pulled on the girls' heart strings with all their might.

The Outfit, in this matter of being faithful to your wife clearly spelled out the ground rules—no cheating on your wife allowed. There's none of this, "I wasn't told, I didn't know," forget about that. You got the word during the ceremony about adultery. You agreed not to commit adultery, and what did you do? You not only crossed the line, you ran across it to another woman as fast as you could.

The Outfit, being an organization that does everything it can to try and hurt someone, on this one, comes out smelling like Mr. Righteous. I know it's hard to believe, even for me, it's a stretch, but you have to give them credit on this one, as at least they start the game holding the women on a pedestal. However, at the end of the game, these guys sure kick the woman a long way off the pedestal.

In the life, a lot of opportunities are out there for Outfit guys to meet women outside of their marriage. Some of these guys jump at the chance for whatever reason to become unfaithful to their wives.

"Bobby, the only place to find action with a woman is in your house with your wife. Your wife is and will be forever and ever number one. There is no two or three; she's it. She's the one you love and protect," Jimmy said. "The moment you become unfaithful is the moment something is wrong at home," he said.

"You gotta fix what's wrong at home or else you will be riding that emotional roller coaster the rest of your life, and that type of stress can kill you," Jimmy said.

"When you look for that type of action outside of your marriage, you better be ready to take the hits from the emotional bullets that are going to be coming your way, and those hits don't go away," Jimmy said.

"I've never seen a guy, yet, who can take the bang, bang, bang of those hits on his soul and come out and still function for the Outfit," he said. "How the hell are you going to lead two lives—one as a married guy and one as a cheater—and not be emotionally torn? It can't lead to a happy life," Jimmy said. "The girlfriend wants you to leave your wife for her, which you're not going to do, so you play a mental game of tug of war with no one being the winner," Jimmy said.

"Guys will act tough and tell you everything is okay, but all you have to do is watch what happens to them as alcohol and drug use increase dramatically," Jimmy said. "These guys have put themselves in the jackpot, and they're running away from a solution," he said.

"Walking the faithful line is the only way to go," I said.

"Exactly, because it seems when depression walks in the store, it buys stupid, and once you start wearing stupid in your life, you can't always return it," Jimmy said.

The Outfit never offered any form of counseling. Their message was if you have a problem, straighten it out in twenty-four hours or else. The 'or else' is the part you never want to venture into. The or else is not being sent to you, it's being sent to St. Matthew's Cemetery for your final problem resolution, clearing your problem slate.

By the mid-1970s, the Las Vegas operation was in full swing. The money was coming in faster than the Outfit could count it. You would think the Outfit would be happy with their take, but to the Mafia kings, enough is never enough; they want more, more, and still more.

A bigger skim of money was planned to include not only the Outfit run hotels, but ones run by Cleveland, Detroit, and Kansas City crime families.

At that time, money that was collected from the casinos, according to the Nevada Gaming Commission, was to be weighed on scales that would show a dollar amount. Coins from the slot machines were really what the state was trying to get a handle on. A representative from the Gaming Commission had to be present when the money was weighed. The scales in those days were not digital. The Outfit decided they would skim more money from the scales, and a plan was devised to do that.

The scales were going to be recalibrated, so when the Nevada Gaming Commission employee approved what he thought was the correct dollar amount on the scale, that was not really true.

The scales were brought back from the El Casa, Monroe, and Terrablanca hotels to Chicago. Substitute scales were put in their place to be used to count the money. The scales from the Outfit hotels were the test scales. Once they were recalibrated and up and running in the hotels, then other hotel scales would be recalibrated. Jimmy was told to have the scales fixed. He took them to Victor Gebring, who owned a store that sold and repaired scales. Gebring's brother Larry was an Outfit fence of stolen goods, so in a way, Jimmy was keeping the business in the family.

Jimmy told Gebring how he wanted the scales fixed, and Gebring said he could do it. Jimmy wanted the scales to show more than they actually did. One hundred dollars of coins would show two hundred dollars instead. The Outfit would skim the difference. The Gaming Commission representative had no idea the scales were rigged and would approve what he read on the scales. So now, besides skimming money from the count rooms, the Outfit skimmed money from the scales.

Once the scales were ready, they were taken back to Las Vegas to be installed and the fun began. As the Outfit saw how well the skim operation worked with the scales in their hotels, the scales in other crime family hotels were rigged the same way. For the next five years, the scale skimming in all the hotels netted nearly thirty million dollars for the Outfit and other crime families. This action was the beginning of the end of the Outfit's Las Vegas operation. The Feds decided to form a joint task force with the State of Nevada's Gaming Commission investigators, and declared war on the Outfit and the other crime families, notably Cleveland and Kansas City, who had partnered with the Outfit. Their sole purpose was to drive the Outfit and other crime families out of Las Vegas permanently.

Jimmy was opposed to this additional skimming plan from the beginning, but it was not his call to make. Joe Aruti, who was running day-to-day operations for the Outfit following Dean's death, and others decided this was what they wanted to do and there was no changing their minds. *Why, Las Vegas was full of chances for the Outfit greed to extend itself,* they thought. The gold will become more golden was their motto. Who's going to stop us, they bragged amongst themselves.

The one thing about greed, it sticks to you so that you never can escape it. You just want more air to fill the balloon until the balloon bursts with a loud bang, and greed tumbles to the ground, pulling you down with it.

"There were too many pieces of the pie that you had to cut," Jimmy said. "The more guys involved, the more chance of something bad happening, which is exactly what happened," he said.

"I told Joe to keep it strictly within a tight bunch of Outfit guys. Don't let other cities get involved with us in this type of skim," Jimmy said. "Joe wouldn't listen. His eyes were full of greed," he said. "Joe's eyes had so much greed in them there was enough greed to fill a third eye," Jimmy said.

"With so many guys involved, and the Feds breathing down their necks, someone would get caught on something," Jimmy said. "Bobby, remember, the Feds could dangle the punishment that was in the RICO Act over someone and that person would crack and rat out everyone else for a plea deal from the Feds," Jimmy said. "Once the Feds get one rat, there will be more rats willing to talk, and whoever's left is going to go down real hard," he said. "The Feds hold all the cards, and with the rats helping them, they come up with a winning hand," Jimmy said.

I looked at Jimmy and could see the disgust on his face as he was schooling me on how an operation can fall apart. The teacher was telling the student you can swallow a piece of pie at one time, but too many pieces of pie at one time will choke you. The scale skimming choked the Outfit's Las Vegas golden goose to death.

I'm not saying the Feds could have been kept out of this family photo. Once the Feds throw their resources at you, you're generally going to lose this game. It stands to reason, when it's their bat and ball, what chance do you have? The Feds become relentless until you are locked up. Their mindset was getting the Outfit out of Las Vegas. The Feds always have the advantage, because they have unlimited access to taxpayers' money when it comes to going after organized crime members.

The Feds were able to develop their rat network against the Outfit and others. Grand juries handed down indictments nonstop in Chicago. Outfit guys and others involved in the scale skimming operation in Las Vegas were arrested and charged with criminal acts under RICO. Trials were held, and the Feds got convictions on those who were indicted. The Feds' actions in Las Vegas started the downward slide of the Outfit.

Sure, there was still an Outfit left after the convictions, but there was an enormous gaping financial hole without the Las Vegas Outfit's books. The Outfit could never fill the financial hole it was left with. Had Dean Dragonetti listened to Jimmy about setting up a drug operation, there would have been more than enough money coming in to cover the loss of the Las Vegas money. Well, it didn't happen.

All Jimmy could do was watch high-ranking Outfit members and others from crime families in Cleveland and Kansas City glumly go off to prison. Jimmy, other than having the scales fixes, had no involvement with Las Vegas. When the money came back from Las Vegas to Chicago, Tommy Guiti, an underboss for Joe Aruti, received the money. Guiti would distribute the money on Joe's orders to whoever was to get it. The Feds could never tie Jimmy to Las Vegas, so he was never indicted. He stood on the sidelines and waved goodbye to his criminal buddies.

The Outfit hotels Monroe, El Casa, and Terrablanca were seized by the Feds and later auctioned off to corporate gaming companies. Las Vegas turned into a corporate town, leaving its mob beginnings behind in the desert.

By the mid-1980s, the last actual boss in Las Vegas, the Outfit's Frank "Fat Frankie" Caputo was convicted on racketeering and murder conspiracy charges. Caputo had been working at the Shoreline Hotel, a smaller place in which the Buffalo New York Condible crime family had partnership with the Outfit. In the early 1990s the Feds got indictments and convictions of the Condible crime family members. The Shoreline was torn down by the new corporate owners, and a bigger hotel/casino was built.

Following the Caputo conviction, the Outfit's Las Vegas operation was buried in the desert by the Feds. Nearly thirty years after it began, Las Vegas ended, thus, ending a flowing money stream that dried up and which the Outfit could never replace. The final outcome was Feds won/Outfit lost.

There was this myth I would hear on the street time and time again, that the Outfit would never touch drugs. Well, first of all, let me end that myth. There were members of the Outfit who were involved in drug trafficking from the time I was a little boy. While the elders did ban it, that did not stop some guys from putting drugs on the street and making a buck off of their sales. You see, any time the Outfit can make illegal money on anything, they will do it.

If the Outfit could get Santa Claus to be a mule, and drop off drugs to people's houses, they would do it. Hell, if Rudolph the Red Nosed Reindeer got indicted on a drug conspiracy charge, the Outfit would tell Rudy to keep his mouth shut if he wanted to see another Christmas.

Jimmy had a drug plan that would have made the Outfit more money than any local or Las Vegas gambling operation could ever think about. The plan was to have begun in the early 1960s. By the late 1960s, with the anti-war movement protesting the Vietnam War, the dope operation, which would have been up and running for a few years, would have swept up those dope smoking college kids; the money brought in would have made the Outfit's most lucrative enterprise, no doubt about it.

"I presented the dope plan to Dean in about May of 1962," Jimmy said. "We would have guys buy the dope, you know, marijuana and heroin in Mexico and drive the dope up to Chicago," Jimmy said. "I mean, I guess we could have tried to grow the marijuana in Chicago, but we would have needed lots of greenhouses to grow the stuff because of the weather. Maybe for a while we could get away with it, but I have the feeling someone, maybe under pressure from the Feds, would rat us out. Jealousy also plays a big part in things, because with having so many marijuana plants around, someone would feel they deserved more money. So, someone would be unhappy, thus, becoming a potential rat," he said. "Drugs, like anything else, have to be as discreet as possible," Jimmy said. "Once the Feds get involved, they're looking for a drug ring to bust, which is no good for business," he said.

"In Chicago, once the dope came to the US from Mexico, we would have used women as the mules, the couriers, and drop off the dope in various locations to Outfit dealers," he said. "The women would have been dressed up in business-type clothes, nice skirt or dress, high heeled shoes, practical type jewelry—nothing flashy or gaudy—stuff that would complement their outfits, makeup, the whole bit so the women would have looked like they're going to work," Jimmy said.

"You want that professional look for the women so they don't draw any attention from anyone. If a cop on the beat sees two guys on the street, one with a haircut, clean cut look, a suit, shined shoes, carrying a briefcase, and the other looking like a bum, who do you think the cop is going to pay attention to?" Jimmy asked. "Same with a professional looking woman, no one thinks she's carrying dope," he said.

"The women would have picked up the locked briefcases with the dope inside, except they wouldn't have known there was dope in the cases. The women would be told they were functioning as messengers with documents in the cases," Jimmy said. "We would work out a financial arrangement with them for their services," he said.

"The Feds wouldn't be looking for a broad to be involved in drug trafficking," Jimmy said. "They're figuring, maybe, one wiseguy is passing the drugs to another wiseguy, and that's how the Feds would conduct their investigation, looking for wiseguys," he said. "The Feds would spend their resources chasing guys, because there are no broads in the Outfit, so how could a broad be involved with this type of stuff," he said with a smile.

"We would have the women do everything at night—go to a park, a warehouse, even a church could be used," Jimmy said. "They would meet a guy who was dressed in a coat and tie so he would look like a businessman carrying a briefcase," he said. "Hell, business guys carry briefcases every day, so nothing would look out of order," Jimmy said.

"Yeah, but what if the Feds are tailing a guy?" I asked.

"No problem. We will use someone in the guy's family or maybe an Outfit guy to go to the destination to pick up the case," Jimmy said. "The case is locked, so no one knows what's inside of it except the guy who's supposed to get it, so it wouldn't matter who was involved in the transfer with the woman," he said.

"How's the woman going to know if he's the right guy she's passing the case to?" I asked.

"The guy will...uh...have a phrase to use like, 'The sauce is good tonight,' and since the woman will be told what the phrase is, once he says it, she'll give him the case," Jimmy said.

"Yeah, but how do you know you can trust the woman?" I asked.

"She'll go to one of our businesses—construction, trucking, vending machine, bars, restaurants, nightclubs, you name it—any one of our businesses that we run and pick up the case," Jimmy said. "At that point, she'll be told where to go and what the phrase is," Jimmy said. "We'll lie to her and tell her she's going to be bonded, because of the sensitive material in the case. That'll make her feel important enough that she's in some secret, specialized work and she'll trust us," he said.

"Don't you think she might get a little suspicious with the drop off or phrase?" I asked.

"She'll be told we're in a highly competitive business and we must be very discreet with our clients' information," he said.

"Yeah, but…," I said.

"If she gets too curious and starts to stick her nose into someplace it doesn't belong, she'll get a free one-way trip to Gondere's, all expenses paid, never to be seen or heard from again," Jimmy said.

"I figured besides the streets, we would hit the gay bars and clubs, plus the straight bars and clubs with the dope," Jimmy said. "Eventually we would add cocaine and other prescription drugs like amphetamines," he said.

"Sort of like diversifying a drug portfolio," I said.

"Sort of," he giggled.

"I figured the total drug operation conservatively could bring in fifty to a hundred million dollars a year, maybe…possibly…probably even more," Jimmy said. "You gotta figure Vegas, Florida, maybe Canada, all places we have tied to or could establish ties to, would expand the drug operation," Jimmy said. "We could have, with the dope money, brought in more money or as much money as everything else we were involved with," he said. "Dope gave us options that were unlimited. Anything is possible with dope. You could develop your own operation all over," Jimmy said.

"Drugs would be all year round. It's not seasonal, like a sports betting operation we got in Chicago," he said. "Sure, we got Vegas all year round for gambling, but the drug money would beat the Vegas money within no time," Jimmy said. "Like any operation, it would take some time to get going, but once we got it going, man, it would really catch fire and take off," Jimmy said.

"How did Dean respond to you when you met?" I asked.

"Dean and I met at Chateau D'Ville, and I explained the plan in detail to him. I told him when the dope came up from Mexico that we would step on it, I mean, cut it up into smaller quantities, but sell it at the same price as if it was a full quantity," Jimmy said. "Dean chuckled when I told him the Feds would be pissing in their pants trying to figure out what's going on," he said.

"The Feds ain't going to be looking for a lady to be involved with a drug operation, no way, forget about it," Jimmy said.

The Outfit, like any other mob organization, is strictly male, so I was thinking Jimmy's plan had possibilities. And the more I thought about it, some damn good ones at that. Dean wouldn't walk away from the money, I reasoned. How could he? But that's the thing about life. A sure shot can go sour in just a couple of spoken words.

"After I finished explaining the whole plan potential and all, he looked at me for a couple of seconds, sorta somber like," Jimmy said. "Then he unloaded. 'Well, yeah, Jimmy, that's a good plan, but it's not right for now,' Dean said. 'I mean, uh, we're just not going to do it,' his voice getting louder and direct. 'I don't think it's the right fuckin' thing for us. Uh, we're not going to fuckin do it, you understand? You get it, Jimmy?' he said. He was getting hot about it, so I figured just let it go," Jimmy said.

"Okay, Dean," I told him, "you're the boss, and it won't happen unless you want it to happen," Jimmy said.

"Fine. I don't want to hear about this drug shit anymore. That's it, we're done talking about drugs," Dean said.

"Fine," Jimmy said.

Dean was the type of guy who ate the same thing every day. He only put gambling, loan-sharking, extortion, money laundering, labor racketeering, and other basic Outfit activities on his plate. Had he expanded his illegal culinary tastes a bit to include drugs, he would have found drugs to be a very pleasurable financial taste that his palate would have enjoyed. Sometimes it pays to add one more ingredient to the sauce.

"The funny thing, Bobby, is while the elders in the Outfit banned drug involvement for mob business, plenty of guys were drug traffickin' on their own, making quite a bit of money," Jimmy said. "We could have had a drug network which would have been coordinated with everyone," he said. "There would have been no independent guys on their own running around making drug money for themselves," Jimmy said.

Like with everything the Outfit did, they would set up these fences with rules, and guys would jump over them and do whatever they wanted. No one ever got whacked for selling drugs, because as time went by, more guys saw the big money that could be made from drugs and participated in the drug trafficking.

Knowing the Outfit as I do, the elders would not want a gang war to erupt as the elders would probably be the targets. The younger guys, seeing the money that could be made from selling drugs, would have had no qualms about clipping anyone who would try and stop them. So, in the case of drugs, the elders were paper tigers saying one thing, but not doing anything to back it up.

In, maybe, 1972 or 1973, I'm not exactly sure, Dean had a meeting with Jimmy about a business matter when all of a sudden, out of the blue, this is what he said. "Jimmy…uh…I uh…want to apologize to you about the drug plan," Dean said. "It uh…uh…really was a good plan and we…uh…should have used it. You were right, especially in the late '60s with all those college kids smoking pot," Dean said. "Hell, my own nephew Vinnie got busted for smoking pot in college," he said. "That would have been another source we could have tapped," Dean said.

"No, you were right. The money would have been huge that we would have made," he said. "I mean…uh…uh…look, other guys were making drugs part of their operation. We could have cashed in," Dean said.

Getting someone in the Outfit to apologize about something is like the federal government lowering your taxes. When does that happen? Jimmy knew he could have thrown Dean's mistake right back in his face and make it stick, but why light a fuse at this point?

"Yeah, well, you made the decision that you thought was best at the time, so we just move forward, that's all," Jimmy said.

"I know, I know, but I just wanted you to know that your plan was a big time money maker and even the great Dean Dragonetti fucks up once in a while," Dean said.

The Outfit, being so hell bent on violence to achieve whatever they wanted, sometimes did not always see the big bright picture of fortune staring them in the face. Thinking something through was not always a commodity that the Outfit kept in stock. Hurt for today, kill for today, that was more their credence. What could have been with drugs was never to be.

The drug tree that needed to have been planted at the time was never done. All the Outfit had to look at was barren land, no drug forest covering every square mile of land that would have produced wealth and prosperity year after year for these greedy souls.

Our friends, the politicians, provided the Outfit with employment and government contracts to Outfit-controlled companies on the state, county and city level. The politicians did not provide these Christmas gifts out of the goodness of their hearts. They expected an envelope full of holiday cheer, better known as the Franklins, as in one hundred dollar bills.

If you were a member of the Franklin club, which meant on cue one hundred dollar bills, saying, "Yes, sir," and filed straight into a white envelope given to the politician for services rendered, politicians provided the perks to you that went along with the membership. Being employed by the state, county, or city, and sometimes double dipping being employed by the city and county at the same time and receiving a check while you never showed up for work, was a popular perk, as you can imagine. Getting a state, county, or city contract for a company with Outfit ties, who then hired an Outfit guy as a consultant who never burned up any calories since he never did any work, was another widely given perk.

Democratic State Senator Danny "Mumbles" Marino was a powerful political force in Illinois politics. Not only was he a state senator, and the ward committeeman of the 12th Ward Regular Democratic Organization, but as a lawyer, he sat on the Democratic Judiciary Slating Committee that slated who would run not only for Cook County Circuit Court judge, but who ran for the Illinois Appellate Court and Illinois State Supreme Court judgeships.

So now you can see how our friends, the politicians, and our friends the judges were happily politically married, election after election, with the Outfit becoming proud in-laws who knew their children would grant any of their legal wishes and make justice skip and dance to their tune.

In Chicago politics, each ward has an alderman and ward committeeman. The alderman takes care of the needs of the ward, while the ward committeeman handles the politics of the ward. The committeeman doles out the patronage jobs and is involved in the slate making process of candidates whom the Democratic Party will support in the primary and general election. Both are elected to four-year terms at different times. In some wards, both jobs are held by the same person.

There are fifty wards in Chicago, thus, fifty committeemen sit on, in this case, the Cook County Democratic Central Committee, which is involved in slate making during election years. There are also thirty Cook County Democratic suburban, known as township committeemen, who sit on the Central Committee. These eighty members endorse a slate of Democratic candidates for various political offices. Since Chicago had the highest number of Democratic votes cast more than any other Cook County municipality, it had the juice to get its candidates always slated.

Depending on how many Democratic votes a committeeman got out in a ward or suburban township in the Democratic primary, was the factor determining how much juice he had with the Central Committee.

Mumbles had two hundred fifty patronage jobs in his ward organization. Come Election Day, those political soldiers were out hustling votes for Mumbles as they knew if they didn't bring in the vote count Mumbles was looking for, their political jobs could disappear. With high Democratic vote totals in the primary in a weighted vote count, he had a lot of juice on the Central Committee.

To the Outfit, it never mattered whether you were a Democrat or Republican, as long as you hummed their theme song. That's all they cared about. Since Chicago is heavily Democratic, the Outfit makes nice with the Democrats. In Mumbles ward organization, he sponsored some Outfit guys for various state, county, and city jobs. The difference between them and the other political workers in the ward organization was they never had to worry about losing their jobs. Their jobs were guaranteed by a higher calling—the call the Outfit would make if someone tried to screw with them. The call that would make your teeth chatter on a cold Chicago day. You never wanted to get that call. With the Outfit political guys, whether they worked a precinct or not, their votes were simply marvelous, doncha know.

Phil Grego was a member of Mumbles' political organization. Greco was a lawyer who was the President of the 12th Ward Regular Democratic Organization. He worked for the Chicago Park District representing them on misdemeanor-type cases. As you can see from his assigned legal work at the Park District, we are not dealing with a legal scholar with eyebrow raising legal competence. Greco was a political hack, an educated one, but still a political hack.

After graduating from law school, Greco twice took and failed the examination for the Illinois State Bar to become licensed. Greco, after trying to pass the bar examination the legit way, decided it was time to use Outfit juice. Greco was the nephew of William "Willie Wonder" Messeto, a vicious Outfit loan shark. He called his uncle, and the juice all of a sudden started to flow.

Uncle Willie called Mumbles for help. Being the wonderful, kind uncle we all longed for, he told Mumbles that if he helped his nephew get his legal license, the next time Mumbles ran for re-election as a state senator, he would not have any opponent. There isn't a politician I have ever known who didn't like running unopposed in an election. Hearing that comforting music, made Mumbles reflect. Uncle Willie's newfound political friendship insured stability in Mumbles' political career. Well, so much for reflection. "I'll help your nephew," Mumbles told Uncle Willie, as reflection was told to leave the room.

Mumbles met with Greco one night in the ward office. He told Greco he spoke with Uncle Willie and would help Greco.

"Phil, the next time you take the bar exam, write down on a piece of paper the test booklet number and give it to me," Mumbles said.

"Okay, Mumbles," Greco said.

As Phil Greco walked into the test room to make his third attempt at passing the Bar exam, he gazed around the room at the other people also there to take the test. They had studied hard taking a Bar review course to prepare themselves for the test. He saw anxiety on their faces, waiting for the proctor to pass out test booklets.

Look at these chumps. They're sweating bullets over this test. Me, I got it made in the legal shade. After today, I'm a licensed lawyer. Test? What test? his royal cockiness thought.

He calmly took his seat so he could kill time. No need to panic, as he knew he was different from everyone else in the room. He had juice and they didn't. His passing was guaranteed. It didn't matter how he answered the questions, because he already passed the test.

Now one else in the room knew the ending of this fairytale except Phil Greco. Greco tapped his pencil on the desk as he opened his booklet and filled in answers to questions he could care less about. He waited until the proctor was not facing him, and then he wrote down the booklet number on a scrap of paper he brought with him. He sat in his chair killing time, waiting for a few people to turn in their test booklet before he turned in his. *No sense drawing attention to myself by being the first one to finish the test*, he thought.

Greco sat for about an hour and a half, and after a couple of people turned in their booklets, he turned his in. He walked out of the room praising himself. *Congratulations, Phil. You did a great job on the test. Good luck with your legal career*, he snidely said to himself.

A few days later, he gave the piece of paper with his booklet number on it to Mumbles. A score of 70 was needed to pass the test.

Two months later, Greco got a letter from the State of Illinois, telling him he passed the Bar examination and was now licensed to practice law in the State of Illinois. He was told when the swearing-in date would be, and the letter also contained his state license number, which is needed when an attorney files court documents.

By reaching out to a political friend, the Outfit got Greco's law license for him. The friend used his juice, which held up Greco's right hand when he was sworn in several weeks later to begin practicing law. Mumbles had the test booklet pulled, rescored it to an 80, and Greco, thus, became a recipient of the 'It's who you know, not what you know' award given out by the Outfit to people who best exemplify being a fake or a phony, and the winner is...

The Outfit always took the shortest route to get what they wanted. Since Greco had an uncle who was a made member of the Outfit, he was qualified to use the relative's special treatment card. This card was good any time a relative had to weasel out of doing something the right way and did it the wrong way, but still was treated as if he did it the right way, like passing the Bar examination without passing the Bar examination. Oh, the joy of being an Outfit relative, when just that little bit of tilting the playing field in your favor can make you stand shoulder to shoulder with the righteous ones who tried to play by the rules. With his head up and shoulders back, an Outfit's relative can now see that in the land of the free and the home of the brave, cheating and correctness can shake hands, forming a détente between illegal and legal. "Wow, it's great to be an American living in this great country," Greco rejoiced.

Rule on, Outfit, your rules give you the benign power over what is just, what is right only to you and for your benefit every step of the way. There is no thought of compassion or feeling for the hardworking souls who pay their taxes, go off to war when called, and teach their children that the right way to do something is the honorable way to do something—no slithering under the door to get what you want. It's the way God would be proud of you. Let the suckers build the pot, the Outfit says, as it spits in your face.

The clock of virtue is ticking. Outfit, your violent, devious, uncaring, maniacal ways will be to hear the alarm go off one day that you won't be able to shut off, and then you will get the crap kicked out of you by the enforcer, who is above us all.

In his next election for his state senator seat, Mumbles had a Republican challenger. The week before the election, which was after the time period in which the Republicans could have replaced him on the ballot, the challenger announced he was withdrawing from the race. He told the media it was for health reasons. Mumbles now was unopposed and got reelected.

It sounded to me like the poor fellow came down with a touch of Mafia-itis. Now, if not treated, the person can be in a life threatening state, which could ultimately result in life's bye-bye stage. The proper medical term is putting yourself in the jackpot. The good news is that if the person takes the prescribed medication, which is to keep your mouth shut and lay low, the condition will disappear, and normal activities such as staying alive can be resumed.

The symptoms are very recognizable, so I will describe them to you, just in case you think you have them. When you answer the ringing of your doorbell by opening up your front door, and Big Louie and Guido—one holding a baseball bat and the other holding a steel pipe—are standing there looking at you, that is when the symptoms of Mafia-itis can be triggered. Sweating, your body starts shaking, rapid heartbeat, a dry mouth gets drier, and wondering where the priest's phone number is to schedule last rites are some of the symptoms to watch out for to avoid getting Mafia-itis. Stay away from the Outfit, as they are extremely contagious and pose a serious health risk to you.

Phil Greco, after becoming a licensed attorney, joined Mumbles' 12th Ward Regular Democratic Organization, where Mumbles sponsored him for an attorney's position with the Chicago Park District. Greco became a precinct captain in the ward organization, working his precinct, hustling for votes in every election. While Greco knew with his Outfit juice he didn't have to worry about losing his job, he wanted to advance in the organization, so he worked his precinct hard in trying to carry it as big as possible.

Greco had an overwhelming Democratic precinct, so carrying the precinct was never really in doubt, but Greco took no chances. He was visible in the precinct all year round, not just around elections. He could get someone in his precinct a garbage can. He could get a tree trimmed for someone in the precinct. Besides the weekly garbage pickup, he could get someone in his precinct a bulk pickup, if they needed. Need an abandoned car towed in the precinct? He could do that. As a precinct captain, Greco doled out favors to his precinct voters who responded by supporting his candidate by a wide margin. His high Democratic vote totals kept him in good standing with Mumbles.

Besides hustling for votes in his precinct, Greco, like all the other precinct captains in the organization, were given tickets to sell for the various ward functions, which were fundraisers for Mumbles. There was a winter dinner, a spring dinner, a golf outing, and ads that had to be sold for the 12th Ward advertisement book, to name a few of the fundraisers.
Mumbles determined by a precinct captain's salary how many tickets to give the captain. Any ticket not sold had to be bought by the captain. Greco sold tickets wherever he could. At work, in the precinct, to friends and relatives; anywhere Greco could sell the tickets, he would.

For the next twenty years, while maintaining his precinct, Greco worked his way up the ward organization ladder. From becoming the ward secretary, then the ward treasurer, and finally president of the ward organization, Greco cultivated his own juice over the years, which would benefit him. To get ahead in Chicago, you need the juice to be the 'who you know' and not the 'what you know.' Someone could be hired for that part of the job.

After working twenty years for the Park District, Greco, while not eligible to draw a pension because of his age, thus, was eligible for a pension when he reached the required age. Greco had developed a good working relationship with Mumbles and went to see him about becoming a Cook County Circuit Court judge. This is what Greco envisioned for himself, a judgeship. It would be nice to hear, "Judge Greco, your table is ready," at a restaurant. It would be nice to be called Judge Greco at a wedding reception. It would be nice to be called Judge Greco and asked your opinion about free trade. It would be nice to be called Judge Greco, period.

Thursday night the ward office was open, so Greco decided it was time to launch his boat in Lake Michigan, and see if the lake's waves could carry him to the judgeship he coveted. He called Mumbles earlier in the day and said he wanted to see Mumbles that night in the ward office.

It was about 8:30 P.M. when they met.

"Danny, I'm interested in becoming a circuit court judge," Greco said.

"Phil, is this what you really want at this time of your life?" Mumbles asked.

"Yeah, Danny, this is what I want now," Greco said. "I've been working for the Park District for twenty years beginning as an Attorney III with your help, and also with your help, I was promoted to Attorney II, Attorney I, and my current position as a Senior Attorney," Greco said. "I am very grateful for all your assistance throughout my career at the Park District," he said. "I could freeze my pension until I am 55 years old, then I could begin to draw it," Greco said. "I am ready to move on with my legal career and, for me, that means becoming a judge," he said.

"Phil, you've been a loyal member of the organization, carrying your precinct in every election you worked in since you started for me," Mumbles said. "You've been the ward's legal counsel and have become the president of the ward's organization," he said. "It would make me proud to see you slated as a judge," Mumbles said. "There is a price for this, though, and it'll be 15 Gs to become slated as a judge on the Democratic ticket in the primary and general elections," Mumbles said.

"So, the money insures that I'll be slated along with other Democratic judicial candidates on the ballot for the primary and general elections?" Greco asked.

"Yes, you would be," Mumbles said.

"I'll get you the money," Greco said.

"Okay, but I have to have the money in hand first," Mumbles said. "Once you give me the money, I'll nominate you for a judgeship before the Democratic Judicial Slatemaking Committee, which I have a lot of juice with," Mumbles said.

"I understand," Greco said.

There is kind of an unwritten rule that when you are slated to be a judge by the Democratic Party, your sponsor presents your political credentials, such as the years of service to a political organization, the various positions held in the political organization, carrying your precinct election after election for the slated Democratic candidates, and loyalty and dedication to the political organization by volunteering your time to work on the annual Christmas party and summer picnic. These are the selling points used by the sponsor.

"Bobby, what about his being a lawyer? Why isn't that mentioned?" you're asking me. Well, the very last thing a sponsor says is and they're a lawyer and that's it. I'm telling you, a person's legal credentials mean zero. It's what you've done for the political organization; that are your credentials.

Greco walked out of the ward office as if he was floating on soft, comforting air. A stiff, cool breeze did not penetrate the warm tingling feeling he was getting in his body at that moment. With Mumbles' support and being slated by the Democratic Party, winning the primary and general election was just a formality. It was a political done deal. A judgeship Chicago-style was waving to him at the end of the block. All he had to do was get the 15 Gs and he would be walking down the block with his arm around the judgeship's shoulder.

The problem was Greco did not have the 15 Gs. Being married with children did not leave him with much of an opportunity to build up a savings. Trying to get a bank loan meant putting up the house for collateral, and if he missed a bank payment for some reason, the bank could foreclose on the loan. *He and his family could be out on the street, so a bank loan was too risky*, he thought.

For the next two weeks, Greco thought about other possible options, but none of them seemed to be able to provide the needed money. He realized that if he wanted to be a judge, the only person who could give him the money was his Uncle Willie. Uncle Willie was the option he would use, he told himself. He called Uncle Willie, and they arranged to meet near the tennis courts at Taft Park.

It was a sticky Friday morning with the temperature expected to be 95 degrees that day. They met and sat on a bench, about to have the 'nephew is coming, hat in hand, for financial help from his uncle' talk.

"How ya doin', Phil? What's my nephew up to?" Messeto said.

"I'm actually doing fine, Uncle Bill," Greco said. "Uncle Bill, I've got a shot at becoming a Cook County Circuit Court Judge. Mumbles Marino will get me slated, but he wants 15 Gs up front before he will do anything," Greco said.

"So, you're telling me you need 15 Gs," Messeto said.

"Yeah, 15 Gs," Greco said.

"Now, you know, Phil, I run a business of loaning money out to people like yourself who don't have the money they need for whatever the reason. I don't know, and I don't care why they need the money. I just loan it to them as a business loan," Messeto said.

"I got it," Greco said.

"I'll loan you the 15 Gs at a monthly interest rate of three percent. You gotta start making monthly payments when I loan you the money. We'll work out a number that you can handle each month," Messeto said. "So, are you okay with the terms of the loan?" he asked.

While this was not exactly how Greco thought he would get the money from Uncle Willie, if he wanted the judgeship, which he did, this was the game he would have to play with his uncle.

"Okay, Uncle Bill. I guess if those are your terms, then I will accept them," Greco said.

"Good. I'll get you the money by next Wednesday. We'll meet here at the park again. It's very quiet in the late morning, as you can see. No one really around, so, yeah, we'll meet here," Messeto said.

"Phil, once you start paying on the loan, don't miss a month making your payment. You don't want to get your uncle mad," Messeto said with a hearty laugh that made its point. "I mean, do you think an uncle would hurt his nephew? Well, before answering, remember Uncle Willie is an Outfit uncle with Outfit privileges." Greco shook his head from side to side. "Yeah, I kind of thought that's how you would answer."

"Don't worry, I won't make you angry. You're my favorite uncle," Greco said.

"I better be," Messeto said jokingly, as he put his arm around Greco's shoulder and gave him a playful squeeze—not too hard, not too soft—just the type the Outfit gives its victims.

"See you next Wednesday," Greco said.

Messeto nodded his head up and down, acknowledging he would see his nephew next Wednesday.

There's an old saying, you've heard it, I've heard it, and probably nearly every human being on this Earth has or will hear it at some point in their life, that blood is thicker than water. Well, with the Outfit, when it comes to money, they drink all the water, not a drop left for you, and your blood is what will wind up spilling over the curb if you do not pay them the money owed to them, so they can continue to guzzle the water. No tap water for them; they buy the best.

Greco was treated like any other paying customer by Messeto. He had no special standing as Messeto's nephew. Pay or you might be walking with a limp for a while was how Messeto marketed himself, even to Greco. By accepting Messeto's loan terms, Greco walked through the door marked. You have now entered and joined being in the life. Being a judge meant Greco would now have to do what the Outfit wanted, for whoever they wanted in the court room. Being in the life, while it got Greco the judgeship he so coveted, it also made him into an Outfit-controlled peon to be legally used and abused, whenever his master wanted.

The next Wednesday, Greco met with Messeto at Taft Park and got the 15 Gs. He called Mumbles to let him know he got the money and to set up a meeting, so he could give Mumbles the money.

"Danny, this is Phil Greco. I'm calling to let you know, I'm ready to expedite that matter we talked about," Greco said.

"To its conclusion?" Mumbles asked.

"Yeah, to its conclusion," Greco said.

"Okay, meet me at the Chateau D'Ville Thursday night about 10:30 P.M. in the back part of their parking lot," Mumbles said.

"I'll be there," Greco said.

They met and Greco gave Mumbles the money. A few months later, Greco was slated for a judgeship. With Democratic Party support, Greco won the primary election in March and was elected that November as a Cook County Circuit Court Judge.

In December, Greco was sworn in as a judge, thus, beginning his first term not only as a judge, but as one of the Outfit's judicial friends.

The cases that were assigned to Greco that did relate to the Outfit were mainly driving under the influence or possible assault cases. Greco knew what the Outfit giveth, they could taketh. He routinely dismissed the cases for lack of evidence, or because the complainant did not show up in court. Maybe, once in a while, he would find someone guilty and make them pay a fine just to make it look like he was legit.

By the time he got reelected to another term, he learned how to play the legal game. He met and made friends with a white envelope filled with cash. Greco set his dollar figure for cases he would fix, and the lawyers who practiced before him knew it was in their best legal interest to associate with Greco's new best friend, the white envelope. The white envelope was a very loyal friend and made sure Greco was taken care of. Case after case, the white envelope, as a trusted friend, always put Greco in a happy state of mind. Cash can make a blue day turn into a rip roaring, 'glad to be alive' day by being part of the friendship club.

Over the years, covering many cases, numerous white envelopes became Greco's new best friend, each and every time. There was one case that defined Greco's judicial career in which even his dear friend could not erase the memory of it.

It was after 2 A.M. on a Tuesday when Raymond "Baby Ray" Iaculle Jr. left Kelly's Bar. Ray Jr. was the son of Raymond "Big Daddy" Iaculle Sr., who ran a gambling, loan-sharking, and prostitution operation on the Southeast Side of Chicago that stretched into Hammond and Whiting, Indiana, for the Outfit.

Ray Jr., when he became drunk, was a mean and belligerent drunk. From experience, I had to pull him out of a couple of places, as it would not have taken much longer before a brawl would have taken place. Come to think of it, even when sober, Ray Jr.'s personality mirrored his intoxicated state—mean and belligerent.

Yet, women were eager to go out with him. I guess for some reason unknown to me, these women either were attracted to his poor behavior or scared. I was never quite sure which one it was.

Chicago Police Officer Terri McSherry was working the midnight shift that Tuesday evening in the 30th District. She was a five- year veteran, who loved being a cop. She had a kind nature and always wanted to help people. By joining the police department, she felt she could make her dream a reality by making the world a better place, even if it was only for one person. Making a person's life better by her actions was what she thought about every day as she started her shift.

Her regular partner Jason Laskowski, a three-year veteran, was off completing his furlough and would not return to work until Saturday. He had gone on a fishing trip to Minnesota with his future father-in-law and a couple of friends.

The fishing trip was all Laskowski talked about, so Terri hoped he would catch a lot of fish and then shut up. They worked well as partners, and she was looking forward to his return.

Terri was working a one-person car that night as she made a left turn on to Kerry Avenue. In front of her was a car that was going twenty-five miles per hour and weaving from side to side.

She put on her overhead lights and adjusted her rearview spotlight to shine on the car.

Ray Jr. glanced up, saw the police lights shining on him and, after driving another block, pulled over to the curb. Terri used her lapel radio to call in the license plate numbers to see if there were any outstanding warrants on the driver of the car. There were no outstanding warrants, so she got out of her patrol car and walked over to talk with Ray Jr.

Ray Jr. saw her walking toward him in the left side mirror. He was not in a cooperative mood. In fact, he felt very hostile. He hated cops. By mixing alcohol and anger, he became very toxic toward her. He rolled down the left side window; he was going to be ready for her in his own way.

Terri just approached the left door of Ray Jr.'s car and was about to ask him for his driver's license when he slowly opened the door. As Terri stood in front of the door, Ray Jr. swung it open forcefully, pushing the door with both hands so it struck Terri's body.

Ray Jr. jumped out of the car as Terri was knocked off balance, grabbing her and throwing her down to the ground with him on top of her.

He had a short, muscular, stocky build, and he started to throw one punch after another into her face. The punches were coming rapid fire— bang, bang, bang—into her face. As hard as she tried to get him off her and defend herself, the punches were coming too fast and too hard, causing major trauma injury to her face. The punches weakened her to the point she was defenseless against their onslaught. Blood began stampeding out of what would be a broken nose. Overwhelming, sharp, jagged pain was coming from what would be a broken jaw.

Ray Jr. got off her, stood up, and began kicking her in the face, shattering both cheek bones. Her face was swollen, and it had a mangled, monstrous Halloween mask-like look to it. Her eyes were barely open as they were swollen and started to close. This was not a happy face, but rather a disfigured mass of torn apart, blood-soaked skin that was totally unrecognizable to the human eye.

Ray Jr. turned away from her for a second, and then he turned back and began swiftly to kick her on the right side of her body, causing her right kidney to become lacerated. He turned her over, continuing his assault on her body by kicking her, ultimately breaking two ribs.

He finally stopped the thuggery on her body. He began to get back in his car when another car was slowing down behind him. He started his car, gunned it, and sped off.

The driver of the other car saw some of the license plate numbers on Ray Jr.'s car, but did not get all of them. He did recognize the make of the car.

The driver got out of his car and, seeing Terri's body, rushed to her. He used her lapel radio and called for help for a fallen officer. She laid there motionless, moaning, blood drenching her face and uniform. She was in extreme, intense pain. Her savagely beaten body was white hot with pain. She was slightly coherent, and the driver who would testify at her trial said the sight of her hideous face made him feel as if he would vomit.

Upon receiving the call, police cars raced down Kerry Avenue at exceptionally high speeds coming to aid a stricken fellow officer. Some had to turn away as they saw in front of them Terri's gruesome, broken, distorted face with countless injuries. Some openly wept at the body's mass destruction caused by the ultra-crazy man Ray Jr. The officers prayed for her as the paramedics rushed her to the hospital.

Sergeant Kevin McCarthy, Terri's sergeant, rode in the ambulance with her, holding her left hand with his left hand, peering over her, never taking his eyes off of her. He placed his right hand over the cross he wore around his neck, praying to the Almighty for her to live. McCarthy would testify at the trial that in his twenty-six years on the police force, he never saw such a destructive beating as what Terri had gotten. The nervous eyes of the paramedics and sergeant spelled out the story of violence before them.

The ambulance—with lights blazing and sirens howling—rocketed down Kerry Avenue, arriving at Gilbert Memorial Hospital in six minutes. Hospital personnel had been called and they had a bed waiting for Terri in the emergency room. Paramedics, as quickly as their legs could carry them, transported

Terri to the emergency room with Sergeant McCarthy charging right behind, as close as he could be.

While examining Terri, Emergency Room Dr. George Pfeiffer noticed on top of her forehead a purplish discoloration and immediately ordered an x-ray of Terri's brain. The staff, under Pfeiffer's direction, worked as quickly as they could to stabilize Terri's falling blood pressure. After seeing the x-ray, Dr. Pfeiffer called Dr. Stephen Jankowski, a neurosurgeon, at home and told him Terri had a small blood clot in the brain. Jankowski told Pfeiffer he was on his way.

Terri's family had been notified and her mother, father, sister, and brother were in the hospital's waiting room, waiting to hear something from a doctor on her medical condition.

The hospital's lobby became very congested as officers filled the hallway, waiting to hear how Terri was doing. They were there in spirit to be Terri's police support, to bolster her fight for her life. Some officers prayed, while others stood with a cup of coffee in hand, blankly looking at other officers who had the same blank, nervous look of despair pasted to their faces.

Nurse Judith Stokley yelled at Terri. "C'mon, girl, fight! C'mon, Terri, fight for your life! You can do it, Terri! Don't stop fighting," Stokley pleaded as she watched a monitor.

Stokley was a proud black woman who sang every Sunday in her church's choir. She sang the gospel hymns that are sung every Sunday in black churches in Chicago. To Stokley, the hymns were convictions of being the type of person God wanted you to be in time of need. That's why Stokley became a nurse. For as a nurse, this child of the church could express the kindness, the goodness, and the strength of love in her heart for those who needed it the most. She was repaying God for his teachings of the need when called to stand strong with those people whose lives are moving toward becoming extinct.

She took Terri's white hand and held it with her black hand. She swallowed hard and said, "Terri, I'm with you. In beating death, remember, two always beats one on the scoreboard of life." Stokley refused to let go of Terri's hand. Every ounce of love in her heart was being transferred from her heart through her fingers into Terri's hand. Her love of life was what Stokley fed to Terri's soul. To love life, you have to be alive to capture those moments of happiness and joy that are the components of a loving life.

Stokley watched the monitor and saw Terri's blood pressure tick slowly upward. She smiled and, in a low, quiet voice, started to sing one of her church hymns. She sang in reference to God as he provided her with the love that reached into Terri's veins of life and brought her from the back of the line to the front of the line.

"Thank you, God," Stokley purred. "See, Lord, we saved another one. The girl's going to live," Stokley inwardly cried out.

Dr. Pfeiffer would always say when the situation called for a hero, he turned to Judy. Stokley felt that, emotionally, if black and white hands held each other, both hands would unite as problem solvers, and the world would be a better place to live. Maybe she's right.

Dr. Jankowski, after looking at the x-ray and conferring with Dr. Pfeiffer, decided it was time to talk with the family. He met with them in the waiting room. Terri's father put his arm around his wife's shoulder and held her tightly. Sergeant McCarthy, a former Marine who won a silver star for valor in the Korean War, with both his hands, held Terri's mother's hand firmly, but compassionately, as the hard core ex-Marine was digging in for an emotional battle of nerves.

The waiting room was packed with police brass and fellow officers. The hallway was packed with officers listening and hanging onto every word spoken by Dr. Jankowski.

The silence was deafening. No one moved; everyone froze in their spot. Dr. Jankowski told the family and fellow officers that Terri had a small blood clot in the brain. While it was not life threatening, there still was a concern that it could travel deeper into the brain. He said Terri required surgery, which he and his surgical team would perform after he left them. He told them the surgery would be four to five hours.

Dr. Jankowski then talked about the horrific trauma injuries to Terri's face. He told the family and others that a plastic surgeon would evaluate her and make the decision on the surgical procedure required. He said it appeared Terri would need multiple plastic surgeries in the coming months, because of the amount of needed reconstructive work the plastic surgeon would have to do.

Terri's mother, her eyes blanketed with moisture from the tears she was shedding, asked Dr. Jankowski, "How's my baby?"

"When Terri first came in, her blood pressure was dropping, but Dr. Pfeiffer and his staff stabilized her to where I can operate," he said. "Her vital signs have greatly improved, so I would say at this point she's doing as well as expected under the circumstances," Dr. Jankowski said.

Dr. Jankowski and his young assistant Dr. Cary Mandeloff scrubbed for surgery. Dr. Mandeloff was a brilliant young surgeon, who during his medical career would make his mark as a world-renowned neurosurgeon, specializing in spinal cord injuries.

As the doctors entered the operating room, there was someone else who had also scrubbed for surgery. He would stand next to Dr. Jankowski, advising him about the incision that needed to be made. He would guide Dr.

Jankowski's hands during the delicate surgery. He would show Dr. Mandeloff how to avoid damaging the artery in the brain. This person was trained in saving lives, so Dr. Jankowski never once questioned what he told him during the surgery.

Terri's soul could see who it was and, after the blood clot was successfully removed, said, "Thank you, God."

The family and police officers were given the good news about the blood clot by the doctors, but, for Terri, her medical needs were really just beginning. The next several months brought a total of six more surgeries that were required and done by Dr. Paul Fanovich, a plastic surgeon, who did the reconstructive work on her face. Dr. Fanovich, as well as Dr. Jankowski, would testify at the trial about the medical procedures they had to perform on Terri. They would also testify what caused these traumatic injuries to Terri.

Ray Jr. turned himself in accompanied by Thomas "Tommy" Calzone, his lawyer, after waiting more than twenty-four hours. The police had checked the tape of Terri calling in Ray Jr.'s license plate numbers to see if he had any warrants. They were hot on his trail looking for him. Ray Sr. was also with his son.

A bond hearing was scheduled for the next day, so Ray Jr. spent the night in Cook County Jail. The next day the judge, who would be presiding over the trial, the Honorable Phil Greco—it's okay, you can laugh—set bond at two hundred thousand dollars. Calzone, after Ray Jr. had previously pled not guilty to all charges, asked and received a bench trial from Greco. Calzone told Greco that Ray Sr. would post the necessary ten percent, which came up to twenty thousand dollars. Ray Jr. walked out of court to wait for his trial.

Tommy Calzone was a top criminal defense lawyer, who was very well known in Chicago for his legal expertise. He sat on several corporate boards of some of Chicago's major corporations. Tommy was no stranger to Outfit cases, as he previously defended some of the boys. While Tommy had a criminal practice in which he had other clients, mob cases were still a big part of his practice. Tommy, as a lawyer, was smooth, real smooth, in a courtroom. The Outfit doesn't hire ambulance chasers to defend them. They hire the best money can buy. Tommy Calzone had a lot of juice that other clients could not resist. Hiring Tommy as your lawyer gave you a secure feeling, because Tommy knew the Outfit. So, at a cocktail party, you could name drop. "I've hired the mob lawyer Tommy Calzone," you would tell your friends, hoping they saw you as a big shot, who, in some perverse way was associated with the Outfit.

It had been almost three years since the beating of Terri McSherry, and finally the trial was set to begin in Cook County Circuit Court. Ray Jr. was charged with multiple assault charges, all felonies. He sat at the defense table with Calzone, a cocky look on his face. He told Calzone he felt like a million bucks today. You could see the juice oozing out of his body.

I went to the trial. The Cook County Criminal Circuit Court Building is located on 34th Street and Nowels Avenue. When referring to any cases there, the residents just called it the 34th and Nowels.

The building had a gritty exterior. The granite stone were decaying off the façade, and they sure could use a good polishing. Each granule of the stones showed the age of so many criminal cases that were tried there. The stones were as worn out as was the justice system inside the building.

The case was held in a courtroom on the 16th floor. I walked up to the defense table where I wished Ray Jr. good luck and said hello to Tommy. I took my seat a few rows back. Ray Jr. had his cheering section behind him. His father, Ray Sr., mother, two brothers, his wife who was expecting their first child, some more relatives, and a couple of guys from Ray Sr.'s street crew were seated in the first two rows behind Ray Jr. I got up from my seat and figured I better pay my respects to Ray Sr. and company. I walked over, extended my hand and before I could say a word, Ray Sr. got out of his seat and stood up.

"Bobby, gee, thanks for coming," Ray Sr. said, as with both of those large meaty hands of his, which did a lot of beatings in their time, took my right hand. Those large powerful fingers that damaged many faces over the years engulfed my right hand, shaking it up and down.

"Good luck, Big Daddy," I said to him.

"We're going to need every bit of it," Ray Sr. said. I then kissed Mrs. Iaculle on the cheek, wishing her well, and did the same with Ray Jr.'s wife. I shook hands with everyone else, expressing to them my hope that Ray Jr. would be acquitted.

I went back and sat down. There's an old Outfit custom that at a trial you always put on a face that you are supportive, even if you're not. The reason for this little love fest is you don't want your non-support to be a reason to get whacked. Like I say, I've seen people get whacked for minor things at times, so I played it cool rather than be called 'that mother who didn't even wish me good luck at my trial' by someone. Keep in mind, we are not always dealing with normal; we're dealing with Outfit normal, which is a galaxy away from what the really normal people subscribe to.

Across the aisle from me was a sea of blue. Every seat was occupied by either an off duty Chicago cop or one who was attending the trial before going to work. They all were in uniform except for Terri's husband, Alex, a nine-year veteran of the force, and her partner at the time Jason Laskowski, who wore suits with ties. Alex and Laskowski sat in the row behind the prosecution table.

The prosecutor was Assistant Cook County State's Attorney David Chopak, a sixteen-year veteran of the office. In opening statements, Chopak told Judge Greco, who since it was a bench trial would be both judge and jury of the case that he would prove beyond a reasonable doubt that Ray Iaculle, Jr. willingly and knowingly committed the assaults he was being charged with against Chicago Police Officer Terri McSherry.

Tommy Calzone, in the defense's opening statement, claimed Ray Jr. had fallen asleep for a moment behind the wheel after a long day of work and that's why the car weaved. As for the injuries, they were caused by undetermined elements, he said to Greco.

Ray Jr. was a truck driver for the City's Water Department, a job he got through his father's juice with Mumbles. Half the time he never showed up for work, yet on the 1st and 16th of every month he was paid in full. Maybe Tommy was referring to all those missed work days Ray accumulated as being equal to one long workday. Outfit math doesn't always correlate to the math we all learned in school. With the Outfit, it's always addition, never subtraction when it's for their pocket. If you don't add their money correctly, you will be physically the one who will be subtracted.

The trial was to last three weeks. The prosecution would call twenty-five witnesses, plus enter numerous photographs of Terri's injuries taken at the hospital as evidence. Chopak brought in Terri's bloody uniform and put it on display over a chair. Every day of the trial, Chopak would have the blood stained uniform on a chair directly facing Greco.

Chopak was going to have to rely on the testimony of the witnesses, specifically the medical personnel, as his main source of evidence. There were no witnesses who saw the beating, and Terri did not have any recollection of the event.

Drs. Pfeiffer, Jankowski, and Fanovich all testified the extent of the trauma injuries that Terri received were consistent of those seen when a person is assaulted. The doctors all explained the types of trauma injuries Terri had received, citing the photographs taken as examples. Tommy did not cross examine Drs. Pfeiffer and Jankowski.

I sat there thinking Tommy has got to have something up his sleeve. He's just letting the doctors have a free pass. When it came time to cross examine Dr. Fanovich, Tommy bore in on him.

"Dr. Fanovich, you have testified to the extent of the trauma injuries, but can't trauma injuries occur in a different way?" Tommy asked.

"Yes," Dr. Fanovich said.

"Isn't it possible Officer McSherry forcefully pulled Mr. Iaculle out of his car, a struggle began, and Mr. Iaculle, who weighs two hundred pounds, was on top of Officer McSherry as she fell face first into the street's cement?

Isn't it possible that due to the weight of my client on top of Officer McSherry, her facial injuries were involuntary in nature in that her body could have turned at that moment and she self-inflicted those trauma injuries to herself?" Tommy asked.

"Well, those trauma injuries are not consistent with ones you get from a fall," Dr. Fanovich said.

"So, you are testifying under oath that you can get trauma injuries from falling," Tommy said.

"Well, yes, but..." Dr. Fanovich said.

"But you did not see how the trauma injuries occurred because you were not there when they took place, so you cannot say with 100% accuracy this is how Officer McSherry got injured, can you? Is that not correct, Dr. Fanovich?" Tommy said.

"That is correct, but I would..." Dr. Fanovich said.

"You only saw what you saw from photographs and medical language accompanying the photographs after that fact. You were not in the hospital that night, so your assessment of Officer McSherry's facial condition came more than twenty-four hours later, is that not correct, Dr. Fanovich?" Tommy said.

"That is correct," Dr. Fanovich said.

"So, since you were not at the scene to see how the actual trauma injuries occurred, and you were not at the hospital that night to examine Officer McSherry, you looked at photographs. Therefore, you can only speculate how the trauma injuries occurred, and you cannot say with 100 percent accuracy how the injuries really occurred, can you, Dr. Fanovich? Is that not correct?" Tommy asked.

"That is correct," Dr. Fanovich said.

"Your Honor, I have no further questions for the witness," Tommy said to Greco.

"The witness is excused," Greco said.

A dazed, bewildered Dr. Fanovich left the courtroom. While the trauma injuries appeared to be able to stand on their own merit as credible evidence for the prosecution, Tommy was at least able, by his questioning of Dr. Fanovich, to raise a doubt about the injuries. Tommy was able to imprint a question mark, maybe a small one, but a question mark nonetheless about how the injuries really occurred. To me it was obvious the injuries occurred from the beating, but I'm not the judge.

Terri finally took the stand as a prosecution witness. Under questioning from Chopak she said she saw Iaculle's car weaving and since the car was weaving, she had probable cause to stop his car. She testified she suspected the driver was intoxicated. Chopak played the tape in which Terri called in the license plate numbers to dispatch to check for any open warrants. Terri confirmed that was her voice on the tape.

Chopak questioned Terri about whether, during her five years as an officer, was it her experience that when she stopped a car for weaving if, in fact, it turned out the driver would be charged with driving under the influence.

"Yes," Terri said.

"So at that point, when you saw the car weaving, there was enough probable cause in your mind to warrant a traffic stop?" Chopak asked.

"Yes," Terri said.

Since Terri had no recollection of the beating, Chopak avoided any questions about that subject.

Terri was to be the last prosecution witness to be called, and it was now time for Tommy to cross examine her.

"Officer McSherry, how big of an area was Mr. Iaculle, by your account, weaving in?" Tommy asked. Raising his right arm up to chest level and using his right hand, Tommy made large weaving motions at first, and then he made small weaving motions. "Well, Officer, was it large or small weaving?" he asked.

"I remember the car was weaving, but I cannot recall the size of the weaves," Terri said.

It had been twenty-six months since the horrific beating Terri had gotten from Ray Jr. She had just returned to light duty three months ago. The department felt it best if she was transferred to another district. So, at the time of the trial, she was working the front desk in the 26th District.

I watched Terri struggle with Tommy's questions. She was desperately trying to remember the facts that would nail this bastard to the wall, but her mind, at a certain point, was a blank—just a big, empty desert with her memory not knowing which direction to turn to.

"Officer McSherry, did Mr. Iaculle's car weave sharply or uncontrollably in any direction?" Tommy asked.
"I don't recall," Terri said.

"Officer McSherry, did Mr. Iaculle's car slightly veer off in any direction?" Tommy asked.

"I don't recall," Terri said.

"While you have testified under oath that you saw Mr. Iaculle's car weaving, you have no recollection and cannot say with veracity to what extent Mr. Iaculle's car was weaving. Is that not correct?" Tommy asked.

"That is correct," Terri said.

"Was Mr. Iaculle ever given a field sobriety test by you?" Tommy asked.

"No," Terri said.

"Was Mr. Iaculle ever given a hospital blood test to check his alcoholic level?" Tommy asked.

"Not that I am aware of," Terri said.

"So, Officer McSherry, even though you thought you had probable cause to stop Mr. Iaculle for some undetermined type of weaving of which you have no recollection, the fact remains you don't have any proof Mr. Iaculle was intoxicated, do you?" Tommy said.

"I do not have any proof," Terri said.

"There was no field sobriety test, nor was there a hospital test to confirm if Mr. Iaculle was intoxicated, so he never was charged with driving under the influence, was he? Is that correct?" Tommy asked.

"That's correct, he was not charged," Terri said.

"Do you have any recollection of how you were injured, Officer McSherry?" Tommy asked.

"No," Terri said.

"So, at this point, you cannot say if you were struck physically either by punching or kicking?" Tommy asked.

"That is correct," Terri said.

"Your injuries, Officer McSherry, could have been self-inflicted. You might have fallen backwards, and as you were falling your body turned, falling face first into the cement," Tommy said.

"The injuries were not self-inflicted," Terri said, sharply looking directly at Tommy.

"Officer McSherry, you have testified that you have no recollection of how you were injured. Can you provide any information to the court that Mr. Iaculle assaulted you, thus, causing your injuries?" Tommy asked.

"No, I cannot provide any information," Terri said.

"Thank you, Officer McSherry," Tommy said. "I have no further questions for the witness, Your Honor," Tommy said to Greco.

"The witness is excused," Greco said.

Terri left the witness box, looked at her husband, lips pressed together then gave him a shrug, and raised her eyes indicating she tried her best. Her husband gave her a thumbs up with his right thumb.

"Your Honor, I'm making a motion for all charges to be dropped against Mr. Iaculle as the state has not proved its case beyond a reasonable doubt," Tommy said.

"Put your motion in writing and get it to me after court today, as I will rule on it tomorrow," Greco said.

"I'll have the written motion to you after court today," Tommy said.

Court, as it did every day, ended at 4 P.M.

Tommy wrote his motion and went to Greco's office at about 4:30 P.M. "Hey, Pisano, how you doing?" Tommy asked.

"Good!" Greco said.

"I have my written motion to drop all charges against Raymond Iaculle Jr. for you," Tommy said.

"Fine," Greco said.

"You know, Philly Boy, I can feel this one in my bones that my guy is going to walk on all charges," Tommy said.

"Just leave the motion. I can't talk about the case now, so I'll see you in court tomorrow," Greco said.

"Sure, fine. Okay, I'll leave the motion. See you in court tomorrow, Your Honor," Tommy said.

In court the next day, Greco denied Tommy's motion to drop all charges against Ray Jr. The prosecution then rested its case. The defense rested its case as Ray Jr. was not called as a witness and neither was anyone else. Closing arguments began the next day.

The prosecutor, David Chopak, told Greco that the photographs of what Terri looked like after the beating by Ray Jr., and medical witnesses who testified showed to the court that Raymond Iaculle Jr. did, in fact, assault Officer Terri McSherry. According to Chopak, the state proved beyond a reasonable doubt that Ray Jr. should be convicted of all charges. Chopak said there was a preponderance of evidence presented to the court that clearly showed Ray Jr. was guilty of committing the charged crimes.

The defense lawyer Tommy Calzone told the court that since Officer McSherry could not testify to the type or pattern of the weaving car driven by Raymond Iaculle Jr., nor was there any evidence of him being intoxicated, probable cause was not in evidence to convict.

Tommy said Officer McSherry testified she had no recollection of how she received her injuries, so he asked the court for a direct acquittal on all charges against Raymond Iaculle Jr. as the State did not prove its case beyond a reasonable doubt.

Chopak, in his rebuttal, said the doctors who testified all agreed that the injuries suffered by Officer McSherry were not self-inflicted, but rather the injuries were administered by a person. "That person, Your Honor," Chopak said, pointing to Ray Jr., "is sitting in this courtroom. The State is asking the court for a conviction on all charged counts as the State has proved its case beyond a reasonable doubt."

Had this been a jury trial, the photographs and doctors' testimony would have made it very difficult for Tommy to make a 12-member jury believe the injuries could not have been self-inflicted. The severity of the injuries logically could not have been self-inflicted. Trying to convince 12 people is a lot harder than trying to convince one that Ray Jr. played no part in the injuries to Terri. However, this was a bench trial in which all logic gets thrown out the window.

After Chopak finished his rebuttal, Greco announced the next court date would be in three weeks, and at that time, he would make public his verdict.

After court ended, Ray Sr. went to a pay phone and called Jimmy to find out if he was available for the two of them to meet tonight. Jimmy suggested that they meet at Mickey's, an ice cream parlor, tonight at 8:30 P.M. Jimmy kidded with Ray Sr. that he had a taste for a root beer float, and he would be the big spender and buy Ray Sr. a banana split. Ray Sr. giggled and said that sealed the deal.

Ray Sr. and Jimmy met at a far back table in order to have some privacy.

"You got juice with Phil Greco, right?" asked Ray Sr.

"Yeah, I got juice with the Honorable Judge Phil Greco. He's been taken care of before. He's a friend," Jimmy said.

"Well, from your experience, what it is it going to cost? I mean, look, Baby Ray screwed up, but I don't want him to go to prison, so give me a number," Ray Sr. said.

"This is a heater case, so you got to figure 5 Gs for this one," Jimmy said. In Chicago speak, a heater case is a high-profile one with a lot of media coverage—the case that makes the 10 P.M. news. The beating of a cop by an Outfit guy's son doesn't get much hotter.

"So, I'll get you the money, and you'll get it to Greco, then the fix will be in, and Baby Ray walks. Is that how it plays out?" Ray Sr. asked.

"Yeah, that's the game plan," Jimmy said.

"How soon do you need the money?" Ray Sr. questioned.

"Well, we got some time, since the verdict won't be announced for three weeks, so get me the money...say a week from today. Does that give you enough time? Once I get the money from you, I'll see Greco," Jimmy said.

"Yeah, sure, a week from today. Yeah, I'll have the money," Ray Sr. said. "I'll have a couple of my boys beat some extra money out of a guy who owes me a few bucks," Ray Sr. said wryly.

"Just tell him he's donating to a worthy cause," Jimmy said.

"Yeah, he's helping a needy family member," Ray Sr. said, laughing so hard he could barely contain himself.

"You'll let me know after you see Greco? I just don't want anything to get screwed up," Ray Senior said.

"Sure. Sure, look, you're a father and I'm a father, so I fully understand your concern, but don't worry, everything will go smooth," Jimmy said.

"Okay, thank God for juice," Ray Sr. said.

"Never hurts to have it," Jimmy said.

"Thanks for everything, Jimmy. I know I'll owe you on this one," Ray Sr. said, as the two of them got up from the table and shook hands.

"I'll be holding your marker," Jimmy jokingly said.

"Thanks again. See you, Jimmy," Ray Sr. said.

"See ya, Big Daddy," Jimmy said.

The next week Ray Sr. delivered the five Gs needed to Jimmy. Jimmy called Greco, and Greco told him to come to his office on Thursday at 5 P.M. Here's where juice and justice go out on a date together.

On Thursday, Jimmy put the five Gs in a white envelope, rubber banded it, and headed out to see the Honorable Judge Phil Greco.

"How are you doing?" Jimmy said, as he met Greco and his office.

"Good, Jimmy, and you?" Greco said.

"Couldn't be better, Phil," Jimmy replied. "Phil, I'm here to see you about Ray Iaculle Jr.'s case," Jimmy said. "I know this is a heater case and it's going to cost more than our usual cases, so I'm going to give you five Gs to see to it Ray Jr. walks," Jimmy said, looking dead center into Greco's eyes. Jimmy then pulled out the rubber banded white envelope and tossed it on the desk in front of Greco.

Greco started to finger the rubber band slightly, snapping it against the envelope. "It'll be $7,500 for this one," Greco said.

"Like I said, I know this is a heater case, but we ain't going up on the price. It's going to be five Gs and that's it," Jimmy said.

"When Ray Jr. walks, there's going to be a hell of a lot of heat, and I feel that $7,500 is a more appropriate amount, considering what's going to happen later," Greco said. "This isn't some DUI case in which you give $500 and that's it. No, I mean, let's not kid ourselves. A cop did get beat up, so I can't treat this case like some average assault case," he said. "The cops in the media will be pitching a bitch all over the place about my decision to acquit Ray Jr. I need more compensation," Greco said.

Jimmy looked at the rubber banded white envelope on the desk. He picked it up, held it, then flipped the envelope back on the desk. This was not the first rubber banded white envelope Greco received, nor would it be the last. He knew the rules of being an Outfit friend. This was one friendship you never wanted the Outfit to end.

"Five Gs, you want to count them, go ahead, but that's all you're getting. So say thank you, and I'll be on my merry way," Jimmy said.

Greco looked at the envelope again. He took off the rubber band and took the money out of the envelope. He fingered the $100 bills, then fanned the Franklins out on the desk. He eyeballed the money, did not count it, and then he put the money back in the envelope. He kept a poker face the whole time. Then he spoke.

"I don't need to count the money, as you have always given me the amount you said you did all the other times. Your word is good with me, it's just I think for this specific case it warrants a little more money and I…"

Jimmy cut him off. "What you have now can always be taken away from you later," he said. "Judges come and judges go," Jimmy said, narrowing his focus on Greco. "When you come up for a retention vote, and if you don't have the party's backing, well, it stands," Jimmy began to say.

"Thank you," Greco said.

"You're welcome," Jimmy said, as he reached across the desk to shake hands with Greco.

"Ray Jr. walks," Jimmy said.

"Ray Jr. walks," Judge Greco said.

Well there you have it. Now, you and I, plus the Iaculles, Jimmy, and the Honorable Judge Phil Greco know the fix is in. Keep this info under your hat, don't tell your relatives or anyone else; mum's the word. You've got to sit in the courtroom like you don't know Baby Ray's going to walk. Act surprised when Greco announces the verdict. I'm trusting you guys on this one.

Jimmy called Ray Sr. and told him to meet him by the tennis courts in Simms's Park at 3 P.M. the day after he saw Greco.

"Hey, Jimmy, everything cool with the judge?" Ray Sr. asked, as they sat down on the bench.

"The fix is in. Greco's going to let Ray Jr. walk on all charges. It's a done deal," Jimmy said.

Ray Sr. looked at Jimmy for a moment, then reached over and hugged him. "This means a lot to me. Even though he did wrong, he's still my kid. I got to protect him," Ray Sr. said after he released Jimmy from the hug.

"Sure, Ray, you did what any father would do," Jimmy said, as both men stood up. "Well, like I said before, I know I owe you big on this one, Jimmy, so I'll be seeing you. Take care," Ray Sr. said, shaking Jimmy's hand. Both of them walked away from each other to their cars.

Juice and the justice system will continue courting each other in the near future. Their relationship has been arranged just like one in the old country. They both want the same thing. Justice closes her eyes to the illegal overtures juice makes to her until she hears what the 'how much' is going to be. Once she finds favor with the how much, she opens her eyes, and bats them at the legal light of the law. She hears no evil, sees no evil, and speaks no evil. As she is prompted by the how much, her voice rings out to those sitting in the courtroom pews, "Walk, walk free my son. Your privilege erases any crime."

She administers the wrong, not the right. Juice paid for freedom, justice gave freedom away without ever asking for a moral receipt. They both got the freedom they desired—one never caring how it happened, the other not caring why it happened.

The three weeks passed, and Ray Jr. was about to hear his fate in Greco's courtroom. The same people who attended the court proceedings before were in the courtroom again. The boys in blue were pressed together on one side of the courtroom, while Ray Jr.'s supporters were on the other side. Terri was not in the courtroom, as she had gotten very depressed after she testified, because she could not remember the pertinent details of the case. This frustrated her as those details pertaining to her she felt would have strengthened the case against Ray Jr. While she was feeling better, she decided her mental sanity needed to be kept away from the courtroom. She had some long bouts with depression following all her surgeries. She felt one more round might be one round too many.

Ray Jr. fidgeted in his chair. He looked at his watch several times, waiting for Greco to appear from his chambers. *Let's get this charade over. It's time for the movie to end,* Ray Jr.'s thinking. *For chrissakes, you're wasting my time,* he told himself.

The courtroom became very quiet, a stillness of silence prevailed as Greco walked in and took his seat. Remember you guys, don't say a word; just sit there and watch and be surprised like everyone else when you hear the verdict, okay? Good, you got it.

"The defendant Raymond Iaculle Jr. has been charged with multiple assault charges," Greco said. He ticked them off one by one.

"The court has based its verdict on the matter of whether the State proved beyond a reasonable doubt that Raymond Iaculle Jr. committed the charged assaults against Officer Terri McSherry. It's the court's opinion that the State was not able to prove beyond a reasonable doubt that Raymond Iaculle Jr. committed the charged assaults against Officer Terri McSherry. The State could not prove beyond a reasonable doubt if the weaving of Mr. Iaculle's car was by intoxication or simply the fact that Mr. Iaculle fell asleep behind the wheel. Since there was no field test to determine the alcoholic content, nor was there a hospital blood test to determine Mr. Iaculle's alcoholic content, there is reasonable doubt whether Mr. Iaculle's blood level was beyond the legal limit to operate a motor vehicle in the state of Illinois. So, there is a doubt about probable cause."

"The State could not prove beyond a reasonable doubt that Mr. Iaculle assaulted Officer Terri McSherry, as there were no witnesses to the alleged assault, nor could Officer Terri McSherry under oath recall how she got the injuries," Greco said. "Dr. Fanovich, testifying under oath, while offering his medical opinion that the injuries were inflicted by someone, did not rule out that trauma injuries can occur from falling, especially if someone, during a struggle, falls on top of someone," he said. "The State did not prove beyond a reasonable doubt how Officer Terri McSherry's injuries really occurred. The State only presented a possible theory on the injuries, but no actual evidence to validate their claims," Greco said.

"Therefore, the court acquits Raymond Iaculle Jr. of all charges brought by the Cook County State's Attorney's office to this court," Greco side. "Mr. Iaculle, you are free to go," Greco said.

Greco banged his gavel and said court was adjourned. Okay, you guys can relax. Take a breath. It's official, Baby Ray walks.

Cook County Sheriff's deputies, who were seated in the back of the courtroom, were summoned by Greco to escort Ray Jr. out of the courtroom and building. They quickly came forward and surrounded Ray Jr., and got him out of the courtroom.

As Ray Jr. walked by me, he gave me one of those 'okay it's all over' winks. The kind of a wink that tells you there's no problem here, because I knew I was going to walk on all of the charges.

"See ya, Bobby," he said to me as he passed by.

"See ya, Ray. Good luck," I said.

Ray Sr. and the rest of the family, after hugging and congratulating themselves, walked past me. "See ya, Bobby," Ray Sr. said, "And say hello to your dad."

"See ya, Big Daddy," I said.

While Ray Jr. was being taken out of the courtroom, the sea of blue across the aisle erupted. The quietness which was there just moments before was washed away by a rising tide of nastiness. The sea of blue now began churning in waves of anger, crashing against the walls in the courtroom. The voices of the waves grew louder and louder, splashing defiantly over the gallery. For those who were sworn to serve and protect the citizens of Chicago, the waves of anger rose to dangerous levels.

Booing started from the sea of blue followed by, "This case was fixed," and, "The fix is in," poured out of the mouths of many officers as Greco started to leave the bench. Jason Laskowski leaped out of his seat, jabbing his right index finger directly at Greco, and with all the exploding alpha male rage running out of his body yelled at Greco, "You fucking piece of shit. You mother fucking piece of shit." Terri's husband, Alex, tried to calm Laskowski. Alex's expression was one of shock. How could the court rule against Terri? How could a thug go free were the headlines plastered across his face.

Greco walked out of the courtroom never looking back at the verbal assaults that were being hurled at him by the Chicago Police Department.

Laskowski sat down, head bowed down, looking straight down at the floor. Alex put his arm around Laskowski's shoulder, "It's okay, it'll be okay," he whispered into Laskowski's right ear.

"How did it happen, Alex? The evidence, the testimony, everything pointed to Iaculle assaulting Terri. How the hell did it happen? Iaculle should be sitting in county jail right now," Laskowski said dejectedly with complete despair in his voice.

Alex, fighting back tears, said, "I don't know. I just don't know how it happened."

Officer after officer came up, first to Alex then Laskowski, saying how sorry they were about the verdict to each of them. They then filtered out of the courtroom one by one. The sea of blue started coming down, the waves of anger were no longer present in the room. The levels of the sea of blue were restoring to normalcy. The sea of blue would now go back to serving and protecting the citizens of Chicago, remembering the great storm they encountered, but that they were not able to change the impact of the storm on one of their own.

Laskowski and Alex walked out of the courtroom, heads down, downtrodden and defeated, wondering if they would ever find the piece of the puzzle that didn't fit and make it fit.

I walked up to Tommy Calzone who was still sitting at the defense table, shook his hand, and congratulated him on his victory—a tainted victory, but a victory nonetheless.

"Thanks, Bobby. I guess I had to earn my money somehow," he laughed. When a trial lawyer goes to court his hourly rate is double. Tommy's office rate was $400 an hour, so it became $800 an hour for court time. So, in three weeks of work during the trial, Tommy pocketed almost 84 Gs. Not bad for a case that was won before it started.

"You walking out?" Tommy said to me.

"No, I'll be here for a couple more minutes," I said. As he put his papers in his briefcase and then got up to leave Tommy said, "Good seeing you, Bobby. Say hello to your dad for me. I guess we'll probably be running into each other again. See ya."

"See you, Tommy," I said.

I looked at the benches in the gallery. "You guys just saw the way justice works in this building," I said. I thought I was the only one left in the courtroom, until I remembered. I turned and looked at the empty benches in the gallery.

You guys can go home now. You've seen it; the show's over. Hey, don't give me those looks, you knew coming in today the case was fixed, so don't give me the evil eye. I told you what was going to happen and it did. If you're pissed off, then piss on the Honorable Judge Phil Greco, he's the one who acquitted Baby Ray, not me.

This isn't some television cop show or movie. What you saw today is the real deal. I know, for those of you who have never been in a courtroom, maybe you were thinking it was going to miraculously have a happy ending for Terri. Someone was going to come forward with new evidence that would convict Ray Jr. Well, I am sorry to rain on your parade, but this is justice Outfit style. They pour the juice, and their friends' thirsts are quenched.

Alright, you guys, get out of here, you'll be late getting home and I don't want you to miss your bus or train. I'm leaving. I know you're disgusted with what you saw in the courtroom today, but in Chicago, you always gotta pack the juice wherever you go. You never know when you're going to have to fill someone's glass with it.

I walked out of the Cook County Criminal Court Building, 34th and Nowels, like I would so many times in my life, as I would see case after case in which an Outfit guy wound up having supper at home, not in the Cook County Jail. When it was an Outfit case, I would watch the Outfit pull out a block of ice, pour a little juice on it, put it on top of the case, and all the charges melted away. Once again, the lawyer firm of hear no evil, see no evil, speak no evil won another case and made sure the Outfit boys were home chewing on some pasta drowning in sauce, watching themselves on the 6 P.M., news walking out of court a free man. They chewed up the pasta like they chewed up the legal system.

"There's a big difference between the justice you're supposed to get and the justice you actually get, Bobby," Jimmy said. "Justice sits in the middle of a teeter-totter with the nobodies sitting on one side and the somebodies sitting on the other side," he said.

"The nobodies, nobody cares about them. They might not have enough money to hire a good lawyer, so they are given a public defender, who might have a ton of other cases they are handling. They don't have the resources to defend the nobody. They can't hire an investigator to check things out, so that nobody gets what he pays for, which amounts to nothing," Jimmy said.

"The somebodies, they'll have the money to not only hire a good lawyer, but one who's got the juice. Especially the somebodies who have a case at 34th and Nowels, then their justice sure as hell won't be the same as the nobodies, as the juice will be the game changer," Jimmy said. "The nobody can only look at the somebody, shake his head, sigh, and say to himself, 'Where is the justice?'

"Bobby, I know that's not what they teach in school. They teach about justice being blind, being fair to all," Jimmy said. "But, in Real World 101, justice gets tilted every day. It ain't blind. Justice is pushed to the somebody with juice who can throw a couple of bucks into a judge's pocket. The judge takes care of the somebody; the somebody takes care of the judge. Juice asks justice to dance, and once that happens, Bobby, the band never changes the tune. Juice and justice just keep on dancing the same old song," Jimmy said. "Juice makes that teeter-totter slippery, and pretty soon justice starts sliding toward the somebodies. Depending on the amount of the juice, the teeter-totter board tilted toward the somebodies becomes excessively sticky, and justice and the somebodies become bonded so tightly together that they never can be pried apart. Once the juice saturates justice, juice never has to worry about how justice will decide the fate of someone. Fate is the easy part of justice's job. The hard part is making God believe so."

"The somebodies fall once in a while," I said.

"Sure, sure they do, but that's when the Feds go after them. When that happens, it becomes a whole different game with different rules," Jimmy said. "Then justice puts on a mask of self-righteousness with the Feds lurking behind. The Feds become the guys in white hats who are going to ride into Dodge and clean up the varmints," he said. "Look, we got Feds on the payroll, so they get some dirt under their fingernails. It's just the judges being appointed for life feel more secure," Jimmy said.

"So, the Fed judges can put the hammer down on a somebody if they want, because you're stuck with them for life," I said.

"Can a Fed judge be reached? Yeah, just like anyone else, but they've got to be more discreet than a judge at 34th and Nowels," Jimmy said. "Once a Fed judge becomes our friend, he loses his legal virginity. His independence is blown into Lake Michigan. We bought him, and we own him," Jimmy said.

As it turned out, the Outfit didn't have much success at winning friends and influencing people among Fed judges. After being convicted of whatever charge or charges by the Feds, a lot of the boys were put in the federal penal system. The Fed judges didn't do the Outfit any favors when they became incarcerated. The federal prison cells had no juice policy, and the boys mouth sure got dry fast.

In Chicago, when you invite people over to your house for a barbecue, just make sure when you're cooking justice to dap a little bit of juice over the justice. The meal will not only taste yummy, it'll keep you out of jail.

Jason Laskowski, Terri's former partner, retired after 31 years of service, mostly as a detective assigned to the burglary unit. He was awarded the

Chicago Police Department Medal of Valor, which is the highest award in the department that an officer can receive for an act of heroism.

There had been a rash of commercial burglaries on the Near North Side. Laskowski and his partner Thomas Fainen observed some lights on in an appliance store one evening after the store was closed and decided to see what was going on inside the store. When they came to the front door, they noticed the window pane above the lock was broken. They entered the store, guns drawn, and on more than one occasion announced they were the police, telling whoever was in the store to come out with their hands raised over their heads.

They cautiously walked down the aisles, Fainen slightly ahead of Laskowski. Near the aisle for electrical supplies, the two perpetrators, who had been hiding in the aisle, saw the officers and opened fire at them. Fainen was hit in the neck, face, and head and died instantly. Laskowski was shot in the right shoulder, but returned fire, killing one perpetrator and severely wounding the other. Laskowski called for help on his radio while holding the wounded perpetrator at bay, pointing his gun at him until backup officers arrived.

Laskowski kept looking back over his shoulder at Fainen. "Tommy, Tommy, you okay?" he called out several times. *Please, Tommy...please, Tommy, answer me,* Laskowski said to himself. There was never going to be a response from Fainen. He was now another Chicago cop who died in the line of duty doing a job not many of us could do. Detective Thomas Fainen—a 14-year veteran, married with three children—would now be transported by the angels to that special resting place in heaven where the honorable and brave Chicago police officers, who run to danger while others run away, and give their lives, too, paying the ultimate price for trying to make Chicago a safer place by serving and protecting every day, can now be at rest, lying in a state of tranquility.

The difference between the Chicago cops on the Outfit's payroll and the rest of the Chicago Police Department officers is very simple. One group put their dignity up for sale and the other group never did.

The second perpetrator shot by Laskowski was permanently paralyzed from the waist down, as his spinal cord was damaged from the shooting. He was convicted four years later of first-degree murder in the killing of Detective Fainen and sentenced to life with no chance of parole by Circuit Court Judge John "Maximum John" Gliebarski. Gliebarski, along with Judge Sol "Put 'Em Away" Pearlstein, were two tough sentencing judges the Outfit always tried to avoid.

Laskowski recovered from his shoulder wound, received the Medal of Valor, and continued to be a fine, dedicated officer during his years of service.

Alex, Terri's husband, retired after 20 years of service as a neighborhood community relations officer in the 13th district. He worked as a police liaison with community groups, local businesses, schools, and citizens of the 13th district.

David Chopak, the prosecutor, left the Cook County State's Attorney's office to become a law partner with...surprise, surprise...Tommy Calzone. Tommy always had a knack for buying off the opposition.

Raymond Iaculle Jr. continued developing his skills as a juice loan collector for his father Ray Sr. When Ray Sr. died from kidney failure, Ray Jr. took over the family business, and brought his son Raymond Iaculle III into the life.

Ray Jr., in the 1990s, was convicted by the Feds on racketeering charges, and Ray III pled guilty to drug trafficking charges. Ray Jr. was sentenced to 15 years, and Ray III received a nine year sentence. Ray Jr., who put himself in the jackpot when he assaulted Terri McSherry, was able to get out of the jackpot by climbing down a slippery ladder covered in juice that was being held by the Honorable Phil Greco. With the Feds, Ray Jr. never got out of the jackpot.

Rising through the ranks to become a lieutenant, Terri McSherry retired after 30 years of service. As Terri patrolled the streets of Chicago, she would drive slowly, going block by block, checking every corner looking for the justice she never got.

Judge Phil Greco was a Cook County Circuit Court judge for 25 years until he retired. He and his wife moved to Clearwater, Florida, where he had purchased a two-bedroom condominium with cash.

Often when moving from one residence to the next, we have accumulated things that we look at and decide we no longer need and throw them out. Greco was cleaning out a file cabinet in his basement and came across things that he no longer needed and decided they should be thrown out, as he wasn't going to need them in Clearwater.

White envelopes and rubber bands were not going to Florida. He put them in a garbage bag and started humming *God Bless America*, the song that we all learn as children. Greco's version was "God Bless the Outfit," because without, them, he might have achieved the unthinkable—a backbone. Greco, who would be receiving a judicial pension from Cook County along with his Park District pension, was glad to put his previous life in the garbage bag. The Honorable Judge Phil Greco had a very dishonorable judicial career.

The one common denominator that all mob families had, no matter if they were located in Chicago, New York, New Jersey, Philly, Boston, Detroit, Buffalo, or Cleveland, etc., etc. was the control of the local unions in the area.

Mob controlled unions provided the crime families with money and jobs. The money came from what the labor bosses could siphon from the membership dues and from overcharging contractors on the actual number of hours worked on the job by a union member. The extra hours were called 'phantom' hours. The time sheets would show union employees working more hours than they actually did.

The money from the phantom hours would be skimmed. Some of it would go to the mob bosses, while some of it would go to the pockets of the union bosses. Every two weeks, mob bosses would get their payoff from the union bosses. Conservatively guys like Dean Dragonetti and Tony Galante raked in $60,000-$70,000 a month just on the union payoffs. The number could be even higher, considering Chicago is a big union city with lots of unions to be controlled.

I went many, many times with Jimmy as he collected money from the union honchos for Dean and Tony. The amounts were set amounts, so there was no discussion about what would be paid. Twice a month, Jimmy would go to the designated unions to get the rubber-banded white envelopes, which were bulging with the cash inside them. The labor bosses were a mixed bag of guys. Some were related Outfit guys while others acted like they were related to Outfit guys. They always treated me nice, always offering me a piece of chocolate or knowing I was a Cubs fan, getting me tickets to a ballgame. Thinking back, I guess they had no choice; they certainly did not want to get on Jimmy's bad side by not treating me square. No one wanted to be an ex-union boss.

The jobs provided by the unions put food on the table and paid the bills for the rank and file Outfit boys. When union workers had to be hired for various construction jobs, Outfit guys were hired first, then other union employees were hired, as needed. I should say the payrolls of the construction or demolition companies, thus, became padded with Outfit guys. The hard-working legit union worker had to work twice as hard on the jobsite, because a no-show Outfit worker never showed up to work. The legit union worker, without knowing it, was working for himself and the ghost workers.

The Outfit guys got full paychecks and, in some cases, got some credited overtime. I guess by staying an extra hour at the mistresses place during their supposed work time, they were credited with an hour of overtime. I'm surprised Outfit guys didn't put in for mileage to and from her place.

Besides getting whatever the union prevailing wage was at that time, the Outfit guys got medical insurance for themselves and their families. As with other chicanery committed by the Outfit, someone else picked up their tab. The contractor had to pay bloated payrolls of Outfit guys, which increased the cost of doing the job. Whenever a construction job in Chicago was bid on, either for the private sector or for the city, county, or state, all the bidding companies knew they would have to build the price the Outfit costs into the job.

It's just the way business was done in Chicago, because you did not want the Outfit to come looking for you. I'll tell you right now, the boys are not going to offer you milk and cookies when they see you. They will be serving you some hurt and pain, from the top of your head to the bottom of your toes, and these will be the leftovers that stay in your body for a very long time.

In Chicago, there is the political patronage used by the politicians to hire people, and then there is the union patronage used to hire Outfit guys and make everyone one nice, happy family.

When the Outfit gets something for nothing, they are so overcome with joy and contentment that they will do anything for you. Try and make them break a sweat or even show up to work, and the sky becomes pitch black; booming thunder can be heard throughout the work area. The question is how far away are the baseball bats that will be used to represent their point of view on your body. I could hear the crashing sound of the baseball bats getting louder and louder. So play nice, children, or else daddy's going to put a big pain all over your body and still collect his check.

The three strongest unions in Chicago that had the deepest ties to the Outfit were run by the three Doms. Dominick "Big Dom" Caponera was the president of the Operating Engineers Teamster Local 650, and Dominick "Little Dom" Scavanello was the president of the Electrical Workers Teamster Local 834. The most powerful of the three was run by Dominick "The Quiet Dom" Quintoni. Quintoni was the president of the Laborer's Union Local 929. Every construction related type of work in Chicago and the suburbs needed laborers. So what I'm telling you, is that without the laborers, there would be no major construction work done anywhere.

Quintoni was a close ally of Jimmy's, so the juice was rather quick between the Outfit and Local 929. Quintoni, because of the large union membership, provided a large amount of the money to the Outfit higher-ups and jobs to the Outfit rank-and-file. A certain amount of money was skimmed off the dues that the union members had automatically taken out of every paycheck. Other money came from the 4% street tax the Outfit imposed on construction jobs. This form of an insurance policy provided by the Outfit assured a construction company there would be no problems concerning the job. Since the Outfit was the only one who could cause a problem, in Outfit logic, they were ensuring a company that the Outfit would protect the company from the Outfit. I'm sure that the wizards of Wall Street would consider this type of an investment AAA rated.

I remember being a little fuzzy on the street tax concept until Joseph "Crazy Joey" Letolle explained it to me. "Bobby, think of a street tax like the Feds watching the Feds," Letolle said.

Letolle was an Outfit guy who was part of a union goon squad. They were the muscle who would explain physically to your body how the street tax worked in case you had any questions. A punch in the ribs sure helped to improve your knowledge about why the street tax was such an important business tool. Who better than Letolle could school me on such a wonderful investment?

"Here, Bobby, I'll break it down for you," he said. "It's dinnertime; you're going to stuff your face. You look at the food on the plate and you put some of it on your fork. You look at it again. You bring the fork full of food up to your lips, open your mouth, swallow the food, and from that point it's up to the stomach to watch out for the food," Letolle said. "See, Bobby, the whole time you have been eyeballing the food, protecting it, watching out for it, making sure no one tries to swipe a meatball off the plate, because if someone does try to grab a meatball, it'll be fuck them. You know what I mean," Letolle said.

"So a street tax is really about protecting a meatball," I said.

"Exactly," Letolle said.

For the rest of my life I looked at a meatball in a new vein. A meatball, upon my contact with it, would be treated with the utmost respect and held as one of the crown jewels in our society. From now on, it would be by appointment only, strictly at the convenience of the meatball that two dear friends will reflect on life's philosophical inner workings together before the meatball glided into my stomach at Panto's Restaurant. There are certain Outfit nicknames that precisely fit the person, as evidenced by Mr. Letolle.

There were many times I went with Jimmy as he collected the street tax from construction companies. In the case of Local 929, most of the time Quintoni would send out Arnold "Arnie Boy" Compabellini who was the B. A. (Business Agent) for Local 929 to collect the street tax for the Outfit. Sometimes Quintoni would visit a job site and personally collect the money. Compabellini was Quintoni's cousin, so Quintoni entrusted him with this responsibility, feeling confident that Compabellini, being a blood relative, could be trusted to keep Quintoni from being caught.

Each month Compabellini would visit the job sites where Local 929 had laborers working and pick up the money that was due. The payments were based on the number of months in the contract that it would take to complete the job. If the contract called for a completion time of 24 months, then the 4%, which was figured on the gross amount of the contractors who were being paid, would be spread out over the 24 months. Most of the construction work was for state, county, and city so the awarded amount of the contract was public record, and everyone knew what the contractors were being paid.

A construction job that was not for a governmental body required a little more research. Since basically the same contractors were used for government and non-government jobs, the information was not that difficult to obtain. The Outfit sales force was trained in using the direct approach. If they ran into a bulky construction company executive who was not as forthcoming with the gross dollar amount of a private industry job, they brought along an approved Outfit sales piece of equipment. The street tax collector would take out brass knuckles from his coat pocket.

"Sir," he would say, "I'm asking the dollar amount of your job for my friend here, and he's the type of friend with a very short temper. So, maybe, I didn't hear you; could you repeat the dollar amount again so my friend can hear you, too?" the street collector said, while starting to put his fingers through the brass knuckles. The company executive, who thought he was going to take a stand against the Outfit, gave up the idea as he realized the company dental insurance plan was not going to pay for the dental work he was going to need. He meekly told the tax collector what the dollar amount was going to be for the work done. The tax collector, while putting the brass knuckles back in his pocket, told the shaken executive, "My friend says it's always nice to make a new friend, especially when you can live to enjoy your new best friend."

Besides the street tax money, Local 929 would load up their payroll with Outfit guys who, with the exception of some who actually showed up during the hours they were supposed to be working at a job site, were off working on Outfit business. These guys were ghost payrollers. To make matters worse, these guys bragged about being no-shows, as if it were a work habit you wanted your kids to emulate.

I remember one laborer by the name of Alfred Mazaforti who was supposed to be sweeping the downtown streets in Chicago as an employee of the City's Department of Public Projects. His job was to manually sweep a designated area downtown.

Mazaforti was an associate member of the Outfit, along with being a member of Local 929. One Tuesday morning when Mazaforti was supposed to be working his city job, he was working another job. He went into a Hobart, Indiana, jewelry store, robbed the store of some of its contents, and brutally pistol whipped the clerk along the way.

Following an investigation by the Hobart Police Department, Mazaforti was arrested and charged with crimes connected to the case. The investigation found out about his employment with the City of Chicago, and the district attorney in Hobart checked with the city about Mazaforti's employment for the day in question, which was the day of the jewelry heist. The city checked the time sheet for the week, which was signed by Mazaforti and his supervisor Jeff Alscott, and saw for that Tuesday Mazaforti signed in the hours he worked as 7 A.M. to 4 P.M. Mazaforti's regular hours were 7 A.M. to 3 P.M., but I guess the streets must have had a lot of debris, because in the overtime column, he wrote one hour of overtime.

Such a hard-working, dedicated employee should calm the anxieties of the Chicago taxpayers who might be wondering if their tax dollars are being spent wisely on the services they're supposed to get.

Fear not, my financial fanatics, here is a city employee who somehow works two jobs a day, one legal, one illegal, and, yet, he managed to drag out his soul with every ounce of moral clarity one could muster under these extreme mental hard work hardships, gasping for every breath of air, one hour of overtime,. Be proud taxpayer warrior nation, as your role model stands tall in your eyes.

Put your right hand over your heart and along with me say God Bless the Outfit. We are indebted to you for your providing us taxpayers with a public employee who truly defines the Chicago style.

You would expect that Jeff Alscott, the supervisor who signed Mazaforti's timesheet would be fired for approving a phony, incorrect timesheet. However, in Chicago where juice rules, this is not the case. In Chicago, everyone knows someone, and if they don't, they better find that someone.

Alscott was put on administrative leave by the city for 29 days with pay. There are several reasons why this happened, but one reason covers all of them, his cousin Mike Farley is a Democratic State Representative.

When Alexander Graham Bell invented the telephone, his first customers were Chicago politicians. You see, a phone call is always made when someone is in trouble to get them out of trouble, and could never have been made without Mr. Bell's invention. After hearing from Cousin Jeff who needed his help, Farley called Mayoral Assistant Karen McViceroy. Farley told McViceroy that the revenue-sharing bill pertaining to Chicago was coming up for a vote in the Illinois House. Farley said it would be a close vote, so if the mayor wanted his vote, Cousin Jeff had to be taken care of. One thing about Illinois politicians, their votes could be bought at wholesale rather than retail.

I always felt if Illinois politicians were put on commission, Illinois taxpayers would get better accountability. I know that and fifty cents will get me on the bus. Well, a fella can dream can't he?

Cousin Jeff was taken care of, and Farley voted for the bill. After coming off the 29-day leave, part of which time Alscott spent sunning himself on the Florida beach and enjoying a family vacation with his paid leave, he thought about his wonderful city job. He was given a transfer to the Department of Street Management with a new title, but no supervision. The city has a penchant, at times, to promote the bad employee over the good employee. Alscott's new title paid $5,000 more than his old title.

Alscott was now in his fifteenth year of service with the city and was eligible for a 5% longevity raise. His new supervisor had Alscott's personnel file pulled so he could see if there was any paperwork in the file that would be a reason for Alscott not to get his longevity raise. There was no paperwork in the file showing his 29-day paid leave. The file included an excellent rating from a previous supervisor, but no mention at all of the leave. Alscott's file had been taken care of Chicago style. The supervisor, with no reason not to, approved the pay raise for Alscott.

On some hot summer day while working on your tan at one of the Chicago's beaches, if a bottle with papers folded inside of it washes up to the sand from Lake Michigan, open the bottle with extreme caution. The lost papers inside of the wet bottle will be very sticky with juice.

Mazaforti, following a phone call from Quintoni to Alderman Charles Balsamo who called the Mayor's office, was suspended with pay pending the legal outcome of his trial in Indiana. For the next 18 months Mazaforti, who was out on bond, got paid from the city of Chicago for not working.

Mazaforti was convicted of armed robbery and felonious assault and was sentenced to 12 years in a maximum state prison in Indiana. The city fired Mazaforti, and now there was a job opening to be filled for a manual street sweeper. Since the title was a union title, the city had a list of people who were graded qualified to be on the list. The city began to call in the people who were on the list for an interview.

The city finally chose their candidate for the job, but when it was learned he was not on the list, Quintoni called Balsamo, who had sent the candidate in for the interview based on Quintoni's recommendation to get the candidate on the list. Basamo called the Department of Personnel and spoke with a deputy, and the candidate was put on the list.

The candidate was hired and told when to report to work.

You don't have to scratch your heads trying to rack your brain about this one. You know the candidate. Sean Mazaforti, the son of one Alfred Mazaforti, who happened to be Edward "Bucky" DeVollo's driver, was deemed the most qualified candidate by the city. DeVollo had a gambling and loan-sharking operation in the Near Southwest suburbs. Again, listen to the choir, there is no such thing as juice. It doesn't exist. Sean got the position on, what's the word, merit—Outfit merit.

Joe Borganna, who owned J & H (for Joe and his wife Harriet) Construction Company was a guy from the neighborhood. His father, Joe, who everyone called Big Joe, drove a United Parcel Service truck for a living. He instilled a strong work ethic in his son, and raised him to believe that by working hard, loving your family, and being a good Catholic, you would have a fulfilling life.

Every Sunday morning, at 10 A.M., Big Joe and his son Joe would be at Mass in Our Lady of Perpetual Worship, listening to the sermon of Father

Tom, and praying to the Almighty for his wisdom and guidance. Big Joe's wife, Lucy, died shortly after giving birth to Joe from complications due to the birth. Big Joe never remarried, choosing to raise Joe as a single parent. There was no greater love for Big Joe than his son. Joe was his world.

When Big Joe went to work, his sister Robin came over and took care of Joe. Big Joe was the type of guy who had to be really, really sick to miss work. He believed that by working hard and playing by the rules, God would reward you. By working as hard as he did, Big Joe felt his reward was Joe.

Joe was an altar boy at Our Lady of Perpetual Worship, and at that point in his life had strong ties to the Catholic Church. Joe tried his very best to be a good practicing Catholic. He followed and maintained good principles of the Catholic Church in his daily life. Joe had a Catholic education starting in elementary school and then on to St. Leonard's, where he attended high school. Joe was the second baseman on the school's baseball team.

When Joe was 16 years old, he went to a dance at the Fieldhouse in Kelton Park. The Fieldhouse was located in Kelton Park and was part of the Chicago Park District, and Joe grew up playing sports inside the Fieldhouse's gymnasium. During the summer months, he and his friends played baseball on the diamonds at Kelton Park. He felt very comfortable in his surroundings and was looking forward to going to the dance.

It was at the dance he met Harriet Taublomenti, a 15-year-old high school student at Queen of All Mary, who also lived in the neighborhood. Joe saw her, liked what he saw, and went over to her. He asked her to dance, and she said 'yes.' From that evening forward, they were boyfriend and girlfriend. "Bobby, I just knew she was the one for me. Those big, beautiful brown deep set eyes were just too good to give up. Yep, I knew she was the one," Joe told me years later.

Harriet liked Joe's strong character, and the tenderness and respect he gave her. "Bobby, right from our first date, Joe treated me like a queen. He not only respected me, but he had such wonderful manners for such a young guy. Yeah, I knew he was the guy for me," Harriet told me years later. She wasn't going to let Joe slip away, as Joe's type don't come around too often.

Following graduation from St. Leonard's, Joe went to Barton Trade School to learn to become a carpenter. After graduating, he began serving his apprenticeship as a carpenter. He worked with experienced carpenters on different types of jobs as he began to develop his skills.

Joe was a clean-cut, nice Italian guy, the type a girl can't wait to bring home to her mama to get the stamp of approval. Harriet was a cute, kind, generous, clean-cut, nice Italian girl, who any family would love to have as their daughter-in-law.

Joe and Harriett came out of the same mold. So, after Joe finished his apprenticeship and was working as a full-fledged carpenter, he and Harriet got engaged to be married. Everyone in the neighborhood who knew them had the 'I knew it' look on their faces and congratulated the wonderful couple.

In raising Joe, Big Joe told him to stay away from some of these future Outfit guys that lived in the neighborhood. "If you play with dirt, you get dirty," he would tell his son. "Be a good Catholic, follow the teachings of the faith, which has no place for the criminals," Big Joe would say. While a couple of guys, who later wound up in the Outfit attended St. Leonard's, Joe, other than saying hi in the hallways of the school, did not engage himself with them.

Since Joe kept his distance from those future criminals, he never knew anything about being in the life.

By the time he was 30 years old, Joe decided he wanted to start his own construction company. He had three daughters ages six, four, and two, so there were a lot of mouths to feed and the pressure of starting a new business meant financial uncertainty in the Borganna household.

Joe talked with Harriet, and told her being a carpenter was okay, but his dream was that he really wanted to own his own construction company. He wanted her approval, as Joe Borganna loved his wife and family, and would not make a move without Harriet's okay. While Joe's love for Harriet was deep, his respect for her was immense.

"Baby, to chase a dream you have to have a dream, and if this is really what you want in life, then start chasing it," Harriet said, then she kissed him on his lips. A wide broad smile rose from Joe's chin up to his forehead. He had gotten what he wanted—Harriet's backing—and now he was ready to lace up the athletic shoes and chase a dream.

While working as a carpenter, Joe had built up an excellent reputation as a worker with his bosses. So, when he started to make the rounds of various companies to begin to try and get business for his company, the results were positive. Joe formed a small construction company with a crew of guys he knew, so this way he had a crew in place, ready to go to work immediately on the job site.

Joe obtained small jobs that while they didn't pay a lot of money, gave him the opportunity to show the kind of work his company was able to do. He promised the companies that if they were not happy with his work, he would redo his work for free to satisfy their needs. It was a bold promise to make, as Joe had no idea if his crew would go along and redo a job and not get paid for the time.

Fortunately, Joe did not have any unhappy customers. He made sure the crew understood that the quality of the work was the signature of the company. It was the main priority on the job. The quality of the work was Joe's selling point as he could have potential customers go see his previous jobs and, thus, his work was his sales force. He monitored the crews' work very closely and when he was away from the job site to try and get new business, he made sure his foreman Tony stayed on top of all the work-related matters. "Tony, once you lose track of the details, you're going to lose business," Joe would say to him. "When you are starting a new business, your reputation for performing the job correctly is critical if you want to stay in business."

While the crew members were not in the union in the beginning, Joe paid them the prevailing wage a union member would get paid. Since jobs were so small, there was no pressure from the Laborer's Union Local 929 to hire union members. During the next few years, as the jobs got bigger, Joe had to hire from Local 929. His current crew decided to unionize, and they joined Local 929. Joe knew by having to hire guys from Local 929, they would influence his crew to join Local 929. Since he was paying the prevailing wage, Joe was not cheating anyone out of money, and he understood the workers wanted other benefits that the union could provide. There were no hard feelings on Joe's part when the crew unionized.

Up to this point, all of Joe's jobs were for private companies. He had never done any government work. There was a big sewer replacement job coming up for bid in the city of Chicago. The job was going to be for three miles of sewer replacement on the South Side, 83rd St. to 107th St. on Reno Avenue. The job was budgeted for $6 million.

Joe decided to bid on the job. His company had done small sewer replacement jobs for private companies on their own property. He devoted a lot of time in the evenings and weekends to filling out the necessary forms the city required for the job and prepared his proposal in the hope of winning the bid. He checked and double checked his calculations to make sure they were correct. With the city, all the *I*s had to be dotted and *T*s crossed. Since Joe did not have juice with a politician, there was no room for mistakes. Jobs like these in Chicago are generally awarded to the politically connected companies. A game is never played on the drawing board; it's played on the field, and you never know what can happen.

Joe made sure he had the proper insurance bond required by the city ready to submit with all of his other paperwork. The day finally came for Joe to submit his bid package to the City for the sewer replacement job.

"Good luck, and here's a kiss to help you," Harriet said, as she kissed Joe on the cheek just before he left for the bid opening at City Hall.

"Thanks, Hon," he said.

While driving downtown to City Hall, Joe hoped his submitted bid would win the job, as this project could give him more capital in his business to pursue more governmental jobs that were available.

There were several rows of chairs facing an elevated platform area in the City's Department of Purchasing bid room where the scheduled bids not only for the sewer job, but other related city work would be read. Joe sat down after turning in his big package to a clerk. While he didn't know any of the other bidders personally, he recognized Billy DeFamilia of the DeFamilia Construction Company. Billy owned the company, and DeFamilia did a lot of city work.

At 11 A.M., no more bids could be accepted and a Contract Forms Specialist started to read the bids. There were seven companies who bid on the sewer work. DeFamilia was the low bidder followed by J & H and Elliot Construction. The top three low bidders were asked to remain in the bid room, and everyone else left.

The three low bidders were told their bids would be reviewed and evaluated and written notification would be sent to each company advising the status of their bid.

Joe wondered, how did DeFamilia always seem to win so many construction bids from the city? What Joe didn't know was Billy's father, Donald "Donnie Jacks" DeFamilia, who was listed as a company director, was an Outfit fence, who particularly fenced stolen jewelry, but also high-end items stolen by the Outfit. So, DeFamilia had the political juice with our aldermanic friends, especially Aldermen Cal Lynch and Alphonse Lastore.

DeFamilia greased them with money and they, in turn, greased the bid process in DeFamilia's favor. All Billy DeFamilia had to do was lowball his bids and turn in his bid package and his friends would take care the rest. Whenever there was a construction bid opening that DeFamilia bid on, Billy would show up and give that phony surprised look of 'gosh, I really won as the low bidder?' He had the technique down to a science.

Joe drove home and gave Harriet the bad news that he wasn't the low bidder. He was the second lowest bidder behind DeFamilia who would probably get the job.

"Hon, you tried your best," she said, as she put her right arm around his shoulder. "Maybe next time."

"Yeah, maybe next time," he said dejectedly.

Joe always tried to play by the rules he learned from Big Joe, but these rules conflicted with Outfit rules played by DeFamilia. The Outfit rules started and ended with we win every time, you lose every time. Got it? Nearly four months later, Joe and Harriet were watching the 10:00 P.M. news when the lead story came on. Donald DeFamilia and his son Billy were indicted by the Feds for tax evasion and money laundering pertaining to the DeFamilia Construction Company.

Both father and son were shown in handcuffs doing the perp walk into the Federal Building. Joe looked at Harriett, and Harriett looked at Joe, both blurting out the same thing at same time, "We won."

A week later, the City sent out a letter to J & H Construction Company, telling them DeFamilia had been disqualified from the sewer job and J & H, being the second lowest bidder, would get the job. Joe called Harriet with the good news. Joe then bowed his head down, saying a prayer to the Almighty and thanking him for the blessing he bestowed on him.

Within the next few months J & H started working on the sewer project. Joe called Local 929 as, due to the size of the job, he would need to hire more laborers.

At the end of each day of the job, Joe came home happy as his company was growing, and this, in turn, would provide more security for his family. He wanted Harriet and the children to reap the benefits of his success. Whatever would make Harriet and the children happy, would make Joe happy. His family meant more to him than anything he could ever attain in the business world. His world was filled with his family. Maybe this would be the time when good Joe beats the bad Outfit. Then, maybe not.

Several weeks into the job, a black Buick pulled up and parked near the job site on 83rd St. and Reno Avenue. A man got out of the car. He asked one of the workers where was Joseph Borganna, and the worker pointed Joe out to the man. The man walked over to Joe and introduced himself.

"Mr. Joseph Borganna, I'm Dominick Quintoni, president of the Laborer's Union Local 929. How are you today?" Quintoni said.

"Fine, sir," Joseph answered.

"Mr. Joseph Borganna, I see you have a big sewer job," Quintoni said, his head looking around the job site.

"Yes, yes, I do," Joe said.

"Well, Mr. Joseph Borganna, have you thought about making…say a 4% donation, based on the gross amount of $6 million, which is what your contract is for, to the union to make sure everything runs smoothly on the job site? I mean, you never know what can happen on a job; all sorts of things. I mean, are you sure you even have enough laborers on the job?" Quintoni asked.

"What is this, some kind of a shakedown?" Joe angrily said.

"Why, Mr. Joseph Borganna, of course not, I wouldn't even think of such a thing. It's just that we would always be available to help you if a problem occurred. That's all I'm saying," Quintoni said.

"Sounds like a shake down to me," Joe said.

"No, no, Mr. Joseph Borganna. All it would be is a strictly voluntary donation on your part. It's your decision. If you choose not to make the voluntary donation, there will be no hard feelings. Local 929 will be there for you regardless," Quintoni said.

"Still sounds like a shakedown to me," Joe disgustedly said.

"Well, Mr. Joseph Borganna, why don't you think it over and I'll come back a week from today. Okay?" Quintoni said.

"It'll still be a shakedown next week too, but okay. I'll think about it," Joe said.

"Good, Mr. Joseph Borganna. I'll stop by next week to see you," Quintoni said.

Quintoni went back to his car, but instead of driving right away, he drove up to Joe and rolled down his car window. "Harriet is a lovely woman, and your kids are precious," Quintoni said to Joe, as he then rolled up his window and sped off. It was the old Outfit zinger used by Quintoni. Throw in the family as bait and the undecided become the decided.

Joe looked at the car and instinctively started to run after it, but stopped after few steps, realizing the car was long gone.

"Boss, boss, you okay?" Tony, the crew's foreman said as he ran up to Joe.

"Tony, come in my office," Joe said. Joe had a small trailer set up as an office on the job site. As he and Tony walked into the trailer, they begin to talk.

"That guy, the president of Local 929 is trying to shake me down for 4% of the gross amount of the contract."

"Four percent is a pretty penny," Tony said, whistling.

"Then, on top of that, he mentions my wife and kids," Joe said to Tony. Joe's eyes were blazing with smoking hot intensity. He wanted to get his hands on Quintoni, and he wanted to do it right now.

Tony, at this point, let Joe talk; he didn't say anything back, yet.

"That motherfucking bastard has the gall to threaten my family," Joe said with his right finger jabbing into his chest. "I'll kill the son of a bitch. I swear, Tony, I'll do it," said Joe. "No one, and I mean no one, is going to use my family as leverage against me. No fucking way is that going to happen. Jesus Christ, who the hell does he think he is, Tony?" Joe said. "His penis is going to be hanging on a lamppost on Reno Avenue, I swear to God, Tony. I'll do it if he threatens my family," Joe said.

"Is he coming back?" Tony asked.

"Yeah, he said next week he's going to stop by," Joe said, as he started to control his red hot motions.

"Okay, boss, calm down. You'll think of something," Tony said.

"Yeah, yeah, I know, but when he started talking about Harriet and the kids," Joe's eyes started to get moist around the eyeballs, and he took a hard swallow in his throat.

Tony took Joe's right arm and held it with his right hand. "It's okay, boss. It's okay. Everything will work out. Don't let this get to you," Tony said.

"Thanks, Tony," Joe said as Tony released hold of Joe's arm.

Joe took out his handkerchief and began dabbing his eyes, keeping the moisture from becoming a waterfall.

"I'm going back to the crew. Don't worry, boss, my lips are sealed on this one. No one's going to know about this, at least not from me," Tony said.

"Okay, yeah, keep an eye on those guys and thanks again for hearing me out," Joe said.

While still at work, Joe could not stop thinking about Quintoni. The thought of having to pay a street tax kept smacking in his brain between thoughts about Harriet and the children.

At home that night after dinner, Joe sat down with Harriett after she had the children go play in their rooms so they would not hear the conversation in the front room of their house. He told her about the day's events with Quintoni. It was not an easy conversation for Joe, as Harriet could see the hurt hanging all over Joe's face. She took both of his hands and held them with hers as he spoke.

"I just don't know what to do," he said, as he completed the day's story about Quintoni.

"Joe, look, somehow, someway you are going to get through this. We are a family, and the kids and I are 100% in your corner," Harriet said.

"It's just when he talked about you and the kids, it got to me," Joe said. Harriet could feel the tightness in Joe hands. Those hands of strength were ready to defend the family.

"Joe, I'm thinking your dad grew up with Jimmy Williams, didn't he?" Harriet asked.

"Yeah, so what?" Joe said.

"There's always these stories in the neighborhood that Jimmy Williams is connected, you know, involved with the Mafia," Harriet said. "I don't know if these stories are true, but he knows you. Maybe you can talk to him. I don't know, what do you think?" she said.

Joe paused for a second and didn't respond right away. "Yeah, my dad would tell me how he and Jimmy growing up would knock heads against each other playing softball or touch football on the schoolyard by Reeves Elementary School, which they both went to," Joe said. "Yeah, I know Jimmy, of course, through my dad," he said. "You're right, I think my dad has Jimmy's phone number. I'll call my dad," Joe said.

"Joe, why don't you go see your dad in person, tell him what's going on, or else he's going to start worrying about you," Harriet said. "With these stories floating around about Jimmy's connections, you don't want your dad's mind playing tricks on him, making him think you're going to join the Mafia or something," Harriet said.

"You're right, babe. I'll go see him," Joe said. "We know who the smart one in the family is," Joe said with a smile on his face as he looked at Harriett. "You're the brains and I'm the brawn," Joe said as he left. He then kissed her on the lips, holding the kiss for a few seconds with her. The kiss was a good kiss—light, but firm…direct, but tender…appealing, but fluffy around the corners. From the kiss, Harriet knew Joe was being Joe, and he was going to be okay.

Joe went to see his father the next evening after having dinner with his family. He told Big Joe about Quintoni's conversation with him, and how he thought by talking to Jimmy Williams he could get some guidance on what to do. With all these rumors about Jimmy being with the Outfit, Joe told his father maybe Jimmy knows of something to get Quintoni off of his back.

Big Joe, as he listened to Joe speak, had that worried look in his eye—the type a father gets when he hears his child has a problem. Big Joe swallowed a little harder when he heard the problem. His hands started to shake a bit, trembling from the fear of the unknown. Joe, seeing this, took Big Joe's hands and held them in his hands, as Harriet did for him.

"Pops, don't worry. Everything will be okay. You'll see," Joe said. Joe looked at Big Joe's hands, the hands that held Joe when he was a child; the hands that would comfort Joe during his youth; the hands that patted him on the back when he did good and scolded him when he did bad; the hands that would teach Joe about love, compassion, and understanding to define Joe's character; the hands that taught Joe to respect a woman, to believe in himself, and to hold the virtues of being a Catholic next to his heart. Big Joe's hands now were tired, but in Joe's time of need, still provided the ageless support a father gives a son. Joe held Big Joe's hands, as he felt the consummate love a father gives a son.

"You're my kid," Big Joe said, as the tears started to form in his left eye.

Joe hugged his father, and kissed him on the side of his head. "Pops, you're my father today, tomorrow, and forever. I love you so much and respect you for everything you've done for me. It's just I need to be held right now. You've always been there for me, and I know if you could fix this, you would definitely do it. Quintoni, I'm sure, is somehow tied to the mob, and maybe Jimmy can help. I'm not saying Jimmy is with the mob; I don't know that, but I've got to find a way to get rid of Quintoni," Joe said.

Big Joe cast his eyes on his son. His son, while a man and not a little boy anymore, was still his son. He hugged Joe back, and said, "We'll put this bastard in his place. You watch and see," then he kissed Joe on his cheek. Big Joe wiped away the tears, went to the bedroom and got his black address book, which had Jimmy's phone number in it.

"Jimmy said if I ever needed something to call him. Well, we need something, so go call him," Big Joe said. Joe wrote the number down on a piece of paper. They both walked to the front door. Big Joe opened the door. Joe said goodbye to his dad and started to walk out.

"Wait a second," Big Joe said, and Joe turned around. Big Joe wrapped his massive arms around Joe. Father and son stood outside in the night air.

"Listen, God," Big Joe said, as he looked upward in the night sky, "we've been good Catholics, and that's got to count for something. I'm telling you, God, no one is going to hurt my kid. Either you stop it or I will. I swear, I will do whatever it takes, but no one is ever going to come between me and my boy, not in this lifetime. Oh yeah, and have a good night, God," Big Joe said.

After Big Joe finished speaking, he dropped his arms from holding Joe, walked into his house, and closed the door. Joe stood outside, looking at his father's house, reflecting on what his father just said to God. Joe then said a prayer and crossed himself. Joe took out his handkerchief and wiped away the liquid that was forming a tear in his right eye. Some people wondered where Joe Borganna got his wonderful love of family. Tonight the answer was revealed.

Joe felt very awkward in calling Jimmy Williams. He really wasn't sure how to express himself, what to say, how to phrase the words to Jimmy. Maybe Jimmy might take what Joe was saying the wrong way and blow up at Joe. Since Joe was not totally sure if Jimmy was part of the Outfit or not, he didn't want to offend him. One wrong word and Joe might be in more trouble than he was potentially in already.

It's just that it was less than a week until Quintoni would come back to the job site to see Joe, so Joe had little time to waste. He made the call the next night.

"Hi, Jimmy, it's Joe Borganna. You know, Big Joe's son," Joe said.

"Hey, how you doing? How's your family?" Jimmy asked.

"I'm fine and so is my family," Joe said.

"What, your old man wants to get another crack at me in a softball game in the schoolyard across from Reeves Elementary School?" Jimmy said jokingly.

"No, no," Joe said with a hearty laugh.

"How's that son of a gun doing? He's feeling okay?" Jimmy asked.

"Dad's fine. He sends his best to you," Joe said. "Jimmy, I...uh...talked with Dad about...uh...what I'm going to tell you, and he thought maybe I should call you. Uh...maybe you can help me, or know someone who can help me," Joe said. Joe was fumbling, tripping, stumbling trying to be extra careful in picking his words in talking to Jimmy.

"Joe, look, there's a reason you called me. I wasn't born yesterday. I hear something is bothering you in your tone of voice. Let's hear it," Jimmy said.

"There's this guy, Dominick Quintoni, president of the Laborer's Union Local 929, who I believe is trying to shake me down for money," Joe said.

"Never heard of him. Go ahead and continue," Jimmy said.

"He's asking for something called a donation of 4% of the gross amount for a sewer contract job I'm doing for the City on Reno Ave.," Joe said. "Quintoni said if I give him the money, there will be no trouble on the job. I'm not sure what this is about, but it sounds like he is shaking me down for money, like I guess protection or something," Joe said.

"Yeah, sounds like it," Jimmy said.

"So, I called for your advice on what to do. Quintoni brought up Harriet and the kids. He didn't threaten them, but I think he was using them as leverage to get the money," Joe said. "Jimmy, no one is going to fu..."

"Joe, it's okay, I got the picture of what's going on. Don't upset yourself," Jimmy said. "Well, look, Joe, how about I come over to your house this Saturday at 2 P.M. to talk about this? I don't know if I'll be of much good, but maybe we can figure out something," Jimmy said.

"Oh, that's great, Jimmy. See you Saturday," Joe said.

Jimmy couldn't tell Joe he not only knew Quintoni, but Quintoni was his ally. If he did that, Joe would figure he and Quintoni were working together against him. It was best to let Joe think Jimmy didn't know Quintoni, and for Jimmy to work an angle so that would help Joe, and keep Quintoni in the dark, so he would never expect Jimmy was even involved in pulling strings from behind the scene.

A false step here, and Joe would put two and two together and know Jimmy's in the Outfit. If that happened, Jimmy had no credibility in Joe's eyes and Joe might do something stupid, like talk to the Feds. Then Quintoni will want to have Joe whacked. Jimmy was not going to let a lot of negatives parade down the block.

Jimmy had too many hard fought softball games with Big Joe to have to look him in the eye if something bad happened to Joe. This would be like a hot apple pie with everyone getting a slice of the pie, and no one knowing who baked the pie. Joe would get his slice like everyone else.

It was a windy, warm Saturday afternoon when Jimmy arrived at Joe Borganna's house for their meeting. "Hi, Jimmy," Joe said as he opened the front door.

"Hey, Joe, nice to see you," Jimmy said, as they shook hands at Joe's front door.

"Come on in. Let's go to the den," Joe said.

As they walked into the den, a small room on the first floor with a television, a light brown couch, a small table with two chairs, and mahogany colored shelving on the wall, Joe asked Jimmy if it would be okay for Harriet to sit in on the meeting. Jimmy understood that since Joe had the type of marriage in which he always talked things over with Harriett, having her at the meeting would make Joe feel more relaxed. Also, Joe wouldn't have to repeat what was said at the meeting to Harriet, since she would be there, and when they talked later, the conversation would center on what Jimmy told them.

"Yeah, sure. Get Harriet," Jimmy said.

Harriet walked into the den, as Joe got her from the dining room. She sat on the couch next to Joe and held his hand. She held his hand during the entire meeting. Dominick Quintoni was not going to be hurting only Joe. He now was up against the Borganna family, as by holding Joe's hand, Harriett was showing her everlasting love and support for her man. The Borganna family was united and ready to punch back.

"Nice to see you, Harriett. Are you sure you had children, because you can't tell with the nice figure you have," Jimmy said. Harriet giggled, "Thanks, Jimmy, and it's nice to see you."

"I've been thinking about what you told me, Joe, about this guy Quintoni, and I think I've got a way out of this problem for you," Jimmy said. "You've got a trailer set up on the job site which functions as your office, right?" Jimmy asked.

"Yeah, I do," Joe said.

"Okay, well on Tuesday, when this guy Quintoni comes back to see you, I'm going to be parked in my car on the opposite side of the street from the trailer," Jimmy said. "You leave the back door of the trailer open," he said. "When Quintoni gets out of his car, I want you to touch the top of your head with your right hand, got it," Jimmy said. "That will be my signal to go into the trailer. Now, I'm going to be facing the wall, not looking out of the window," he said. "Depending on which way the window's facing, I'll take either my right or left hand, and cup it against my chin. All you'll see from the outside is a profile of me sitting in the trailer. You and Quintoni won't see my face," Jimmy said.

"You'll look at the window and then turn to Quintoni after he asks you if you have decided to make a donation. You tell him that an FBI agent is in your trailer right now asking you if anyone has been asking you for a street tax on the construction job your company is doing," Jimmy said. "Then, you'll point to the window, telling Quintoni, 'See, there's the FBI agent,'" he said. "You'll tell Quintoni you told the FBI guy no one has asked you for any street tax money," Jimmy said. "Then, to pull Quintoni's chain, you'll tell him maybe we can get the FBI agent to make a donation to Local 929. Let's go talk to him," Jimmy said.

"This guy Quintoni won't want any part of no FBI agent," he said. "I'm telling you, while he ain't gonna like it, he'll leave and it'll be bye bye to the donation," Jimmy said.

As Jimmy spoke while sitting on the chair, he lowered his eyes to see Joe and Harriett, who were sitting on the couch holding hands. The display of emotion by both of them was felt by Jimmy. He thought *here are a couple of nice, clean-cut Italian kids with a beautiful, loving marriage, and indirectly the Outfit was trying to fuck him up. Nope, it's not going to happen,* Jimmy's brain retorted. *The Outfit can go find someone else to play there 'let's see whose life I can screw up' game.*

The Borganna's have a tight bond of trust and respect, and if the Outfit thinks they can crush that bond with one powerful blow of their hand of might, which devastated so many others, their attempt will be broken by a force even stronger than their own—the force of uncommunicated love, which every successful relationship has. This type of love is not a human being that the Outfit can punch in the gut or kick in the ribs. The Outfit cannot see this type of love, and they stand helplessly in a circle while this type of love circles around them, peppering them with jabs of love, something the Outfit does not know how to defend.

So start walking, Outfit, because the Borganna's love will break you into jagged pieces of weakness. You are weak, Outfit, against the one power you cannot control, the power of love. You cannot bully, scare, or threaten anyone who embraces love. Go away from the Borganna's as quickly as possible, or else you, Outfit, will be ensnared in love and the unthinkable might happen, you might develop feelings of love in that cruel, vile heart of yours.

When Joe heard Jimmy's plan, he was ecstatic. "Wow, do you really think this will work?" Joe asked Jimmy. Before Jimmy could answer, Harriet chimed in. "Is Joe going to be safe? Will Quintoni retaliate? I'm scared," she said. Harriet's face showed the outward concern that was being generated by her inner feelings. She was tense from head to toe, and her body language pulled no punches. She held Joe's hand tighter while waiting to hear Jimmy's response.

"You know, Harriett, when I hear FBI, that scares the crap out of me. Joe, does it scare the crap out of you?" Jimmy asked.

"Yeah, Jimmy," Joe said. "Harriet, does it scare the crap out of you?" Jimmy asked. "It sure does, Jimmy," Harriett said.

"Quintoni is no different than you or me. It scares the crap out of him," Jimmy said. "I don't know if he's tied to the Outfit or not, but he knows once the FBI starts digging on you, they don't stop until they have all the information they want," Jimmy said. "So, Quintoni won't want the FBI investigating his business; no one wants the FBI checking them out," Jimmy said. "That's why I think the plan will work, as Quintoni will back off once he hears the FBI is sniffing around," Jimmy said.

"Joe, just play it cool with this guy. Don't lose your temper or anything like that. Stay calm, and I'm telling you, Harriett, everything will work out for the good. You'll see," Jimmy said.

Harriett felt relieved. The volcanic tension building in her gut, which was working its way up through her lungs to her throat, suddenly was washed away. Jimmy's reassuring words hosed down the fears she was speculating might become real. If something happened to him, how, oh how could she live without her Joe?

"So, we got a plan, Borgannas?" Jimmy asked. Both Joe and Harriett nodded together in unison, showing their agreement.

"I've never seen anyone in law enforcement scare the crap out of you," I said to Jimmy. "We've got friends with the FBI, Chicago Police Department, Cook County Sheriff's Department, and Illinois State Police, so how could you tell Joe and Harriet the FBI scares the crap out of you?" I asked. "It doesn't make any sense. How many times have I seen you make the phone call to someone in law enforcement to get someone off our backs? A lot," I said. "How many times have I seen you pay off someone in law enforcement to get whatever the hell you want? A lot," I said. "So weren't you misleading Joe and Harriet?" I asked.

"Bobby, in the game of life, if someone comes to you with a problem, you got to make them feel that you understand their problem and work on a solution, so there will be no problem," Jimmy said. "Quintoni is trying to put Joe in the jackpot. Well, you got to use a reverse move to put Quintoni in the jackpot, if he don't back off," Jimmy said. "But to do this, I gotta make Joe and Harriet believe their pain is my pain," he said. "So, by doing that, I win over their confidence, and my plan makes them feel like now we got a way to get rid of Quintoni. It's just making the play when the play has to be made, that's all," Jimmy said.

"Sort of like a commandment, deception supports reality, another form of the Outfit religion, I suppose," I said.

"Yeah, Bobby, think of it as you're trying to screw me into the jackpot, but I'm going to screw you into the jackpot first. And, if I got to play with some words, so be it. Remember, it's the final score on the scoreboard that counts in the game of life, and you want to be the winner and not the loser," Jimmy said. "No one ever remembers the losers, just the winners," Jimmy said.

"Bobby, to make someone believe in you when they come to you with their problem, you got to act like a winner," Jimmy said. "People want to associate with a winner. Don't forget that. So, when you help someone, make damn sure you got a plan that's going to be a winner," he said. "In the game of life, there's going to be times when you have to accept a loss. That's okay, but never except losing. Trace your steps back to see how you lost, and if you can turn the loss around the next time," Jimmy said.

In the Outfit, losses were not accepted, so I understood why Jimmy was telling me about wins and losses in the game of life. To help Joe Borganna, Jimmy had to portray himself as a winner. If not, Joe would never have believed in himself enough to carry out what Jimmy wanted him to do.

Years later when I got my college education and entered the workforce, I looked out of my office window in the street one day and I realized us college guys often thumb our noses at guys who make a living working on the street. But, Jimmy taught me the street sure had a lot more answers to life's problems, if we only would listen.

"Okay, Joe. Good. I'll see you Tuesday morning," Jimmy said, as he got up from his chair. Joe and Harriet stood up. "Thanks, Jimmy," Joe said, shaking Jimmy's hand. Harriet hugged Jimmy, thanking him for his help.

Monday morning, Joe kissed Harriett goodbye and got into his car. As he drove to the job site, he started whistling a confident tune. It was a light, breezy 'I feel good' type of tune. Joe felt a lot more confident in dealing with Quintoni since talking to Jimmy on Saturday. Nothing could go wrong...or could it?

Arriving at his usual time, about 7:30 A.M., he parked his car behind the trailer. As he got out of his car and walked to the front of the trailer, all he heard was quiet—no voices, no cleaning of equipment, no nothing. Absolutely nothing—not one sound could be heard at the job site. *This couldn't be. No construction site is ever this quiet; never ever this quiet,* Joe thought. He only saw his crew's foreman Tony, and no one else.

"Hey, Tony, where is the crew? It's too early for them to be on break," Joe asked.

"Beats me, boss. I just got here about five minutes before you. I don't know where everyone is," Tony said.

Joe's face became stiff as he started to pace around the empty job site. Construction jobs like this one require a bank loan for startup capital, and you're paying a certain amount of interest on the loan. The bank expects its money from you, and if the job isn't completed on time, the city could withhold paying Joe, so where's Joe going to get the money to pay the bank. An idle job site isn't helping the matter. No work means a day behind schedule.

"I'm going to call the 929 and see if they can tell me what is going on," Joe told Tony.

"I'll walk around the site. Maybe someone left a note or something," Tony replied.

Joe went in the trailer and called Local 929. A voice answered, but only kept telling Joe over and over, like a squawking parrot, "I don't know, I don't know, I don't know," when Joe asked why his laborers did not report to work today. Joe hung up the phone, his face warm with anger.

Who should he call? What should he do? Joe slumped in his chair, pointed his head downward toward the floor, shaking it from side to side. *I don't understand why this is happening. I never had this happen to me on any other previous job,* Joe said to himself. What caused this to happen? Right now the job had to be shut down—no laborers, no heavy equipment operator, and no other union personnel were there to work.

Joe decided to call Jimmy for help. Maybe Jimmy could explain to him what was going on. Joe's voice was frantic in his call to Jimmy. "Jimmy, no one is here, Jimmy. No one came to work today. I'm shutdown. There's no one here to work," Joe said in an emotional, tension-filled voice. "It's not good, Jimmy. It's not good," Joe said in desperation.

"Wait a minute, Joe, don't worry. The workers will be back on Tuesday," Jimmy said. "Joe, this is just a ploy by this guy Quintoni to show you he's got the muscle and show you if you don't make your donation to him, he'll shut your job site down," Jimmy said. "It's strictly a scare tactic on his part, one that is older than dirt that he is using on you to get the money from you," Jimmy said. "The guys will be back tomorrow, you'll see," he said.

"Really? You really think that's all this is? Are you sure? How do you know the guys will be back?" Joe asked.

"Lucky guess," Jimmy said. "Go home, Joe. Tomorrow will be a better day. I'll see you tomorrow," Jimmy said.

Joe called Harriet and told her about the day's events. She agreed with Jimmy that tomorrow would be a better day. "Joe, so far it seems Jimmy knows what he's talking about, so we have to trust him," Harriett said. "It's no use worrying about something you can't control, Joe. Let's let this thing play out, okay, honey?" she said.

"You're right," Joe said. Joe felt more reassured that things would work out in his favor after he talked to Harriet. Yeah, tomorrow would be a better day.

Joe told Tony to go home and he would see him tomorrow. "Don't worry, boss. Maybe it was a 24-hour flu or something. We'll be okay tomorrow," Tony said.

"Yeah, we'll be okay tomorrow," Joe said.

Joe decided to make a stop at Our Lady of Perpetual Worship before going home. A little prayer never hurt in a moment like this, and for Joe, he needed to call the bullpen and bring in the strength of his faith as additional backup for tomorrow. I always respected Joe for the commitment he had to his faith. He wasn't a part-time Catholic just showing up for Christmas and Easter services. Joe stuck the Catholic faith to his soul and incorporated the faith in his daily life's activities. If anyone tried to live the life the way the 'Good Book' taught it, it was Joe.

I never had a lot of religion in my life. Jimmy was a missing Protestant, who never went to church. Karen, who was raised a Catholic, had been, maybe, a quarterly Catholic at best, going to Our Lady of Perpetual Worship just enough so Father Tom didn't forget her name. Karen grew more religious after my sister Mary moved out.

Mary was nine years older than me, so after graduating high school, she moved out. She moved into an apartment with a girlfriend and got a clerical position at a downtown store. Mary and I were Baptized, and we both made our First Communion at Our Lady of Perpetual Worship, which I guess qualified us as Catholics.

One thing about Jimmy, he always respected everyone's faith. "Everyone's faith is important to them," he often told me, "and no one's faith is any better or worse than anyone else's, so always treat people of different faiths with respect and dignity."

"Bobby, we all pray to the same God, except we all like different ice cream," he would say. "I like chocolate, Karen likes vanilla, your friend Jeff Greenberg likes strawberry, Mr. Saccopous, who owns Greek Tony's Restaurant, likes peppermint, but it's all still ice cream, only different flavors," Jimmy said. Jimmy never cared if Karen wanted to raise Mary and I as Catholics. He told her he was leaving the religion up to her.

After Mary moved out, she didn't have much contact with the family, especially Karen. She didn't talk to Karen that much. I know it hurt Karen, but Mary had her reason. Mary, while not knowing for sure what Jimmy's involvement was with the Outfit, sensed something and didn't want to be around it. Before she moved out, she said to me, "Bobby, when your time comes, move out. I think Daddy is with the Mafia, and mom knows, but won't say so to confirm it."

I looked at Mary, and I didn't have the heart to tell her she was right. I knew at nine years old, with Jimmy taking me places to see what he did with people, that Jimmy was part of the Outfit. I figured I'd just keep quiet and listen to her. She was my sister, and I wasn't going to hurt her feelings.

About a year later, Mary met a guy who was a musician, and I think he thought of himself as the next Elvis Presley. They started dating, and he talked her into moving to California with him as moving to California was going to put him on the road to stardom. Mary had fallen for the guy. She believed what he was telling her was the truth. It became another story of how love pulls the shade down on reality.

Mary came over to our apartment, and told us she was moving to California with Elvis Jr. I remember Karen sitting on the couch, being very still, and Jimmy just looking at her, not saying a word as she told us about the move. It was the last time we saw Mary in person.

She went to California and lived with Elvis Jr. The next time we heard from Mary, she called to tell us she was pregnant, which was about two years after she moved. Mary had a little girl, but six months later, Elvis Jr. left Mary and baby Elizabeth, never to be seen again.

Mary let us know she was moving to another part of California to try and start a new life for her and Elizabeth. She didn't tell us where she was moving and that was the last time we ever heard from Mary. Karen started to go more regularly to Sunday Mass at Our Lady of Perpetual Worship. She prayed for Mary and Elizabeth at every Sunday service she attended.

Was it guilt that made Karen go to church and pray to the Almighty to watch over Mary and Elizabeth? I can't say, but what I can say is that she never stopped loving Mary and Elizabeth. The church became Karen's special place to seek salvation for losing touch with Mary. Karen, to express to the Almighty her sorrow over losing a daughter, released her inner feelings of a need to regain the spiritual love she never would have with Mary. The situation with Mary never changed. God listened to Karen and his listening provided Karen with comfort and compassion, knowing someone understood that a parent never stops caring about their child.

When Jimmy, and later Karen, died, I thought of Mary, wondering how she and a grown Elizabeth were doing. I was never able to tell Mary about the death of her father and mother, as I had no contact phone number or mailing address. I still love Mary, even to this day. And, though I was nine years old at the time she moved out, she and Elizabeth will always have a permanent residence in my heart. Love ya, Sis.

As Joe walked into the sanctuary at Our Lady of Perpetual Worship, he saw a big, broad shouldered, burly type of man sitting in the first pew facing the altar with his head bowed down, hunched forward, and his hands clasped together in front of him. Joe walked slowly to the front of the sanctuary, measuring his steps, not wanting to disturb the man. Upon getting close enough, he could hear what the man was saying.

"Lord, you gotta help my son. My son needs your help with a serious problem, Lord. Ever since my wife died shortly after having given birth to my son, I have raised him to be a good Catholic. I never remarried. I gave all my love and devotion to my son. He's been the best son a father could ask for and now he's got his own family, and loves his wife and their kids beyond belief. Lord, he needs you. He needs your wisdom and guidance, but most of all he needs your presence. He needs to feel your presence in his soul. Dear Lord, protect my son. I love him so much."

Joe just stared at the man for a moment, then he said a prayer to himself, crossed himself, and turned and carefully walked to the back of the sanctuary. Before leaving the sanctuary, Joe looked up toward the ceiling and said, "Lord, I love him so much."

Tuesday morning Joe left for work at his usual time. Harriett kissed him goodbye and told him everything would work out for the good. Joe gave her a weak smile and walked out the door. He was quite apprehensive about what was going to happen that day at work. Would there be a crew at work? Would Quintoni show up? Would he be able to pull off Jimmy's plan? A lot of questions swirled around in his head, but none that he could answer right now. As he started his car and put his hands on the steering wheel, he put today in fate's hands.

Upon arriving at work, everything looked normal. The crew was there just starting their workday. Tony ran up to the car. "See, boss, I told you everything would work out," Tony said. "The full crew is here, ready to work," he said. "It's going to be a good day. I just know it," Tony said.

"Right," said Joe.

Joe went into the trailer to wait for Jimmy. Joe had some paperwork on his desk. He picked it up and then put it back down on the desk. He wasn't able to concentrate on the paperwork. He took a pencil from the desk drawer and started tapping the pencil on the papers. He was trying to control his emotions, waiting for Jimmy. He looked at his wristwatch often wondering where Jimmy was. A few minutes after 8:30 A.M., Jimmy parked his car and walked to the trailer.

"Morning, Joe, everyone showed up today?" Jimmy asked as he walked in the trailer.

"Yeah, they're all here," Joe said.

"I'm going to sit by this window," Jimmy pointed to a window facing west, "just like we talked about. When Quintoni comes, you point toward this window where I'm sitting, telling him an FBI agent is sitting inside the trailer. Got it? I just want you to be clear on what you gotta tell Quintoni, okay?" Jimmy said.

"Yeah, I'm okay. I'm all set," Joe said.

"Good," Jimmy said, "and then you go into the rest of your spiel," he said.

"Right, got it," Joe said.

"I know you've got a little bit of the butterflies in your stomach; that's okay and that's normal. Just stay calm and keep the conversation short. You'll do fine. We'll have him out of your hair, don't worry," Jimmy said.

"Thanks for having the confidence in me, but what if Quintoni doesn't bite on the FBI story? Then what do we do?" Joe asked.

"Don't worry; Quintoni not only will buy it, he'll swallow everything you tell him, and he'll be gone, never to be seen again," Jimmy said.

"I know you know what you're talking about, but how do you know for sure Quintoni will bite?" Joe asked. "Lucky guess," Jimmy said.

A few minutes after 9 A.M., Quintoni's car arrived at the job site with Quintoni sitting in the backseat. Joe saw the car and told Jimmy Quintoni had arrived. Jimmy said, "Go get 'em, kid," and gave Joe a thumbs-up. He then took a seat near the window as Joe left the trailer to go meet with Quintoni.

Quintoni, this time, had brought along two union goons. Pat Devlin, who was the driver, and Jim Sheridan, who rode in the front seat passenger side. They were brought along by Quintoni to show his muscle. Sheridan got out and opened the back car door, and Quintoni got out.

"Well, good morning, Mr. Joseph Borganna," Quintoni said. He looked around the job site. "Heard you had a little problem here yesterday. Everything okay today?" he asked.

"Everything is fine," Joe said.

"Glad to hear it. See, that's what I mean, a donation to 929 would have, most likely, kept that little problem you had away from the job site, and you wouldn't have had a delay in your schedule," Quintoni said. "See, that donation will get you the full support of 929, and prevent not only that little problem you had, Mr. Joseph Borganna, but any other related little problem that just might pop up," Quintoni said. "In Chicago, it's always good to be able to count on a friend to keep everything fine," he said.

"Everything's fine," Joe said.

"Well, Mr. Joseph Borganna, have you made a decision about what we talked about last week? You know...the donation?" Quintoni said. "Oh, yeah, how are Harriett and the kids? You're so blessed to have a wonderful family," Quintoni said.

Joe kept his composure and, boy, it sure was hard for him to do it, but he did it. There was something big time he really wanted to tell Quintoni, but he knew he had to follow the script, which he did.

Joe turned sideways, raising his right arm and pointing with his index finger toward the trailer. "See that guy sitting by the window? He came in a few minutes before you did. He's an FBI agent and he's asking me if anyone has come to the job site and tried to extort a street tax off of the gross dollar amount of the city contract I have," Joe said. "Of course, I told him no one has bothered me," he said.

"Of course," Quintoni said.

"He said I should let him know if someone comes by asking. Maybe, we should go talk to him about the donation you want from me," Joe said.

Jimmy did not look out the window. He just kept his pose, so Quintoni could not see his face.

"That won't be necessary," Quintoni said. "Okay, Mr. Joseph Borganna, I have no more business here with you." Quintoni inwardly was seething, but he turned and started to walk back to the car where Devlin and Sheridan had been standing outside along the side of the car. He turned his head back and without saying a word, gave Joe a chilling, 'cut to the bone' stare.

"Goodbye, Mr. Dominick Quintoni," Joe shouted at him. He then walked briskly back to the trailer. There was a bounce to his step, his heart was tapping a lively beat, and he had a victory-type broad smile on his face. He walked like a winner, he carried himself like a winner, and he believed he was a winner.

"Whew, that was tough," he said to Jimmy once inside the trailer. "I had to control myself as a couple of times I was ready to let him have it, especially when he mentioned Harriet and the kids," Joe said.

"You did fine," Jimmy said, as he shook Joe's right hand with his.

"Do you think he'll make any trouble?" Joe asked.

"No, he doesn't want the Feds poking around in his business. I'm sure you won't see him again, asking you for any street tax donation," Jimmy said.

"I don't know how to thank you," as Joe hugged Jimmy. "Just make those phone calls to Harriet and your dad, telling them everything is okay," Jimmy said.

"Will do. Will definitely do," Joe said.

"Take care, Joe. I gotta go," Jimmy said.

"Sure, sure, you're really something," Joe said.

"You didn't believe Quintoni was through with Joe, did you?" I asked Jimmy. "No, I never did, but I couldn't let Joe know that," Jimmy said. "Almost a week later, Quintoni called me and I pretty much knew what he wanted to talk about, even before we met near the baseball diamond at Robinson Park," Jimmy said.

It was a nice sunny day when Jimmy and Quintoni met at Robinson Park, but for Joe Borganna, dark clouds were starting to form around him. These dark Outfit clouds can be very ominous when they roll all in. The white clouds ran for cover when they saw the Outfit clouds building over Lake Michigan, starting to thrash their way through the sky. Panic-stricken, the white clouds looked to the sun for support, but were rebuffed. The clouds started moving en masse away from Chicago. They looked over their shoulders and saw the powerful, muscular Outfit clouds punching, elbowing, kicking, and shoving their might against a defenseless sky. The white clouds retreated to a safe sky somewhere far from Chicago where they could have fun and frolic in a blue, serene, cloud-friendly sky. They let the Outfit clouds blacken the sky, taking over the blue sky, forcing the hue to turn midnight black, extorting the blue sky to relinquish its neutrality. There was no more safe blue sky. The blue sky waits in line like everyone else for the Outfit clouds to decide to move on to someone else's sky. The blue sky wonders what destruction the Outfit clouds will direct toward someone in their wrath. Will there even be a sky left, the white clouds and blue sky chatter to themselves.

"Jimmy, you know the city gave a big sewer construction job on Reno Avenue to a J & H Construction Company after the DeFamilias were indicted," Quintoni said.

"I heard," Jimmy said.

"Well, I go over to the job site to meet with the owner, Joe Borganna," Quintoni said. "You know the guy? Ever heard of him?" Quintoni questioned.

"Nope. Never heard of the guy," Jimmy said.

"I talked to him, you know, about a donation of 4% off of the gross amount of the contract," Quintoni said. "Give him the line about things staying smooth on the job, the whole bit," he said. "Then I tell him, I'll come back in a week to get his answer," Quintoni said. "Before I'm going to see him, I make sure none of the union guys show up for work that day. I shut him down for a day. Sort of...uh...to teach him this is what can happen to you if you don't play ball," Quintoni said. "See, I've given him time to think it over, put some icing on the cake for him to see our muscle," Quintoni said. "So, I go back the next week to see him and lo and behold, a goddamn FBI agent is sitting in his trailer, is what he tells me. I look at the trailer and sure enough the motherfucking FBI is sitting by the window," an irritated Quintoni said.

"Is that so?" Jimmy said.

"Yeah, then this asshole, Borganna, tells me the FBI is asking him if anyone is coming by, asking about a street tax, trying to extort money from him for street tax," Quintoni said. "Can you believe this shit?" Quintoni said.

"So, then what happened?" asked Jimmy.

"Borganna throws out some bullshit that, of course, I don't believe, that he told the FBI no one has come by and asked him for any money," Quintoni said. "I figure he ratted me out to the FBI and is fingering me for shaking him down," Quintoni said. "That motherfucker, we've got to have him whacked as this will put the word out on the street that when Dominick Quintoni or one of his boys come to see you, you better do exactly as you're told or else. Otherwise, you're going to become the 'or else,'" Quintoni said.

"Dom, look, we got a look at the whole picture, not a snapshot," Jimmy said.

"What do you mean?" Quintoni asked.

"I mean, this is a new job and the Feds pretty well know how the game is played. They knew DeFamilia Construction was paying off to cover the street tax," Jimmy said. "But, the Feds never had the evidence to go after them for that," he said. "They knew the money was going from one hand to the other, but you gotta be able to prove it in court," Jimmy said. "No proof, no case," he said.

"So?" Quintoni said.

"So, maybe someone is tipping the FBI that something is going on, on Reno Avenue, and they're just checking things out. This Borganna guy could very well be legit and is just an innocent bystander. Get my drift?" Jimmy said.

"So?" Quintoni said.

"So, whacking Borganna would be a bad thing as then the Feds would be looking at you. Remember, people saw you at the job site, and would rat you out to the FBI by telling them you talked to Borganna," Jimmy said. "The FBI, they ain't stupid. Once they hear you, Dominick Quintoni, talked to Borganna, they're going to figure you were there looking for money for the street tax," Jimmy said. "Then they'll start investigating you. Do you want that?" Jimmy asked.

"No, but I'm losing a fucking hell of a lot of money, so when you come to collect money for Dean or Tony, what am I going to give you? What, am I supposed to walk around with my finger up my ass?" Quintoni said. "I don't want any trouble with the higher ups, Jimmy. If they don't get their money, hell, they might have you arrange for me to be whacked," Quintoni said.

"This Borganna guy, leave him alone. Stay away from him," Jimmy said. "The FBI now knows him, and who knows if they don't go back and visit him again, asking him about the street tax, if anyone tries to collect it," he said. "How many times are they going to keep coming back, if he keeps telling them 'no' to their same questions? Not too many," Jimmy said. "As long as you stay away from him, the only thing he can tell the FBI is one word and that's 'no,'" Jimmy said.

"The Chicago Police Department's Narcotics Unit very soon is going to make a big drug bust," Jimmy said. "One of the guys in the unit, Keith Stanley, is one of our friends. He called me and asked me if I wanted him to grab some dope during the bust. The conversation was all in code, talking about his family, things like that in case the Feds were listening. So, everything is cool between me and Stanley," Jimmy said.

"Tell me how much money, Dom, were you going to get from this Borganna guy and I'll have Stanley take not only the dollar equivalent, but take more than you need so you can sell the extra amount on the street and make yourself some extra bucks," Jimmy said.

"What are we talking about?" Quintoni said.

"Well, these guys do between $200,000 to $250,000 a week in the city and northern suburbs in dope sales," Jimmy said. "Stanley told me they store bricks of heroin in a warehouse. He'll be at the warehouse with some guys while other guys will be arresting the drug ring guys at their houses," Jimmy said.

"Is this guy sure about the warehouse?" Quintoni asked.

"According to Stanley, they got an undercover narc inside the ring, so yeah, he's sure," Jimmy said. "See, if Stanley grabs a few bricks during the bust, who's going to know?" Jimmy said. "Once they get the dope to the station, it'll be inventoried and stored as evidence in a lockup area, so he can't take anything then. During the bust things get a little chaotic, people aren't always paying attention, so a grab is easier," Jimmy said.

"Did Stanley say if the horse is 100% pure stuff? I don't want any tainted stuff," Quintoni said.

"No, he told me it's 100% pure. Supposedly it came to Chicago through Mexican sources. So, when you step on it before you sell it, you can get the customers what they think is pure, but it is really blended," Jimmy said. "Look, once these dopers put the stuff in their body by injecting it with a needle into some vein, snorting it through their nose, or whatever way, they will be high and won't know what the hell kind of stuff they got," Jimmy said. "What the hell, if the stuff is 100% pure, it might kill 'em, so in a way, we're keeping them alive by blending the stuff," Jimmy said.

"Makes sense," Quintoni said.

For you clean-cut types out there who have no experience with street drugs, stepping on it means cutting up the dope into so many kilos, and then put a small amount of white powder into the kilos, which is the blending. The customer is paying a top buck for what he thinks, in this case, is pure heroin or it could be at some other time cocaine, peyote, or some other street drugs. It's the same procedure, the blending that is used for any street drug when sold. When it's been blended, more kilos or grams are sold to a wider amount of customers, who unknowingly pay big bucks for a lesser quality of dope, thus, the profit is a lot bigger for the seller.

Think of it as making a bowl of soup, then keep adding water to stretch the life of the bowl. Sure, the soup gets weaker, but you keep selling the soup, passing it off as right out of the can. Since everything is illegal, the sellers are conning the buyers that the dope is legit, and the buyers are conning themselves that it is. One is a thief, who is only concerned about making money; the other is concerned about feeding an addiction. In this case, two wrongs still make a wrong.

Now don't start messing around with street drugs. You guys just stick to legit drugs prescribed by your docs. I ain't going to be responsible if someone acts like a goof. Remember, there is a reason street drugs are called dope. Don't become one.

"Dom, then after you sell the dope, you can get the Outfit higher ups the usual amount of money they get from 929. They don't care where the money comes from, and then you can make some side money for yourself," Jimmy said. "Then you don't have to be bothered with what's his name," Jimmy said.

"Borganna," Quintoni said.

"Yeah, right, Borganna," Jimmy said.

"Jimmy, you're a lifesaver. That's why I talk to you," Quintoni said.

"I'm always available," Jimmy said. "I'll get in touch with Stanley once you give me the number. Don't wait too long," Jimmy said.

"Give me 24 hours and I'll get back to you," Quintoni said.

"Fine," Jimmy said. "So, we're through with this guy, what was his name?" Jimmy said. "Yeah, we're through with him," Quintoni said.

Joe Borganna was washed, rinsed, and dried clean by the Outfit, and he came out smelling like the proverbial rose with his feet not even touching the ground and he never knew a thing happened. How did this all happen? Mr. Jimmy Williams created a three act play using Joe Borganna against Dominick Quintoni. Act I was the plan; Act II, the enactment of the plan; and Act III, the plan behind the plan. Jimmy made Joe believe the plan about the FBI agent would work and scare off Quintoni. Jimmy then took the FBI plan and used it to save Joe's life. Jimmy knew Quintoni had to back off Joe, but he still needed money for the Outfit. Jimmy knew about the drug bust that was upcoming, so that became the plan behind the plan. Joe is happy, Quintoni was happy, no one got whacked or investigated by the FBI, and Jimmy, well let's say the art of illusion was another skill he added to his Outfit resume.

Joe and Harriet didn't need to know the details of the inner workings of the Outfit playing *Let's Make a Deal* among themselves. All they needed to know was the Outfit was out of their lives. Just a couple of nice, clean-cut Italian kids who could now go ahead and raise their children to be wonderful human beings like their mom and dad. The Outfit would leave the Borganna household alone now, as they would take a stroll down the block, looking to prey on their next victim. The next nice clean-cut Italian kids might not be so lucky.

"Bobby, there are some times you can make one plus one equal three and help someone, and there are other times you can only make one plus one equal two and take your medicine," Jimmy said. "When you're in the life, sometimes the victim has to be a victim or else you will become the victim," he said.

"So, you gotta trade off someone's life, at times," I said.

"Yeah, Bobby, that's what you gotta do," Jimmy said.

"So, if Quintoni didn't buy into your drug plan and wanted Joe whacked, you would have arranged it once the order was given to have him whacked?" I said.

"Yeah, Bobby," Jimmy said.

"So, all this bullshit with you and Big Joe about softball in Reeves Elementary School yard, you still would've had Joe whacked?" I asked.

"Yeah, Bobby," Jimmy said.

"So, how in the hell could you face Big Joe if you met him on the street, knowing you had his son whacked?" I asked.

"I'd say sorry to hear about your loss, because, Bobby, this is why I want you to see all sides of being in the life, so you'll know what you're getting into," Jimmy said. "Being in the life is not chocolate filled Saturdays," he said. "It's knowing how to survive in a world in which violence plus violence equals violence, and feelings and emotions about friends are always left out of the equation," Jimmy said. "In the life, Bobby, you never want to add two negatives together, because there's only one answer and that's death. You know, Bobby, math is one subject the Outfit is pretty good at," Jimmy said, with the slightest of smiles on his face. "In my life I learned the members of the Outfit were math scholars, they understood street math with razor-sharp precision."

Edwin "Eddie" Scofaro was the president of the Steamfitters and Pipefitters Union Local 250. Scofaro, who along with his slate was running for re-election, was a close friend of Vincent "Vinnie G" Gatto. Scofaro and Gatto had been boyhood friends ever since they grew up together on the South Side on Granite Avenue, which was four blocks from Haller Field where the Chicago White Sox play. Each one of them went into a life—Gatto with the Outfit, and Scofaro with the union.

Gatto was a street enforcer for Louis "Babe" Tamica. Gatto was given the hard-to-collect, delinquent, overdue accounts in which guys owed Tamica money related to gambling, loan-sharking, drug money, and business loans. These types of accounts were given to guys in the Outfit who were so violent in nature that other Outfit guys just shook their heads at the mention of their name. When Gatto came a-knocking on a client's door with a baseball bat in one hand and a black jack in the other, he was there to do some serious physical knocking on the client's body. When a client heard Gatto was coming to see him, he begged, borrowed, and cried to family and friends to get some money to give to Gatto. A partial amount of money was physically a lot better than no money. While Gatto wanted full payment, he accepted the partial sum and threatened, snarling with foam coming out of his mouth like a wild creature in the woods, confronting his prey at the client's telling him next time payment in full or he would take the payment physically from the client's body.

Gatto was so close a friend to Scofaro that Scofaro hired him as a $45,000 a year consultant for Local 250. Gatto supposedly was to consult on pertinent and relevant union issues pertaining to the union members of Local 250.

The key word here is 'supposedly.' Gatto never attended any local, state, or national meetings or conventions representing Local 250. Gatto never submitted one report on any pertinent or relevant union issue. Gatto never met with any union members of Local 250 to discuss pertinent and relevant union issues. Gatto never turned in a written report or verbally advised Scofaro on any pertinent and relevant union issues relating to Local 250. Gatto never attended any meetings with other Chicago unions in which he represented Local 250 and spoke on their behalf. Gatto never submitted a report to the trustees of Local 250 to advise them of pertinent and relative union issues. Gatto never attended a meeting with the trustees of Local 250, where he spoke to them about pertinent and relative union issues concerning Local 250.

So, if you walk like a union ghost payroller, talk like a union ghost payroller, and act like a union ghost payroller, you must be a union ghost payroller, correct? A union ghost payroller in a Chicago union? You've got to be kidding me! Bite your tongue. Forget about it. That doesn't happen in Chicago…wink, wink. Man, Chicago is the city that works. The question is, for whom?

You can see how valuable Gatto was to Local 250. Scofaro was so concerned about Gatto maintaining good health, he had Local 250 pay for health insurance for Gatto and his family. The union membership of Local 250, who only went out every damn day busting their asses installing and repairing equipment for heating, cooling, ventilating, and refrigerating systems in dark, dirty, filthy, grimy, often deplorable working conditions, with God knows what in those pipes, I'm sure they thought about their friends. With blackened hands and clothes filled with soot every day, besides being physically exhausted at the end of the day, I'm sure they were glad to know Gatto was on the payroll as a consultant, looking out for their best interests on pertinent and relevant union issues for Local 250.

There was one union member who actually did care about the members of Local 250. He cared about who was hired by Scofaro and how the dues money was being spent.

Jack Worthington had been elected four years ago as vice president of Local 250 by a scant five votes over Scofaro's candidate. The vice president's race was the only one Scofaro lost. Scofaro demanded and got a recount, but Worthington got the Feds to monitor the recount to keep Scofaro from stealing the election, which had never happened before in Chicago. Sure, just like you can see the waterfall in the Mojave Desert. Worthington's lead held up after the recount and he was declared the winner.

Worthington had been a union member for 27 years, working just as hard as everyone else on their jobs. He was tired of getting the runaround from Scofaro when he asked questions about the union finances. He decided to run for vice president of Local 250, and campaigned hard, telling the members of Local 250 he would work hard for them, asking the tough questions and not give lip service to pertinent and relevant union issues, but actually caring about someone else to make sure they work for the best interest of the union membership. Worthington ran as the membership's candidate, not someone who was a Scofaro lackey, a toady who impersonated an elected official.

After being elected vice president for the next four years, Worthington kept asking those tough questions of how Scofaro conducted union business. He kept submitting resolutions, never giving up and generally being a prickly thorn, sticking Scofaro. Since Scofaro controlled the elected union leadership, Worthington could only be an army of one. Everything he tried to do was either deferred to a committee or defeated by a voice vote. Worthington, while frustrated, never gave up his quest for a clean union, and not an Outfit-controlled union. He still badgered Scofaro at nearly every meeting; poking and picking away at what he felt were unjust actions that did not benefit the rank and file.

Worthington, now four years later, decided he was going to run for president of Local 250. He felt he could convince the membership that a change at the top was necessary to stop the corrupt acts of Scofaro. In talking with the members, he received encouragement to run for president. "We hear you, Jack." "It's time to kick Scofaro out." "We're behind you," the rank and file told him. Worthington's campaign slogan was: Back Jack - It's time for a change.

Worthington wanted a clean union, one that was fair to all its members, instead of one that Scofaro took care of his chosen few, who not only got a piece of the pie, but came back and got seconds, while everyone else waited in line for their meager first and only slice. He listened to the rumbles of discontent he heard from the members of Local 250. He promised that, if elected, their voices would be heard loud and clear.

Help him start a new day; help him make a transparent union, not a back room dealing union; help him make a union we can all be proud to say we are members; help him kick out the Outfit, whose hands wound up Scofaro, who then became their puppet. Help him make a union that becomes known for fairness to all. Help him by electing him president of Local 250, Worthington yelled at the members.

"Run, Jack, run," they chanted, straining their vocal cords, yelling, screaming so loudly their voices awakened Scofaro.

Scofaro, for the first time since becoming president, had a challenger. When you have had things your own way for many years, you want things to continue favoring you and your allies. Opposition was a threat to not only Scofaro, but also the Outfit was threatened. If Scofaro loses, the Outfit loses. They lose money, jobs, and power—the three things you never want to lose with the union; losing Scofaro for the Outfit meant losing their conduit to the union so they lose juice.

The advantage Scofaro had over Worthington was Scofaro had a consultant on the payroll, one who was adept at consulting on pertinent and relevant union issues, and an election for the union presidency was just such an issue.

Scofaro called Gatto. A meeting was arranged between the two of them to take place at the union hall on a Sunday afternoon when no one else would be around to hear what they discussed.

"Vinnie, this goody-goody Worthington, we've gotta get rid of him. He's stirring up the members about changing how we conduct union business," Scofaro said.

"No, we can't have that, Eddie," Gatto said. "Things gotta stay the way they are," he said.

"Worthington is not the type of guy you can buy off," Scofaro said.

"These goody-goody types never are," Gatto said.

"We'll try this first. We'll see if we can pin something on him so he'll drop out of the race," Gatto said.

"If that don't work, we'll have to do something to him," Scofaro said.

"Whacking him presents another problem," Gatto said. "The cops will start sniffing around, maybe subpoenaing the books to see if Worthington knew something about the way things are run around here," Gatto said. "I mean, if it comes down to it and we have no other option, yeah, we'll kill him," Gatto said. Gatto, being a street enforcer, was not immune from using violence. That's his bread-and-butter on the street, but right now violence was only the B plan. "A lot of eyes watching the election."

Gatto knew business as usual could not be business as usual. It was too risky to take Worthington out…better to try and use a plan to get Worthington out of his own accord. With the right plan you can inflict enough pain to get someone to do something they vowed they would never do. You can always whack a guy, but since there is no statute of limitation on murder, that would hang over your head forever. Who wants to go to prison when they're 70 years old?

"What we're going to do is, I'll call Ernie Marciano and get one of his girls," Gatto said. "We'll make a phony telephone call to Worthington, using one of our political friends, Congressman Steve Dubinski, and pretend his office is calling Worthington," he said. "The caller will tell Worthington the Congressman wants to meet to tell him he's planning on looking into the mob's possible control of Local 250 and would like Worthington's input," Gatto said.

"Dubinski's office will tell Worthington he's got a meeting downtown, and they should get together at the Cleveland Hotel about 8 P.M. When Worthington comes, the broad will pretend she's Dubinski's secretary and prepare him a drink. She'll put some sleeping powder in the drink," Gatto said. "We'll have someone there move him to the bedroom once he's asleep and we'll take pictures of her pretending to make love to him, but she'll make it look real," he said. "It'll be like love without love," Gatto said. "She'll be naked and he'll have his clothes off in bed, and she'll make it appear to be having sex with him. She'll be in different positions with him, and we'll be snapping away getting enough pictures that will tell the story we want to tell," Gatto said. "Also, we'll spread empty beer cans around the bed and get pictures of what looks like a night of drinking and sex," he said. "After the pictures are developed, I'll get them to you and you can go from there," Gatto said.

"Vinnie, that's why you are the consultant," Scofaro grinned.

Gatto called Ernie Marciano and told him he needed one of his girls who could play the part of a secretary. He didn't want a chesty chick who might arouse suspicion in Worthington's mind, that she didn't look the type to be a secretary. He told Ernie what he wanted in the girl and what was expected of her concerning Worthington. Ernie told Gatto he understood and would send over a girl who would be right for what Gatto wanted. They agreed upon a price of $300 for her services. For her part it was just another sex-type job, but with no sex between her and the client ever taking place.

A few days later, a girl Ernie sent over came to see Gatto. As soon as he laid eyes on her, he knew she was the girl he wanted. She was a demure brunette who looked like she just walked out of secretarial school. She definitely would suffice as a secretary.

"Introduce yourself to Jack Worthington as Patty James, Congressman Dubinski's secretary," Gatto said. "Tell him the Congressman called and he said he's running late, and I should offer you a drink in the meantime," Gatto said. "Worthington is a beer drinker, so we'll have a six pack in the refrigerator. Oh yeah, before we go on, when you get to the Cleveland, look in the lobby for guy wearing a White Sox cap. He'll be one of my guys, so walk up to him and tell him you're the relief pitcher. That will be the password for him to take you up to the room," Gatto said.

"Okay, back to Worthington. From what I've seen when I've been in his company he is a one beer man, so I'll tell you what we're going to do with the other cans," he said. Gatto gave the girl a blonde wig. "Here, use this wig only after you see Worthington has passed out after you put the sleeping powder in his beer," Gatto said. "I don't want him to recognize you after the pictures have been taken. My guys will be there to move the body into the bedroom and will undress him. I want you to empty the rest of the beer cans in the kitchen sink and bring them to the bedroom," Gatto said.

"I want the empty cans in the pictures so it'll look like Worthington is drunk," Gatto said. "Put a couple of the cans on the bed, maybe one on the nightstand, you know, spread them around, making Worthington look like he has been drinking and having sex," he said. "We're going to show another side of Jack Worthington that no one has ever seen," Gatto said. "Then, after you spread the beer cans around, put on the wig, get on top of Worthington. He'll be on his back, so your face won't be showing to the camera. You kiss, caress him, and move your body kinda up and down on him like you're having sex. You know, the whole bit," he said. "After taking those pictures, you switch positions with him. You'll be on your back and the boys will put him on top of you, and again, you act it out like you and he are having sex," Gatto said. "You gotta make it look like a Hollywood movie, like it's all real, but in reality there ain't no sex between you and him, but we got to get everyone convinced he's boozing it and screwing you," Gatto said.

"The pictures will be shot showing much more of him than you, but there will be enough of you showing Worthington looking like he's having sex with you," he said. "Once we shoot enough pictures and we're done, you'll give the wig to one of my guys and he'll give you an envelope with the agreed-upon amount of $300," Gatto said. "Whatever financial arrangement you got with Marciano is between you and him. I got nothing to do with that," Gatto said.

"Look, this better go right. We've only got this one chance with Worthington, so no screw-ups," Gatto said.

"Don't worry, Mr. Gatto, everything will be done exactly as you want it," she said.

"Good, that's what I want to hear," Gatto said.

Worthington arrived a few minutes before 8 P.M. at the Cleveland Hotel. The Cleveland was an older hotel, but well maintained, clean, and comfy, and had an established clientele who appreciated its professional surroundings. Most people who stayed at the Cleveland were business people who came to Chicago from out of town on business. The rates were affordable and the services were good. The Cleveland was close enough to downtown where, at night, the business boys could loosen their ties and visit some of the local establishments.

Worthington was very eager to meet with the Congressman. *Finally, someone was going to look at the shenanigans that were going on at Local 250,* he thought. Worthington was confident that after they talked, the Congressman would become his ally after their meeting. The Congressman would get a federal investigation going against Local 250 after hearing what he had to say regarding how Scofaro was running the union for the Outfit's benefit, he reasoned. *There is just too much dirt in Local 250 for the Congressman not to want to get to the bottom of it,* he told himself.

The girl opened the room's door upon hearing a knocking on the door and looking through the peephole. She introduced herself as Patty James, the Congressman's secretary. Worthington then introduced himself. They both walked into a room much like a living room. She sat on the couch and he sat on the chair. They made some small talk and she told him the Congressman called a few minutes ago and said he was running late. She laughed when she said to Worthington, "The Congressman didn't want you to think we are bad hosts, so I should offer you a drink. I have wine, liquor, and beer. What's your poison?" she joked, with Worthington.

"A beer will be fine," he said.

"I'll be back with it," she said.

She went into the kitchen and got the beer out of the refrigerator. She put the sleeping powder into a glass and then poured the beer over it. She took a plastic spoon she had brought from her purse and stirred the beer so it mixed with the powder in the glass. She dried the spoon and put it back in her purse.

"Here you go, Mr. Worthington," she said, as she handed him the beer. She poured herself some wine in a glass, just enough to clink Worthington's glass and say cheers. She was playing the role of the secretary to a hilt. Now she sat back and watched Worthington start to drink his beer. Soon he would be fast asleep and the Outfit would finish off his hopes to become union president.

She brought her legs up under her while sitting on the couch. She listened as Worthington talked glowingly about his wife, Maureen, and their children. He couldn't stop praising Maureen for being the best wife a man could have and how she was such a great mother to the children. His family meant so much to him, he told her. She could tell he was not only a good husband and father, but a sweet, kind gentleman.

She thought to herself, *guys like him are few and far between. He's quite a catch for any woman.*

Worthington continued to drink his beer and talk about why he was running for president of Local 250. He said he was a man of conviction, that he stood for honor and integrity.

She thought, *if only, well business is business, and things must be taken care of. A job has to be done with no distractions.*

After drinking more than half of his beer, Worthington started to feel drowsy. "I guess all the campaigning I've done has made me feeling kind of sleepy," he said.

251

"Go ahead, finish your beer. Maybe you just need to get some more liquid in you," she said in a soft, but instructive voice.

"Yeah, you're probably right," he said, as he drank the rest of the beer.

Within about 10 minutes after finishing his beer, Worthington started to close his eyes as he began to nod off. She got off the couch and put one of the couch pillows behind Worthington's head so he could be in a more restful state. She didn't want his head to start snapping back. *Let him rest comfortably*, she thought.

For a girl who earned her living working horizontal, she showed compassion to Worthington. I've always felt God gave most women a compassion gene in their DNA. He left it up to them when to activate it. Some women activate it, some don't. The reason he gave women the compassion gene was he trusted them to have babies.

Let's face it, if God trusted men, they would have the ability to child bear. Well, they don't because God gave them other responsibilities to perform. As Karen often told me, "God knew better than to trust a man becoming pregnant. Hell, they can't even put the dirty laundry in the laundry bag half the time, so you think God has any confidence they could carry children? No way."

She took Worthington's empty beer glass and her wine glass into the kitchen. She washed the glasses and she took out the other beer cans from the refrigerator, opening and emptying them into the sink, and washing the beer down the drain. After she finished, she went back to check on Worthington in the front room.

His head was against the pillow and his eyes were closed. He was breathing normally. She took her right hand and slightly shook his left shoulder to see if he was asleep. There was no body movement; he just remained still. She took her right hand and lifted his right forearm from underneath, slightly away from his leg. She released her hand slowly and his arm fell back by his leg. Again, he showed he was in a deep sleep. Seeing that he was not going to be awakened, she went and put the empty beer cans in the bedroom.

She walked over to the door that connected to the next room and opened it. Inside the room were two of Gatto's boys—Richard "Chico" Kuzak, a bookmaker, and Ralph "Fat Ralphie" Tamberetti, a street enforcer. Also in the room was Lou Merdici, a trustee of Local 250 with the camera.

"Look, he's ready. I'll go put on the wig and you take care of him," she told Kuzak and Tamberetti. They went to get Worthington while Merdici took the camera and went to the bedroom.

Kuzak and Tamberetti carried Worthington into the bedroom, where they put him on the bed. They went through his pants pockets to look for his car keys. In the left pants pocket, they found a parking ticket and car keys on the key ring for a Chevrolet Chevelle. Since the hotel had a small visitors' parking section underneath the hotel, Worthington's car would not be hard to find.

They undressed Worthington down to his birthday suit. They removed his socks also as they wanted him completely naked. No reason to draw any conclusions in the pictures other than Worthington was having sex in bed with a woman other than his wife. His being naked in the pictures would confirm his intent and the sexual actions between the two of them.

She came back into the bedroom with the blonde wig on and started to take off all of her clothes. "Oops, I forgot something in my purse," she said, as she had stripped down to her panties. "I'll be right back." Merdici turned to Kuzak and Tamberetti. "I think you guys should be in the living room," he said. Merdici was not some professional photographer who was used to taking pictures of naked women. He felt uncomfortable with Kuzak and Tamberetti in the bedroom watching what was to unfold.

"I know she's a pro and all, but you know, her and a john one on one. Maybe she might feel uncomfortable with you guys watching, I don't know. I'm just saying," Merdici said. "We don't want her to tense up or anything because it might show up in the pictures," he said. "If we screw this one up, then Vinnie will have our asses," Merdici said.

"Hey, and miss the show?" Tamberetti laughingly said. "Wait a second, Ralphie, Lou's got a point. We've only got one crack at this. We can't mess up," Kuzak said. "Okay, Louie, you get to be alone with the happy couple. C'mon, Ralphie, let's go. We'll wait to hear from you, Louie, that it's okay to come back. If you need us, we'll be in the living room," Kuzak said.

"Darn," Tamberetti said, snapping his right middle finger and thumb together. "I guess I'll just have to wait until the movie comes out," with a smirk on his face.

"I'm only shooting one roll of film, which is 24 exposures, so it shouldn't take her long to do," Merdici said.

"Alright, for chrissakes, a guy can't even have a little fun," Tamberetti sarcastically said, as he is and Kuzak left the bedroom.

She came back into the bedroom. "I didn't want to forget this," she said. She then unwrapped a condom. Even though Worthington, who now was on his back fast asleep in bed, would never penetrate her, she didn't want to take any chances. Looking at Merdici, she said, "He shouldn't be aroused because he's asleep," but with a wink directed at Merdici, "I might be better than I think," she said with laughter in her voice.

Merdici's face produced a half smile that was tainted with the red color of embarrassment. Merdici was married with three daughters and was not comfortable shooting pictures of a naked man and woman, whether it be pretending or not, having sex. He thought of his daughters and what if someone was taking pictures of them doing what Worthington and this woman were doing. While it disgusted him, and this was something he didn't want to do, he had no choice and had to do it. If he didn't do it, who knows what would happen, so you do it.

She put the condom on his penis and took off her bra and panties. She lay on top of him while allowing his face to be shown and positioned herself so the lower part of her body was close, but not touching his penis.

Merdici put a couple of empty beer cans close to them and then he started taking pictures of those, and the other cans on the nightstand. He then began to take pictures of the two of them appearing to be having sex. She moved her body into different positions while on top of him. She asked Merdici if the positions looked okay. He never told her 'no,' and Merdici kept on taking the pictures, letting the pro do her job.

After shooting about half of the role of film, she got off him. "Let's take the rest of the pictures with him on top of me," she said. "Get the other two guys back to turn him so he'll be on top of me," she said.

Merdici went and got Kuzak in Tamberetti to move Worthington as she suggested. Kuzak and Tamberetti lifted Worthington up enough to put him on top of her at a slight angle. The pictures would make it look like Worthington was completely on top of her, but in reality, that was not the case. Kuzak and Tamberetti left the bedroom.

She animated herself by holding Worthington, putting her arms around his shoulders, playing with his hair, kissing his lips, and squirming with her body against his. She did a lot of this to make it appear the two of them were not only having sex, but were enjoying the sex. Actions were being captured on film, adding to the authenticity of having sex without having sex. Doing sex is what she did for a living. She was a pro who could deliver sex for real or fabricated to make it look like sex was taking place when it wasn't. Worthington was a sleeping student and she was the teacher of sex making. It looked like the student knew more than the teacher.

The Outfit, who were dropouts in the educational system, would teach Worthington that trying to take away control of one of their unions would get him a failing grade. The academics administered a kick to the groin as extra credit to you to make sure you never took the class on trying to buck the Outfit again.

No one, after seeing the pictures, would doubt the two of them were not only having sex, but having so much sexual fun. The pictures would show two consenting adults carrying out their sexual pleasures in the most tantalizing ways. The pictures would show two bodies enjoying sex as one, meshing together to allow sex to transmit from one to another. "Well, I've got one more shot left," Merdici said to her. He waited to see what she was going to do. What was she going to do in the last picture that would seal the deal against Worthington? She reached out with both hands and slid slightly below Worthington's face so he was nearly looking in her face.

She turned her head to the right and told Merdici to get ready. She looked back at Worthington and picked up his arms, placing them around her shoulders. She brought his face to hers and gave him a powerful earthquake type kiss, pressing her lips against his, holding the kiss while Merdici took the picture. "Okay, were done. That's it for the pictures. Well, I could feel the floor move on that kiss."

"Yeah, you sure are good," Merdici said.

"It's what I do for a living, but thanks," she said, as she wiggled out from under Worthington and put on her bra and panties. She went to the bathroom and got a washcloth and removed the condom from Worthington. She rolled up the washcloth with the condom in it and left it on the bed.

She took off the wig and put it on the bed. She then went into another room to get dressed. After she got dressed, she came back into the bedroom. Merdici reached into the left-hand upper pocket of his sport coat that he was wearing and gave her an envelope with three $100 bills in it.

She accepted the envelope, looked inside it, and said thanks to Merdici. She walked out of the bedroom followed by Merdici. She got her purse from a hall closet, put the envelope in her purse, and put on a light blue spring jacket.

"Nice working with you," she said to Merdici, as she extended her right hand to him.

"Likewise," Merdici said, as he took his right hand, wrapped it around her hand and slightly shook her hand, then releasing her hand slowly with his fingers.

She turned to Kuzak and Tamberetti and said, "See ya." Kuzak gave her an acknowledged nod while Tamberetti just looked at her with no change of emotion. She walked out the front door. As she walked down the hall to the elevator, she prepared herself to get ready to go back to be one of Marciano's girls again. This assignment was over and it was time to get back on her back to earn a living. The pro pressed down on the elevator panel and waited for the elevator to reach her floor. The pro turned and looked back at the room she left. The pro was still a woman with emotional feelings, regardless of what she did for a living. Her eyes glued to the front door of the room. Someday I'll meet my own Jack Worthington, a man whose heart is strictly for me, live a life every girl dreams about, and make love to my own Jack Worthington for free. *Yes, somewhere out there in this big world is my own Jack Worthington*, she thought.

Merdici, with Kuzak and Tamberetti, went back to the bedroom. Merdici told Tamberetti to get a plastic bag from the bathroom garbage container, which he did. Merdici threw the rolled up washcloth with the condom, plus the wig, in the plastic bag and put the empty beer cans in the brown paper bag, which they were in when bought at the liquor store. "I'll take care of this stuff later," he said, while holding the plastic and brown bags and said to Kuzak and Tamberetti, "you take care of Worthington." Merdici picked up the camera from the bed. He put the bags down, as he put the camera in its case and then put the camera into the pocket of his raincoat. He picked up the bags and went and sat on the couch in the living room.

Kuzak and Tamberetti dressed Worthington, who was still pretty much asleep. Kuzak took Worthington's car keys. "I'll be right back, Ralphie. I'm going to the basement to see where Worthington's car is," he told Tamberetti. "Once I find the car, I'll drive it right up to the freight elevator so we can put Worthington right in it," Kuzak said.

"Take your time, Chico, he ain't going nowhere," Tamberetti said.

Kuzak found Worthington's Chevy Chevelle, got in and parked it near the freight elevator, leaving the doors unlocked. He then went back upstairs.

"Lou, you go get the freight elevator, hold it open, and me and Ralphie will put Worthington in it," Kuzak said. "Can you go drop off the room keys for both rooms in the downstairs lobby?" he asked.

"Then I'm done, right? You guys will get Worthington home," Merdici said.

"Right," Kuzak said.

Merdici went to get the freight elevator. "Ralphie, once we put Worthington in the front passenger seat, I'll drive him home with you following me," Kuzak said. "Give me his wallet and I'll check his driver's license for his home address," he said.

"Okay," Tamberetti said, as he reached into Worthington's back pants pocket, pulled out his wallet, and showed Kuzak Worthington's driver's license. "I know where he lives. I'm going out in the hall and see if Lou got the elevator," Kuzak said.

Kuzak went into the hallway and saw Merdici standing in the elevator, motioning to him to bring Worthington. Kuzak nodded his head 'yes' to Merdici. Kuzak went back in the room. "Come on, Ralphie, let's grab Worthington and get out of here," Kuzak said.

Since Worthington was not in any condition to walk, yet, Kuzak and Tamberetti carried Worthington to the front door. "Hold it, Ralphie, let me check the hall to make sure no one is there," Kuzak said. Kuzak carefully looked right then carefully looked left. "Okay, Ralphie, the coast is clear. Let's swing his body a little bit and I'll shut the door as we go," Kuzak said.

The room was about four rooms away from the freight elevator, so they didn't have to carry Worthington very far. Once inside the elevator Tamberetti, who had been holding Worthington from underneath his shoulders while Kuzak held his legs, slowly lifted Worthington up so they could prop him up against one of the elevator walls and hold him against it. "Okay, Louie, let's go," Kuzak said to Merdici, once Worthington was in position.

When the elevator got to the basement, Kuzak and Tamberetti walked Worthington a few steps to Worthington's car, each guy holding Worthington under each of his arms. They put him in the front passenger seat, so his head was back against the head rest. His car had seatbelts, so they strapped him in.

"I'll drop the keys off and tomorrow I'll take the film to Vinnie. See ya," Merdici said to them.

"See ya," Tamberetti said. He cupped his hand to his mouth and said, "Louie, it looks like you found another profession."

Merdici walked away, raised his arm and waved it, never looking back. This is one night in the life of Lou Merdici he wanted no kudos for. Merdici rode the passenger elevator to the lobby. "Turning in Mr. Smith's room key from room 410," Merdici told the clerk. "The room has already been paid for," he said.

"Hope Mr. Smith enjoyed his stay at the Cleveland," the clerk said.

"Yes, he found it very restful," Merdici said.

"You're right, the room has been paid for, so have a good night," the clerk said.

Merdici walked out of the Cleveland into the blackness of night, quickly walking to his car, never wanting to see the Cleveland again, as tonight's memory can never be deleted. It would be a permanent resident in his subconscious while he's alive and who knows after that.

Kuzak started the car and put the headlights on. He checked Worthington's seatbelt one more time before he pulled away to make sure Worthington would not plop around in the car. The concern for Worthington's safety is heartwarming. Yeah, right, like anyone gave a whistle about Worthington's health up to this point. What if the sleeping powder didn't agree with Worthington? What was the assigned brain trust going to do? As usual, they probably would've used the standard Outfit waste disposal service. Another body would've been dumped in Lake Michigan with nary a concern about keeping the lake pollution free. The only environment the Outfit was concerned about was a Fed free environment.

Kuzak pulled out of the underground parking area with Tamberetti following behind in his car. Kuzak drove carefully, obeying the speed limit, as he did not want to get stopped by the cops. Worthington was starting to get restless as the effects of the sleeping powder were beginning to wear off. Kuzak reached Worthington's street in the middle-class neighborhood on the northwest side of the city. As he approached the driveway, Kuzak shut off the headlights. Kuzak pulled slowly into the driveway, slowly stopping the car and then turned the engine off. Tamberetti parked on the street next to the driveway, turning off the headlights, but keeping the engine running so he and Kuzak could make a fast exit.

Kuzak looked at Worthington and shook his head sideways a couple of times. Good luck explaining this one to the missus, Kuzak thought. Kuzak got out of the car, walked over and sat in the front passenger seat of Tamberetti's car. "Okay, Ralphie, hit it. Let's go," Kuzak said.

Tamberetti looked at Kuzak. "Hey, Chico, was it really worth it for Worthington to run for union president?"

"Well, he fucked himself up royally with his wife with the pictures. I don't know; I just can't see it. You know what I mean?" Tamberetti said.

"Ralphie, Vinnie pays us to do a job. We ain't thinkers, so if Worthington put himself in the jackpot, he's only got himself to blame. We're just paid help, you got it? So, unless you got to go to driving school to learn to drive this thing, let's get going," Kuzak said.

"Yeah, yeah, I got it," Tamberetti said as he then drove off.

An hour and a half later, while sitting in his car, Worthington started to awaken. As he tried to stretch his arms out, he realized he's wearing a seatbelt. He clicked the seatbelt and stretched his arms upward. He rubbed his eyes and reached over to take the key out of the ignition. Still very groggy, he moved his head slowly from side to side, trying to come to. He pulled on the inside door handle and opened the car door. As he got out of the car, he held onto the door to balance himself. He started to walk, his steps were wobbly, while his feet shifted from side to side. He nearly stumbled, but he grabbed the stairway railing leading to the house and steadied himself. He walked on the stairs carefully, putting one foot then the other on each step until he reached the top. He dug into his pants pocket for his house keys. He fumbled with them, finally opening the front door.

Maureen, who could not sleep, her body tossing and turning all night long, heard the front door open. "Jack! Jack, is that you?" she called out. She got out of bed. "Jack? Jack!" she yelled, as she approached the top of the stairs leading to the second floor where the bedroom is.

He grunted out, "Yeah, it's me."

"Jack, are you all right?" she nervously asked, as she turned on the lights in the downstairs hallway. "What happened? Why were you so late? Did you go to the hotel for your meeting?" she questioned, as she walked downstairs to meet him.

"Right now, I'm so exhausted; I feel like I've slept, but haven't slept," he said. "I know that doesn't make a lot of sense, but I just want to go to bed and put my head on the pillow and fall off to sleep. I'll talk to you in the morning," he said.

"Okay, Jack, sure. We'll talk tomorrow. You just get some rest. The main thing is you are home," she said.

Worthington trudged up the stairs, holding Maureen's arm. He flopped into bed not even bothering to change into his pajamas. He fell asleep in his street clothes at 4:30 A.M.

The next morning, Jack awoke at 10:30 A.M. He showered and went downstairs to the kitchen. "Hi, sweetie," Maureen said, as she went over and kissed Jack on the cheek. "Feel better? I'll fix you some bacon and eggs," she said.

"Sounds good. That'll hit the spot," Jack said.

"I'm still a bit groggy. I feel like I've been drugged. I just can't put my finger on what exactly happened last night," he said. "I remember going to the hotel and meeting Dubinski's secretary. I think her name is Patty," he said. "She said the Congressman called and was running a bit late, and then my mind draws a complete and total blank about what happened after that. I have no recollection of meeting the Congressman or, in fact, how I got home," he said.

"Maybe, if you call the Congressman's office you can start to backtrack from there and, maybe, then you can recall what happened last night," Maureen said. "Sure sounds strange to me," she said, shaking her head from side to side.

"That's what I was thinking of doing. So, after breakfast I'm going to call Dubinski's office and get to the bottom of this," he said.

Eating breakfast, Worthington tried to put the pieces together of what happened last night, but he was missing too many to complete the puzzle. After breakfast he called Dubinski's office, figuring they would provide the missing parts to the puzzle.

"Hi, my name is Jack Worthington. I had an appointment with the Congressman to meet at the Cleveland Hotel last night. Can you check his appointment schedule to see if he had me scheduled? I met with his secretary, Patty, at the hotel," Worthington said. The female voice who answered the phone told Worthington to hold on. She then came back on the line. "Sir, I checked the Congressman's appointment schedule and you were not on it."

"The Congressman's office called me about scheduling a meeting between the Congressman and myself about activities taking place in Teamster Union Local 250. I was going to provide him with information about the local," Worthington said. "Can I speak with the secretary, Patty?" Worthington asked.

"Sir, we do not have anyone working here by the name of Patty. His secretary's name is not Patty," the female voice said.

"But I met with Patty at the Cleveland Hotel last night. In fact, she said she received a call from the Congressman and he was running a little late," Worthington said.

"Sir, neither the Congressman nor any of the Congressman's staff were at the hotel last night. Is there anything else I can help you with?" the female voice asked.

"No, I guess there's nothing else. Thanks," Worthington said in an uncertain quizzical voice. Worthington hung up the phone, knowing exactly what he knew before he made the call, which was exactly nothing. He sat by the phone on a chair, more bewildered than before. This was very perplexing to Worthington, as none of it made any sense to him. Worthington was a logical man trying to trace illogical events.

He looked at Maureen. "Honey, something happened at the hotel last night, but I can't put my finger on what happened there and that bothers me," Worthington said. "Maybe, if I just put it behind me, it'll come to me what happened at the hotel," he said.

"That's right, honey, no need stressing yourself out about it. I'm sure in time everything will come back to you," Maureen said.

Ten days after Worthington's drugging and picture taking at the Cleveland Hotel, Gatto now had the developed pictures of Worthington and the phantom Patty James. Gatto called Scofaro to set up a meeting. The meeting was set for Friday morning at Scofaro's office.

"Hey, Eddie, got 'em. Here they are," Gatto said to Scofaro, as he walked into the office. He handed Scofaro an 8.5" x 11" brown envelope with all the pictures. Scofaro looked at each picture, not really saying anything, yet. Gatto stood patiently, waiting to hear what Scofaro was going to say about the pictures. Gatto looked in Scofaro's eyes to see if he could read some type of sign. The longer it took Scofaro to respond, the more restless Gatto got. *Maybe, Scofaro was unhappy with the pictures. Maybe, he wanted different pictures*, Gatto was thinking.

"These pictures are fine, Vinnie, just what the doctor ordered," Scofaro laughingly said to a much relieved Gatto. "I'll call Worthington and arrange a meeting with him," Scofaro said. "These pictures, once Worthington sees them, should knock him out of the box for the presidency," Scofaro said.

"If not, then we'll go the other route," Gatto said. The other route Gatto was referring to was the tried-and-true Outfit way of having Worthington's legs broken if he didn't drop out of the race. The threat of violence is what keeps the Outfit in business. It's their own winning formula that never fails to get the results the Outfit wants.

"No, I don't think we'll have to do that. These pictures speak for themselves," Scofaro told Gatto. "Worthington will buckle. He's got too much to lose if these pictures come out," Scofaro said. "Once he's in the jackpot, how's he going to explain this, not only to the other union members, but his wife?" asked Scofaro. "Vinnie, I'm telling you, Worthington will cave in," Scofaro said.

Gatto shrugged his shoulders, "Yeah, I guess you're right, Eddie. I mean, you know the guy better than me. But I'm only saying, if he don't get out, we'll get him out," Gatto said. "I know what you're saying. Believe me, I got it, but in this case I don't think we'll have to use that stuff," Scofaro said.

A meeting was arranged between Scofaro and Worthington at Scofaro's union office for Thursday, late in the afternoon. After speaking with Scofaro, Worthington wasn't sure why Scofaro wanted to talk to him. *Maybe's Scofaro is going to drop out of the race. Wouldn't that be nice,* Worthington thought.

Worthington arrived at Scofaro's office for the meeting. He sat across a large walnut colored desk with Scofaro looking straight at his face.

While opening the brown envelope with the pictures, Scofaro said to Worthington, "Jack, I'm really surprised by this. I never thought of you is this type of guy," placing the pictures on the desk in front of Worthington.

"Wait a minute. What are you talking about?" Worthington said as he looked at the pictures.

"Why, Jack, look at the pictures of you and another woman, not Maureen, making love. What were you thinking?" Scofaro said in a mocking tone of voice.

"Hold on here, you set me up!" Worthington snapped at Scofaro.

"Jack, how could I have set you up?" Scofaro said. "I wasn't wherever this took place. Someone put this envelope in the union mailbox. You were there. Isn't that you, Jack?" Scofaro said.

"Yeah, that's me, but I don't know that woman. I've never seen her in my life," Worthington angrily said.

"Well, Jack, it seems to me that these pictures show a definite lack of not only good judgment, but morals, which would make you unfit to be president of the union," Scofaro said.

"So, that's what this is about. Trying to get me to drop out of the race," Worthington said.

"Jack, once the union members and the media see this…and, of course, your lovely Maureen sees this, she will be deeply hurt," Scofaro said. "How do you think anyone would trust you to be president? I mean, the president must be of sound judgment and good morals," Scofaro said.

"Something you have neither of," Worthington said.

"Well, Jack, I think it's best for everyone if you drop out of the race," Scofaro said.

"I'm not a quitter and I'm not dropping out, no way. I'm in this race until the end when I will win it," Worthington defiantly said. "These false charges will not stop me," Worthington said.

"Sure, Jack, if that's how you want it. It's just when everyone sees these pictures, you're going to have a lot of explaining to do, not only about you and this woman, but about your drinking problem," Scofaro said.

"Drinking problem?" Worthington said.

"Those pictures of the beer cans in the bed and on the table by the bed. Don't tell me you weren't drinking," Scofaro said.

"Someone put those beer cans in the bed and on the table to make it look like I was doing a lot of drinking," Worthington said. "It's obvious this is a big frame up to get me out of the race," he said.

"Do you have any recollection of that night, anything at all?" Scofaro insincerely questioned Worthington.

"None. I draw a blank," Worthington said.

"See, that's my point; you were so drunk that night, that's why you can't remember anything that happened. Maybe the pressure of the election is getting to you. I know you're a good man and will do the right thing," Scofaro said.

"The right thing is I find out what happened that night to clear my name from this garbage," Worthington said. "To my dying day, I will never believe that I wasn't framed with someone taking pictures of me doing something totally out of character for me to get me out of the race," he said. "Right now I can't point a finger at whoever did this, but I will do my best to find out who the lowdown, lowlife is who did this to me," Worthington said.

"You're going to have to explain not only cheating on your wife, in which you got caught, but your drinking problem is also a problem that needs explanation," Scofaro said. "Let's face it, Jack, with all this explaining you have to do, when will you be able to campaign?" Scofaro asked.

"Look, this conversation is pointless. I was set up with this woman and I was set up with the drinking," Worthington said. "I'm done talking with you," Worthington said as he got up from his chair, turned his back on Scofaro, and walked out.

After Worthington left, Scofaro chuckled to himself. He looked at the pictures and figured he planted enough doubt in Worthington's mind that the seeds of loyalty to his wife and children would gain strength every second, every minute, every hour, and every day. Eventually, the seeds would grow strong enough and Worthington would have to decide which family gets his loyalty, his own or the union.

The days following his meeting with Scofaro were the most difficult in Worthington's life. It became a mental tug-of-war with Maureen and the kids pulling on family emotions saying, 'Jack, we need you,' and the union pulling, saying, 'This is our chance to be free. Jack, we need you.' Back and forth, Worthington went from side to side. The mental ping-pong was wearing him out. Maureen and the kids, yes…the union, no; the union, yes…Maureen and the kids, no. Right punch followed by left punch, followed by left punch followed by right punch—his mind taking shot after shot. The clock was ticking, not much time left. Judgment day just got off the bus and was walking toward him, and there was nowhere to run and no place to hide.

He didn't tell Maureen about his meeting with Scofaro. It went against his nature, as he and Maureen talked about practically everything. Whether it was about the children, or buying a new car, they talked. Their marriage was one where everyone's opinion mattered and was heard. This was different, because he knew as much as he tried, these false accusations would still hurt her, so he had to decide on his own what to do. If he stayed in the race, Scofaro would release the pictures and that would cause pain and suffering for Maureen. He thought she would believe him once she would hear his side of the story…or would she. Maybe she would think the man she married was not really the man she married. Maybe he changed and became someone else.

His chances for winning the union presidency once the pictures became public would greatly decrease, most likely no chance, in fact. To the union members, he would go from honest Jack to sleazy Jack, and who votes for someone like that? Then another problem was the timing; when would Scofaro release the pictures? If it was a few days before the election, Worthington wouldn't have enough time to make his case to the members that he had been framed. Jack Worthington was a proud man, an honorable man, who believed in fairness, equality for all union members, and was going to have to decide which side of the street his loyalty stood on.

If this was Hollywood, they would come up with a righted ending to this movie. Forget about Hollywood, we're talking about reality here. This ain't a movie. This is Chicago, where a thumb to the eye, elbow to the ribs, and a knee to the groin are the keys to victory. Someone for real will get hurt unless they read the memo. It's about the Outfit controlling a union, doing whatever it takes to stay in power. Chicago style is we don't play fair, we play to win, doing whatever to whomever, whenever. In Chicago, if you can't stand the heat, you better hightail it out of the kitchen, because we're going to burn that mother down, then you'll have to eat in our kitchen and pay oh so dearly for our juice.

"Maureen, I've been thinking, this presidency would be upsetting to the family," Worthington said. "I would be putting in long hours trying to straighten out the mess Scofaro left me," he said. "I'd be coming home late and it wouldn't be fair to you and the kids to have a part-time husband and part-time father. Besides, physically, it would be very exhausting and I would probably be emotionally drained, as well, and I'm no spring chicken," Worthington said.

"Jack, this is all you have talked about, wanting to make the union not only a better place to work, but fair to all the members," Maureen said. "Stop the corruption, spend the union money the way it's supposed to be spent, a union not for a few, but for all. These are the things you told me comprise your dream of making a union everyone can be proud to be a member of. Don't give up your dream, don't do that," she said. "Me and the kids, we will sacrifice whatever it takes for your dream to come true," Maureen said. "You've worked so hard all these years in the union; the members need you to be the president," she said. "Please, just think it over," Maureen said.

Worthington held Maureen's hands with his own. He pressed her hands firmly. "I knew from our very first date you are the right one for me and you are just as right now for me, but as the man of the family, I can't put my ambition ahead of what's best for the family. I'm going to drop out of the race tomorrow," Worthington said.

"Jack, are you sure this is what you want? Are you really, really sure?" Maureen asked.

"Yes, honey, I'm sure this is what I want," Worthington said. Decisions like these never come easy. Here you are one minute fighting for something you believe in and the next minute the Outfit is telling you to stop fighting, stop caring, you're worthless. Just punch out at quitting time and leave us to run the show. The pecking order is you're a peon; we're the powerful. Got it, buddy? Your inclination is to fight back. It's pretty hard to do with an empty gun and someone else holding the bullets. It's easy to Monday morning quarterback and say Worthington should have fought like a man for his principles, but then again, our body wasn't the one the Outfit would come looking for if Worthington stayed in the race.

The next day, Worthington announced that for personal reasons he was dropping out of the race for union president. He made it sound like he was dropping out for health reasons, but was never specific about any medical reason. His supporters were stunned as they had no idea Worthington was quitting the race. They were as surprised as everyone else was. Following his announcement, Worthington went to the pension board and filed his papers to retire at the end of the month. He just didn't have the heart to be working with the union members after he felt he let them down by dropping out of the race. He didn't want to face them and be around to watch Scofaro win another term and keep the union functioning on what was best for Scofaro and friends, not the members. Worthington did what he had to do so Maureen and the kids would not be hurt. While he took care of his family, his eyes would moisten when he thought about his other family—the union family, he never took care of.

Following his retirement, Worthington, a few months later, got a job with a construction company as a job cost estimator. He would start a new work life trying to distance himself from the union, but found he never could forget or really want to forget how the Outfit muscled him out.

When Scofaro and Gatto heard Worthington had dropped out, they hugged and back slapped in Scofaro's office. They congratulated themselves on a job well done.

"The guy was no good. He was trying to reform something that was running just fine. Who the hell needs him," Gatto said.

"Yeah, just a goody-goody type who we showed ain't that good," Scofaro said in a cocky voice.

"Yeah, a JV player trying to play in the major leagues who thought the clean union was the way it was supposed to be. What a fucking fool. Who needs that shit?" Gatto said. "Some guys, I guess, have to learn the hard way," Scofaro said.

"Yeah, now he can go be a Boy Scout somewhere else," Gatto said. They decided to go to Dickie's, a neighborhood bar, for a drink to celebrate reducing the union membership by one. Scofaro and his complete slate were reelected to another four-year term.

I remember an alderman's kid who was running for eighth grade class president at St. Isaac for the Apostle. The kid's father was called to school by the principal. It seems that while the kid won the election, he had more votes than there were eighth grade students.

In the principal's office, the father got the kid to admit he offered some seventh graders free ice cream cones at Mikey's if they would vote for him. The principal gave the kid a one-day suspension and made the kid who finished second the class president. As they walked out of the principal's office, the father put his arm around his son's shoulder and said with a smile on his face, "That's my boy, a chip off the old Chicago political block."

Elections in Chicago are taken very seriously by the participants. They use every trick in the political playbook to win at all costs. Elections in Chicago are not for the faint of heart. It can be brutal and possibly deadly. Elections in Chicago mean one thing and one thing only, the winner has the juice.

I don't care if the election is for president of the United States, president of the union local, or president of an eighth grade class, the winner pours the juice in a glass and passes out straws to the chosen few to sip some juice through the straw. The juice might be running a Democratic ward organization in Chicago and getting someone's brother-in-law a cushy government job. The juice might be hiring an Outfit consultant to work for your union on pertinent and relative union issues, except the consultant never seems to find any pertinent and relative issues to work on. The juice might be promising ice cream cones to seventh graders to illegally vote in an eighth grade class election, thus, teaching children in true Chicago style a vote bought is better than a vote earned.

Elections in Chicago have one campaign slogan that fits every election, no matter what level of election, and that is if you want the juice to continue to flow, vote for me. We're very good at winning elections in Chicago. We're also very good at never letting the cup become empty and run out of juice.

The Outfit has always been involved in elections, which only benefit them. Since elections in Chicago are the second oldest profession, closely aligned to the first, the Outfit passes their experience from one to another. Like the oldest profession where you pay for what you get, the taxpayers in Chicago pay a heavy price for the political juice that only a trickle will ever taste.

It's often been said in Chicago that when asked what people want for Christmas, they ask for their political Santa Claus to leave a little juice in the fridge. It leaves a very chilling effect on your morals.

"Dammit, this still leaves a bad taste in my mouth," I said to Jimmy. "I know, Worthington had his family to consider, but nothing is ever going to change unless someone tries to make it change," I said. "Worthington was a man of principles, but why did he roll over to Scofaro without at least a fight to the finish? I know the pictures would have come out, but come on, not everyone is stupid enough to believe this was not a setup. Sure, some people would have voted against him because of the pictures, but a lot of the members knew Worthington was not this type of man and would have voted for him. Maureen knew what type of man she was married to. She would never believe what was in those pictures for one second. Yeah, I'm not saying she wouldn't, at first, have been hurt, but after the initial shock, she would realize that for this to be photographed, someone had planned this against her husband. Unless you're making a porno movie or kinky sex tape, who photographs two people making love unless it's a setup? The more she would have peeled back the onion, the more this thing would've smelled. You always told me, the first day you run from a problem, you'll be running the rest of your life from the problem, so why doesn't that apply here?" I asked Jimmy.

Jimmy looked at me, not answering me right away. Finally he spoke. "Bobby, in life we have some sure bets. If you live long enough, you grow old;

it's a change we can't stop. Monday comes, Monday goes, then Tuesday comes, Tuesday goes; we have the seasonal changes that occur every year. We go to work, we get paid. All these things, we know there's no guesswork, these are all sure bets. But it's the unknown things that give people fits."

"Until the Cubs play their baseball, they don't know what the outcome is going to be. They can talk all they want about the game in the clubhouse before the game, but none of the players know for sure who's going to win or who's going to lose until the game is played. Worthington never knew for sure how the members or Maureen would react once the pictures became public. Worthington never knew for sure if he had the votes to win until the election was held. One thing Worthington knew for sure that he could count on was the Outfit put him in the jackpot and everything turned negative from that point forward if he stayed in the race. The Outfit let him see the next day's story before everyone else did.

"Maybe Worthington fights his way out of the jackpot, maybe not," Jimmy said. "Elections come, elections go, but at the end of the day, Worthington took the sure bet, having his family there for him over the election, which was the unknown," he said. "I'm not saying what you said is wrong, Bobby, and I'm not saying what Worthington did was wrong, I'm saying someday you will have a family of your own and you want them to be your sure bet against any unknown," Jimmy said.

After getting married and having my own family, there were situations that made me think of Jack Worthington. Maybe, I was a twenty-something punk kid spouting off to Jimmy about Worthington making a grandstand play to change the union, replace the wrongs with the rights, but being married with kids, I got what Jimmy was saying. Boy, did I get what he was saying.

Jimmy was an Outfit guy involved in all these criminal activities. He arranged for guys to be whacked among the many hats he wore. Yet, he was still my dad, teaching me about life, how to live in it and survive. He used his lifetime of Outfit experiences to teach his son not his way, but the right way of living a life. I wonder if he would have been the Outfit's dad, if certain people's lives would not have worked out better. I always loved you, Pop. I just never told you how much.

If you're married to an Outfit guy, maybe there was a good solid reason you married him and the physical part does not count. The physical part, while important, is only a sliver of the relationship. It's the part of the relationship after the physical that determines whether a relationship floats or sinks. If it's not a strong foundation, thick concrete of values of why you married the guy in the first place, you better have Jesus's home phone number handy to make that call for help. There will be a time when you, as a woman, will be on the empty street of life looking in all directions, waiting for someone to be driving a Chicago Transit Authority bus to get you home safely. Well, honey, it ain't gonna happen. His Outfit life has left you in a desolate outpost where your screams for help are only heard by you and no one else. So, you better wipe away those tears and start walking, because only you and you alone will find the salvation required to allow you to function as a responsible human being. Each step will build the strength of your character, each step will empower you to exercise the will of survival, and each step will build your moral character to put your family on your back and carry them through the troubled waters you must wade through. And, each step will walk you down a path of courage and conviction that, at the end of your journey, while you might be battered, you might be bruised, but your spirit will now pack a punch that will knock out any evilness that challenges you. You have met your foe and won by winning the greatest of them all, your self-respect.

Tommy Calzone, like a lot of parents who have more than one child, had some intuition—call it a parent's sense—which one of the children is going to be the successful one. While they love all their children, there's one that stands out among the rest. There's one child who radiates the glow of success, the one a parent looks back at and always knew would set the world on fire.

Melissa was Tommy and Roberta Calzone's middle child. The older daughter was only interested in thumbing through the latest fashion magazines to see what the current style of dress, hairstyles, and makeup was. She always wanted to look good and get the boys' attention. She had two failed marriages that produced three children. While she received some child support, Grandpa Tommy wound up paying most of the bills that were incurred. Tommy would joke with me that he'd be practicing law into the next century to support the oldest daughter and her three kids. The high legal fees he charged were based on the monthly note he had for his daughter and her kids. She worked the counter at a cosmetic store, not earning enough money to support her and her kids. She never amounted to anything.

Tommy's son, his youngest child, drank too much and couldn't keep a job. With Tommy's juice, the son got plenty of jobs, but every job he felt was beneath him. He would tell his boss that he should have a more important job at a substantially higher salary. Most of these jobs lasted, if he was lucky, about a year. Tommy laid down the law to him that he's got to work, and while he went from job to job, I'll say this about him, he wanted to work. He wasn't the type to sit around on his behind and just be a freeloader.

He had girlfriend after girlfriend, going through them about as quickly as the jobs he couldn't hold. Though he finally got married and had a child, that marriage failed because of his immaturity in being able to function as a husband and a father. He just couldn't stop his infidelity of going to bars and meeting women for horizontal exercise. He had another child with a woman, but he never married her. While Tommy had laid down the law about working, when it came down to it for his son's daughter from his marriage, Grandpa Tommy still threw a few bucks his granddaughter's way. A grandpa is still a grandpa when it comes to his grandchildren. The son, he never amounted to anything.

While the Outfit needed Tommy as their lawyer, Tommy needed the Outfit equally as much as without these lawbreakers, his grandkids would financially suffer. There are those that say crime doesn't pay. While it might not pay for the person who commits the crime in the form of incarceration, but it sure pays for the person who, without the crime, would have no job to pay for his grandkids' fun.

Melissa was the smart one of her siblings. She was on the honor roll in elementary school at St. Anne's and in the National Honor Society at Queen of Maria High School. She graduated from the University of Illinois with honors, getting a degree in economics.

With Tommy applying his juice, Melissa got a job in downtown Chicago at the Federal Reserve working on economic forecasts and trends.

She attended Northwestern University at night, studying for her master's degree in economics. Melissa was well liked, not only by her co-workers, but her boss, who besides liking her, saw her potential to excel at the bank. Success, or so it seemed, was following success. After about 18 months on the job, she got a promotion making $3,000 more a year.

Through it all, Melissa kept a level head. She never bragged or made sure you knew about her academic achievements. You would never know from her about how well her career was going at the Federal Reserve Bank. Melissa could have, but was never one to toot her own horn. She let her actions speak for themselves. She was a sweet, kind, smart, down to earth girl—that prototype that every parent hopes their son will marry. While Tommy never bad-mouthed his kids, he had thought he caught lightning in the bottle with Melissa, and she would make up for the other two failures.

I would always see her with a smile on her face, always seeming to care more about others than herself. She volunteered, caring more about others than herself. She volunteered at Our Lady of Perpetual Worship, tutoring kids with their studies and worked on projects that helped the needy and less fortunate of our society. I thought she had a nice figure, but she would tease me and say her hips were too wide. I liked her, Jimmy liked her, Karen liked her, Dean Dragonetti and Tony Galante liked her. Everyone who met her liked her. If a friend was sick, she went over with a container filled with soup to make sure the friend would not dehydrate. People mattered to her and there were never enough hours in the day when it came to helping someone in need.

The type of girl Melissa was came out of the womb that way. You are either born with her personality traits or not. You don't train someone to be good. It comes from within from birth. The situations in a person's life will bring out the goodness they carry in their soul only if the goodness is there to begin with. Everyone who knew Melissa knew she was genuine, not a fake.

Victor Lanzo, one of Tommy's legal clients for the longest time, had his eye on Melissa for his son Peter. Victor Lanzo had a string of mob adult book stores located on the Near North Side of Chicago, a couple close to downtown and others in unincorporated areas near the southwest suburbs. He made and sold adult pornographic movies with his partners being the Outfit. The films would be sold and distributed to mob adult bookstores in Indiana, Michigan, and Wisconsin. Lanzo also had a small sports betting and loan-sharking operation on the Southwest Side of Chicago, which supplemented his income.

He was an associate member of the Outfit, who benefitted from having their street enforcement in getting the movies distributed from Point A to Point B. Lanzo was responsible for getting the movies made, but like any other type of movie, needed it to be sold and distributed to make money and this is where the Outfit came in. The Outfit had the juice with other adult bookstores to make them buy the movies at the price the Outfit set. The adult bookstore owners, while at times grumbled about the price, pretty much had to accept it. By not accepting the Outfit prices, the stores knew the Outfit would reach into their bag of violent tricks and pull out the one best suited to get their point across. Someone gets beaten up or a store gets firebombed, things that if you deal with the Outfit, you better read the fine print of their contract. So, the stores knew it was better for business and their own personal safety to just say, 'Yes, master,' and move on.

Pornography was a big moneymaker for the Outfit when you look at the cost of making an adult movie. The movie's budgets were low as the salaries paid to the actors and actresses were not high. The movies, a lot of the times, were shot in a warehouse in California where some cheap-looking furniture was brought in to make it look like the action was taking place in a home. The production crew was not paid union scale…far below it. For a lot of the production crew, they were either in between movies, waiting to be hired for their next movie, or unemployed, so they were glad to get the work and the income that went along with it.

The actors and actresses were unknowns just trying somehow to get a foot in the entertainment door, even if it meant being in an adult movie, so they were willing to accept any salary offered to them. They were mainly in their early 20s and just wanted to be part of Hollywood somehow. Years and years later, maybe if they got in the real movies, they were embarrassed when some Hollywood gossip columnist would find out about their porno acting days and write a story about those days. They would, at first, deny ever doing porno, but a persistent columnist would somehow get a copy of one of the movies and threaten the actors and actresses that if the columnist didn't get inside stories from them for columns about the Hollywood stars they dealt with, the columnist would expose their backgrounds to the public. The columnist was blackmailing them and, at that time, no one wanted their porno background exposed. So, they played ball with the columnist. The columnist and the Outfit unknowingly had something in common—acting in a criminal manner makes work a whole lot easier.

The profit margin on the Outfit's porno business was very high 60% to 70%. Sex always sells, no matter what; it just takes on different forms depending on what technology is available. For Victor Lanzo, financial bad meant good, smut meant dollars in his pocket...ah...showbiz the Outfit way made sex sit at the same table with a Fortune 500 Company discussing a bottom line, though the Outfit's looked better in a bikini.

One of the sidebars to the Outfit is their involvement in matchmaking. It's not uncommon to see arranged marriages between Outfit members. Kids whose fathers are Outfit members will be introduced to each other in order to marry within the Outfit family. It'll look like a boy meets girl type of romance, but what the kids don't always know is the two fathers have had a sit down meeting to arrange the future of their sons and daughters. By arranging a marriage, the two fathers are arranging the potential of any business deals between the two of them. As in-laws, the deals could always be thought of as a way to help the married couple. The fathers would not be competing against each other, but rather, making a deal that would benefit them and the kids, each side having an equal stake in the deal.

But, like anything else the Outfit gets involved with, there are successes and disasters. For the Outfit being a matchmaker was not about putting two people together to enjoin them into a loving family. No, it was about a couple of street crews working out some illegal activity based on the fact that their kids are married to each other and because of this, one father would avoid being whacked by another father since they were in-laws and wouldn't want the kids hurt by their actions. Everyone could be one big happy family unless the kids get divorced. Then you better put on your gym shoes, sneakers, or whatever you call them, and run for cover, churn those legs as fast as you can; run, baby, run as the fathers' no-longer-family will be deciding whose blood will be splattered on the street. You want to run away saying you're

Switzerland, because once those bullets start flying, anyone and everyone could become a target and I have, yet, to see anyone reason with a bullet. It's all about street business, baby, and who runs it.

Victor Lanzo decided it was time to play matchmaker for Melissa and his son Peter. He was going to have a party at his house on Saturday night and invited Melissa over with the intent of meeting Peter. Melissa had seen Peter before, holding a casual conversation with him, but she did not know him at all. While guests were invited, they were only there as a backdrop. It was Melissa and Peter that were center stage at this affair. Victor had scheduled them as the main event. Victor was hoping that through his connection with Tommy Calzone, he would become a happy father-in-law and proud grandparent.

Victor was willing to spread his juice over what he wanted—a beautiful wedding at Our Lady of Perpetual Worship for a prince and princess. This was the one movie he really wanted to make and it would never go on sale. It would be strictly for his own private enjoyment.

Peter "Shorty" Lanzo, who was 6'3" tall, had a very lanky build, almost a string bean look that gave the appearance of a pencil with an eraser. Melissa would tease Peter, at that time, about looking so vertical with no horizontal meat on his bones.

Shorty had graduated from Loyola University in Chicago with a degree in business administration. He went to Loyola Law School for one year, where he made the grades, actually doing well, but never went back for the second year. It was a mistake, which proved to be a bigger, very costly mistake later on in his life.

Shorty was a pleasant kind of guy who, at times, could turn on the charm and spread it across the audience right in front of him. There were times when I had to remind myself, *Don't forget, Shorty's in the Outfit*. He didn't fit the cocky, arrogant, do you know who the fuck you're dealing with, violent stereotype of Outfit guys I knew. He had brains. How he used them, well, was another story. He could talk to people in such a way that they never felt he was talking down to them. Shorty could have eaten at the table of success, but he bit off more than he could chew.

He was a loyal, loving son and that was the problem. I was a loyal, loving son to Jimmy, but I understood from a very young age what Outfit life was all about, and the all about part had the capability of blowing up your life into jagged fragmented pieces with its consequences. Shorty, like most sons, had been sheltered from a functioning Outfit life, so he didn't know what the hell he was getting into. I'm sure he had an idea, maybe, a pretty good idea what Victor did for a living to pay the bills as Shorty was not stupid. But, Shorty had no experience, and while guys in the Outfit often learned by trial and error, it could be the error that could be deadly. The draw of the Outfit, standing across from Shorty on the bad street with their outstretched arms, hands reaching across 'good street' to pull you in became too tempting a life for Shorty to turn his back on. The Outfit put the hook in him and now he was going to become one of them. He was going to work side-by-side with his father and make him proud of his Outfit son.

Victor never came right out and asked Shorty to join the Outfit, but he didn't try and stop him, either. For most of the sons of Outfit guys, their fathers never explained to them what mob life is all about. Fathers would say, "Okay, you want to get in the business," and their sons sort of drift into it. Now, some sons in their teens begin Outfit pre-school. They steal or as it's known in the life, boost cars, do stickups, and begin to do burglaries. So, by the time they're 16 years old, if they're even in high school, they drop out and are ready to begin their Outfit internship.

Victor, in his own way, felt satisfied with Shorty in the life, knowing there would be a Lanzo running the family business after his departure. The handing over of the family business from the father to son meant a line of succession would continue the flow of illegal money to keep the Outfit viable. The son would maintain an allegiance to the only family that mattered—the Outfit family. Running the family criminal business supported the lifestyle the Outfit wanted…not asked for, but expected.

With Shorty's willingness to enter the life, Victor became his son's field training officer, showing and teaching Shorty all the nuances of the smut business or, as Victor referred to it, an organization keeping people working and off of welfare. I never saw being in the life as a purely economical benefit for taxpayers and neither did the Outfit. The smut business was just another criminal activity in a long list of criminal activities carried out by the boys from Chicago.

Melissa, though, was no stranger to Outfit types, since her father represented them as legal counsel. She met many of them and their families. However, meeting someone and working with someone is a whole other chapter in our personal life's stories. Yet, to Melissa, Shorty seemed different, maybe, because he was a college graduate, more polished, who could use his brains rather than his fists. He wasn't a high school dropout street thug bully with the mental capacity of a ping-pong ball. She knew Victor was in the life from her father's legal work, but when she met Shorty at the house party, the Outfit, being in the life, everything related to organized crime had no bearing on the guy standing in front of her. He was a man. She was a woman. The emotion said it all.

Even though he towered over her 5'4" frame—5'6" in heels as she would laughingly say—their eyes, even though coming from different heights, never left each other. She focused on him. He focused on her. While they were just making small talk, as couples do when they first meet, their connection grew stronger with each spoken word. The words started to connect, each one of them to the other.

Far off in the corner of the room, Victor stood, arms folded across his chest, watching the young couple intently. He watched his juice saturate. The young couple was emotionally making their own movie. As Victor watched each frame of their movie, a confident smile crossed his face, as he nodded his head approvingly up and down to what he was seeing developing between Melissa and Peter. *The prince and the princess are going to become the ideal couple*, he thought. *Matchmaking isn't so tough as long as you mix the right juice*, he reasoned.

Shorty asked Melissa out for a dinner date on the following Saturday night. She gladly accepted his offer and their first date was booked. The rest of the evening, while now anti-climactic since they scheduled a date, still allowed for a foundation to begin to be built between the two. They were still getting to know each other like two professional boxers in the first round of a fight, lightly sparring with each other, verbally looking to see what worked and what didn't.

Melissa talked about how much she enjoyed her job at the Federal Reserve Bank, finding the work challenging and mentally stimulating, and she had great co-workers. She was very animated in her voice inflection when talking about work—always positive, upbeat, and actually kind of refreshing to hear. Shorty was vague about his work, saying he was learning about film from a guy, but never got specific about what Victor was teaching him. He diverted the subject from their conversation, just moving on and talking about something else. Melissa never pressed him about his work, she just let the conversation continue to flow upstream, letting him row the verbal boat in whatever direction he wanted. She saw no reason to look for an undercurrent, as she was interested in the man, not his work.

"Melissa should have pressed Shorty about his work," I said to Jimmy. "Then she would have been able to decide if she wanted to pursue a relationship with a guy who was going to be in the life," I said.

"Bobby, Shorty would have lied to Melissa anyway, even if she pressed him," Jimmy said. "Men are fishermen when it comes to relationships. They only put so much bait on the hook to catch a woman. Too much bait will fall off the hook, and if a man wants to catch a woman, he just wants to dangle enough bait to wet the woman's appetite to keep her interested and wanting to know more about him. By her wanting to know more, means the relationship will have to continue, possibly growing to something more serious, and the man has accomplished what he wanted all along to hook her for himself," Jimmy said.

"What about women? C'mon, they go fishing, too," I said.

"Absolutely, women go fishing, but with a woman, it's physical bait that they use," Jimmy said. "Men use accomplishment, things they can brag about, where women will be concerned about how they look, what image are they portraying to the man. The bait for women becomes the right dress, the right purse, the right shoes, the right jewelry, the right lipstick, and put this all together with the appropriate smile and when to use it. And, a woman's bait can be very eye catching to a man. Men are visual. Once they see it, they want it," Jimmy said. "Women can keep their bait fresh and men have to leave some bait off the hook in order to avoid becoming stale," he said. "Two different approaches, hoping for the same end result in relationship fishing," Jimmy said.

"So, using your analogy about fishing, shouldn't Melissa have done a little more fishing about Shorty's work? I mean, if she had more knowledge about what he really did, maybe she would have backed away from him and saved herself a lot of grief later," I said.

"Bobby," Jimmy said, "with a smile, some people catch a fish, smell a stink to it, and throw it back into the lake, and start the process again while others catch a fish, smell a stink, but keep the fish, hoping in time the stink will go away because they like the fish and really want to keep it." Melissa was looking to catch that love fish and pretended the stink was never there. Melissa never smelled the fish.

The dinner date between Melissa and Shorty led to a movie date, which led to going to a Chicago Cubs baseball date, which led to getting tickets to see a play at a downtown Chicago theater date, which led to going out for lunch and spending the rest of the afternoon at the Chicago Art Institute, walking around looking at beautiful pictures, with Melissa telling Shorty information about the painting and painters date. Shorty was impressed by Melissa's knowledge in the art world, as he felt quite proud to be with her. One date continuously followed another. They were both growing to like being with each other. Their strengths were bouncing off each other in a positive way.

"Right, Jimmy, isn't that how love works?" I said.

"Sure does, Bobby. That's how it works," Jimmy said. "You meet someone and you can't stop thinking about them. You wake up in the morning thinking about them, you go to sleep at night thinking about them. So, you want to wrap your arms around their soul so tight they'll never get away.

"See, if they get away, Bobby, you're going to be waiting on the street corner a long, long time before someone like that comes along again, if ever," Jimmy said. "Sometimes, you only get one chance to make that first impression, a lasting impression; otherwise, you might never leave the street corner. Got the picture, kid?" Jimmy said.

"Yup, the picture's in focus," I said

The relationship between Melissa and Shorty bonded stronger over the next several months. A year would pass and the inevitable was coming. A relationship, which had been percolating for beyond a year, had reached its zenith and was ready to spill over into the next level. Shorty had reached the eventful day with ring in hand. He was going to propose marriage to Melissa that night at dinner. Earlier in the day, he went to see Tommy at his law office to get Tommy's approval to marry Melissa. Tommy said 'yes' and gave Shorty a big welcome-to-the-family hug.

That night after dinner at Jensen's Restaurant, Shorty told Melissa how much he loved her. He told her since he met her and had been dating her, how much better his life had been. He told her how smart she was and how much she had elevated him by showing him things he never had much interest in. Finally, the moment arrived, and Shorty reached into the upper inside pocket of his sport jacket and pulled out a small light blue box. He opened the box in front of her.

He took the ring out of the box. The diamond ring was pear shaped, a little less than three carats, and was a sparkler. The restaurant lights glistened on the diamond, giving it a magical hue for a magical night.

"Melissa, will you marry me?" Shorty asked, looking directly into Melissa's eyes.

"Yes, yes I will, Pete. Yes, of course I will marry you," Melissa said as she lunged toward Shorty and kissed him on the lips. Shorty took Melissa's left hand and placed the ring on her finger. The diamond ring now placed, Melissa and Shorty were one. Happy days were coming...or were they?

In love, Melissa made what was to be the worst mistake of her life. She said 'yes.' When a woman falls in love with an Outfit guy, a message gets sent Airborne Express to the woman's brain to blank out the fact the he is in the Outfit, and what life would be like married to an Outfit guy. Outfit, what Outfit, you love him and he loves you. That's all that matters. If anyone else tries to tell you different, screw them. Forget about it. We're going to have a normal, healthy life together because I love him and he loves me. Well, if you believe that one, I can get you a good deal on snow tires for your winter vacation in Hawaii.

Melissa had the all-encompassing love stars in her eyes, which blinded her reality vision. She never thought about what if Shorty was in the life and the effect of being married to a criminal would have on her life or the lives of her four children. She never thought how her life would change the day Shorty was handcuffed, arrested, and walked out of their house by the FBI.

No, at this very moment, with a diamond ring on her finger, she just saw a long-lasting life with the man she loves. Nothing was going to disrupt Melissa's life, as at this moment, she was feeling love, a warm, balmy wind blowing from the south, brushing up against her body. Life was going to be such a high being married to Shorty that when one 24-hour day ended, she was giddy thinking about the next 24 hours and how rewarding being with the love of her life was going to be. Melissa was already counting the days until she became Mrs. Lanzo. In Chicago, we have the changing of the seasons. While Melissa was content in the warm love winds penetrating her body, with time, a biting, freezing, arctic wind would be howling from the north, causing a change in lifestyle. The Feds were coming.

Karen, Jimmy, and I were invited to the wedding. We went to the wedding ceremony at Our Lady of Perpetual Worship. It was a lovely ceremony, officiated by Father Tom. The church was packed and everyone saw a beautiful bride and groom express their love to each other through the vows they had written for each other. Many in the audience dabbed their eyes with Kleenex as the vows were so heartfelt, they struck a chord with the guests.

Following the ceremony at Our Lady of Perpetual Worship, the reception was held at Château D'Ville. The numbers swelled at Château D'Ville, as people who didn't attend the church ceremony came for the reception. There were nearly 600 guests attending this mammoth event. Château D'Ville had two large connecting banquet rooms that were used and the guests went back and forth between both rooms. The best of Chicago and the best of the Outfit were represented at Château D'Ville. It was interesting to watch and see the people with the financial muscle who could make things happen by beating back all the competition in the same room as the Outfit, who had the physical muscle to make things happen by beating you and having no competition.

The Governor of Illinois sent a telegram, wishing Melissa and Shorty happiness on the beginning of their new life together. The Outfit was represented by Dean Dragonetti and someone half his age, a young blonde female who, for all I know, could have been selling Girl Scout cookies last week, wearing a dress with a plunging neckline that kept on a-plunging all night. Tony Galante was there with his wife, Rena, and Tony's bodyguard Frank "Frankie Flinch" Passanacco. Frankie Flinch's right shoulder had this built-in tic movement and you weren't sure if he was coming after you or not. The shoulder would flinch at you, scaring the hell out of you because, you know that saying about a bad guy that you wouldn't want to meet in a dark alley, you wouldn't want to meet Frankie Flinch in any alley—light or dark, period.

Frankie Flinch had this exceptionally hard muscled body. Even if you brushed against him, it stung. His body's muscles not only had muscles, but I think he carried some extra muscles in his back pocket for back up. The only thing you had to tell Frank Flinch about someone was beat him bad and you never had to review his work. In his lifetime, Frankie Flinch killed, maybe, 11 guys and, if you were able to talk to the victims, they would probably have said 'praise God,' thanking him for allowing them to be killed rather than beaten.

Jimmy, Karen, and I were standing next to Dean Dragonetti and the juvenile, who I guess was of legal age, but because of the age difference with Dean still looked like his daughter, were making small talk. Tony Galante, Rena, and Frankie Flinch came up to us.

I stretched out my arm to Frankie Flinch after shaking hands with Tony. "How ya doing, Frankie?" I said. Frank Flinch looked at me, nodded his head in a form of acknowledgment, did not shake my hand, and walked behind Tony.

"Bobby, when I told Frankie you would be at the reception, he got excited and couldn't wait to see you," Tony said. As you can see, Frankie Flinch was probably so overwhelmed to see me the words got stuck in his throat and he couldn't talk. *Ya right, Bobby. Come up with another one*, I thought. *Just be grateful he didn't talk to you with his fists. That's a conversation you can do without.*

Ernie Marciano walked in with one of his girls as his date, saying his wife was ill. I didn't recognize her at first since she was standing upright, a position I was unfamiliar seeing her in. Maybe Mrs. Marciano came down with a touch of the HC flu virus. Known as the husband-cheating flu strain, it seems to affect Outfit wives at any time during the year. Since the Outfit men are the carriers of this strain, the only known cure for the Outfit wives is to get a divorce. The symptoms will leave your body quickly; however, there is one side effect I need to mention. You could become DOA and I don't think you have to give the layman syntax on this one.

There were two photographers at the wedding reception; one on the inside hired by Melissa and Peter to capture the memories of a special night for them and their guests. Snapping away at the festivities that surrounded this royal event, the photographer interjected himself with family and friends, being able to take their pictures at a moment of fun and frolic. The photographer, at a later time, would look at the developed pictures and see a good time was had by all.

The photographer on the outside of Château D'Ville was hired with taxpayers' money. He was employed by the taxpayers to also take pictures. Except his pictures were of specific people who were attending the reception. The photographer was an FBI paparazzo. He was an agent, who along with a couple of other agents, were assigned to gather information on known Outfit members. The pictures could be used at trials when the Feds, as part of prosecution of the Outfit boys, were trying to show associations with other known Outfit guys.

The FBI paparazzo sat in a car with the other agents, clicking away every time a known Outfit guy walked into the Château D'Ville. The paparazzo used a telephoto lens on the camera, as the FBI car was directly across from the Château D'Ville. Most of the time, the Outfit guys were not paying attention to the fact that they were going Hollywood, as the boys referred to the picture taking sessions. If the boys actually saw the paparazzo, they would try and either cover or shield their faces. They weren't going to make it easy for the paparazzo, if they could help it.

As Chris "The Beast" Sampelli was about to walk into the Château D'Ville with his Lana, he turned his head and looked across the street at the blue Chevrolet parked with people sitting inside. He stared at the car and his Outfit mind told him there was paparazzo inside, taking pictures of the Outfit guys. He turned away and then turned back looking at the car one more time.

"Everything okay, Chris?" Lana said.

"Sure. Sure, baby doll. Everything is okay. Let's go in and party," Chris said. When Chris walked in, I saw the look on his face and knew everything was not alright.

"Hi, Chris. Hi, Lana," I said to both of them.

"Hi, Bobby. Where's your old man?" Chris said.

"He's over there," and I pointed where he was talking to Dean and Tony.

"I'll be right back, honey," Chris said. "I'm going over to say hi to the boys."

Chris left us, and I said, "You look very sharp tonight, Mrs. Sampelli. The dress is lovely."

"Oh thank you, Bobby. You're always such a gentleman," Lana said. In my opinion, Lana had the best legs north of Milwaukee. I made sure I tried extra hard to look into her face, but those legs sure had an extra appeal to them. Strong, but not too strong; muscular, but not too muscular; just enough to make you drop your eyes, look at them, and dream. With her being married to the Beast, you knew you were only going to be a casual observer of those healthy legs because you wanted your legs to remain healthy also.

"How ya doing?" Jimmy said to Chris.

"Great, Jimmy, just great. Say, I'd like to talk to you," Chris said.

"Okay, c'mon over here," Jimmy said, as the two of them walked away from Dean and Tony to an area in the banquet hall where they could talk privately.

"You know the FBI is outside taking pictures," Chris said.

"Yeah, I saw the blue Chevy parked across the street and figured it was them," Jimmy said.

"I'm damn tired; everywhere I go, it seems they're going Hollywood on me," Chris said. "Well, I've had it with them, and I'm going to fuck with them, sort of get back at them," Chris said.

"Maybe you've become their new heartthrob," Jimmy said with a smile on his face.

"Tell them they can go throb this," Chris said, while he took both his hands with his thumbs out, pointing downward at his crotch.

"Okay, just be careful whatever you're going to do," Jimmy said.

"Nah, I'm just going to give them a taste of their own medicine," Chris said.

Chris took a paper cup from a waiter, drank the champagne, and headed out to visit the FBI. He walked up to the driver's side of the blue Chevy and started knocking on the window. "Come on, I know you guys are in there," he said, banging his left hand on the glass and holding the paper cup in his right hand. Finally, the window rolled down.

"Can I help you, sir?" the FBI agent said.

"No, Mr. FBI, I'm going to help you," Chris said. Chris proceeded to lower the zipper on the front of his pants and urinated into the paper cup. "I'm buying. Here's something for you to drink while you're taking the fucking pictures of everyone tonight," Chris said. "It'll go down real smooth for you fucking assholes. Go ahead. Take a picture of this you scumbags," he said.

Chris, who had zipped up his pants, walked by the hood of the car and placed the paper cup on the hood. He then glared at the agent, turned, and started to walk back to the Château D'Ville, talking under his breath, calling the FBI agents a bunch of cunts. The FBI agent who was the focus of Chris's tirade was sitting solemn in the car. After Chris left, the agent turned to the paparazzo and said, "I guess he was having a bad day."

When Chris came back inside the Château D'Ville, Jimmy asked Chris if everything was okay. "Yeah, Jimmy, everything is fine. I just pissed on some FBI shit," Chris said.

Victor Lanzo walked around the banquet room like a proud peacock. He had put a brown paper shopping bag behind Melissa and Shorty, who were in the receiving line, and then took his spot next to his wife in the receiving line. He mindfully watched as the well-wishers came up to the receiving line, hugging and kissing Melissa, and the women, at least, doing the same to Shorty, while the men shook Shorty's hand and put a white envelope with a gift inside in Shorty's hand. Shorty turned and put the envelope into the paper bag. The line of well-wishers grew and so did the number of white envelopes in the paper bag. Like a Chicago snow day that starts out with a few snow flurries and gradually grows into bigger flakes where some real accumulation starts to take place, the white envelopes were accumulating quickly in the brown paper bag.

Jimmy, Karen, and I were in the receiving line. I watched as Jimmy gave Shorty an envelope, which he put in the paper bag. The paper bag was filling out much like a pregnant woman with the envelopes starting to push out the sides of the paper bag. The only difference was this baby wouldn't require years of love. It provided instant love as soon as Melissa and Shorty opened the envelopes. The bride and groom collected $125,000 from the minions.

Whenever I've gone to an Outfit wedding, it's been interesting to watch people pony up those white envelopes, everyone hoping the white envelopes they give would put them on the future juice list. You never want to be left out in the cold in Chicago as your lips get awfully dry without the juice.

Nick Rosentino's band played well into the night. I think Nicky was afraid not to keep on playing. It was better to be told, "Okay, Nicky, one more time and that's it for the night," rather than just playing for the night. Well, Nicky had a contract, so did Victor. Victor might wave the Outfit wand, conducting trunk music with the band members being the only ones listening. After the Outfit clipped someone, they would put the body in the trunk of a car and say, "Well, now so and so can now listen to trunk music."

Angelo "the Lunatic" Easoli, a juice collector, when collecting a juice payment would ask the person what type of music he liked. He would then tell the person if he didn't pay what he owed

The press had always dubbed Cook County Circuit Court Judge John McHollister "Honest John" for his hard-hitting sentencing and what seemed to be his impartiality in his courtroom. McHollister was on the dance floor, dancing with his wife, humming a tune Nicky Rosentino's band was playing. He looked in Dorothy's eyes, enjoying the dance with her. He and Dorothy, who were both good dancers, glided onto another part of the dance floor.

As McHollister turned Dorothy, he looked in the direction of Ernie Marciano's substitute date for the supposedly sick wife, who saw McHollister. She raised her right hand and started giving him the friendly 'Hi, Johnny' wave, not the type of wave you use to hail a cab. She knew McHollister and he knew her. Honest John didn't feel too honest at that point. She walked around the outside of the dance floor, smiling at him, still giving him a wave. McHollister frantically kept turning Dorothy, trying to keep her from seeing the paid sexual help.

"Boy, you're really doing a lot of turns tonight, honey," Dorothy said.

"If you don't mind, honey, I'd like to take a break," McHollister said.

"Sure, honey, we can dance later," Dorothy said.

Wow, isn't it nice to see how these lovebirds throw around so much honey that it's drawing a bee. McHollister left Dorothy and made a beeline toward Miss Sub.

"What are you doing here?" he asked, as they walked outside, going behind the Château D'Ville. When they walked out the front to head to the back, the FBI paparazzo said to his partner, "Isn't that Judge McHollister? What do they call him, Honest John? What's he doing here? And, that sure doesn't look like his wife."

"Okay, go ahead take a picture. We can send him a copy for a scrapbook," the partner said.

"It makes you wonder why he's here at an Outfit wedding. Obviously, as a guest," the paparazzo said.

"Maybe, Honest John is not the honest saint the press makes him out to be," the partner said.

"Yeah, the honest judge might have a little dirt on his sleeve. I think we better keep this picture I took in the file. It might come in handy later," the paparazzo said.

Sometimes a picture can tell a story that changes your life. You might lie about the facts, but the picture doesn't.

McHollister and Miss Sub talked in an alley behind the Château D'Ville. "I can't be seen with you. Do you understand that?" McHollister said in a pointed and firm voice.

"Sure Johnny, don't worry. I'll be cool and keep my distance so your wifey doesn't get suspicious," she said. "It's just I'd rather see you holding me on the dance floor instead of your wife," she said with a coy teasing smile.

"Look, it's not that I don't want to be with you. I do," he said. "I pay you a good buck to keep me sexually happy and you do that very well, but I got an image to protect and if Dorothy finds out, I'm screwed royally," McHollister said.

"So, I'm just hired help? What am I, Mother Vagina to you?" she playfully teased McHollister.

"No, no. I didn't mean that," McHollister said.

"Okay apologize," she said kind of controlling McHollister.

"I apologize. Look, I gotta go back in, so please let's not let our ships pass in there okay?" he said.

"Sure, Johnny. I'll just watch from a safe distance," she said. "See you same day and time next week, as usual," she said as she kissed him on the cheek.

"Yeah, normal schedule next week. See ya," McHollister said.

He went back inside and met up with Dorothy. "I got a little fresh air. Ready to go back on the dance floor," he said.

"Absolutely," she answered, "let's go out there and show them how it's done."

McHollister's ship, in a few years, would start sinking, as it began to leak and take on water. The leak was caused by choppy water, courtesy of the Feds. The Feds built a case of McHollister having a long-standing relationship with the white envelopes full of his favorite color green to fix cases. McHollister would go down with a smile on his face, as well he should—he paid a good buck for it.

After the last well-wisher passed through the receiving line, Victor Lanzo went over to Tommy Calzone. He shook Tommy's hand, thanking him for giving Shorty permission to marry Melissa. Two proud father-in-laws, arm-in-arm, congratulating each other on the union of their two kids.

"I guess were kinda family now," Victor said.

"I guess so," Tommy said.

"Good, does this mean I'll get a family discount on my legal bills for the future?" Victor joked.

"It depends on which side of the family we're talking about," Tommy deadpanned.

While playfully squeezing Tommy's neck, Victor said, "What are you changing jobs, going from law to comedy?" Tommy just grinned as he knew representing the Outfit boys always meant a ton of repeat business. Tommy never had to look for business. The Outfit, conducting their own monkey business, provided it for him.

Jimmy just got off the dance floor after dancing a slow dance with Karen. She draped her arms around his shoulders and he had his arms around her waist, barely moving on the dance floor, but speaking volumes for love with their body language. I didn't remember if I ever saw Mom and Dad dance before. They were so much in love, both just looking in each other's eyes, not paying a bit of attention to the music coming from Nicky Rosentino's band. I watched two lovers who had been in love with each other every moment they had been with each other continue to express their love for each other in the greatest love story ever.

I wondered if Mom really knew what Dad did for the Outfit, would she maintain that everlasting love she had for Dad. When a woman marries an Outfit guy, that part of the wedding ceremony talking about for better or worse is very meaningful. I suppose, in the marriage there is some better 'hey, I'm trying to be positive here, so give me a break,' but the worse...oh, the worse, will only get worse over time. The woman thinks she has only married an Outfit guy, but what she will find out in time is she married the Outfit life and things will get progressively worse over time.

For Melissa Lanzo, her wedding day would be the high point of her life with Shorty because the low points would descend on her, washing away the vows she took with Shorty in becoming husband and wife. Shorty's vows with the Outfit, unfortunately, are the only ones that matter.

Karen went to talk with someone. I still had McHollister on my mind. There were some in the media who speculated that Honest John might run for Cook County state's attorney and, if successful, possibly governor.

"Was he always one of our friends? Was he always dirty? Did he always have his hand out?" I asked Jimmy.

"Yes on all of the above," Jimmy said.

"But he…" I began to say.

"I know, Bobby, his image and how he really is never meshed," Jimmy said.

Publicly, he was honest, forthright, and gave everyone the impression he was a straight arrow, but the trouble was the arrow had a bend in the middle. McHollister lived a two-handed life. On the one hand, he gave the impression juice had no claim in his court. No matter who you were—rich man, poor man—you got the justice you deserved from him. He portrayed himself as legally fighting for the little guy. That's why the media loved him, calling him Honest John.

On the other hand, a long time ago, he became the Outfit's boy in a courtroom. Jimmy said, "Remember, Bobby, McHollister even running for judicial retention after his term is up, he is slated by the Cook County Regular Democratic Organization. Without party support, he could run as an independent, but he won't have the precinct captains getting votes for him," Jimmy said. "Our friends, the politicians, could sink his ship at any time. Once McHollister started playing ball with us, we owned him," Jimmy said.

"I know, but it's just disheartening. You think you have a hero wearing the white hat and then you find out when he thinks no one is looking, he puts on the black hat, being a bad guy like everyone else," I said.

Jimmy, looking in my face, said with a laugh in his voice, "Bobby, Superman died a long time ago. If you want a hero, become one. When I got married and had a family, I tried my best to be their hero by leading with actions that they could be proud of. I wasn't perfect, just like any other mortal. I had faults, but my wife and children were always my heroes and I never lost sight of that throughout the years."

The wedding cake was being cut and pieces were given to the guests as the reception was drawing to a close. Victor joked that the guy on the cake who represented the groom was too short to be Shorty. Victor also said the guy was too clean-cut, maybe he was the FBI, so you guys better watch what you say; he's probably wearing a wire. Everyone laughed on cue…they better.

Victor gave Nicky Rosentino the eye, and Nicky closed out his performance with the song *Love Is a Many Splendored Thing* as the new Mr. and Mrs. Lanzo danced their final dance of the night, ready to begin life as a couple who dreamed of a life filled with happy children, a fun world, a safe world, a world that brought daily sprinkles of love scented with a rich tangy sweet emotion that would stick to their souls for a lifetime. Were these things just inflated delusional thoughts? I guess we'll find out when God opens the envelope and announces the winner is....

The bride and groom finished their dance, said their goodbyes to the guests, and left the Château D'Ville to begin their new life together as Mr. and Mrs. Lanzo. Oh, yeah, I forgot to tell you, when Melissa threw the bouquet of flowers, Shorty's Aunt Carmen Biscoline, who's been married three times, caught the bouquet. She was also a Cubs fan, so maybe the two go together.

"Wow! That was a great wedding. The food, the band, everything was great— a perfect sendoff for a prince and princess to live happily ever after," I said to Jimmy.

"We'll see, Bobby. We'll see," Jimmy said to me.

What's with this 'we'll see' crap I'm thinking? How could something go wrong for the perfect couple in having the perfect life? I asked Jimmy that question.

"First of all, nothing is perfect, Bobby, as far as life goes," Jimmy said. "I know Shorty is a college grad and Victor is showing him the ropes in the smut business, but will Shorty be a street graduate? That's the question hanging on the cliff," he said. "There are going to be times when Shorty will have to make the play when the play has to be made; in the life, he's gonna have a problem within the Outfit. If he isn't capable of making the play when the play has to be made or just doesn't do it, he'll put himself in the jackpot," Jimmy said.

"If you make a mistake with the Outfit, you gotta cover it up real fast. It can't linger," he said. "You might have to point the finger at someone who is not even at fault, but you need a fall guy, so there he is," Jimmy said. "Maybe he gets whacked, maybe he don't, but you covered up the problem so no one in the Outfit looks at you as the problem," he said. "As long as the Feds aren't sniffing around Shorty, he can keep Melissa in the dark about being in the life and they can go on living that storybook life. If the Feds start closely checking Shorty's dance card, things could spill over into his personal life. Then Melissa starts hearing things and starts firing questions at Shorty because she doesn't want to wind up in the jackpot herself.

"Melissa's no dummy. She's gonna want to know what Shorty's doing that the Feds are looking at him, because remember, Bobby, she's got kids to protect beside herself. So, like I said, Bobby, we will see," Jimmy said.

While Jimmy gave you the whole story, I knew Jimmy had an idea or kept a plan in his back pocket concerning the story or subject matter he was talking about. He never let you know what was in his pocket until he wanted you to know what it was. He didn't play it close to the vest. He wore the vest.

"Bobby, never show your full hand, only what's necessary to win," Jimmy would tell me. "Use that extra bit of knowledge to gain an advantage with someone. Always keep a door open for yourself. Never back yourself into a corner because then you'll be in the jackpot." he would say. "If a guy thinks he's the smartest guy in the room, let the fool think that; let the suckers build the pot for you. Then you go in, make the play when the play has to be made, and grab the pot. The smartest guy in the room will be looking for a buck and you'll have it," Jimmy said. "Then, he's got to come to you for a buck and then you, not him, write the financial lyrics to the song. Mr. Smart Guy ain't so smart now, is he? He's gonna have to pay for the money you took from him, so who's the smart guy?" Jimmy said. When the Feds would send an Outfit guy away to college, Jimmy would tell me 'nothing wrong with being a high school graduate,' with a wink of his eye.

After coming back from their honeymoon in Northern California, Melissa went back to earning legal money at the Federal Reserve Bank and Shorty went back to earning illegal money from the smut business. Melissa was glad to be back at work, seeing her co-workers. In the next two years, she received a promotion and seemed to be heading higher at the bank. Her next move would be to a middle management supervisory position. The bank saw her potential and had no qualms about moving her up the corporate ladder. No matter what position she held at the bank, she maintained a friendly disposition with everyone along the way.

Tommy taught her if you have friends, they can help advance you, not only on the job, but in your personal life, so be careful where you step. Don't step on people because once you make an enemy, you always have to look over your shoulder to watch out for them, Tommy would tell her. Melissa listened to Tommy and followed his fatherly advice. Shorty listened to Victor's advice and followed it. Gee, I wonder whose advice was best. Well, I'll let you decide.

Before they got married, Melissa and Shorty discussed having children. They both went through the premarital counseling session at Our Lady of Perpetual Worship offered by Father Tom. They both told Father Tom they wanted children in their married life and were looking forward to raising children. Father Tom told them that since they were both good Catholics, the children would be raised in a loving, religious, spiritual way and he wished them the best. Everyone bowed their heads as Father Tom said a prayer asking God to watch over this family. God heard the prayer and he turned to the Feds and said, "I guess you'll be watching over Shorty's other family."

It was late in the afternoon on a Wednesday while at work that Melissa received a call from her doctor's office that the test result came back saying she was pregnant. "I'm pregnant. I'm really pregnant," Melissa excitedly said to the doctor's nurse who called her.

"Congratulations, Mrs. Lanzo. Yes, you are pregnant," the nurse said.

"Thank you. Oh, my God, thank you so much," Melissa said as she hung up the phone.

A female co-worker who sat near Melissa came by. "Melissa, I heard what you said. You're pregnant. How wonderful," the co-worker said.

Melissa stood up and said, "I'm really pregnant," in a happy dazed kind of way. The co-worker and Melissa hugged. "I can't wait to get home and tell Pete. I know he'll be thrilled and so excited about becoming a father," Melissa said.

As soon as Shorty walked in the house, Melissa, who had been waiting for him, took his hand. "Pete, come here. Sit down," she said, as she led him to the couch in the living room. Still holding his hand while they sat on the couch, Melissa said, "Pete, I have the most wonderful news to tell you. I heard from the doctor's office this afternoon and they told me the test result confirmed I'm pregnant."

She then put her arms around Pete's waist and put her head slightly sideways while laying there waiting for his response. Hearing that he was going to become a father was not exactly what Shorty wanted to hear at that moment. *Maybe in a year or two, but not now* he thought. Shorty put on a brave front for Melissa. Saying you want kids and then having them, for some people, is like talking the talk but now can you do the walk? Shorty was stumbling and trying to maintain his balance after being hit with a verbally gusty wind from Melissa.

"Baby, that's wonderful. I just don't have the words to express my happiness about becoming a father," he said, as he then bent his head down and kissed the top of her head.

"Oh, I know you'll be a great father, just a great dad. I bet now that I've told you, you can hardly wait," Melissa said.

"Hardly," Shorty said, as he put his arms around Melissa's shoulders.

Now not only would Shorty have to worry about supporting this future family, but he still had to worry how he was going to support his other family. With your family, you worry about the children sleeping through the night. With the other family, you worry about never waking up.

During Melissa's pregnancy, she found out she was going to have twins, as it turned out, a boy and a girl. As much as she wanted to continue working at the bank, she knew that was not possible, having to raise two children. She and Shorty talked it over and they decided, in the best interest of the children, Melissa would stay home and care for them. This was one of the few times they would be in total agreement in their marriage.

Regretfully, after the birth of the twins, Melissa called her boss and told him she would not be returning to work. He told her she was an excellent employee and that he would miss her. He wished her well and if she changed her mind about work, he would have a position for her. Melissa thanked him and felt very good about herself after hearing her boss's compliments. She was really looking forward to motherhood.

She was a wonderful, loving mother, not only to the twins, but when her other two children were born—a girl and a boy—she gave them the same amount of love. There was no doubt about it; Melissa was the dominant factor in the children's lives. Years later, all her children thanked her for being their mother and doing an outstanding job of being a parent.

While she was home raising the children, Melissa threw herself into charitable work at Our Lady of Perpetual Worship. Everything at home seemed to be going well with the children. Shorty was doing well financially. There was food on the table and the bills were paid. Melissa, having that active mind, found Our Lady of Perpetual Worship to give her mind an outlet and allow her brain to exercise her thoughts.

At the church, she organized the yearly food drive, contacting the major grocery chains to assist her. She organized the Christmas clothing drive, contacting major retail stores for assistance, calling radio stations to publicize the clothing drive, used political juice to get the City of Chicago to establish drop off points where clothing could be donated, and she got the professional sports teams to support the clothing drive. She organized the spring dinner dance, which was a fundraiser for the church. She organized the church's first after-school program, where children could be involved with sports and other activities to keep them occupied until their parents could pick them up.

She organized a voluntary 'meet a neighbor' program where youngsters met with senior citizens to learn important life experiences and to offer and develop friendships. Both groups benefited by the program. The elderly, with their life experiences, could turn the clock back and look at life through the eyes of the youngster. The youngster gained valuable experience projecting their lives through the eyes of the elderly. Both could bridge the gap between young and old—each one showing the other that both, no matter what age, never stopped learning about life.

Father Tom joked that he was putting the paperwork through to get Melissa promoted to Assistant to God because of her contributions to Our Lady of Perpetual Worship. Every activity that Melissa organized was wildly successful beyond all expectations. More food, more clothes were received by the church than any previous year. As Father Tom would say, Melissa had a golden mind that sure turned her projects into gold. While raising the children, doing all these charitable things at the church, and being a caring wife to Shorty, she didn't have the time to think about what Shorty did to earn his money or what he told her he did to earn this money.

When a woman is married to an Outfit guy, there is a standard operating procedure that is followed. He tells her what he wants to tell her, which is very little of how he earns his living. The kids know nothing at all about their father's type of work. All they know is he leaves in the morning at some point and comes home at night, sometimes very late at night. He gets paid for doing something and no one is quite sure what he's doing.

He never talks about business at home. Outfit business remains outside the house. It never gets a place at the dinner table, nor is it invited over for a glass of wine. Outfit business, if known, brings questions—questions that are best left unanswered a couple of blocks away from the house. Questions that can breed more questions, for the family in the house, if they want to remain a family, need never be answered. Secrecy is the Outfit's middle name. If no one knows anything about what you do, no one can rat you out. So, when it comes to an Outfit guy's personal family, mum's the word about their so-called profession.

In some cases, the Outfit guy has what is known as a front job and that's what his family thinks he does for a living. A front job could be on a government payroll—either for the state, county, or city—and sometimes the guy could be a double dipper on more than one government agency. It was not uncommon for a guy to be a ghost worker for the city and county at the same time.

One of our political friends would get the Outfit guy a position out in the field. The title could be a field tech, field rep, or field coordinator. Nobody saw the guy or knew what he did, yet, his title was in the budget and he got salary, health benefits, and if he worked (and I use the term loosely) at least 20 years, a pension.

Another type of front job was being on a union payroll or being on the payroll of an Outfit-controlled construction company. These types of front jobs were similar to government jobs in the sense that guys were ghost payrollers. Whereas in the government jobs, taxpayers pay the freight for Outfit workers who don't work in the union or construction type jobs, companies pay the freight for the no-show Outfit guys. No matter how you slice the bread, the Outfit eats the slices and never breaks a sweat, and either taxpayers, private industry, or both pay for the right of never getting a slice. Just another example of let the suckers build the pot then you take it for yourself.

To the wife and family, all of these front jobs are sounding legit, so why would they question what the Outfit guy tells them. If he doesn't have a front job, the Outfit guy will invent some type of job to snow the family. He'll turn on the snowflakes and tell the wife it's a job where they pay in cash. The truth of the matter is he doesn't really earn his money from front jobs or made-up fairytale jobs. He earns his money in any number of illegal ways.

Open the Outfit menu and place your order today. I have a taste for gambling. Could you put the loan-sharking on the side? Oh yeah, hold the money laundering, too. Drink? Yeah, aggressive drug trafficking. There are two selections that are on the Outfit menu seven days a week. You can always order beatings and murder, if you're looking to burn up some calories.

With the family of the Outfit guy, thinking the leader of the house is putting his nose to the grindstone to earn a living, happiness reigns supreme in the house money coming in, financial problems staying out. I would say probably 99.9% of Outfit families function this way. No one knows anything or wants to know anything. Jimmy was the one in a million, as he wanted me, starting at the age of eight and going forward, to see the totality of what being in the life really was all about—no television or movie concepts about the mob—just the facts, man, just the ice cold, bone-rattling, nauseatingly truthful facts of how the underworld tries to get a social standing by inflicting their criminal ways on people who want to criminally party with them.

Many a time I prayed to God to ask him to stop some physical and/or emotional pain being doled out by the Outfit. Please, God, just make it stop. Stop whatever pain I was seeing right in front of me. God would tell me, "Bobby, by seeing the sharp jagged bent edges of being in the life, the naked angles that have to be played, there is only one solution—never go into the life. For, if your eyes don't see it, your brain won't feel it," God said. No Outfit guy wanted their kids to know what being in the life was all about. This might be one of the few times when I can say Outfit guys were normal in their thinking. To Jimmy, me seeing everything in the life was normal. To me, when I went away to college, I got a bachelor's degree in a recognized field from an authentic college after four years of study. When Outfit kids I knew later went away to college, their education was in a federal facility being measured by years being served for a conviction. Who was the better teacher?

Shorty initially told Melissa that he made industrial films that in some situations could be used for corporate and educational training purposes. Maybe by watching one of Shorty's training films, it would help you pass Sex 101. Pay attention, guys, otherwise you'll be going to summer school.

Did Melissa really believe Shorty when he told her that he did legit work? Who knows. Melissa was sharp, but maybe she believed Shorty because she wanted tranquility in her family's life. Frankly, unless someone could prove differently, her man was like any other hardworking husband trying to give his family the security all families desire. However, there was someone out there lurking who would prove Shorty wrong.

The children were not quite teenagers when Victor died in his sleep from the heart attack. Shorty then assumed leadership of Victor's operation. He decided to expand the business. He expanded the business more heavily into child pornography. Child porn was a huge moneymaker because there's always lots of pedophiles in this country who will spend some bucks on watching little kids do things adults might not even think of, let alone do. The profit margin on making child porn was high, maybe 65% to 70%. Production costs were cheaper than adult porn—much smaller payroll.

I can hear your outrage. How could someone do this to children? Child pornography is a vile, sick, heinous, dirty thing to do to God's precious little angels. There is nothing more repulsive than using sparkling beautiful children to make a buck. The Outfit never had any morals about how they treated human beings before, so you can't expect them to care about the defenseless little ones who have no one to protect them now. No one will speak up for them; no one will be their advocate. As long as there is a buyer for this disgusting crap, it'll be made…and the beat goes on.

The Outfit has that one code and one code only, and it is can we make a buck off of whatever it is. Since the Outfit is always doing an illegal dance, the coed will have a partner for every tune played. The coed will never have to be asked to dance by anyone, as the Outfit's criminal activities will keep the coed on the dance floor all night long.

Shorty held his daily court at an Italian social club called Bambino's. Bambino's was a two-story building on the west side of Chicago, where Shorty and his crew would meet to talk about mob business. There were a couple of tables on the first floor where guys would talk and play cards. There was a small bar area with a refrigerator nearby. Some Outfit wannabes would drop by to either talk to or play cards with crew members.

On the second floor was where Shorty would hear from his crew about how things were going out on the street and also where he gave orders to the crew. The crew was composed of six guys, though there were a couple of other guys, who while not part of the crew as members, were involved more directly with Shorty himself.

Money collected by the crew from gambling, loan-sharking, and the smut operation was brought to Bambino's and given to Shorty. Maybe 40% of the money went for payroll and the remaining 60% went to Shorty. Some of his money went for operating expenses, especially legal fees, but there were other operating expenses that Shorty had to pay for, especially concerning the smut business. Shorty still made a real good buck for himself, so he brought home enough money to cover household expenses, which avoided any questions from Melissa.

Bambino's was owned by one of Shorty's street crew members Angelo "Big Ang" Fairene—a 6'1", 240-lb. hulking menace of a man—who, unless you paid him monies owed, never smiled. Fairene had jet black hair and, with those evil eyes, looked like all the bad guys you would see on television. Fairene was a fists first kind of guy where he liked to beat you, then he would let you speak, if you could. It was pretty tough to talk with a mashed face and aching body, so the victims rarely said much. If Fairene was in a good mood, he would only use his fists, but if he was having many of those 'forget about it' days he would take out his feelings by kicking the victim anywhere on the victim's body.

Nothing was off limits from the victim's head to his toes. It was like you wind him up and watch him turn loose and drop bombs on the victim with his forceful feet. Fairene would end his attack by asking the victim if he wanted more. Sometimes, Fairene would answer his own question, "Oh, so you want more," and then he would throw in a couple more kicks for good measure. He then would yell at the victim, "Are you happy now?" In his mind, Fairene was just using good old mob etiquette by entertaining his guest, making him feel right at home with these Outfit social graces. Fairene was such an outgoing host to the victim, wasn't he?

Fairene was Shorty's most loyal crew member. Fairene would always say, referring to Shorty, "Whatever the boss wants, that's what we would do." Shorty trusted Fairene to the point where he made him his confidant about the running of street operations by the crew. Shorty made Fairene his captain and gave him a lot of authority over the street crew. Everyone on the street always said Shorty and Big Ang were as close as brothers. In a way, they were brothers, as both of them committed criminal acts in tandem. You couldn't separate the two of them on that count.

Fairene mainly was involved with the distribution of adult and child pornography in the city in the southwest suburbs to adult bookstores and dealers, who sold this type of smut to subscribers. When Corral's, one of the adult bookstores Fairene sold to, bought bootleg adult movies, he wanted to take action against them, but he had to clear it with Shorty at Bambino's.

"We gotta problem with Corral's," Fairene told Shorty.

"How do you know?" Shorty said.

"Cause Richie the Pig told me," Fairene said. Richard "Richie the Pig" Paublete was a street hustler. Fairene used to pay him a couple of bucks to keep his eyes and ears open on the street and let Fairene know what was happening. Paublete was always selling something hot on the street. It could be jewelry, it could be clothes, it could be a television, or it could be anything hot that he bought from the Outfit boys, who obtained the items using their preferred five-finger discount.

Paublete was in Corral's one day, and he overheard a conversation between owner John Dorben and some guy Paublete didn't know. The guy told Dorben he could get him bootleg adult porn movies that would be cheaper than he's paying for them now. Dorben asked the guy, according to Paublete, if the quality of the films was good. The guy told him they were as the copies were made from a store-bought original.

"Richie said he watched the guy go to his car, open up his trunk, and bring back a couple of copies," Fairene said. "Richie said Dorben took the copies and went to the back part of the store in a room to check out the copies. Richie said Dorben said to the guy after coming back from the room, 'When can you deliver?' and the guy said, 'Give me a couple of days,'" Fairene said. "Richie said Dorben said, 'That'll be fine, as I'll sell out my remaining stock first, but I'll shelve yours in the back until my stock is gone, then I'll start selling your stuff,' he told the guy," Fairene said. "Richie said they agreed on a price cheaper than what we sell to Corral's," said Fairene.

"How much cheaper?" Shorty said.

"Richie wasn't quite sure, but it sounded like maybe 20% cheaper than our stuff," Fairene said.

"Yeah, it sounds like we gotta problem here," Shorty said.

"Boss, look, I'm not telling you what to, but we can't let this guy, this mamaluke, this goof, run around to other stores we sell our movies to and undercut our price," Fairene said. "We gotta make an example of Corral's so everyone on the street we deal with knows we mean business if you buy from someone else," he said. "We gotta hit Corral's hard," Fairene said. "If you think this is the right thing to do, give the order and we'll light up Corral's," Fairene said. "Besides, I'm sure this mamaluke has visited our other stores already, so in a way, we're playing catch up trying to nip this thing in the bud before it hurts us in the pocketbook," Fairene said.

"Big Ang, you got the order. Take a couple of guys from the crew and light up Corral's," Shorty said.

"Okay, boss. That's all I needed to hear. That's what you want and that's what we'll do," Fairene said.

"This is where Shorty screwed up," I said to Jimmy.

"Yeah, this is the difference between a college education, which is theory, and a street education where you peel back the layers until you get to the real story," Jimmy said. "First of all, Shorty should not have taken Richie the Pig's story at face value," he said. "Richie is the type of guy who will tell you it's Tuesday when everyone knows it's Wednesday. The calendar says it's Wednesday, the daily newspaper says it's Wednesday, the radio announcer tells you it's Wednesday, and here comes Richie the Pig telling you it's Tuesday," Jimmy said. "Then Richie will say, 'For five bucks I'll check it out for you and see if it's really Tuesday or Wednesday," Jimmy said. "You don't take the word of the street scammer like Richie without checking it out," he said.

"I ain't saying, Bobby, Richie is right. He could be right, but you gotta research this. Don't just give a fuckin' order on Corral's before you're sure of the facts," Jimmy said. "Once you got enough information, you have the owner Johnny Dorben come to Bambino's for a one-on-one sit-down. You lay out the story chapter and verse to him that if he buys from someone else, he'll be out of business," Jimmy said. "Then you get out of your chair, walk behind Dorben, and put your hands on his shoulder, and tell him, 'Johnny, I really like you as a person, but if you pull this shit and buy from someone else…well business is business…and you know we always mean business when it comes to our business,'" Jimmy said. "Then you take your hands off his shoulder, take a couple of steps back, but don't say anything, yet. Just stay quiet for a bit, let Dorben digest what you just told him," Jimmy said.

"Then you say to him, now standing in front of him, 'Any questions, Johnny, because the only question for you is how long do you think your life expectancy is going to be if you cross me?'" Jimmy said. "Then you put your eyes right on Johnny's face, don't say another word, let everything melt on his brain, and just keep looking at him. Then stick your hand out to shake his hand and say to him, 'Deal or else,'" Jimmy said. "He'll shake your hand. What else is he going to do? Then after the handshake, you walk him to the door and tell him this is the first and last time we're going to have this conversation, Johnny. It's up to you, because if by some remote chance this happens again, you've got a nice family, and it could be pretty lonely coming home every night to an empty house, which you caused to happen," said Jimmy.

I looked at Jimmy and Jimmy looked right back at me. All I could think at that point was wow, oh wow, how Jimmy, without missing a beat, had this all figured out.

"Bobby, it's still about the money. You want to keep it flowing," Jimmy said. "Now, maybe, in some cases, you would light up Corral's—you might not have a choice—but it would have been to Shorty's benefit if he took a little more time to find out whether he could keep the money coming from Corral's or not, that's all I'm saying," Jimmy said.

"I wouldn't be too trusting of Big Ang, either," Jimmy said.

How so? I thought. Big Ang was Shorty's guy and he seemed so loyal to Shorty like he's tied to him.

"Bobby, if something happens to Shorty, say the Feds start climbing over him, who becomes the capo of the street crew? Not me; not you; but Big Ang," Jimmy said. "Big Ang comes in and wants to go after Corral's solely on what Richie the Pig is telling him. It's like…bam…we gotta do something real fast to Corral's," Jimmy said. "I know that's how Big Ang works on the street—punch once, punch twice, no questions asked so no answers given," Jimmy said. "But what if Big Ang got ideas about becoming the capo of the crew, taking over the business on the street?" he asked.

"So, he gives Shorty some uncorroborated story from a guy Big Ang pays to bird dog what's happening on the street, so how legit is that?" Jimmy asked. "Big Ang could be setting Shorty up for a fall by laying it on real thick that they gotta go after Corral's," Jimmy said. "See, Bobby, Big Ang backs Shorty into a corner by telling him they gotta keep the guy who's undercutting their price on the movies from going to any other store to undercut the price, thus, forcing Shorty to give the order to light up Corral's," he said.

"So, later on, if something goes down on Shorty, Big Ang throws up his hands and says, 'See, it was Shorty who gave the order, not me,'" Jimmy said. "Big Ang comes off smelling clean like a baby's ass because he's pointing the finger at Shorty," Jimmy said. "Look, Shorty doesn't have Victor around anymore to wipe his nose when it runs. The thing is, Shorty is still wet behind the ears learning the business," Jimmy continued. "In the life, you gotta remember, Bobby, what did I always tell you about a story?" Jimmy asked.

"There are three stories: your story, my story, and the truth," I said.

"That's right, because guys in the life are constantly lying to you and giving you bullshit," Jimmy said. "So, unless it's a medical emergency where you gotta make a decision right now, when you deal with guys in the life, don't rush to judgment about what they tell you. Put it in neutral and start researching what they're telling you," Jimmy said.

"What did I tell you about a mother's love?" Jimmy said.

"If your mother says she loves you, check it out," I said.

"Right," Jimmy said with a smile stretching across his face.

"So, are you saying like, maybe, Shorty put himself in the jackpot because of his order on Corral's?" I said.

"You're learning, Bobby. You're learning," Jimmy said.

About 10 days after Shorty gave the order to hit Corral's, Fairene acquired the needed explosives. Corral's was not just going to be torched, it was going to be blown apart. The explosives Fairene got were powerful and toxic, so the message left by these explosives would be the Outfit's greeting to other adult stores that it would be very prudent on their part to continue their business with the Outfit rather than get a personalized greeting hand delivered by the boys.

Fairene chose two crew members to help him carry out the hit on Corral's—Jimmy Quartino, who was a 19-year-old punk with a smart mouth who was the gofer for the crew, but dreamed of a bigger role with the Outfit and John "Johnny Stut" Guissepe. Guissepe, when he talked, especially if he was nervous, had a slight speech impediment; he would stutter. It wasn't pronounced unless you really paid attention when he was talking. Guissepe was a quiet guy, who wore glasses, and his job with the crew was as a bookmaker. Behind Guissepe's back, guys would mimic Guissepe's stuttering, but they never did this to his face, and their reason for not doing this in front of him was…well, let's say, they wanted to grow old.

One Saturday night, Guissepe, his wife, sister, and brother-in-law went to Tokyo Joe's, a Chinese restaurant near downtown. The brother-in-law, who had this superior attitude, started to berate Guissepe at the table for not taking his wife on a vacation. The brother-in-law bragged about the vacations he took Guissepe's sister on. Then the brother-in-law, to top it off, pretended to stutter, and said, "I don't know what you really do for a living, but whatever it is, you don't make enough money," and he tried to emphasize the word money in his made-up stutter. Guissepe just looked at him, but he didn't say a word. Guissepe's sister immediately changed the subject.

A few days later, maybe three or four, the brother-in-law, who owned a hardware store, kissed his wife goodbye and went to work. No one has seen him since that day. When Shorty's crew heard about the missing brother-in-law, from that point forward, the crew never performed in front of Guissepe, they performed in private as sometimes the audience didn't like the show.

With explosives in hand, Fairene, Quartino, and Guissepe set out one night to school Corral's that you never screw with the teacher. It was well after closing when the boys broke into Corral's, going through the back door, and then set up the explosives in the store. Once the timer was set for three minutes, the boys quickly exited the store and went back to their car, which was parked a safe distance away, to watch their work. When the timer went off, a deafening roaring blast occurred inside Corral's. The store was engulfed in roiling hot flames and a fire spread throughout the store.

The boys took off in the car as their criminal work of art was on full display for all to see. They drove off laughing, telling each other they showed Corral's who was boss. "You feel you can stand up to the Outfit, then we'll knock you down like anyone else who gets in our way," the boys said to each other. "You want to be COD with us, then we will be DOD (destruction on delivery) with you," the boys exclaimed.

Within seconds after the blast, a neighbor's dog started barking at the top of his lungs. This woke the neighbor who looked out his bedroom window to see a smoking building in which flames were shooting a bright orange hue into the jet black night sky. He ran to his kitchen phone, dialing the emergency number to call for the fire department as quickly as his fingers let him. By the time the fire department came, which was within a few minutes, Corral's was completely destroyed. After the fire was put out, an arson investigation was ordered. Two days after the fire, the fire department ruled from its investigation that Corral's had been firebombed and, indeed, arson had been committed.

When an adult book and movie store is firebombed in Chicago, the local FBI takes an interest because of who the culprit generally turns out to be. I'll give you a hint, someone with a vowel at the end of his last name, who belongs to an organization, who doesn't play nice with others.

The firebombing of Corral's, which was ordered by Shorty, got the attention of the Feds. They started their investigation, putting the name of the person who they knew to be involved in adult and child pornography at the top of their list. Shorty Lanzo, go to the front of the class.

The Feds knew Shorty and the crew conducted business at Bambino's, so they got a court ordered wiretap to be used to listen to phone conversations coming in and going out. The most prominent person who, at that point, the Feds heard was Fairene. The Feds recorded quite a few hours of Fairene discussing crew business, particularly the firebombing of Corral's, among other things. The FBI started to tail Fairene, watching his comings and goings, and also photographed him talking to known Outfit members.

One of the conversations that the FBI listened to was between Fairene and a dealer about the delivery of some child pornography. The FBI followed Fairene to where the drop off was going to take place. The FBI took pictures of Fairene talking to the dealer. While investigating the dealer, the FBI found out this dealer was under investigation for income tax evasion. The Feds got a court ordered wiretap for the dealer's home phone.

They heard a conversation in which the dealer called from home and spoke with Fairene at Bambino's, telling him he was going to Wisconsin to sell and distribute adult and child pornography to an adult bookstore in Milwaukee. Upon hearing this, the FBI Chicago office contacted the FBI Milwaukee office, telling them about their investigation of the dealer. Both Chicago and Milwaukee coordinated a plan to arrest the dealer.

The Chicago FBI followed the dealer to Milwaukee one Saturday afternoon and, along with Milwaukee FBI, arrested the dealer in the adult bookstore with the pornography. The dealer was taken back to Chicago where he was held for a bond hearing in the MCC. The Metropolitan Correctional Center in downtown Chicago is close to the Federal Building where the bond hearing was supposed to be held.

The dealer requested his lawyer, and in their presence, the Feds told them besides probably being charged with income tax evasion, the dealer was going to be charged with crossing a state line to sell and distribute pornography. They played the tape of the dealer talking to Fairene at Bambino's about going to Milwaukee to sell the pornography, which the Feds said additional charges would be pending for conspiracy. Another tape was played in which the dealer and Fairene talked about receiving pornography through the mail, thus, charges were pending on mail fraud. The Feds then turned up the heat by saying they were developing a racketeering case against the dealer. They told him if he didn't cooperate, he could be looking at 20 years, if convicted.

The dealer asked to be alone with his lawyer to confer about his case. The Assistant United States Attorney and the FBI left the room. In less than a half hour, the dealer's attorney told the Feds the dealer would cooperate in exchange for a lesser sentence that both lawyers would negotiate over the next several months. The Feds accepted the deal.

The dealer's apartment, courtesy of the FBI, had audio and video equipment installed, which would be used to incriminate Fairene. The dealer, over the next several months, had numerous conversations with Fairene. He got Fairene to talk about not only the crew's illegal activities, but specifically about the firebombing of Corral's. Fairene said that Shorty detailed a plan to firebomb the adult bookstore as someone was selling bootleg movies cheaper than them and Shorty didn't want this to spread to other adult stores they dealt with. "I approached Shorty about hitting Corral's, but Shorty gave the order to firebomb the building," Fairene said. The Feds recorded enough conversations between the dealer and Fairene that were incriminating enough to get an arrest warrant for Fairene.

When the Feds would come early in the morning to arrest one of the boys, Outfit guys referred to that type of an arrest as the Feds making a coffee run, which was the case on an early Thursday morning at about 6 A.M. when the Feds came to Fairene's house and arrested him. Once downtown in the MCC, Fairene said he wasn't talking until his lawyer came. Fairene's wife, upon the arrest, called Fairene's lawyer to tell him Fairene had been arrested by the FBI.

Once the lawyer arrived, the Feds played selected tapes for Fairene and his lawyer. Fairene sat dumbfounded as he watched himself on tape and heard himself say the things he said. Fairene's face tightened up as he was watching himself basically convict himself on the tapes. The Feds gave Fairene's lawyer a copy of the indictment with the charges listed. The Feds pointed out to the lawyer the big charge for firebombing Corral's, a mandatory minimum sentence of 30 years. If convicted on that charge, Fairene was looking at a minimum of 30 years and the judge could sentence Fairene to a lot more than that, if he wanted to. Putting that charge together with the other charges of conspiracy to sell pornography across state lines, income tax evasion, mail fraud, and racketeering—all carrying multiple counts if convicted—Fairene was never coming home from college.

The Feds then threw out the safety line to Fairene, as they usually do. Those three little words 'if you cooperate' were thrown into Fairene's lap. Fairene started to snarl, but his lawyer cut him off. Fairene's lawyer, Tim Dickerson, told the Feds he wanted to confer with his client. The Feds left the room.

"Ang, the tapes we've seen are very incriminating, and the FBI has a lot more tapes they will use against you in a trial. I can go ahead and enter a not guilty plea at the arraignment. The Feds will ask for no bond and probably get it. You'll sit at the Metropolitan Correctional Center over a year until the trial takes place. While I can attack the credibility and motive of the government witnesses, the fact is the jury is going to remember what they see and hear on the tapes," Dickerson said. "While I can say you were just shooting your mouth off on the tapes, I don't believe the jury will buy it," Dickerson said.

"What about entrapment?" Fairene said.

"The US Supreme Court has ruled on numerous entrapment cases, generally siding with the prosecution. This case would not fall under entrapment guidelines set forth by the Supreme Court," Dickerson said.

"I'm not a rat. I ain't going to rat out Shorty," Fairene angrily said.

"Ang, even if the judge gives you the mandatory minimum of 30 years on a convicted bombing charge, he'll be giving you additional time on the other charges, if convicted," Dickerson said. "You could be looking at 40 to 55 total years, which you have to serve 85% of the time," he said. "That's only if you get the minimum on the bombing charge. If the judge wants, he could go as high as 60 years max just on the bombing charge," Dickerson said. "So, you have to think about what's at stake," Dickerson said.

"I'm not a rat," Fairene said.

"Ang, you gotta think about your family. It's really possible you might be in prison the rest of your life and never see your family again. No holidays. No birthdays. No graduations. None of those family events ever again. They will be missing you and you will miss them," Dickerson said. "With full cooperation, I think I could get you a plea deal of between 48 to 60 months as you would have to plead guilty to lesser charges," Dickerson said. "Maybe I can get the Assistant US Attorney to give you under 48 months. I'd have to see how bad he wants Shorty and the crew. Whatever I get you, you will have to serve 85% of your sentence," Dickerson said. "If you want to go to trial, fine, then we'll do that. Then I'll go ahead and prepare a defense. It's your decision," he said. "I'm just advising you of your legal options, but you're the client, so it's your call on what you want to do," Dickerson said.

"I'm not a rat," Fairene said.

I know you guys are probably thinking this guy Fairene is hardcore to the bone and he'll never rat out Shorty and the crew. The Feds might as well forget about it with Fairene. He'll never open up his mouth. Well, Mr. I'm Not a Rat became a big one as not only did he rat out Shorty and the crew, but he sang to the choir about two bookies who weren't even part of the crew—Steven "Little Stevie" Armani and Guy "Numbers" Elate were later indicted and convicted of gambling charges.

"Who would ever think Big Ang would turn out to be a rat?" I said to Jimmy. "Here's a guy who, if he physically ran headfirst into a building, the building would get hurt," I said. "He's a brute. No way do you figure a tough guy like Big Ang ratting out Shorty and the crew," I said. "I mean Big Ang was Shorty's right-hand man. He seemed so loyal to Shorty," I said.

"Bobby, while being a rat is considered the worst thing a guy in the Outfit could be, and guys get whacked for sure if they rat, sometimes the guy gets whacked if he's suspected of being a rat. You gotta look at Big Ang's situation," Jimmy said. "He's not going to get probation or community service if convicted after a trial," Jimmy said. "He's going to be separated from his family, possibly forever," Jimmy said. "He ain't going to be graduating from college," Jimmy said.

"Some guys can handle being away at college, seeing none of their family, and others can't," Jimmy said. "I ain't saying it's okay to be a rat. It's just you gotta do what's best for you," he said. "Who's to say if it was Shorty in the jackpot, he wouldn't rat out Big Ang? Don't trust anyone, because when they're in the deep stuff up to their eyeballs, it becomes who's going to survive over who," Jimmy said.

"I suppose you're right," I said to Jimmy.

"I guess guys talk about loyalty to the Outfit, but does what it comes down to is that they are going to be loyal to me, myself, and I. Screw everyone else if they suffer. So what, I'm okay and that's all that matters. I got the best deal for me," I said.

The more I saw of being in the life, the more I realized it is like a game of dodgeball. You're running, ducking, trying not to get caught by the Feds or whacked by the Outfit. You are trying to step gingerly around the criminal acts that you are part of in order not to blow yourself up and become an Outfit casualty. Loyalty is supposed to be your safety vest, protecting you from the ills of being in the life. However, for some guys in the life, loyalty is a figure of speech like saying, 'I'm a good citizen.'

When the Feds coming to barter with you all of a sudden, loyalty is just a bargaining chip you put on the table to improve the deal you ultimately get from the Feds. You sell loyalty to the Feds to give them who they want. Loyalty is cheap when it no longer has any personal meaning to you. You become a rat, and then you carry around the feeling of *oh, well, better him than me*. So, loyalty ranks right up there with being second. It's used to take down number one, then once that happens and Mr. Big is gone, loyalty gets thrown where it always belonged—in the garbage.

"Bobby, in the life, you never can have a one size fits all mentality," Jimmy said. "You gotta be flexible and adapt to what you see coming around the corner," Jimmy said. "When you don't see something, then you go along, you know, businesses as usual, but once you see what's coming at you, you gotta make the play that has to be made for that situation," he said.

"Big Ang is in the jackpot; sure, he put himself there, but the fact is the Feds got their own jackpot they'll put you in," Jimmy said. "Their jackpot has two locked doors—one saying good, one saying bad," he said. "It's up to you what door you want the Feds to open up. You make a deal with the Feds, they'll open the good door. You want to go to trial and roll the dice, fine, but if you lose, then they open the bad door," Jimmy said. "See, Bobby, the Feds at that point aren't looking to make a deal unless you got something they can hang their hat on," he said.

"Being in the life is changing," Jimmy said. "The Feds are pushing harder and you ain't got nothing to push back with other than giving the Feds what they want to enroll someone in college," Jimmy said. "You can't live in the past. You gotta deal with what's right in front of you," Jimmy said. "The past is only a memory and Big Ang didn't want any memories," Jimmy said.

"Bobby, you got a good heart," Jimmy said to me, as he put his arm around my shoulder. "You must have gotten it from Karen because you certainly didn't get it from the old man," he said with a smile on his face. "It bothers you Big Ang became a rat. I can see it," Jimmy said. "You want everything to be on the square. I understand that, but if you can find a life in which that takes place, let me know," Jimmy said. "What have I always told you about business?" Jimmy said.

"If it's something important to you, keep it to yourself and never tell anyone then you'll never get hurt," I said.

"Well, when Shorty took Big Ang into his confidence and told him things, maybe some things he had to tell him, maybe some things he shouldn't have told him," Jimmy said. "Once Big Ang got a line on Shorty, he knew which buttons to push like the firebombing of Corral's," Jimmy said. "He pushed Shorty into it and Shorty never thought about how this would play out in the future," he said. "So, when the Feds nabbed Big Ang, he knew he had the trump card to protect himself," Jimmy said. "He was going to protect himself as much as he could by putting the knife in Shorty's back," he said. "He figures if the roles were reversed, Shorty would put it in his back," Jimmy said. "At any time, Bobby, you gotta watch what you tell people—the less, the better," Jimmy said.

"I know, but if you're loyal to someone, logically why would you turn on them?" I said.

"Bobby, logic and survival walk on different sides of the street," Jimmy said. "Logic is the theory of the game and survival is winning the game and when the Feds are your opponent, you always play to win, Bobby, because they're doing the same," Jimmy said. "In life, Bobby, no one remembers who came in second place. Only the winner is remembered," Jimmy said. "Big Ang wanted to be the winner. The cost to Shorty was never factored in," Jimmy said.

I thought, maybe, if Jimmy had schooled Shorty on Outfit ways, things would have been different. However, since Victor was his teacher, Shorty used Victor's ways and never would have listened to Jimmy. Shorty was a college grad who thought he knew it all. There was one part of the all he didn't know and wasn't going to be able to take a refresher course—the part where the Feds attack you from all angles because they got better resources than you.

After Fairene decided to cooperate, the Feds installed audio and video equipment in Bambino's. As they always do, the Feds coached Fairene on what they wanted him to talk about. He wore a wire. Fairene, while saying he would cooperate, was not happy about ratting out Shorty and the crew members, but he had no choice other than going to trial, which even his own lawyer was not in favor of.

The Feds started recording hour after hour, day after day, week after week, month after month of Fairene's conversations with the crew and Shorty. You could hear on the audiotapes, the crew talking about gambling, loan-sharking, and the firebombing of Corral's. The crew responded back in conversation incriminating themselves. You could hear on the audiotapes, Shorty not only talking about the same subjects, but also talking to Fairene about adult and child pornography, and if he had to order another firebombing of another adult bookstore, he would do it just like he did at Corral's.

The FBI continued recording for months, as they were listening, parked in a van about two blocks away. The FBI would just shake their heads at how freely everyone was talking and helping to build the case against themselves. One FBI agent said to another, "They're convicting themselves and we're not even breaking a sweat over this case." The FBI agents heard Jimmy Quartino brag about the firebombing of Corral's, how he really enjoyed showing any other adult bookstore this is what would happen to you if you screwed with the Outfit. He talked about his role in the firebombing at Corral's. The FBI agents heard John Guissepe talk about how Corral's, by purchasing movies from someone other than the Outfit, got what they deserved. He talked about his role in the firebombing of Corral's.

The FBI, after recording conversations between Fairene, Shorty, and the crew for nearly a year, decided it was time to play the pertinent tapes for the Assistant US Attorney. He concluded he had enough evidence to take before a grand jury to seek indictments against those individuals who incriminated themselves by talking about criminal activities. The Assistant US Attorney decided it was time to call for a grand jury.

Jury summonses are mailed out to people just as are notifications for Circuit Court jury duty. You are told to report on a specific day to the Collins Federal Building in downtown Chicago. A grand jury could be impaneled for 18 months, but they only meet once a week. In this case, it was every Wednesday. You filled out a questionnaire and the Assistant US Attorney would interview you. If chosen, you would be part of a grand jury that usually has between 16 and 23 other jurists. Your responsibility is to hear the evidence and determine if people should be charged with crimes; if so, they're indicted for these criminal acts. You don't determine guilt or innocence; that is up to a trial jury.

The grand jury is a prosecutor's theater. He is running the show in the courtroom as there are no defense lawyers present in the courtroom. They can wait outside the courtroom and, many a time, I stood out in the hallway with defense lawyers as Big Louie, or Rocco, or Guido came out of the courtroom to confer with their lawyers. The grand jury hears what the prosecutor wants them to hear about the case, so it's all one-sided and that's why it's very rare for a grand jury not to indict someone, as they do not hear the other side of the case. But, this is the legal system. It's legit, but rigged for the prosecutor to win the indictment. The legal system only wants a grand jury to decide if the acts warrant a trial and someone should be charged for something that the legal system says is criminal.

The prosecutor presented his evidence by showing selected tapes of Shorty and the crew, along with witnesses subpoenaed to testify in this case—adult bookstore owners and others who were criminally involved with Shorty and the crew. An Internal Revenue Agent assigned to the IRS Criminal Division testified that during audits of Shorty and the crew's tax filings over the last few years, earned income was not reported, as required.

A little more than a year later, after hearing the prosecutor's evidence, the grand jury returned a sealed indictment against Shorty and the crew. The US Attorney then must make a decision whether to open or leave it sealed; the Assistant US Attorney has no say about opening or not opening the sealed indictment. It's up to his boss, the US Attorney for the Northern District of Illinois to make the decision.

We all know no US Attorney is going to let his Assistant US Attorney conduct a grand jury probe into Outfit activities for practice. The US Attorney opened the indictment, which was a racketeering case under the RICO Act with umbrella charges of gambling, loan-sharking, selling and distributing pornography across lines, tax evasion, and one more charge of firebombing of Corral's. The US Attorney authorized that after getting arrest warrants, Shorty and the crew be picked up by the FBI and US Marshal's office, as now the fun would begin.

For those US Attorneys in Chicago with political aspirations, for let's say governor of Illinois or being a United States senator, arresting Outfit guys became a staged circus. The media was notified about the arrests of Outfit guys so camera crews from the various television stations filmed Outfit guys handcuffed, doing the perp walk, while they were escorted by the grim-faced FBI agent, clutching the guy's arm, walking into the Collins Federal Building.

The US Attorney would hold a press conference, generally about 11:00 A.M., announcing the indictments of the arrested Outfit guys. The US Attorney would peer out, making eye contact with the television cameras, talking about how he had now taken mob criminals off the street and how these arrests were a blow to mob operations; just another political speech to make the US Attorney look like he was tough on crime to the voters. This dog and pony show would be seen on all the television stations that had 10:00 P.M. newscasts. Thousands of voters would see the US Attorney tell them they could feel a bit safer, knowing he had locked up these big, bad Outfit guys.

These political speeches the US Attorney would give, press conference after press conference, didn't cost the US Attorney a dime. Every time he spoke at a press conference, it was free publicity for a future run for office. There was one group of Chicagoans who watched the 10:00 P.M. news, saw the US Attorney talk about justice being served, and then walked over to their window to look out on the street. They didn't see Outfit guys dealing drugs on their street corner day after day. They didn't see Outfit guys driving down their street, shooting innocent people for no apparent reason. They saw guys selling drugs on their street corner night after night. They saw gangbangers drive down their street and shoot innocent children as young as six years old who were just playing in front of their house. When these Chicagoans looked out on their street, they didn't see any justice prevailing. When they went back and looked at the rest of the 10:00 P.M. news, they didn't see the US Attorney talking about the arrests of any big, bad guys on their street. Their street doesn't count because you can't make any future political hay off some every day drug deal or drive-by shooting. They just don't have the political bite like a mob arrest. The media becomes the US Attorney's ally, as they usually place mob arrest stories as one of their top stories.

So, the people in those Chicago neighborhoods, who for decades have seen the same crimes occur over and over again, you guys have a way out of this life. Encourage Outfit guys to move into your neighborhoods. Maybe the city will give the guys a break on their real estate tax. With Outfit guys living on your block, you will see law enforcement on every corner and you might just be able to have the same life every other Chicagoan has in his or her neighborhood—a good safe one.

If an Outfit wife is not sure about what her husband does for a living, one knock on the door by the FBI will make everything crystal-clear what an Outfit hubby really does for a living. The knock on the Lanzo door that Thursday morning was going to change the lives of Melissa and the children forever.

The FBI, along with the US marshal's office, made their early coffee run around 6 A.M., not only at the Lanzo house, but other crew members' residences. Dean Dragonetti used to call the arresting Fed officers punctual pricks. The Feds make these early coffee runs to take the defendant out of his house before most people are up and about. Get it in, get out is what the Feds say to themselves, as they don't want any neighbors to know what's going on. So, if you're a bad guy, you better go to bed early each night, get your rest, because the Feds are early birds.

Melissa awoke to the doorbell ringing. As she went downstairs in her pajamas, she heard knocking on the door. Shorty was starting to awake upstairs in the master bedroom. She pulled the curtain slightly back as she peered out the downstairs window and saw several cars parked in and near her driveway. She opened the front door slowly, and some men in FBI and US marshal's office jackets were standing right in front of her.

"Good morning, Mrs. Lanzo. I am Paul O'Connor, Special Agent with the Federal Bureau of Investigation and I'm here today with other agents and the US marshal's office personnel to arrest Mr. Peter Lanzo on the charges listed in this arrest warrant I'm holding," O'Connor said. O'Connor then handed the warrant to Melissa.

Melissa, still trying to shake the sleep out of her eyes, said, "What do you mean you're here to arrest my husband?" her voice shaking, a slice of a quiver running through it. "Why, Pete makes educational and training films for a living. There's gotta be a mistake," Melissa said in a hostile, defensive voice. "No, no, you must have the wrong Peter Lanzo. Are you sure you have the right man?" she said.

"Yes, Mrs. Lanzo, we have the right man. We're here to arrest your husband based on an indictment handed down by a federal grand jury on the charges spelled out in the arrest warrant. May we come in?" O'Connor said in that typical, calm FBI voice they use like they're a neighbor trying to borrow a cup of sugar, when really they're screwing with your life big time.

Melissa skimmed the arrest warrant. "This is impossible. This is not Pete at all. Okay, come in." Melissa really wanted to say, 'No, you can't come in,' but she knew the Feds could slap their handcuffs on her, and charge her with obstruction of justice. Hey, she wasn't a lawyer's kid for nothing. "Please, wait here. I'll go get him," she said, while everyone was in the front hallway downstairs.

"We'll have to go upstairs with you, Mrs. Lanzo," O'Connor said.

"Okay, I'll take you to the master bedroom upstairs. My kids are still sleeping," she said.

"We will be as quiet as possible, Mrs. Lanzo, not to disturb the children," O'Connor said.

"Thank you," Melissa said.

Once upstairs, everyone walked to the master bedroom. Shorty was already up and was getting himself cleaned up. After Melissa went downstairs to answer the knocking on the door, Shorty got out of bed, looked out the bedroom window, and saw the Feds were here to arrest him.

"Pete, the Feds are here to see you. They've got an arrest warrant. What the hell is going on?" Melissa said.

"Yeah, I know. I looked out the window. I'll be out in five minutes," Shorty said.

"What do you mean you know? You knew the FBI was coming?" Melissa sharply said.

"Hon, just pull out a shirt and pants from the cabinet. I'll be right out," Shorty said.

"You didn't answer me, Pete. You knew the FBI was coming?" Melissa said.

"One more thing, hon, pull out my black shoes. I'm just about through in here," Shorty said.

When a man gets caught by a woman doing something he's not supposed to be doing, he goes into the 'three D' mode: deflect, deceive, and deny. Shorty would eventually use all the Ds with Melissa, but with the Feds looking at his face, deflection would have to be used right now.

Melissa's emotions were reaching the boiling point, but with FBI Agent O'Connor seeing and hearing her body language, she had to keep what she really wanted to tell Shorty to herself.

Shorty came out of the bathroom wearing a sparkling white T-shirt and white boxer shorts. He surprisingly had a slight smile on his face as O'Connor introduced himself and told Shorty why he and the other agents were there. Here's where Melissa thought Shorty would strongly deny the charges because, in her mind, he wasn't with or part of the Outfit, that's why this must all be a big mistake. Shorty never made that denial.

Melissa walked right behind Shorty, as he was buttoning his dark blue, long sleeved shirt. "Pete, what is this all about?" Melissa said. "Am I having a bad dream or what? Tell me this is all a mistake, that they have the wrong guy," she said. Shorty said nothing as he put on his dark charcoal gray slacks.

"Hon, can you reach into that drawer and get me a shoehorn?" Shorty asked Melissa. Melissa gave Shorty not only the shoehorn, but a look that had deadly force behind it and wanted to inflict some pain on the man she married, for better or worse. For Melissa, there was a whole truckload of worse yet to come.

"I think I need a cup of coffee about now. Can I get you a cup, Mr. O'-Connor?" Melissa said.

"No thank you, Mrs. Lanzo," O'Connor said.

Even in a first-class crisis like this, Melissa had manners with a guest. Maybe one she didn't care for, but still a guest nonetheless.

"Melissa, look, just call your father and tell him I've been arrested by the Feds, okay?" Shorty said. Melissa heard Shorty, but did not speak to him. She was thinking *you son of a bitch, you goddamn son of a bitch. You won't even answer me about what is going on. Now you want to use my father to pull your chestnuts out of the fire go*. At this point, Melissa got control of her heated, but understandable emotions. There was a lot at stake here concerning her and the children, so it's best for everyone who's affected by this shocking event if I turn the flame down a bit, she reasoned.

After Shorty got dressed, FBI Agent Thomas Greiswell placed Shorty in handcuffs and advised him of his rights. Shorty acknowledged that he understood what his rights were.

"Where you taking my husband?" Melissa asked O'Connor.

"He will be transported to the Metropolitan Correctional Center downtown where he will be processed," O'Connor said.

"Melissa, call your father," Shorty said again.

"Don't worry about it," Melissa sarcastically said.

Shorty, escorted by the FBI, walked out of his house at 6:45 A.M. to be transported to the MCC. I'm sorry; no guns blazing, no TV cop show surprises where there's some kind of fake shootout between the FBI and Shorty's crew. None of that stuff. This is how the FBI works. I've seen it on the occasions the FBI took Jimmy downtown for questioning. They're polite and strictly business when they come to screw with you.

Everything with the FBI is by the book. This is our job and your job is to cooperate. Nothing personal, but we don't like you and you don't like us, but we both know the way the game is played. So, everyone makes pretend nice with each other for a while, and we all go forward to begin playing the legal game of 'I caught you, now it's your legal move as to what happens next.'

After Shorty left, Melissa called her father. "Daddy, Daddy, this is Melissa. The FBI just arrested Pete. They're taking him downtown." Her voice was choppy, an uncertain edge to it and hitting those fear octaves, just plain damn scared. Just thinking of what Melissa was mentally going through during the call scares the crap out of me.

"Okay, okay, honey. Please, don't worry. I know this is very unsettling for you, but, please, I don't want my little girl to worry. I'll get dressed and go downtown to the MCC and find out what's going on," Tommy said. "Don't worry. I'll call you once I've got all the facts. Just don't say anything to the children. Why worry them. Okay, love you," Tommy said.

This wasn't Tommy's first visit to the MCC, but it was different now, as he was going to defend the husband of his daughter and the father of his grandchildren. Shorty was not some Outfit defendant who he was not personally attached to. Shorty was personal to Tommy, as he was family, husband, and father all rolled into one.

Once downtown, Tommy met with Jeffrey Zellerbach, the Assistant US Attorney who was going to be the prosecutor. Zellerbach spelled out the charges on the indictment. He gave Tommy copies of the indictment and the arrest warrant. Besides the charges in the indictment, Shorty was charged with running a criminal enterprise. All of these charges meant, if convicted, Shorty was eligible to be sentenced under penalties of the RICO Act.

Zellerbach told Tommy the arraignment was that afternoon with Federal Magistrate Lorna Taylor and he would be asking for no bond. He advised Tommy he would be forwarding to him copies of his evidence, including specific surveillance tapes recorded by the FBI.

Tommy told Zellerbach he wanted to meet with Shorty and Zellerbach arranged a room so they could confer. A US marshal would be positioned outside the room. While waiting for Shorty, Tommy reviewed the evidence except the tapes, which he would have to play back at the office. Tommy knew as a defense lawyer who has defended Outfit guys before, the tapes become your number one concern. A jury sees and hears them and digests the subject matter. The tapes are often what a jury asks for when deliberating the guilt or innocence of the defendant. They want to hear right from the guy's mouth what he is saying, which helps them make a decision. In this case, Shorty and the crew said some powerfully incriminating things. Tommy would have to chisel away at what the jury sees and hears from Shorty's mouth. He's hoping he can convince the jury they're just watching a movie, just a made-up fantasy, but no real truth spoken by Shorty.

The Feds were able to build a racketeering case with the umbrella charges of gambling, loan-sharking, selling and distributing adult and child pornography, plus the firebombing of Corral's with Shorty's help. The jury was going to see on those tapes that Shorty was his own worst enemy. If loose lips sink ships, then Shorty sunk a boatload of criminal activities as far as the eye can see and the ear can hear.

Tommy met briefly with Shorty. As Tommy talked about what evidence he had seen so far concerning the case, Shorty sat quietly in his chair. "We're going to plead not guilty, right?" Shorty said after Tommy stopped talking.

"Yes, I'll enter a not guilty plea, but I'm going to tell you, Pete, the Feds have a lot of evidence, not only in witness testimony, but in those taped conversations you're having with your crew—Fairene primarily—but that will make this a more difficult case," Tommy said.

"Yeah, I know, but you're a good lawyer. You'll figure out a way to beat this rap," Shorty confidently said.

"Well thanks for the compliment, but...and you're the client, so it's your decision to make...but do you want me to work on the plea deal for you?" Tommy said.

"No way, plead not guilty. I'm going to beat this sucker," Shorty said.

"Okay, I'll request bond for you. At the arraignment, we're going to plead not guilty. I'll see you at the arraignment."

"Okay, see you there," Shortly said.

Shorty was in a pensive mood after talking with Tommy. He didn't seem surprised by the government's case. He felt Tommy would poke holes in the government's case and he would be a free man, laughing in the face of the Feds, as he left Collins Federal Building.

"I'll call Melissa, just to update her," Tommy said before he left.

"Fine," Shorty said.

Shorty was returned to a holding area while he waited for the arraignment. Tommy called Melissa, who was anxiously waiting at home. He methodically explained what Shorty had been charged with and what the potential penalties were if Shorty was convicted. Tommy told her he was reviewing the evidence the government forwarded to him.

"Child pornography...what, are you kidding me?" Melissa lashed out. "We've got kids of our own. How could he do something like this?" she said.

"He told me he was making industrial and educational films. What the hell is this all about?" Melissa said.

"Melissa, these are just allegations at this point. That's all they are right now," Tommy said.

"Right now, I'm so angry at Pete, I could scream," Melissa said. "Daddy, how could he? Child pornography? Who in their right mind does that to children? Maybe I just answered my own question. Was Pete in a right frame of mind?" she said, as her voice started to crack from the stress. "What about these other charges—gambling, loan-sharking, and firebombing some adult bookstore? I know you told me," Melissa said, as she began to sob.

"Corral's," Tommy said.

"Yeah, Corral's," Melissa said. "Oh, Daddy, what am I going to do?" Melissa said in a voice that was filling up with tears. "God, what did he do to me and the children?" she said in a weepy voice.

"Melissa, please, please don't cry," Tommy said. "I don't know why Pete did what he did, but I'm going to review all the evidence and see what type of defense I'm going to use when we go to trial," he said. "We're going to plead not guilty at the arraignment this afternoon and I will ask for bond, though, I'm not too optimistic bond will be set," Tommy said.

"As far as I'm concerned, he can rot in the MCC," Melissa said with a still tearful tone.

"Melissa, honey, please don't cry anymore. Don't worry, you still have Mom and me 100 percent in your corner and I will support you anyway I can through this terrible time, along with supporting the children," Tommy said, as he was trying to control his emotions before Melissa, but inside his emotions were scorching with anger at Pete for putting his baby girl and grandchildren right in the eye of the storm. Boy, did he want to poke that eye.

"I'll call you after the arraignment, okay? But, please, promise no more tears. You have to be powerful for your children. They need you very much for support, comfort, and to know they are in a safe environment," Tommy said.

"I promise, Daddy, for the children. I promise," Melissa said. She exhaled air from a very agitated nervous system. "Yeah, call me," she said.

"Love ya. Don't worry, everything will turn out okay. Just don't worry," Tommy said.

Melissa's brain talked to her nervous system. "Look, you've got to calm down. I know you're upset, but you'll create other physical problems for Melissa," the brain said to the nervous system.

"Upset, that's putting it mildly. I'm so pissed off at this mother fuckin' son of a bitch poor excuse of a man right now. I want to beat the shit out of him," the nervous system said. "Here he's got a wife who loves him, adores him, and gives him more than 100% emotional support, besides raising their children to be good, kind, loving human beings. So what does this scumbag do? He picks these criminal Outfit ways over his wife and children," said the nervous system. "This rat bastard, this lowdown, lowlife; he's lucky I'm not his nervous system. He'd better lace up his gym shoes because I would put him on diarrhea patrol; he'd be running so fast to the toilet the friction would cause his undershorts to catch on fire," the nervous system said.

"This goddamn bastard will find out real motherfuckin' quick that he's dealing with one, in using your term, brain, highly upset Italian nervous system that's going to put his motherfuckin' ass in a sling for what he's doing to Melissa and the kids. Fuck 'em," the nervous system said.

"I know you're really upset," the brain said to the nervous system, "but for Melissa's sake and the sake of the children, you gotta turn the thermostat down on her emotions. If you keep generating emotional heat to Melissa, she's going to wind up in a depression," said the brain. Then she won't eat, she'll act listless, get run down mentally and physically, and ultimately the children suffer, as they won't have a healthy mom to count on," the brain said. "You and I both know that if Melissa goes to the doctor what he's gonna say; he's going to say it's nerves. So, cool it," the brain said to the nervous system.

"Yeah I know," the nervous system said. "I'll cook a pot of sauce. Cooking relaxes me and when I get frayed, I eat. It's just Shorty put Melissa in the jackpot, while not legally, definitely emotionally, and that was totally uncalled for. He's a..."

"Don't use the bad language," the brain said.

"...a bad and poor example of a human being," continued the nervous system.

"Good, now you're making progress," the brain said.

Melissa, while not feeling her best, felt better after talking to Tommy. She was able to release the inner toxic feelings she had about Shorty. By releasing those feelings, Melissa would now be able with clear and precise thoughts start to think about her and the children's future. While not having a definite roadmap to lay out future plans, Melissa had at least faced the reality of the world she was now living in. The days ahead would often be dark and scary, but by uncorking her bottled up emotions, her mind was now free to think about what will be, not what was.

At the arraignment, Shorty, Jimmy Quartino, and John Guissepe pled not guilty to all charges. Tommy and their lawyers argued for a very low bond for each. Zellerbach countered that Shorty and the crew were threats to the community based on the pending criminal charges. Zellerbach played parts of two selected tapes, where Fairene talked to Shorty and then the crew about what should be done to a guy who hasn't paid his loan-sharking interest payment. Shorty and the crew's responses were very graphic as what should physically be done to the guy.

The Federal Magistrate Lorna Taylor didn't seem particularly interested in giving anyone not only a low bond, but any bond at all. Her face stoic, she was going through paperwork concerning the case. Her head was bent downward as, while the lawyers spoke, she signed some legal papers.

She raised her head and spoke. "There will be no bond for any of the defendants," Taylor said. The defendants will be held over for trial at the Metropolitan Correctional Center until the trial date is set by the presiding judge assigned to the case," she said in plain matter-of-fact tones of drama in her voice. Tommy told Shorty he would be in touch with him, as Shorty and the other defendants were returned to their assigned cells in the MCC by the US Marshal's office deputies.

Tommy called Melissa. "No bond, honey, for Pete. He's going to be held at the MCC until his trial, as he pled not guilty to all charges, thus, a trial will take place," Tommy said. "I'm sorry, he won't be coming home tonight," Tommy said.

"Who wants him?" Melissa said. "The MCC is a good place for him right now. Maybe it'll give him time to think about what he did to his family," she said. "Right now, I'm so mad at him, I don't even want to see him, as I don't even know what I would say to him," Melissa said in a more controlled voice. "For the life of me, I don't understand why he didn't think about what he was doing and how it was going to impact me and the kids," Melissa said. "I'm going to be honest with the kids. They're not babies. It's better they hear it from me than some kids at school, who might be mean and taunt them. I'm going to tell them their father was arrested and what he's being charged with. No sense lying to them, as one lie leads to another, then another. I won't do that," Melissa said.

"Honesty is the best policy. I know it's going to hurt to tell the kids about Pete's arrest and charges, but that's how Mom and I raised you, to be honest even when painful, just be honest," Tommy said. "By lying, you'll only compound a difficult situation into one stinking lying situation requiring more stinking lies to cover lie after lie," said Tommy said. Even while saying this to Melissa, it hurt for Tommy to say it. These were still his grandchildren and because of that, this case was hitting home.

Tommy loved and adored his grandchildren like any other grandparent. So, while he was supporting Melissa's decision to tell the children, as a parent, as a grandparent, he was crying inside. For while Tommy legally counseled clients, as a grandparent he was seeking counseling on getting salvation from his soul that his grandchildren would be safe from the falling rocks coming down at them from a very uncertain or uneven cliff of life.

This wasn't some Outfit defendant who hired Tommy to defend him. This was Tommy's own personal Outfit defendant, someone directly tied to and directly involved with Tommy's personal life. Tommy wasn't just defending Shorty, but Melissa and the grandkids were also his clients in this one.

"Maybe Pete wasn't raised to be honest, because he sure didn't show it on this one," Melissa said. "I know you gotta go, so I'll talk to you later," Melissa said to Tommy. "In the meantime, I'm going to work on getting my composure back," she said.

"Okay honey, don't worry, everything will work out. Okay?" Tommy said.

Tommy went back to his office following the arraignment and played the tapes. He watched Shorty and his crew talk their way into problems with Big Ang. He brought his left hand up to his chin and rested it there. The tapes were revealing. There was little left to the imagination as to what Shorty's intent was during these conversations. Tommy peered at the tapes, watching them with a look of disgust, and realized he didn't have much to defend Shorty with. Oh, he'd come up with some type of defense, but would the jury even hear him after viewing the tapes. Would their minds be made up to convict Shorty at that point? Tommy saw and heard Shorty talk about the firebombing of Corral's besides his other operations. As Tommy watched the tapes, he saw Shorty convict himself. Shorty had incriminated himself over and over again on the tapes. While maybe, and this is a big maybe, Tommy might be able to create some doubt in the jury's mind about the prosecution's witnesses' testimony, the tapes had no gray area. In Shorty's own words, he would show the jury he committed the alleged crimes. The tapes were irrefutable evidence.

The case screamed out for a plea bargain. In the next few days, Tommy did talk to Shorty about a plea deal, but Shorty did not want to hear about a plea deal. Shorty was on his high horse and only wanted to know how Tommy was going to get him acquitted on all charges. He flatly refused to consider a plea deal. He told Tommy to prepare for a trial, which Tommy said he would do. Tommy wasn't happy with Shorty's decision to go to trial, so reluctantly he started to prepare a defense.

While Tommy was Shorty's lawyer, he was also a father. He decided after viewing the tapes, he would go to see Melissa just to check on her. She was still his daughter and he was concerned for her well being. Tommy turned off the lights in his office and headed out to visit Melissa.

"Hi, honey. How are you?" Tommy said, as Melissa met him at the front door. He hugged her and gave her a kiss on the cheek.

"Holding on, Daddy, just barely holding here," Melissa said. "I still can't believe Pete was doing all those things you told me he was charged with," she said.

"Well, we'll see. How are you doing financially?" Tommy asked.

"We got $800 in the checking account," Melissa said.

"That's it?" Tommy said in a questioning voice.

"Yeah, that's it," Melissa said.

"You got another mortgage payment coming due. You gotta buy food. You got other household expenses. There are utilities you gotta pay and other bills that have to be paid," Tommy said. "C'mon, look, you need financial help, so I'm going to give you a check for $10,000 to at least tide you over for a while until we can get a handle on your monthly expenses," Tommy said.

"Daddy, I don't want..." she started to say, but he cut her off.

"Melissa, I know you don't want to take any money from me, but you got the kids to take care of on top of everything else and, right now, you don't have any income coming in," Tommy said. "I'll bring you a check tomorrow," he said. "At least you won't have to pay for a lawyer," Tommy said. Melissa smiled, which relieved some of the tension. "See, you look better already, just keep a smile on your face and don't worry, things will work themselves out," he said.

"How bad is it, Daddy, for Pete?" Melissa questioned with tears swelling in her eyes. She still loved the guy and had feelings for him. Realistically because of the tapes, the case is going to be an uphill fight," Tommy said. "I offered to go to the prosecutor to talk about a plea agreement, but Pete said no. I'll fight as hard as I can at the trial, but those tapes put us behind the eight ball," Tommy said. "I can cross examine a human witness and I'm pretty good at raising doubt about the witness's testimony on my cross, but I can't cross examine a tape, so I'll have to come up with something to refute the tapes," he said.

"Well, we'll just have to fight our hardest to win the case," she said. At that point, she was, as they say, cautiously optimistic. Her optimism would dry up and evaporate during the trial.

Presiding Judge Ned Eddick was known as "Ned the Fed" for his 18 years of service as an Assistant US Attorney around Collins Federal Courthouse. Eddick was considered a law and order judge, the type of judge who prosecutors like to argue their cases. Let's face it, judges are like any other human beings, they have their likes and they have their dislikes. Eddick's bench rulings and various prosecution motions, especially new evidence, was it or was it not admissible in a case they were trying seemed, at times, to favor the prosecution. As much as Eddick tried to be fair in his rulings, the fact was that for 18 years, he walked in the prosecutor's shoes, was always looking over his shoulder, and I think at times he took a quick glance over his shoulder before making a ruling. Defense lawyers never questioned his competence about the law. It's just, at times, they felt even the prosecutors were either that good in winning their motions, or a former colleague never forgot his roots and was helping a few buddies out.

Eddick was generally stricter on the sentences he handed out after a jury convicted a defendant. He wasn't like a couple of other federal judges, who you could give some song and dance to and they would give you a lighter sentence, unless the conviction carried a mandatory minimum sentence where a judge had to give a minimum sentence. In these, judges were known as weepers as a sob story would work in your favor.

I remember one judge, Nelson Stainiki. You had to bring an extra hand-kerchief to his courtroom to wipe your eyes when hearing the touching lies come out of the mouths of these professional liars. Stainiki would nod his head while listening to tales of a bad childhood, which forced them, yes, forced them into a life of crime. It's funny how other people had bad childhoods and are not forced into a life of crime. I suppose the criminals are God's chosen crim-inal people. Stainiki's decisions affirmed that.

Shorty knew from Tommy, with Eddick residing over his case, not to expect any breaks, if convicted. Eddick was like any other judge on the day of sentenc-ing; he would let you have your chance to speak in court, if you wanted it. How-ever, his mind was already made up on how much time you were going to get the moment he took his seat on the bench. He just went through the motions of letting you speak with no intention of budging one iota on his decision.

Eighteen months after being arrested, Shorty and the crew went on trial. The trial lasted six weeks. While the Feds called numerous witnesses to testify, they also played taped conversations from Bambino's, where the jury saw and heard Shorty and the crew talking about criminal activities. The Feds also played wiretapped conversations from Bambino's that recorded telephone con-versations between Shorty and Fairene. The video and wiretapped conversa-tions were the cornerstone of the Feds' case against the defendants. The jury saw and heard the defendants play right into the prosecutor's case.

The prosecution team, with lead prosecutor Jeffrey Zellerbach, along with David McArthur and John Gleasen, sat smugly at the prosecution table while the various tapes were played. You could see in their body language they were very confident of winning convictions against the defendants, who just looked at the tapes with an empty blank look on their faces. The defendants did not show any emotion while looking and listening to the tapes.

While the jury of eight men and four women heard various prosecution witnesses testify, the time had come when the Feds were going to call their star witness to the stand. He was the headliner. He was the star attraction, the main headliner that everyone lined up early to see. He was the one who would dot the 'I's and cross the 'T's for the prosecution's case. He was the prosecu-tions legal savior about ready to destroy an Outfit street crew. Big Ang was called as a witness.

He sat in the witness box, his hands clasped in his lap. He wore a dark blue navy suit, and white shirt with a light gray tie, neatly tied. I never saw Big Ang look so dapper. I'll say this about Zellerbach and his team, the time they spent coaching him really paid off, as Big Ang sat remarkably calm and answered

Zellerbach's questions crisply, but very calmly. He was still a warrior, but a trained one. His mouth became the deadly force now, rather than his trademark on the street, his hands.

Melissa sat in the row behind Shorty, her eyes transfixed on Big Ang. Big Ang explained what the defendants were talking about on the tapes. The jury listened very closely, some edging up closer to hear this real life mobster talk about a criminal life that none of the jury members knew anything about. Many of them took notes of the mob speak they heard from the lips of a real life participant in the murky, uncleansed world of the Outfit. To them, it was a foreign language they were trying to understand. To Big Ang, it was, 'Hey, what's your problem?'

As the jurors scribbled notes in their notebooks while listening to Big Ang, his testimony brought a look of disgust to Shorty's face. The look telegraphed his thoughts about Big Ang. *How could he rat out me and the crew?* was blazing across Shorty's brain. *I trusted him like a brother and now he's trying to put a stake in my soul* Shorty thought.

While Big Ang described and corroborated the crew's activities that the jurors were watching on the tapes, Shorty twisted his head first left, then right, continuously denying what Big Ang was saying. *He's trying to make his words sound like the gospel, like that's some sort of pious truth, and it ain't so* Shorty's brain blurted out.

For Melissa to hear about her husband's involvement in the Outfit from Big Ang was stinging and pricking at her morality. This was a side of Shorty she never saw. Melissa looked down at the floor. *Was I that naïve? I'm not a stupid girl. What did I miss?* she thought, as she kept replaying her life to herself. Her life with Shorty, was it just full of false ingredients mixed together to give the impression of a loving family? A love that was tainted with a very dark gutter-like shade attached to it. With the facts now coming out, the love was being thoroughly scrubbed clean and what was left was a slimy base of deceit, not the real upbeat vibrant love required for a happy family life. Love for an Outfit couple is the husband only putting in 50%, but never telling his wife about the other 50%. He never wanted his wife to know the real monster she married.

When Big Ang talked about child pornography as a part of Shorty's business operations, it was something that sickened Melissa. Shorty had his own children, children he saw every day. How could he come home and show love to his children on one hand and be a pornography demon, a purveyor of sick behavior on the other hand, Melissa wondered.

As Melissa sat in the courtroom, she kept thinking over and over that it was all about lies. Shorty deceived Melissa and the children into believing that he was just another straight arrow Joe out there every day working his butt off for them to have nice comforts in life. What Melissa admired about Shorty was he could leave his work at the office and never come home crabby about his job. Now, she learned why he never brought the job home with him. The job was not only criminal, but it was morally a dirty, filthy, scummy way of conducting yourself. Melissa was now glad to have never really known what Shorty did for a living. Such repulsive behavior on his part would have been too much for her to bear.

Telling lies is as common as brushing your teeth for the Outfit. Lies, lies, and more lies run out as quickly as they can from their mouths. It doesn't matter who gets hurt, just as long as they have a lie in their shirt pocket ready to be pulled out and used whenever necessary. The lies provided the Outfit with cover and the more lies they told, the more they believed them.

Melissa was beyond hurt. The reality of Shorty's Outfit life rinsed away those marriage vows they both had taken so long ago. She was getting numb listening to the daily parade of witnesses and tapes that was served up on a criminal platter. Every day of the trial, the more she heard, the harder it became to even look at Shorty. When she did look at Shorty, she wondered if her mind was playing tricks on her. *Was this the same guy I loved, wanted to spend the rest of my life with, grow old, live happily ever after with*, she tried to figure out. She finally came to the conclusion that 'yes', this was the guy she married, but no, this was not the guy she married because while she was truthful about their marriage vows, he was not.

Finally, the prosecution finished questioning their trained seal. It was Tommy's turn to get a crack at Big Ang. While cross examining other witnesses, Tommy was able to raise some doubt about the truthfulness of their testimony in some instances, but with Big Ang, he was a participant in the tapes. The jury saw him talk to Shorty and the crew and now, as a witness, he appeared to be more credible as he was one of the actors. He wasn't talking from outside the house looking in like other witnesses. Big Ang spoke as someone inside the house who was right in the middle of various criminal plots that were taking place.

"The government offered you a nice deal to testify. Didn't they, Mr. Fairene?" Tommy said.

"Yes, they did," Big Ang said.

"A deal that gave you considerably less time than if you were convicted. Isn't that right, Mr. Fairene?" Tommy said.

"Yes," Big Ang said.

"Such a sweet deal that you have no problems today ratting out Peter Lanzo. Isn't that right, Mr. Fairene?" Tommy said.

"I'm no rat," Big Ang said.

"Mr. Fairene, then why are you not sitting at the defense table defending yourself like the other defendants? Because you're a rat. Isn't that right, Mr. Fairene?" Tommy said.

"I'm not a rat," Big Ang said.

"Mr. Fairene, wiseguys like to boast and often lie. Isn't that right, Mr. Fairene?" Tommy said.

"I don't know," Big Ang said.

"Well, Mr. Fairene, let me read back a transcript from a tape where you and Mr. Guissepe were discussing Mr. John Schmidt, a medical doctor who owed a gambling debt and testified earlier as a prosecution witness. You said, 'If we get rid of Schmidt, I could do his fuckin' job,' to Mr. Guissepe," Tommy said. "Mr. Fairene, have you graduated from medical school?" Tommy said.

"No," Big Ang said.

"Mr. Fairene, have you passed any medical boards in the State of Illinois that would grant you a medical license to practice medicine in the State of Illinois?" Tommy said.

"No," Big Ang said.

"Mr. Fairene, do you have any medical training at all?" Tommy said.

"No," Big Ang said.

"So, Mr. Fairene, since you did not answer 'yes' to any of my last three questions, you couldn't possibly do Mr. Schmidt's job as medical doctor, could you?" Tommy said.

"No," Big Ang said.

"Therefore, Mr. Fairene, you lied when you said you could do Mr. Schmidt's job, didn't you?" Tommy said.

"I was just talkin'," Big Ang said.

"Then were you just talking to Peter Lanzo on the tapes? Just making up lies and false accusations about people to Peter Lanzo to make him believe what you were saying was the truth?" Tommy said.

"No, I was being honest with him," Big Ang said.

"Mr. Fairene, didn't you come to court today solely to tell lies about Peter Lanzo?" Tommy said.

"Objection, Your Honor. Counsel is just speculating and has no basis of proof that Mr. Fairene came to court today to not be truthful and forthright in his testimony," Zellerbach said.

"I'll rephrase the question, Your Honor," Tommy said. "Mr. Fairene, in your entire life, have you not lied at least once?" Tommy said.

"Oh, I might have told a white lie, like anyone else," Big Ang said.

"So, the answer is 'yes,' you have lied in your life," Tommy said.

"Yes," Big Ang said.

"Mr. Fairene, then why should we believe anything you are saying today, and I will remind you that you are still under oath; are these just lies or fairytales in your mind about Peter Lanzo?" asked Tommy.

"I am here today to speak the truth about Peter Lanzo and the tapes will confirm that," Big Ang said in a composed manner. During Tommy's cross-examination, Big Ang let Tommy have his theater and calmly answered 'yes' and 'no' to practically all the questions. The Feds trained Big Ang not to get into it with Tommy, fearing he would say something that could hurt their case.

Having seen so many criminal cases over the years, answering 'yes' or 'no' was the best way to respond, unless the question required a more detailed answer. You want to avoid tripping yourself up and jeopardizing your case. A lawyer is a professional 'ask a question' person who does this day in and day out. You are not going to beat them at their own game. So, keep your answers short. Don't give them an opportunity to make you look stupid as a witness.

"I have no further questions for the witness, Your Honor," Tommy said to Eddick.

"The witness may be excused," Eddick said.

Big Ang got out of the witness box and made no eye contact with Shorty. Shorty, though, was making a whole lot of evil looking eye contact with Big Ang. Shorty's eyes were combat ready if Big Ang looked at him. The troops were in place, ready to attack, but Big Ang was escorted out of the courtroom by a couple of very large refrigerator sized US Marshals and Shorty's eyes went on stand down.

The prosecution rested its case. Tommy never put on any defense witnesses, nor called Shorty as a witness. The lawyers for Quartino and Guissepe followed suit and all the defendants rested their cases. Closing arguments followed by the lawyers for the prosecution and defense making their final pleas for guilt and innocence. Judge Eddick gave the jury their instructions.

After six weeks of testimony, a weary jury finally got the case to begin their deliberations. For six weeks, the jury had been sequestered by Judge Eddick and they were ready to decide the fate of the defendant. The jury went from the hotel to the courtroom and back to the hotel for six weeks, and they were anxious to do their job and get back to their families.

After the jurors filed out of the courtroom, Melissa went up to Tommy. The defendants had been removed from the courtroom so Melissa did not have to pass Shorty.

"Thanks, Dad. You were great in your defense of Pete," Melissa said, as she hugged Tommy.

"Thanks, honey. I tried my best for Pete," Tommy said. Tommy sustained his hug. He remembered hugging Melissa when she was a little girl, showing her the love and affection that a father is supposed to do. He remembered hugging Melissa when she was a little girl, letting her know that as a father he would protect her and make her feel safe and secure. So, here in the courtroom, he was hugging his grown-up daughter, making her feel safe and secure.

In an empty courtroom, now far removed from the trial, a father pressed his daughter so close to his body, he could feel the warmth from his body saturate hers. In an empty courtroom, a father recommitted his love to his daughter, building a wall of security around her. In an empty courtroom, no matter what a jury decided, a father is now and forever going to be his daughter's illuminating lifeline—being there for her, helping her walk through the dark passages of her life.

After four days of deliberations, the jury sent a note to Judge Eddick that they had reached a verdict for all the defendants. The families of the defendants were sitting silently in the courtroom. Jimmy Quartino's mother tightly held her rosary beads, hoping to squeeze yet one more miracle from God. It took about an hour to get everyone in the courtroom. Finally, everyone stood as Judge Eddick entered the courtroom and took his seat on the bench.

"Will the marshal please have the jury enter the courtroom?" Eddick instructed the marshal. The jury walked in. They did not look at the defendants. This is usually a bad sign because if the jury looks at the defendants, there's a possibility of an acquittal. No one wants to look in someone's face and give them the bad news. When the jury doesn't look at the defendants, generally, bad news—real bad news—is coming.

"Ladies and gentlemen of the jury, have you reached a verdict on all counts for each defendant?" Eddick said to the jury after they were seated.

The jury foreman stood up and said, "Yes, we have, Your Honor."

The judge asked his clerk to walk over and get the sealed 8½ by 11-inch brown envelope. She briskly walked over to the jury foreman, got the envelope, turned, and walked back to the bench, and handed it to the judge.

The courtroom was still; even the air was quiet. There were no sounds as the spectators started to lean forward to listen to the judge speak. Shorty had his left hand holding his face near his chin, his eyes just gazing in Eddick's direction, with no real focus. They just looked forward, waiting for someone to tell them how they should act. Quartino kind of shifted his weight in the chair; his nerves were churning inside his body. Guissepe played with a pencil on the table. He never directly looked at Eddick.

Jimmy was in the courtroom, sitting right next to Melissa. He held her hand to support her, whatever the verdict was. She weakly smiled at Jimmy, as she looked in his face. It was the 'thank you' smile we give to someone who is there for us when we are about to be surrounded by the blackest of black moments in our life.

Tommy Calzone, while having gone through this moment many times as someone's lawyer, was now going through it as a caring father. He sat erect in his chair, looking firmly into the eyes of Judge Eddick. He hoped for the best, whatever that might be, but he knew on this one, the chances of Shorty going home a free man were dimming with each second. Before Eddick began to speak, Tommy looked at the jury. He looked into their eyes and did not see any sympathy in those eyes. Tommy brought his hands together, holding them tightly together, right hand supporting the left hand, left hand supporting the right hand.

Eddick opened the envelope and starting with Shorty, read every count against each defendant, and the only word he said after that was guilty. The defendants were found guilty on all counts. Shorty showed no emotion, just looking straight ahead. Quartino tightened his lips and slightly shook his head in disagreement. Guissepe looked up briefly, as he continued to play with the pencil. Tommy put his right arm around Shorty's shoulder and whispered a comforting thought in his ear.

As Melissa heard the verdict in the courtroom, she bowed her head, shaking it from side to side, looking directly at the floor. For, as of that exact moment, she no longer was going to have the same life she had before. That life was now history, only a parting memory that was now filed under 'used to be.' Her whole world had been flipped over and the new world she was looking at was painfully raw and sensitive. It was the uncertainty she and the children would face that scared her. Where would the money come to pay the bills and support her and the children in the future? *Daddy can't pay my bills forever* she thought.

Tommy turned and looked at his daughter. He mouthed to Melissa, "It'll be okay." She looked at him and he mouthed to her, "Please, smile." As hard as it was for her to do right now, at least for her daddy, she forced a smile. He winked at her, then he turned and faced forward. Jimmy sat, still holding Melissa's hand for that all-important support during this ordeal.

Eddick asked the lawyers if they wanted the jurors polled and they all said 'yes.' The jurors, one by one, affirmed their guilty votes. After hearing the final juror, Eddick thanked the jurors for their service and released them from jury duty. He said he would advise the lawyers when sentencing would take place. He ordered the defendants held at the MCC until sentenced. They were taken out of the courtroom by US Marshals, handcuffed. Shorty started to look at Melissa, but she looked away from him. Seeing that, Shorty looked straight ahead as he walked out of the courtroom.

Tommy shook Jimmy's hand and thanked him for coming to court and being supportive of Melissa. "Can I walk you to your car, honey?" Tommy said to Melissa.

"If you don't mind, Daddy, Jimmy, could you walk me to my car?" Melissa said.

"Sure Melissa, no problem," Jimmy said.

They walked to the car, Jimmy letting Melissa do the talking. "Well, there's no more doubt whether Pete is guilty or not. The jury answered that one today," Melissa said. "It's just why did he do those things? He is a college graduate. He could have a good job," Melissa said. "He didn't have to ruin our lives...did he, Jimmy?" Melissa said.

"No, Melissa, he didn't," Jimmy said. "Maybe, he just saw the money that could be made from what he was doing, but never thought about the repercussions of his actions," Jimmy said.

"You're right, Jimmy," Melissa said.

"It's like baseball, Melissa. The Cubs and White Sox play a season of games. They win one, lose one, but after each game, they prepare for the next game and don't dwell on yesterday's game," Jimmy said. "Melissa, you can't let what happened today in court weigh you down," he said. "You gotta, for the sake of your kids, think about the tomorrows, not the yesterdays," Jimmy said. "I know it won't be easy because your life got tossed in the air today and...bang...hit the ground, breaking into a million pieces," Jimmy said, "but somehow, you gotta pick up the pieces of your life piece by piece and connect them again to make yourself be the person you deserve to be," he said.

"No one can do it for you. You're working solo on this one, but Melissa, you're a hell of a smart woman. You can do it. If anyone on this earth can do it, it's you," he said. "I'll be in your corner cheering for you. C'mon, Melissa, you can do it. You can turn defeat into victory. If you have no one else cheering you on, you'll have me," Jimmy said.

Melissa stood in front of him; she looked at Jimmy and then threw her arms around him. Whenever we are at that critical moment of our life when it seems a heavy burden has been placed in our path, and we have no way to remove the burden, we desperately search for a hero to help us. We look down the lonely, cold street of life and someone does appear. Someone who by an act of kindness, by an act of sincerity, by any act of thoughtfulness, by an act of wanting to make the wrong right, using words of support, reminding us of our strengths, makes us look into our inner soul. We do not have to hope for a hero. We do not have to pray for a hero. We do not have to buy a hero. The words from that special someone make us look at our personality through a mirrored image, reflecting strength and courage that we've always had but needed to be highlighted with confidence.

The real hero we are looking for is us. We all have that ability to be that hero. It just needs to be brought out in us. Once we realize we are the hero, we can lift life's heavy burden out of our path, throw it on the curb, and continue to walk down the street, enjoying the best life has to offer us. Happy tunes play in our head as we have liberated ourselves from being a weakling into a hero.

Melissa turned and opened her car door. Jimmy helped her in. "Okay, Melissa, we'll be talking. No negative thoughts. Promise, Scout's honor?" Jimmy smiled, as he offered more encouragement.

"I promise," Melissa said. For the first time that day, a real full-blown smile crossed her face—nothing forced, all natural.

Seven months after their convictions, Shorty, Quartino, and John Guissepe were back in court in front of Judge Eddick to hear their fate. Eddick heard from the prosecution, the defense lawyers, and selected individuals, all giving input to Eddick, concerning the sentences of the three. Tommy argued for a three-year sentence, based on the fact that Shorty had no prior convictions and should be shown leniency. Melissa, who was sitting next to Jimmy, was thinking Shorty didn't give her and the children any leniency by his actions. Oh, if she could only be the judge, she reasoned. *I'd give him leniency— a swift kick to...well, I'm a lady, so I'll just stop at that*, she thought.

Lea Quartino, Jimmy's mother, spoke to Eddick. Jimmy was an altar boy at Our Lady of Perpetual Worship and on Sundays, he was an usher helping people to the pews, she said. He's a good, Catholic boy, who would help anyone in need, she said. Jimmy slightly turned his head toward his mother, nodding in confirmation as she spoke. Why, I thought Jimmy might become a priest with his love of helping people in need, she said.

Whether you like the Catholic Church or don't like the Catholic Church, you can sympathize with them, as they are always pulled in on sentencing hearing days to be used like the Outfit guy was a product of the Catholic Church. If the Outfit guy had followed the beliefs of the Catholic Church, he never would be sitting in Collins Federal Court waiting to see how hard the hammer was going to drop on him for being convicted of criminal activities. The Outfit guy would have followed the teachings of the Church to be a good person, a righteous person, a respected person, a man of whom others always spoke in glowing terms. Nope, the dope conveniently forgot the good ways that are taught by the Catholic Church and used the bad ways taught by the Outfit to live his life.

After hearing everyone speak, Eddick asked the defendants if they wanted to address the court. Shorty and Guissepe declined. Quartino stood up and addressed the court. "Your Honor, I am a man of God. Therefore, I have to do God's work and sometimes God's work isn't pleasant," Quartino said. "Sometimes in the name of the Lord, people get hurt," he said. "While I did not try and hurt anyone intentionally, being as it was God's way, someone had to get hurt," Quartino said. Just as that moment, there was a loud, crashing, booming sound of thunder in the sky outside of the Collins Federal Building.

Jimmy whispered to Melissa, "I think that's God's way of telling Jimmy Quartino to sit his ass down and stop using his name to snow the court."

Melissa giggled. It was good to see her giggle. *That's the Melissa I know*, Jimmy thought.

"Mr. Quartino, I think we've had enough religious instruction today. Take your seat," Eddick said.

Quartino was about ready to give Eddick some smart aleck remark when his lawyer took his arm and told him to sit down and calm down. Quartino gave Eddick a look of disgust and sat down. Once a punk, always a punk.

It was now time for the final act in the sentencing hearing to begin. The lead actor, who really was the star of the show, was about to deliver his lines. He was the one on who all eyes in the courtroom focused. He was the one on whose every word everyone would be hanging. He was the one for whom the spectators lined up early again outside the courtroom. The lead actor would close out this tragic comedy and bring down the legal curtain. Judge Eddick began to speak.

"The three defendants have been convicted of very serious crimes," Eddick said. "I do believe that if given freedom, all three of you would go back to some sort of a life of crime," he said. "All three of you are career criminals, who would just continue being criminals, no matter what," he said. "There is no reason why I should waste my time talking to you, as all three of you are part of organized crime and, at this time, will remain part of organized crime and have no interest in what I would say to you," Eddick said.

"I feel all three of you are serious threats to society and must be incarcerated in the federated penal system," Eddick said.

Fed judges always make it sound like Outfit guys are going to knock on everyone's door and do something bad to them. The only part of society who has to worry is the people who deal directly with the Outfit. The Outfit doesn't walk down the street randomly hurting people. Fed judges love to throw out a potential scare tactic as to why someone gets sentenced the way they do.

"I am sentencing you three men to the following: Peter Lanzo, 780 months; John Guissepe, 480 months; James Quartino, 456 months."

Since the Fed judges sentence in months, I'll translate. You don't have to use a calculator. Shorty got 65 years. Guissepe got 40 years and Quartino, the punk kid, got 38 years. The bombing charges alone got Shorty 45 years and Guissepe and Quartino got 30 years each.

"All three defendants will be held at the MCC until the Bureau of Prisons decides what facility each one of you will be placed in," Eddick said. "I will not make any recommendation to the Bureau of Prisons as to where you are to be placed," he said. "If your attorney's want to, they can make a written request and send it to the Bureau of Prisons as to a specific facility," Eddick said.

Generally, the BOP (Bureau of Prisons) has a policy that they try and place you within a 500-mile radius of your home, but if BOP thinks you belong farther away since you are a 'threat to society,' they will lock you up a long way from home. I've seen Outfit guys locked up in Illinois and I've seen them locked up in California. BOP has their own agenda where the boys will go.

"Court is adjourned," Eddick said, as he banged his gavel on the desk.

As Shorty was being walked out of the courtroom, he turned and mouthed to Melissa, "I love you." She looked at him and slowly shook her head from side to side, responding in a 'no you don't' answer to him. Jimmy, sitting next to Melissa, looked at her sad eyes—eyes that still loved Shorty, but eyes that knew a new beginning was to evolve for Melissa. A beginning that would have some very slippery and steep steps to climb, but would be character building for Melissa as while the degree of difficulty would be a challenge for Melissa, reaching the top of the stairs would strengthen her convictions to now assume the leadership role of her family. Jimmy put his arm around her and told her the best is yet to come into her life. Tommy came by and, after hugging, they left the courtroom together.

Weeks later, Big Ang, for his complete cooperation, got a 40-month sentence from Eddick. Like everyone else, he had to serve 85% of his time. His family had been placed in the Witness Relocation Program already and, after getting out of college, Big Ang would be in the program, getting a new identity and living somewhere out West with his family. It was hard for me to picture Big Ang as some guy named Joe Sullivan or whatever his new name would be. Big Ang knew what the alternative was and he wasn't going to let the Outfit cash his chips in quite yet.

The Lanzo family became another family destroyed by the Outfit's ways. They're always the proverbial tornado. They rip through violently altering your family, not for a moment, but forever, and then leave a shredded family behind and you have to clean up their mess after their actions simmer down.

Melissa now learned a hard lesson that when you marry into the Outfit, you better get a full night's sleep and have your eyes wide open. Make sure you look north, south, east, and west because the Outfit has the ability to turn you in the direction that best benefits them. Once the Outfit has now positioned how they want you, they begin to play their game of deceits and lies, and park them on your head, specifically indoor parking in your brain.

No one in this universe is better at making you feel like a million bucks when, in reality, you're only worth a penny than the boys from Chicago. Always remember, ladies, when falling in love with an Outfit guy, they take you for a ride and they never give up the steering wheel.

Jimmy walked out of the courtroom and saw Melissa standing by herself. "Hey, Melissa. Where's your dad?" Jimmy said.

"Oh, he had to go back to the office," she said.

"C'mon, let's blow this joint. No reason to be here now, "Jimmy said.

As they rode down together in the elevator, Jimmy thought about the nowhere street Melissa was on at that moment. The trial was over, sentencing was over, but yet it wasn't over for Melissa.

"I could ask you how ya doin', but I pretty much know you aren't up to dancing tonight," Jimmy said, as he held open the elevator door for Melissa.

They left the Collins Federal Building and walked a few feet away from the building. Melissa turned her body facing Jimmy and began to speak to him. "You know, Jimmy, Pete betrayed the trust I had in him and with this long sentence, most likely I'll never see him again. He's probably going to die in prison," Melissa said. "Yet, there's a part of me—a very small part of me—that still loves him," she said. "I know he'll never be there for me physically and emotionally anymore, that's over; but if he had come to me, talked to me, maybe we could have figured out a different career path," Melissa said. "I really don't have a husband anymore, and the kids don't have a father," she said.

She fiddled with her marriage ring. "Sure, legally, I'm still married to Pete, but our souls are no longer married to each other," Melissa said. "They have been disconnected from each other and in a million years, never can be put back together. The flame of love we had has been doused out for eternity," she said.

Jimmy chose his words very carefully before he spoke to Melissa. Melissa was fragile right now. Her emotions toward Shorty were frayed and heated, at best. Jimmy didn't want to say something that would spark more negativity than was already out there in Melissa's thought pattern.

"Melissa, you just don't erase love like that," Jimmy said, while snapping his fingers. "Love is going to stay with you for a long time," he said. "Like the loss of a loved one, as one day builds on another, you feel relief from your loss, but you never forget the person. You adjust your thought process to soothe the feelings of grief you have," Jimmy said.

"You're going to have those feelings of love. You're going to look at pictures of you, Pete, and the kids, and wonder why things turned out the way they did. That's normal," Jimmy said. "But, the one thing that no court can ever take away from you is that when you walk in your house, you will still be Mom to those lovely children for now and forever," he said. "As tough as things are that you are going to go through, you'll still have your children to pick up after being knocked down," Jimmy said. "A family is always worth fighting for and you are smart enough and strong enough never to stop fighting for your family," Jimmy said. "I will never stop believing in you that you can and will turn bad into good," he said.

"Thanks Jimmy, your words mean a lot," Melissa said. "I remember something you told me when I was in my teens," she said. "You said, 'Melissa, the reason God gave us seven days was you couldn't have seven good days in a row or seven bad days in a row. There will be good days. There will be bad days, but never let one day stop you from living your life the best way you can,'" Melissa said. "I never forgot those words, Jimmy, and how true they were after a day like today," Melissa said. "While today was one of those bad days, the bad streak stops at one," she said. As she held Jimmy's arm, she said, "Thanks, Jimmy, for all of your support through this mess. I don't think I could have made it without you."

"Melissa, you're smart, you'll figure something out to help you go forward," Jimmy said. "If you need anything extra around the house, let me know, okay? Don't hesitate, just call me," he said. "If there's anything else I can help you with, let me know," Jimmy said.

"Jimmy, you've always been so sweet to all the mob wives during their time of need, and that includes me now," Melissa said. "Don't worry, I will call you if something needs your attention," she said. "Karen is very lucky to have you," Melissa said.

"I'm lucky to have Karen," Jimmy said. Jimmy then hugged Melissa and said, "Take care of yourself, kid."

"I will, Jimmy," said Melissa. They then began to part ways.

"See ya, Melissa," Jimmy said.

"See ya, Jimmy," Melissa said.

The one thing I always respected about Jimmy was, as Melissa said, when the Outfit wives needed someone in their time of trouble, he tried his best to be there for them. I'm not going to make excuses or apologize for Jimmy's Outfit life. He, by carrying out an order, disrupted a family's life, so let's be clear about that. He wasn't a 'goody two shoes' as that is not in the Outfit's job description. Yet, he had a sense of trying to keep a family together and whether by helping financially or being a handyman fixing a sink at someone's house, he never wanted to see a family fall apart. While Jimmy could be the problem as to what changed in the family, he was also the solution in trying to piece together something he had broken. He knew the families needed money—that was priority one—but he knew the families needed a friend, a pillow to put their weary head on after a days' worth of crises. He tried to be the friend who created a laugh when needed to break the tension and the friend who held an umbrella over their heads during their times of need. Jimmy was by far the exception, not the rule, when it came to caring for Outfit families.

"How are ya going to help Melissa? I mean Shorty put her in the jackpot. You gotta have something up your sleeve or something you can pull out of your back pocket to help her get out of the jackpot," I said to Jimmy. "What's your plan?" I said.

"I don't have one right now, Bobby," Jimmy said.

"For real? You gotta be kidding me. When does Jimmy Williams not have a plan?" I said.

"Bobby, it's not that simple," Jimmy said. "If I take some money from one thing, I gotta figure out from what operation I can take money to cover the money I need," he said. "I'm not a bank. I still report to Dean, so I gotta keep enough balls in the air to keep everyone happy," Jimmy said.

"Yeah, but you got millions of dollars coming in from all the operations. Couldn't you just take something, say off the top, for Melissa?" I said.

"Bobby, for certain operations, Dean expects a certain gross to come in, so I gotta be careful in where I choose to take the money for Melissa," Jimmy said.

"So you're telling me you're going to let Melissa sit in the jackpot until you come up with some way to get her some money that won't piss off Dean?" I said.

"Yeah, Bobby. I guess that's the plan," Jimmy said. "Look, I'm checking around to get an idea of what the landscape is for her; something will break, I know it," Jimmy said. "She's still got some money left that Tommy gave her, so it's not like she needs money today, but Tommy's got other kids, so he can't just support Melissa. She'll need money. I know that," Jimmy said.

"I can see by your face you're not happy, but Bobby, in the life, you gotta follow certain rules," Jimmy said. "You gotta make sure you don't leave any holes as you don't want to be put in a hole in St. Matthew's Cemetery," Jimmy continued. "I'll get her out of the jackpot, you'll see."

As much as I wanted to disagree with Jimmy, I knew he was right about following the rules when you are in the life. While Outfit rules, at times, were made up as they went along, the rules about money were clear—don't screw with it or we'll screw with you. Jimmy was going to have to find a way to get Melissa money and make sure the Outfit didn't lose a penny.

Melissa went to see Brian Bianchi after someone told her he was taking over Shorty's operation. Bianchi had been a juice collector for Victor Lanzo before going off on his own. He was in the adult porn business, besides selling stolen guns. He had a street crew, which carried out his dirty deeds. Melissa knew Bianchi very well, as Tommy represented him on a couple of minor charges that were dismissed for lack of evidence.

"Brian, you know with Pete going away to prison, I'm going to need some money for myself and the children," Melissa said. "I'll pay you back, but until I get myself situated, I need living money to support my kids," she said. "The money would just be for paying the bills, things like that—no extras, just meeting expenses," Melissa said.

"I'm sorry to hear Pete put himself in the jackpot, but I can't give you any money," Bianchi said, looking at her and speaking in the cold voice.

"It's not a lot I'm asking for, maybe just $5,000, maybe a little less," Melissa said. "I stayed home raising the kids and since I didn't work, I don't have any income," she pleaded. "It's for my kids. I can't keep running to my dad. I swear I'll pay you back every cent I borrow," she desperately said.

"As I said, Pete put himself in the jackpot. You ain't my problem, understand?" Bianchi angrily said. "Look, you got a body. Go out on the street and use it; put on a pair of tight shorts and go out and shake your moneymaker," he said, telling her in a 'that's the way it is' type of voice. "Broads think when they marry guys like us, they'll always get the sweet," Bianchi said. Well, sometimes there's the sour, so since there's nothing else to talk about, see ya," Bianchi briskly said. What Bianchi was telling Melissa was Shorty's gone and no one cares about what he left behind. That's your problem, sweetheart.

Melissa got her education in the fact that, to the Outfit, you only count when they need something from you. Your needs never count to the Outfit. If you want something, you are like yesterday's news—forgotten. 'Stop crying to me,' the Outfit said. 'Mop up your own mess.'

This is unfortunately why I, with very little success, tried to talk either girls going with Outfit guys or guys going with daughters of Outfit guys to look elsewhere for their true love. Not every daughter is a 'Mafia Princess' nor is every son a 'Wiseguy.' It's just that being close to the Outfit through marriage might make you a lot closer than you want to be. I would emphasize if you wanted to marry someone who was Italian, there were plenty of great Italian guys and girls out there to meet.

Italian guys and girls who are smart, wonderful, loving, caring people who would be terrific partners are more than available. There are handsome, good looking Italian guys and beautiful Italian girls who are around every corner, ready to meet you. I would tell you people that if you play with dirt, you will get dirty. But often, I felt my success in persuading people not to marry into the Outfit was about as good as the Chicago Cubs' chances of winning the

World Series. Well, the Cubbies are still trying and so am I, as futile as it might seem. Someday the fortunes of the Cubs and the Outfit will change…yeah right, buddy, keep on dreaming.

Too many times I've seen the bad side effects of what happens when you marry into trouble. Melissa is the example of what happens to an Outfit marriage when bad happens. While Melissa had no way of knowing Shorty would become an Outfit guy since his father's DNA engulfed him, the odds were pretty good that the old apple doesn't fall far from the tree theory would prevail. Shorty's apple nestled comfortably against Victor's tree. But as with any type of fruit, if you leave it out too long, it turns rotten. Every day Shorty was in the life; he eventually turned rotten to the core.

When Melissa got to her car after meeting with Bianchi, which produced zero results for her, she sat down in the front seat, put her head down on the steering wheel, and began sobbing. She raised her head up after a few seconds and decided to seek guidance from the one who has known her for her entire life; the trusted one who has guided her during her most difficult decisions in her life; the one who, maybe, she should have consulted with before marrying Shorty. The one who emotionally held her hand, walking her down the good street of life, letting her see houses that had the lights on, where smiles could be seen through the windows and laughter could be heard. A sense of love was hanging on all the walls. Life's fruits of joy were dry walled around the houses.

This was the life shown to Melissa as the life to live—the one that kept Melissa off of the bad streets where there were no lights on in any of the houses. The houses were strikingly black inside as fighting, yelling, and screaming darkened them so deeply that no ray of happiness could penetrate the evil that lived there. There was no sign of life in these houses, as any type of well-meaning life was squeezed out of them. Raging bad attitudes blockaded the doors, not allowing an expression of love to come in. There were once people living in these houses, families who became so broken they abandoned what should have been a safe sanctuary, but turned into a stench-filled purgatory filled with hate, deception, and deep rooted anti-love soiled in the carpet.

It was time for Melissa to listen to her heart. "Melissa you have one true ally and somehow he's going to help you," her heart said. "Jimmy Williams, he's the one you have to see," her heart said. "Everyone from the Outfit is running away from you. You're a pariah to them, but not to Jimmy because he's not wired that way. Listen to me; I'm not giving you bad advice. Do it for your kids. Do it for yourself. You go, girl," her heart said.

Melissa felt relieved at that moment, as if a deeply guilt-ridden weight had been hoisted off her shoulders. *Things are tough now and will probably get a whole lot tougher, but maybe God has put an angel in front of my face and it's time I open my eyes and see that hand stretching out to help me,* Melissa thought.

Jimmy was always a realist, I'll give him that. He understood that a strong family structure must remain intact no matter how battered it became, no matter how many speed bumps were put in its path, no matter how many hoops the family had to jump through to remain united, no matter how strong were the gusty winds of despair blowing in their faces, what mattered was they were still family. It was a side of Jimmy you would see in which he would come out from behind the curtains and walk to the center stage of life and with his actions, help an Outfit family go from treading water to swim the length of the pool. Maybe, in Jimmy's own way, he was trying to drill out the criminal decay of the Outfit so real families, who were part of the Outfit by association, could chew on the sweets of life and feel no pain. His dialogue was simply put—a family will always be a family and never allow them to miss a loving beat.

Melissa called Jimmy and they arranged to meet for lunch at Caesar's Inn. "Hi, Jimmy," Melissa said, as she sat down at a table where Jimmy was seated. "I'm sorry to keep you waiting. I ran a little late today," Melissa said.

"Nah, don't worry about it. I just got here five minutes ago," Jimmy said as he got out of his chair and hugged Melissa. Jimmy helped Melissa take off her coat and held a chair for her as she had stood up when Jimmy approached her. "You didn't have to stand up, Melissa," Jimmy said.

"Hugs are better standing up," she teased.

While seated, they ordered their lunch, then Melissa spoke. "I met with Brian Bianchi," Melissa said.

"He told you he had no money for you and to use your body on the street. I think the words were 'Go shake your moneymaker,'" Jimmy interrupted.

"Yes, that's exactly what he said. How did you know?" Melissa's big, bright, expressive, brown eyes quickly enlarged as she spoke.

"Lucky guess," Jimmy said. "Melissa, everyone thinks that guys in the Outfit, when there is a problem for a family, they step in and take care of their own. That's a big heavy load of crap," Jimmy said. "When a guy goes away to college, dies naturally or not, the boys are interested in only one thing—how can they take over his action," Jimmy said. "Maybe people watch too much TV or go to the movies and somehow think the mob cares about the guy's loved ones. One day you're Pete's wife; the next day, you're Melissa who? Sure, you'll have some guys use a fake attitude of caring by saying, 'Gee I didn't know it was this bad for you,'" Jimmy said. "What a bunch of baloney. These guys knew damn well it was going to be bad for you because, if you get money from Pete and they are taking over his operations and pocketing his money, where is your money going to come from?" he said. "They're just trying to make themselves sound good, at your expense," Jimmy said.

"Sort of like bad boys trying to be good boys, but are still bad boys," Melissa said.

"See, I told you that you were smart," Jimmy said. "The line Bianchi told you is standard operating procedure for the Outfit. They want to put you outta sight, outta mind," Jimmy said. "You're no longer on somebody street. Now you're on nobody street," he said. "The problem is with that logic, the kids are put squarely in the middle of the street and no one cares what their fate is going to be except their mother, which in this case is you," Jimmy said.

"I feel like I'm standing in the middle of the street with my kids and I don't know which way to turn," Melissa said.

"Melissa, you're one of the smartest women I know. Really, I ain't just saying that to pump you up and to make you feel better. I swear it's the truth," Jimmy said. "So, let's pull back for a second and think about this," Jimmy said.

"Thanks, Jimmy, you just got a way of making a woman feel a whole lot better about herself," Melissa said. "Maybe it's that you know how to turn on a light in a dark place and make it a whole lot brighter," she said.

"Careful, you're starting to sound like Jimmy Williams," Jimmy said. Melissa giggled.

Melissa had eye contact of steel; her eyes were the strongest they had been, as they locked into Jimmy's eyes as he spoke. "You do a lot of good volunteer work at Our Lady of Perpetual Worship and work with the rich people's church, St. Bonaventure the Holy on the Near North Side. You get a lot of these rich people to donate clothes and stuff, so I was thinking— have you ever thought about some type of resale shop business?" Jimmy said. "I'm just throwing this thought out on the table for you to think about," Jimmy said.

"I never thought about it," Melissa said. "I'm really good at getting people to donate things. You might have hit on something," she said.

"It's just a thought. I'm not telling you to do it, but Melissa, you've got a talent for this type of stuff, so just think it over," Jimmy said.

Often during difficult times in our life, while thinking of ways to help ourselves out, we forget to look at the one resource that can help us in our time of need. That is ourselves. We are our own best resource and we don't have to leave the neighborhood when looking. We possess our own talents, yet, we feel we have to look elsewhere to find those talents. We all have those latent talents inside of us and all we have to do is open the door for opportunity and let those talents walk through the door and see the light of day. For those talents, the talents from within are the best talents we could ever find.

Jimmy had heard through the Outfit grapevine, a dealer owed Shorty $25,000. Jimmy did not say anything to Melissa about that.

"Melissa, really think this over. I'm going to sniff around to see if I can come up with some money for you," Jimmy said. "I'll promise to try. I'm not saying I'll be successful, but I'll try for you," Jimmy said.

"You're really serious about this?" Melissa said.

"Yes, yes, I am. I really believe you are smart enough to be a success," he said. "I really believe in you. You're a college graduate. You're very bright and mentally you can light it up. You're a success waiting to happen," Jimmy said.

"Hmm," she answered.

"So, will you at least think about it?" he said.

"Yes, I will," she said. "Thanks, Jimmy. I feel a whole lot better since talking to you," Melissa said.

"Alright, I'll be talking to you," Jimmy said. They parted ways—one to think about the future; the other to create the future.

Joe "Sleepy Joe" Ciparetti told Jimmy about the dealer who owed Shorty money. Sleepy Joe had those sleepy looking type of eyes that when you looked at him, you thought he would nod off any second. I swear, I think Joe could walk and fall asleep at the same time. He worked on stolen cars in an Outfit chop shop, but he was the type of guy who kept his ear to that Outfit pavement. Joe was a street snitch, but Jimmy never called him that. He would tell me Joe was a liaison for corporate communications.

"Bobby, the Outfit is a corporation," Jimmy would say. "You always need someone to communicate important corporate information and Joe Ciparetti plays that role," Jimmy would say to me with a straight face. Jimmy would throw a couple of bucks Joe's way for information. While Jimmy, with a straight face, would tell me Joe's a corporate guy, the fact was he was a street snitch. "Bobby, whether you are in the life or some other life, you gotta be two steps ahead of everyone else and, at times, need an advantage and guys like Joe Ciparetti give you what you need to stay ahead," Jimmy said. "To bring the bacon home, you gotta play every angle and a little advantage never hurts."

Jimmy went to see the dealer. The dealer had bought some adult films from Shorty, but never paid him for them. Jimmy introduced himself and told the dealer he was here today to collect on the debt of $25,000, which was owed to Shorty for his family.

"Shorty's in jail. I don't owe a damn thing to anybody," the dealer said, kind of sneering at Jimmy.

"Yes, you do you owe someone. You owe Shorty's family the money," Jimmy said. "You bought the films, so you gotta pay for them," Jimmy said.

"Look buddy, the deal was between me and Shorty, not no family," the dealer said. "Shorty's in the clink. He ain't getting out anytime soon, so the deal is over. There's no reason I gotta talk to you, so scram," the dealer said in a cocky, arrogant screw you voice.

Jimmy reached into his jacket pocket and pulled out a loaded .32-caliber handgun and stood up. He walked behind the dealer and with his left hand, he grabbed the dealer's throat; with his right hand, as he forced the dealer to turn sideways, he jammed the gun barrel into the inside of the dealer's mouth. Jimmy was from the school that you had to make the play when the play had to be made. "Bobby, whether you're in the life or doing something else with your life, when the opportunity presents itself, you gotta make the play when the play has to be made," Jimmy would say to me. "Maybe you want to invest in a stock that's two bucks a share; you don't invest at two bucks a share and the stock goes up to $100 bucks a share. See, you didn't make the play when the play had to be made and you lost out on making some money for yourself."

Jimmy continued, "You meet a nice girl. You can tell after a few dates she's right for you, but maybe, you don't show her enough love or affection to let her know how much you care for her and…bang…she doesn't want to see you anymore and you've lost her. Had you made the play when the play had to be made, you would still have been together with her and probably gotten married, had kids, and would have had a great life," Jimmy said.

"You're on a job and you feel you've been doing good enough on your job to merit a raise," Jimmy said. "So you go see your boss and you don't act like a goof and start demanding a raise. Rather, you talk about your accomplishments for that year—the projects you worked on, maybe the money you saved the company, all the good stuff you have done that year to self-promote yourself in the boss's eye," said Jimmy. "Maybe the boss will put you in for a raise, maybe not, but by making the play when the play had to be made and going in and talking to the boss, you at least planted the seed of why you should get a raise in his head. By sitting at your desk and not making the play when the play has to be made means you're letting an opportunity slip through your fingers because by talking to the boss, you're telling him what you did this year. Everything is fresh. If you wait until next year to talk to the boss, you can't talk about last year's accomplishments. The boss wants to hear what you are doing for me now," Jimmy said.

"So, making the play when the play has to be made is about timing," I said.

"Yup, it's about timing, but it's the right timing that counts," Jimmy said.

"So, putting a gun barrel in a dealer's mouth is making the play when the play has to be made," I said.

"You got it, Bobby boy. Let's say it brings a new perspective to the conversation," Jimmy said with a sneaky smile on his face.

Holding the gun steady in the dealer's mouth, Jimmy said, "I've got six good reasons why the conversation should continue, but I'm only going to ask you one. When am I going to get the 25 Gs?" Jimmy asked.

The dealer carefully nodded his head in agreement, bouncing it up and down ever so carefully, as Jimmy slowly took the gun out of the dealer's mouth.

"Whatcha say? Can't hear you?" Jimmy said in a mean menacing way.

"Give me a couple of days. Please don't shoot me. I've got a family. Please, please, I beg you. I'll get you the money, just don't shoot me," the dealer said. All of a sudden the dealer was not hard-edged to Jimmy, his tough attitude was washed away by fear. He was melting like a spring thaw. Ah, being the victim sure does change the season for someone. Nothing like a little potential violence to assist in an attitude change, I say.

"Shorty's got a family, too," Jimmy said. "I'll be back in two days for the money. No funny stuff like calling the cops, otherwise, your family's going on the hit parade," Jimmy said. "I want all the money, the complete 25 Gs—not partial payments, got it?" Jimmy said.

"Okay, okay, don't worry. I promise. You'll get all the money, just please put the gun away," the dealer said meekly. This little tale was an example of the difference between the racketeer and a gangster.

"See, Bobby, always remember this, there's a big difference between a racketeer and a gangster. A racketeer always wants to have a sit-down when it comes to making a decision about someone or something," Jimmy said. " 'Let's talk about it,' they'll say and, well, that's okay if you have to do it, like if you're going to whack a made guy, then you're supposed to have a sit-down," Jimmy said. "If someone physically touches a made guy—you know, like in a fight punches him, kicks him, whatever—then you're supposed to have a sit-down as the guy may be a made guy, maybe an associate member for touching a made guy like that automatically gets whacked," Jimmy said. "A made guy can't be fucked with. Even if a made guy does something wrong, he's supposed to get a sit-down," Jimmy said. "Made guys have been whacked without sit-downs and those orders have been given by gangsters."

"If a street crew even suspects the crew boss is a racketeer, they're going to think he's soft, takes too much time deciding something. A crew can sense within time if the boss is a racketeer or gangster. Generally a boss is a gangster, but there are times when some are racketeers," Jimmy said. "It's not that they won't give an order to whack someone. It's just they ain't full of spit and fire like a gangster," said Jimmy.

"Within a crew, guys will start talking among themselves about the boss if they think he's talking too much and not acting quickly on something," Jimmy said. "Talking is okay when necessary. It's just you gotta know your place, where and when, otherwise you can get a reputation you don't want," said Jimmy. "Guys in a crew will say, 'Where's the action? He spends too much time talking, maybe the boss isn't strong enough to be boss,'" Jimmy said.

"A gangster is decisive. He takes action. Bang, something happens and a gangster gives an order for something to be done," he said. "A gangster doesn't wait or care about a sit-down. A gangster does this to keep the crew in line," said Jimmy. "He makes a move, and the crew sees this and respects him for taking action quickly. A crew knows if they fuck up, they better have a damn good reason why or there's going to be action," he continued.

"I ain't going to lie do you, Bobby, a gangster isn't always right. He sometimes jumps the gun on something, not getting the real story, but the story he wants to hear," he said. "Then he makes a quick decision that turns out to be the wrong one and someone gets fucked. This happens more than you think," Jimmy said.

"So, in a person's life, it's better to have balance, in which you take a little time to check something out, to make sure you got the facts right, then you can pull the trigger," I said.

"Exactly," Jimmy said. "You can't overload one side or the other because you're bound to screw up either way," he said. "Look, nobody likes a weak person—not in the Outfit, not anywhere—but to be strong, you gotta make sure you ain't missing something. That's all I'm saying," Jimmy said.

"So, getting back to this putting a gun in the dealer's mouth, you felt your only option was to act like a gangster," I said.

"What other option did I have?" asked Jimmy. "The guy's giving me this tough mouth attitude, so I wasn't going to back off and take his shit. If he talks to me like a gentleman, then it's different; maybe, we can work something out and the gun don't come out of my jacket," Jimmy said. "You see, his tough mouth attitude wasn't so tough with the gun jammed in his mouth. You'll find that in life, Bobby, there are guys that will act tough, but when someone comes right back at them that toughness sure gets lost," he said. "A tough guy's actions will show you how tough he is not how he runs his mouth," Jimmy said.

"In your lifetime, Bobby, you'll come across plenty of big mouths who'll sound tough. Don't worry about them," he said. "Always keep your eye on the quiet ones, Bobby, because those are the ones you never know what they are thinking and...bang...one day they take action and everyone says, 'Where the hell did that come from,'" Jimmy said. "If you decide you want to be in the life, those are the guys who keep the spotlights on because those types of guys go from the unknown to the known in a high-speed deadly kind of way."

Two days later, Jimmy went back to see the dealer. The guy couldn't have been nicer to Jimmy. Three times he counted out the 25 Gs. "Enough already, I see the 25 Gs are here," Jimmy said.

"I just want to make sure you're happy, Mr. Williams. I just want to make sure you're satisfied, Mr. Williams. I just want to make sure we are square, Mr. Williams. I just want..." the guy said.

"Shut the hell up already. Everything is fine. I'm taking the money. I'll see you," Jimmy said.

"Thanks, Mr. Williams. It's been an honor to be in your presence," the guy said.

Jimmy reached the door, turned and let his eyes look at the guy, expressing themselves very clearly and directly. *One more word out of you, buddy, and the next words you'll be hearing will be your eulogy at Our Lady of Perpetual Worship.* Jimmy turned and walked out, shaking his head.

Melissa gave a lot of thought to what Jimmy said pertaining to a resale shop business. Jimmy had been right she reasoned. She was smart and had to earn a living for herself and her kids. Since she loved dressing up herself, maybe a resale shop could become her vocation.

She started calling her contacts from St. Bonaventure the Holy Church. The wealthy ladies from St. Bonaventure the Holy were always looking to update their wardrobes, so they were glad to discard last year's styles. With their social lives chock-full of one event after another, who wants to be seen in last year's style? Since the wealthy ladies from St. Bonaventure the Holy had the money to throw out the old and buy the new, they were not going to be seen on the Near North Side of Chicago wearing last year's style. They wanted to be seen on the Near North Side in the styles everyone was talking about for this year. So, it wasn't hard for Melissa to convince them to empty their closets and she gladly took their clothes.

Her garage quickly filled with clothes. She put the clothes in boxes to store them. As she was having her morning coffee and trying to figure out what to do with the clothes, the phone rang. It was Jimmy and he asked her if he could come over. Melissa told him, "Sure, that would be fine; so, come on over."

"Hi, Melissa," Jimmy said, as he walked in her front door.

"Hi, Jimmy," she said.

"Melissa, I was able to come up with some money to help you out," he said.

Melissa, while dying to know where the money was coming from, decided if she knew zero where the money was coming from, if someone asked her about it, she could honestly say, 'I have no idea.' So she never asked Jimmy where he got the money. "Wow, that's wonderful," she said.

"I'm giving you $25,000," Jimmy said.

"Oh, my God, I'm stunned. I'm at a loss for words," Melissa said. "Thank you. Thank you so much. You must know an angel," she said. Melissa tightly hugged Jimmy. "For me and my kids, this is a godsend," she whispered in his ear. Melissa released him and had a beaming smile on her face. "C'mon with me to the garage. I want to show you something," she said to Jimmy.

Melissa opened up the garage door. "Look at all the clothes you have. So, you have started the business," Jimmy said, as he saw the boxes of clothes.

"Yes," she said smiling. "I thought about what you said after Pete's sentencing. I just can't keep my head in the sand and hope for the best," Melissa said. "No, I've got to try and make an attempt at making a new financial life for me and the kids. I gotta be the responsible one," she said.

"You can't hit the ball if you don't swing the bat," Jimmy said.

"It's on my shoulders to be the breadwinner for the family," Melissa said. "I don't even know where to begin to thank you, Jimmy. Now I can go rent a storefront and really make a serious effort to pursue the opportunity you have given me," said Melissa.

She hugged Jimmy hard, squeezing her arms around him. The hug had strength to it. Its strength came from her sensing that someone really cared about Melissa Lanzo. Melissa knew with the long, long road she faced in starting a new business there would be good days and not so good days that a business goes through. Melissa knew there would always be someone—that one special someone—yelling from her corner to her. "You can do it Melissa, don't quit on yourself. Never, ever stay on the ground after you have been knocked down. Get up please, just get up, Melissa; think things through. Make the play when the play has to be made. You can do it, Melissa," that someone would be cheering for her.

Jimmy was not the type of guy who just had Melissa's back. No, he had her whole body and soul. Jimmy always told me the first day you run from the problem, you'll be running the rest of your life from the problem.

Confront it, challenge it, nail it, kick it in the rear, but never let the problem win in the game of life. It says, 'No, you can't'; you scream back, 'Yes, I can.' It says you'll never make it in life; you say, 'I'll never be counted out. I'll always get up, no your matter how many times you knock me down.'

Jimmy would be Melissa's safety net. Whenever Melissa felt down from the pressures that a business can bring in life, Jimmy would catch her and stabilize her. He would tell her champion players make champion plays and you, Melissa, are a champion destined for greatness. Look in the mirror, Melissa.

There's your only opponent. There's the one stopping you from achieving the great heights you are capable of. There's the one you gotta knockout of your life Jimmy would say.

Jimmy was an associate member of a violent, bloodthirsty organization. The difference between him and the Outfit was they didn't care how they left a victim. They just moved on to the next one. Jimmy made sure the victim could stand on their own two feet.

Melissa's business grew from a tiny storefront operation eventually to three resale stores—one in Chicago and two in the northern suburbs. Melissa made contacts with clothing manufacturers and bought women's clothes—some high-end, like designer clothes, which had minor defects in them. These defects were the reason the clothes couldn't be sold in the manufacturer's stores. Melissa bought these types of clothes cheaply and she priced them at affordable rates. Her stores were busy, as women from Chicago and the suburbs flocked to them. Where else could you buy designer and other high quality clothing for 50% to 60% less then you pay in a retail store? Melissa was making a handsome profit in her stores.

Most Outfit stories usually do not have happy endings like Melissa's. The husband goes away to college and the family is shattered. That's it. No one helps financially. It's see ya, Charlie. You're on your own, buddy. Guys in the life are actors when it comes to helping a family in need. They play the role, as if they really care about someone's family, but the only thing they care about is acquiring the guy's business. They'll give you this look of concern when they see you, but it's all an act to stroke their ego.

I would like to tell you I saw plenty of Jimmy Williamses in the Outfit, but that would be a lie. There was only one Jimmy Williams in the Outfit. So, from your son Bobby, thanks, Dad, for having a heart; even though I knew what you did for the Outfit and you knew what you did for the Outfit, you never took a powder when a family was in need. You never gave a family an excuse not to help them. If you taught me nothing else, you taught me to help someone in need if you can, because you never know when that someone might be you. So thanks, Jimmy, for being the pavement Melissa could walk on, knowing it was secure enough for her to make her 'American Dream' come true. ML, Inc. went from *no you can't* to *baby, look at me now*.

In most businesses, whenever there is a change in management, there are always some new policies that are implemented. With the Outfit, the core businesses remain the same when someone new takes over, but the tricky part is will the management style help or hinder the core businesses.

The death of Dean Dragonetti presented itself as an opportunity to test new leadership. The difference between corporate America and the Outfit is your review period might be 24 hours with deadly consequences if your performance levels are not met. Dean's management style was basically a reign of terror. He had a gangster mentality and he was hardcore La Cosa Nostra. He had a violent mind living in a violent body. He accepted no excuses and no one gave him any. He had a highly explosive temper that caused him, at times, to give Jimmy an order to have someone clipped when they shouldn't have. Sometimes, Jimmy would wait 24 hours after Dean gave an order on someone and go back to talk to Dean about the person. Sometimes, Jimmy could get Dean to rescind the order; sometimes not.

Since everything with the Outfit is about money, Dean made sure everyone knew that money and only the money counted. He allowed no screw ups when it came to getting the money for the Outfit. Jimmy was really the perfect balance for Dean's psychotic behavior. As much as others in the Outfit didn't like Jimmy because he wasn't Italian, no one would dispute his intelligence. While Dean would rant and rave about someone and what should be done to that person, Jimmy would look at the long range implication of Dean's decision for the Outfit. If I heard him say it once, I heard him say it 100 times to Dean, what's best for the Outfit? How does it make them stronger? Will this be a plus or minus for us? That's why Jimmy and Dean got along because Dean, even though he didn't say it, appreciated Jimmy's long-range outlook on things.

"Bobby, if your father was Italian, he'd be running the Outfit," Dean would say to me. For Dean, that was a compliment. When Jimmy was an underboss to Tony Galente, Tony felt the same way about Jimmy.

Dean's death impacted that Outfit because no two bosses are the same and while Joe Aruti had similar approaches like Dean, he wasn't Dean. The Outfit would never have a boss like Dean again. Many tried to emulate him, but none could be him. The hardcore La Cosa Nostra types like Dean were dying off. The Board of Trustee meetings at St. Matthew's Cemetery started to gain more members as the years went by.

Dean was in his late 60s, when one evening he went out to dinner with a woman in her mid-30s. After dinner, he drove her to the Cherokee Motel, which he owned. Dean never spent a lot of time at the Cherokee, as he let Jimmy oversee the motel's operations. Dean got his monthly money from the Cherokee and he was content. He trusted Jimmy's ability to manage the Cherokee and the Cherokee was profitable.

Jimmy always made sure the Cherokee was spic and span. He reasoned a very clean motel would be appetizing to the customers, which it was. Customers felt comfortable in the motel. It was not uncommon for a customer to comment about how clean the place was. On Wednesdays, customers who rented a room got a 10% discount on their bill.

The Cherokee was also a hot pillow place. Mob prostitutes would bring their johns there to perform whatever sexual acts johns were willing to pay for. Hot pillow joints helped the Outfit's bottom line. The rooms could be turned over more than once, thus, generating a lot of income for the Outfit. The Cherokee was not only for mob prostitutes, but you would see Asian businessmen dressed up in their expensive suits, driving their expensive cars to bring their girlfriends during the lunch hour (usually between 12:00 P.M. and 2:00 P.M.). These guys, for the most part, were married and they needed a place far away from their home for their sexual recess time.

The ladies were generally Asian. Some might have been prostitutes, while others were just single women running around with married guys. When you would see the ladies, they wore nice dresses or skirts, high-heeled shoes, make up—maybe they figured by dressing up the package, their lunchtime partners would pay a little more for the product or in the case of the single girls, who were just looking for romance, entice the men to deliver some afternoon delight. I'll give it to the girls, while they looked like teachers or nurses or just regular girls going to work, they knew how to heat up the eggroll for everyone's satisfaction.

After the lunchtime lovebirds left, the beds were stripped down as sheets and pillowcases were changed and the rooms were made ready for the next contestants. Outfit fences would come to the Cherokee in the wee hours of the morning to buy stolen merchandise from Outfit burglars who had hit places earlier that night. The fences would rent a room and at a designated time, the Outfit burglars would show up. At about 4:00 A.M., the Cherokee parking lot filled up with cars containing jewelry, expensive furs, and any other items that could bring in money for the burglars. The fences, after buying the merchandise, would often sell it to retailers, who would sell it to the public. So, it was possible for a woman to have had a mink coat stolen, go to her furrier and without her knowing it, she rebuys her own fur coat, thus, in effect, paying twice for the same mink coat. As you can see, the Outfit believed in giving someone a second chance in life.

The Cherokee, in good business sense, did not have all its eggs in one basket. It had subsidiary action all night long. The revenue on the first floor was running into the revenue on the second floor. They kept bumping into each other hour after hour each night.

Big Steve worked the front desk at night in the Cherokee. Big Steve was a jovial, easy-going black guy who was from the South Side. He was married with a couple of kids. He and I would talk about sports whenever I saw him. He was a die-hard White Sox fan, who would try and convert me into leaving my Cubbies. He would tell me it was a sin to be a Cubs fan in that laughing voice of his. Somehow, I pictured Big Steve slipping a White Sox cap on Jesus' head. He was a good-hearted guy, who would lend an Outfit prostitute a buck so she could buy a pack of smokes from the vending machine.

"Bobby," Big Steve would say to me, "my first name is I hear no evil, my middle name is I see no evil and my last name is I speak no evil." Big Steve, I knew what was going around in his surroundings, but like anyone else who needs a job, he just did his job and went home in one piece. The Outfit boys who visited the Cherokee liked Big Steve and gave him a tip when they left. He treated them with respect and was very courteous to them, thanking them for coming to the Cherokee and saying he hoped to see them soon. I remember a mob burglar Sal Vincanzette, who said to me, "Bobby, Big Steve is a good black." The Outfit was not known for their racial tolerance or even their tolerance for non-Italians, so Sal calling Big Steve a good black was probably something that wouldn't happen again in this century.

Jimmy increased the night room rates on specific rooms to take advantage of the flow of customers, who would be using the rooms only at night. The Cherokee had a few full-time residents, who paid so much a month for rent. They kept to themselves and if they did know about Outfit activities at the Cherokee, they kept it to themselves. They kept their doors shut at night to make sure the Outfit didn't know they existed. Unless they had to go to the front desk to see Donny the day guy or Big Steve at night, they tried to remain as invisible as possible.

The outside of the Cherokee had a high wall around it, so the rooms and parking spaces from the street were obscure. This was another type of Outfit business, in which secrecy helped the bottom line.

The Cherokee was located in the Chicago Police Department's 33rd District. Sgt. Jake O'Fahey was responsible for the police patrol in that beat. He was an Outfit friend, who Jimmy gave $500 a month to make sure the police did not interfere with the Outfit's ability to earn a buck at the Cherokee. O'-Fahey would have a day officer and night officer check in with Donny or Big Steve just for show.

The day officer, George Patalonis, was the skinniest Greek guy I ever saw in my life. You could fit him between two pieces of pita bread and still have room. George was always sociable, loved his wife and kids, and enjoyed being a cop. I don't believe George was on the take, as he would always say to Donny, "Sarge wanted me to stop by and check to see if everything is okay." Donny would say everything is fine and you wouldn't see George until the next day. George had this thing about saying you can't screw up on the job or you could lose your pension. So, I think O'Fahey just made the Cherokee one of George's regular assigned stops, but never gave him any money. George was too paranoid about doing something that could cost him his pension.

Now, the night guy who O'Fahey assigned to the Cherokee was a different story. Michael Laccacini was an Outfit friend, due to the fact that he was the nephew of John Euido, who everyone called JE. Euido was a juice collector for Patsy Sabrufica, and I can tell you after seeing him in action, a man with a very short temper. I saw Euido once walk up to guy, punch him in the gut, then ask him where's the money. He would get physical with people before they had a chance to speak.

Patrolman Michael Laccacini always had his hand out for a freebie. Big Steve always had something on the counter—a candy bar, package of gum, something for Laccacini to take when he came in.

"Hey, Stevarino. How ya doin'?" Laccacini would say when he entered the Cherokee.

"Fine, officer, just fine and yourself?" Big Steve would say.

"Couldn't be better," Laccacini would say. He would then ask Big Steve how things were going there and Big Steve would say well.

"Well, that's good to hear. I guess I'll go back on the street and protect the citizens of Chicago," Laccacini would say with a hearty laugh. That night, Big Steve had a candy bar on the counter and his eyes watched and waited for Laccacini to make his move.

"Okay, Stevarino. Have a good night," Laccacini said, as he picked up the candy bar, started unwrapping it, and walked out the door. Laccacini was his ignorant self, never asking Big Steve if it was okay to take the candy bar or thanking him for the candy bar. Nope, it was what are you going to do about it, call a cop? That was Laccacini's mentality.

O'Fahey never gave Laccacini any money, but what he did do was he arranged to give Laccacini four to five hours a week in overtime. O'Fahey would sign the timesheet marking the OT on the various days. Laccacini told O'Fahey he wasn't going to work the OT, so the OT existed only on the timesheet and the recorded hours were never worked. The taxpayers of Chicago paid for police services they never got. It kind of makes you wonder who was protecting who. Since Chicago cops can keep OT on the books until they retire and then get a check from the city, those overtime hours Laccacini was getting grew and grew month by month. Patrolman Michael Laccacini surely was one of Chicago's finest in the 'unfinest' way.

One night, Dean and his lady friend were in a room near the backend of the parking lot. He sat on the bed as she started to undress in front of him—slowly removing each garment, tantalizing him, teasing him, increasing his sexual temperature to a point where the sexual beast in him would capture his prey. Each button on her blouse she carefully opened up, then giving him a naughty smile, lips pouting, 'there's more to come, baby' type of look in her eyes, all projecting a sexual road they would travel together.

As her sexual séance continued with her skirt dropping to the ground, Dean started to move forward to her. He started to raise his right hand when a thunderbolt of pain hit his chest. He clutched his chest and fell back into the bed, his head hitting the covers and his eyes, wide-open, looking straight at the ceiling. His head turned slightly to the left with no visible body movement. God whacked him as he had done to others.

"Dean! Dean!" she frantically called out. "Oh, my God!" she repeated over and over. She started to shake him. "Dean! Dean, you okay?" she said. Nothing…nothing at all produced any sign of life. She threw her clothes on, threw open the door and ran to the office.

"It's Dean. Something's happened to him!" her voice rising as she spoke to Big Steve. "C'mon!" she said frantically, waving her arms at Big Steve. "We gotta help him! Please, hurry!" Big Steve literally jumped out of his chair and raced to their room with her running behind him.

When Big Steve entered the room, he froze for a second. He regained control of himself and went to Dean. "Mr. Dragonetti? Oh, my God," Big Steve said as he pressed his right thumb into Dean's neck trying to feel a pulse. There was nothing giving Big Steve any hope Dean was alive. With his left and right forefingers, he slowly pushed down Dean's eyelids.

"C'mon with me. I gotta call someone from the office," Big Steve said to the girl.

"Is it okay to leave him here?" she asked.

"Honey, at this point, I don't think Mr. Dragonetti will be leaving anytime soon," Big Steve said.

They went back to the office, she visibly upset, and Big Steve looking for guidance. Big Steve called Jimmy and explained as best he could the circumstances surrounding Dean.

"You did right calling me," Jimmy said to Big Steve. Jimmy told Big Steve to call 911 and tell the operator to send the paramedics. "I'm on my way over," Jimmy said. "Steve, keep the girl in the office. I don't want the paramedics to see her because they'll start questioning her and we don't want that, do we?" Jimmy said.

"Right, Jimmy. I'll keep her in the office," Big Steve said.

"What should I say when they question me?" Big Steve said.

"Just say Mr. Dragonetti stopped by the desk and said he was a little tired and was going to take a nap in Room 116," Jimmy said. "Then say you made a cup of coffee for Mr. Dragonetti and took it to Room 116 and that's when you found Mr. Dragonetti in his current condition, as he left the door slightly open," Jimmy said.

"Golly, Jimmy boy, you sure can think fast on your feet. Don't worry, I'll tell the paramedics exactly what you told me," Big Steve said.

"Good. I'm out the door. See you soon," Jimmy said.

When Jimmy got to the Cherokee, the paramedics were still there preparing to put Dean in the ambulance. "I'm a friend of Mr. Dragonetti," Jimmy said to one of the paramedics.

"Hey, this isn't the guy I read about in the papers, you know with the mob?" the paramedic said.

"What mob? Mr. Dragonetti, who is a personal friend of mine, is a businessman. He owns this motel. I don't know what the hell you're talking about," Jimmy said. "The mob or whatever they call it is a figment of Hollywood's imagination. There's no such thing as the mob," Jimmy said.

"Okay, sorry about that. It looks like he had a massive heart attack and died instantly," the paramedic said. "We gotta take him to Concord Hospital, which is the closest hospital where a doc will have to see him in order for the doc to sign the death certificate," the paramedic said.

"Okay, I'll meet you over at Concord. I'll call the family and they'll probably want me to call Gondere's to pick up the body after all the hospital paperwork is done," Jimmy said.

"Sounds good. I'll see you there," the paramedic said.

Jimmy went inside the office to talk to the woman. "Honey, it wasn't your fault what happened to Dean. It was, I guess, something that was going to happen at some time and it happened tonight," Jimmy said.

She was still visibly shaken from seeing Dean die in front of her. Jimmy offered her a cup of coffee. She took a slow drink out of the cup. She thanked Jimmy for the coffee.

"We will call a cab for you," Jimmy said. Jimmy reached into his pants pocket and pulled out his wallet. "Here's $25. That should cover your cab fare," he said.

"Thank you for being so kind to me," she said, as the coffee seemed to relax her. Her body language had slowed down considerably. She looked and acted more herself. "I just got so scared when I saw Dean fall back on the bed. I didn't know what to do. I had never seen anything like that in my life," she said. "We never touched each other and then boom, he's dead," she said.

"There wasn't anything you could have done to stop the heart attack, but you did the right thing. You ran for help," Jimmy said.

"I know what you're saying is true. It's just seeing someone die like that makes you feel helpless," she said.

"Look, you go home and forget about tonight for the sake of Dean's family. Forget about what you saw here," Jimmy said. "Don't tell anyone you were here tonight with Dean. Forget about it. It didn't happen," Jimmy said. "As far as me and Steve, we never saw you here tonight, right Steve?" he said.

"Right, Jimmy" Steve said.

"I know you can't just turn off in your head what you saw tonight, but each day will get a little easier than the day before," he said. "So, we gotta deal about tonight?" Jimmy asked her.

"Yeah, I'll do my best to eventually put this out of mind, though, it's going to take a long, long time to do that. Yeah, we got a deal," she said.

While she waited inside the office for a cab to come, Jimmy took Big Steve outside. "Steve, you did a hell of a good job tonight keeping things under control," Jimmy said. Jimmy pulled out a $50, folded it and put it in Steve's shirt pocket.

"Jimmy, no. C'mon, you don't have to do this. I was just doing my job. I love working here and Mr. Dragonetti has been very nice to me. He gives me $200 every Christmas," Big Steve said. "He personally comes to see me, shakes my hand, and says 'Steve, you gave me a great year,'" Big Steve said. His face had a proud smile stretched across it.

"I know all about it and like the great job you do all year, but you did a great job tonight," Jimmy said. "You and the missus go out and have some fun," Jimmy said. "Oh yeah, and one more thing," Jimmy said to Steve, "you're no longer the night man. You are now the night manager and you'll be making $65 more a week than you're making now, so enjoy the raise." Big Steve was stunned.

"Jimmy, I…I am at a loss for words. Oh, my God. This…this is so unexpected. Thank you. Thank from the bottom of my heart." A tear started to swell in Big Steve's eye. He hugged Jimmy and then with his shirt sleeve, he wiped away the tear.

"This promotion is well deserved and tonight was an example of the kind of work you've done for us," Jimmy said. "Things could have gotten out of control tonight, but you kept a lid on things and didn't allow any problems to creep in," Jimmy said. "Dean and I have always appreciated what type of job you have done for us at the Cherokee," he said. "So, I talked with Dean and he was in agreement with me about your promotion, so keep on doing the great job you're doing," Jimmy said.

"Don't worry, Jimmy. You'll never get a bad day's work out of me. That I promise and you can take that to the bank and deposit it," Big Steve said.

"You were just protecting Outfit interests with the girl and Big Steve, weren't you?" I said to Jimmy.

"Well, Bobby, it's true. I was protecting Outfit interests at the Cherokee, but I was protecting the girl and rewarding Steve," Jimmy said.

"What, did you pull this little charade out of your Outfit bag of tricks?" I said.

"No, Bobby. As far as the girl, I don't know what Dean told her or didn't tell her, but I know there are guys in the Outfit who would think maybe Dean said something to her about things the Outfit do and aren't going to be happy with her," Jimmy said.

"So, you're telling me someone would want the girl whacked because they think Dean told her something? That's insane. I mean Dean wouldn't tell her anything. You know Dean. He wouldn't talk about business with her," I said.

"Bobby, I'm not saying you're wrong. I agree with you. I don't think Dean would talk about business with her, but it's not about what I think. It's about what someone else thinks," Jimmy said.

"This is unreal. If this isn't nuts, I'll eat my shirt," I said. "How can the girl get whacked over something no one knows if she even knows, what someone thinks she's supposed to know based only on the fact she was Dean's girlfriend? This whole thing makes no damn sense to me," I said.

"Bobby, look, here's an example of what someone in the Outfit would think. The alphabet boys find out about her and go pay her a visit and start questioning her," Jimmy said. It always tickled me when Jimmy referred to the FBI as the alphabet boys. "So before you know it, word gets out on the street who she is and the alphabet boys have gone to see her. Now, she might tell the alphabet boys Dean never mentioned Outfit business and she knows absolutely nothing about the Outfit at all and that could be the truth," Jimmy said.

"However, someone in the Outfit might not buy her story," he said. "Someone might think this broad's lying. So, by getting her out of the picture, no one knows who she is and then no one can reach her and, maybe, hurt her," Jimmy said. "This way, the story on the street will be Dean had a heart attack and no one will know anything else. You see, Bobby, she's just an innocent bystander in all of this, so why put her in possible danger?" said Jimmy. "Sometimes you have to spin a story so someone who has done nothing to deserve it gets out of harm's way or else they become a victim of someone's paranoia," Jimmy said.

"Okay, I can see getting the girl out of the picture because someone in the Outfit will go bonkers if they find out the FBI talked to her, but what about Big Steve," I said. "Was this promotion done just to keep him quiet? I bet you never talked to Dean about promoting him; It was just something you did in the moment, a Jimmy Williams play, to protect the high and mighty Outfit," I said.

"I never talked to Dean about promoting Steve, but I had the paperwork put through to promote him. Dean's death made me tell him a little sooner, that's all," Jimmy said.

"So, you were going to promote Big Steve all along?" I asked.

"Yeah, Big Steve was going to be promoted," Jimmy said. "Steve got the promotion on merit. He's deserving of it." Jimmy continued, "When it's ten below zero in the winter, he's at work. When it's 95 degrees in the summer, he's at work. He never misses a damn day, never takes a vacation. He's very dependable," Jimmy said. "Once I came to the Cherokee and I saw Steve with a can of paint and a brush, painting the front door of one of the rooms. He paid for everything out of his own pocket, so I told him to reimburse himself with money from the petty cash," said Jimmy said.

"You know what he tells me? He says, 'Jimmy, 85% of the game is appearance and the front door just wasn't looking right, and we gotta have the Cherokee looking right because if the Cherokee is looking right, it'll be projecting the right appearance, so customers will want to stay at the Cherokee he said.' He never reimbursed himself. To Steve, working at the Cherokee wasn't a job. He managed the place like it was his own place. Where do you find a person like that?" Jimmy said. "Besides, he got along with everyone and I figured he had a pretty good idea what was going on at the Cherokee, but he had an 'if it's your business and not my business then it's none of my business' mentality. He kept things that didn't involve him to himself," Jimmy said.

"So, putting this all together, I made the play when the play had to be made, and I put Steve in for a promotion. This one didn't require any great consultation," Jimmy said. "Steve got the promotion because of Steve. He made it happen for himself. That's what a good employee does. Put a period on it, end of story," Jimmy said.

"It just seemed like, maybe, you had some ulterior motive for promoting Big Steve, but if you tell me he got it on merit...case closed," I said.

"Thank you, Judge Bobby Williams," Jimmy said, his eyes smiling at me.

Since Dean was Catholic, there would have been at least a one-day wake at Gondere's with a funeral service the next day at Our Lady of Perpetual Worship and burial at St. Matthew's Cemetery. Dean's family did not want a public funeral. They told Jimmy they were not up to a media circus, which they felt would occur at a public funeral. They asked Jimmy to talk to Father Tom and ask him to perform graveside services at St. Matthew's. Jimmy spoke with Father Tom and he agreed to the family's wishes.

Jimmy and I went to the service. As we pulled up to St. Matthew's, there was a beige Ford parked across the street with two guys sitting in the car. "Looks like the alphabet boys are here to check things out," Jimmy said. I turned my head to look in their direction. "Maybe they think Dean's having a meeting with the boys," Jimmy crackled. We walked into the cemetery and spoke briefly with the family. I gave them my condolences as Dean was still their family regardless of what Dean was and, at that moment, deserved the proper respect.

Father Tom performed the service, saying the prayers and trying in his own priestly way to put a positive spin on Dean's life. I stood there respectfully but, damn, it was hard to listen to Father Tom talk about Dean in a way that I knew was not true. I looked at Jimmy for emotional help as Dean was the monster of Chicago—a violent, psychotic person, who wasn't even worthy of being called a human being. He was an uncaged animal running loose on the streets of Chicago, using violence wherever and to whomever he deemed appropriate. He was a madman, controlling the reins of wild, violent, mentally depraved, and emotionally unfit creatures in the Outfit.

Jimmy looked back at me, kind of raising his eyes, acknowledging that what I was thinking of Dean was correct. Nevertheless, for this day, we had to respect the life of Dean for the sake of his family, no matter how much the stinking odor of his Outfit life permeated in his coffin.

As the casket was lowered into the ground at St. Matthew's Cemetery, I watched the burying of an era. The Dean Dragonetti era was over. The Outfit would continue on, but things were not going to be the same, as they never are.

As Jimmy and I walked back to the car, I asked him if he expected changes in the Outfit.

"Bobby, whether you want changes or not, changes will occur because the world changes. Laws change and attitudes change; things might look the same on the outside, but internally there will be changes," Jimmy said. "So, yeah, I expect there will be changes in the Outfit. Whether they are good changes or bad changes, time will tell," he said.

I listened to Jimmy's answer and thought about the new sheriff running the Outfit. Would he leave his own imprint on the Outfit or would he have the old sheriff's ways hanging over his head? Jimmy was right. Time would tell. It always does.

Joe Aruti, with Tony Galente's blessing, took over running the day-to-day operations of the Outfit. Joe had been Dean's underboss and, on paper, you would think for the most part, he would run the Outfit the same way or as close to it as Dean did. What's on paper and what gets translated into working conditions becomes another story.

The Outfit, like your family or minister teaches core values to its members and associate members. Intimidation, threats, bullying, and violence are all handed down from one generation to the next. Deviating from the core values can put you in the jackpot really quick.

Aruti was a stern-faced guy. You really had to earn a smile from him as he did not give them out very freely. If you were lucky, maybe twice a year you would see him smile, maybe. Joe's underboss, Sal Lombardi, just assumed he would be Joe's consigliere. Not so fast, Sal. You're still standing in line and no one has called your number, yet.

Tony Galente talked with Joe Aruti about Jimmy becoming Joe's consigliere. Jimmy knew the operations upside down and inside out, Tony told Joe. "If you want someone else as your consigliere, that's fine, but remember, if the consigliere thinks the boss is not running things right, he can have you clipped," Tony said. "I know from my experience with Jimmy as my underboss...he'll work for you, not against you," Tony said.

"Jimmy's smart, no question about that, and in years since I've known him, he's been nothing but good to me," Joe said.

"Yeah, he knows not being Italian, he can only go so far, but I never heard him bitch about it, not once. He's a great team player and he makes guys look good. It's a knack not everyone has," Tony said.

"Let me think about it," Joe said.

"Okay, Joe. It's your call, but choose wisely," Tony said.

Aruti remembered how Jimmy recommended him to be the Outfit's first Las Vegas guy. He wasn't everyone's first choice, but he remembered how Jimmy stuck his neck out for him and convinced everyone to give Joe a six-month try out in Las Vegas. It was his performance in Las Vegas that caught the bosses' eyes and his Outfit career started to take off from there. Joe never thanked Jimmy to his face for being his juice with the bosses, but he never forgot, either.

"Joe was the type of guy, Bobby, who would roll up his sleeves and do the heavy lifting for you," Jimmy said to me. "I recognized in him that he was not afraid to get his hands dirty, so I pushed for him," Jimmy said. "I knew Joe was going up the Outfit ladder from the beginning. Some guys you can tell right away what their future is going to be," Jimmy said. "So, for whatever it was worth, I showed my loyalty to him by pushing him up the ladder, telling the bosses Joe can do this and Joe can do that. And pretty soon, Joe Aruti wasn't going to be a soldier, he was going to become a capo, a boss eventually over a street crew and that's exactly what happened," Jimmy said.

Aruti called for a meeting with Jimmy. "Jimmy, I want you to be my consigliere, functioning like you did for Dean," Aruti said.

"Before I answer, Joe, what about Sal?" Jimmy wanted to know where Sal was going to fit in.

Jimmy never trusted Sal Lombardi, as Sal was one of those guys who would point the finger at someone, blaming them for something not going right just to protect himself and make Sal Lombardi look good in everyone's eyes. If Sal had to clip someone to make it look like he was the innocent one, he wouldn't think twice about committing murder.

"A real weasel," I said to Jimmy once in reference to Sal.

"Yeah, of the first degree. Never let him get behind you because the knife will get stuck as deep as he can do it in your back," Jimmy would say.

Joe had been around long enough and seen enough to know that while Sal Lombardi talked about being loyal to Joe, Joe didn't know if Sal had his own agenda, an agenda which eventually excluded Joe. With Jimmy not being Italian, he couldn't get Joe's spot. Joe reasoned Jimmy was not going to work a deal with an Italian guy to have Joe clipped. Joe figured Jimmy was too smart to make a deal with someone because once he was hit, they would hit Jimmy next, so why would Jimmy make a deal that ultimately led to his own death? Jimmy would see he was being used and wouldn't make any deals like that. Sal...who knows what he was thinking and would come up with; that's why Jimmy had to be the buffer between Sal and Joe. Joe knew that and wasn't going to call Sal's number to become consigliere.

"Sal's gonna stay right where he's at as an underboss," Aruti said to Jimmy.

"He ain't gonna like it," Jimmy said.

"Well, Sal's got two choices—stay as an underboss or St. Matthew's Cemetery. It's up to him, Jimmy. Who says I'm not democratic?" Aruti said with that deadpan look of his.

"Okay Joe, if you want me to be your consigliere, I accept," Jimmy said.

"Good, Jimmy, we'll make a good team just like you and Dean were," Aruti said. "I'll tell Sal he ain't gonna be the consigliere and he'll remain as my underboss," Aruti said. "I'm gonna have Sal report to you. I want you to keep tabs on him, okay, Jimmy?" Aruti said.

"Sure, will do," Jimmy said.

"If you smell something that ain't right with Sal, I know you, Jimmy, you'll check it out head to toe, front to back, sideways, from every angle. That's how you work, I know that and once you have the information, come to me and we'll talk about it. You okay with all this?" Aruti said.

"You're the boss, Joe. Whatever you want, that's how things will be done," Jimmy said.

With Dean Dragonetti, the Outfit boys knew he was a foul-mouthed, mean, vile, bad son of a bitch with an extensive, violent temper wrapped around his soul. God wouldn't find a special place in Hell for him. He'd put him in the whole damn building. Let Dean Dragonetti have to deal with Dean Dragonetti.

With Dean, the negative adjectives could stretch from Chicago to Canada. The one thing that Dean, generally, did do after all the huffing and puffing was listen to Jimmy. There were times, like with Jimmy's drug plan, that he should have listened to Jimmy, but he listened enough never to go to a federal facility to go to college.

"Bobby," I remembered Dean telling me this, "your old man has kept me out of prison probably more times than I can remember." The last thing Dean did for anyone was to give them a compliment, but with Jimmy, he knew whether he liked you or not. If you were his boss, he supported you. He respected the position. Joe Aruti, while cut from the same cloth as Dean Dragonetti, was made up of different material, and Jimmy knew things were going to be different with Joe.

"Bobby, it's not a question of who's the smartest guy in the room, but who makes the play when the play has to be made by making the right decision when it matters," Jimmy said. "Melissa Lanzo, one of the smartest women I know, could at half speed run rings around guys, but made a bad decision in marrying Shorty. Why? Because Shorty was book smart trying to live in a world that needed him to be street smart to survive, and that's what got him in trouble. Shorty, for that reason, was destined for trouble and, unfortunately, pulled Melissa into the jackpot with him. She suffered because of it. Sure, she became successful later on with her business, and was one of the lucky ones to make it, but she paid a heavy price for her decision to marry someone with Outfit ties who didn't know what he was doing. She thought he was different than his father, Victor, and you saw how that turned out."

"She made a play when a play had to be made, but it was the wrong play because Shorty was really doomed from the start," I said.

"Exactly, because a son can never be his father when trying to run the same business—close, maybe, but never the same," Jimmy said. That was the day I knew I would never be Jimmy Williams.

"When did you see the difference between Joe and Dean?" I asked.

"When it came to becoming a made member of the Outfit," Jimmy said. "Joe decided there wasn't a need for the ceremony anymore, and guys depending on their position were made," Jimmy said. "New York always has a ceremony, but I think Joe didn't want to be bothered with the ceremony," Jimmy said.

"So, under Joe, if you're made, you don't have to first make bones and kill someone, which you had to do before there could even be a ceremony, and you had to have a sponsor to sponsor you in becoming made," I said. "So, if you become, let's say, captain, Joe says you're made and that's it—no ritual, no ceremony. He just shakes your hand and that's it," I said.

"Yeah, that's how Joe wanted it done. If Dean knew what Joe did, he'd jump out of the ground and clip him," Jimmy said.

"I don't understand, Joe was hardcore La Cosa Nostra, a tough guy with a gangster mentality. Why would he change how a guy was made? It just doesn't add up," I said.

"You see, Bobby, Joe never wanted to be compared to Dean and he was going to do something that stood out as something done by Joe Aruti," Jimmy said.

"I guess being made was not important to Joe, so he back-doored it for guys to get," I said.

"Bobby, when you start to chip away at the foundation, what is left?" Jimmy said.

"So, now I see what happened in Las Vegas," I said.

Aruti had been raised with the same Outfit diet everyone is fed. Gambling and loan-sharking are next to God and everything else was just part of the meal. Aruti, like Dean Dragonetti, stayed with the basic Outfit operations and, like Dean, knew drug dealing was being done by some of the Outfit boys but never coordinated it as Jimmy wanted to do, and allowed a potential financial empire never to become an Outfit goldmine. Drug money would have easily eclipsed all the other Outfit financial operations combined.

The big difference between Joe and Dean was Joe figured guys were scared of him. Dean knew guys were scared of him. Joe had a couple of apartments he rented besides his home residence and was constantly shuttling from one place to another. You really never knew where Joe was half the time. You had a hard time getting a hold of him because you didn't always know where he was. It was all a game to keep the Feds guessing where he was at so they couldn't get a line on him. Joe would talk with Jimmy and he would have Jimmy and Sal carry out his wishes.

Joe tried to avoid meeting with guys unless he had to. The street crew bosses knew to go to Jimmy if they wanted something. Where Dean was a hands-on manager, Joe was hands off, unless needed. Any figures he wanted, he had Jimmy get from the boss of a street crew and give to him. If he wasn't happy, then he would call the guy in and let the guy know what was expected.

While the Outfit still functioned as it normally did, if you looked real close, you could see small cracks in the foundation as a breeze of discontent was starting to stir off of Lake Michigan fueled by a strong northerly gust known as RICO. As years went on, after Aruti's reign, the Feds made the cracks wider and wider and started sending more and more guys away to college. At this point in their lives, Outfit guys were not looking to further their education. Some of them joined 'Team America' and became starting players on the 'Rat Squad.'

"How long could the Outfit have stayed in Las Vegas?" I asked Jimmy.

"At least five more years, but Joe didn't listen to me when he wanted a bigger skim; so, Vegas could have lasted longer, but it didn't," Jimmy said. "In 1975, Joe wanted more money from Vegas, so he decided to partner up with other crime families who had hotels in Vegas," Jimmy said. "I told him if he went outside of Chicago, the more guys involved, the bigger the chance someone would rat you out to the Feds," he said. "If you kept it among the Outfit, you could control them. Once you go outside of the circle, you become more vulnerable," Jimmy said.

"Joe was so consumed about money, if he had one dollar, he wanted two; if he had two, he wanted three," Jimmy said. "Enough is never enough for Joe. So, while he heard what I said about not expanding the circle beyond Chicago, his mind had already decided what he wanted to do. Right. 'Jimmy, you're right,' he said to me about not going beyond our guys to skim more from Vegas and then he did the complete opposite," Jimmy said.

Jimmy told me in detail how the Feds got convictions in Las Vegas. "I knew there would be trouble including others and, sure enough, trouble occurred," Jimmy said. "It happened when a guy from the Cleveland crime family, Larry Galbo, ratted us out. The Feds were investigating him and his brother Frank on something else when Larry finds out he's got terminal cancer—I think it was lung cancer," said Jimmy. "So, he makes the deal with the Feds if they go easy on his brother, he'll give them Vegas, particularly the Outfit. So the guy tells the Feds in a video confession, which was used later in Joe Aruti's trial, how Vegas was run by the Outfit, the use of teamster funds to build hotels, how messengers brought back money to Chicago, how the skim worked, and anything else related to the Vegas operation. Jimmy continued, "So the Feds decided with what he was telling them, to go full throttle after the Outfit in Vegas."

"Did the Feds coordinate between Las Vegas and Chicago FBI offices once they got this guy's information?" I asked.

"Yeah, they did, sending agents to Vegas from Chicago to assist in their investigation," Jimmy said. "Also, IRS agents from Chicago's Criminal Division were sent to Vegas to help the Las Vegas IRS office."

"So, the Internal Revenue Service was looking for unreported income, tax evasion stuff besides other criminal stuff?" I said.

"Yeah, that's right," Jimmy said.

"What about the State of Nevada? Did they get involved in all of this?" I asked.

"The state worked with the Feds by assigning state gaming investigators to the case," Jimmy said. "The Feds checked out the investigators carefully before deciding who they would accept," Jimmy said. "The Feds didn't want anyone leaking stuff to the Outfit," he said.

"Wow, so this was a real assault against the Outfit, huh?" I said.

"Bobby, it was the equivalent of D-Day in World War II. The Feds made up their minds that they were going to get the Outfit out of Vegas, and they threw every resource at us. They had to make their efforts successful."

Shortly before the indictments of Joe Aruti, other Outfit boys, and guys from crime families from Cleveland and Kansas City, on a Sunday morning, Tony Galente collapsed at home from a stroke. He died two weeks later. Dean was dead, Tony was dead, and Joe was in hot soup. The Outfit now, for the first time, was back on their heels and they didn't like it, but had no juice to stop it. The Feds pushed their backs up against the wall like no one ever could.

It was the Feds who changed the Outfit's management style. The US Attorney's office in Chicago, by obtaining convictions in the Las Vegas case, gave the Feds confidence to move forward in going after the Outfit in Chicago. The Feds felt that now they were going to try and take away as much power from the Outfit as they could.

The 1980s conviction of Joe Aruti and others was the opening shot fired by the Feds against the Outfit. This was no warning shot fired in Las Vegas. This was a direct hit on the Outfit. Las Vegas ceased to be part of the Outfit's financial domain. After the convictions, the Feds went back into court and seized the Outfit's three main hotels in Las Vegas—the Terrablanca, El Casa, and the Monroe, as part of their forfeiture case against the Outfit. No Vegas money, meant no money for the Outfit to run some of their other operations.

Glen Mannero, who took over the Outfit leadership after Joe Aruti's conviction, was more like a steward than a boss of what was going to be left of the Outfit. The Outfit was alive, but its future health prognosis was one in which they shouldn't be buying too many green bananas from the Fed's fruit store.

"Boy, talk about killing the golden goose. Joe really screwed up in Las Vegas, though. I guess it was inevitable. Vegas was going to end someday as the Feds would close in on something with the Outfit," I said.

"It was a mistake waiting to happen, Bobby, that's all it was," Jimmy said. "There are two types of mistakes—little ones and big ones," he said. "A little one you can recover from. A big one like Vegas you can't because there was nothing financially to replace Vegas. Vegas left a hole in the Outfit's heart that could never be filled. You lose something like Vegas and it takes away from having the money to do things like corrupting our friends, politicians, judges, and cops, among other things," Jimmy said. "Without our friends, where would be? I'll tell you where we would be without our friends, we would have to be like legit, straight as an arrow type of people...that creeps me out," Jimmy said.

By the 1990s, the Feds' mission was to imprison as many Outfit guys as they could. The FBI got guys to flip against their brother Outfit guys, and the guys who flipped, thus, joined Team America. These guys reasoned it was better to go into the Witness Relocation Program and be with your family, rather than sitting in a government facility for the next 20 years thinking about your family. With the cooperation of these guys, the US Attorney's office in Chicago built strong RICO-type cases against various Outfit street crews.

In some cases, the boss of a crew pled guilty and the rest of the crew followed suit so there was no trial. In the cases where there were trials, the US Attorney's office got convictions and lengthy prison sentences. The convictions of the various street crews shrunk the size of the Outfit. As members and associates went off to college, the Outfit had a difficult time replacing them.

Areas that used to produce future Outfit guys changed. Different ethnic groups moved in and they changed the face of their communities. The communities no longer were mainly Italian, the stores on the streets in the areas came in catering to the changing neighborhood and the Italian mom-and-pop stores started to vanish. So, with no one basically coming up to replace their elders, the circle of what could be controlled got smaller as the manpower needed to run things dwindled.

Also in the 1990s, the Feds went after Outfit-controlled unions and corrupt Outfit-friendly politicians. The Feds got convictions of those union bosses with Outfit ties mainly on bribery, mail and wire fraud charges, and the Feds forced other union bosses with Outfit ties to resign their union jobs. The loss of these unions that the Feds targeted eliminated not only a source of income for the Outfit, but jobs for their guys.

As the Outfit connected, politicians were convicted, and the Outfit lost its core piece of leverage in getting away with criminal activities. By losing the corrupt politicians that, in turn, caused a loss of corrupt judges and corrupt cops. "Once we lost our friends, Bobby, we lost our cover. We lost our safety net and we lost what allowed the Outfit to be the Outfit," Jimmy said. Jimmy had a wistful look on his face as he spoke to me. There was still going to be an Outfit left, but it wasn't Jimmy's Outfit. While gambling and loan-sharking remained for those who were left, even those stalwarts of the Outfit world had lessened affecting a disintegrating bottom line. While Jimmy didn't like what he saw happening to the Outfit, he knew he could forever hold on clutching so tightly with both hands that he contributed, even if only a memory now, to make the Outfit the most feared crime family of all.

I'm not saying that the Outfit died, though the Feds sure would have loved to send the flowers for their burial, and that was the end of them. It's just you couldn't run everything like you did before. The Outfit could no longer say to themselves well I'll just send my guy over there to do such and such. They didn't have many guys left to do such and such. When that happened, things start to dry up and before you knew it, that part of the operation disappeared. When you had about 325 guys like the Outfit did in the 1970s and in the 1990s, you're down to maybe 30 or 40 guys, you became limited in what kinds of things you could do. I think by the late 1990s, some television newsie-type women, after the conviction of an Outfit street enforcer, said the Outfit was over.

Lady, I got something to tell you. When, on a Monday morning, an FBI agent assigned to the LCN (La Cosa Nostra) Unit reports for work and his boss calls him into his office and tells him that he and the other agents assigned to the unit are being transferred to other units because there are no more Outfit boys to investigate, then it's over. So, lady, I'm telling you in a nice way to keep the speculations to yourself and keep your mouth shut about the Outfit.

So far there are still Outfit guys out there doing criminal things, so don't start giving the Outfit its last rights. It's still many years away from talking about the Outfit in the past rather than the present. Maybe they're no longer eating a complete meal anymore, but there are still guys out there filling their stomachs with soup and a sandwich and making you foot the bill.

"By the mid-1980s, after Joe Aruti was convicted, Jimmy by his own admission distanced himself from the Outfit. Glen Mannero, who had taken over from Joe Aruti, became the boss over day-to-day operations and his brother Patrick became Glen's consigliere," Jimmy said. "Glen would give me a courtesy call now and then, but he and Pat were running what was left of the show their way. After all hell broke loose in the 1990s with the Fed's action, there were only five street crews left and their bosses were just giving Glen lip service," said Jimmy "They were running their crews pretty much independent of Glen because they knew he didn't have the muscle to enforce things as had been done in the past," he said.

"In a way, I felt sorry for Glen, as he was like a substitute teacher filling in for the regular teacher and the students knew the teacher was just the sub with no power. So, some of them acted poorly in the classroom and got away with it," Jimmy continued. "That's how the street crews treated Glen. Yeah, we'll listen, but we're going to do it our way."

"In your opinion, was Glen more or less just a paper tiger?" I asked Jimmy.

"To an extent, I guess you could say that," Jimmy said. "He still had some guys around him, so it's not like he couldn't have done some things to the street crews, but I think he was shell shocked like everyone else was after seeing the Feds take so many guys down. So, he just circled the wagons with a few things—gambling, loan-sharking, maybe some money laundering, maybe a couple of other things, and just retreated, trying to avoid the shots being legally fired at the Outfit by the Feds," he said.

"So, you saw the handwriting on the wall as for as the Outfit's future," I said.

"The reason, Bobby, baseball is a nine-inning game unless tied so the teams play extra innings, is because the game has to end," Jimmy said. "After Joe Aruti was convicted, for me the game ended. If I continued in the game, most likely the Feds would have gotten me as someone would have ratted me out," said Jimmy. "I wasn't blind. I could see the Feds would throw RICO charges in someone's face and to save themselves, and someone would promise the Feds they would give them Jimmy Williams.

"Glen Mannero and his brother Pat were not going to include me in their plans. Glen and I were never close, so he was going to put his own team in and run things how he wanted to. Sure, I could have helped him because I had the experience, but he didn't see it or want it that way. I'm not complaining about it, Bobby, because I had my day and it was time to walk away from the Outfit, rather than have them walk all over me," Jimmy said.

"The days of loyalty were over, as far as I was concerned. As I told you a long time ago, when the Feds passed this RICO law, eventually things would change and they did. Now you don't know, Bobby, who you can trust and who you can't. You don't know who's wearing a wire and who's not. The Feds throw out these RICO charges and some guys grab the bait the Feds throw out. They'll give someone up just to save me, myself, and I. They're just rats jumping off a sinking ship, in my opinion," Jimmy said.

"But, you're so smart. You evaded them all these years," I said.

"Bobby, you gotta remember this, when you see a change in life, you gotta adapt," Jimmy said. "It's like this computer stuff coming out. That's what the future is going to be. There is never going to be a typewriter world. It's over; forget about it. Those days are past," he said. "This computer stuff buried the typewriter and, as this computer stuff grows, it'll be worldwide and then it'll change everyone's life, you'll see," said Jimmy.

"It's the same with guys ratting out other guys. It's a symptom you can't ignore because more and more guys are doing it. That's today's world," Jimmy said. "With longer prison terms because of RICO and the fact you have to do 85% of your time makes being a rat look very enticing. So, things aren't going back to the old days when everyone kept their mouth shut," he said. "The Feds are like a sexy broad. They tease you enough to make you think your actions justify the means," Jimmy said.

"The Feds always say once you're in the Outfit, you're in for life," I said.

"That's just some damn prosecutor running his mouth in front of a jury, trying to make us look like next to us, the devil is a saint," Jimmy said. "Guys who go away to college and come back after serving their time have a choice," he said. "They can go back to whatever they were doing before or do something new," Jimmy said. "When you get out of the joint, no one is standing outside the prison gates waiting to put a gun to your head to come back to your old life," Jimmy said. "Guys go back to being in the life because they want to go back," he said. "Bobby, did you ever see an Outfit guy having a tattoo stamped on his forehead that said forever?" Jimmy said.

"Not that I recall," I said.

"Look at these guys, Bobby, who rat guys out; once they do that they're through with the Outfit, they ain't going back. They're done with the Outfit. They go into the Witness Relocation Program and they don't give the Outfit their forwarding address. They don't send out Christmas cards to the Outfit boys. No, they have left the Outfit for good. That's it; forget about it. "So you see, Bobby, guys leave the Outfit. Maybe, it's not how they want to leave it, but they do leave," Jimmy said.

"So, my point is, if you want to be in the life, Bobby, that you gotta walk around with your eyes open because the rats will continue to be there in the future," Jimmy said. "They ain't going away. So, if you want to be in the life, you gotta be really careful what you say and who you say it to," Jimmy said.

"Okay, but aren't guys going to be looking for the rats?" I said.

"The Feds move the rats far away from Chicago, maybe Phoenix, Arizona; Tacoma, Washington; Boise, Idaho; Austin, Texas—all places out West," Jimmy said.

"You just rattled off a bunch of places. How come you mentioned them? You know something about the Witness Relocation Program?" I said.

"Lucky guess," Jimmy said.

"So, who runs the program?" I asked.

"The US Marshal's office runs the program," Jimmy said. "A guy gets an FBI handler wherever they're put. The Feds give you a new identity and try to get you a job. I mean it ain't easy. Remember, your family's got to adjust to a new name, new location, and maybe new schools for the kids, so it puts pressure on the wife and kids. If you've got grown-up kids, that's a different story— maybe, they've graduated high school, so they're more mature than preteens," Jimmy said. "They could handle the change a little better, maybe, than the younger ones, though. You never know who handles what best," he said.

"A guy's wife is going to be far away from her family and she won't be able to contact them," Jimmy said. "So, emotionally, she's got to have the mindset that she ain't going to see her mom and dad, or sisters and brothers, and miss out on the family activities and be able to live with that. Besides the family adjustment, there's finding a new doctor, dentist, place to get your haircut—all these things you take for granted in Chicago, you got to start all over with new wherever you live," he said.

"Some people adjust better than others; some never adjust at all and that's where the problem starts," Jimmy said. "Once a guy tells his FBI handler he wants out of the program that is where trouble can begin. Bobby, as long as you stay in the program, you're probably going to be okay," said Jimmy. "The guys you ratted out that are in prison will either die in the joint or be very old when they get out. The longer time goes by, the likelihood of someone looking to whack you lessens with each passing year," Jimmy said.

"One day, you wake up and all the guys that would be looking for you are all gone," he said. "Nobody's left that you gotta fear, so you give a sigh of relief and live the rest of your life not looking over your shoulder anymore," Jimmy said. "Now, if a guy leaves the program, that's when a guy is vulnerable. It has happened—a guy's been whacked outside the program, but if he stays in the program, his chances of living out his life are sure a lot greater," he said.

"A guy's gotta be smart, too," Jimmy said. "Whatever he did in Chicago, he gotta cremate that in his brain. That life don't exist anymore. It's over, so he's got to blend in with the locals," he said. "Also, he's gotta have no thoughts about doing anything criminal in the new area—forget about it. For some guys, the temptation to go back to what they did in Chicago becomes too great," Jimmy said.

"If a guy pulls stupid, Bobby, his old self will appear and, if caught, the first thing the media will harp on is why he was in the Witness Relocation Program," Jimmy said. "Bingo…Chicago knows where you are, then they will want to go rat hunting. A guy is his own worst enemy. Because of his actions, he put himself in the jackpot and has no one to blame but himself," said Jimmy.

"So a made guy, who when they did the ceremony, basically took a vow of loyalty, now becomes a rat," I said. "He took a loyalty oath to the Outfit that didn't mean crap to him. First chance he got, he ratted out other Outfit guys just to save himself. What type of loyalty is that?" I said.

"Bobby, the ceremony to become a made guy meant a hell of a lot more when I was coming up than it did for the guys who followed me. You had to have a sponsor. You had to whack someone to make bones. It was all different then," Jimmy said. "Once Joe Aruti did away with the ceremony and guys got made without it, the loyalty part of what was expected of a guy who got made floated out on Lake Michigan. Because of that, loyalty was lip service; that's what it became," Jimmy said.

"Even with the ceremony, there were guys who weren't loyal in other ways," Jimmy said. "One of the things discussed when the Outfit still did ceremonies, Bobby, was that a guy, once he was made, was told that he had to be faithful to his wife. Infidelity was not acceptable. You were expected to be faithful to your wife. Horizontal dances with another woman were totally off-limits," Jimmy said. "You saw how that worked, but I suppose like everything else with the Outfit, nothing means anything. Guys are barely out the door after completing the ceremony and they're with a broad in a motel room doing two things at once—screwing the broad and screwing their wife," Jimmy said.

"When the Feds put the heat on some made guys, they couldn't wait to run their mouths. For them, it's about self-preservation—their own. Then there are some guys who just won't rat anyone out and will take their punishment and they never say a word. Those are the stand-up guys in the organization," Jimmy said. "The oath doesn't mean anything to the rats. As long as they get what they want, then it's okay in their minds to unload on someone," he said. "So you see, Bobby, that's why you never ever tell something to even one person that could come back and put its hands around your throat. If you're the only one that knows, you'll never be hurt by anyone. Jimmy continued, "Keep the dirty stuff to a party of one with you being the only one invited to the party."

Jimmy was a different type of father—very unique, much different than my friends' fathers. He was always talking to me about the various personalities of guys in the Outfit, which were personalities that people see in their daily lives. So what he was telling me really could apply to anyone's life, not just the Outfit life. We talked constantly about guys who were backstabbers; moody guys; guys who had to be the clowns; guys who painted this beautiful picture of life, but it never stuck to the canvas; guys who were whiners and complainers; guys who always said they'd take care of whatever needed to be taken care of, but never did; guys who were operators, who had their own agendas and tried to make you think they were working in your best interest, but were really working for their best interest; guys who were loverboys, unfaithful to their wives, and never saw how their girlfriends were just manipulating them to get what they wanted out of the deal by using sex as the bargaining chip, giving it out a drop here and a drop there to keep the guy coming back, but getting twice back in the material things they earned, and Jimmy would talk to me about any other type of assorted personality you could think of.

But the one personality he probably spent the most time on, the one he told me to watch with both eyes, the one he said never to let get behind me, the one to make sure I kept in front of me at all times, maybe, the deadliest of all personalities was the guy who said nothing, the quiet one. The guy who had that type of personality...no one knew what he was thinking or what he was planning. "The quiet ones, Bobby, will hit you and you'll say I never saw it coming," Jimmy said. "Bobby, always overestimate the quiet ones, never underestimate them." "With the quiet ones, you never want them to feel no one is watching them because that is when they become toxic and catch people by surprise," Jimmy would say.

"Some people, Bobby, you think you know and then you put them in a situation and they surprise you," Jimmy said. "In the life, not everyone can do other jobs. Bookies don't always have the personalities to be street enforcers and street enforcers don't have the personalities to be bookies," he said. "So, you try and match the skills of the person with the position, but like anything else, you make mistakes with people, you think someone is capable and it turns out they're not. So, Bobby, once you see that you gotta make a move real quick, never delay it or else you're going to wind up putting yourself in the jackpot. I don't care if you're a gangster or racketeer, you act on the guy as fast as you can because the crew is going to see the guy is unsuited for the position and start questioning why the boss is not taking action on the guy," Jimmy said.

"Bobby, as the boss of a street crew, you never want a crew to start to focus on you. You want them only focusing on what their job is and doing the job," Jimmy said. "If they start to focus on you, someone in the crew is going to say maybe it's time the boss should go—that's code for maybe it's time to whack the boss," said Jimmy. "Guys work the angles…always remember that. So, with some guys, you can't let them have time to think because that's when they're gonna put you in the jackpot. Keep 'em busy, even if you gotta make something up for them to do," he said. "This way, you'll live a healthier life or, maybe, I should say you'll live," Jimmy said with a laugh.

I know in his own way, Jimmy wanted to prepare me for life's challenges that I would face in a hard, cruel world in which the weak become puddles, thinking that the world is a soft, velvet kind of place where your neighbors are please and thank you and no cops are needed to patrol the neighborhood. For those do gooder 'every kid deserves a trophy even if they finish last' types, whose names should have been have a nice day imprinted on their birth certificates, when the world jabs their gut with a stick dipped in hateful contempt of their sunny side up dispositions, what are they going to do? When the world says fuck you to them, what are they gonna do?

I'll tell you what the 'oh it's my turn to bring treats for the kids' soccer game crowd' is going to do. They move to the suburbs, vote Republican, complain about the taxes, and stop caring. The shame of it is when you lose a caring person, it's the world that loses, as with the more caring people you have, the more problems you can solve.

Life in the Outfit taught Jimmy that without strength, your character will never be able to stand tall and fight off the adversities of life that you will encounter in a lifetime. He would try and teach me that to survive in this world, a strong character was an absolute necessity. "Bobby," he would say, "when a problem walks in the front door, you never run out the back door because you will be running the rest of your life from the problem. You gotta stand up to the problem. When the world gives you the evil look, Bobby, you gotta spit right in its face, which is a way of telling the world to go find some weakling to bully. If you open up your mouth to me, world, I'm going to rip your lips off," he would say to me, emphasizing the fact that a problem is just another big mouth who needs to be knocked on his ass. "A woman, Bobby, never likes to see a man who's weak and doesn't punch out the problem. They look at a man as a protector and if he ain't protecting them, maybe it's time to get a new protector.

Jimmy, because of his Outfit life, rarely went by the book when he talked about life, doing life, as he put it. No matter how you sliced it, diced it, cooked it, cleaned it, mapped it, or dissected it, the Outfit taught evil, raised you on evil, created evil, used evil to inflict pain and suffering on people, used evil in threats and intimidation, used evil to scare and make people cower, and passed evil down to the next Outfit generation. So, in Jimmy's book that he taught me from, he would always start out using the bad stuff as examples then working up to the good stuff as to what was needed to be done. His life experiences with the Outfit could be seen chapter after chapter.

As I worked my way through adulthood, while I didn't always agree with the things Jimmy told me, his book was sure a lot closer to the real world than any other I ever saw. Jimmy's thing was getting me ready for the real world.

"Bobby, I gotta get you ready for the world," Jimmy would say to me. "This is what fathers are supposed to do, make sure their kids can handle what the world is going to throw at them. The problem is some fathers don't get their kids prepared for the world. They're weaklings themselves and figure let the kid learn on his own, you know, by trial and error," Jimmy said. "Sure, you can let the kid learn on his own, but the kid might make some seriously bad decisions because no one talked to him about life, and that there's always a consequence (good or bad) from the decision you make," Jimmy said.

"I know, Bobby, you didn't have a normal life starting as a kid seeing what you saw in the Outfit life," Jimmy said.

"That's for sure," I said.

"So, if someone wants to throw a shot at me for being a bad dad, fine let 'em, but you got to see life in the Outfit for what it really is. How many Outfit fathers did that?" Jimmy said.

"None that I can recall," I said.

"So, how did the kids who went into the Outfit never seeing anything like Shorty Lanzo wind up?" "Did they have a happy life?" asked Jimmy.

"Hardly," I said. "Why does life in general have to be so hard?" I asked.

"Bobby, it's not that life is hard. It's the decisions about life that you have to make that are hard," Jimmy said. "A kid is in a classroom learning his ABCs, but the teacher doesn't tell him what to do when someone doesn't give him the B," Jimmy said. "The kid don't know what to do at that point. Now the kid is lost in life because he doesn't know how to get from A to C without B," he said. "So, unless someone shows him how to get from A to C without B, the kid starts experimenting how to do it. While some experiments might work, others will blow up in your face," said Jimmy. "That's why someone has to tell the kid which way to go. If the kid don't want to listen and goes another way, that's the kid's decision, but a hell of a lot of bad decisions can be avoided if the kid's old man remembers he's the father, not a friend," Jimmy said.

"A formal education is necessary. People need to be educated. I'm not talking against that, it's just some kid can get all As in all his subjects, but put him on the street and the street flunks him. The street flunks him because he makes bad decisions on life issues, not classroom issues," Jimmy said. "Bobby, remember the classroom doesn't teach you how to avoid being put in the jackpot. Whether you decide, Bobby, to go into the life, to become an associate member of the Outfit or not is immaterial," Jimmy said. "Bobby, your education in the school of hard knocks is ongoing…you never graduate. You learn from each day's experience and that's how you build your life's education," Jimmy said.

"It's your call, kiddo, what you want to do with your life. I can't tell you what to do," Jimmy said. "I can't make that decision for you. You gotta make the adult decision as far as how you want to run your life, what direction it should take, but you never can say your old man didn't prepare you for life," he said.

Throughout my adult years, like everyone else, I made my share of mistakes, but I always would think about the things Jimmy taught me in trying to correct those mistakes. Why I made the mistake in the first place, did I have other options I could have explored, what is necessary to correct the mistake and take the appropriate action to correct it, and what did I learn from the mistake?

"Bobby," Jimmy would say to me, "I can't with 100% accuracy tell you how to solve every problem or correct every mistake you face because a lot of times it will be the situation that you are currently facing that will present life's challenges and you will have to make a decision on what's right for that moment. But, what I can do is give you a framework that can be applicable to a lot of situations," Jimmy said. "Think of it like a salesman. If a guy can sell, it doesn't matter what he is selling—it could be shoes, cars, x-ray equipment, washing machine, pencils—the product doesn't matter because the salesman will use the same selling techniques no matter what the goods or services are," he said. "The salesman doesn't care what he's selling because his success or failure at making the sale will be based on how his selling techniques work with any customer for any goods or services. The principles that I teach you about life can be applied to practically any of life's problems, it's just adapting the principles to whatever problem you face," Jimmy said.

I never thought that much about it as a kid when I saw the Outfit life and then continuing in my teen years and in my 20s. But, I had the best dad in the whole world because he loved me so much, he didn't want me to get beaten up by the world. He loved me enough to make sure by seeing the bad, I would know what the good in life really was.

By knowing what the good really was, it would be genuine—not some artificial, fake feeling to me. The good would not be some temporary feeling that would quickly pass through my body, but a sincere enrichment of what life had to offer. The positives, the warmth of success were the lights glowing from the good. Yeah, life could be damn good and there are a lot of damn good people in life.

As for me, Bobby Williams, I graduated in the early 1970s from a small college in Michigan with a degree in English. I got a job with Copeland Advertising in downtown Chicago as a junior copywriter. A few years later, while assigned to an account, Copeland hired a public relations firm to work on the account. That is how I met Linda Swanson.

Linda, a cute brunette with laughing eyes, was assigned to the account. Linda, who was a graduate of the University of Illinois with a degree in public relations, I could tell from our first conversation, was a very bright woman. We had worked together on the account for about three weeks when I got up enough nerve to ask her out for lunch. She gladly accepted and from that lunch date, I knew she was the right one for me.

During lunch, I found out she was as big a Cubs fan as I was, so I got tickets for a game. She accepted my request to go to the game and we had a great time, which would have been a better time if the Cubbies had won, but still, I was with her and that's what made the time great. Years later, she recounted details of the game while I only remember looking into those big, beautiful, brown eyes and talking a lot to her. I learned that women never forget—boy, they never forgot. So, my male species out there, when dealing with a woman, don't screw up on her birthday, Mother's Day, Valentine's Day, holidays, or any other day that's important to her because she will not forget and unless you want your brain turned into mashed potatoes by her rapid fire memory recalling your screw ups going back at least 40 years at some point, it's imperative you take care of your one and only, as even God lays low when the ladies start recalling.

We started dating and each date was better than the previous one. We had a lot of similar interests and we really seemed to enjoy each other's company. Sex was good with Linda as we both derived the same pleasures of the intimacy that we had with each other. I'll tell you, though, I knew it was serious with Linda and me as one day we were going to lunch downtown, walking down Gallagher Avenue on a nice spring day, when I held Linda's hand. We both looked at each other hand-in-hand and felt it was right between us. Her body language and mine at that moment put the stamp of approval on our relationship. From that moment forward, we were inseparable.

Two years later, we were married and it was the best decision of my life. Jimmy and Karen liked Linda from the first time they met her and both of them were happy that we united as one. I told Jimmy and Karen that I was getting married to Linda, Jimmy hugged me and Karen kissed me on my cheek. Boy, did it feel swell to have my parents support my decision.

"She's a wonderful girl. You made the right choice. You'll have a good life with her," Jimmy said.

"Thanks, Dad, for the vote of confidence," I said.

After telling them, I sat down with Jimmy in the den and we both agreed it was best that we just stick to the story that he had a union job and let his Outfit life be forgotten. I wasn't sure, at first, how Jimmy would take to my suggestion about making his being in the life nonexistent. Jimmy handled it like a pro. "Bobby, remember how I taught you to keep something important to yourself and never tell even one person so you never will get hurt?" Jimmy said. "Well, this thing about the Outfit life I had is important to you and it'll be kept between you and me," he said. "Nothing will pass my lips about the Outfit. I'll keep it to myself. You've got my word on it," Jimmy said.

"Thanks Dad," I said.

True to his word, Jimmy went to his grave and never said a word about the Outfit to Linda, the grandkids, or my in-laws— no one heard anything about the Outfit from him.

I remember going with Linda, her parents, Jimmy, and Karen to this mob movie *Top Boss*. It was one of those movies everyone was going to and talking about. I was a little hesitant to go, but I figured if I said 'no' Linda might start questioning me, so since I didn't want to talk about why I didn't want to go, I said, "Sure, it sounds great, let's go see it," when she suggested it.

We went to a Sunday 2 P.M. showing and had reservations later for dinner at a real nice restaurant called Sunny's Delight. After the movie was over, as we walked out of the theater, my father-in-law turned to Jimmy and said, "Boy, what a life to be in." I froze for a second. *What is he going to say?* I thought.

"Gee, Art, I'm glad I'll never have to find out," Jimmy said. The air came back into my lungs. My heart went back to its normal rhythm, the beats were in sync.

"Well let's all get ready for a great meal at Sunny's," I said, changing the topic real fast. Jimmy winked at me.

"So Art, how's the hardware business going?" he said. I relaxed immensely as like with the Outfit, Jimmy knew how to switch gears.

I never wanted Linda to know that Jimmy was in the Outfit or what he did for the Outfit. I was afraid it would jeopardize our relationship if she knew and I would lose her. When you have something good, you don't want to lose it and Linda was beyond good, so good I might never meet someone like her in my lifetime. So, I just kept my mouth shut about Jimmy's criminal activities.

It wasn't long after we were married that our oldest daughter was born and 25 months later, our second daughter was born. Our oldest daughter is a nurse who is married to a doctor and they have a daughter. Our youngest daughter is a manufacturer's sales representative for a women's clothing company and is married to a guy who is an electrical engineer. They also have a daughter. Linda and I are blessed with two beautiful granddaughters. Our daughters were raised by a wonderful mother and they turned out super.

I helped Linda when I came from work giving them baths, helping feed them, reading stories to them at bedtime, going shopping for the groceries, and helping out wherever I could. But Linda deserves the credit for the way the girls turned out. Linda gave up her career and decided to stay home to take care of the girls. She spent the bulk of their formative years raising them while I was at work. She spent more time with them than I did for that reason. The wonderful women they became and the wonderful mothers they will become came from Linda and the outstanding role model she was to them. That's why she deserves the gold star above her name.

As far as the discipline went with the girls, we worked together. If the girls came to me looking to overrule what their mother told them, it wasn't going to happen. I had pat answer for them whenever they came to me. When they told me what Linda told them, I responded, "What did your mother say? Well, then, that's how it's going to be, case closed; next case," was my answer.

As a parent, I realized when the girls were born, Linda and I had to be a team and not individuals. There were times I didn't always agree with what Linda was telling the girls, but the girls were never going to know that. I always backed Linda up in front of the girls. They were not going to see a divided household. The girls would only hear one decision and, thus, not think they could get their way with one parent or the other. In private, away from the girls, I would express my opinion to Linda about something she said to the girls and she would tell me why she told them what she had. It was our own meeting of the minds which sure saved a lot of battles from happening. I think the strategy worked out pretty well as when people met our girls, we received many compliments on them. When we received those complements, I would raise Linda's right arm and say, "Congratulations, champ, we're all lucky to have you in our lives."

I must have been about 38 years old when I changed jobs and left Copeland, where I was a senior copywriter. I got a job with Brockton Publishing Company. Brockton owned a chain of weekly newspapers in the northern suburbs. I became their feature writer, covering the areas where the papers were being published. It has been a great job because the stories I wrote about were diversified. They could be about community people, community businesses, and community events, which because of the diversification, kept my writing skills sharp. I wasn't covering the same old territories over and over again, trying to come up with a new angle to write about. With the Brockton papers in so many communities, it allowed me to maintain a freshness to my writings.

I have talked with Linda and I'm going to retire next year. I will have been with Brockton 28 years at the time of my retirement. It's time to turn the page and enjoy my golden years while my health is good. I've seen too many people die on the job. Linda and I have talked about taking a summer trip to Finland, Norway, and Sweden after I retire. It should be a fine trip and I'm looking forward to it.

Jimmy died in 1998 from colon cancer. He fought as hard as he could over the two-year period. The cancer had spread to other organs and for the last nine weeks of his life, he had to have a feeding tube in him. I went to see Jimmy the day before he died at Sawyer Hospital. I had been going to see him regularly. His two-year bout with cancer was drawing to a close. He was very weak, barely getting out the word 'hi' to me. He was drifting in and out. His eyes were closed most of the time. Other than the 'hi,' he never spoke another word to me.

I pulled up a chair right by his bedside and, with my right hand, I held his right hand. I told him how much I loved him and appreciated him and, in his own way, he was the best dad a son could have. The words didn't come easily as I remembered what he made me see. The violence, the corruption, the criminal life was his way of educating me to the world. While I know that's not what a kid needs to see in his life, but in my adult years, I realized he truly loved me and didn't want to see me hurt by naivety when it came to the Outfit. As I held his hand, I thought would I do what Jimmy did to me—make me see the Outfit work in full force, never skipping a criminal beat—if I had a son. I realized I would have done the same damn thing he did. I would want my son's eyes to be as open as mine were in seeing what being in the life meant and what was required to maintain that life.

I was only going to stay a few minutes, but I held his hand for an hour. Every time I wanted to let go, I couldn't. I just sat there with him. We never spoke a word to each other. A son was watching his father's era pass right in front of him. I looked around the room for compassion, but it was still—nothing was moving. I looked back at him, knowing that soon, very soon, a son's darkest moments were going to be delivered to his soul by the death of his father. A son would no longer have his father for guidance, as now the son, hopefully, had learned enough from his father to have the strength, courage, and conviction of making the right decisions at the right time and the capacity to love to use those things in his everyday life. For while the sun will rise a little higher, easing the loss a son feels for his father, each day the son's brain will have a special reserved spot set for eternity for the love a son has for a father.

I looked at Jimmy's hand and remembered how he held my hand at the beginning of my life as a little boy while crossing a street. Now, I was holding his hand, but he was crossing his final street at the end of his life.

After an hour, I got up and pushed the chair to the side. I bent over and kissed Jimmy on the cheek and thought *thanks for everything you did for me, Dad*. I looked at him one more time and gave him one more kiss on top of his head, thinking this one is from your son Bobby with love that will never be surrendered, Dad.

As I left Jimmy's room and started walking in the hallway, I felt a drop in my eye. My eyes are raining with moisture. I walked as quickly as I could to the elevator. I didn't want anyone to see the moisture in my eyes. *They just wouldn't understand* I thought. "Never get caught in the Outfit's rain, always get out of the rain," Jimmy would tell me. Once inside the safety of the elevator, I felt out of the rain and it was okay for the tears of love to celebrate the life of Jimmy Williams. A father leaves a legacy to a son and Jimmy's legacy that he left me was, "Bobby, truth beats denial every time."

Karen wanted graveside services to be held for Jimmy at St. Matthew's Cemetery. So, Father Francis Shannon from Our Lady of Perpetual Worship, who was the main priest at the time, agreed to perform the service, even though Jimmy was not Catholic. He did it as a favor to Karen, who regularly attended Sunday services at Our Lady of Perpetual Worship.

It was a cool breezy day as besides Karen and myself, my daughters and sons-in-law were also at St. Matthew's. Karen did not want anyone from the Outfit at the service, but by that time, there weren't many guys left from Jimmy's era. They were either dead or locked up for life. A couple of the younger guys, who knew Jimmy through their dads, Tony Blattine and Angelo Carasapa, did send flowers to the house with the note wishing Karen and me well.

After the service, Karen said that she wanted to be with Jimmy one more time. I told everyone to go back to their cars and we would be there shortly. Everyone left except Karen and me, as we watched the cemetery workers lower the casket into the ground. I reached over and held Karen and she, in turn, held me. While we were still a family, we were without our leader.

"I loved him so much," Karen said, as she began to sob.

"So did I," I said.

"I'll miss him so much," she said.

"So will I," I said.

"I know his life was difficult for you, Bobby, and your sister Mary, but family, us, we always came first to him. He loved us all with all the love he could squeeze from his heart and I'm saying that as God is my witness," Karen said. "There was none better than Jimmy. He was the best," she said.

"The best," I said.

As we held each other, two souls who relied upon their leader for moral strength, we both were trying to find the path that would lead us to having internal peace and the fortitude to be leaders in our own way. We wouldn't have Jimmy shining the light, showing us what direction to go in life. We would now replace Jimmy's light bulb with our own, confidently knowing his training that he has given us will let us turn on our light bulb and let our own brightness be our guide to a happy life.

Karen looked up towards the sky. "I know, God, Jimmy lived in a terrible world and probably did terrible things to people, but he really was a good man. I know death is punishment for his sins. Please be merciful to his soul. Please, Lord, I beg of you," Karen said.

"Everything will be reviewed," God said.

In 2003, Karen died of heart failure. While there is no medical proof of this, of course, I wonder if Karen didn't die from a broken heart after Jim died. While she would tell me life goes on after Jimmy died, I'm not sure if her heart believed that. She always went to St. Matthews's Cemetery on Jimmy's birthday, their wedding anniversary date, and Father's Day to visit his grave. I guess a love never dies for the one you love.

Karen was a good mother to my sister Mary and me, considering she had a very difficult life with Jimmy being in the life. The FBI coming to see him on numerous occasions was stressful for her as she didn't know if they were just questioning him or were going to arrest him. Mary and I saw the FBI come to see our father, so Karen couldn't hide that from us. Karen, in her own way, tried to raise Mary and me in a normal household, which was governed by the un-normal life Jimmy led.

I'm glad for one thing that, at least, Jimmy and Karen were around to see their beautiful grandchildren. Linda always made sure to invite them to any of the children's activities, especially as they got older. Linda believed and, rightfully so, that grandparents should be involved in their grandchildren's lives. She believed that grandparents' love was a vital part in their grandchildren's development as human beings. Linda would say to me a home without love is an empty home and home can never have too much love from the parents and grandparents. Both sets of grandparents were invited to our home for all the holidays that families get together for. See, I told you, Linda was the smart one.

So, you're thinking Bobby never went into the life and never became involved with the Outfit. It's true, I never went into the life because I never bought into the notion that being in the life was going to give me the type of life I wanted. Seeing the life as I did, brought me to one conclusion, that if you were looking for trouble, being in the life would gladly give you the opportunity to pursue trouble as a vocation. My name is Bobby, and I wasn't looking to change it to 'Trouble.'

I'm not God. I don't judge anyone's decision to become an Outfit guy. If a guy feels a life of crime is what he wants to do with his life… fine, it's his decision. No one is ever forced to go into the life. That's a decision they have clearly made on their own. If he feels this is how he's going to earn a living and support a family, he and he alone is the only one making the decision to enter the life.

I remember something John "Johnny Shakes" Qualacine told me. "Bobby, no one ever puts a gun to your head to go into the life, so until somebody does, don't beef about it," Qualacine said. Johnny Shakes was right. Being in the life was strictly voluntary. No one was drafted or coerced to join the Outfit or else something bad would happen to you. You made that decision and if you are comfortable with committing criminal acts to put a roof over your family's head and food on their plates, so be it. Just don't come beefing to me about the Outfit. Think before you act.

However if you are in the life, there's one thing you are responsible for and that is screwing up your family big time if you get caught by the Feds. They suffer as much as you do, probably more. If you go away to college, at least you have a roof over your head and three square meals a day. That's not a guarantee your family has. Can they pay the mortgage or buy food for the kids? That is the unanswered questions they face as no one is giving them a written contract saying somebody will guarantee that the money to take care the monthly expenses will be provided for the family. If you're in the life and are single, then you're only responsible for yourself. If you are married, your lifestyle as a criminal has impacted innocent bystanders who are dragged into this swirling, unchartered world that you have left them. You put them in the jackpot.

The movies and television never show what it's like for a mob family when the man of the house is in the federal facility. They only show you some glorified shoot 'em up Hollywood version of the mob. When was the last time you saw in the movie or television show the family receiving a letter telling them when they will be evicted because the mortgage wasn't paid or the letter the family gets saying if the car note is not paid by a certain date the car will be repossessed? Don't think too hard on that one.

The tears the family shed are not only for you, but for themselves. What happens to their lives? Have they just become change on the dollar which is pocketed and no one looks at or gives a damn about? All they feel is the loud, ear piercing, crashing thunder of uncertainty reverberating in their half-starved souls. Scary ghouls of negativity dance in their heads. A positive mental attitude is not allowed on this dance floor because there is none at this time. The thumping, cascading, negative beat of *what am I going to do, how am I going to survive, to where is the money we need going to come from* bounces from side to side in their brain. They dance alone on the dance floor. No one asks them to dance.

There is no outstretched hand touching their shoulders offering help, direction, and guidance for them from a non-caring world. They stagger aimlessly, trying to balance their minds to start thinking about their future now that the criminal storm has passed over their mental house. As they shuffle down the block of life without their warrior to lead the tribe, they know they can only knock on one door for help. Every other door and every other house will be closed to them.

With all their strength, a trembling hand, a hand that holds no hope in it, a hand that feels no sensation of a better time ahead in it faintly knocks on the door. The door opens and a voice calls out, "Come in, you are always welcome in the home of the Lord." It's that voice of safety we all turn to during our darkest moment. It's that voice we call out to when in a bleak moment it's us against the problem and we need emotional, structural support to keep from caving into defeat. It's the voice we do not have to pay for. It's the voice that welcomes a weary body drained of life and aching legs that since losing its leader have made the family enter a journey having to walk through the ashes that were once their lives. Lives that had a semblance of the family balance. Dad went off to work whatever that meant, kids went to school, mom stayed home and was a mom. This was the life a family knew, the structure they felt safe in. Now a legal sledgehammer has completely bashed in the family section, decimating every brick that built it.

It's a voice that only knows the positive. It's a voice that will douse the flaming fires of the life you once lived burning right before your eyes. It's the voice that will soothe the anger raging in your body because the loved one was a criminal who deceived every family member, hurting them and stealing from them their daily life routine. The loved one, with his criminal ways, ignited the blaze that left an unforgiving hole in the threads of their lives, values, and self-worth.

It's the voice that will be waiting for them on the corner and when all other voices are silent, it will be the voice that takes those trembling hands of uncertainty, holds them firmly and strong, walking them across the street of evil onto the street of good. It's the voice that never sleeps. It's available 24 hours a day, 7 days a week for the family. It's the voice that understands any language and it doesn't need a translation to grasp the fears and the spoken word. It's the voice that forms an umbrella over the heads of the families, protecting them from the driving negative thoughts that the dark rain clouds of life are sending down and driving in torrents on them.

It's the voice that not even the Outfit can intimidate or bully, for it always stands strong, no matter who tries to silence it. It's the voice of experience, being able to untangle the knots of despair and turn back on the electricity of hope for you, telling you a better day is coming, even while you are in a weakened emotional state.

It's the voice who says, "Yes, my child, come in to my house, leave the double negative of fear and being scared of the unknown in life on the front porch." It's the voice that has never changed over the centuries. It has been and always will be the smoothly paved road that leads you to a happier life by pushing you, cajoling you, and believing in you to find that new life. It's the voice that allows you to collect your thoughts and to develop a new plan for your life. It's the voice that will make you a better, stronger person in being able to deal with life's distractions. It allows your soul to bench press the problem completely out of your body.

You will thank the voice for being that one multi-shining light of belief in you when everything in your life was nothing but total darkness with no happy faces to look at. While your loved one has been convicted of a crime, you no longer remain convicted. You are free, man; you are free. The voice is really the voice within us all. It just waits to be called upon by its master. Each and every one of you has the voice, and never be afraid to use it at a time in your life when the odds appear to favor the house. You can beat the house by turning on your internal voice and listening to its positive feedback. You are a winner; you just have to believe it.

There's a motto in the Outfit that everyone can be bought for a price. In Outfit logic, it's just finding the price then...bam...I've got you doing what I want you to do. On countless occasions, I was with Jimmy and watched him give our friends—the corrupt politicians, the corrupt judges, the corrupt cops, Cook County Sheriff deputies, state police of Illinois, FBI agents, and other corrupt human beings–that the Outfit reached out and touched with their white envelope filled with the price. Jimmy called it their birthday money, but I often wondered how many birthdays does a person get a year. No ever refused the envelope, not one time that I saw. Not one time did anyone tell Jimmy, "No thanks, whatever I did for you came from the goodness of my heart."

Corruption is void of any heartfelt feelings. It only takes what it wants and it never gives back anything worthwhile to society. It was always, "You got my money?" Jimmy would be asked and Jimmy would say while giving the guy the white envelope with the exact amount of money in it, "Go ahead and count it." The guy would take the envelope, open it, sometimes count it, or sometimes just finger the money. "Looks okay to me," he would tell Jimmy, his eyes doing the happy dance now that he's got the extra money to spend on the lifestyle born out of corruption. While the faces of the people Jimmy paid off would change, the connection would remain the same.

There was one thing that the Outfit couldn't buy and it kept them scratching their heads trying to figure out how to buy it. That was a person's dignity. A person's dignity is never really for sale. Sure, I know there are people who will compromise their dignity for the almighty buck, but you can never put a for sale sign on what makes a person tick. For the Outfit, getting most people that they would come in contact with to sell their dignity was easy, maybe, too easy. The Outfit's well-deserved reputation made most people cave in to the Outfit's demands. But, when they met a guy who would not sell his dignity, this befuddled them because they didn't see this happen much, so they were not that adept at how to handle the guy. They would press the 'we will use violence on this guy if he doesn't play ball' button, which was always their time honored way of handling the situation when things weren't verbally going their way. Thinking *if I threaten the guy he'll say fuck the dignity I'll do what you want*, the Outfit felt they had the winning hand.

However, with some guys, threatening you to dance after feeling the baseball bat beat still didn't play out. Their dignity was just too damn important to them. The Outfit always had their toughest days on the street when it came to trying to win friends and influence people who had the stiff moral character to say no to the Outfit. There were some guys who did pay a price for holding on with both hands to their dignity, but at least they made the Outfit work for it.

It is dignity that allows a family of an Outfit guy to rebuild their life one daily brick at a time, as painful as it might be. Dignity is the baseline of the person's character. That is the moral traffic cop, directing a person's behavior. When an Outfit wife has to tell the children we are starting over, she must first believe it herself. Her dignity must be strong, decisive, and forthcoming. Your dignity must be a leader, not a follower, during this time. As she looks into her children's faces, she must reassure them that though their father is not in the house now, the house will remain strong. She must hug her children and tell them they will stand together. "We will stand tall and no one can knock all of us down at once. We will not be divided. We will be a family." she will tell him. "Kids, we are a family and families that work together get ahead together." she will say. Her dignity will teach the children that through the bleakest of days, it will be their dignity that will march them forward to better days. She will lead them by example.

The movies and television never show you the effects of what happens to a mob family when Dad goes away to college. That wouldn't be glamorous for viewers to see. Nope, let's just show lots of shooting and killings. That's what we will feed to the public. The comeback of a mob family is because there is one star in the family who makes a comeback possible. The mother of the family is the star of the family. Championship players make championship plays to win a game. The same can be said about mothers. Time and time again I would see Outfit women rise to the occasion and assume the leadership role in their family following a husband being convicted by the Feds.

When I was younger, maybe in my teens, I didn't give much thought to the role an Outfit wife plays in her family without her husband. As I got older, I realized the women's importance in that role. While I would offer my support as Jimmy did, I realized much later in life that Jimmy understood the complete depth of the kinds of support an Outfit wife needed. Me, at those times, I was a tagalong being there physically, but not understanding or wanting to understand what the women were going through at those times.

I often reflected back on those days and used those days as a learning experience to be the best possible husband I could be to Linda and the best possible father I could be to the girls. Like anyone else, I'm not perfect but I didn't grow up in a perfect life, either. The Outfit women taught me that caring for your family is number one in the playbook and there are no other options. There's a reason God created women to be mothers. To all the mob wives and all other mothers, let them all bask in well-deserved praise as their star power extends throughout the world.

Looking back at my life, I had a front row seat to being in the life. I was in the life without ever being in the life. Me, Bobby Williams, I saw it all. Every part of the Outfit business passed right in front of my eyes. I sat on the reviewing stand, watching the criminal parade march by me one by one. The criminal acts committed by the Outfit were all dressed up, clean shaven, looking spic and span as they walked by me. "Hi Bobby," they would say to me as they walk by me. "See how respectful and honest we look, Bobby? Come on and join us. You'll have loads of fun," they would say. Their idea of fun never, at any time, put a smile on anyone's face. Their idea of fun was how much mental and physical pain they could inflict on you. Not my type of fun.

The Outfit life Jimmy had and wanted me to see forced me to grow up differently than all the other kids in the neighborhood. I never had a bicycle to ride like the other kids did, so I could never take a bike ride with them. I could never share with the kids in the neighborhood the criminal things I was seeing. I had to keep everything to myself just like Jimmy told me to. There were some things, boy, I really wanted to tell the kids, but I couldn't and who knows, maybe they would have thought I was making stuff up just to sound like a big shot. None of the kids knew what type of life I was really having. When I was with them, I just went along with the flow. The fact was, while my age indicated I was a child, my mind was that of an adult. With the other kids, I pretended to be a child like them, talking about things children talk about at the age when I was with them. When I was away from them, driving with Jimmy to observe something illegal being done somewhere, I went back to my adult ways. Mentally, I was never really a kid, only playing an undercover role of the kid when I had to. Actions taken by adults on adults in the Outfit that I saw, never allowed me to think like a kid. I saw adult things, so I thought like an adult, because with the Outfit, they were not about child's play. To avoid problems with them, you needed to think like an adult, or they would physically beat you like an adult.

While in elementary and high school, there were a lot of times my mind was not in the classroom. I would hear what the teacher was saying, but my mind was far, far away from the classroom. I would think about what I had seen the day before—watching Bobby "The Bottle" Bariviolo, a juice collector, beat a guy who owed juice on a gambling debt with a baseball bat, and it wasn't even baseball season; Jimmy paying off Tommy the cop not to show up in court on an assault charge against Nicky Cocolante, so it could be dropped; Jimmy paying off Fat Jack, a politician, to get a zoning change for a mob run business that made pinball machines; and Jimmy paying off Chicago Police Department Captain Everett Malone to leave bars alone that had video poker machines being used by the bar patrons in 38th police district. There was never a week that went by that I didn't see something illegal occurring in the Outfit's classroom.

The formal education that I was getting in the Chicago Public School system was important for my intellectual growth. The formal education I was getting from the Outfit would teach me what was bad in the world I was going to live in and how to recognize it. While I was learning how to live in a society from my classroom studies in the Chicago Public School system, by broadening my intellect, I also was learning from my Outfit education how to survive in society. I guess, in a way, I had it over the other kids in the neighborhood as I was getting two types of formal education— one legal, one illegal.

Seeing what I saw—the violence, the scheming, the lying, the cheating, the white envelopes, the juice being poured for clout, and all the other criminal activities associated with the Outfit—made me become a grown-up in the child's body. Was I mature enough to handle what I was seeing in the Outfit world at the ages I was seeing things? Of course not, but I learned maturity real quick as I saw the same things occurring day after day. I was maturing at a lightning fast pace. I had no choice. I didn't have time to be naïve in a child-like way and wonder what the world was really like for a kid growing up. The movie was playing out in front of me, but I knew it was no movie I was watching. It was the real sordid underworld of one of the most feared mob organizations known to mankind, performing their skullduggery on the unsuspecting ones who were foolish enough to involve themselves with these maniacal thugs that I saw for real day after day. I couldn't run from them. I couldn't hide from them. All I could do was watch them. Oh, I would see those guys plead their cases about why they couldn't pay the money they owed on gambling, loan-sharking, illegal drugs, and a whole host of other things they owed to the Outfit. The Outfit was the judge, jury, and executioner. It was like one-stop shopping, but they always handed down the same ruling—pay up or else.

So, growing up, I was doing this balancing act. Honesty, kindness, and being a good person sits on one side of the teeter-totter and the Outfit with its slanted criminal actions on the other side. Back-and-forth I went, seeing one side then the other, one day swinging one way, the next day swinging the other way. I had no guidance; no one put their arm around my shoulder and said, "Bobby, it's going to be okay. Things are going to be okay." It was left up to me, Bobby Williams, to reach in the grab bag and pull out the type of life I wanted.

While the sights and sounds of the Outfit were stinging, it made me realize later as an adult that the world is real with its own vibe and not a place you created in your head of how you would like it to be. The world has pimples. It's a place where we live with three stories—yours, mine, and the truth. Good and bad play together in the world's park. At times, the world defies the things your parents taught you, school taught you, and your house of worship taught you. But through it all, the world will always allow you to make a decision on what type of person you want to be and what type of life you want to live. The world turns over the keys to the life you want to live to you and it's up to you to open life's door and move forward. But remember one thing when deciding whether to live a good life or bad life—check in the mirror and see if that person agrees with your decision. Through it all, I learned while criminal life is and always will be part of the world, that's not the only room in the building. The building has more good rooms than bad and the people are the ones who prove it.

People make the world a much better place to be than we could ever imagine, even with the bad that tries to undercut the good. Never give up on people, as they will never give up on you. While there is bad among us and no one knows that better than me, the numbers of good far exceed what the eyes can see. They're your family, they're your neighbors, and they're strangers we don't even know; yet, at some point in your life they will perform acts of kindness toward you. The size of the kindness does not matter; what counts is the act of kindness is running expressly from their heart to yours.

Tons of people have said to me, "Bobby, you gotta write a book." Maybe someday I'll put my thoughts about my life as an Outfit observer on paper. Ah, what the hell, who would care? I probably couldn't even sell one book. Well, maybe someday, I'll have the guts to do it.

When I look in Linda's eyes, when I wrap my arms around her, when we hold hands while walking in the mall, I am forever grateful this is the life I chose. Being with Linda and the girls has been a dream come true for me. It's been the greatest love I could have ever asked for. Sure, like any family we have had our fights, arguments, and disagreements over things. A lot of times it was pretty petty stuff, especially with the girls during the teenage years. Linda and I worked together so there was only one decision to be made. Sometimes we were a little easier on the girls and sometimes we stuck to our guns. We all survived; the girls turned out great. I couldn't be more proud of them. I know they will provide a safe, loving home for our darling grandchildren.

If any one of you is thinking about going into the mob's life, think about something else. If you decide you want to be in the life, I say God bless. You have my condolences and the jackpot is waiting for you.

Lin, is that you calling me? Sure, I won't forget to go to the cleaners to pick up our stuff when I'm out.

Well, I gotta go. Linda wants to go to a movie this afternoon, so I better get moving, so I'll be back on time. It's a movie were an FBI agent goes undercover to infiltrate a mob family. Everyone has been seeing it but don't worry, when Linda asks me how I liked the movie, I'll tell her it was great. In this case, I really will be watching just a movie where when 'The End' appears on the screen, it really will be the end.

Printed in the USA
CPSIA information can be obtained
at www.ICGtesting.com
LVHW021502220224
772537LV00001B/102